DUNCTON QUEST

Spindle got to his paws and backed a little in awe.

'Who art thou?' he asked, again in the old way. 'From where hast thou come?'

'We have come from Duncton, which is one of the Seven Systems,' replied Boswell. 'To Uffington have we been bound these many long and troubled years. I am myself of Uffington. I am a scribemole. My name is Boswell and we will do you no harm.'

Then Spindle simply stared at Boswell, all his feigned aggression gone and replaced by a look on his face of pathetic vulnerability as if, after many years of being brave, he had finally admitted that he was much afraid, and much alone. His mouth trembled and his eyes filled with tears, and then he lowered his snout into his front paws and began to sob with such sadness mingled with joyful relief that tears came to the eyes of Tryfan as well.

William Horwood was born in Oxford in 1944, and brought up on the south-east coast of England. He went to Bristol University, where he gained a degree in Geography, and worked as a journalist for ten years, becoming a features editor with the *Daily Mail*. His first novel *Duncton Wood* (1980) became an instant bestseller, and started his career as a full-time writer. Since then he has published *The Stonor Eagles*, *Callanish* and *Skallagrigg*, and he now lives on the Kent coast.

Also in Arrow by William Horwood

**DUNCTON WOOD
THE STONOR EAGLES**

Duncton Quest

The Duncton Chronicles 2

William Horwood

ARROW BOOKS

Arrow Books Limited
62–65 Chandos Place, London WC2N 4NW

An imprint of Century Hutchinson Limited

London Melbourne Sydney Auckland
Johannesburg and agencies throughout
the world

First published in Great Britain by
Century 1988
Arrow edition 1989

© 1988 by William Horwood

Photoset by Deltatype Ltd, Ellesmere Port
Printed and bound in Great Britain by
Courier International Ltd, Tiptree, Essex

ISBN 0 09 960620 8

Contents

Prologue

Tryfan was born of Bracken and Rebecca, whose tale is the first part of Duncton's history. The great task that they began, which was to show allmole the Silence of the Stone, bold Tryfan now continues.

For he grew to have faith and strength, and was entrusted with the task of accompanying old Boswell, holy mole, White Mole, safely back to the Holy Burrows of Uffington. And with Boswell to take the seventh Stillstone, the last one, to its rightful place so that the true silence of the Stone might be heard. So they set off from Duncton Wood in hope and faith.

But even as they left, the chill winds of the Word were already spreading across the land, whispering falseness to the weak, giving corrupt succour to the lonely, confusing the minds of the lazy, filling the void in the hearts of the faithless, offering power to the clever and astute.

With the coming of the Word shadows lengthened over moledom, faster and deeper, engulfing even Uffington, and it became lone Tryfan's great and terrible task to lead those few who had the strength on a quest to protect the light and silence of the Stone against the shadows and the corrupted ones who came.

Few moles to the many, and led by one who held no power but that which comes from a spirit of truth and love. One who was hunted and reviled, cast out and punished. One whom the very Stone itself seemed to wish to crush to nothingness.

This book is Tryfan's story and tells how the Stone demanded of him a courage, a purpose and a faith rarely wreaked of anymole. It tells of how Tryfan became the greatest scribemole of his time, and of how his work, his loyalty and his love prepared the ground for the coming of one who could call out to all moles from the Silence, that they might know what it was that Tryfan and his followers had sought with such courage.

So all you who once made a blessing upon Bracken and his Rebecca, share now in a petition for their son Tryfan; watch over him through the light and darkness of his journeying; help him with your love, and pray that he may return home at last, safeguarded.

PART I

Return to Uffington

Chapter One

March; and a cold north wind blew across the scarps and vales of Southern England, scurrying old leaves under hedgerows and into the newly opened entrances of tunnel and burrow. It tore at tree-buds and flurried the black feathers of sheltering rook. It whipped the stiff dead winter grass, and flayed the bare soil of ploughed fields. The land seemed withered, and all on it huddled miserably, waiting for change.

Among the rising heights of the grey beeches of the small copse which stands near the eastern foot of the great scarp of Uffington wherein the Holy Burrows lie, that same wind twisted and turned in the leafless branches, then whined low among the surface roots, sending a shiver to the snout and a shiver to the heart of any creature that might be hiding there. Like vole or squirrel, fox or subtle stoat.

Or mole. . . .

Two moles crouched in the poor shelter of a beech tree's surface roots, silent and close. One was Tryfan*, son of Rebecca and Bracken. His full dark fur had a hint of the beauty and strength that had been his mother's; his eyes and stance had the purpose and courage that had taken his father far, far from Duncton Wood and back again, through danger to body and spirit into a final silence with his mate which all moles desire. Yet Tryfan was still young and his stance had the impatience and uncertainty of youth, and he held his talons tensely as if expecting attack.

The second mole was old Boswell, most revered and mysterious of all the scribemoles of Uffington, finder of the seventh Stillstone. In all the annals of moledom, none

*Tryfan is pronounced 'Triffan'.

has more honour than him. His name was spoken – will always be spoken – with reverence, and to this day many a mole touches his left paw with his right when a storyteller first mentions the name Boswell. For he was crippled as a youngster and lived his life lame, and for this reason needed help and protection on his journeys as a scribe-mole. By the time Tryfan first knew him, which was in Rebecca and Bracken's final days in Duncton Wood, Boswell was old indeed, his face lined and, in repose, weary. But his eyes were ever full of care and love, and when he was comfortable and had fed, then he would smile and look about him with the eagerness of a pup; and when he spoke his voice was gentle and unhurried, as if time itself waited on him.

But now, crouched beneath the rising escarpment to Uffington, Boswell seemed fatigued, though an observant mole might have seen that even if his eyes were only half open as his snout extended over his good paw, they were watchful: the eyes of a wise mole thinking. Tryfan, who crouched at his side and a little behind, looked restless and impatient, a young adult male doing his best to keep his energy and purpose in check; waiting, as a young adult should, upon an elder. While before them rose the hallowed heights of Uffington's great chalk escarpment, which they must climb before their journey's end.

Long, long had they journeyed, Boswell and Tryfan, for from Duncton Wood to the Holy Burrows of Uffington is many a molemile, too many to count but in the cycle of seasons and passing of moleyears. And the Stillstone Boswell carried beneath his right paw was burdensome, as true Silence may be.

'Still it blows, still it comes, even here in the very vale of Uffington,' whispered Boswell, dimly snouting up to where the branches of the tree bent uneasily, and to where the sky beyond was grim grey with uneasy cloud.

'But spring's stirring underground,' said Tryfan, trying to sound cheerful as he hunched his flanks against the cold and sought to keep the wind off Boswell. 'We've had some good days and weeks, the snow has gone, and so will this wind.'

Boswell only shook his head in doubt, and Tryfan had to admit to himself that in all the long moleyears of their journey this frightening wind had rarely eased. It had been relentless and bitter, and had come to seem like a warning, a wind of danger and wrong purpose. A north wind which carried trouble before it, and stirred faction and dark change wherever it had been. A wind ancient in its dark impulse, deep in its dread effect. A north wind of warped spirits, and one which seemed to want to accompany them even to Uffington itself.

Their journey had been by the ancient secret ways known only to scribemoles, above the vales and avoiding contact with other moles. For Tryfan had had much to learn of scribing and the love of moles, and Boswell preferred solitariness and silence for his teachings, and, as a White Mole, was too conspicuous to be comfortable with other moles unless they were used to him. Indeed, in the one system they had come upon, which was three-quarters empty from the same plague and fires that had devastated the Duncton system before Tryfan was born, the few moles there had flocked to touch Boswell, as if he might heal them of the unease that had cast its shadow upon all systems these many moleyears past. Tryfan had had to rescue him from their attentions and firmly guide him back to the old tracks.

It is a hard lesson for a mole to learn that happiness and contentment, care and love, are experiences which pass like the summer breeze through a sun-filled vale, now here, now gone; and a mole had best enjoy them while he may. The rest – the memory, the hopes, the regret – are but echoes of the happiness that was or the glimmering of love that may be again.

So there came a time when Tryfan looked back on those moleyears with Boswell, regretting that he had not realised at the time how content he was, and excited, too, to be travelling in the company of one who taught him so much, with such kind and easy grace.

They had not travelled quickly, for Boswell liked to dally here and there, teaching his disciple the patience and the peace that comes with being still.

'It does not matter what you contemplate provided it is something important,' Boswell would say.

'Such as?' Tryfan had asked eagerly in the early months, snouting around as if he might find something important there.

'Well,' said Boswell, 'almost anything is important except yourself, but few moles find time to think of anything else.'

Boswell had laughed a laugh that in time had made poor Tryfan angry, for however hard he tried it seemed impossible not to think of himself, or of things or hopes or dreams or ideas that wilfully attached themselves to 'himself'.

But then, when Tryfan was quite sure how very hard it was to contemplate something 'important', Boswell took him up on to the surface one day in January to watch the changing light of day through snow. A contemplation that Tryfan became so absorbed in that when it was done, and Boswell ordained that they could return underground and eat, it seemed that a whole day had passed in what, to Tryfan, seemed a few moments. That was the first day that Tryfan had ever felt free of himself and began to hear the sound of Silence. The first time he saw he had contemplated something 'important'.

In such quiet ways did Boswell teach him to know how to be at peace with himself so that, as their journey progressed, Tryfan learnt how a mole might meditate and carry always with him something of the Silence of the Stone.

'Can a mole ever hear the Silence fully?' Tryfan asked one day. 'Hear it, and still be alive?'

Boswell thought for a moment and said, 'Yes, yes a mole can, and perhaps a mole has in the past. It is the greatest thing to which a mole can aspire, to be at one with the Silence. I believe a mole will come who is of it.'

'The Stonemole you mean?' said Tryfan quickly, referring to the legendary mole who, the stories said, would one day come and free moles to hear the Silence for ever. Of *him* Boswell rarely said anything at all, except to say that he would come one day, and that would be a day indeed!

'Ah, no, I am not talking of the Stonemole – his task is different. Through Him will all moles learn to have faith that they might hear the Silence, as scribemoles have faith. No, no, after Him one will come who will have found Silence. Soon after Him . . . yes, yes, Tryfan, soon then one will come. I know it will be so. . . .'

Old Boswell lowered his snout when he said this and seemed suddenly tired, perhaps more than tired, and Tryfan saw an unusual weariness in his eyes. He turned away, and went off a little by himself muttering as he went, 'One will come then, yes, one must come then.' His voice seemed filled with sad hope and Tryfan, surprised at this sudden vulnerability in his master, went to him and touched him.

'Can I do anything?' he asked softly, and Boswell turned to him and stared at him and his old eyes filled with tears.

'No, no, Tryfan, you learn well and you give me love and support. Out of faith one will come, after the Stonemole, after that and then I . . . then I . . .' and Boswell wept. And as he wept it seemed the very tunnels wept, and the trees and grass above, and moledom itself, and Tryfan was distraught as well.

'I don't understand – ' he began. 'I don't . . . I can't. . . .'

'I know you can't,' said Boswell at last, and in his eyes now was tenderness for the young mole, and love for him, and understanding, and Tryfan wept in his turn.

After that Boswell said no more, and for hours he was silent, contemplating some great sadness or joy, his body

7

crouched and hunched, and his faded patchy fur ravaged as if he carried the whole of moledom in himself and was waiting until somemole came to help him.

Many times in that long wait did Tryfan of Duncton start forward towards Boswell, but always he stopped, sensing that for now his task was only to watch over him from a distance, helpless before the great trouble and struggle that seemed to have set upon him. Then dawn came, warmth, another day, and that unresolved shadow seemed to pass back into the darkness and confusion out of which it had come.

In such ways Tryfan learned that there was more to a White Mole than the simple goodness that was all most other moles saw in him, and if Boswell seemed weary at times it was less because of his age than because there was much in moles that might weary a mole who has known Silence. And, so long as Tryfan was able to see that Boswell's care for other moles and his tolerance of the weariness they sometimes brought him was the result of the love he gave to them, so he came to love Boswell more, and might one day love other moles as well.

But there were things Boswell chose not to talk about, in spite of the hardest questioning from Tryfan, and one of them concerned the task that Tryfan himself might be given should he ever be allowed to be a scribemole. For Tryfan knew that all moles, whether scribemoles or not, have tasks ordained by the Stone, the fulfilment of which expresses the fullest potential of their strength or their intelligence, or simply their ability to live. For scribemoles, however, the tasks may be more formal, and in the gift of other more senior scribemoles to ordain until the time comes when a scribemole's task is self-ordained, a solemn undertaking indeed, demanding – as it seemed to Tryfan – weighty consideration and self-knowledge.

Of this, even if it were true, Boswell would say little and answer less, observing that the sooner Tryfan stopped worrying about his task the sooner he might be ready to fulfil it. Yet in the final molemonths of their journey, when they came down from the chalk heights to the vales and met other moles once more, he could not but notice that Boswell directed him humbly to learn what he could of everymole and what concerned them, as if, in that direction, his task might one day lie.

As they had neared Uffington, one theme more than any other had run through the chatter of moles they met: the coming of the 'Word' which was seen as a message of strength and power, hope and security in a troubled world. Yet its existence, its very meaning indeed, was no more than a rumour among moles, and one that for a long time Tryfan assumed to be but the idle gossip and hope of moles who, having been afflicted by plagues and fire, now projected their hopes of the future in the coming of a deeper wisdom than the Stone itself, and called this wisdom the Word. It *was* coming, many a mole told them as they neared Uffington. 'Aye, and when it does all will be well again, and these Stone-forsaken northern winds quite gone and spring return!'

So moles did say, hunching against the bitter winds that seemed to afflict a mole wherever he turned in those dark days, as bitter snout-shrivelling wind as ever was.

Then too, in those post-plague days, there were many rumours, telling of dark, dangerous moles travelling from the north of which the wind was the harbinger, casting fear into moles' hearts and making many a system, already decimated and afflicted, places of fear and unwelcoming to travellers like Tryfan and Boswell. But Boswell did not dismiss this kind of gossip as mere superstition.

'The Word?' said Boswell. 'Yes, it's coming. Not too soon, I hope, for you have much to learn before that.' But more he would not say, leading Tryfan back one last time to solitary routes as if to protect him from other moles and further knowledge of those lengthening shadows in which rumours of danger and the Word were intertwined. Then, somehow, in those final weeks of travel Tryfan came to see that whatever his task was it had to do with the coming of the Word, and that it was awesome, and that he had much to learn if he was to fulfil it; and that Boswell would reveal its nature to him when the time was right. . . .

In the last days of their journey, Boswell had begun to talk to him differently, saying, 'You must tell them . . . You will show them . . .' and even, 'Your task may be to make them see . . .' as if all that he had taught Tryfan had been only so that he, Tryfan, might pass it on. As if *he* might be a teacher as Boswell was. And this troubled Tryfan, for the whole history of the journey, so far as his learning was concerned, was the discovery of how little he knew, and how little he had to say to other moles. Which, when he admitted it to Boswell, the scribemole laughed aloud at saying how true but how hard *that* truth was to teach!

So, in a spirit of humble confusion (as Tryfan was later to describe it), and after some last weeks of complete seclusion from other moles and with the north wind blowing cold and bitter as ever, they had reached at last the eastern end of Uffington. . . .

. . . And thinking of the journey past and the task that might be ahead of him, Tryfan began to see that Boswell's hesitation to start the final climb to Uffington might simply be reluctance to admit that the journey was finally done, and that change might be upon them.

'We had better move,' said Tryfan staring once more about the copse in which they had taken stance. 'The morning is advancing and there are rooks about.'

Rooks are more irksome than mortally dangerous to moles, but since the last stage of the journey would be on the surface – there being no communal tunnels up to Uffington – Tryfan preferred not to be the object of the curiosity of rooks or any other avian. Rooks bring kestrel, and kestrel may bring hunting owl; and hunting owl is death. Yet still Boswell did not answer, or even stir.

'What is it, Boswell?' asked Tryfan irritably. 'You've been crouched there brooding since dawn. Can't we just get on with it? If you want food before we go I suppose I can find a worm or two about here. . .' He looked reluctantly around the bleak copse, whose bare chalk surface was littered with beech leaves and was unpromising for worms, and, thinking the better of delaying their start further, he hastily added: 'But surely the scribemoles will have food aplenty up in the Burrows?'

Tryfan had often daydreamed of the welcome the scribemoles would give them, and he knew that of all their number Boswell must now be the most honoured and the most revered. The more so because, after so many decades when it had been lost, he was bringing the seventh Stillstone back at last, whose return would herald the coming of Silence for allmole who sought it.

'What is it?' Tryfan asked again, but gently now and with more respect, coming closer and trying to do what Boswell had taught him to do: listen truly to another mole's heart. For impatient though he was, Tryfan loved Boswell as his father Bracken had, more than the world, more perhaps than the Stone itself, and he would have run any risk and faced any danger, even death itself, to protect and honour him. Such had been his task when they set off from Duncton Wood, and though they had faced owl, water, fox and twofoots, and risked crushing at the black rush of roaring owl whose shining eyes can mesmerise the unwary, yet Tryfan had boldly protected old Boswell and grown from youth to warrior mole in the course of that journey. And wise mole too, who knew when to give Boswell space. So now Tryfan sighed, and settled down beside the beloved scribemole, to let him explain in his own time why he had stopped.

Sensing which, Boswell stirred and scratched himself, fretting at the lichen on the root at his side and snuffling half-heartedly at the humus of leaf and bark and twig. No worms there, just dank wetness.

'I'm not sure, Tryfan, but I fear . . . I sense . . . I know not . . .' and his voice trailed away to nothing, as the grey roots of the tree in whose protection they were hiding turned and twisted and lost themselves in the earth about them. 'Or, rather, I know only too well,' he added.

Above them, high in the trees, the March wind caught again at sharp young buds and shook them with memories of winter. Then it turned and swirled and redoubled its strength, to catch at the litter of leaves beneath the trees, and pull coldly at Tryfan's strong fur, and the ragged white-grey coat of Boswell. Tryfan shuddered and said, 'Surely we are so close now that we are within the protection of Uffington. In only another hour or two and we'll be there, Boswell, safe and protected. Can't we talk then?'

'Ah! Yes! We can talk then, I suppose, but it may be rather too late. There are things I must tell you before. . . .'

'Before what?' asked Tryfan in frustration at Boswell's unusual reluctance to say what was on his mind.

'Tryfan,' said Boswell, his voice such a whisper that he seemed almost to be speaking to himself, 'I am reluctant to move because I fear this journey's end will bring our parting. I have tried to teach you what I know but there is so much more . . . The truth is I don't want to let you go!'

'But I'm not going! I don't want to. I want to stay at Uffington and learn to be a scribemole. Is it that I have failed in that, being good only as a warrior for your protection?'

Boswell put his paw to Tryfan's and said, 'No, no that is far from the truth. You have learnt much of scribing, much of ancient lore, and you have learnt well and truly. Already you . . .' he stopped again, snout low, tensely listening. 'Trouble. Grief. Pity. Can you not feel them in the ground? They will mean that we must part. I fear that.'

Tryfan snouted about and said firmly, 'I sense nothing of the sort. That's just your usual doubts and fears, Boswell. Old age!'

Boswell's eyes smiled. Sometimes Tryfan forgot himself and spoke as a son might, but Boswell did not mind, though he affected a certain disapproval. And it was true: he was not as strong as once he had been, old age brought aches and pains . . . and unnecessary doubts. There had

12

been many times on the journey to Uffington when it had needed Tryfan's youth and confidence to carry them forward. White Moles are not infallible.

Boswell peered about him and said, 'Well, I fear I am right this time. For one thing I am surprised that scribemoles have not already come out to meet us, for surely news of our coming precedes us. For another . . . well . . . the very soil itself feels troubled. The roots, the trees, the wind.'

'That's just the beginnings of a storm, and so the sooner we – '

'Yes!' said Boswell rising suddenly. 'It may well be the beginning of a "storm". An ancient storm and one that will plunge all of moledom into darkness before it is done. But you are right. We had better get on and confront whatever we must in the Holy Burrows.'

'But it can only be a welcome, Boswell.'

'Can it?' said Boswell, his bright eyes turning on Tryfan's. 'Feel the ground, Tryfan, feel it!' And Tryfan snouted low and felt the ground as Boswell had taught him to, clearing his mind of the excitement of arrival and the expectation of the good things to come, and he sensed at last that it was 'troubled'.

'Yes, I sense it,' said Tryfan. 'What is wrong, Boswell?'

'I don't know,' Boswell replied simply.

'And why must we part?'

But Boswell did not reply. Instead he irritably set off, limping rapidly ahead with the energy that always surprised Tryfan. With barely any hesitation, and with the escarpment rising to their left, he took them on a route that went by hedgerow and long grass, in the shadow of ancient lynchets and across the dry valleys that ran down off the scarp face.

Boswell stopped only once, pausing briefly in a small wood that edged on to a way up a valley that cut up into the escarpment above them, and muttered, 'The Blowing Stone, that's up there. If this wind rises and veers west we will hear it before long. From here Uffington really begins.'

13

'Yes!' exclaimed Tryfan, a tremor of excitement in his voice because he could now feel the power of the Blowing Stone which was part of the Uffington legend, and had given sanctuary to many a mole, including his own father Bracken.

'Can't we just visit the Blowing Stone?' said Tryfan as Boswell started off again. He regretted saying it the moment he spoke because Boswell turned sharply to him and said, ' "*Just* visit it?" That you cannot do. It is an object of reverence, not idle curiosity.' Then he hurried on, and Tryfan followed behind, looking humbled, but watchful as well for they were on open ground now with the great sky wide above them and he was beginning to feel, as Boswell did, that the air about them was troubled indeed; and by something more enduring than a bitter north wind.

★ ★ ★ ★ ★ ★ ★

Halfway up the steep chalk escarpment that forms the north edge of Uffington Hill, the ground levels off to the east and forms a great field of pasture. To the right, the west, the escarpment steepens and it was at this stage in their long ascent that there came to them, strong even against the wind, the odour of death. With it came a curious whining sound, sharp and strange, and a rasping or rattling of metal on wood. The combined effect was chilling and seemed to cast a darkness on the light of day.

They stopped together and took shelter in some long grass.

'Stay here. I shall go forward,' said Tryfan with authority, to which Boswell raised no objection. It was Tryfan's task to see to such matters of danger, and one he did well. Though if he ever imagined that Boswell was waiting in suspense for his return during these reconnaissances, he would have been mistaken – it was Boswell's habit, at such moments when he could do nothing useful, to crouch comfortably down and meditate, muttering a rhyme or invocation to himself, or even humming some scribemole song.

14

But he had barely got started before Tryfan was back, his face shocked.

'There is no living mole about, alien or otherwise. So of such we need have no fear. Nor any other living creature except for rabbits out on the pasture. But there is something, Boswell, something terrible. You had better come and see.'

Tryfan led him up the tussocky slope towards the pasture. The odour they had smelt before was clearer but not much stronger – a dry, grim smell. Then ahead were the rising wooden posts of a fence between which stretched barbed wire.

It was from there, as the wind swept by, that the high whining sound came. Closer to, the wire vibrated savagely, seeming to give malevolent voice to the wind, turned its bitter sweepings into part moan, part howl and part scream. An effect which would have had anymole looking sharply over his shoulder as if expecting attack from an enemy.

But though this was bad enough, what was worse was the grim sight that had so shocked Tryfan and brought him running back to Boswell. For impaled on the barbs of the bottom rung of wire, their back feet just touching the grass below, were the bodies of two moles. Wind-bleached bones pierced through their dried skin and fur and their talons pointed up in arcs of agony to the barbs on to which they had been impaled, each one through the snout. The strong north wind swung them back and forth on the wire to give them an obscene semblance of life. The ear-rending windsound seemed like the echo of their screams and final moans.

Boswell said nothing but, advancing slowly along the wire, examined them. Finally he pointed mutely at their paws, each reaching up to the terrible barbs as if . . . if. . . .

'They were impaled alive,' said Boswell quietly. 'Each of them hung here alive.'

For a time Boswell said nothing but then he turned to

15

Tryfan who saw that his eyes were filled with tears. Behind him hung the moles, and beyond that the rising downland heights of Uffington Hill, above which the sky was angry and bleak. For a time he could not speak. But then, as Tryfan went forward to comfort him in his evident distress, he turned back to the moles and whispered, 'These are scribemoles of the Holy Burrows. From their worn talons and the greying fur they were old, too old to live in a normal system, especially in such stressful times as these.'

'But how could they be so impaled?' asked Tryfan.

Boswell shrugged. 'I have heard of such a thing with twofoots, trapping creatures live and then putting them on a wire like this. But that is usually near a wood and involves other creatures such as crow and vole. Here, alone, like this . . . I fear. . . .'

'Yes?' said Tryfan.

'Othermole.'

Tryfan gasped in disbelief and horror. Other *mole*?

'Do not think that mole would not do this as well. The records show that snouting such as this has been done by mole.'

'Whichmole?' said Tryfan, his voice shaking.

'In ages past. As punishment. On barbs of blackthorn, or even wire where it hangs low enough, as here. It is the cruellest death. It is a punishment best not survived, for moles so hurt would be in living death.' Tryfan knew why, for a mole's snout is more than smell, it is touch and sight as well. If a snouted mole survived he would be so badly maimed he would be defenceless and lost. Only in fights to death do moles talon – thrust at each other's snout.

'But on *scribemole*?' wondered Tryfan.

'Well . . .' hesitated Boswell, staring again at the bodies and then out over the vale of Uffington and north beyond it. 'There are few records, but in the northern reaches of moledom, where the ground rises to impassable wormless moors, others live who are not believers in the Stone.'

'Grike moles, giants!' said Tryfan. 'Such as my mother told me stories of. Stoneless moles.'

'Aye, some call them grikes,' said Boswell. 'But among themselves they use another name.'

'Which is?' asked Tryfan impatiently.

'They are moles of the Word,' said Boswell looking bleakly at the snouted moles. 'This is punishment by the Word.'

Tryfan was aghast, for all that he had heard moles say of the Word was hopeful and promising. Not like this. Then he felt stricken with awe, and the sense of what his task might be became clearer. He said nothing but went closer to Boswell.

Boswell seemed unaware of his disquiet, but continued his account of snouting. 'We know that these grikes punished visiting scribemoles with snouting. Of that, sadly, there are records through the ages. No southern mole has been there for many tens of years, more than a century perhaps, for the reign of plagues has been long and has weakened moles as it weakened other creatures, and the scribemoles had enough to do in the regions of the Seven Systems. But I cannot be sure. This may be an accident of some kind to do with the wind, it may be twofoots rather than mole. But it is ominous, and makes me worry even more at the sense of trouble I feel about Uffington.'

'They have been there a long time,' said Tryfan eventually.

'Nearly a full cycle of seasons, certainly long before Longest Night.' Boswell's voice was cold now, assessing the evidence. His tears were gone.

'These bodies have dried in strong sun, such as we had soon after we left Duncton Wood. That, followed by the freezing weather for so long, has helped preserve them.'

'Why did owls not take them?'

'The power of scribemoles is great and fearful to other creatures, even hunting owls. How else have scribemoles survived their traditional journeys to the Seven Systems and beyond?'

Boswell turned to the killing wire and raised a taloned paw and began to chant.

> *What is their death, oh stone?*
>
> *Death of toil and of repentance,*
> *Death of joy and of peace,*
> *Death of grace and of forgiveness,*
> *Death of hope and of despair.*
>
> *Grant them what there is in death oh Stone:*
> *Silence.*

As he spoke this last solitary word the sound of the wind in the wire seemed to die, and from off to the east came a different sound, deeper and reverberant. To them it came in a deep note, and then again, and then once more. It was the haunting sound of the Blowing Stone.

'May they know the Silence of the Stone,' said Tryfan softly.

'May it be so,' concluded Boswell.

Even as he said it a storm of wind broke about them with a roar, and then across the face of the escarpment; it battered at the uprights of the fence, stressed the barbed wire between them, and swung the bodies of the moles ever more violently until first one and then the other fell off the barbs to break across the grass; the bones and fur lifted like feathers and were blown away with the wind. Tryfan watched this in wonder, though he had little doubt that it was quite in Boswell's power to so provoke the wind and release the moles from their torment in death.

'Come,' cried Boswell above the noise of wind. 'We will find an entrance to the Holy Burrows.'

'But what will we find there? And what of the greater trouble you spoke of?' shouted Tryfan back.

'We shall find whatever it is that the Stone wishes us to find,' replied Boswell.

Then they ran on uphill and even as the wind seemed to redouble its efforts to pull them from the steep side of the escarpment and hurl them to the vales far below they found a tunnel entrance and entered it, to make their escape into the silence of the most sacred burrows of moledom.

Chapter Two

The tunnel they found themselves in was narrow, but dry and made in the old way, its walls arching elegantly upward and its roof well finished. In consequence it had a pleasant airiness of sound, absorbing the wind-stresses from the grass above, though the whining of the barbed wire was carried down into the soil by the fence posts and was loud, its vibration unpleasant to the paws.

The floor was dusty and in places covered by black and withered grass roots which had tumbled from among the living ones lacing the ceiling and higher sides. These had a pleasing green-white colour which combined with the grey of the chalk to give the light in the tunnels the peaceful hallowed quality for which Uffington was famous.

But it was evident to both of them that nomole had passed this way for many a month, though vole and weasel had both left spoor at the entrance, probably while sheltering from a predator. In the tunnel itself the chalk dust was thick on the ground and in wall crevices, so that as they went along their coats became white with it.

'This is quite a place, Boswell,' whispered Tryfan as the old mole hurried on ahead. 'It turns even a novitiate like me into a White Mole in no time at all. As for you, you'll disappear altogether if you get any dustier!'

'That is my ultimate intention, as a matter of fact,' said Boswell, 'to disappear altogether! But it is taking time; and so are you with idle chatter. Come! There's a worm-rich stretch higher up and since I know it's food you're after we'll stop there to feed and rest before venturing on into the main system.' He laughed gently, instinctively speaking softly, for, apart from a natural reverence for the place, they both knew that in tunnels such as these talk travels, and neither could guess what dangers lay ahead.

So they went steadily and cautiously uphill through tunnels that became progressively bigger and more airy. They had a sense of ancient holiness and here and there the chalk was carved with ancient script. Sometimes, too, the tunnels seem to have been especially aligned with the great flints that the chalk held, stones with which Tryfan was familiar from the Ancient System in Duncton Wood, but these in Uffington were on a more massive scale. On their convoluted surfaces, and across their polished faces where they were broken, sound seemed changed and lost, echoing away to come back minutes later from other flints.

More than once Tryfan started back into a defensive stance, mistaking the echoes of their own pawsteps for attacking moles and finding that he was raising his talons to his own shadow. It needed an effort of concentration to keep a sense of direction, but Boswell had trained him well and he did not lose his way when Boswell went ahead too fast and was out of sight for a while.

Eventually Boswell stopped. 'We're nearing the main system now,' he said in a low voice. 'So we will go even more carefully.'

'In case there are alien moles about?'

'That, and the fact that these are the Holy Burrows. Respectful quiet is expected from all moles here. From scribemoles, silence, unless speech is essential, which it rarely is. But just ahead we may eat and rest, and pause awhile. I suggest, Tryfan, that you do as I do and think a little upon our journey past and find strength for the days to come.' Boswell's 'pausing awhiles' were his term for meditation, and Tryfan knew it could take hours. He resigned himself to a long wait.

Soon after this the soil darkened and the chalk fell away beneath them: they had run into a deposit of clay and flints which was replete with food and comfortable burrows.

'Guest quarters,' whispered Boswell. 'Your father once stayed here.'

Tryfan found food and they settled down to crunch a

21

few worms and recover from the shocks and effort of this final stage of their journey.

'Think a little upon our journey,' Boswell had said . . . but now they were here, and they were safe, Tryfan felt tired, terribly tired, and as Boswell began a formal meditation Tryfan found his thoughts drifting, despite all he could do, with his body warm and his talons relaxing, as around him the White Mole's thanksgiving for a safe homecoming seemed to fill the old place with images of the moleyears of travel and toil it had taken them to get here, and replace them one by one with the light of Silence, as if those dangers had not been.

'A scribemole does not dwell on dangers past, or dangers yet to come; nor on what might be or might have been. A scribemole strives for the Silence that is here now for all to hear. But at a time of homecoming a scribemole thanks the Stone for the grace of returning and so now I thank the Stone . . .' Boswell's words were half instruction, half prayer but Tryfan began to have difficulty hearing them, for around Boswell was a light, white and pure, and Tryfan wanted to reach his whole body into it.

'B – Bos – B – ' But Tryfan seemed unable to say Boswell's name.

'Sleep now, Tryfan, sleep and rest, for you have completed your task and brought me home to Uffington safeguarded. Now your new task will begin and you will need strength for the trials ahead that you will face alone.'

'New task . . . alone . . .' Boswell's words sounded a note of alarm in Tryfan's heart in the moments before sleep, or a dreaming unconsciousness, overtook him. Certainly afterwards Tryfan never quite knew if he slept or not. He remembered being unable to move, unable to speak, unable to be anything but at the centre of images that Boswell conjured up about him with his incantations and thanksgivings.

He sensed that Boswell was near him, touching him, and that there was a deep Silence over the burrow out of which came Boswell's voice. . . 'He has learnt worthily,

Stone, but he is young. He knows not yet what he already knows and so he will feel fear and suffer doubt and loss. But he is the one I have found and on whom thy burden will rest. Guide him, give him strength, let him hear, let him. . . .'

And Tryfan wanted to raise himself from his waking sleep and ask Boswell or the Stone or whatever it was that spoke, ask him, ask it . . . 'Bos – B – ' but his talons were as weak as a pup's and his eyes could not see as that voice repeated, 'Sleep, rest . . .' and Tryfan *was* a pup again, running up the tunnels away from his siblings and out into the sunlight of Duncton Wood whose scents were warm with summer, whose light was dappled and fresh, whose trees were comforting and whose Stone stood high in the centre of the Ancient System. There was Rebecca his mother and Bracken his father and Comfrey his half-brother to go and see . . . but Tryfan chose instead to wander free in that great wood until one day when he was older his path turned to the Stone, before which he crouched in awe wondering if he could dare think that he, Tryfan, might become a scribemole: 'Why does a mole have to travel so far just to find himself in the same place?' he had asked the Stone later, when he had matured; and it had been then that Boswell had found him. And now, he was there again, and sensed the wonder of Duncton Wood about him, its green old vales and its rich pattern of tunnels which were his own, and he felt content that he was of it, and it forever of him; but he felt finally a sadness that he had to leave it, and a deep desire that one day the Stone might allow him to return and not rove again from the system he loved.

* * * * * * *

'Wake up, it is time now; time for us to go on.'

Boswell's voice was normal again and the burrow filling with dawning light, but Tryfan still had difficulty emerging from the deep warm reveries into which his rest had sent him. The trees of Duncton and a past that seemed so long ago rose still about him, but fading now, drifting from his reach.

23

'B – Bos – Boswell,' he managed to say at last. 'Will I return to Duncton Wood safeguarded?' Even as he spoke it his eyes were full of tears, for he suddenly missed the place where he had been born, missed it as if only at this moment, so long after leaving it, did he feel it had been taken from him.

'Well? Will I?'

Boswell stared at him, his bright eyes distantly troubled.

'You will have much to do before that. Before then you will return but only to recover yourself and those who may be with you. But yes, one day you will return finally to your home system, as each mole should.'

'Will you be there, Boswell?'

'I will always be there,' said Boswell quietly. 'For I will be with you. . . .'

'No, will *you* be there?'

'If you have faith in the Stone, and if you can see me, then I will be there.'

'You're sad Boswell, and on all our journey you have never been that. Until . . . yesterday, by those snouted moles.'

'Our journey together is over now, so I am sad. A White Mole has feelings, you know.'

'I know,' said Tryfan. 'Have I slept long?'

'Night has passed, day has come.'

'I wanted to keep awake. You were saying blessings and prayers that I should know.'

'Why should you know them?'

'If ever I am to become a scribemole. . . .'

'Feed now, and groom,' said Boswell, refusing to respond to this at all, 'and we will go.'

Then Tryfan was fully awake, never more so, full of energy, and, after due pause for a thanksgiving for the day to come, as Boswell had taught him, he rose and said, 'Now, I suggest I go ahead for we cannot be sure whatmole may be here and whether they are friend or foe.'

'I have heard none,' said Boswell.

24

'H'm,' said Tryfan doubtfully, for Boswell being old was inclined to miss the subtler sounds and vibrations. In any case, there was confusing windsound now about the tunnels, whispers and echoes that might be mole, or might be dustfalls.

'You stay just behind and guide me by touch whether to go right or left, for you know these tunnels,' said Tryfan firmly. 'We had better not risk talking.'

So, close as shadows, Tryfan began their advance into the Holy Burrows, not in triumph and celebration as he had always hoped, but in silence and with caution, lest there was danger for the mole whose protection he still felt was his task.

At first the tunnels seemed little different than those they had lately been following; a little wider perhaps, a little more worn. But soon they subtly changed, their walls being polished with great use and age, their floors shiny with the passage of a hundred thousand talons and there was about them an awesome sense of reverence and peace. Their pawfalls echoed softly ahead, and above them ran the air currents of a system designed in ages past by moles who knew how to set an entrance and make a turn so that a tunnel was in balance both with itself and the system of which it was a part. Though of *this* great skill Boswell had observed more than once that tunnels and systems, however cleverly they may be designed, are likely to be only as harmonious as the moles who make them.

They passed several passages off to right and left, the portals richly embossed and decorated in a way Tryfan had not observed before. There were, too, at regular intervals, slipways up to the surface, whose windsound was gently controlled by the earth and chalk above them. Once or twice they heard the soft stomp of sheep's hooves above; and once the patter of rabbit. Each sound was well conveyed, as it should be in a well-made system, but with such precision that Tryfan could scarcely believe it.

The tunnels themselves were deserted and, as they had been throughout their progress on Uffington Hill, dust-covered. They came across only one roof-fall, and that a minor one.

Tryfan stopped finally only when he came to a major junction, turning to Boswell to whisper, 'Which way here?'

'Left is the Chapter Burrow, right goes to the communal tunnels and the Holy Library,' Boswell replied. 'Go left.'

The tunnel ahead was narrower than before, and dark, and some natural caution had Tryfan proceeding with special care. There was something about the air currents that suggested blockage ahead, or a mole lying in wait.

The tunnel turned ahead of them and they slowed, stopped, and listened. There was no sound, and the ground ahead was dusty and showed no tracks, but even so Tryfan raised a paw silently to indicate to Boswell that he intended going ahead alone, and then advanced, taking the tunnel's turn carefully, ready for attack.

The currents of air above him were confused, and whatever was blocking the tunnel seemed near. Gathering his courage together Tryfan advanced rapidly round the turn to where the tunnel straightened and stopped quite still, unable at first to make sense of the grim sight before him. There was the portal that led into the great Chapter Burrow, but beneath it, turning, broken, wretched, crouched . . . or lay, the remains of a long-dead mole. But more than that: from the disposition of the body, from the fact that the skull – 'head' was too generous a word for so perished a thing – lay some way from the trunk, and one of the back paws was some way to the other side. The mole had not simply been killed: it had been ripped apart.

From the fur, which was well preserved on one side, it was obvious that the mole had been very old, and whatever mole had killed him had done it cruelly with a ripping blow to the belly and others that had severed the head and paw. Boswell came softly along behind Tryfan to observe the scene for himself.

And there was worse. Beyond this mole, who seemed to

have been retreating into the Chapter Burrow, Tryfan and Boswell saw more, piled into grotesque attitudes of violent death, and two against a far wall appeared to have been taloned where they crouched.

Boswell said nothing, but stared at these horrific sights, reaching out instinctively to touch Tryfan, as if, in that touch, there was affirmation that moledom was not only filled with cruelty and death but held life and goodness as well.

Then they heard a sound: a sudden running, the hint of talons scampering on dusty chalk, and they froze and waited, but it did not occur again.

'Rabbit? Vole?' said Boswell, adding almost light-heartedly, 'irreverent as ever they were!' It was almost as if, the shock of the murdered scribemoles before him, he was trying to ignore it.

'Ssh!' whispered Tryfan, alert and listening. Then, when the distant sounds had ceased, he whispered urgently, his voice shocked, 'What's happened here? What is all this?' He moved forward and pointed wearily to yet another body, barely aware that Boswell did not seem surprised.

'It is of the Stone,' said Boswell cryptically.

They turned out of the Chapter Burrow and started back the way they had come and then on to find the tunnels leading to the Holy Library, advancing down them cautiously lest they find other bodies. But their caution, and reserve, did not last long for soon they did find others, and from now on, wherever they went, they seemed to find the bodies of murdered scribemoles. Whatever and however the massacre had taken place it has been ruthless and sudden. There seemed to have been little attempt to escape.

So widespread was the evidence of death that soon both began to get used to it. Perhaps fortunately the bodies were now dried and odourless, though here and there near entrances was evidence of predation from outside. Stoat or weasel, perhaps.

More than that, there was recent life about, for they could see that the floor had been recently crossed, and recrossed. A mole, or moles, and they had dragged something through the tunnels, though nothing as big as a mole's body which, in the circumstances, might have been logical. But the only talon marks they found were of solitary moles, vagrants probably, who must have made their way into the system in the recent past.

'They are still here, somewhere,' said Tryfan, 'for these are fresh tracks. But at least the talon marks are those of a weak mole or moles.'

Boswell agreed. And, more relaxed, said, 'Let us go to the Library itself now, though I doubt after this that there will be much to see. Perhaps, though, we can recover something of the books there. . . .'

'Nomole would dare damage such relics,' declared Tryfan, shoulders hunching for a fight.

'We might have said nomole would touch scribemoles. But moles have. Moledom is not changing, Tryfan. It has changed.'

At Boswell's direction Tryfan, still cautious, led the way out of the main complex of tunnels and the communal burrows to the one that he said led off to the Library. As he turned into it he stopped suddenly and pointed. The tracks they had observed earlier were very recent here, and there was scent of life.

With Tryfan taking the lead and hunched ready for mortal fight if such was necessary, they advanced down the tunnel, the air heavy with tension. It was a rougher tunnel than some of the others, more ancient, and with the tension was mixed a deep awe, for Tryfan knew that at last he was near the fabled Library of the Holy Burrows, the greatest repository of records and folios in the whole of moledom. This was the very intellectual heart of the scribemole's life, from down here all the greatest scribings were said to have come, or been done, through the long ages of mole.

Suddenly the hushed and tense silence was broken in a

28

way so dramatic and unexpected that it had them stopping still immediately and crouching low, looking at each other in surprise. For, at first distantly and then rather louder, came the welling sound of pawsteps accompanied by voices. It was so unexpected that for a moment they could not tell from where it came, but then it clarified, the echoes much less, the sound dying for a moment, and they knew it came from the tunnel ahead, where the Library lay.

Then louder again and frightening, the sound of talon tread, of paws marching, and a roaring as of many voices. Tryfan immediately hunched back protectively with Boswell behind him, pushing him almost into the wall and looking behind to consider their best line of retreat.

'If I was alone, Boswell, I might go quietly ahead and see what I can see,' whispered Tryfan. 'One mole always moves better than two. But my task is still to get you to a place of safety. It's no good unnecessarily – '

As he spoke the approaching sounds grew louder still and Tryfan began to try to herd Boswell away as if he were a family of pups.

But Boswell was not moving. Not that Tryfan expected him to show fear – he seemed to have forgotten how to feel such a thing decades ago – but at least he might have a sensible concern for his own life.

'The sounds have not actually materialised, have they?' he said calmly. 'In fact they seem to be dying away again. Strange that!'

Tryfan looked at him quizzically, and more so because he was smiling slightly.

Then, thinking swiftly, and looking much calmer himself, Tryfan said, 'Fine, then we'll pretend to retreat!' and with that he thumped his paws and rattled his talons on the tunnel floor, even shouting out in a fading kind of voice: 'Come on, let's get out of here.' And then they froze into silence to see what happened.

Ahead of them the tunnel turned out of sight, the turn demarcated by an abutment of flint. Beyond it, Boswell had said, was the final few feet of tunnel to the Library portals.

There was silence for a few moments, and then, briefly, a final roaring of rushing moles and warlike voices all of which came to an abrupt stop and once more did not materialise. A long silence followed, in which Tryfan hardly dared breathe. Then, beyond the tunnel turn there was the slightest movement, so slight indeed that it was evident only from a marginal change of the air current over their backs from the top of the tunnel.

Then there was the shuffle of timid talon on chalk. Then a sigh and cough, rather nervous. Then a muttering by mole, solitary mole, very solitary mole indeed, and a gulping sound as of timid, solitary, nervous mole summoning up courage to move down the tunnel towards them.

Tryfan began to move forward himself, so smoothly and with such grace that he was like a fox in the final moments of taking static prey. The shuffling head became bolder and a voice said, 'Better take a look old fellow. Come on, just round the corner. Just to check they've gone.'

Tryfan stopped still, only feet from the turn. The shuffling approached. They heard breathing, nervous and short. Then a humming as of a mole trying to make himself believe there is nothing to be afraid of.

Then round that flint came a whisker, then a snout. Rather a thin one, rather long.

Then the voice again, preceded by a sniffing and a snouting. 'Mole was here. I can smell mole. Good smell that. Gone now.'

Then the snout came forward again and beneath it a thin paw of weak talons. Tryfan had shrunk back into the wall of the tunnel to take advantage of the great flint's shadow. Boswell was further back, his already pale and now very dusty coat making him hard to see.

Then the mole's head and upper part of his body came into view, a weak-looking thin-looking mole doing his very best to be bold and resolute.

30

'Gone they have and good riddance. Up to no good. Bet they were scared.' Sniff sniff. 'But it's good to smell mole. Mmm. Wait! May come back! Gone but may return. Well, old fellow, you'd better do one more.'

The mole disappeared back around the corner, or at least his front half did, and there was a brief scratching of talons and, to Tryfan's astonishment, the threatening sound of an army of moles surged up again before suddenly dying away and the mole muttering irritably to himself: 'Oh bother, I've broken my talon!'

Tryfan advanced round the corner and saw the mole beside an extraordinary scribing on the wall, down which presumably he had dragged his talons and produced the sound.

'Greetings!' said Tryfan calmly.

'Oh!' cried out the mole. 'Oh!' And turning round saw Tryfan's large and menacing form and nearly tripped over himself in his alarm. Tryfan backed respectfully away and to his surprise the mole advanced upon him, crying out as boldly as he could, 'And well you might! Retreat! Get away before my many friends, who are *very* close behind me, come and kill you. Yes!' But Tryfan merely stopped, and immediately the mole did the same.

'Retreat!' he said again, a command no doubt meant to be threatening but which came out more like a mole choking on a dead worm. He gulped and stared along his thin snout at Tryfan and said, 'Whoever you are you're not coming past me. I've got a whole army of moles behind me. I'm their. . .' He looked down at his unwarlike paws and pale talons. '. . . er adviser. Take my advice and go away. Don't push me too hard for I am a killer! Yes indeed!'

'What is thy name?' asked Boswell from his more distant shadows.

'Oh!' and then, 'oh dear!' exclaimed the mole, turning and tripping over himself at this new threat. 'Two of you eh! Two against the many. Brave moles indeed!' He turned and looked back over his shoulder and shouted,

31

'Stay back, do not kill them! They are merely foolish wanderers and are retreating.' Then, turning his voice into a conspiratorial hiss, he said, 'I suggest you go while you can. The moles behind me are wretched killers, every one. Murderous.'

Boswell said, 'We are both of us well aware that there is nomole behind you. We come in reverence and friendship to the Holy Burrows.'

'A likely story, but this is as far as you come. Go away now, like the good harmless moles you appear to be.'

He managed a sickly smile, eyeing appraisingly Tryfan's huge shoulders and massive talons.

For reasons of his own Boswell stayed where he was.

'Well, we're not going,' said Tryfan, 'and we mean you no harm. So answer my friend's question: what is your name?'

'Courtesy demands you tell me yours first,' said the mole with as much bold dignity as he could muster, which was not much. And yet Tryfan began to see that there was about him a courage a mole should respect.

'My name is Tryfan and I am of Duncton Wood.'

'And whither are you bound?' asked the mole in the traditional way, speaking now less tensely. Tryfan noticed that he had a refined scholarly voice, and though it seemed nervous it was more a habit of speech than real, for the mole fixed him with a steady gaze.

'To here were we bound.'

'How long thy travel?'

'Six years our travel,' said Boswell from behind Tryfan. The mole looked at them. 'And *thy* name?'

But Boswell did not reply, nor appear yet from the shadow he was in.

'No, *thy* name, for you have mine,' said Tryfan firmly.

'Spindle, that's me,' said the mole. 'Yes, Spindle.' Repeating it rather doubtfully as if he did not quite believe in his own identity any more. He looked at Tryfan and settled down on to his paws.

'There aren't any moles behind you are there?' said Tryfan, just to make sure.

'No. Not one. You're the first moles I've seen in three years. Since Longest Night in fact. And a fine time you've chosen to come. Could have done with some help in January and February. Bit late now.'

'Impressive, that sound you made,' observed Tryfan.

'Yes indeed, those scribemoles knew a thing or two.'

'Knew?' said Boswell from the shadows.

'All gone now,' said Spindle. 'Gone to the Stone. Not one left. Didn't you see them? Murdered, everymole. Terrible. Can't move the bodies myself.'

'You've been moving something,' said Tryfan. 'We could see the tracks.'

'Books,' said Spindle. 'Those that are left. To safety. Before the grikes come back. Though whatmole can read them now I know not as all the scribemoles have gone.'

'No,' said Boswell with sudden authority. 'Not all gone. One or two are left.'

'Not so,' said Spindle firmly. 'The last were snouted moleyears back. You can still see their bodies on the pastures.' He added with sudden hope, '*Aren't* they the last then?'

Boswell came slowly out of the shadows and shook himself free of dust and grime. As it cleared they saw that his coat seemed yet whiter, and that there was about him, enhanced perhaps by the great sense of age and history of the burrows in which they stood, a power and holiness which nomole could deny.

Spindle got to his paws and backed a little in awe.

'Who art thou?' he asked, again in the old way. 'From where hast thou come?'

'We have come from Duncton, which is one of the Seven Systems,' replied Boswell. 'To Uffington have we been bound these many long and troubled years. I am myself of Uffington. I am a scribemole. My name is Boswell and we will do you no harm.'

Then Spindle simply stared at Boswell, all his feigned aggression gone and replaced by a look on his face of pathetic vulnerability as if, after many years of being brave, he had finally admitted that he was much afraid, and much alone. His mouth trembled and his eyes filled with tears, and then he lowered his snout into his front paws and began to sob with such sadness mingled with joyful relief that tears came to the eyes of Tryfan as well.

After a while, his face fur now quite wet with tears, Spindle looked up and tried to speak, eventually managing to say in a whispery broken voice, 'Are you really Boswell. *The* Boswell?'

Boswell nodded and smiled, and went forward and laid his paw on Spindle's paw, and then briefly caressed his face.

'I have heard of you many times,' said Spindle, regaining his composure a little. 'Oh yes, many, many times. And I have prayed that a mole such as you might still be alive, but I never thought, I never . . .' and once more his voice broke, and he wept.

'Well, now thy wait is over, good Spindle, and thy fear can be at an end,' said Boswell gently. 'Thy loneliness is no more and it will never return.'

Tryfan listened in silence, for Boswell spoke with power and respect and the gentleness of one who heals another.

Poor Spindle, who had been so determined a moment ago to defend the Library against them, now seemed to lack the courage even to look into Boswell's eyes.

'This is a mole of very great courage and strength,' Boswell whispered to Tryfan. 'We are well met and the Stone's will is done.' And in that moment, with Boswell's voice powerful about them, Tryfan knew that somehow the task he was to be given was inextricably bound up with Spindle, and so he too went forward and touched paws with him, as if only by touching might all three affirm that they were really together and well met.

Spindle finally said, 'You see I have waited for your coming, though I did not imagine it would be Boswell himself who would come. I said – ' And there was still a slight sob in his voice. – 'I said to the Stone after the scribemoles were killed or snouted, "I'm asking you to

34

send me help. You promise to do that and I'll stay and do what I can." '

'What did the Stone say?' asked Boswell.

'Not a lot,' said Spindle so naturally that Tryfan wanted to laugh and cry at the same time in sympathy. 'Nothing to tell the truth. Dead silence in fact.'

'So why did you stay?'

'Nowhere else to go. I'm a mole from the south side of Uffington and we used to serve the scribemoles. Most of my system perished with the plague and the few who survived that were killed by the grikes. Nomole left to tell me what to do. And anyway. . .' He looked up for the first time. '. . . I knew the Stone was listening though there was silence. I knew somemole would come. I trusted the Stone to do things right,' he said simply. 'And here you are! Better late than never!'

'I think you have much to tell us, Spindle, and there is no better place to tell us than in the ancient Library. So lead us there and on the way show my young friend Tryfan how you made the sound of an army of moles.'

Spindle rose up again and led them back the way he had come. As he passed a curious carving in the tunnel wall he rasped his talons over its indentations and around them the sound of mole started, an army of moles, paws a-marching.

'Clever, eh?' he said.

'Er, yes,' Tryfan had to agree.

'Scared the living daylights out of me first time I discovered it,' said Spindle shortly. 'They call it dark sound. All the moles of old could make such scribing, and we have the classic text on the subject, and that's survived at least.'

'Scribed by Scirpus,' said Boswell.

Spindle nodded quickly and continued down the last part of the passage and passed through a rounded and unimpressive entrance into a great and magnificent burrow which stretched right and left and straight ahead as far as the eye could see. Here and there, with no regularity at all, its chalky roof was supported by great black flints. There were shelves, row on row of them, but they were empty and broken, and on the floor of the burrow, wildly scattered about except in a few areas where Spindle himself had cleared up the mess, were the fragments and parts of broken bark books and records, scrolls and folios. The great Library of the Holy Burrows had been desecrated and destroyed.

'Not a lot to see,' said Spindle. 'The grikes did much damage. Dear me, yes they did.' Then with a sigh walked aimlessly back and forth quite bereft of words.

Boswell took all this in quickly, touched a few remnants that lay nearby, and then turned to Spindle.

'You had better tell us what happened,' he said.

'That's a tale and a half,' said Spindle.

'Then there's no better place to tell it than here and one day, perhaps, Spindle, the words you speak will be scribed in their turn,' he said, looking meaningfully at Tryfan. 'So tell of it well and of your part in it, and with truth. Let it run its natural course.'

'That I will!' said Spindle, responding to Boswell's instruction. 'From my heart to thy heart I tell it, truth by truth as I saw it and may it one day be known to all moles.'

With which he settled down amidst the debris. Then, with a final look about them as if to confirm that they were indeed alive and he was not alone in the Holy Burrows anymore, he took a deep breath, scratched himself once or twice, peered here and there for inspiration, and then began to tell them of the disaster that had overtaken Uffington of which he, Spindle, who never thought he was much of a mole at all, was the sole living survivor.

Chapter Three

'Of Seven Barrows am I, which is one of the systems on the southern side of Uffington and has long provided moles as worm-finders, tunnel-makers and clerics to service the scribemoles,' began Spindle.

'My mother had to send one of us up to Uffington the June before last Longest Night and, as I was not much of a one for fighting or defence she sent the weakest – me!' He peered at his paws and shrugged his thin shoulders apologetically.

'I was put into the service of the scribemole Brevis who was new to the Burrows. His only question was whether or not I had faith in the Stone.'

'And your reply?' asked Boswell.

'I said I had,' said Spindle quietly, with a look of absolute faith in his eyes, and gentleness, too. 'I was born in the shadow of the Holy Burrows and there are many Stones about the downland of Seven Barrows. As a youngster I used to hide from my siblings among them. They protected me and I knew their strength. I know the Stone exists.'

Spindle spoke these words fervently. Boswell nodded encouragingly and looked at Tryfan, who saw he was well pleased with the answer.

'My master Brevis had only recently completed his novitiate and been ordained a scribemole, and I was pleased to be put with one of the newer members of the community. Not that he was especially young, however, for he had come to his vocation late in life and had made his own way from Buckland, a system to the north of Uffington. But he soon became a good scribe and scholar, his paw being a fair one, and he was kind enough to teach me a little of scribing so that I might help him in the

37

Library – something other scribemoles rather frowned on. But though I could not read well, nor fully scribe, I could scriven notes for him and find texts as well, and this was to come in useful after the grikes had done their terrible work.

'So, as well as I could, I did what I was asked to do and though others were better than I he never complained nor harried me. As summer advanced I grew to like my new place and the tasks I was set, which were varied and involved travelling about Uffington on Brevis' business. Being naturally curious, especially about the way the tunnels were made – for they were much grander than those I was brought up in – I got to know them well. This knowledge, and the fact that of all moles there I was attached to Brevis, later saved my life.'

Sprindle paused briefly and he sighed. The tale he was telling was clearly burdensome to him and revived memories of a mole whom he had grown to respect and perhaps love – a feeling Tryfan understood from his own time with Boswell – but which he had been able to forget in his long isolation these past moleyears. Then he settled down again and began to tell of how news of the grikes first reached Uffington, and of their subsequent arrival, and the brutal destruction they wrought.

* * * * * * * *

The earliest rumours of the coming trouble reached Uffington in August, when travelling moles from the systems to the north arrived and confirmed what had followed in the wake of the plagues that had troubled moledom for many years: the coming of a new terror in the shape of grike moles.

The plagues themselves had caused division in Uffington, some scribemoles saying that their most ancient task was to heal, and that allmole would benefit if the scribemoles were seen to be fearlessly going out to bring help and preach the Stone's Silence. But others, and they were the more dominant, said the role of the Holy Burrows was to set an example by prayer and learning; the plagues were, surely, a punishment for moledom's loss of belief and faith in the Stone over the past decades. The scribemoles need do nothing; the Stone would decide the future.

Spindle's master Brevis was one of the spokesmoles for the former group and argued for scribemoles going forth and doing healing work –but the final word was with Medlar, the Holy Mole, who had aged in recent moleyears and in that hour of crisis erred to caution and non-action. So, along with the heat of that summer, dissension, uncertainty and a fatal paralysis came to Uffington.

Then, in August, there began to come to the Holy Burrows ominous stories that missionary moles of the long disregarded Word were rapidly spreading from the north in the wake of the plagues and were now within reach of Uffington itself. Three of the seven Ancient Systems – Caer Caradoc, Stonehenge and Rollright – had already been taken over and the scribemoles in the Burrows began to feel that they were gradually being surrounded.

These invading moles were called 'grikes', though what the derivation of this name was, none at Uffington, not even the oldest scholars, was able to establish. All that was known, from the ancient reports, was that the original grikes were dark of fur and snout, clever, lithe of body and strong. They had little humour but much self-confidence, the frightening confidence of moles who know they are right, and were inclined to talk calmly but forcefully. If provoked they did not hesitate for one minute to fight, and to claim as they did so that right must be on their side.

Grikes, it seemed, were not believers in the Stone and despised those who were. They were, rather, followers of the 'Word' and it was their duty to preach the Word, to convert moles to it, and to make Stone-believers see the folly of their ways, however it had to be done.

The Word was not unknown to Uffington. Although its disciples evidently believed that it was of divine origin, scholars in the Holy Burrows had established decades before that the Word was the work of a corrupt and evil scribemole of early medieval times whose name was Scirpus. From a system in the north had he come, a young, unlettered mole driven by faith in the Stone to make his way alone to Uffington. There had he learned scribing, and become a great scholar whose commentary on the early Treatise of Dark Sound remains a classic of its kind. But his interest in this dark side of the Stone had deepened and become obsessive, and his work had lingered too long in the Stone's shadows and the darkness that surrounds its light. Scirpus, the records showed, grew impatient and disenchanted with the existing teachings at Uffington, and, claiming revelation and enlightenment he scribed the infamous Book of the Word. This strange, obscure text, which expounded a mixture of dark love and ominous prophecy, was essentially one long blasphemy against the Stone. It claimed that the Word came first and would be last; that the sound of Silence was dark sound; that moles must atone in blood if they are to be saved of the Word; that to deny the Word is to deny Truth and should be punishable; that it is the first duty of moles to teach the Word for the good of moles; that the Word is the Truth.

His position at the Holy Burrows unfortunately gained considerable credibility by the actions of the eccentric Holy Mole of that period, Dunbar. Until Scirpus' emergence as the author of his own evil Book, Dunbar had been an exemplary scribemole of great achievement and courage. He had travelled far and wide, but had himself come to Uffington from the north as Scirpus had, and this perhaps gave them a common sympathy.

In the weeks after Scirpus presented his Book of the Word to the Library and invited other scribemoles to read and comment on it, Dunbar remained silent, despite the storm of anger and acrimony the Book immediately created among other scribes. Contemporary reports make clear that Dunbar never gave his full approval of the Book, but he did not demand that Scirpus be forced to withdraw it, saying only (to quote a historian of that troubled period), 'Cum broders, by the pawe him tak, for dirk and drublie hertes need loffe. Yef youe doo nat then so shall I! Fro this youre lackelufingnesse cums alle our trublie now and I will staye namore but traveyle fro hir.' And when, much shocked – for Holy Moles, once appointed, had never left Uffington before, and Dunbar's unique decision to leave is one of the great mysteries of the Holy Burrows – his colleagues asked him where he would go, he said he would go with Scirpus, to debate more with him, and if he did not prevail on him to change his views he would be 'nought and nowhedyr' – be nothing and go nowhere.

He was as good as his word, and when Scirpus left, the venerable Dunbar went with him, disputing questions of Dark Sound and the Word all the while. Naturally the decision of so revered a Holy Mole to leave encouraged other moles to follow him, and some scribes and many eager young novices went as well.

Contemporary accounts, based on the reports of a scribemole who had gone with the original party but who later left it and after a number of moleyears returned to the Holy Burrows and did penance, say that they took with them copies of the Book of the Word and the Scirpuscan commentary on the Treatise of Dark Sound. It seems that the party stayed together as far as the Rollright System, which is to the north of Duncton Wood. Scirpus had by then won many of those who had gone with Dunbar over to the way of the Word: there was a dispute, a fight, and only by the loyalty of moles close to Dunbar did the old mole escape. In the confusion the single scribemole who subsequently got back to Uffington escaped as well, but he was soon parted from Dunbar and on his own.

The mystery of where the Holy Mole and the pawful of moles with him subsequently went was not solved until some centuries later, when more adventurous generations of scribes established from place-name evidence and oral stories that Dunbar, or a mole remarkably similar to him, travelled eastwards, in the direction of what story-telling moles fancifully call the 'Empty Quarter', but whose proper name is the 'Wen' which in Old Mole means a malignant growth on the flank of a body, or the side of a tree. A growth that has a life of its own, and drains the life from that on which it grows. Malignant, parasitic . . . and odiferous, for when it breaks, the smell of a wen was believed to be fatally poisonous to mole.

To the east, it was said, such a place existed, where nomole could live because the noise, the dangers, the very air itself was unpalatable and dangerous to mole. There, it was said, twofoots and other great vile creatures roamed of whom the many grim tales were the stuff of which a young mole's nightmares are made; and it was the home of the roaring owls.

'But where is it *exactly*?' a youngster might ask his parent, looking fearfully over his shoulder (for such fears always lie behind a mole in the shadows outside a snouting's range).

But the answer was clearer than that: to the east of the most easterly of the Seven Systems, which is Duncton Wood, a mole gets progressively nearer the Wen, but he had best never get anywhere near where it actually starts. . . Which was answer enough.

It was towards this supposed place that, much later, travelling scribemoles, bravely reporting on the state of moledom, established that Dunbar had travelled, and probably taken with him a copy of the Book of the Word. Certainly enough records were left behind in the eastern systems to trace his route, until at last specific record of him was lost, replaced instead by stories and legends that he had gone ever more eastwards and was lost for all time in the darkness there. Of his final end, or that of his followers, none knew, but few doubt that it was terrible and grim, and that the fatal Book he carried, and the knowledge he and his few followers had, was forever lost as well.

Why he took the Book of the Word with him, or whether he took any other book, is never told in the legends of Dunbar, though it is hinted at in the most

42

famous of them, which suggests that somewhere in the heart of the Wen he hoped that the infamous Book would be kept until 'the schism is complete and ended'. And when that happened a mole would come forth from the Wen who would bring peace to moledom, and a sacred knowledge, and a hope for all moles.

So Dunbar went from history, to remain only in memory as a mole who established a race of mythical Wen moles, beings who live in a place that nomole can reach, far to the east, where to breathe the air is death for a mole. Of course there are many legends of the Wen, and the notion that special moles survive there is a common one, as, too, is the idea that one day, from such a place, a great saviour will come at a time when the shadows are long and dark over moledom and he is most needed. Whatever the truth of that, the legend concerning Dunbar was right to talk of a schism, for many date the beginning of the decline of the faith in the Stone in moledom from the Scirpuscan revolt and Dunbar's strange departure from Uffington.

Indeed, something is known of the fate of Scirpus, that most dark of moles. After the split from Dunbar he trekked northward, back towards the system from which he came, and so charismatic was his leadership that many joined him. His trek north became a march, which many joined, and he led them to a place which lies beyond the Dark Peak and the inhospitable moors where nomole had lived. Yet there Scirpus brought his followers, a place of enormous tunnels and rushing water, and dangers uncharted. It had no name, but in time moles gave it one after the mythical evil system of legend and story, where malevolent giant moles were said to roam: the System of Whern.

It was there that Scirpus developed the first Scirpuscan Community, and it became notorious for its harsh discipline and punishment. There he first tried out ideas later incorporated into the set of principles (which he later called a Rule, the Rule of the Word) by which systems should be ordered, establishing clear hierarchies (which are anathema to faith in the Stone) and punishment to death for transgressions of the Rule – such punishments as snouting which no true believer in the Stone could even contemplate practising.

There, so it was said, Scirpus scribed anew his Book, but adding to it dark prophecies which forecast the end of the Stone and the ascendancy of the Word. Trouble would come, and strife, doubt and argument; then fear and a final decline of faith in the Stone. Plague would come, Uffington would be destroyed and then moles would Atone at last, and under the direction of a great leader the Word would be the saving of moledom.

So scribed Scirpus, and through the decades the memory of him waxed and waned. From time to time followers of Scirpus emerged from the north, usually in the wake of periodic plague, claiming the hour of the Word had come. Some for a time ran their own systems as Scirpuscans, where the dark arts of the Stone were said to be practised, and where the Word was preached. Scribemoles had over the generations bravely investigated the Scirpuscan movement in the north –'bravely' because many did not come back – and in the time of the Blessed Arnold of Avebury, one of the longest serving Holy Moles, a successful war was waged against them. They were routed from their new systems and driven back to the very edge of Whern itself, and up into its bleak and wormless heights. Whether or not any survived, none knew for none dared follow them, and whether they reached the notorious system of Whern again, if such existed, none knew either.

Nor did there seem need to know, for Scirpus and his followers were forgotten in the centuries that followed. So much so that, when the Stone did go into decline, few remembered the dark prophecies. Nor did many connect the coming of the plagues with any chronology of doom for moledom. Moles in danger of their lives, their systems in collapse, do not dwell long on memories of a sinister medieval scholar, and a Book all copies of which were thought to have vanished long ago.

So when stories of the grikes came at last to an already enfeebled Uffington, none there immediately associated them with Scirpus, even when it was said that these grikes preached the Word.

But then, at the end of that August, there came to Uffington two direct accounts of the methods these northern missionaries were using – one from a devout female of the Lovell system, which lies north of the Thames; a second from a youngster who, somehow or other, had reached the Holy Burrows, and who came from Buckland, the system of Spindle's master Brevis.

Both moles reported that the grikes massacred any who did not agree to follow the Word, and even though, out of fear, moles agreed to do so, many were terrorised or given 'Atonements' which involved physical abuse.

When the grikes had come to Buckland, they had killed many moles, forced others to convert to the Word, and then driven the few braver moles who refused to concur with the Word up the slopes above Buckland to Harrowdown, a small adjacent system known for its devotion to the Stone.

There, on the pretext of some ultimate transgression, the grikes snouted all the moles, using the barbs of the wires that surrounded Harrowdown Copse. The youngster managed to hide and then escape, making for the distant Holy Burrows as the only possible sanctuary he could trust. But his memory of the sight and sound of such horror left him in such fright and despair that he shook constantly, and could not be left alone. He died three weeks after reaching the Holy Burrows.

Naturally the scribemoles were distressed at these stories, but none more so than Brevis. He and six others decided to defy the edict of Medlar and set out to investigate what was happening, each travelling to a different system. They agreed to return before the end of September and then prepare a report for the Holy Mole on what they had found. In the event, only one of them was ever heard of again, and that was Brevis. . . .

But before that, while Brevis was still away and before the full significance of the grike rumours was really understood at Uffington, two travelling moles arrived at the Holy Burrows whose coming was more ominous than could ever have seemed possible at the time.

According to Spindle's account, they gave false names on arrival, and the unsuspecting scribemoles, welcoming anymole who might give them information about what was going on in the outside world, accepted them rather too readily. Historians since then have added the fanciful report that the Blowing Stone sounded deep warning notes on their arrival, though Spindle did not remember such a thing. But it might well have done, for those moles that came to Uffington were none other than Weed, agent and adviser to the highest grike leadership; and the female Sleekit, as cunning, scheming and askew a mole as ever lived below ground, or on its surface.

The two claimed to be on a Stone pilgrimage and to have travelled from a system some way to the north. The Holy Mole saw them and was impressed by them. Weed already had some scribing, though of a crude kind, which he said had been taught in their system more than a generation before by a scribemole of Uffington who had come there and died in it. Yet one or two of the scribemoles were doubtful of them, and Spindle overheard them expressing concern about Weed's script which had deviations of an unfamiliar and sinister kind which they did not like. What these were Spindle himself could not properly know, not being a scribemole, but he afterwards remembered, when he had to handle some of Weed's work and his talons ran over it, there was a certain cruelty in the style, a leftward slant, a hint, even, of dark sound.

Of the two, Weed, as moles later knew him to be, was the dominant. Physically he was not immediately striking, being of average build and having motley fur. His snout curved a little to the left, which gave anymole talking to him the feeling that he was turning all the time. He smiled a lot, and his eyes seemed warm unless a mole could catch them unawares (which was very difficult) and see that when he was not engaged with another mole, and thought he was quite alone, they were as dark and cold as pure flint. A curious thing about him was this: when he ate worms there was not a single sound – not a crunch, not a suck, not a lick. One moment the worm was there, pink and succulent, next thing that worm was gone.

But the most disconcerting thing about Weed, which all moles who got to know him reported on, was that it was hard, however much a mole might suspect him of evil and duplicity, not to like him. Those eyes, though cold, had intelligence, even humour, and he had a quick wit and winning way and, as fast as another mole might think, Weed gave the impression without saying or doing very much, that he thought faster, and knew more.

When Weed wanted a mole to talk – and Weed was a mole who positively thrived on information, gossip and rumour – he would say 'Yes?' in a way that was difficult, if not quite impossible, not to answer without giving more away.

'This way here, now that's the Lower Route, yes?' he might typically have asked – for he had a great desire to know all the routes and ways into and out of the Holy Burrows, which moles more worldlywise than the scribemoles of Medlar's time might well have recognised as reconnaissance.

'Yes?'

Why yes of course it was, *that* one the side route, and *that* one the middle lower route and and and . . . and then, when the poor questioned mole thought he had completely finished and had nothing more to say at all, Weed would wait until the silence got embarrassing and then say, 'Ye. . .es?' and somehow a mole could not help adding more, even things he had forgotten he knew, just to fill up that unbearable silence on the far side of which Weed waited, his eyes so pleasant.

Sleekit was a different kind of mole and as a female her admission into the Holy Burrows caused some consternation. There were precedents, however, for travelling females accompanied by a male were allowed to stay in the visitors' burrows, and even, if the Holy Mole was willing, permitted to view some of the communal burrows and meeting places.

Sleekit was the kind of female whose elegance of fur and carriage, and annoying calmness of voice, was such that other females are intimidated by her while males, impressed by an outward show, tended to be struck speechless or fawning in her presence. Other wiser moles might have seen beyond her elegance to the strange mix of coldness and vulnerability it sought to hide. She was sharp of tongue, and clever, and moles watched what they said in her presence. Her real role – one of the select sideem of the grikes, watchers and schemers and spies – could not possibly have been guessed at the time she arrived in Uffington. But the scribemoles, with the exception of a few of the more worldly ones, were so impressed by her good looks and her seeming interest in what they did that they almost fell over themselves to inform her of their ways and the work they did; and well, very well, did she mask her true intent, which was to complement the information that Weed was gathering about what texts they had, where they were kept, and what the scribemoles' routine was.

Yet where Sleekit went, discord among males always followed, especially among celibate males such as scribe-moles. The older they were the worse it became, for there was something about the way Sleekit came close to them, looking so vulnerable and innocent, that stirred in them feelings and produced actions which they themselves, jostling in a rivalrous kind of way for her attention, might have called fraternal, or avuncular, or possibly paternal, but which, in truth, went beyond the acceptable bounds of all three.

Insidiously, like the spread of rotten root disease beneath a raft of mat-grass, the divisions and ructions in Uffington that preceded Brevis' departure, seemed to deepen with the arrival of Weed and Sleekit.

Not that any mole then saw that they caused it – indeed, none would have guessed it. For were not the newcomers most ardent in their worship of the Stone, and most respectful (especially that young and most caringly intelligent female), and willing to learn?

Were they not also charitable and balanced in their views on the invasive grikes, suggesting that, after all, the stories had been exaggerated and the grikes were a lot better than they seemed? The rumours were unkind and unfair. The grikes were hospitable and learned and lived by a code which, if other moles abided by it, was just and probably sensible for the rougher and more dangerous systems they came from. What was more, they seemed to have evolved a way of dealing with the plague based on strict observance of worship and cleanliness . . . All of which was just what the scribemoles wished to hear, assuaging as it did their doubts about what was going on in moledom, and giving support to the prevailing view that the grikes were not a real threat at all and scribemoles were best advised to do nothing. So, unknowingly, the scribemoles allowed two leading grikes into their midst, a spying sojourn broken only when suddenly, unexpectedly and dramatically, Brevis returned.

It was in the middle of September, and he came up the slopes from the north, tired, badly cut about with talonthrusts, and looking as if he had aged a cycle of seasons. Yet he insisted on an immediate audience with the Holy Mole himself. In the course of it he not only gave the most dire warnings of the grikes, and much evidence of their ruthless cruelty, but learned, to his horror, of the fact that two strange moles had been admitted into the Holy Burrows . . . moles whom he was able immediately to identify from hearsay as Weed and Sideem Sleekit.

But too late: Weed and Sleekit had gone, leaving grim evidence of the urgency of their departure. A cleric, Fawn, and a scribemole, Weld, were found dead on the westside, as cleanly talon-thrust to death as moles might be. Murder expertly done. They must, surmised Brevis,

49

have become suspicious and tried to stop the two fleeing grikes. Yet even faced by this evidence, the scribemoles led by Medlar would not act, for was there not some other explanation possible, and might the two not have been killed by other moles, unknown?

'No!' declared Brevis.

'It is possible!' said the intellectual scribemoles, unwilling to believe that their judgements could be so wrong, and therefore to admit that preparations for defence might now be wise. So, in that prevarication, the fate of the scribemoles of Uffington, and perhaps of the Holy Burrows themselves, came to be sealed.

Yet the story that Brevis had to report was stark and to the point. The grikes had crossed the Thames to the north of Uffington and were rapidly taking over all the adjacent systems to it. It was easy for them to do so since most of the systems had been decimated by the plague.

Whether or not they had used gentler methods of argument and persuasion to convert systems earlier in their campaigns he did not know, but their strength had become so great that they proceeded now with speed, efficiency and brutality. Most moles in a system were so cowed by moleyears of privation and disease that they did not argue when the grikes arrived, and those that did and refused to subject themselves to Atonement and Instruction in the Word were systematically starved, terrorised, broken and re-educated. The few that stood up to such treatment were snouted publicly or, in some cases where conditions were right, drowned by enforced burrowing in mud. In each case a system's takeover was prefaced by some random snoutings, as if to show everymole that the grikes meant business.

Brevis reported that the grikes were well-organised and disciplined. There was a system of guardmoles, elders and eldrenes – female elders. Their method was to take over a larger system and herd the remnants of smaller systems into it. Since almost every system had plague dead who had been left to rot where they died and their tunnels sealed off, the grikes had a policy of clearance carried out by 'clearers', usually diseased, demented or vagrant moles ostracised and feared by others. These lived apart in 'congregations' and cleared out a system by taking corpses to the surface. The grikes used clearing as a punishment, knowing that many clearers soon died of plague or developed other diseases.

Brevis, who, at great risk to himself, had infiltrated his home system of Buckland, and had even begun to receive instruction in the Word, had succeeded in establishing what the aims of the grikes were in coming to Uffington: nothing less than the destruction of faith in the Stone.

And if Uffington had indeed unwittingly played host to grikes like Weed and Sleekit it was important that they did something *now* warned Brevis. Invasion was probably imminent. . . .

But incredibly, the ever-cautious Medlar insisted on a written report before elder scribemoles could consider what action to take . . . and only Spindle knew the full depth of Brevis' anguish. To leave the Holy Burrows in defiance of the Holy Mole was one thing – indeed, Boswell himself had done it on occasion – but to lobby for action before an elder meeting and against a Holy Mole's clear directive was another. So for two days and nights Brevis worked to scribe his report.

Spindle later remembered the near desperation with which Brevis laboured, knowing that each extra moment that he took was another moment lost, each extra minute and each hour . . . and in the only brief time he took off, he had warned – indeed *ordered* – Spindle that if the grikes came he was to flee immediately, and if he was caught he must, however much he disliked doing so, pretend to reject faith in the Stone and accept the Word.

The warning was just in time, and Brevis' great fears fully justified. Up the northern slopes they came, across the western heights, through the eastward tunnels, by way of the southern vales; dark they were and silent, ferocious in their assault, efficient in their attack, ruthless in their

51

killing. Few questions, little mercy, and their purposes quite clear: to find the original Book of the Word that was believed to be still in the Holy Burrows, to trace a mole called Boswell, and to so decimate Uffington that it could be a place of reverence no more.

They used two poor tortured scribemoles to identify the other moles in their effort to find Boswell, moles who were reluctant at first to name their brothers but who did so when their eyes and ears and genitals were pierced with talons until those two screamed out that they might be put to death, so great was their pain and suffering. Oh yes, they were put to death all right: for those were the two who, so much later, Boswell and Tryfan had found hanging in a snouted death upon the barbed wire on the surface.

A few, including Brevis and Spindle, escaped the first attack. Spindle was soon separated from the others, caught, and, when it was discovered he was not a scribemole yet knew the tunnels well, he was spared. As for Brevis and the others, they were undoubtedly caught and killed, for Spindle heard it braggingly spoken of by the grikes, of how the escapees had been found near the Blowing Stone and there savaged to death and left for owl fodder. (A fact which, sadly, Spindle was later to confirm, for he saw what remained of the bodies themselves, though so broken and eaten were they by then that he could not recognise them individually.)

But that was later. First Spindle and other clerics had to suffer the scrutiny and cruelty of the grikes, as they interrogated them all, killing some quite arbitrarily. Spindle himself pretended to simplicity and a willingness to believe in the Word, and he was spared. He was asked many questions about the Library and the location of other libraries if such existed. He knew of none and gave little away. Again and again he and other clerics were asked to look at the bodies and see if they could see the mole Boswell – and it took a long time before the grikes were convinced that long ago Boswell had left for Duncton

Wood and had not been heard of for many a moleyear. The grikes were not forthcoming about why they wanted to find Boswell, but it was clear they wanted him alive.

They seemed concerned, too, to find the copy of the Book of the Word which the Library was supposed to contain, but none knew of it, and it was not found. They seemed uninterested in anything else, for they were brutish, unsophisticated moles, intent only on killing.

Yet a few days later, reported Spindle, other more senior moles arrived at the Holy Burrows, among them Weed himself and Sleekit, and others Spindle did not know or even see. These, it seemed, were displeased by the extent of the destruction of the Library and ordered recriminatory punishment. Weed's personal guardmoles killed several of the grikes who had led the attack on Uffington. It seemed that Weed felt there might have been some purpose in keeping the Library intact.

When those days of death and anarchy were over, the grikes, and the few clerics remaining alive, left Uffington to travel south-westward to Avebury. This they targeted as the next ancient system they had to take, leaving Siabod to the far west and Duncton to the east. Their intention, as Spindle discovered it, was to use Avebury as the centre from which to consolidate their gains in the west and then to return to Uffington for the Spring Solstice and ensure its final demise by celebrating dark rituals there before leaving it to a final abandonment.

Whether the two remaining ancient systems of Siabod and Duncton Wood had been taken by the time Boswell and Tryfan reached Uffington, Spindle had no idea. But he had little doubt that in time they would be, unless a leader could be found among the believers in the Stone who could rally support and resistance among those who still had faith.

* * * * * * *

This was Spindle's terrible tale and when he had finished it he crouched in silence. Boswell had explained some of the import of what he had said but Tryfan, until now, had stayed silent, listening.

'But your own escape,' he asked at last. 'How did that happen?'

Spindle grinned. 'My apparent weakness and insignificance has advantages, one of which is that guardmoles and others do not think I will even try to escape. What is more, I knew these tunnels and those at Seven Barrows well, and it is possible, when large numbers of moles are on the move, to go unnoticed. So, quietly and I think unseen (for none came in pursuit), I left them.'

'What did you do when they had gone?'

'For days I did nothing,' said Spindle, his voice barely a whisper as he re-lived the shock of what he had seen. 'There were one or two other survivors but they spoke not to me, nor I to them. Then they were gone. But I . . . I know not. I could only think to worship the Stone and, just as I did when I was a pup, I went down to the Stones near my home system of Seven Barrows and they gave me sanctuary. I asked for guidance. I passed Longest Night alone. I spoke what invocations I could and then I knew what I must do. Was I not a cleric of the Holy Burrows, was not my task there?'

He stared at them both and they saw in his eyes the terrible courage he must have needed to do what he then did. Alone, afraid, without hope, he went back into the tunnels of Uffington and made his way past more tortured death than anymole should ever see, and reached the Library.

'What did you there?' asked Boswell gently.

'I began to gather what whole books remained and took them, one by one, down to Seven Barrows and there I have hid them lest the grikes destroy more on their return . . . and then, you see, I had . . . I had . . .' But he stopped and despite pressing from Tryfan would not say what he had been going to. Instead he continued, 'It has taken me all these moleyears to do this task and I have done my best. Often have I prayed to the Stone for help, but when vagrants have come by I have not trusted them. You are the first . . . but you are too late! The Spring Solstice is almost on us and I fear the grikes will soon be back. This journey today was to have been my last, for there is not much more left that is complete. But when I heard you I thought . . . that you . . . I feared.'

'And yet you sought to defend the Library by yourself,' said Tryfan with considerable respect in his voice.

'It was my task,' said Spindle.

'But there was more, was there not?' said Boswell strangely.

'I don't know what you mean!' said Spindle rather too quickly and looking much afraid.

'You were going to talk of it just now,' said Boswell gently, 'but fear stopped you.'

'I – I – ' whispered Spindle, his flanks trembling, his eyes wild with fear and dread.

'You need not have been afraid of us,' said Tryfan.

'It isn't you,' said Spindle, his voice almost hysterical now. 'It isn't you, it's them. I can't. Not again. I can't. . . .'

Then Boswell smiled and touched Spindle once more, and took his paws, and as the Library filled with peace and light Tryfan remembered Boswell's words when they had first met Spindle. 'This is a mole of very great courage and strength.' And he remembered, too, the sense he had had that his own life would be bound up with Spindle's and as Spindle had trembled so now did Tryfan, for he felt his real task was beginning, and that it was great and difficult, and he might not have the strength or faith for it.

'You have not told us all, have you Spindle?' said Boswell, his wise old eyes intense upon poor Spindle, who, for his reply, could only bleakly shake his head.

'Not all,' he whispered.

'Tell us,' said Boswell.

'I – I – ' began Spindle once more, his suffering almost palpable about them.

'He said I mustn't tell anymole, not anymole at all, not until . . . I mustn't, I mustn't, I mustn't!' And as his voice rose towards hysteria again – as if by shouting repetition

he might drown out Boswell's query, and even his gaze –
Boswell reached his paw under the fold of skin beneath his
flank and slowly took out the Stillstone he carried there
and placed it on the ground among the three of them.

Tryfan, who had not seen the Stillstone since Boswell
had taken it up from beneath the Duncton Stone so many
moleyears before, gazed on it in awe. For his part, Spindle
seemed struck speechless with fright, but it was clear that
he knew what it was. But to any other mole watching, their
response might at first have seemed strange, for the stone
was nothing at all, barely more than a pebble, smooth in
parts, rough in others.

But then from it there began to emanate a light, and
then around it a sound of such beauty that a mole who had
faith would know he was hearing, or beginning to hear,
the sound of Silence.

'Take it up again!' cried out Tryfan.

'Hide it!' said Spindle.

But Boswell only looked from one to another, as if – as
Tryfan already feared – they were both involved in
whatever it was that Spindle was so reluctant to talk about.
Then Boswell turned his gaze on the frightened mole and
said in a voice that seemed to vibrate down the tunnels of
history, and beyond them to an undecided and uncertain
future yet to come, a voice of awesome power, 'Thy task is
great, Spindle, and in time thy name will be honoured for
what thou hast already done, and still must seek to do. But
now thy own long agony of struggle and loneliness is truly
over, your burden will be shared and taken on by others
beyond the realm of Uffington, to those who must choose
for themselves if moledom is to be a place of darkness and
dark sound, or Silence and light.

'So now, brave Spindle, most worthy mole, tell us what
it was you really saved.'

For a moment more Spindle said nothing as the light of
the Stillstone of Silence played around them. Then he
whispered, 'Take it up again, Boswell, only thou must see
it, hide it from us . . .' and Boswell did so. Spindle turned

56

to Tryfan, as if it was to Tryfan that he had to answer the question, and said, 'I would rather show you than tell you.'

'Then show us,' Tryfan found himself saying, as if he was in charge, and old Boswell, whose disciple and protector he had been for so long, was moving aside for him to be master now.

'I shall,' said Spindle, 'yes, yes, I shall . . .' and there was relief in his voice as, the light of the Stillstone fading around them, the cleric mole turned from the ruined Library asking them to follow him, that he might show them what it was that he had saved.

Chapter Four

The journey to Seven Barrows was long and tortuous, and all underground. Spindle led them in silence most of the way, only talking to give them directions round some difficult obstruction, or over awkward roots.

After an initial run of rising tunnels, the route was gently downhill, running with the dip of the chalk and retaining for a while that same airiness and majesty of light which characterised the tunnels in the heart of the Holy Burrows. Then they changed as the chalk dipped away beneath them and they continued on into the darker, moister overlay of clay with flints. In places they passed beneath woodland, for the tunnels were bounded by the roots of gnarled oak and beech, and the roots carried down into the tunnels that same windsound of the cold north wind which, it seemed to Tryfan, he had been battling against for long years past.

They had set out in late afternoon, just as a murky dusk had begun to fall, and when darkness came two hours later they stopped. Spindle found them food, which they ate in tired silence, and then they slept, the wind a dull roar overhead. When dawn came, and as the tunnels began to fill with light, they groomed, ate some food, and then set off once more.

Boswell chose to take up the rear, and though the pace was quite fast he seemed to have no trouble keeping up with them. Every time Tryfan looked round protectively to check he was all right, Boswell was limping steadily along just a little way behind, nodding and smiling at them to continue as they were. Of the three of them, he seemed the least worried and most relaxed.

Spindle went steadily on, and it seemed extraordinary to Tryfan that so paltry looking a mole had managed to carry books from the Library along a difficult route like this day after day, all by himself and without much hope that the task would be successful. It was obvious that Spindle had qualities of strength and endurance along with his obvious intelligence and resourcefulness which made him a mole worth knowing. But more than that, thought Tryfan, who had seen so few moles these past years, he liked him: there might be something comic about Spindle's awkward, slightly nervous gait, but he was likeable, and in his own serious way a caring mole.

This feeling of liking and respect mingled now with growing curiosity as to what it was that Spindle was going to reveal to them, a curiosity the greater because Tryfan sensed that Boswell himself in some way already suspected what it was. At the same time, as the tunnels moved once more into a rising strata of chalk, though of a more friable kind than that which caps Uffington Hill, there came to Tryfan the strong feeling that they were now moving towards a Stone, for the ground had that nearly imperceptible vibration or hum which a Stone always gives it. Then Spindle stopped, and Tryfan saw that the tunnel forked to right and left.

'Down there,' explained Spindle pointing leftward, 'leads to the system of Seven Barrows itself; this way leads to the Stones.' His face was suddenly clear of worry and doubt, and he looked like a mole who was glad to be on his home ground once more, among familiar tunnels that bring back memories in which, for better or worse, his security lies.

'Shall I tell you what happened? Now? Here?' he asked Boswell doubtfully.

'You decide,' said Boswell, who did not seem much interested. Ever since they had met Spindle, Boswell seemed to prefer the two of them to make decisions, as if he desired that what happened should remain beyond his control or influence: it was for Tryfan and Spindle to make their own minds up about what they did, where they went, and what their tasks might be.

'Well,' began Spindle hesitantly, 'maybe it would be best . . . Yes! I shall show you the Stones first and then I'll show you . . . yes that's best.'

He turned into the right-paw tunnel, went along it for a while and then took a slip route up to the surface to a sight that Tryfan never afterwards forgot. For the early morning had advanced just far enough to bring the day to that point of change when the long reaches of night were forgotten, and the dawn is past, but the light of the sun is bright enough only to hint at the beauty in the grass and trees that the full light of day will bring. Indeed, its light among the dewdrops gives the sense that the best, the very best, is yet to come.

But there was about that particular morning far more. For though a chill north wind still blew, now, after so very long, there was the hint that spring was nearby, not far over the horizon, and it quickened a mole's heart to know it, and made him desirous to stretch the chill of the winter out of his shoulders and flanks, and to shake the lingering cold from his paws and snout, and think of the good things to come as March ends and April begins, bringing with it the yet warmer promise of the month of May to come.

So each in his own way snouted joyfully up at the sky, where for a time that morning streaks of blue ran beyond the driving clouds, and they peered this way and that as if, very, very soon now, they sensed they would see the world anew.

It was only after this pleasant and promising interlude was over that Tryfan began to take in the scene about him, and see how fine and splendid it was. The more so that good Spindle, quite overcome, it seemed, to be in a favourite place of his with moles he trusted, was humming to himself a wormful song and seemed for the time being to have quite forgotten the object of their journey.

Tryfan saw that they were halfway up the slope of a southward-dipping vale whose lines were gentle curves, subtle and aged. Near and far rose Stones, not in any obvious order of circle or line, but spread out across the vale, here and there, like friends that have paused awhile on a common journey to contemplate a springtime view. The Stones, big and small, many fallen and a few erect, stretched away as far as the eye could see.

The colours were, for now, March-dull: the bare earth brown or shining grey where wet chalk stained it. The grassy places were still dominated by the dried-out stalks of the previous autumn, while the distant copses of trees, still leafless, were dark and rather ominous. But below them, where a stream ran, was a line of greener grass, but that was all. No sound, no life but for the wheeling of rooks darkly on the grey horizon, and the grey-white flutter of black-headed seagull over a distant field. And. . . .

'What is it, Tryfan?' asked Spindle, using Tryfan's name for the first time, and coming close, as one who trusts another will.

Tryfan's head was tilted a little on one side as if trying to hear again something he thought he might have heard before.

'I thought it was the call of lapwing,' he said quietly. 'The last time I heard that was a full cycle of seasons ago over the Pastures alongside Duncton Wood! Now that's a sound that heralds spring!'

'It does!' said Spindle. 'That and the lark which rises over the chalk and drives a mole mad if he's not got his paws on the ground and in a good mood!' The two moles laughed, shared laughter, and Boswell, behind them, was glad to see them together, and to feel in his old bones the energy they had, and the promise they felt. And he whispered an invocation for them that they might find courage and true purpose in the days and months to come, and trust each other.

Tryfan and Spindle, flank to flank, did not notice him at all, but instead looked excitedly about them, for spring was imminent in the air, still just beyond reach, but *there*, near, coming: and this bitter wind would stop.

The two wandered, chatting a little, out over the

surface, leaving Boswell in the protection of the tunnel entrance while Spindle pointed out the features of the place. There were a few taller standing Stones among the many there, but most were small, like a scatter of scree or debris across the lovely curving vales and hills, running east and west, north and south, fields on fields of sarsen stones. Most strange, most wonderful. In places there were shallow pits in which tiny stones seemed to have collected and no grass grew. In other places the sarsen stones peeped out of the soil, like the tip or flank of giant buried Stones. While here and there, near and far, rose the Stones themselves, guardians of those slopes and vales. It made a mole want to wander forever among them, and wander awhile they did, passing among the fallen smaller stones, and staring up in reverence at one of the bigger ones still standing.

'Oh! There you are, Boswell!' Tryfan said more than once, for Boswell, having been left behind, seemed to have caught them up again and even been waiting ahead of them. More than once that happened! Boswell watching over them, content.

'What a strange place this is,' said Tryfan, 'a mole loses all sense of direction. I could have sworn you were behind us Boswell . . .' But Boswell was gone, and only Spindle was there, oblivious it seemed of these confusions. Or used to them, more like. But eventually, one way or another, they all joined up together again and took a stance out of the wind. The early promise of the morning had died a little, the distant streaks of blue sky had gone, the north wind was freshening again. Spring was going to bide its time a little more.

'What is this place called?' asked Tryfan.

'I don't think it has a name. When I was barely more than a pup I came to this place alone, and rarely saw another mole,' said Spindle quietly. 'I would explore the ways among the Stones and sometimes go into the tunnels that moles of Seven Barrows delved long ago but no longer use. They are wormless now, and ruined, but they still give a mole shelter from rain or curious kestrel.'

'How many Stones are there here?' asked Tryfan.

'Nomole knows or will ever know,' said Spindle. 'Not for want of trying to find out though! I've started counting them many times but a mole grows tired . . . too many here! Too many to count!'

'But the standing Stones,' said Tryfan. 'Surely those you could count.'

'That's what I thought,' said Spindle, 'and I can tell you how many there *aren't*. Not less than six no more than seven!'

' "Not less than six nor more than seven?" ' repeated Tryfan, his face puzzled. 'You mean there's either six or seven?'

'Yes I do mean that,' said Spindle.

'Well, which is it?' said Tryfan.

'Come and see for yourself,' said Spindle with the weary patience of a mole familiar with a problem which he knows another is going to find impossible to solve.

He led them underground, through tunnels ruined indeed, for many of the chambers were open to the skies, or had fallen in and a mole had to climb out on to the surface for a time before picking up the tunnel's line again. They soon came to the buried flanks of one of the standing Stones, the one Tryfan presumed they had already passed, judging from the direction in which they approached it. Then another – the green rust-yellow side of the sarsen stone familiar to Tryfan from the Duncton Stone. And a third, its sides rising high above them before the roof closed in, and the tunnel curving away around its edge so that a mole going round it, as they did, could not quite work out its subterranean dimensions or shape.

'How many so far?' asked Spindle.

'Why, three of course,' said Tryfan.

'Perhaps,' said Spindle strangely.

So they progressed through more tunnels, the next two Stones being further afield and the route they took confusing, for they crossed and recrossed themselves more than once.

63

'Must be a better way of visiting each of them underground than this,' grumbled Tryfan.

'Must there?' said Spindle.

Each of the bases of the Stones was quite distinct, in colour or shape, and each had a tunnel that went right round them and then onwards, though never straight on but, rather, at a swinging angle that made it hard for a mole to judge quite where he was relative to the others.

Finally they had visited the base of seven Stones and touched each one, feeling its humming height rise above them up through the soil and on towards the sky, sentinels to the faith of moles, emblems and harbingers of Silence. Spindle brought them back out on to the surface.

'So,' said Tryfan as they took a route to the surface, 'seven in all. Why not say so immediately? No point in making a mystery where there is none!'

'Yes, I quite agree,' said Spindle, 'except that . . . er . . . well. See for yourself!'

They had surfaced through some gravelly soil and now found themselves some way to the west of where they had first gone underground, with the standing Stones at varying distances all around them.

'There you are,' said Tryfan easily, 'one, two, three . . .' But his voice began to falter. 'Four, five, six . . .' he concluded, turning around again and staring at each of the Stones in succession. 'Well I've made a mistake that's all. There were seven, weren't there?'

'Underground there were,' said Spindle. 'But, here, on the surface, one's gone missing.'

'That's ridiculous,' said Tryfan impatiently. 'Look. One, two, three . . .' but however many times he counted them, and from whichever direction he started, and even when he went here and there checking what he saw and *even* (finally) when he went underground once more to count them subterraneously again, he could not find the seventh Stone on the surface, nor work out which of the seven underground ones was 'missing'.

When he was tired, confused and ill-tempered and had

rejoined the other two (who had long since crouched quietly to munch worms), Boswell looked uneasily about them, and spoke almost for the first time that morning.

'Perhaps now is the time for you to tell us what more you know, Spindle,' he said.

The wind about them stirred and seemed troubled and urgent, the day more cloudy above, the air sharper once more, and there were slight spits of rain in the air. Then Spindle began to tell them.

* * * * * * *

It was in the middle of the attack by the grikes on the Holy Burrows when, in spite of every effort he and his master Brevis could make, the two of them became separated. Faced by an onrush of grikes, Spindle had turned down a tunnel and run, and found that Brevis was no longer with him.

But in what Brevis must have realised might be a final separation, the scribemole had thrust something into Spindle's paws. He only looked at it a little time later when, finding himself in some nomole's land of quiet in the assault on Uffington, he found he was carrying the report Brevis had been scribing. It seemed to him then that nothing could be more important than that he did not allow it to fall into grike paws, and so, harried and chased and in danger of his life, there seem to have been born in Spindle, but a humble cleric, the conviction that he must save what texts he could from the Library itself, and not just the one he found himself carrying. Knowing the tunnels as he did, he was able to make a cautious way towards the Library through tunnels filled with mayhem and slaughter. Somehow, miraculously as it seemed to him, he reached it, and found it so far intact. There were a couple of elderly scholars posted at the portal protecting it and when they saw him they allowed him in. Shortly afterwards grikes approached and the scribemoles ordered him to retreat into the deeper recesses of the Library. It was then he heard dark sound for the first time, for the guardians of the Library must have used their talons on the defensive scribing by the portal which was later to confuse Tryfan for a time.

But the ruse worked only for a short time and the grikes charged in, and Spindle saw, from where he was hidden, the killing of the two moles and the terrible destruction of the Library as more grikes came in and began to pull down the Rolls and break the ancient bark books of Uffington.

Spindle knew that he would soon be found, and had no doubt that he would be killed. Yet even then, driven by an impulse he did not understand, he sought to hide the text Brevis had entrusted him with by burying it in a dusty shadowed corner of the Library.

The grikes did not seem to suspect that other moles might be in the Library and so did not set about searching its nooks and corners, or its darker recesses, preferring instead to systematically work their way along its shelves, embayment by embayment, destroying all they saw.

So Spindle was able to work undisturbed as he burrowed deep and put first Brevis's text and then other ancient texts into the hole he made. In this way he had managed to hide nine or ten of the most ancient-looking books he could find before the grikes, perhaps hearing his movements, became suspicious and began searching for him.

He might then have been found, but their attention was diverted by the arrival of a few scribemoles making a belated and futile attempt to save the treasures that their forebears had protected for so long. During this brief diversion Spindle was able to bring down a wall adjacent to a stack of books and bury them as well, if not completely at least enough to make it look as if they were not worth digging out again merely to destroy them.

So, bravely, unable to escape, Spindle did what he could to save the books of the Holy Burrows knowing all the time that the outcome of his actions would probably be his own death.

Soon the grikes put down the scribemole counterattack and turned back to finding him and now, mortally afraid, poor Spindle retreated into ever-more obscure corners of that great Library, clambering among the shelves, scurrying between walls, desperate, in what he believed to be his final moments, to put off death a few moments more.

But to no avail. A shadow loomed behind him, he turned to face it, and two grikes were bearing down upon him, their shouts murderous and frightening. It was in that moment, as their talons raised upon high, ready to come down on the shadowy movement which was all they could see of him – for that part of the Library was dark indeed – that Spindle felt a paw at his flank, and heard a voice. A gentle paw, a gentle voice, yet strong, very sure, more certain and safe than anything he had ever known, such that he felt what he afterwards could only describe as the sense of coming back to his home burrow, where no harm could befall him.

That voice said, 'Spindle of Seven Barrows there is something more for you to save than these old texts. Now come, come with me . . .' and he turned and he saw a mole about whom such light shone that he was dazzled at its brightness, and felt that he was nothing before it. Behind him, as if at a great distance, he heard the grikes confused and in disarray, shouting that they had seen a mole but lost him and making recriminations against each other.

Then he saw the face of the mole who had touched him, the eyes shining with love of mole. They were the eyes of a female who seemed young, barely more than a pup, and yet in her presence he felt safe and unafraid.

She took him, as it seemed, even further into the corner into which he had retreated, and from there to a chamber in which lay, in no particular order, six books. And on each was placed a stone, small and seemingly inconsequential. And in that chamber was a light and a sound more beautiful than any he had ever seen or heard, and that young female was everywhere it seemed.

'You will take the Books, Spindle, and you will hide them where they will be safe, with all the others that you find and collect. You will hide them so that future generations may find them, which they will. These stones you will take as well, but throw them amongst the pits by Seven Barrows, where all moles may see them but only moles who are ready will know what they see. There they will be safe until the time is right that they be taken up at last.'

'But what books are they? And what stones?' he managed to ask.

And she laughed, a laugh of such pleasure and joy that Spindle, even when he became very old, never forgot it, and ever desired to hear it again.

'It is better that you know not their names, or what they mean. Your task is hard enough without that, good Spindle.'

'How will I know where to take them?' he asked.

'You'll know, you'll know. . .' she said, laughing again.

'Well,' he declared, seeming to recover himself a little so that his normal curiosity got the better of him, 'if those stones are what I think they are then there should one day be seven of them, for aren't they the Stillstones the scribemoles have always guarded?'

'Perhaps they are!' said the young mole playfully.

'And those the Books for each one?' he added.

'More than likely,' she said.

He peered more closely at them, and she did not stop him, and then he ran his clerical paw – trembling no doubt – over them but the script was medieval and beyond his kenning.

'When shall I start to remove them?' he asked.

'Whenever you like, provided you can avoid the moles of darkness on your way.'

'Well if they are the Books and Stillstones I think they are then there's one I'd prefer to carry first, and that's the Book of Fighting! It'll protect me, won't it?'

'In a way it will. But your faith in the Stone will protect you more. Good luck, Spindle, worthy mole! Good luck!'

'But – but you – will *you* come back?' he had asked finally, fearing her departure.

'Oh yes,' he remembered her saying, 'yes, for you I shall . . .' and she was gone, and her light and beauty with her, and he found himself crouched in the Library, and a grike ordering him up.

'Little bastard,' said the grike, in the charming language that they used, 'come with me *now* . . .' and he was dragged out of the Library and before another grike who had at his side a broken, pathetic, tortured scribemole Spindle knew. And this creature simply shook his head and whispered, 'He's Spindle, he's a cleric, he's not . . . he knows nothing, nothing . . .' And so Spindle's life was saved.

Yet there was more to that moment than that. For as the scribemole said, 'He knows nothing . . .' he raised his agonised gaze to look in Spindle's eyes and even as Spindle knew that he *did* know something, something important indeed, something that was the most important thing there was to know in the Holy Burrows, he knew that the broken scribemole saw it too, and was glad that his suffering was not in vain, and the Stone's will might yet be done.

After that Spindle remembered little, but that he was harshly interrogated and eventually, along with others, taken south-westwards from Uffington at the beginning of a trek to Avebury. It was then he escaped, made his way to the Seven Barrows, and wandered about for days, perhaps weeks, among the Stones that had given him sanctuary when he was a young mole. But whatever else he might have forgotten he did not forget the young mole who had found him in the Library, and revealed the Books and the Stillstones, nor the task she had given him.

So it was that Spindle of Seven Barrows, a mole who was 'not much of one for fighting or defence', began his great task of carrying, without help or encouragement from anymole, in an isolation impossible to imagine, among burrows haunted by memory and death, those books he could salvage from moledom's greatest Library, and most onerously of all, six of the seven great Books, and all but

69

the last of the Stillstones whose secret place he had been shown.

Through those long and tortuous tunnels from Uffington to the Stones of Seven Barrows he carried them, starting in November and continuing for four moleyears through to the following March. Whatever mole it was had come to him, whatever it was she had shown him, it was not a dream or a vision: the Books were there, and the Stillstones, terrible for a mole to contemplate, nearly impossible to carry. Seven Stillstones, seven Books made, all but one have come to ground . . . and then the names of the Stillstones, one by one . . . of Earth for living, of Suffering, of Fighting, of Darkness, of Healing, of Light. . . .

These six, one by one, good Spindle had to carry to safety before the grikes came back, and with them the Books. And so he had, each one seeming a greater burden than the last, and with the dreadful fourth one, of Darkness, he all but succumbed to its might, but the light of his great faith carried him through.

Down to the Stones he took them, hiding the Books in a chamber of his own finding, and hurling the Stillstones out on to the surface among other stones, so doing as the young mole whose name he did not know had told him. Until early in March his task was finished, and he slept and wandered in utter fatigue for many days. Then a new energy came to him and, knowing the Spring Solstice was coming, he spent a final few days searching the Library and taking what last significant fragments and folios he could, and hiding them where he had hidden the Books.

'And where is that? Are you going to show us?' asked Tryfan at the end of Spindle's strange story.

'Of course I am. I can't go through the rest of my life being the only one who knows, and if I can't trust a White Mole and his disciple who can I trust?' said Spindle.

With which he took them back underground, in and around and among the tunnels they had been through before and by others they had not noticed, until down there somewhere, deep across that legendary vale, in a place that only moles of faith and courage will find, Spindle led them to a chamber lined with stone, made by twofoots in the centuries before mole memory, and showed them the result of his courage and long industry.

There were eighty-seven complete books and a further sixty major fragments. As he could not read scribing very well, Spindle had little idea what he was rescuing, but he had tended to go for older books which he could recognise by the colour of the bark and the style of scribing.

Boswell stared at the great array of books – carefully ranged and stacked, and went to them and touched them. Many were the treasures there, including a number of the historic Rolls of the Systems, which are the accounts of travelling scribemoles of the different systems they visited and reported on.

But most important of all there were the six Books, scribed at different times, starting with the oldest of all, which is the Book of Earth, and scribed, it is said, by Linden, who had loved Ballagan, first mole, whose talon strikes upon the very Stone of Stones had made the chips which are the seven Stillstones.

Boswell looked briefly at the six Books, touching them lightly, and inviting Tryfan to do the same, that he might know the feel of these Books, each written in a different age, by moles – White Moles – who had reached enlightenment.

All there but the last Book, the Book of Silence. And Tryfan saying nothing, for he knew that in their final moments, before the Silence took them, his parents Bracken and Rebecca, had given not only the seventh Stillstone to Boswell, but the Book of Silence, or its secret, as well. They had understood that he was the mole who would scribe it.

Now Boswell crouched before the six Books, his snout low, and his flanks pale and worn.

'Will you scribe the last Book?' asked Tryfan boldly. 'Will you, Boswell?'

'Each of the Books marks a stage in the maturing of mole,' replied Boswell, 'and many moles have had to struggle to make such moments possible. Now the last Stillstone is nearly come to ground, as the ancient text puts it, and already the Book of Silence is being scribed. I have been scribing it a long time, Tryfan, such a long time.'

'But I haven't seen you scribe, except for teaching me, in all the years of our journey to Uffington.'

'Haven't you?' said Boswell. 'Well, I have been, and for a long time before that. Yes, yes, a long time now. I hope that one day you'll know it.'

There was silence among them and they contemplated Spindle's great work of rescue. Then Tryfan asked Spindle, 'Where did you hide the Stillstones?'

'I didn't hide them,' said Spindle, 'I did what that youngster told me and put them with ordinary – '

'But where?' said Tryfan urgently.

'Well . . . er . . . it's hard . . . you see. . . .'

'You haven't forgotten!' said Tryfan, appalled.

'I don't think I ever knew, as a matter of fact,' said Spindle defensively. Then, turning from the chamber and leading them once more to the surface, he waved the talons of his right paw somewhat vaguely over the slopes and vales of Seven Barrows.

'I brought the first Stillstone up here and thought I *would* try to put it somewhere where I could find it and I *thought* I had – well I threw it in a stonepit and watched it carefully but I couldn't exactly be sure that the one I thought it was *was* the one it had been . . . so then when I brought the second Stillstone, and it's no good looking so disapproving, Tryfan, because the Stillstones aren't exactly fun to carry even if they are small and I doubt *very* much if you would have done better even if you are stronger than me because there's something about them that weighs down a mole. So anyway . . . I got the second one and took it to the same stonepit except that I wasn't sure by then if that had been the one I threw the first one in . . . and by the third I was utterly confused, and by the

72

fourth, which was no joke at all being the Stillstone of Darkness, all I wanted to do was get rid of the thing and I can't remember much at all about the last ones. . .' He tailed off.

'Well, it sounds a bit pathetic to me. You're sure you don't know exactly where they are?' said Tryfan suspiciously. But Spindle gave him such a look of hurt honesty that Tryfan apologised and then fell silent.

'All I do know,' said Spindle finally, 'is that each of the Stillstones went in a pit near one of the six Stones, which has an obvious kind of logic, I suppose. It's the sort of thing the Stone would make a mole do!' He laughed, a little ruefully.

'Well!' said Tryfan, exasperated. 'Well!' And turning to Boswell he looked at him for some kind of support, or comment, but Boswell gave none, but instead scratched himself, hummed an annoyingly cheerful tune quite out of keeping with the sombreness of the occasion, and then found some food and ate it.

'Sleep seems to be in order,' he said. And, settling his snout along his wrinkled paws, he closed his eyes and started to snore.

And Tryfan and Spindle eventually settled themselves in companionable proximity, and lay staring at the fall of night, listening to the eternal north wind, their minds racing with all they had been talking about.

★ ★ ★ ★ ★ ★ ★

'By the way, Spindle,' said Boswell, who woke bright and early the following day, 'do you happen to know if Brevis named the leader of the grikes in that report of his?'

'Yes he did. But anyway he told me,' said Spindle. 'I know the name of the leader whom the others obey to the death and believe to be the mole Scirpus prophesied would come back to lead the Word to final victory over the Stone.' A look of fear and dread crossed Spindle's face.

'Well, what's he called?' asked Tryfan.

'Oh, it's not a male. The grike leader is a female,' said

73

Spindle. 'And I saw her, too, just once. She was . . . she. . . .'

'Well?' said Boswell.

'Dark. Strong looking. Her eyes . . . were . . . fierce. I saw her, just for a moment. I shouldn't have done, I know that. She was darkly – um – ' He looked down at his paws with embarrassment.

'Yes?' prompted Tryfan.

'Beautiful,' said Spindle. 'I mean she . . . she did not look evil. And yet there is something about her to make a mole afraid. Oh yes, terribly afraid. But she was – '

' "Beautiful",' mimicked Tryfan. 'Sounds to me you find all females beautiful. Probably haven't seen enough of them.'

'And her name?' said Boswell cutting across Tryfan's remark.

Even as Spindle said it, Tryfan had the strange and frightening feeling that Boswell already knew it, and had known it all – all of this terror and destruction – and there was in his eyes, and about his whole stance, a sense of expectation, as if time had turned to a point he, Boswell, White Mole, had long waited for.

'Her name,' whispered Spindle, as if merely uttering it would bring the walls of the chamber crashing down upon them. 'Her name is Henbane.'

The very name seemed to call forth a hush of dread in the chamber they were in. With some difficulty Tryfan turned to Boswell and said, 'You look as if that was a name you expected to hear? Do you know of this Henbane?' He tried to sound calm and yet was filled with a nameless dread that turned his stomach and seemed to leave a dark singing in his ears.

Boswell stared at each of them in turn.

'Yes, I know of her. A long time ago your father Bracken fought with a mole who had taken over Duncton Wood. An evil mole, and a mole of more power than Bracken could have known. His name is Rune.'

'*Is* Rune?' said Tryfan, surprised. 'But did not Rune

perish over the high cliff to the eastside of the Ancient System on Duncton Hill?'

'I said,' repeated Boswell, his white fur curiously filled with light, 'that Rune was a mole of power. More than power: he is a mole who is a Master of Dark Sound. He survives, as I survive, beyond due years. He has his task as I have mine.'

'And what of this Rune?' said Tryfan, trying to appear indifferent to the claims of evil power in a mole he thought his own father had destroyed.

'Henbane is Rune's daughter,' said Boswell quietly.

'Rune's daughter?' repeated Tryfan, aghast. 'And of what system is she?'

'Oh, I know *that*,' said Spindle. 'Henbane is of Whern.'

'But – ' began Tryfan horrified, for he had thought Whern was only a dark place of legend, not real, not extant.

But even as he began to react to Spindle's extraordinary claim that a leader from Whern had been to the Holy Burrows themselves, the tunnel was filled with the distant drumming of paws, as of many moles travelling out on the surface – confident moles, strong moles, moles filled with zeal and led with power.

Tryfan's natural protectiveness immediately took over, and, ordering the other two to stay still and quiet, he went out on to the surface to see what he could.

Moles. Many of them. Advancing among the Stones steadily and with dark purpose. Not searching, nor tunnelling, but heading back north the way they had come: heading for Uffington. The grikes had returned to the scene of their cruellest destruction.

Tryfan went below ground and looked at Spindle and Boswell. No words were spoken, nor needed to be: as the drumming of pawsteps continued for minute after minute and hour after hour, they knew that the Spring Solstice was on them, and the hour of a bloody Atonement had come.

Chapter Five

They stayed close and silent in the chamber, fearful of being discovered, but as dusk fell it became obvious that the grikes were on the march, and not searching for enemies.

Tryfan went up again to see what he could observe and the other two soon followed. The initial drumming of confident pawsteps had thinned, and they could see why. The first wave of moles must have been grike guardmoles, but now there were other moles, captive moles, pitiful moles. The ill, the weak, the aged, the defiant . . . in groups they came, herded and bullied along by grikes who seemed never happier than when giving commands, never more delighted than when drawing blood with their talons. Time and again Tryfan saw these wretched moles raise weary and frightened eyes, and heard more than one say, 'That must be it, that's Uffington.'

But they spoke not with hope or delight, as such moles would once have spoken, but with fear and dread, and Tryfan guessed that they knew, or had been told, that at Uffington they would suffer and perhaps die. They had a role to play, and a terrible one, for it was ritualistic and sacrificial, and they were its forfeits.

It was hard to gauge their numbers and Tryfan soon gave up trying, but certainly there were many of them, more moles together than any of them had ever seen.

'More than likely they've gathered others to their numbers,' said Tryfan, 'and will be moving on from here to Buckland, as your master Brevis suggested in his report. Well, for now, this is as good a place to stay as any. We're more likely to be seen moving than staying still.'

'Is there nothing we can do?' said Spindle.

'Nothing that won't get us killed,' said Tryfan firmly.

'The Stone will find its own way of dealing with these grikes, and if it includes me in its scheme I shall be well pleased!'

'What are we going to do when they've gone?' asked Spindle, looking worried.

'Get Boswell to safety,' said Tryfan, speaking almost as if Boswell was not there.

Boswell had settled down and was examining his worn talons and toothing them clean, first this way and then that, as calm as ever in a crisis in which he could do nothing.

'Humph!' was all he observed as the other two discussed his safety.

But when darkness fell, and the pawfalls above petered out and were replaced by a strengthening wind, he said suddenly, 'Is there a moon up, and if so what is it?'

Tryfan went to look.

'High,' he said. 'The Solstice will very soon be on us. Tomorrow or the next day. Hard to make out the moon clearly, but the light's enough to see the nearest Stone.'

'We're nearly finished here then,' said Boswell, sounding pleased. 'Very nearly now, Tryfan.' And the way he looked at Tryfan, with compassion and with love, sent a pang through the young mole's heart, and the premonition he had of a future separated from Boswell came back to him.

'We'll get you to safety,' he said hunching his shoulders aggressively. 'When it's safe we'll leave southwards, away from Uffington, away from the grikes.'

'No Tryfan, we will not. Your future lies northwards. And yours, Spindle, yours too. Now sleep both of you and I will wake you when the time is ripe. Soon now, very soon . . .' And his voice was soothing and sleep-making, and the two moles, tired from the grim excitements and discoveries of the past few days, slipped into slumber, the one weak-looking, scholastic and physically uncertain; the other powerful and sure, his fur good and his face maturing now into that of a mole who might in time be a leader of moles of the Stone.

Unseen, Boswell watched over them, his eyes kindly and concerned, and a silence came to their refuge, deep and good. At last, when the two moles were asleep, Boswell whispered prayers and invocations, and quietly left them to go out on the surface.

The moon, which had been masked earlier, was clear now, but occasionally high cloud drifted across it, too thin to obscure it, but making a halo that seemed to encircle the sky above where Boswell crouched.

About him the stonefields stretched out dark in the night, but the taller standing Stones caught the moon's light, their sides pale and green and rising against the sky and stars. Grass stirred softly and was still; then stirred again.

Far below, near where the river ran in the darkened vale, an owl shrieked briefly, and another answered it, far away. There was movement in the grass across the vale, and then it was gone, and Boswell sighed. Far, far away, slowly, a roaring owl crossed the vale in the night, its eyes bright for a moment before it turned away, its gaze sweeping some trees, then shining for a moment towards the sky before the gaze and the moan of its call was gone. Grass stirred nearby again.

'Mole,' he whispered, and then, more softly still, 'Mole. Yes, yes, mole. Your time is come.' And the moon's light was on old Boswell, and his fur was white.

He turned, and limped back as if he carried a great burden, and then he reached the burrow leading to the chamber and went below; while on the surface the Stones seemed hushed and reverent, turned in a way towards the place where he had been. The wind veered, whispered change, and from somewhere near or far, there was laughter of mole, young and joyful and. . . .

. . . And Spindle stirred. Turned in his sleep, snouted up as if some dream was waking him and then stretched out again as Tryfan, the stronger in waking, moved closer to him in the sleeping, and seemed more protected by Spindle than his protector. And then, when they were still

78

again, Boswell took out the seventh Stillstone and laid it on the chamber floor before them and its light came and was on them all.

'Tryfan! Spindle! Wake now, wake.'

They woke as if they had never been asleep, and looked in awe at the Stillstone, and at Boswell who was beyond it staring at them.

'The time is come,' said Boswell simply. 'Now Tryfan, take up the Stillstone. You, good Spindle, follow me now, and attend us.' With that Boswell left the chamber.

Panic gripped Tryfan and he stared speechless at the Stone, and then at Spindle.

'You must,' said Spindle, 'you must do as I did. Think of the Stone and reach out your paw, think. . . .'

'Come on, Spindle, Tryfan must make his own way now!' called out Boswell, and premonition became terrible certainty in Tryfan: he was going to be separated from Boswell, lost to him as he had been lost to Duncton Wood. Then Tryfan settled his paws on the ground, as he had been taught, and stared at the Stillstone, as Boswell had taught him to stare at many things, and the panic quietened and was nothing, and the sadness too, and he was still.

Tryfan of Duncton took up the Stillstone and, though he gasped with a kind of pain at the touch of it, burdened suddenly, and old, and staring after the others as they went out on to the surface and wondering where he would find the strength to follow them, yet he did so, thinking of nothing more than the Stone, and the Silence beyond it.

As he began to climb up out of the chamber towards the surface, the Stillstone was like a cloud of knowing on him; but of a knowledge that seemed too great for mortal mole to bear for it reached up to the stars, and down into the earth, and along, tunnel by tunnel, system by system, to embrace all moles, and more than moles. It was knowledge of suffering and knowledge of love, and it tore at Tryfan's body and his heart, filling it with jagged light and

79

pain, and he wanted to cast it from himself for it was too much, too great; and yet it was too precious for him to want to cast off, or even to turn from. So that his eyes filled with wonder, as if he could see a beauty of Silence about him, yet his body was weighed down, and his paws shaking, and his snout humble. So, racked, breaking yet exalting, Tryfan of Duncton reached the surface and sought out where Boswell and Spindle had gone. They turned to look back at him and seemed a great distance away, and white, shining white, figures in a moonlit world of rising Stones and night landscapes.

'Come, Tryfan, come now for time is short,' said a voice which he supposed was Boswell's, though the old mole seemed disconnected from the words. Then other sound, building like the billowing of clouds above, storm clouds perhaps, yes yes yes, dark they were, sound that grew louder and he could not bear it. The mounting sound of Silence.

'Boswell!' he cried, 'I can't – '

'You must!' said Boswell. 'Of all moles, you must.'

'Where?' asked Tryfan, for there was somewhere where the Stillstone could rest, he could rest, he could find peace and not this resounding Silence in which he felt so isolated and lost, so wonderstruck and fearful that he would lose it, the thing that caused him suffering and bliss.

'Think of the Stone,' said Spindle like a parent to a pup.

Stone. There. Somewhere. The seventh Stillstone and Tryfan held it from him and dared to look at it and into its light and for a moment he was still and heard the Silence as if he were part of it, and it was his own.

Then its enormity came in on him again, and was too much for him to bear, and he ran past them, across the surface in the night past one Stone and then the next and on, now here now there, huge movement in the night as in a dance of seasons, and past the third Stone and the fourth. His body was of the Silence now, large perhaps, small, he neither knew nor cared, he was running unseeing but knowing, sure now.

Past the fifth and on hugely to the sixth and laughing, dancing, the great moon swinging to the Solstice point as he turned and called out, 'See the seventh Stone!'

Then Tryfan of Duncton stood in the moonshadow of the seventh Stone which neither he nor Spindle had been able to see before, and which was not there now but for moles that could see, and he turned and raised his paw, and high towards a pit of smaller stones he threw the Stillstone, an arcing crescent in the night, over the moon perhaps, among the stars and then down to the ground before them, the sound of Silence falling, somewhere. Many moles saw that moment as a shooting light in the sky, many that, in time, Tryfan and Spindle would meet. Some were moles of the Word, and they would meet them soon indeed. But others were moles of the Stone, humble moles, moles beset by doubt and loss, and they saw that seventh Stillstone light that night of the March Solstice and their pulse quickened, and in their hearts was born the hope that change was coming, good change, for which perhaps they might be needed, however weak, insignificant or oppressed they seemed. Then the light was gone leaving only a memory in the night sky, and wondering moles with a secret in their hearts.

While at Seven Barrows Spindle cried; watched the Stillstone arc and cried out, 'There!' His talon pointed to where it fell.

Somewhere there, just before them, it was done, the Stillstone gone to ground. And dark returned.

But moments later a dull, deep moan that rose quickly to a mighty roar came from a little to the north, carried on that too-familiar bitter breeze: the sound of many moles, dark moles, dark sound. Then Tryfan and Spindle instinctively came close, each protective of the other, and above them, the shadow of the seventh Stone cast beyond him across the grass and towards where the Stillstone lay, Boswell, White Mole, great mole, awesome and commanding in his strength.

'Tell of this night,' said Boswell. 'Scribe of it that

allmole may know that here the Stillstones lie, waiting, for there are the chosen generations and the time is come for them again. Scribe of it, saying that all moles may seek the Stillstones and they may take them up if they have the strength.'

'Will there be such moles?' whispered Tryfan, for he felt the weight of the Stillstone of Silence upon him yet.

Boswell nodded. 'The first always find it hardest, as you have, Tryfan and Spindle, for the hardest thing is having faith to do what has not yet been done. So, a first pawstep is hard, and a first hello; a first healing is difficult and a first fight. Over the centuries moles found and carried the Stillstones to Uffington. Now you two have brought them finally to ground. Others will take up the burden you carried the easier for knowing that you carried it.'

'And where will they take the Stones?' wondered Spindle, frowning, for he liked to find a problem and ponder its solution.

Boswell smiled, his eyes alight with love and care for each of them.

'They will take them to a system where a mole is,' he said, 'a mole whose laughter and joy you have heard, Spindle.'

Then Spindle's eyes opened in wonder, and he lifted his snout a little as if to scent out such a wondrous system, and the moon shone on it, and caught his fur. He remembered the young female in the library.

'But where is that system?' asked Tryfan. 'Is it the Wen? Is it Whern? Or is it far afield like Siabod?'

'Lead moles to the Stone as I have taught you and you will find it, Tryfan. Tell them of the Silence, teach them to have courage in the face of darkness and doubt, lead them wisely and with love, prepare them for the coming of one who will cry out from the Silence that they might hear it as you have.'

'The Stonemole?' whispered Spindle, who knew the legends well enough.

Boswell nodded, weary now.

'Is that the mole I saw?'

Boswell's eyes lightened for a moment and he said, 'Oh no, no, I think she was not the Stonemole. She was – she was . . .' and Spindle leaned closer, for there was a yearning in him to know the answer.

Boswell stirred restlessly, beset suddenly by other concerns, but then some desire in him too took his attention back to the waiting Spindle, and his eyes softened once more. 'She was the hope of Mole, of all of us, and she will come, Spindle, and then others will know what to do, moles, ordinary moles, and they will know always that the Silence may be theirs. Yes! Always! And then I. . . .'

'What will you do then, Boswell?' asked Tryfan, and he came forward and touched Boswell, for the White Mole was weary and tired, and sad too. 'What, Boswell?'

Boswell smiled ruefully. 'Don't know. Not sure. Old fool. Foolish fool. I – ' but Boswell did not look old. As he wept suddenly, and Tryfan held him in his strong young paws, it seemed to Tryfan that he held a pup beneath the stars, and a pup that was lost. He sensed that in this moment his future lay.

Then the surface was touched by distant and ominous vibration and the strange moment passed as Boswell turned sharply from Tryfan, his tears gone, and said, 'Now we must leave. The grikes are searching for us.'

'We *must* go southward now,' said Tryfan.

Boswell shook his head and pointed a talon northward, towards Uffington.

'Your way, like your enemy, lies there, Tryfan, and you must take it.'

'But . . .' began Tryfan.

Boswell laid a paw on his and said, 'You brought me safely to Uffington, now I must show you "both the safe way from it and set you on your path. No "buts" Tryfan, no doubts, Spindle, the Solstice has come, the Stillstones are placed and now the difficult dawning begins, but each of you is prepared as best you ever can be for what is yet to come. But at least I can give you my safe guidance across Uffington and set you on to the northward path.'

'But you're coming with us!' said Tryfan, more as a command than a request.

'Follow me,' was all Boswell said for reply, and he led them silently northward, and a grey dawn light touched their flanks as they went.

* * * * * * * *

They found a pall of evil over Uffington as they made their way into its tunnels and then by secret careful ways to the heart of the Holy Burrows themselves.

Most of the moles they had seen making passage the day before seemed to have passed on again, leaving behind only a few guardmoles in charge. Yet a few was quite enough.

The three moles saw darkness and savagery, for the rituals of the March Solstice are savage indeed among the grikes, who make killings and snoutings then in the name and honour of the Word. First of miscreants, then of the aged, then of the useless ill, and finally of the weak ones of new litters. Such moles are sacrificed, cast outside the Word by murder and torture, barbed on thorns and wire, snouted savagely. But worse than that, their deaths are used to defile the ground on which they are made: at Uffington they desecrated the tunnels of the Holy Burrows whose majesty was belittled by their blood, and whose peaceful tunnels were stricken by their screams and torture-wrought blasphemies against the Stone that protected them not.

Blood red was the colour of the evil that had come to the Holy Burrows as the grikes ritually desecrated that ancient place, leaving the wounded and the crushed to crawl hopelessly along the ancient tunnels into the darkness of their death.

The sights that Tryfan and Spindle saw then they never forgot, and they might have been filled with hate but that Boswell said again and again, 'Remember the grikes *are* moles, they are but moles. As there is light, so there is

84

dark. Remember my words and judge them not, Tryfan. Lead others not in hatred against them for that is the way to darkness. Rather, lead them towards the Stone, remember, remember. This will be the hardest thing but it is the most important.'

Then Boswell turned to Spindle saying, 'Remind him, help him to remember, forgive them and the light of Silence may be thine, and those that follow you.'

But it is hard to forgive. In one place, out on the surface, they found an old male taloned in the chest and left to die amongst others already dead.

'What moles are you?' asked Tryfan, who had gone to the mole to see what he could do for him, for Tryfan had been taught healing by his mother, and had learned more of it from Boswell.

'Of Avebury,' the suffering mole gasped, 'all of us. The grikes took over the system and then at the beginning of March we set off here, and many of us died on the way. Many others they have killed. They brought us here but they might as well have killed us there! Avebury is no more. All are gone.' And so the mole rambled, putting a paw to his wounds but unable to stop the blood which pressed out between his talons and on to the grass in which he lay. They stayed with him till he died.

So, apparently unseen, they crossed through the Holy Burrows, Boswell seeming to want them to see the ruin of the place that they would not forget.

But late in the afternoon of the second day, a guard-mole caught sight of one of them, others reported the suspicion that alien moles were about and soon it was clear that the grikes were in pursuit of them, for parties were routinely working their way through tunnels and on the surface with such method and efficiency that they were driven out on to the surface, away from tunnel entrances, surrounded by the sense of remorseless quartering of the high ground of Uffington all about them.

The parties communicated with each other by an

ominous drumming on the ground, staccato and irregular, and Tryfan, as the strongest of the three and their physical protector, was now very worried. By nightfall they found themselves crouching near the highest point of Uffington Hill. While to the north, beyond the approaching searchers and far below them, the Vale of the White Horse stretched into darkness, eerily visible sometimes when the cloud briefly cleared and the moon emerged at its brightest. Around them the grass flurried with the breeze that drove the night clouds, and the gusts were getting stronger. Change, always change, coming to Uffington; change coming to allmole. And then, low and distant, the Blowing Stone sounded – a single sombre note from out of the western darkness.

'You know where we are?' said Boswell suddenly.

'Of course I do,' said Tryfan rather tetchily, for he felt they had been led into unnecessary danger. Neither Stones nor Stillstones to protect them here; just themselves and they were three against many.

Boswell's old voice was calm and gentle about them. They had been facing north, towards the ever-cold wind, but now he turned his back on it and surveyed the nightscape of Uffington beneath which lay the Holy Burrows.

'Here have the great traditions and secrets of the scribemoles been kept, the rituals been enacted, the disciplines been undertaken; here an important part of the spirit of moledom was nurtured and the Silence of the Stone heard. Here. . . .

'Here,' whispered Boswell again, his voice filled with a gentle sadness, the sadness of an open heart that gives; a sadness that has longing in it, great longing, aged longing, that reached to those times Tryfan had imagined himself to be travelling down, and forward too, a little impatiently. To the time Tryfan had sensed as well was coming. . . .

'Here, now,' said Boswell. Now. And Tryfan looked about him in wonder. *Now*. And for a moment he understood that word, of the way that Boswell uttered it and in it he knew no fear, and knowing no fear he heard a Silence, great and good, burgeoning all about him so that he sighed and tears came to him. The Silence was now and in the being of it completely, where a mole is not himself any more, nor even a mole.

Then he looked around, a little embarrassed, at Spindle who to his astonishment he saw was yawning and scratching himself.

Then Spindle sighed too.

'I'm tired,' he said. 'Too much excitement, too little food, too much travel. Too much danger. I think we should run for it while we still can . . . but if you two are going to talk about it I'm going to have a sleep.'

Which, to Tryfan's astonishment, he did.

Then Boswell said, 'Honour him, Tryfan, for Spindle will always be at your side to love and support you in your task. The Stone has found him for you, as the Stone found you for me, to be a good companion, to learn and to teach me when I had forgotten what I knew, to touch me with talon and heart, faith and hope. So will loyal Spindle be with you when you need him and when you cannot or will not accept help from any other.'

Boswell reached out a paw and touched Tryfan gently on the shoulder, and drew him a little away from where Spindle slept. The ground was stealthy with vibration, and the air over Uffington heavy with darkness.

'It is nearly time now, my dear Tryfan, for you and I to part.'

Tryfan tried to protest, but Boswell's touch on him tightened as he stilled him and said, 'You have learnt what I have taught you well. . . .'

'But I know so little,' whispered Tryfan. 'Hardly a thing! I can barely scribe, and there is so much more to know. . . .'

'Then knowing that, you know much indeed,' said Boswell. 'Now listen to me, and listen well, for there are teachings a mole must utter but once lest too much is lost

87

in the telling. It is in the doing with awareness that the learning comes. You say you have learnt little, well, let us see what this "little" is!'

Boswell laughed suddenly, in that joyous way he sometimes did in which he seemed a pup again, and Tryfan smiled as well, remembering suddenly the first months with Boswell when again and again he had asked him to teach him something – *anything* – and Boswell had laughed and told him he had started doing so already and one day Tryfan would know it.

'But what?' Tryfan had asked.

'You'll know when you stop trying so hard to learn!' Boswell had said and now, *now*, Boswell was asking him, 'So what have I taught you?'

Perhaps Boswell's voice was raised a little then, perhaps it was not a night to sleep, for unseen by either of them Spindle stirred, and his eyes opened, and he saw them close and heard them talking as he lay still, listening. He suspected that Boswell knew he heard, and was sure that the Stone did, but it was right that he did, for through him the first teachings of Tryfan, the greatest teacher of his generation, might one day be known to allmole.

'What have I taught you?' repeated Boswell.

Tryfan settled quickly down, grounding each paw one by one as Boswell had taught him and said with confidence, 'To think true thoughts, a mole must learn not to think at all!' Boswell had once told him, mysteriously as it seemed then, 'Ground the paws, one, two, three, four, use the paws and the feel of the earth to forget the troubled mind, the tired body and the doubting spirit – all misguided, all unreal! Ground the paws with mindlessness and true action comes! But ssh! Don't tell anymole!'

Now Boswell was crouched before him, and Tryfan, placing his paws in that special way he had done a thousand times before was thinking of not thinking, and thinking that. . . .

'Tryfan!' called out Boswell suddenly and sharply. 'State the First Teaching!'

'The First is that where my paws are, where I am, there is goodness and light, right there!' said Tryfan, a part of him astonished at his own words, another deeper, truer part not surprised at all. 'The light is waiting to be seen, right here, here! And it is that good light that makes a mole laugh out loud because he made such an effort to see something always before his snout.'

Boswell nodded, grinning, as if happy, at last, to share a secret he had wanted to speak of.

'And then?' he said.

'The Second Teaching is that a mole who believes that defending his burrow, his system, or even his life, is more important than putting one paw in front of the other towards the Silence of the Stone, is a mole afraid. And a mole afraid is a mole in fear, and a mole in fear cannot fully see the light. So the most important thing is where this paw goes next.'

Tryfan raised his right paw and looked at it, grinning too, the paw raised between them like some object that was waiting to be told what to do.

'And where does it go next?' asked Boswell.

'Here,' said Tryfan, putting it back down in exactly the same spot from which he had raised it. 'To moledom's most distant burrow and back!'

'Quite so,' agreed Boswell. 'Fear makes a mole take short steps, fearlessness brings the greatest steps of all: from light to dark and back again. Fear is grey and cloudy, a muffling of sound, a dimming of light and shadow, a half-life of tentative steps, each one harder than the next.'

They were silent for a time, paws grounded, sharing Teachings that the great scribemoles kept secret only because their simplicity deludes a mole into thinking they can be learnt, as worm-finding can be learnt. But these were teachings a mole *becomes* . . . and Spindle heard them, and knew them to be so.

'And then for the Third?' asked Boswell.

And then, and then . . . 'A mole cannot learn alone. He

must know another, and others too, perhaps, and so far as he opens his heart to them so is he able to learn.'

'It is so,' said Boswell. 'For this reason have novice scribemoles always been placed with a master, who teaches them by word and by deed. Who the master is is of little consequence if the novice is willing to learn. It is a question of having an open heart that may feel all the beauty and the love and the sadness that is there where a mole places his four paws.'

'For the Fourth,' continued Tryfan, wondering at where his words came from and thinking that perhaps it was some magic of Boswell's who was in some way really talking, 'there is discipline. At the centre it is, for the fourth is centre to the seven, three one way, three the other. Discipline forms the walls on either side of the way that leads to Silence and itself is neither the way nor the light, nor even important. Discipline is not the impulse to move along the way, and is therefore of no value in itself, but it stops a mole from straying off the path.'

Boswell nodded, and touched Tryfan gently once more, as if to remind him that a mole is more of a mole if he touches another and to acknowledge that his words showed he had learned much, and was ready to teach now in his own turn.

'I have instructed you in discipline, and you know what I know. Discipline comes from the practice of prayer and meditation, at the centre of which is the Stone and its Silence. Such discipline is like walls indeed, but invisible walls, silent walls, powerful walls, which give a mole security to resist the clamourings that seek to divert his attention as he follows his proper way. Meditation is not a closing up but an opening out, and a mole should do it with his eyes open to the world about him. It is easy enough to shut yourself away, and sometimes important too. Why, I myself shut myself away in a silent burrow nearby this very place. But true meditation is now and always now, whatever else a mole may be doing, and it encompasses those around him. A mole who would be disciplined should contemplate his four paws on the ground. That is the true scribemole's way, *your* way.'

'But I'm not a scribemole!' said Tryfan rather alarmed, but Boswell waved him silent, and then nodded for him to continue what he had been saying before.

'The Fifth,' said Tryfan with a little hesitation, 'the Fifth . . .' And before him came the memory of old Boswell's special love of the rising sun before which he would crouch, his eyes open, his glance going this way and that to enjoy the morning spectacle of life reborn to light, of joy and colour replacing dark and shadow. '. . .The Fifth is to find the way that leads to the great eastern sun and away from the dark of the setting western sun. Most moles chose the shadow of setting, unsearching but for cover, unseeing but for dark, where the eyes and the mind play tricks. But with the rising sun comes light and truth, and only in that way may the Stone be truly seen, its Silence truly heard. Awed but not afraid should a mole be of such light, this you have shown me.'

Boswell nodded, and together they were silent for a while, contemplating the Fifth Teaching that Tryfan had uttered, and feeling that great light in their hearts. For a mole should know that when Tryfan spoke of the eastern sun he meant a sun far greater, far brighter than the real one. He meant one in a mole's heart, whose place and glory is found only through a devotion to the way, and an avoidance of the tempting shadows along its route, which indiscipline makes seem real and worthy refuges, when really they are traps and tunnels with no purpose.

Yet, when Boswell spoke, and he did so very quietly, he brought Tryfan towards a strange reality indeed. 'Yes, yes,' he said, 'this great light awaits all moles, but few know it, and fewer yet are ready to believe it. You must show them, Tryfan, show them by a journey, and a journey that will be to the east, towards that rising sun. Yes, that will be it, so all moles may know. To the east they wait for you, moles of the past, and moles of the future: a journey that will bring more in its wake than you can ever know!'

Tryfan tried to interrupt him, but Boswell waved him silent again and continued, though now speaking so low that it was almost to himself, as if he doubted that even Tryfan, whom he had trained in the ways of meditation and scribemole wisdom, and loved as his own pup, would fully understand what he was saying.

'But you must not forget the west, where darkness is and where Siabod, the strangest and darkest-seeming of the Seven Systems is. To there your father went, and of there is your name made. From there will shadows come, subtle clever shadows that seem like light, but a light whose bright reflection is lined with the black of the eyes of a mole whose spirit is dying. In Siabod Rebecca gave birth to sons, your half-brothers. They and their kind are your kin, Tryfan, and they will come now, for Rebecca's love is in them, and great Mandrake's strength, and something too of Bracken's faith, and the moles that follow you will need them.

'But beware of their anger and power, Tryfan. Watch for them and seek to turn the shadows they bring into great shafts of light: for a loving mole learns to turn darkness to light and to turn the misdirections of moles back towards the Stone. Yes, yes, listen for them, for they will come and as your journey to the east will make a legend that moles will not forget, so will their coming out of Siabod and the shadows and light your brothers bring make a legend too, yes, yes. . . .

Spindle listened, eyes wide with wonder, for he thought of himself as but an ordinary mole, and after so many years of being by himself, company was strange, but company that spoke so awesomely – as if a book was in the making – was strange indeed. More than that, it had his talons itching to scribe something of it all, and wishing that he could scribe at all. Just a few scrivenings, and his own name, but he might have made an attempt at 'TRYFAN' and at 'BOSWELL White Mole', for, to Spindle, much more than to Tryfan, there was a power in the scribing itself. And 'TRYFAN' and 'SPINDLE' and the memory of the great night sky and the wind in the grass of Uffington Hill would be enough to remind him of this to which he was witness.

The excitement of it all must have made him stir for the other two heard and Boswell stopped speaking and the two of them acknowledged Spindle's presence. Then Boswell moved closer to Tryfan and said, 'So, you have spoken the first five Teachings, but the last two . . . well, now, mysteries indeed!' Boswell laughed, laughter like a pup's rose into the night. Somewhere in that Tryfan saw on into the next teaching, and words for it began to form into a feeling so palpable that he tried to reach forward for them. 'And the Sixth is – it is – it . . .' But it slipped away, beyond his reach, and he had a moment's sense that beyond it, unseen but felt, was something more, a Seventh, a last one, something of the Silence but not the Silence, something he knew, yes, yes, yes, he *knew* and it was there, Seventh and last, last to first, there all the time, embraced within words that Boswell had spoken, embraced within himself, something . . . and it was lost again and he felt a loss terrible and deep, and shook, and wept, staring at Boswell, tears on his face fur.

'What are the last Teachings?' he whispered. 'What is the Seventh?'

'Not yet, mole,' said Boswell gently. 'Not yet. But your heart knows them, as it always has, before you knew me. But you have forgotten and those last Teachings I will bring you again in time.'

'You're going, aren't you?' said Tryfan, concerned and calm at the same time, knowing now for certain that his training was at an end, though he felt he knew so little, except the grim fact that he had been trained to confront the moments that were coming.

'The Boswell you know is going,' said Boswell, '*must* go, yes, yes, yes, *must* go. Remember the Five Teachings you have uttered, and seek the last ones on your way.'

The Five Teachings? What had he said? Tryfan found he could form no words at all in his mind, nor remember quite what he had said. Instinctively he looked round at

93

Spindle, and Spindle nodded as if to acknowledge that he had heard and between them both they would find them again. At the sight of which friendship Boswell again laughed with delight, and they might have joined in but Boswell's voice rasped and cracked and he began to cough and splutter.

'Age!' he grumbled. 'Old age!' But when he had gathered himself together he said, 'So you think you have forgotten already! Wonderful! Perfect!' And Tryfan laughed too, because, after all, such teachings were not of the mind but the heart, waiting there to be drawn out by whatever mole he met was ready for them. That was *obvious*, and for no good reason that was what seemed funny about it. It was all so simple. A mole becomes the teachings and so can never forget them, even if he has difficulty remembering them as words.

'Have you finished?' asked Spindle.

'None of us has finished,' said Boswell.

'Well, if I'm not mistaken the grikes are getting nearer.' And it was true enough, the ground was heavy with their pursuit.

'Yes,' said Boswell, 'maybe you're right. Better get on with it. But we'll need your help, Spindle.'

'For what?' asked Spindle, looking pleased.

'Vouchsafing,' said Boswell shortly.

While Tryfan looked puzzled at this, Spindle, who clearly knew what Boswell meant, looked alarmed.

'But I'm not . . . I mean I'm just . . .' And he looked about him, nervously grooming his face fur and trying, as it seemed, to smarten himself up a bit as if he expected to go before an audience of moles.

Meanwhile Tryfan looked from one to the other, not understanding at all, but before he could say anything Boswell had taken a stance before him and as he raised his good paw it seemed that around them was a light of stars.

'Now listen, Tryfan, and listen well,' said Boswell. 'And you, Spindle, be witness to what I will do, for there will be a time when moles will doubt what Tryfan is about

94

to become, a time even that Tryfan himself will doubt; and you alone will remember what happened this night and that Tryfan took on a task which, if the Stone grants its fulfilment and he has faith, will make his name honoured over moledom as long as there are moles to tell stories and remember the truth. So listen, and watch, and do not forget.'

So Spindle, not a scribe, and feeling humble before such learned moles as these, crouched low to listen and watch. 'There will not be time to repeat myself,' continued Boswell, turning back to Tryfan, 'so remember. Many years ago you asked if you would ever be a scribemole and I replied, "One day, perhaps". You have learnt much with me, you have honoured me, and more than that you have honoured the Stone. You have learnt to read and to scribe, the first mole I know who has done so outside the Holy Burrows. But I have long believed – feared, perhaps – that there was a reason for this and now – ' And Boswell looked around as if to see the danger of the grikes they could all sense was so near. ' – Now I think I understand the Stone's purpose. Only I know you can scribe, Tryfan, and Spindle, is a witness and a worthy mole. Yes . . . yes that's it . . . none other knows than us. And for the time being it may be best if no other mole does know. Your life and the Stone's future in the heart of all moles may depend on it. Yes that's it: *will* depend on it.'

'But I'm not a scribemole yet Boswell,' said Tryfan puzzled, 'and I can never be until I have served my time in the Library and been initiated as anciently proscribed before the Holy Mole and in the presence of the ancient books within the Silence of the Stone. The Library is no more, nor the scribemoles and so I can never be one myself.'

'Let the Stone judge your worthiness,' said Boswell. 'Becoming a scribemole in the old way is not your task.'

'My task is to protect you, Boswell.'

'Your task is to serve the Stone which will protect us both,' said Boswell softly. Was it, then, a trick of that strange light in the sky that made Boswell's fur seem to grow brighter and he himself to grow about them?

'Come closer,' he said, reaching out to Tryfan, 'and be not afraid for me or for yourself. Listen now, for the first part of your journey is finally over and you have honoured your task and the Stone. Listen . . .' and the white light gathered ever more around Boswell as he began to speak the words that Tryfan realised with alarm make the novice who hears them forever a scribe.

> *Stone, give him thy strength*
> *Stone, give him thy wisdom*

'No Boswell, no! I am not worthy,' Tryfan whispered in awe. 'Not yet. Not yet.'

> *Stone, give him courage, give him purpose,*
> *Stone, direct his long journey,*
>
> *Silence, to hear*
> *Silence, to listen*
> *Silence, to know*
> *Silence, to love*
>
> *Stone, help him always.*

'Do you, Tryfan, vow always to scribe true?'

'Oh Boswell, how can I be worthy?'

'Do you, Tryfan, vow always to scribe true?' repeated Boswell.

After a long pause Tryfan whispered, 'I do,' his voice seeming removed from him, as if it was not his own.

'Do you, Tryfan, vow to seek Silence?'

'I do.'

'Do you, Tryfan, son of Rebecca, son of Bracken and sponsored by myself, Boswell of Uffington, vow to follow the hardest way, which is the scribemole's way: which is to love the unloved, to love where love seems lost, to love where love would have you die, to love yet not possess, to love when love is not returned, to scribe with love what truth you know, and be guided in all these things by the Silence that is of the Stone?'

Tryfan bowed his head and whispered, 'I do.'

Then Boswell spoke these ancient words:

> *Stone, accept Tryfan of Duncton as a worthy mole,*
> *Stone, help him always.*
> *Stone, embrace him with thy Silence.*

For a moment the only sounds they heard were the distant running of pursuing pawsteps, and the wind in dry grass, and then even those sounds faded as Silence fell, or seemed to fall upon them, so deep and pure that time itself was banished from that place. Each one there seemed still as the Stone itself, and Tryfan entered the stance of meditation which is what all scribemoles enter upon their ordination. And over them the moon circled and the Solstice came, and the stars shone bright, and the northerly wind, strong for so long, faltered and then was gone.

Until a distant dawn came, and Boswell stirred and stretched and reached out a paw to Spindle, and finally to Tryfan.

He said calmly, 'Now, Tryfan, you and Spindle must go.'

'But where do we go?' asked Tryfan miserably. 'And from what do we flee?'

'You flee from faith in mole before faith in the Stone; faith in dark before light; a lust to hear the dark sound and not the true Sound of Silence. Like the north wind it has come even to Uffington, turning the hearts of moles bitter and frozen, mean and lost. It is the dark side of the Stone made real and it is on us.' So spoke Boswell.

'Go now to other systems, with Spindle as your companion, listen and watch and speak little. Go to the old places, the places of legend and power where the spirit of the Stone will survive, for now it will be needed. Go to

Nuneham, to Rollright, to Siabod and to the distant northern systems. Follow the way the Stone leads you. Go to south and north, to east and west, go where true moles live and seek out their help.

'Return to Duncton Wood and save its moles for they are chosen to love the Stone. Lead them, Tryfan, to a place where the grikes cannot reach them; to the difficult places, even to the empty quarter in the east which nomole has reached for generations. There, perhaps, this evil will not penetrate and perhaps, perhaps . . .'

'But I am not trained, not worthy, I am nothing.'

Boswell embraced him. 'You are worthy. May the Silence of the Stone be thine.' Then, turning to Spindle, he said, 'May thy loyalty be a standfast to Tryfan, may thy good humour be his friend and may thy faith be to him a star which shines when his, for want of strength or faith, grows dim. May the Stone protect thee, Spindle, and guide thee true always.'

Poor Spindle! The words seemed like great cries of light across the dark sky and he was overawed by them.

For a final moment there was once more Silence so deep that Tryfan and Spindle were lost in it, and felt tears well up in their eyes as if, after a long journey, they had come home, and in that place it seemed that Boswell was around them and everywhere, each strand of his fur a shaft of light which sprang from Silence into Silence and mole was one with One, and all was now and evermore.

'Who art thou?' Tryfan asked of Boswell in awe, for surely this was no ordinary mole who gave them love as if he was father and mother of allmole.

'I am what you have made me,' whispered Boswell into the great grey dawn, 'and I will be what you may do.' But his voice, his distant travelling voice: was it but wind in the grass? And the light about him but the last of the moon and the first of the rising sun?

Then all changed, and Tryfan's paws were firmly on Uffington Hill once more with Spindle and old Boswell to protect, and danger was theirs. The grikes began to drum the ground to signal the resumption of their search. Moles were on the hill above them and rustling on the slopes below.

'Listen,' said Boswell urgently. 'Listen and obey. Our long journey has been but a preparation and strengthening. You cannot stay in the Holy Burrows as you had hoped. You must flee the danger I must face alone for now, while you protect for us who are old and for you who are young, and your pups, moledom's faith in the Stone. Take it up in your paws, be its guardian and its saviour.'

Then Tryfan leaned forward, and opened his mouth as if for one last time to protest. But Boswell's gaze stilled him and he said instead, 'I will. With Spindle as my witness and my guide, I will.' As he said this there was a flash of lightning, white and searing, which tore across the dawn sky and was followed immediately by an enormous burst of thunder that shook all of Uffington Hill. And then, even more strange, a flash of darkness, as if, for a moment, the very sun itself was in eclipse.

Then out of that darkness, even as it was gone and dawn on them once again, there came a great shout from the hill above them, of a voice as beautiful as cruel ice caught by a chill winter sun:

'Boswell!'

It seemed to come out of the lingerings of the thunder itself as the shape of mole loomed there, as black as night and as powerful. And whisperings, as of many moles, evil incantations and invocations. 'Boswell, I know you are down there in the grey light of morning! My guardmoles will find you!'

The voice was now deep and powerful; female and frightening. The image above terrifying in the unnatural dark which the presence of alien moles had brought to the slopes.

'Flee now before they see you, find a place of safety,' whispered Boswell. 'Find others you can trust, learn to lead them as once your father had to learn, tell them what you know, teach them, Tryfan.'

'But where shall I find them?'

'The Stone and your heart will guide you . . .' But even as he spoke that darkness on hill above him moved nearer, and with terrible weariness he turned upslope towards where that first fearsome calling of his name had come from.

'Boswell!' the voice said again. 'Welcome!' And as they all looked towards where the voice came from it seemed that the massing clouds of a storm was a great rearing of evil darkness on the crest of the hill above them, and there was the sense of talons darker than night itself, and of a power against which even the light of a White Mole seemed weak.

'Go now, Tryfan, leave me to the Stone's protection. Let Spindle lead you west towards the Blowing Stone, for it will give you sanctuary and time to find a way to escape.'

The shapes loomed down nearer towards them, strange in the sinister light over Uffington.

'Boswell!' the voice was louder, clear, female.

'Tryfan, we *must* go now. Now, Tryfan!' Spindle whispered.

They could sense the female coming nearer them and a dread was on Tryfan and Spindle and they dared not look to the hill above any more.

Boswell touched Tryfan once more, a last time, and murmured the ancient journey blessing upon him and said, 'You were trained better than you know, better than I know. You carry forward the love of Bracken and Rebecca whose power will be in you and give you strength. And I led you to thoughts whose wisdom you will in time understand. All this and the Stone will be your strength. Go now, beloved Tryfan, for I have taught you all I can and you must face the freedom that waits for all moles.'

'And you – ?' asked Tryfan, his voice filled with agony.

'I shall send one to come after me and he shall have strength, for he will be of allmole's faith.'

'What will his name?' asked Tryfan.

'His name will be for allmole and forever, his name, his – ' And over Boswell was a suffering.

Then Tryfan did have faith, and knew that one day what Boswell said would be, would be. Yes, yes, it would. The sound of pawsteps was closer, the paralysing heaviness of evil was almost on them.

'Come *on*!' beseeched poor Spindle.

Then Boswell turned up the hill, his frail form enshadowed by the storm above, tiny and pathetic against the darker shadows that rose and ranked up about him on the hill, of moles whose presence was dark and whose purpose was evil.

'Welcome back, Boswell of Uffington!'

The voice was laden with such power and grim threat that Tryfan was unable to control the rising terror he felt as, stumbling and tripping on the grass and soil in his haste to escape, the freezing wind across his face, he turned and ran with Spindle at his side.

Even as he did so he heard that voice call out to Boswell, 'At last you come, last of the scribemoles. Welcome Boswell, old fool. Welcome!' And there was a laugh as of a thousand moles which echoed across the hill of Uffington.

'Yes, I have come, Henbane,' they heard Boswell say. 'I have come.'

Last of the scribemoles! Except for he himself, Tryfan, who was nomole and nothing, a failed guardian, a coward to run . . . Were he and Boswell the last?

Then Tryfan heard no more, but stretched out his paws as Spindle led him towards the distant Blowing Stone.

'His name will be for allmole and forever,' had been Boswell's final words to him and in that promise he felt the love of Boswell in him and for him, and he sobbed with grief and fear as he followed good Spindle, both pushing themselves on, the sound of pursuit close behind. But what was he? Nothing. Not holy. Unholy. The one over whom history and storytellers would surely shake their heads and say, 'He failed.'

'Stone, help me me now for I am unworthy, help me,' he cried out as he ran.

'Come on, Tryfan!' called out Spindle ahead of him, and together they went on. While around them all they could hear was the sound of pursuit, sinister and sure, and rain in the wake of thunder, and wind from a dawning sky carrying the sound of their own desperate, tired paws on the ground ever onward as behind them the darkness and danger of Henbane engulfed Boswell into its evil.

Chapter Six

Moles pursuing close behind, dangerous with intent. Others somewhere in the grass at their side, more skulking on the steep slope of Uffington Hill above. Hidden ahead. Running, pausing to snout them out, getting nearer. Hunting, searching, chasing. A bitter, dangerous dawn.

The grass wiry and difficult, cold-wet with dew; and the wind harsh across their snouts, the ground sloped and awkward, the route exposed. And Spindle was losing pace ahead. . . .

'Go faster Spindle, faster!'

'Doing my best,' panted Spindle.

'Where are you heading for?'

'Away to the east and then round in an arc to the south. Know the ground there.'

'Lead us to the Blowing Stone.'

Spindle slowed suddenly and half turned as he ran, crashing through the grass ahead in his confusion. 'Can't go there. Not me. Not allowed.'

'It's sanctuary for true mole,' said Tryfan. 'Everymole knows that.'

'I'd be scared there!' said Spindle.

'We'll be dead anywhere else!' replied Tryfan. 'Now lead on as fast as you can!' And with Tryfan almost herding his companion ahead of him they fled on into the morning wind as around them the sense of pursuit quickened.

'They're making for the Blowing Stone. Can't have that. Cut the buggers off. Yes, yes, yes. . . .'

Grike voices shouted around him, hard and short of vowel, with a male one more commanding than the others, all contorted by the wind.

Tryfan fought against his instinct to burrow to the

tunnels he could sense in the ground beneath: but wise moles do not seek escape into strange systems if they can help it, for once there a mole is easily trapped. Tryfan slowed the pace to give Spindle time to catch his breath while he interpreted the vibrations at his paws.

'Can't have that,' the grike leader had said. Why should they be so concerned by the Blowing Stone? Tryfan did not know, but if they were then that seemed the best place to be going. He was encouraged by the fact that he seemed able to sense the direction in which they should go, his limbs growing heavy the moment he drew off what seemed to be the direct line to the Stone. Perhaps he should trust himself to take over the lead now and he could probably set a better pace than Spindle.

The wind dropped suddenly and the grass was quiet. Silence. Pursued and pursuers were still and listening for the others' sound, waiting for somemole to make a move.

Still, still, be still, Tryfan commanded himself, his heart thumping so loudly he was sure they would hear it; his fear the greater because they had not yet had a single glimpse of their pursuers, unless they were the frightening silhouettes that had ranked beside the great female who had 'welcomed' Boswell. Their vibrations told him only that they were big and they ran fast. . . .

And *below* as well. Somewhere in tunnels below they were coming. Panic began to overcome him as he crouched silently with Spindle heaving and puffing with effort at his side, wondering what to do. He looked at Spindle and saw that his flank was shaking with fear.

'We'll soon be safe,' said Tryfan reassuringly, pleased to see that Spindle responded by becoming calmer at his confidence and wishing he had more faith in himself.

'Close in, lower down. Yes.' The commanding voice was suddenly loud again, and nearer, somewhere just above them on the slopes. Then, suddenly, drumming, then silence. Then drumming from their left, short and staccato. Near. Then more drumming, urgent and frightening. Like a hare but sharper. Then more, ever nearer. And the skulkings of mole below, listening for them above. Then that mole drumming. Then a fourth; then the first again.

Signals. They were using sound and vibration to coordinate their encircling of them and to paralyse them into inaction.

Suddenly, without hesitating longer, Tryfan rose from where he had crouched and with a whispered, 'Follow close behind me!' to Spindle, he raced ahead with no further thought of concealment, for he sensed that in moments more they would be discovered.

A female rose ahead of him, big and strong, but he was moving fast and was able to talon-thrust her out of the way and with a further shout of encouragement to Spindle they raced on by as she screamed a warning to the others behind them. He ran on, held back from going at his fastest pace by Spindle who was now panting desperately with tiredness, but watching ahead in case other grikes were lying in wait. Unless they reached sanctuary soon they would be caught, and the quest Boswell had sent them on ended before it began.

The ground rose a little and became hard to traverse, and their pursuers began to catch up again as poor Spindle's breathing became progressively more desperate and laboured. Though Tryfan sensed now that they were near the Blowing Stone, each step forward seemed to push it further away. So near now surely, but so difficult to reach, so near. . . .

'Go . . . on . . . Tryfan. You . . . go . . .' It was Spindle, slowing now, unable to continue, and Tryfan turned and saw him stumble to a halt, and behind him, bearing down fast, three moles, big and certain in their stride.

Spindle looked back at them and then forward to Tryfan, and cried out, 'Don't stop for me, not for me. You go on!' But before Tryfan could even think of what he was doing he had stopped, turned, and moved back to protect Spindle from the onslaught of the grikes. Powerful was he then, his flanks well formed and his shoulders huge and his talons expertly raised as he stood still and steady to defend his new friend, his mouth a little open and his eyes wary.

The leading grike came straight for him and Tryfan easily sidestepped him and powered him on over his right side, away from Spindle. Then the second, whose talons met his with a crash, and the third . . . and the fight turned into a grapple, and Tryfan knew that they were lost when he saw more coming, and encircling them.

'Let go!' It was Spindle, objecting. 'You let go. We've got a whole army of moles just waiting to attack, yes we have!'

Tryfan stopped struggling and the grikes pulled off immediately, eyeing Spindle with amusement as he talon-thrust feebly at the air and chattered on about the moles who would rescue them.

'All right, that's enough. We're caught.' Spindle was silent immediately, glancing quickly at Tryfan in surprise, for there was still confidence and purpose in his voice as if he still believed, even now, that they would escape.

The grikes did not attack more but rather grasped them firmly, three to each one, as a seventh, the female Tryfan had struck, joined them, shouting, 'Quick, quick, get them away. Move, move, *move* . . .!' As they harried them both away the grikes looked fearfully over their shoulders towards the Blowing Stone which, Tryfan now saw, was but a few moleyards away. They had been caught only seconds from what might have been safety. The great Stone towered over them, dark against the white morning sky and Tryfan could sense its power, and understand the grikes' fear of it.

He slumped on his shoulder, playing for time. Spindle, quick as a flash, started to limp.

'Ow! My paw hurts,' he whined convincingly.

'Come on, come on, *come on*,' urged the grikes, pushing and shoving them back the way they had come.

Tryfan opened his mouth to protest, to argue, to delay,

106

but then he stopped. On the slopes above them another mole had appeared, different from the rest. He had eyes that smiled inappropriately, eyes that appraised, and a curious stance such that he seemed to welcome them yet knew he had power over them. His snout was curiously twisted to the left. His mouth was a little open revealing teeth of yellow sharpness.

'That's Weed,' whispered Spindle between wincing sounds of feigned pain, for he was maintaining the fiction that his paw was hurt.

Tryfan saw that Weed stared at them with a curious weary indifference as if, now that they were caught, they were nothing, and would never be anything again.

'We reached them just before the Stone,' said the female who seemed the leader of the pursuit party.

'That's good then,' replied Weed. 'Well done indeed. Praise be for the saving of their souls. They will Atone and be forgiven.'

Weed came nearer to them and the little party stopped, though the leader still looked back fearfully in the direction of the Blowing Stone.

'What is your name?'

'Tryfan,' Tryfan replied boldly.

'You will obey, Tryfan, and you will not run from yourself anymore. Nor will your friend. We will help you be forgiven.' Weed smiled suddenly, and there was something callous in the warmth of his eyes that chilled Tryfan.

'Forgiven for what?' said Tryfan, hunching forward for a fight. The talons of the others restrained him painfully.

Weed eyed him and said nothing, as if nothing was worth saying.

One of the others said, 'We must get him away Sir, away from that Stone.'

Weed smiled slightly, his teeth glinting, his eyes colder still.

'The north wind is still, the Stone will not sound again quite yet.'

'The Stone will sound forever!' shouted Tryfan, struggling to escape the henchmoles' grasp.

'In that case we had better get you out of here, had we not?' said Weed, laughing slightly. 'Get them underground,' he ordered the others. 'Get them to Atonement. There's an entrance a little way on. Use that.'

But as they set off back through the grass, the wind freshened and dark wild clouds turned and rose in the sky above them.

'This place – ' said one of them, looking up for a moment and then back at the Blowing Stone. 'It scares me.'

'Say the Word then,' muttered another. 'That's the best,' and they all chanted a song-prayer in deep voices, as if by doing so they would stop the wind itself.

But over their voices came a low moan, indefinable, vibrating. . . .

'Come *on*!' they shouted at them, fear in their voices, even Weed joining his talons to the others as they pushed Tryfan towards an entrance.

Tryfan said again, desperate now to gain time, 'Where are you taking us?' But their reply was to harry them faster along and quicken their chant.

'Stone,' cried out Tryfan from his heart, for he knew he was being taken somewhere, or to something, terrible, 'help us now!' He turned to look at Spindle whose earlier bravado had turned to fear, and saw the beginnings of a submission that comes with great tiredness.

'Stone!' he began to cry out again, but as he spoke the very words were torn from his mouth, the sky darkened, the wind was suddenly gusting strong and the moaning sound that worried the moles turned into a deep and sonorous note from the Blowing Stone behind them.

The moles about him hesitated and stopped, their mouths began to open in distress, their teeth to snarl as if to bite themselves, and their talons were wild against the sky and ground as if to stop the sound. Even their leader seemed caught in confusion while on the slopes above

Weed's smile was gone and there was a desperate surprise in his eyes.

'The Blowing Stone!' one managed to cry in fear.

'Come *on*!' cried out another, but his voice seemed suddenly tortured as the Stone sounded again, even more powerfully, and Tryfan saw them confused all about him, Spindle included.

Instinctively in that moment of panic Tryfan took his chance. He pushed himself clear of the moles nearest him and, as they seemed to go yet wilder with distress, pushed through to grab and support Spindle with his right paw. Then he turned back towards the Blowing Stone. At first Spindle was moaning in distress as well, but as they got nearer he seemed to gain strength once more and, no longer needing support, ran alongside Tryfan. Their paws felt light on the ground, their snouts were full to where the sound came as ahead they saw the great Stone loom up, forbidding but certain, powerful but benevolent, and they ran forward to its sanctuary.

So confident were they that they dared turn round to look back at their captors and were astonished to see how far they had travelled. The grikes were scattered on the slope beneath them, only Weed seeming capable of watching after them through the sonorous soundings of the Blowing Stone. To him Tryfan shouted, 'Tell your Mistress I shall return for Boswell. May she never dare harm him or *she* will "Atone"!'

His words were carried out before him, booming and resounding with the great notes from the Stone behind. He stared for a moment longer, saw Weed turn away in confusion and then with Spindle at his side, Tryfan entered the worn area of grass at the ancient Stone's base, and reached out to touch the Stone itself.

It rose out of sight to the sky, worn and pock-marked with time, the strange holes and fissures in it that were the source of its sounds were black in its grey-green mass.

A peace and silence came on them. Spindle said, 'I'm tired – and scared!'

'You did well, Spindle, and we are safe now. The grikes will not venture here. We will rest and then leave Uffington.'

So there, in the shadows and dry grass at the Stone's base, Tryfan and Spindle squeezed into shelter, and with their minds whirling with tiredness and relief, wonder and fear, they watched out over the slopes.

The wind died, the notes sounded no more, and from the ground through his paws Tryfan could feel the vibrations of frightened moles, escaping moles, until he felt them no more. Then as the day advanced they crept into the darkest recesses of the Stone's base, with still-wintering ladybirds in the cracks above their backs, and fell into a deep sleep, safe in the Stone's protection, flank to flank, snout to snout.

Chapter Seven

When Tryfan awoke in the dark shelter of the Blowing Stone, he knew immediately that something had gone, something familiar and disliked. Even something feared.

He stirred and snouted about in puzzlement, going out from beneath the edge of the Blowing Stone into the light. And, oh! he sighed, breathed deeply, and stretched out as if to touch the world about him with each of his four paws in turn.

For where the day before – no, the months and mole*years* before – there had been cold, and bitterness, and withered vegetation beaten by a wuthering wind, now there was warmth and the scent of spring. Not the hint of it in distant light, which they had seen a few days before, but spring itself, all around, in scent, and sight and smell and excited growth and busy callings of birds, and the scurrying of insects; here, *now*!

He snouted higher into the air, his eyes alight, not knowing which way to turn so promising did every scent and sound seem to be; so very welcoming was everything to mole.

Then he called out, 'Spindle, Spindle!' to wake his friend and show him things to give a mole pleasure.

But Spindle slept deeply, and though he stirred and groaned comfortably at Tryfan's call, Tryfan fell silent once more to let him sleep on and turned back to the springtime.

The dawning sun was casting its warm rays over the slopes about him. Early morning mist clung to the deeper, danker hollows of Uffington Hill and drifted up weakly from among the beeches on the slopes far below.

From somewhere down there he heard the busy cawing of rooks and then, as the sun gained in strength, and the mist cleared to reveal a world of life and gentle colour that stretched as far as the eye could see, there was a rising of wings nearby, and he heard the first sweet shurrlings of skylark overhead.

Yet even as he relaxed into it there came over him, for the briefest of moments, dark panic as he remembered Henbane and Boswell and all of it, all that darkness and trouble. He snouted in the direction of Uffington Hill above him, then crouched back again, and knew that his task was not there now.

Boswell had told him to journey away, to seek others' support and to teach them what he knew. What he had seen of the grikes, and what Spindle had told them, was enough to make Tryfan believe they had had a lucky escape, and one that was not of their own doing but the Stone's. That same Stone that ordained the seasons, and the compass, if not quite the direction of moles' lives.

Now. . .? Now they had little time. The grikes would be after them again, and the best way he could help Boswell was to do what he had told them to and be guided by the Stone.

He moved a few steps further away from the Blowing Stone and turned to face it. As he did so, and the sun began to warm his fur pleasantly, he felt the distant vibration of mole and knew he and Spindle must soon travel down-slope to the Vale of Uffington and from there make their way to safety.

Spindle stirred, looked up, saw Tryfan, came out and settled his snout on his paws for a moment and declared, 'Blessed be, but the spring has come!' Then, humming with a kind of tuneless good cheer, he busied himself looking for some food, quietly leaving Tryfan to his contemplation of the Stone.

Tryfan looked up at it, composed himself as Boswell had taught him, and whispered, 'Stone, Boswell made me a scribemole but I am not worthy. He entrusted me with the task of leading moles towards the Silence, but I have not Silence. He told me to journey, but I know not where.

So now I ask for your guidance and entrust my life to you.'

Then he lowered his head humbly and prayed to the Stone to give them both strength and purpose.

Nomole knows now how long his meditation lasted, but he felt no fear as he heard the grikes approaching from across the slopes. Before the Stone a mole's time is his own.

Tryfan finished his contemplation and muttered, 'Well if I'm a scribemole I had better start scribing!'

'Have some food,' said Spindle behind him, where he had been patiently waiting, and they ate the food he had found.

Tradition has it that it was after that, in the shadow of approaching danger, that Tryfan scribed the first of his great invocations, using the bare earth on which he stanced, since he had no better. He scribed fast, with great concentration, and when he had finished he ran his talons quickly over the words repeating them to himself.

Spindle meanwhile watched with excitement and awe, for he had never seen scribing done in the open under the sky. The scribemoles of Uffington did it in burrows and tunnels, in shadows, secretly, as if it was something to keep to themselves and show nomole else. But here Tryfan seemed almost to rejoice in scribing in the open before the sun, and sharing it with another. It seemed to him as if Tryfan was talking to the earth itself and that if the Stone had given him the task of helping this mole of all moles then it was one he wished to do well.

'What's your scribing say?' he asked, crouching back in silence, and Tryfan spoke the words he had scribed:

> *Oh Stone,*
> *In our deeds*
> *In our words*
> *In our wishes*
> *In our reason*
> *And in the fulfilling of our task*
> *In our sleep*

In our dreams
In our repose
In our thoughts
In our heart and soul always
May the wisdom of love,
And thy silence, dwell always in our heart

Oh in our heart and soul always
May thy love and thy Silence dwell.

They stayed in silence some moments more before Tryfan turned to the Stone, stared a final time up at its great heights, which were now golden in the morning sun, and then with a nod to his companion, led them off out of the eastern reaches of Uffington to start the journey Boswell had commanded that they make.

'Whither are we bound?' asked Spindle, who had taken a position just a little behind Tryfan.

'To Buckland near the Thames where the scribemole Brevis first went, and from there we must, before continuing our greater journey, make for Duncton, for I would see it once more before we travel onward. Moles there can be trusted, and they are led by my half-brother Comfrey and he should know our purpose. Perhaps there we may find moles to help us on our quest, for then it is northward we must go, where evil and disruption come from, to there we must take the healing lessons of Silence.'

Without saying more, they moved on quietly down-slope away from the Holy Burrows, leaving the scurryings and searchings of the grikes behind them, never looking back, but trusting that the Stone would protect Boswell whom they left behind, as it would protect them as they journeyed on.

* * * * * * *

A short time later, as the great shouts of searching mole played harshly over the hill, a solitary mole, dark and female, her great shadow a menace to that spring morning,

114

her cold black eyes an enemy of light, reached the Blowing Stone and approached it without fear.

Her talons shone blackly in the morning sun, her fur glittered like coal, her gait was calm and smooth. This was Henbane, dread Henbane of Whern, daughter of Rune. Out of evil cometh evil.

Behind her, to her right side, came a mature male of presence: Wrekin. To her left was a mole of turning snout and cunning eye: Weed of Ilkley, mole of influence.

'The mole Tryfan and that cleric made straight for this Stone fearlessly,' said Weed. 'Our guardmoles could not pursue them, and nor, for that matter could I.'

'Boswell's strength must have been with them,' replied Henbane with soft menace. 'Yet are you sure this Tryfan is not a scribe?'

'I am sure as a mole can be,' said Weed, who did not have it in his watchful nature ever to reply 'yes' or 'no' to a question when ambiguity would do as well. But it was true enough: he was as sure as a mole could be that Tryfan was not a scribemole. Then, by way of explanation, he added, 'He was still too young, and anyway there would have been no time or opportunity to ordain him. Now there are no scribemoles left to do it but for Boswell, and he is in our sway now.'

Henbane went forward and saw the scribing Tryfan had made.

'Well, it seems that Boswell must have come this way for he left scribing on the ground.'

She read it, curve by curve, paw touch by touch, eyes alert. Weed watched her for any reaction: his life was service to Henbane, his pleasure was knowing her mind and influencing it, at which he was better than anymole living.

'What is it? What does it say?' he asked. 'A curse perhaps?'

'Nothing so dramatic. You should know by now that scribemoles don't curse! These scribings are but weak dreams and frail hopes.' She laughed, the same laugh

115

Tryfan had heard. Wrekin laughed in dark sympathy with her; and their laughs together were like the menace of nightshade and its shadow, and in their way as deathly beautiful. Weed's eyes and yellow smile never left Henbane. Wrekin, a heavy mole with lines of anger and purpose to his face, looked out over the Vale of Uffington.

'What have you to say, Wrekin?' asked Henbane.

'I say the mole Tryfan is cursed and that he and his weak friend will be found. They will Atone; the Word's will be done. I have already deputed guardmoles to send descriptions and warnings out so that, if they escape us here, they will be found when they venture to other systems. I like not to know that moles have been to the very centre of our activity and gone free.'

'It is well, Wrekin. Your thoroughness pleases me. And what of Boswell? What say you now a night is past and torture seems to pain him not?'

'I say you should eliminate Boswell without further delay. Kill him while he is in our power. Living he is something the Stone followers can yearn for, dead he will be forgotten.'

'And you, good Weed, what do you think?' She moved nearer to Weed, her eyes softening a little. It was plain that while she respected Wrekin she liked Weed more.

'That Boswell be kept alive of course,' said Weed promptly. 'Turn him from the ways of the Stone, make him Atone, and if my judgement of what a White Mole means to these southern moles is right then you could do nothing to dispirit them more.'

'You're wrong, Weed,' said Wrekin angrily. 'Alive, a mole like Boswell will always be a threat. Dead, he – '

'Will be a martyr,' said Weed dismissively. 'You warriors see things too simply in dark and light, in life and death. But let the WordSpeaker decide.'

Henbane turned and looked briefly at him, pleased at the deference to her power. She liked flattery, she glowed before it as quickly as she slid into destructive anger when she was denied. Weed smiled at her, enjoying the sight of

116

her. Despite the evil that she was, Henbane's dark grace has become legendary among moles, and though by then the fur round the corners of her eyes was creased yet she still had the grace of mature youth, and there was about her, hidden deeply it is true, some touch of a shattered innocence – as if even as an adult, and a malevolent one, some part of her had not quite let go of the good spirit of a mole who was once very young and, if only for a moment, has had a glimpse of good light she could never quite forget.

But as it was, only Wrekin was there, and twisted Weed, who saw other, darker things. For indeed Henbane's fur had a curious shining darkness to it, as if reflecting the ominous light that fills great storm clouds after their rain has passed and the sun is behind them, trying to break out; when she turned, darkness seemed to turn with her, and imminent murderous storms to be returning again.

At that moment, to loyal Weed, Henbane looked as harmless as she ever did. As she reared up and stared down the slopes towards Uffington Vale, her instinct correctly told her where the fugitives had gone, and said, 'We will find this mole Tryfan soon enough. He cannot go far without discovery. He will be a goodly catch who may show us ways of trapping Boswell himself into Atonement so that the Word may be known to all moles.' Then her tone changed into command: 'Silence now,' she said, 'I wish to scribe the Word.'

Weed backed away, smiling; Wrekin stood respectfully to one side.

For a moment Henbane stared up at the Stone. There was no fear in her eyes, nor a fur's hair of doubt in her stance. Then she laughed and with one mighty sweep of her talons she scratched down the full length of Tryfan's words again and again and again, her eyes red with sudden anger, and destroyed them.

Then she looked up fearlessly at the Stone and scribed these words:

Wherever the Stone rises the Word rises higher.
The Word is more powerful than the Stone.
The Word is truth, the Stone was dreams.
The Word is
the Stone was.

The Word will be for evermore.

Then she added one last line:

Henbane scribes it

'Blessed be the Word,' she said.

'Blessed be!' intoned the other two obediently.

But Wrekin was bored: a fanatical believer in the Word, yes, but in the Word as action, not ritual. There was something wild and unruly about these rituals of Henbane, something emotional, something that had no place in the regular routine he followed at sunrise and sunset, of repetition of familiar words of the Word; something that set his mouth in the grim line of unspoken distaste. All the shouting, all the crying, all the bloodied talons and the snouting. Unruly. Inefficient. Unmilitary. The job could have been done as well without all that.

But Weed did not think so. He watched Henbane now, as he so often had in the dramatic moleyears past, and wondered at the dark, destructive energy in her that had driven guardmoles south and all but destroyed faith in the Stone, which had once dominated all of moledom. Of the so-called seven Ancient Systems two only now remained unravished by the agents of the Word. One was Siabod, which was judged to be of no account – judged, that is, by Wrekin and the other fighters who had decided their time was better spent where there were more moles to fight.

The other system was Duncton Wood of which all moles knew, for a great tradition seemed to attach to it, and there were stories of the moles there being chosen of

118

the Stone, to lead and resurrect its glory. Henbane had left that system until last, principally because access to it was difficult since it was surrounded on three sides by the River Thames and on the fourth by a roaring owl way. It was, too, the most easterly of the Seven Systems and until the recent takeover of Avebury and the Holy Burrows, the forces Wrekin led were too dispersed to mount an attack so far to the eastside of moledom.

Nor was there much to conquer beyond it, for there the desert of the Wen lay, whose only interest for grikes was that into its deepest interior the mole Dunbar, a one-time supporter of Scirpus himself, had gone into retreat. For modern grikes there would be nothing there except legends of survivors and a few abject and snivelling ignorant moles of the kind who know no better than the marginal territory they choose to inhabit. The Wen was of the twofoots now, and closed forever to mole; and Dunbar's descendants, if there had been any, must long since have died, or been dispersed.

So Weed stared at Henbane as she meditated, smug in the privilege he felt to be so close to the mole so many held in awe. Yes, yes, privileged: she had powers and energies more than he had ever had, and, though he could outface her when he needed to, he knew that she must never know – or be certain – of the awe and fear he sometimes felt in her presence. She had a ruthlessness at times that took his breath away – and might one day take his life as well, as it had taken the life of many a mole who had offended her.

Since she had come south, Henbane seemed to be fascinated by these great stones, though he personally felt uneasy in their presence, and just the memory of the sound of the Uffington Blowing Stone – which had confused him the day before – set his teeth on edge and had him worrying now that the wind might start up again. It hadn't seemed to disturb Wrekin quite so much: no imagination that mole, just a fighter. Well, the fighting time would be over one day and Wrekin would find he had less power when Henbane had less need of him. Yes, yes.

Meanwhile, Weed had been worried by Henbane's awe of the Stones and had sent word northward by way of the sideem, to great Rune himself. Revered Rune, indestructible Rune: Weed's real master.

But now, in the presence of this Stone, Weed was thinking that Henbane seemed peaceful and there is something about her . . . something . . . But how can a mole as turned and slanted, askew and twisted as Weed hope to see aright the light of the Stone in so dark a mole as Henbane? Weed could not understand the nature of that distant thwarted light in Henbane he only dimly saw; for it was this that gave him unease, and had decided him to send reports North, and to think that the time was surely coming when Henbane must be persuaded North once more. Now they had captured old Boswell, whom Rune had expressly ordered should be brought to Whern alive, there was little enough to hold them back – except the taking of Duncton Wood, and perhaps an assault by some of Wrekin's more stupid guardmoles upon the distant Siabod.

Henbane stirred, looked up at the Stone, briefly touched the scribing she had made and then, with a sigh – a passionate sigh almost – settled down again to her meditation.

Weed looked at her, and he supposed he lusted after her, though Word forbid she should ever guess that. His pleasure was in finding other males for her and watching her sidelong as she greeted some new young male warmly (Weed knew the type well, and even had the sideem watching out for them: young, large but innocent, and above all fresh and clean) and heard what stumbling words he had to say as she took him into her confidence, flattered him, won his trust and longing, looked at him and his body with a sideways glance (as Weed looked at Henbane now!).

Then she would ignore the prospective new male utterly for a time, and let him suffer doubt (which is the ingredient that makes lustful longing grow) as she thought of decisions she must make – important strategic decisions for moledom – before she gave her attention again to the smaller, intenser, desires she would fulfil.

Weed had often seen such males waiting, but envied them not. Their moment came, and then it passed leaving their seed to pulsate, wriggle and die in the sterile desert that Henbane was and surely always would be. She was not born to pup, beautiful though she was.

Weed the procurer pitied her poor consorts, for afterwards they would be given over to the eldrenes, old shrivelled haggard moles the lot of them, and then those young males were made to die. Dreadful deaths usually, which Henbane liked to watch privily from some dark corner as if this punishment was a final secret lust that she permitted herself.

Weed shivered and stared at her flanks, and wondered if one day she would decide that he knew her rather too well. Well, it was a risk worth taking, and a challenge to be clever enough to escape her talons and at the right time to fade away into the obscurity from which he had so successfully come to travel at Henbane's side, trusted and listened to. . . .

For, of all things, Weed was a realist and knew that finally, when all ended, Henbane was but a mole, and all moles die. The Word? The Stone? The sky? The moon? Weed sneered in the darkness of his heart at all of it as he paid lip service to the Word. Finally, when all was said and all quite done, a mole would die and then there was . . . nothing. And so, as Henbane meditated, Weed pursed his mouth and sneered not at Henbane but at everymole else who chose to make her great, and did not know – nor could not – that she was but mole, made in a moment's calculated lust, between two moles whose secret Weed alone knew.

* * * * * * *

Henbane of Whern was littered of Rune out of cruel Charlock, two moles whose deeds were dark enough to make night seem day, or sunshine cold as winter twilight.

121

Moles who know the first part of Duncton's history know Rune well enough, and turn in nightmare despair to think of his vile deeds. On his return from the south, and after his ascension as Master of the Sideem, a role he achieved with the connivance and treachery of Charlock, he took her to mate, the bitter selfish painful mating of two whose spirits for good are withered, and whose spirit for evil is greedy. Passionless passion, talons that hurt, teeth sharp to mating's flank; eyes lustful for the deed not the idea. Rune and Charlock, aye, those two mated: nothing good to come out of them.

Months later, when Charlock was fat with young and ready for pupping, Rune took her to the most secret of the dark caverns of the High Sideem in Whern, where subterranean waters run and the life is white for lack of sun. Then on to the Rock of the Word itself. There Rune watched over the pupping. With short screams she did it, as if she objected to being so used, and he stared at the pink blind things, caressing them with his powerful paws and talons, holding their veined gasping heads between his talons, sensuous, smiling at their bleats with cold assessment.

'Not this one,' he said softly, 'and nor this, Charlock.'

'No,' she whispered evilly. Maternity was not her way.

'Nor this,' he said dismissively of a third, pushing it aside, his talons drawing blood on its frail flank. The pup was feeble and wan.

Two remained, a male and a female.

'Only one we need, just one,' he purred, taking the male and holding it up. Blind and trusting, it quested its soft small snout to his cold strength. He looked at it with distaste.

'I think not, Charlock. No?'

'No,' she hissed, agreeing. She bit the pup to death.

'But this one,' he said gently, pointing at the female remaining close to her. 'Yes, yes this one must be the one. Yes?'

'Yes . . .' purred Charlock contentedly, staring at the

tiny grey-pink female and watching her turn weakly from the two of them and seem to wish to go her own way. Some say that then, at that dark hour of that poor female's birth, even into the fast darkness of the high tunnels made by the sideem of Scirpus, light came, sudden and sharp. Shining in a single white stream from some moving gap in the roof far above, down, down in a shaft into the great pool of blackwater that forever forms at the base of the Rock of the Word. Down came that light, for a moment blinding Charlock and Rune, who started back, while the young female, her eyes not yet open, sensed something more beautiful than she could know and feebly sought it out. Colours there were in that moment in the hidden blackwater of the pool, and reflected light, that put forever a beauty into that mole's face. And more than that it left behind an impulse, however weak, however seemingly lost, that one day, at one moment, just fleetingly, might be manifest in a single act of goodness from one who seemed evil incarnate.

Then the light was gone and darkness returned and Rune and Charlock were their evil selves again.

'So, let this one live,' said Rune, 'but kill the others too, as you did that other. Let their blood bathe their sibling's head.'

Charlock smiled and bit their heads that their blood might stain the body of their only living sibling, and then she carried them out to the surface for owl fodder, leaving the remaining female lone and bleating in the nest. Rune watched her, hunched vilely over her, father to daughter, male to female, horrible and obscene.

Charlock returned, laughed, called the bleating pathetic female 'my pretty', snouted Rune aside and curled a thin teat to the pup's mouth.

'She's strong,' whispered Rune.

'Comely she'll be,' said Charlock.

'Mine,' said Rune.

'Yours *and* mine,' said Charlock.

'Yours until she's nearly ripe, then mine,' allowed

Rune. Their voices were like the sheenings of the mating of adders in a single shaft of light.

'Teach her dark things and to trust nomole, teach her strength of purpose . . . Tell her not that I am her father, but teach her to respect and desire the Master of the Sideem,' said Rune.

'You?'

Rune nodded: 'She must never know.'

'I will teach her to love the Master of the Sideem,' agreed Charlock.

'Not "love" Charlock, desire. She shall desire him and I shall take her, yes?'

'Thou shalt Rune,' whispered Charlock, eyeing the young female with malevolent pleasure. 'She shall desire the Master before all other males. She shall not know he is her father. She shall be worthy.'

'If she is not, I shall kill her,' said Rune.

'She will be, Rune.'

'I think she will.'

Charlock put a talon to the throat of the chosen pup, and pushed it in until the skin almost broke and the pup made vestigal efforts to escape, the milk of its vile mother on its mouth, the blood and brains of its siblings on its paws.

'Have no fear Rune, she *will*.'

Rune stared at the pup, his eyes bitterly bright, his talons caressing her fragile flanks, his stance strangely lustful, seeing all in that burrow, even the hatred in Charlock's eyes: of him and his lust, of their daughter. And he laughed.

'What shall we call you?' he whispered.

'Henbane is a pretty name,' said Charlock, smiling darkly.

'Henbane,' repeated Rune, 'is good. Oh yes, yes: Henbane. Take her from here, let nomole know who she is, least of all the sideem for I will have her WordSpeaker one day and will not have her harmed.'

'Until she is nearly ripe I'll keep her.'

'And then I want her.'

'Yes, Rune. And I?'

'You?' said Rune, and shrugged indifferently. 'You have played your part for the Word, and pupped the mole who will take the Word into the whole of moledom. I will send two moles I trust to guard you both southwards. They will say nothing, but even so, Charlock . . . kill them.'

Charlock's eyes glittered.

Then Rune was gone, and soon Charlock left too, taking the pup out of the reach of the dread sideem to a place to the south of Whern, called Rombald's Moor, where once the great molegiant Rombald lived. There, on that wormless fell where only cripples and idiots eked out a life, Charlock killed Henbane's two guards, and lived to raise the pup alone, teaching her the dark arts through the moleyears unto her ripening. No friends but her mother had she, and her mother taught her to brook no denial, that she was the best and worthy of the best. And the best she would have, which was in the power and right of the Master of the Sideem.

When her first spring approached and Charlock saw she was nearly ripe and questioning, Charlock took males to herself, and let Henbane hear her sighs to make her desirous and jealous.

'I want them too,' said Henbane.

'No, not yet, my darling. Not for you. Unworthy these. Only the Master of the Sideem for you!' So Henbane learned her place was high, and she had contempt of the males her mother had, and was allowed to see them die. That was where she learnt to lust and kill.

While Henbane gained in size and beauty in those moleyears of her youth, Rune strengthened his power over the sideem and widened their purpose. While Slithe had still himself been Master he had sent the young Rune south, no doubt hoping he might be lost there, for the plagues were rife then and no grike had ever set off to report on the Seven Systems and returned. But Rune did return and his vision had been widened by what he saw, and he told the sideem that the time to take the Word southwards was coming, and the ways of the sideem in Whern, which were rigid and inward-looking should be over. So he had returned, and that was when he took one of Slithe's young mates, Charlock, to himself and used her to learn the secrets of Slithe, and pup the mole Henbane.

But Charlock told this not to Henbane.

'Thy father loved you not, hated you, despised you, rejected you,' she said, never saying his true name. 'But the Master of the Sideem you will love and cherish. One day he will be your guide and your helpmate, and he will teach you the Word.'

That day came. And Rune, knowing, pondered long on which of the sideem to send southward to Rombald's Moor to bring back Henbane. Clever he must be, and cunning – for Charlock might not easily say farewell to the child now nearly ripe.

Rune finally chose not a sideem for this task. But another, one with twisted snout, one very loyal indeed, loyal as decay to a corpse. A young mole called Weed, born of Ilkley, and clever and cunning like all moles from those parts. Loyal to Rune, subservient, efficient, clever at not seeming too clever. Weed it had been who delivered Slithe for snouting; Weed had turned traitor on traitor and made each reveal the other; Weed knew much and kept his mouth shut. Weed could dissemble to anymole and win their cautious trust, and Weed would win Henbane's and betray her to Rune alone.

Yes, Weed was the one. He travelled south, found Charlock and Henbane, he told them he was sent by the Master himself and he counselled Henbane before they left. Counselled her so well that Henbane killed her own mother, not ever knowing that her father had a paw in it through Weed. Weed smiled to see surprise in Charlock's eyes before her sudden death. Charlock had taught Henbane her arts too well.

'But – ' was all Charlock managed to say, but the look

of surprise, dismay and betrayal on her face – Rune would enjoy Weed's description of that.

So, with her mother's own blood on her talons, Henbane left with Weed.

'You are going too fast,' said Henbane.

'Then faster shall I go,' smiled Weed, and did.

'There is not enough food here,' said Henbane.

'Then less shall you have!' smiled Weed, and took what food she had from her.

'I need more sleep!' said Henbane. To which Weed did not reply, but let her sleep.

But when she was in the deepest way of sleep he woke her roughly, saying, 'Then less shall you have!' And forced her to travel on.

So Weed prepared Henbane for the rigors of the sideem and in doing so won from her a curious loyalty, as those who are tormented learn to love their tormentor.

Rune was well pleased at what Weed had done, making him counsellor to Henbane; to prepare the ground for her journey south.

Of Rune's vile using of Henbane we shall say little. But he took her as father should never take daughter, and her not knowing who he was and, being trained well by Charlock, she wanted more and more. And sometimes he gave it and sometimes he did not. Dark, dark the glitter in his incestuous sadistic eye; black, black the lust that drove his talons into Henbane's flanks; bleak, bleak the feeling in Henbane's heart when Rune said, at last, having taught her the Word, that she must travel south.

'I do not wish to go,' she said.

'It is the Word's will,' he said.

'I do not wish it.'

'Nor to be WordSpeaker?' he said. 'For Scirpus wrote that a WordSpeaker would come who was female and would take the Word into all of moledom.' Rune smiled to see ambition and power light Henbane's eyes.

'But to be WordSpeaker is hard,' said Henbane. For such a mole must learn the Book of the Word from first to last, the only mole who knows it all but for the Master, and he – or she – must repeat a quarter of the book each solstice.

'It will not be hard for thee,' smiled Rune. Nor was it. For Henbane went into seclusion in the high tunnels and there was taught the Book by the Keepers, the twelve moles who each know a portion of the Book, one for each moleyear of the cycle of seasons. Then Henbane made her recitation in the presence of the twelve and Rune declared her WordSpeaker.

'What is thy will, Master?' she asked of him afterwards.

'Southward thou wilt go, with Weed as thy adviser and a mole of thy own choosing as leader of your guardmoles. And you will destroy the followers of the Stone even unto the Holy Burrows themselves. To the Seven Systems you will go and they shall be made desolate of the Stone and the Word will hold sway. Do it now.'

Desolate was Henbane to leave the Master she loved and who had taken her, but she was WordSpeaker now and holder of Rune's dream to conquer moledom, and she was the one chosen to bring at last to fruition the great work Scirpus had begun.

'One more task you will perform. There is a mole, Boswell. Find him and send him to me.'

So Henbane left Rune and the sideem of Whern, with Weed as her adviser. She made Wrekin leader of the guardmoles and wise was that choice, for nomole in the history of moledom has organised so few to defeat so many. And then, following in the wake of the plagues, she took over the enfeebled systems of the Stone until she reached the Holy Burrows themselves, leaving only Siabod, away to the west, and Duncton Wood, so far untouched. . . .

'For thee I do it, Master,' whispered Henbane now, staring up at the Blowing Stone with hatred. 'Soon now my task will be done and you will allow my return to thy side. Soon now . . .' and Weed, who had never been a father, could not hear in her voice the entreaty of a pup who desires to be loved.

Weed only saw her stir, and heard her whisperings. Long had been her meditation, and long his own. She nodded to him and to Wrekin, and then, like the shadows of clouds over a summer field, they made their way back towards the Holy Burrows of Uffington.

PART II

Buckland

Chapter Eight

Spring is a testing time for travelling moles. Males are allowed to watch over their females' litters only from afar and, resuming their old burrows, incline to be murderous to usurpers of their territory and argumentative with passers-by.

Females are best left alone where they have littered, for they are jealous of their tunnels and vicious for their pups. A sensible traveller makes a lot of noise so as not to take a mother by surprise and risk attack. He leaves the easier worms alone for mothers to find.

But the world is delightfully busy, the soil is warm again, and everything is astir. Worm and beetle roam aplenty, easy prey to teeth and talon. But owl are hunting for their young, and fox, and badger too *and* stoat, so a wise mole keeps his snout low, his talons sharp, and his ears ready for the shish of winged death and the over-ground rustle of the furred hunter.

For all that, a confident mole in spring travels with excitement as his friend and adventure as his mate, and traditionally finds welcome enough if his approach is right. For males, though tetchy, like to pass the time of day and grouse, while females are happy to talk with strangers who steer clear of their space and nestlings; and all want to find out what news there may be abroad and establish whither a traveller be bound.

At least that's how it used to be in the southern systems before the plagues and the coming of the grikes, when moles were untroubled by doubts and bitter memories of death and loss.

'But two moles travelling?' declared Tryfan doubtfully one day. 'A bit of a problem, Spindle, if we're to avoid investigation. We'll need some kind of story to explain what we're about.' He paused and thought a little before adding, 'I suppose I could be a herbalist – even the grikes will have a use for them, and I learnt a lot from my mother Rebecca and my half-brother Comfrey, who is healer still to the Duncton Wood system. You can be my assistant.'

Spindle looked about him uneasily, for they had travelled a good distance since they had left the Blowing Stone a week before, and had come off the chalk on to the clay vales to the north. The vegetation was different from anything he had ever seen. There were all sorts of shoots above ground and roots below which he knew nothing about, while some, like the delicate roots of harebell and the sturdy windings of knapweed, so useful to support tunnels in dry and friable soils, seemed scarce hereabouts and he missed them.

'Well,' he said finally, sounding as positive as he could, 'so long as nomole asks me to name the plants I'll get by, and I can learn their properties soon enough.'

Their alibi, however, was not to be tested quite yet, for it seemed sensible to Tryfan that once clear of Uffington and the possibility of pursuit they should rest in some deserted place, where they could enjoy the advance of spring, recover from the sudden flight from Uffington, build up their strength, and take advantage of swifter journeying once the warm dry weather of late April came. By then, too, mated moles would not be aggressive, and crossing their territory less of a problem.

No records exist of the place the two moles stayed, though many systems north of Uffington have been anxious to claim the honour to themselves.

Some say it was in the wetlands of the Lyford system, others that it was further west at Charney, birthplace of Skeat, one of the Holy Moles Boswell knew. A few believe that Tryfan travelled further north than that, given special swiftness by the Stone's grace, and was at or near no less a system than Pusey, ancient and good.

But scholars ever wish to travel over the barren ground

of surmise and make of life a guessing game. For moles who seek the silent centre of Tryfan's life it is enough to know that they found a goodly place, worm-rich and quiet, empty of other moles because of the plague, and there lived out the remaining weeks of March and the first half of April until the warmer days of early summer came.

They learnt to live in harmony with one another. Freed of the self-imposed tasks they had had before and able to make their days their own, they had the space to come to terms with the grim moleyears they had each, in their own way, lived through. Spindle put on weight, though never in his legs, which remained as elongated and thin as ever. At least he did not look quite so hunted and pathetic as when Tryfan had first seen him.

Tryfan aged a little and gained the authority that always comes when a mole leaves another he has relied on, and learns that he must go out into the world, taking responsibility for his own place in it, and perhaps for others too.

Certainly in those molemonths Tryfan himself seemed to grow stronger and more impressive, his coat a glossy dark now and his snout mature and purposeful. He had, though he was not aware of it, an air of calm – the calm that came with the faith that had been his inheritance from Duncton Wood, and which Boswell had nurtured so well in him.

Nomole knows now how much Tryfan suffered from the loss of Boswell, but Spindle sensed it and was careful to help the young scribemole all he could – checking tunnels, worm-finding, clearing and maintaining; and by being quiet in those long periods when Tryfan wished to meditate and do those rituals which scribemoles must.

The two moles shared a communal burrow and came together there to eat and talk quietly of the day's doings. It was Tryfan's habit to start their meals with a grace, such as scribemoles normally speak, and he would vary them according to his mood.

Some days, when he was cast down by the loss of

135

Boswell and worried for him, he might say the grace his father Bracken taught him:

> Be with us, Stone, at the start of our feast
> Be with us, Stone, at the close of our meal.
> Let nomole adown our bodies
> That may hurt our sorrowing souls,
> Oh nomole adown our bodies
> That may hurt our sorrowing souls.

Yet as spring progressed and summer came upon them, whatever crises Tryfan was passing through seemed to be over and he began to speak more positively of the future, and to invoke gladness and joy in graces that, later, Spindle remembered with love, and himself used on occasion:

> Give us, O stone, with the morning meal
> Health to the body, joy to the soul
> Give us, O Stone, of the final worm
> Enough for our need in the silence of sleep
> To the greedy, too much
> To the austere, good humour
> To the wasteful, no second chance
> To the unloved, thy love
> That all may eat and be well blessed.

What Spindle did not yet see, or rather comprehend, was the weariness that was with Tryfan at times in consequence of the burden he felt Boswell had put upon him – a burden to quest for something he did not really understand: a quest for Silence, a quest to prepare the ground for a mole or moles that were coming and would bring the wonder of that great Silence to allmole.

What Spindle did know, however, was that at times Tryfan was troubled in sleep, tossing and turning and mumbling about a white light he had seen and which was on him, over him, and Boswell was lost in it and needed help. At other times, Spindle knew, his talons thrashed this way and that, seeking to cast off from him some burden too great for a mole to bear. Sometimes then, in those dreams, he called Boswell's name, and sometimes tears were there, and then Spindle suffered too, his brow furrowed in distress, watching over Tryfan though never afterwards saying anything.

It has to be said too that Spindle, cleric though he was, and scholarly though his nature, had, through the moles he had known at Seven Barrows and from his master Brevis, learnt something more of the world than Tryfan had been able to while in the company of Boswell. So Spindle, inexperienced though he was, knew that spring was a time for mating, and if sometimes Tryfan was out of sorts and irritable it might have to do with the lack of female company; indeed the lack of *any* company but his own and Spindle's. As for Spindle, now that the Stone had sent him from Uffington and since he had taken no strict vows as Tryfan had, he saw no good reason why a bit of consorting and canoodling might not, of a young summer's evening, be in order, and good order too. So . . .

'Whither shall we be bound when we leave?' Spindle began to ask in mid-April, when the birds of hedge and copse were busy with their nestlings, and the ground was alive with the green growth of plants.

'I know not,' said Tryfan, 'but the Stone will guide me.'

'When?' asked Spindle impatiently.

'I cannot know that. But soon now, very soon. Are you restless of this place?'

'Yes,' said Spindle simply. 'Not exactly full of moles is it? Bit on the solitary side. Not much life, if you know what I mean.'

'Have you been bored, Spindle?'

'No, only lately. When the cold side of spring is over and the early summer sun starts lighting up the entrances once more, and other creatures are about, then a mole wants to busy himself and say hello.'

137

Tryfan laughed.

'Does he?' he said.

'Or she!' said Spindle with a sideways glance.

'She?' said Tryfan frowning.

'Well . . . yes. I didn't expect to mate after Longest Night, nomole to mate with. And now I'm your companion I don't suppose there'll be time for that sort of thing even if the season is right. But I wouldn't mind saying hello to a female or two!'

Tryfan looked at Spindle's thin fur and awkward paws, and the way his eyes were both humble and intelligent, and declared in some surprise that 'the thought never crossed my mind.'

'Ah well, Tryfan, you're a scribemole, aren't you? And celibate. Mind you, I'm not saying the thought might not cross your mind, but not quite the thing, is it? Not that the moles in Uffington were perfect in that respect. There was always a bit of wandering down to Seven Barrows in January and who's to say what goes on in tunnels in deep winter, or from where a litter comes? Not me! Suspiciously intelligent some litters in Seven Barrows were, considering that the local males themselves were never famous for their quick wits and repartee! Thick as lobworms, in fact. Why, some say that I myself might well have been fathered by a scribemole!' Having announced which he fell silent, blinked, and then looked rather smug.

Tryfan stared at him for some time, and finally said, a little stiffly, 'I don't know what you're talking about, Spindle.'

Spindle laughed and then stopped suddenly.

'Not yet you don't, but you will!'

'H'm,' said Tryfan and went off in a most unscribemole-like huff to meditate, except that the thoughts he had were too confused and mixed up to be called contemplative.

Females? He hadn't thought about them until now. Other moles? Society? Mixing? Tryfan wished his mind were his own but sometimes it did not behave as if it was, and the thoughts of the Stone he wished to have were not there.

It's time we got on with the journey, he said to himself eventually, and from the way he suddenly felt light-hearted, and the sudden singing of the birds and warming of the sun, and the exciting sense that beyond this forgotten place where they had been staying awhile there was a whole world to explore whose excitements and challenges were barely known . . . from all this, Tryfan might reasonably say, as he did to Spindle, that the Stone was telling him at last it was time to move on and that in a few days they would go.

The night before their departure the two moles crouched on the surface in the darkness and watched the moon rise and light up the vales over which, in the days and weeks to come, they would travel.

'Is it true a scribemole like you can read the ways of the Stone?' asked Spindle, staring out into the darkness and wondering about the world beyond them.

'Anymole can, it's just that I've been taught how to be still enough to do so easily.'

'Well I couldn't!' said Spindle.

'You could more easily than you think! You could scribe as well come to that. It's just that moles like to make a mystery of things, and then they can't do them.'

Spindle's eyes lit up. 'Now there's a dream, to scribe like a scribemole! I know what *I'd* scribe.'

'What?'

'History, that's what. What happened in moledom, when and why. Very interesting that, to scribe the things that moles say happened and then work out if they really did happen that way! Differences you see, the accounts all have differences. So where does the truth lie, Tryfan?'

'In moles' hearts I should think,' said Tryfan. Then he said nothing for a while, for history did not much interest him; it was the now that Boswell had taught him to take notice of. He tried to relax and feel the vibrations of the Stones near and far, a pattern of feelings that Boswell had taken pains to teach him. But it was hard at first because the power of nearby Uffington and the Blowing Stone was so strong, and made stronger on this line because beyond them was the great Avebury system whose stones are famed over moledom.

'I don't know anything about the systems beyond Uffington, except a few names,' said Spindle a little wistfully.

'I know them only from other moles who have travelled, as my parents did, and as Boswell has,' replied Tryfan.

'Make a tale of what you know then,' said Spindle, for he was a mole who liked to talk on a clear night, and would himself make a tale of anything.

So Tryfan told how, long ago, he had learnt from Boswell the directions of the seven Ancient Systems, and of the Stones that mark not only their location, but the communal ways between.

Each system has its own feel which is like a distant call, almost a vibration, he explained, and within the orbit of the Seven Systems each one could be felt, the changes in their relative strengths and tones being a scribemole's guide to where he was, and where he was heading.

Of the Seven Systems only one, the grim westerly system of Siabod, lies beyond the reaches of the three Rivers. These are the Thames, river of light and dark; the Severn, river of danger, which a mole must cross to reach Siabod; and the Trent, river of no return, beyond which, Tryfan had been told, lay territories unrecorded even in the Rolls of the Systems, except for those stories associated with Scirpus and the system of Whern.

Tryfan remembered his mother Rebecca telling him of the North and tried to remember it for Spindle now: 'Nomole can know what lies in the northern ranges, a land bleak of worm and dank of soil, where if moles live they know not of the Stone, or of the sun in summer. There the ground freezes up with cold and the tunnels, if they could be made, would burst with ice and crush a mole as if he never was.'

Bracken had said the same, adding that it was a place of giants and of fear. Yet a mole's heart quickens to hear the stories of the North, where the First Moles lived, who were made of the sparks hammered out by Ballagan when he smote the Stone in his time of doubt – smitings that finally produced the seven Stillstones; and the many legends of giants and snakes and natural dangers like the ice and the roaring mud; and the rain that eats a mole's skin and poisons his soul.

'If mole has been there, he or she has not come back to tell of it,' Boswell told him, 'but there is not a system that does not have its moles who have left to find the North, or legends of moles that have come back.'

Of all this Spindle knew something, but was glad to crouch low in the May night and hear Tryfan's account.

'And what of the places you were told of as a youngster?' asked Tryfan in his turn, when he had finished.

'I heard of Siabod, that's a system and a half that is. Wouldn't want to go there in a hurry! And the others of the Seven, including your own Duncton Wood. But what used to give me nightmares when I was a pup was my father's stories of the Empty Quarter known as the Wen which Boswell himself mentioned before we left Uffington.'

Tryfan nodded, settling down, for it sounded as if Spindle knew something of that and desired to tell of it.

'Yes,' continued Spindle, 'that's a place where the great Thames is swallowed underground and nomole lives.'

'Nomole?' said Tryfan, surprised, for he had heard that mole did live there, legendary mole.

'Well, that is to say, nomole lives there now I should think. Might have done in the past. Systems come and go. Sometimes moles used to come to Uffington from the distant east and they had tales of the Wen.'

'What is it exactly?' asked Tryfan.

'A twofoot system, not for mole. A place of rushing sucking water and disease. Rats black as night and the roaring owl, and fire at night so the sky is lurid with it. Nomole there!'

141

'Bracken said there might be,' said Tryfan. 'He said
. . .' and suddenly an early memory of his father came to
him and, in the darkness, Tryfan smiled a little sadly, for
his father had meant much to him, and when he was young
had told him a tale or two up by Duncton's great Stone on
such nights as this one.

'My father believed it was the place of the roaring owl
and all the roaring owl ways lead there, and they have
tunnels larger than the greatest Stone and there is the
march of twofoots all day long. There the old moles live
who speak the old language, and everymole can scribe – '

'Everymole?'

'Yes. There are no scribemoles, but everymole must
learn. From there the scribemoles first came as the grikes
have come now, to interpret the Stone to mole and teach of
the Silence that may be found.'

'So your ancestors came from the Empty Quarter!' said
Spindle, a little light-heartedly.

'And yours.'

'And our cousins may still be there! With roaring owls
for friends, and rats for good company!'

'You may laugh,' said Tryfan, 'but did not Boswell say
we might go "even to the Empty Quarter"?'

'Yes, but. . . .'

Tryfan smiled in the dark.

'But nothing,' he said with as strong and humourless a
voice as possible. 'I hope that you remember your task is to
keep with me.'

'But, Tryfan . . . you're not . . .?'

'The Stone will guide us,' said Tryfan with a maddening
calm, 'and it will lead us to where we must go.'

'It's getting cold,' said Spindle to change the subject.
'When will we set off, and for where?'

'Dawn for Buckland,' said Tryfan distantly. 'Dawn
. . .' and he hunched forward, snout a little to one side,
moonlight in the fur on his back, eyes enshadowed, his
voice strange suddenly.

Just below them there was a short bark and a shrill

squeal, and a fox paused for a moment, rabbit in jaw, and stared up in their direction before slinking into the darkness of a ditch. Downslope to the right a tawny owl called sharply and both moles instinctively moved nearer together, flank to flank.

Tryfan shivered suddenly, frightened perhaps by the prospects of journey and responsibility before him. Spindle tried to comfort him.

'Boswell said this was your task. I heard it. Good Boswell said I was to go with you, and I shall, though I am shaken with fear sometimes and won't be much good to you when you need strength, or quickness, or rituals. Won't be much good at all, I'm afraid. But I can find worms, I can make a tunnel the proper way, and, and . . . I'll never leave you, Tryfan, so long as you need me.'

And he paused apologetically, as if this, which was all a mole could give, was not enough.

'You have forgotten what Boswell saw as your greatest strength,' said Tryfan, his voice stronger for Spindle's encouragement and trust. 'You have not mentioned your faith in the Stone; that may, at times, be your greatest gift to me.'

'I have that and will not lose it.'

'Whatever happens?'

'No, never,' said Spindle firmly. 'Not so long as the memory of Boswell and what he said to me lives, not ever. Now, Tryfan, you had best sleep through these last hours of the night.' And together they crept underground to their burrows, and slept the light and troubled sleep of uncertain travellers on the eve of a journey, who do not know their journey's purpose, or where its end might be.

Chapter Nine

'What are your names and whither are you bound?'

The voice that challenged them came from the shadows of a wide part of the communal way down which they were travelling. It was from a confident male, and one who knew how to take a firm stance without unnecessary aggression. Tryfan went on ahead of Spindle and saw that the mole was powerful of haunch and that his fur caught the entrance light healthily. His gaze was indifferent and untroubled, that of a mole who feels secure in the organisation behind him, but there was something flat and emotionless about his voice which reminded Tryfan immediately of the guardmoles who had held them briefly at Uffington.

It would have been a dim mole who could not see that he had no intention of letting travellers pass by without checking on what their business was and where they were going. It seemed certain that they had reached the edges of the notorious Buckland system. . . .

They had learnt much of Buckland in the eight days since they had left their place of refuge and gone forward on their journey once more, and more, too, of the grikes' cruel ways. All of it confirmed the grim report which the scribemole Brevis, Spindle's master, had made before he had disappeared and probably been killed during the grike invasion of the Holy Burrows.

It seemed that when the plagues came, Buckland, a worthy enough place though Stoneless, had been hard hit and many had died and been sealed in. When the grikes took it over they decided to use it as one of their key systems, mainly because of its convenient location at a junction of ways leading to north and south, and to east and west. Just a little to the north of it was a crossing over the Thames, made by twofoots but reputedly ancient, a way moles and other creatures could use in relative safety from roaring owls, often a hazard at river crossing points. Roaring owls are jealous of such points and guard them well, crossing and re-crossing them constantly and blinding moles with the light of their eyes, or fuming them, if they fail to crush them on their onward rush. So a system with a safe crossing over a major river often prospered, and such seemed to be the case with Buckland.

They were informed that Buckland was to be a centre for guardmole training and much clearing and tunnel repair had been done in preparation for its inauguration at Midsummer as a working system. Indeed, so the rumours went, Henbane of Whern herself was to visit the system then and preside over the rituals the grikes favoured for Midsummer's eve.

'Rituals?' Tryfan had asked.

But the responses to *that* question among the moles they met were furtive and uneasy, muttered whispers, fearful glances. Aye, rituals, snoutings and killings and that. Punishments and Atonements. From Midsummer on, they learnt, Stone believers were to be outcast.

'Outcast?'

'Where do you two come from that you ask such questions?' somemole Tryfan was treating had asked suspiciously.

'Herbalists like us are more concerned with finding plants than worrying ourselves over-much with these goings on,' Tryfan had replied carelessly, digging his talons in extra hard to the mole whose shoulder he was healing. 'We've come from east of Fyfield way and the grikes have not done much there yet.'

'Eastward'll be the last push, praise the Word!' said the mole. 'Ouch! That hurts, healer!'

'Relax mole!' said Tryfan. 'Now, tell me about being outcast. We feel we've been such all our lives, eh Spindle?'

'Yes Benet,' replied Spindle, using the name they had decided to give Tryfan.

'Outcast moles may be killed by any who meet them, or taken to guardmoles who have rights to kill them as they will. Not to do so is a snouting offence in itself. To be outcast is to be dead, for a mole cannot hide from the Word,' said Tryfan's patient grimly. 'I wouldn't want to be a Stone follower and anywhere near Buckland at Midsummer. It'd be a snouting for sure!'

So they had journeyed towards Buckland, bit by bit learning what they could of the grikes. So that when they finally arrived there and were challenged by the guard-mole at the entrance to the Buckland system Tryfan had their answers ready. . . .

'Of Fyfield am I,' said Tryfan, choosing a system near Duncton which he knew to be extensive and where the plagues had been especially bad. He knew his accent gave him away as a mole from the systems east of Uffington but the chances of meeting a Fyfield mole who might challenge him were probably low. If he did he would just have to bluff it out by pretending to be from the outliers – those areas adjacent to major systems in which more idiosyncratic moles like to live. As it was, the guardmole did not seem to react or to wish to question his claim so he continued with his story. 'My name is Benet. My companion is a vagrant and simple, but of use to me.'

'Of use?' asked the guardmole.

Tryfan shrugged. 'A healer am I and I know of herbs, and he finds them well. And what is more – ' Tryfan laughed – 'he finds worms and I can eat them well!'

A brief obligatory smile went across the guardmole's face at this pleasantry and so, seemingly satisfied, he turned from Tryfan to Spindle.

'Your name?'

Spindle gawped at him stupidly, wiped his snout messily on his flank, peered at his talons and said, 'They do call me Spindle. They do call him Benet. What's your name?'

The guardmole recoiled a little at this rudeness but

then, dismissing it, said to Tryfan, 'Well, Benet, you have done wisely to come here. Healers, genuine healers that is, are in short supply and always needed when the Word has come. Are you of the Word?'

'Never was much of one for all that business, the Stone, the Word, and that,' he said slowly, adding indifferently, 'It's all one to me.'

'Well, you are obviously not initiate,' said the guardmole. 'But the eldrenes will see to that! A mole who is not of the Word lives against the Word and that is wrong, and by Midsummer it will be an outcasting for moles who have not Atoned. You have time enough. We don't hold it against southerners to have been of the Stone if they're willing to change their ways and learn the Word, may its power be praised.'

The mole paused, looking from one of them to the other.

'You always travel together?'

'Yes,' said Tryfan, puzzled by the question. 'Why, is . . .?'

The mole smiled, a little too positively, and, shrugging, raised a paw and said, 'It's nothing, no, no, nothing.' He paused again. 'You're a healer, you say?'

'Yes,' said Tryfan.

'Of Fyfield?'

'I have said so.'

'And where have you come from?'

'Wandering, here and there.'

'Well, well, it is good. You are welcome. But take care to become initiate. The eldrenes will help.'

Tryfan relaxed for the guardmole seemed satisfied, though for a moment his questions had expressed suspicion. As Tryfan looked suitably apologetic he wondered why the idea of the 'eldrenes' – who were presumably no more than female elders – left him feeling uneasy.

'Moles who do not learn the Word,' the guardmole was continuing pompously, 'are a source of trouble and concern. They are outside all systems and after the

147

Atonings of next Midsummer then such moles will be reviled and punished, hunted and driven from security into loneliness, and lost. The WordSpeaker says this must be.' The lecture ended there except for a final 'Merciful is the Word', spoken rather tonelessly, as if the guardmole was repeating words he had learned by rote. His eyes expressed little emotion and certainly no warmth, love and charity, the impulses that might be associated with 'mercy'. Tryfan was beginning to get the measure of grike guardmoles.

'WordSpeaker?' repeated Tryfan doubtfully. 'We're just simple moles of a system hit by plague and find all this hard to understand. The Word I know, but the "WordSpeaker"?'

'You southerners are ignorant,' said the guardmole dismissively. 'The WordSpeaker is Henbane of Whern, Word be with her, and she will honour us with a visit before long – which is why we are recruiting moles, even doltish herbalists, to get the system ready. Buckland is to be the mission centre for the final push to the east, to Duncton Wood and beyond to the very edge of the Wen.'

'Ah, yes,' said Tryfan, sounding as stupid as he could and thinking that this was useful information. The Wen was the same place as the 'Empty Quarter' that Boswell had mentioned in their final moments together on Uffington Hill. But more than that, when the guardmole mentioned the name, Tryfan felt that stirring of power come to him and a certainty that their way must lead into the Wen.

Spindle, perhaps sensing that the time had come to move on, looked about unhappily and declared in a loud voice, 'Time to move! Food!'

The guardmole seemed to lose interest at this point and, evidently satisfied with their story, said, 'You stay here and I'll fetch a mole to take you to the visitors' burrows. You'll stay there a day or two, be interviewed by an eldrene, and then be allocated a task within your competence.'

148

The guardmole left them briefly, and quickly returned with an abject looking male.

'This one'll guide you,' said the guardmole shortly. 'No talking, pausing, eating, fouling, or wandering. And don't surface. The guardmoles patrol and have orders to talon anymole they find on the surface without permission. It's for your own good: there are a lot of owls about.' With that they were dismissed into the Buckland system. Their guide looked at them briefly and muttered, 'The Word be with thee,' before leading them into the tunnels.

They were too intent on following their guide into the tunnel, which grew suddenly rather dark and unclear, to notice a female who appeared from a concealed side entrance near the guardmole and, like him, watched after them.

She was slim but somehow more impressive than the guardmole, but there was little doubt about whichmole had most authority.

'Whichmole's their guide?' she asked, her voice clipped and cold.

'Ragwort. He's trusty enough, Sleekit. A bit dim but he knows this infernal system better than most.' The guardmole stopped speaking and waited for her to reply, obviously in some awe of her.

'I like them not, I trust them not,' said Sleekit. 'They were not nervous enough. You did well to detain them with questioning. They may be the ones we seek, or they may not. "Benet", "Spindle" – the mole we seek is named "Tryfan". The White Mole Boswell told us that much. But the second we have no name for. These two seemed unsuspicious and it is best they remain so.'

Sleekit thought for a moment and then spoke a quiet instruction: 'Send word of their descriptions by the northern route and put a watch out for them. They must not be alerted that they are under surveillance, but neither of them must escape or be killed. They may have information of something we are looking for. I will follow behind them. Take that order now.'

Sleekit followed on down the tunnel the way Tryfan and Spindle had gone, while the guardmole rapidly went by another route until he found a colleague.

'Another alarm,' he said heavily. 'The sideem thinks a couple of moles I just let through may be the ones there was a fuss about a while ago. They seemed all right to me, just a bit ignorant. But you know the sideem, especially Sideem Sleekit. Take the usual password for watchout and give them these descriptions. . .' The two guardmoles talked a little longer and then set about their tasks.

★ ★ ★ ★ ★ ★ ★

For a time Tryfan and Spindle followed their guide directly north in good but mundane tunnels, but then they turned west into what was obviously an older part of the system. The tunnels were more winding, the soil darker, and they both felt more at home. Their guide slowed a little and Tryfan took the opportunity of asking him his name.

'Talking's not allowed,' replied the mole.

They travelled on in depressing silence a little longer until Spindle said, 'I'm stopping for food!' He had seen a wormful tunnel and turned into it. The party came to an abrupt stop.

'You're not meant to,' said the guide wearily.

Tryfan shrugged. 'He's rather . . .' He shrugged again and smiled.

'Oh,' said the guide apathetically. 'Yes. Well, all right. But if some guardmoles come we had better move right on.'

'You're not a guardmole then?' asked Tryfan.

The mole grinned a little ruefully.

'Me? I'm just . . . a mole.'

'Nomole's just a mole,' said Tryfan almost to himself, crouching down as Spindle tucked into a worm.

The guide seemed surprised at this response. 'A mole's just a mole in *this* system, you'll soon find that out,' he said.

Tryfan turned full on him and gazed at him. He felt the

150

power of the Stone in himself and so, evidently, did Spindle, for he turned from taloning the roof for more worms and watched Tryfan.

'What is thy name?' asked Tryfan softly.

'It's Ragwort, but . . .' His voice faded weakly. His eyes were wide on Tryfan.

'Then remember, Ragwort, that no Word nor Stone, nor anymole but thee can say truly what thou art or might become.' Tryfan seemed angry and Ragwort backed away from him in awe. 'There will come a time when thou must stand firm and say, "I *am* and nomole may gainsay it," and so long as you talk weakly of being "just a mole" so long off is that hour.'

Behind them in the tunnel they had journeyed down, the sideem female, who had followed them, listened intently, looked thoughtful, and then purposefully went off another way.

'What was that?' said Spindle suddenly, looking back the way they had come, and attuned to subtle noise from moleyears of being alone in the Holy Burrows.

'Nothing. Surface noise,' said Ragwort.

But Tryfan was not so sure either, and moved quickly back down the tunnel. There was nothing there and nomole in sight.

'Nomole there,' said Tryfan returning. 'It was nothing but nerves.'

He seemed suddenly weary and crouched low and said no more. Spindle brought him food. Ragwort settled a little way off, thoroughly unhappy and trying to summon up courage to speak but failing to find it.

Eventually Tryfan turned on him again and said, more gently now, 'If you've something to say then say it. I'll not harm you.' But Ragwort only shook his head, and said apologetically that really they ought to be moving otherwise they might be found and he would be punished by the eldrenes.

'Who are these "eldrenes" anyway?' asked Tryfan getting up to move on.

151

'They're the female elders who run the system and instruct the initiates.' said Ragwort. They – '

But there was the sound of movement ahead and they all three fell silent as they advanced on their way. A guardmole was crouched impassively in a major side route and watched them pass. Further on another waited too, this time blocking the way ahead. Ragwort signalled to them to stop and indicated a new tunnel that went off to the east, sloping down a little. An angled unfriendly tunnel cut into the hard subsoil. They stopped in the entrance.

'There's to be an Atoning,' whispered Ragwort. 'That's why there's a lot of guardmoles about.'

Before they could ask what he meant there was a heavy rush of air from the tunnel and a huge guardmole appeared followed by a frail looking mole, half-starved it seemed and his fur ragged. Two of his talons were bloody and broken and there was a look of despair in his face. Behind him, and driving him on with vicious talon-thrusts, came another guardmole.

'Come on, come *on*!' shouted the second one. 'The eldrene Fescue does not like being kept waiting.'

The prisoner mole stopped for a moment very near Tryfan and Spindle, and he seemed for a moment to seek them out, to gaze at them, as if sensing there were still at least a few moles who might help him. Tryfan instinctively pushed forward towards him, and only Ragwort's restraining paw prevented him from making a gesture of rescue that might easily have endangered them all.

Then the moment passed, the mole was driven on down the tunnel ahead of them, and after a short interval they were allowed to proceed.

Ragwort led them on, slowing because others were ahead of him. There was a curious mood about the place, full of light cheer and dark laughs, excited, unkind.

'What's going on?' Tryfan demanded of Ragwort, pulling him to one side to let others pass.

'Trouble,' said Ragwort. 'Best to keep your snout low. Best not to notice.'

'Where are they taking that mole we saw?'

Ragwort did not answer the question directly but said instead, 'There's things go on here. . . .'

'Th – things?' asked Spindle. Suddenly the atmosphere of Buckland seemed dark and ugly. Guardmoles seemed to be watching them from the shadows. They felt entrapped and threatened.

'Disappearances,' said Ragwort shortly.

'And snoutings?' asked Tryfan.

'There's things worse than snoutings,' said Ragwort, 'and places that are punishments in themselves.'

'Such as?' asked Tryfan.

'Where clearers are, which in this system means the Slopeside.' He said 'clearers' with a distaste and fear, as if the very word itself tainted the mole who spoke it. 'Take my advice and stay away from the Slopeside. Hardly anymole knows the half of what goes on up there, and the deaths that result.'

'But clearing's an honourable enough task,' said Tryfan, surprised. Clearers are moles, usually first-years or weaklings, who sort out and repair roof-falls and damage in the summer tunnels, and open up the deeper winter runs when the first cold comes and the worms go down.

'To be a clearer in Buckland is to be as good as dead.'

'Why? What do they do?'

'They clear plague corpses and open the seal-ups. But it's not what they do, it's what they catch doing it.'

'Is that mole going to be taken to the Slopeside?'

Ragwort hesitated before answering Spindle's question, his eyes uneasy, and Tryfan knew that he wished he could say 'yes' – but the fate of the mole was likely to be swifter and more final than that.

Before he could answer, however, they were pushed on by moles coming from behind into the rush and crush of moles at the entrance of a great communal tunnel, and it was evident that they had arrived very near the centre of the system, and at a time when something unpleasant was apaw.

Moments later, still carried along by other moles, they entered the main communal burrow itself, a huge cavernous place in which they suddenly had space as Ragwort led them hurriedly around the back of a mob of moles that faced the east end of the chamber. They saw that the place was supported on one side by the thin shining roots of birch, and shored up on another by honey coloured brecchia stone. The air was clear and well controlled and the acoustics dampening, so despite the large number of moles congregating the place was quiet.

Ragwort took them round the edge of the chamber, well clear of the main concourse and they had the chance to take it all in. The grikes were obvious enough, being squatter and darker than the others, and carried themselves with confidence and power. They talked in twos and threes, and passed by with a certain bravado, and Tryfan noticed that other moles got out of their way and avoided their gaze.

'What the hell you staring at? Eh?'

Tryfan turned quickly and found himself facing a large grike whose right front paw was already on him, the talons sharp.

'Well?'

'I was just . . . looking,' said Tryfan weakly, controlling the anger he felt at this rudeness.

'Say "Sir",' said the guardmole.

Tryfan stared at him and received a buffet for his insolence.

'I was just looking, Sir,' he said.

'Watch it, mole, or my friend'll have you,' laughed another guardmole unpleasantly. The first one turned and they all saw Spindle rearing up aggressively, as if ready to come to the aid of Tryfan.

'Very frightening!' said the guardmole sarcastically, and with a swift lunge winded Spindle who fell sideways. Other guardmoles saw it and laughed.

Ragwort ran quickly forward.

'Sorry, Sir,' he said. 'They're new to the system and not even initiate.'

'Well bugger off and don't poke your snouts about here again until you are,' said the guardmole, moving away.

A little shaken by the suddenness and violence of this encounter, the three of them regrouped.

'Grike guardmoles!' whispered Ragwort. 'They're the worst.'

They advanced on round the great burrow and were about to turn out of it down another tunnel when Tryfan became aware of a flurry and hush at the far end of the chamber, where roots supported the roof. He paused and turned but could see little because of the many moles between. Ragwort whispered urgently, 'Come on, we must get on!' But Spindle had stopped as well.

'What's going on over there?' asked Tryfan.

'It's the Atoning of that mole, but we mustn't stop for it,' said Ragwort.

But Tryfan had come to Buckland to find out what he could of the grikes, and that was what he intended to do. In any case, the attention of everymole there was suddenly taken up by moles arriving at the far end of the chamber; nomole seemed bothered by the three of them, and the bullying grike guardmoles had gone down to get a better view.

As he watched, two old and dried-up-looking females of severe unsmiling mien entered at the far end of the burrow where the others were waiting expectantly. Other moles seemed respectful of them, falling silent as they came near and casting swift, nervous glances at them as if awed but curious. Tryfan saw one of the guardmoles who had threatened them earlier so aggressively lower his snout in submission as they went past him.

'They are the eldrenes,' whispered Ragwort nervously.

The two eldrenes settled down, their backs to the great enshadowed roots behind them, which stretched up into the darkness at the top of the chamber and plunged down behind them into its floor.

Although there were two of them, the moles there had eyes for only one – the older, greyer, more grizzled of the two. Her mouth was downturned, her eyes narrow and suspicious, her stare chillingly cold. Her paws were strangely angled as if, in puphood, she had suffered some disease that had left her with a minor spasm in each paw. So they were like hooks beneath her, and their talons seemed longer than normal, shiny grey and curved. She seemed to crouch as if in continual pain, a pain that tainted her face with cruelty and a desire to punish others.

'Whatmole is that?' asked Spindle.

'Eldrene Fescue, most feared of all the eldrenes in moledom,' whispered Ragwort who, having failed to get his charges to leave, had reluctantly joined them. None of them saw a guardmole watching them carefully from the shadows. 'She was in Rollright before but has been sent on down here to get the system in shape before Longest Day. That means snoutings by all accounts.'

There was a sudden hush in the chamber as Eldrene Fescue began a whispered meditation to herself, the words indistinct.

'Merciful is the Word,' she said finally looking up at them all, and several moles in the crowd called out, 'Aye!' and 'Praise the Word!'

'Merciful is the Word,' repeated Fescue cutting across their voices, her own voice a chilling pained whisper again. And then she signalled to one of the guardmoles, and the wounded, abject mole they had seen earlier being driven down the tunnel was brought into the chamber and paraded in front of the eldrenes.

As he came in, with a guardmole on either side of him, a low and horrid murmur passed among the moles, the sound of contempt, and anger, and murderous intent. The sound, and the way the eldrenes leaned forward and stared mercilessly at the mole, sent a chill over Tryfan's fur and he felt he was watching something a long way away, something horrible, something he could not stop: darkness was on him and he sensed that in Fescue's presence he was the witness of evil; and worse than that, by being there

156

at all and doing nothing he was in some curious way a partner to it.

Yet though he tried to speak, tried to go forward, he was quite unable to, for cast upon him with the sense of evil was the discovery of fear, deep and jagged in him, impaling him to the very soil where they crouched – terror for himself. Yet he watched, while at his side Spindle, unable to look at the horror that was so clearly about to come, had closed his eyes and was desperately whispering an invocation to the Stone, asking its aid and mercy.

'What is the mole's name?' asked Tryfan of Ragwort.

Ragwort shrugged and shook his head.

'He was found wandering and talking of the Stone. There are many such. They have lost their minds and are too unfit to become initiate. They are either sent to the Slopeside or, if they are articulate and refuse to acknowledge the Word, then they are snouted.'

'But what is his name?' asked Tryfan again, for suddenly it seemed important to know. Then Eldrene Fescue began speaking.

'I do not propose to waste much time on you, mole, for you have told us you will not Atone and you have not been willing to confess of the Word.'

The mole held his snout low and looked at nomole.

'It is still not too late, for the Word is merciful. Atone, mole, and thy life will be spared.'

Then the mole spoke, his voice weak and yet his words very strong.

'I am of the Stone,' he said. 'So was I raised and so will I die. And the Stone will be merciful upon thee!'

The eldrene's eyes flashed with anger.

'Mercy is not thine to give,' said Fescue, 'nor thine to invoke, nor ever to have without the Word's will. Wilt thou Atone?'

'I am of the Stone,' repeated the mole.

'Then the Word will give thee one last chance. Thou will be marked among the moles here, witnesses of the Word who desire that you join them.'

157

'Aye,' muttered the moles in the chamber in a way Tryfan could hardly call welcoming.

'What is this "marking"?' he asked Ragwort as Spindle continued his prayers, his eyes shut to the proceedings before him.

'You'll see,' said Ragwort. 'And if he's brought anywhere near here, whatever you do, mark him. It is punishable not to.'

As he spoke the mole was taken bodily from behind by two large guardmoles and paraded around the chamber. To his horror Tryfan began to see what a marking was, for each mole that he was led past or proffered to, thrust or stabbed at him, not heavily but enough to hurt and draw blood.

'Atone!' they cried out as he came to them, and this cry turned into a chant, louder and louder, as the mole was successively marked by them. Until, as he was brought to where Tryfan waited, it was clear that the pain of the markings was great – but more than that, the pain of being so outcast and rejected was great, for the poor mole had begun to cry deeply and terribly as the chant around him grew ever louder: 'Atone! Atone! *Atone!*' and the markings turned his feeble body into a run of blood and wounds and each new touch was torture.

Spindle suddenly turned from Tryfan's side and fled out of the chamber, and Ragwort followed, but something kept Tryfan where he was even though the mole was now very near him and would soon be proffered to him and he would have to mark him too.

'Stone, guide me,' whispered Tryfan. 'Help me have courage, show me what to do, Stone . . .' And then the mole was before him and his tears of loneliness in the agony of his final punishment were on his face, and behind him, staring at Tryfan, were the exultant sadistic eyes of the two guardmoles, shouting and chanting.

Then Tryfan went forward, reached out a taloned paw and speaking low but clearly so that only the mole himself might hear, while appearing to strike him as well, Tryfan said, 'The Stone is with thee, mole, and now thou can hear its Silence, now its Silence is thine, listen mole listen. . . .'

For a moment the mole went still, then he looked at Tryfan and he saw faith in the Stone in Tryfan's eyes, and love, and knew he was not alone of the Stone, and as he passed on the guardmoles were astonished to hear him cry out in a voice suddenly strong, '*I am of the Stone!*' Then as more moles marked him he seemed to feel it not, his voice strong and praising the Stone, his very existence suddenly an affront to all there such that their chant became angry and changed now to, 'Kill him! Snout him! Make him die!'

So the clamour passed from Tryfan and back to the part of the chamber where the eldrenes waited, and as the mole seemed to find ever greater courage in the face of the death that faced him, and feel their blows no more, Tryfan seemed to shake and tremble in agony, as if he was taking the mole's blows for him.

Indeed it did seem so for Spindle, watching from a side tunnel, saw Tryfan rear up and his mouth open into a cry of pain, though if he did cry out nomole heard it or noticed it for the chanting and clamour was great now, and all eyes were on the final fate of the mole.

'Kill him that the Word may show him the mercy in death he could not accept in life,' said Eldrene Fescue.

Then all was blood and final horror as one guardmole held him and another pulled back his huge paw, extended his sharp talons and plunged them forward into the nameless mole's snout and eyes. Then, as the grikes roared out their approval and the mole arced into one last spasm of life before death, Tryfan, unnoticed at the back, screamed out, his fur shining with dark sweat and his breath fast and agonised, and his eyes full of tears.

Hurriedly Spindle and Ragwort came for him, and dragged him away and out of the chamber before others saw him in the terrible state he was in.

As they took him down the tunnel they heard a final roar, murderous, evil, cruel, as the moles behind them

159

watched the nameless follower of the Stone die, and in the exultant silence that followed, Eldrene Fescue's voice whispered, 'Merciful is the Word!'

While behind the three hurrying moles a mole came as well as a voice. Elegant she was and female; watching darkly.

'Follow them,' she whispered to the guardmole who had been watching them throughout.

'Yes, Sideem Sleekit,' said the guardmole.

'And watch *that* mole well,' she hissed coldly, pointing a talon after Tryfan as, hunched and nearly helpless, he was carried away from the communal chamber by Spindle and Ragwort.

Chapter Ten

By the time Spindle and Ragwort had got Tryfan through
the tunnels to the visitors' quarters of Buckland he was in
an even worse state of collapse than when he had left the
central chamber. He seemed deeply troubled, and in pain,
his fur sweating profusely and his talons weak. Ragwort
was very frightened, as if it were all his fault and he would
be punished. He had also become aware that a guardmole
was following them and was convinced that he would be
killed. Spindle, too, was concerned, for though he
understood that Tryfan's state was to do with the evil they
had witnessed in the communal chamber and his touching
of the mole, he had no idea how to comfort Tryfan, who
seemed to hear nothing that was said to him but, rather,
was lost in some suffering beyond them all.

So, greatly troubled, they arrived at the visitors'
quarters, where Spindle immediately sought out a dry and
comfortable place where Tryfan could lie down and sleep.
There he led him, gently pushing him down and staying
with him as he passed fretfully into slumber.

It was only then that Spindle was able to look round and
observe the communal burrow they were in more closely.
It was foul and ill-kempt, and there were two other moles
huddled in a far corner watched over by two guardmoles,
one on duty near the entrance through which they had
come, and the other guarding what appeared to be a
surface entrance. The nearer of the guardmoles came over
and spoke to Ragwort who, after briefly explaining who
they were, and that 'Benet' had been taken ill, said a quick
goodbye to Spindle, looked worriedly at the stricken
Tryfan and left after muttering a final whispered wish that
they might meet again.

The guardmole turned to Spindle in a friendly enough way.

161

'You're to stop here for a night or two and then you'll be taken to Eldrene Fescue to be given your task. Not the most salubrious of places, this. Punishment duty for us! But feel free to help yourselves to the food, such as it is.' Nearby was a crude larder of decapitated worms, some writhing in the dark, but several already dead and unappetisingly still.

'You two best rest and keep quiet,' he concluded. 'Don't bother us and we'll not bother you. If you do need something just give a shout. My name's Alder and my mate's called Marram.' Alder was a big mole, and strong, and though his head and flanks were scarred and pitted from fighting, he had a friendly face and cheerful eyes, and he looked at a mole directly. His friend Marram was a little smaller, though still large and strong enough, and looked more concerned with life than Alder did: rather serious, perhaps. Spindle felt that, judging from the other guardmoles they had met, they could have done a lot worse.

'Can we go up on to the surface?' asked Spindle, indicating the surface entrance Marram was guarding. Marram came over and joined them and said immediately, 'No, you can't do that. You shouldn't have a need to, and anyway, your friend doesn't look up to much.'

'My friend might like some fresh air,' said Spindle.

'There's owls about up there, and if they don't get you the patrols will,' Marram said. 'Best stay here.' He looked forceful, and Spindle knew they had no choice but to do as he said.

As if to take Spindle's mind off the freedom the surface represented, Alder pointed an indifferent talon at the two moles in the far corner. They seemed miserable and tired, and looked grubby and abject.

'Don't mind them, they're vagrants waiting for instruction or Atonement.' Even from where he was, Spindle could tell from their stance and the subjected lie of their paws and snouts that they were apprehensive, or worse. One of them, a young male, looked briefly over towards

162

them and then away again. The other, a female, appeared weak and restless, probably ill.

The guardmoles returned to their stance and had a quick whispered word with each other, looking over at Spindle and Tryfan, Marram looking worried, but Alder waved a friendly talon in their direction when he saw Spindle watching, as if to reassure him.

Some hours later, when dusk was creeping over the surface and the burrow was getting dark, Tryfan, whose sleep had been restless, fell still as if, finally, peace had come back to him and his breathing became deep and steady. Spindle continued to watch over him with protective concern, though to anymole else it would have seemed it was the thin and gaunt-looking Spindle who need the protecting, and the young and powerful Tryfan who would have provided it.

Then suddenly Tryfan stirred and opened his eyes, and stared with affection on Spindle, who immediately went to get him some worms which, despite their poor quality, Tryfan ate hungrily, as if he had not eaten for days.

'You know, Spindle,' he said eventually, 'it was the fact that that mole had no name. No name. Nomole knew who he was, or where he came from. He could have been anymole . . . anymole.'

Spindle noticed that Tryfan's voice had changed, though perhaps the full impact on Tryfan of the torture and death of a mole they had witnessed was not clear yet. But his voice was deeper, older, and there was to his stance the sense that he now accepted a responsibility and purpose he had not been able to before.

'I shall not forget that mole, not ever in my life,' said Tryfan, 'nor the fact that I was afraid to help him.'

'You could have done nothing, Tryfan, nothing at all except get yourself killed, and me as well. Even as it is we are not exactly what I would call safe!'

For a time Tryfan was silent, thinking about it all. Then he said, 'I know that is true, but I also know that there was something wrong about what we did and something right

163

about what the mole did. He said simply, "I am of the Stone", and the grikes could not stand that he did so. He had no name . . . no name. The Stone wants us to know something of that, something very important, but I don't know what it is. When I touched him I felt the power of the Stone in me and though I could not hear the Silence myself I know that through me he heard it, and in giving him that way to the Stone I took upon my body the pain he had. It was hard, very hard, and I have been somewhere that one day I will have to find the strength to go back to.'

For a moment Tryfan's voice trembled, and Spindle moved closer to him.

'I was there near, I was watching you, and I was frightened too, Tryfan, but I would not have left you and I never will.'

'I know you were,' said Tryfan. 'I knew that all the time you were there, and your faith was there. But something . . . there is something I don't know about it all, something that I must learn. "I am of the Stone," that's what the mole said. And I do not even know his name.'

Seeing them talking, though their voices were low, Alder ambled over and joined them.

'It's not too bad here,' he said, 'and it won't be for long for you. Just a day or so. We've got another three or four days of this ourselves until those two get taken for instruction, always assuming that female makes it. She's not well. You two to be initiated?'

Tryfan said he was not sure. He thought so probably.

'It's a doddle if you keep your trap shut. Listen right, do as they say, and a mole like you with a bit of sense to him will get a good billet and easy worms.'

' "Billet"?' repeated Tryfan, nodding in a friendly way at the guardmole. They kept using words he did not understand.

'You know, burrow; what a mole lives in. Billet's what we call it where we come from.'

'Where are you from, then?' asked Spindle, always curious, for he was a collector of information, and curious about the whys and wherefores of other moles and their systems.

'North,' said Alder unhelpfully, and they noticed for the first time that he had the same shortened hard accent as the other grikes they had met, and a slight defensiveness beneath his natural friendliness. There was silence.

'North?' repeated Spindle, frustrated at the short answer.

Alder relaxed again, as if pleased that they were interested. 'Came down with the second push after Henbane left. Sent off by Rune himself we were.'

'Did you see him?' asked Tryfan, coming closer.

'Did we *see* him?' he repeated slowly. 'Well, that would be hard to say exactly, wouldn't it? Whern's a dark sort of place where the shadows are confusing and a mole does well to keep his snout low and his thoughts to himself. There was a mole up there, old and with fur that shone like I've never seen, all dark and glittering, and they said he was Rune and I stole a quick look but I was scared . . . we all were. "That's Rune!" somemole said, and I was willing to believe it, the burrow felt so . . . so *important* with him in it.'

'Did he say anything?' asked Spindle, fascinated.

'A bit, but I can't remember much. Angry he was, his voice suddenly rising loud and he said the time had come to go south and take the systems that were ours by right. Death to the Stone followers, he said, and then he was silent, and that's the bit I remember best.'

'The silence?' whispered Tryfan.

Alder nodded. 'Terrible it was, him just up there with his coat all darkly glittering and silent, like sharp talons are silent, and it seemed to last forever; and then he was gone and we knew where we had to go, and what we had to do.'

He pulled himself up short as if surprised to find himself speaking so much and then, to change the subject, looked over at the two moles in the corner appraisingly. '*They* won't be up to much if you ask me. Nice for a show at

165

Midsummer but that's about it. Eldrene Fescue's not one to tolerate weakness, know what I mean? I served with her at Rollright, and I'd say if they put one paw wrong, and with Fescue all it takes is to breathe wrong once, and they'll be sent up the Slopeside or snouted sooner'n you can say "dead"!' He thought this very funny and laughed loudly. The male mole looked nervously over towards them, and then back to the female, moving closer to her as if to protect her from the guardmole's laughter.

Alder wandered off and took up his station again at the entrance as Tryfan pondered what he had said about Rune.

He and Spindle settled down as night fell, affecting indifference to the other moles while looking carefully about and considering what their options might now be.

From the thumping and shuffling overhead and the pulling up of grass it was not hard to deduce that cows were grazing above and that they were beneath some pasture land, or very near it. Probably adjacent to it, decided Tryfan, for the rotten base of a fence post thrust down on one side of the burrow formed a buttress to the surface entrances, while spreading across the ceiling were the roots and tendrils of giant thistle and broom, such as grew in the wasteland between pasture and wood. A good place for exits and entrances and one which often defined the boundary of a wood-based system. But Tryfan had not seen or smelt evidence of woody tunnels and guessed that much of the system lay beneath untended scrubland, offering its young the opportunity of expanding up into woodland or down to pasture. The 'Slopeside' was presumably the area that stretched up under the wood-land, and Tryfan, a woodland mole, felt an instinctive interest in it, however grim might be the dangers it harboured. He missed tunnels which held the sound and complexity of tree roots and disliked the straightness and sterility of these lowland systems.

With such thoughts, and following Spindle's lead, he had a little more food and then went back to sleep.

Shortly afterwards, from the shadows of the entrance through which they had come, there was a sly dark movement, and Sideem Sleekit emerged. The guardmoles immediately crouched to attention saying, 'Word be with thee.'

'And thee,' said the sideem indifferently. 'Any problems?'

'None, Miss.'

'Keep them here without fail. It'll be a snouting for you both if you lose them.'

'Don't worry, Miss, we've warned them off the outside already. Er . . . whatmole are they?'

'Stone followers,' said Sleekit. 'Watch them carefully. Your names?'

'Alder,' said the one who had talked about Rune.

'And mine's Marram, Miss,' said the second.

'I'll not forget,' said the sideem. 'Until morning, then. Now rest easy.'

'Aye, aye!' said Marram.

They breathed more easily once she had gone.

'Wonder whatmoles they really are,' said Alder, who had an intelligent and interested face and was obviously a mole who wanted to know things.

'She said they were Stone followers, didn't she? That's all we need to know. Now you take the first night watch and let me get some rest,' said Marram turning away to sleep.

Alder settled his snout on his extended paws, and fixed his gaze on Tryfan's sleeping face, and afterwards, long, long, afterwards, when he was an old mole with memories of great things to tell his grandchildren's pups, he remembered how, as he gazed on that mole he was guarding, his heart seemed suddenly beset by a blizzard wilderness, caused perhaps by being asked about where he had come from and why, and he had a longing he could not account for to know of the Stone which was said to be so bad. And then, he said, he found that the eyes of Tryfan (as he later knew him) were open on him, staring at him, and he could not look away and he swore, though it was a strange thing to remember, that Tryfan came over to him and said, 'Why do you punish Stone followers when they cause you no harm? Why?' Yet when Alder found courage to look again he only saw Tryfan asleep, and his eyes closed. Then Alder seemed to see before him all the many sufferings and torments of Stone followers he had witnessed and knew that the mole was near him then and willing him to remember. And Alder was ashamed.

Then, try as he might not to, for he had taken the watch, he slipped into sleep. As dawn came, and as he turned to check the mole who troubled him so much was still there, he found that Tryfan was there at his side, and there was nothing in the burrow but him, and his gaze upon Alder, and Alder was afraid.

'Come,' said Tryfan, 'for I have something to show you.'

And Alder, unprotesting, driven by something in the mole's terrible strength and sadness, followed him; and they went to the surface.

It seemed to Alder then, as he ever afterwards remembered it, that the rising sun was in the tunnel ahead of the mole and its light was all around him and there was something he would see and he was afraid of it; for it made him cry, and he was a grike, a Northerner, a campaigner, and he was only doing his job. . . .

Tryfan led him out on to the surface and, avoiding the patrols, they went a good way through and under the protection of straggly gorse and broom to a clear patch in whose centre, near another entrance, lay the body of a mole. Marked was he, terribly, and his snout crushed, and he lay curled into death, his mouth a little open. Dew had formed on his fur and the sun's dawn rays were caught in it. It was the mole who had been killed the day before.

'Do *you* know his name?' asked Tryfan. 'Do you?' And he stared down at the mole, his snout low, and he wept before Alder and Alder stared at him, his world suddenly numb to him, and he saw the pity of the mole that had died.

'Why do you punish Stone followers, Alder?' asked Tryfan again, but repeating his name this time. 'Tell me, why? This mole was a follower of the Stone, and so am I, and in punishing us you punish only yourself. Why do you do it?'

'But I . . .' But there was nothing he could say, for Tryfan looked at him with an open heart, and he could not bear the stillness there.

Then Tryfan turned from him and went back and crouched by the entrance to give him time for his own thoughts. Alder stayed where he was, staring, and he saw in that nameless mole who had been killed by the grikes the day before, the tens, the hundreds, the thousands that had died in the long march of the grikes to the south.

'But I . . .' Alder's mouth trembled, and he heard their cries again, around him, the many, the nameless many, and he felt ashamed and he was blinded with tears.

Then he turned, his body heavy, his paws aching, and he saw Tryfan waiting for him.

'What shall I do?' asked Alder.

'Listen for the Silence of the Stone,' said Tryfan, and his eyes were like the sun on Alder.

'Whatmole are you?' asked Alder in a whisper. 'Whatmole?'

'I am nomole,' said Tryfan, 'but there is one coming before whom you will forget all others and he will be of the Stone's Silence. And you will know him, and help him.

'You have courage, Alder, for you have slept and now you have dared to waken. And before the day of thy life is done you will see the mole who will lead you to Silence.'

'What is his name?' asked Alder

Tryfan turned and looked back at the mole who had been killed the day before and said, 'We of the Stone call him the Stone Mole but his name I know not. Nomole knows it yet. He is nameless and unborn.'

'But he will come?'

'Yes,' said Tryfan, 'he will come. And you will know him.'

Then they returned to the sleeping chamber, again without encountering a grike patrol, and none other there, not even Spindle, knew where they had been, what they had seen, or what Tryfan had said.

★ ★ ★ ★ ★ ★ ★

Even so, during the day that followed Spindle was much puzzled, for Tryfan was silent and barely stirred, and the guardmoles seemed to have had an argument, for the one called Alder was silent too, crouched, his snout along his paws, and though his colleague Marram seemed to try to talk to him yet he said nothing. As for the two vagrants at the end of the chamber, only the male moved, carrying food over to the female and grooming her with a touching care.

Then when the male asked if he might go to the surface for some fresh air, although Marram said no, the guard-mole Alder suddenly turned and said, 'Let him!' and it was an order that anymole would have been afraid to disobey. So, unaccompanied, the male went to the surface, from where he soon returned.

It was all a puzzlement to Spindle, for there seemed to be something in the burrow that he could not name or see, but which was there, something peaceful. And Tryfan knew of it; and Alder. And, and. . . .

It was not until late evening of that day that Tryfan stirred once more, saying suddenly that they might as well find out what they could about the two silent vagrants in the corner. Moles like to know the gossip and what goes on. Spindle agreed with this happily, for it suggested that Tryfan was coming back to normal. They approached the male and, since a traditional greeting seemed out of place, simply said, 'Hello.'

'Are you going to instruct us?' asked the male. His voice, like his body, was thin and unsure of itself. His eyes were filled with apprehension, but Tryfan noticed that even so he moved in front of the female, as if to protect her.

'We're new to the system,' said Tryfan in a low voice. 'We've only just arrived.'

The male stared uncertainly at him.

'What's your name?' he asked.

'My name doesn't matter for now,' said Tryfan gently.

'Oh,' said the male, staring at Tryfan and Spindle, and then over to Alder and Marram who were watching them all.

'I'm not a grike, if that's what you're thinking,' said Tryfan, indicating the two guardmoles. 'We're just visitors, herbalists in fact.'

'Ah,' repeated the male, relaxing a little.

'What's your name?' Tryfan asked.

'Pennywort,' said the mole, adding apologetically, 'That's unfortunately what they called me. Stone knows . . . I mean goodness knows why. Silly name.' His speech was a lot more lively than his looks.

'Pennywort,' repeated Tryfan, laughing slightly and approaching nearer. He felt himself warming to Pennywort for there was something open about him even if he seemed nervous and awkward in his stance, his talons fidgeting and his snout unsure. But he seemed to want to speak.

'Yes?' said Tryfan encouragingly.

'Well . . .' There was more hesitation, another glance at the guardmoles, and then a lowering of the voice. 'Well . . . you laughed. They *never* laugh. Not at the right things anyway.'

'Oh,' said Tryfan, considering this. Certainly there had not been much mirth about the grikes at Uffington, nor those moles he had seen in Buckland's central burrow.

'Where are you from?' asked Pennywort.

'Fyfield,' said Spindle quickly, for Tryfan seemed slow to reply. It seemed to Spindle that Tryfan was reluctant to maintain their disguise or tell a lie. Considering the careful story about being travelling herbalists they had prepared, this was a change indeed. But Spindle was right: the experience in the central chamber had deeply affected Tryfan. He was somehow stiller, more certain. It was as if he had learnt something important and that the knowledge of it would always be with him.

'Fyfield's to the north isn't it?' said Pennywort.

'North east,' said Tryfan.

'A goodly system I've been told.' Again Tryfan was silent.

'Yes,' mumbled Spindle for him.

'Where are you from?' asked Tryfan.

'No system with a name. South of here, near Basset.'

'Both of you?' asked Tryfan, looking at the female.

'My sister and I.'

Pennywort turned to the female and Tryfan looked surprised. The female was clearly a Longest Night older than her brother.

'Different litter, same parents,' explained Pennywort reading his thoughts. 'Both dead in the plague which came to us late a Longest Night ago. Thyme – that's her name – raised me. She's ill now so I'm protecting her. When the grikes came we kept to ourselves but we were flooded out of our burrows in February so we travelled to better ground. Met two other moles and joined them and then we ran into the grikes. Fighting. The two with us got killed. They could have killed us but they didn't. Brought us here. Waited now for days. Thyme's very ill but they won't bring a healer. They say she can't have one until she's initiate and accepted the Word. But I know her. She won't do that. Not ever. She won't.'

Pennywort gazed at his sister who lay with her eyes closed, her mouth open and her breathing laboured. Her fur was matted and her paws limp and colourless, one bent back under her. Occasionally she moaned.

'I don't know what to do,' said Pennywort finally and Tryfan saw he was close to tears. He had spoken rapidly, as if he had had nomole to talk to for a long time. Then he added: 'I don't know what's wrong with her,' he said. 'It's got worse since we met the grikes.'

'Where were you bound?'

'To find a Stone for her to touch!' said Pennywort. 'None near Basset, but I thought there might be one here somewhere. I wasn't sure . . . And now they won't let us go away.'

Tryfan looked at Thyme again. But then, as he moved a little closer, Pennywort came aggressively between them again.

He stared hard at Tryfan.

'Are you of the Word?' he asked. 'No disrespect, but if you are I would rather you didn't touch my sister.'

'I have said that I am not,' repeated Tryfan reassuringly. Thyme turned uncomfortably in her half-sleep, and Tryfan could smell her sickness, but it did not repel him. Some words of Boswell were sounding in his heart: 'A scribemole's constant task is to love, and to love the weak before the strong, the sick before the well. This is most hard, Tryfan, and takes many years to accomplish, for a mole is attracted by the light which he thinks he sees in the strong and the healthy, and he seeks to avoid the dark he imagines in the sick lest it attach itself to him. Learn to love them and to see the light they hold . . . for if you do it will shine brightly in your heart and lighten your way.'

Tryfan stared at Thyme but could see no great light there: only suffering and illness and the smell of despair and, perhaps, death. But then, for the briefest of moments, the sense that he was of Rebecca, who had herself been a healer, came over him and, quite forgetting the front of indifference he had been maintaining, and ignoring the possibility that the guardmoles in the distance might become curious, he reached out to touch her. Pennywort faltered and then moved to one side.

Spindle came closer too and stared down at her.

'Is there anything you can do?' he whispered to Tryfan. 'For she seems a worthy mole.' But he needed to say no more, for Tryfan was already stancing himself over Thyme, and bringing his paws to her and there was stillness about him now which Spindle recognised as that of a true scribemole.

As Tryfan touched Thyme's flank he felt within himself the power of the Stone and it was as if his body was shaken with her sickness and he too was ill. He felt her suffering as he had felt the pain of the nameless mole the day before.

173

Would it then always be so hard to be a healer? Was this what his brother Comfrey felt?

He turned to Pennywort and said, 'I remember a blessing my mother used to say.'

'It is not allowed. They'll stop you,' said Pennywort, looking nervously towards the guardmoles. Indeed, Alder, who had been watching them from across the burrow, got up and began to come purposefully towards them.

'The guardmole Alder's coming!' hissed Spindle.

But Tryfan ignored this warning altogether and, to Spindle's surprise, when Alder reached them he was not aggressive.

'Better you than me,' he said mildly. 'Could be residual plague she's got. We never wanted her in here in the first place. But – ' He shrugged. 'I don't suppose a bit of old-fashioned laying on of paws'll hurt anymole. The eldrenes should have sent somemole here before this so I'll not be reporting what you do.' Alder went off and engaged in conversation with the other one on the far side of the burrow who, it seemed from snatches of conversation they heard, was not quite so keen on a healing going on, old-fashioned or not.

As Tryfan turned back to Thyme, Spindle too went close to her, and with such concern in his thin face that Pennywort moved not a talon to stop him.

It was at this moment that Thyme, perhaps feeling Tryfan's presence, opened her eyes and found she was looking into the eyes of Spindle. She was too weak to recoil from the stranger.

'It'll be all right,' faltered Spindle. 'My friend will help you.'

She tried to speak but could not, and Spindle said softly, 'Now don't you say a thing. My friend . . .' And he looked round at Tryfan with appeal in his eyes. '. . . knows what to do.'

The Stone grants to all moles the capacity to heal, though few know it or, if they do, honour it. Until then

Tryfan had done little more than touch other moles in friendliness, but now he felt at last the sure calm nature of healing, and understood the effort it required.

As Tryfan's paws touched Thyme's flanks, he found himself whispering of seven moles, seven Books, seven Stillstones and as he did so, as the Stone's grace is sudden and always unheralded to mole, power was there and light and Tryfan began the task for which his life so far had been the preparation.

He seemed quite unconcerned by the presence of others, friendly or not, and no longer adopting the low concealing voice he had first addressed Pennywort in, he began a healing chant Rebecca his mother had taught him:

> *May Stone's silence be thine*
> *And well and seven times well may you become*
> *The warmth of the Stone be about thee. . . .*

He spoke powerfully, and everymole in that burrow knew instantly that something strange and powerful was apaw. Hearing his voice the guardmoles looked round: 'healing' was one thing but this was much more than that and now the guardmole Marram started to come across the burrow to tell him to stop.

> *The warmth of the Stone be about thee*
> *The shadow of Stone to protect you*
> *From the crown of thy head*
> *To the soles of your paws*
> *The light of the Stone for your health. . . .*

'One of the guardmoles's coming again!' cried out Pennywort, instinctively moving closer to Thyme to protect her. But Tryfan had neither thought nor eyes for anything but Thyme, and simply continued chanting the invocation in an ever-more powerful voice so that the walls and ceilings of the burrow seemed to shake with change and light:

175

The light of the Stone for your health
And the love of the Stone for your eyes.
And well and seven times well may you become

'Alder, he speaks in awe of the Stone!' cried out Marram in fear.

'Yes,' said Alder, 'yes . . .' And there was joy in his voice to hear Tryfan's words and he made no attempt to stop them, nor to help Marram to do so.

'He must be stopped!' shouted Marram, running forward again.

But when he reached Tryfan all his talons could do was flail the air powerlessly as if upon a fortress of light no dark talons could destroy.

Tryfan ignored him utterly, his paws on Thyme as the fur on his back and side matted with sweat in his effort to invoke the powers that a healer must. Around him was light, and darkness too, effort and trouble, and all there felt the sickness in Thyme as if it was a haunting of their making which only together they might exorcise.

'Help me!' cried out Tryfan suddenly. 'You must all help me!' His voice thundered about the burrow, and whatever protest Marram had been making, and any doubt that Pennywort had had, were forgotten as the moles ranged behind Tryfan, staring and helpless as Thyme lay writhing in distress now, and shivering, and Tryfan tried to hold her, as if her very life was caught between the light he held and the darkness all about.

'Help me!' he cried out urgently again. And then he began to mutter desperately, as if his own strength was beginning to fail and the healing still not done, 'Seven moles come, seven Books made, seven, seven . . . We need another, Spindle. We need one more. Six here only, six including Thyme. Spindle, help me.' And as Spindle, desperately uncertain what to do, reached out a paw to touch poor Thyme as well, and the others joined their paws together too, Tryfan sighed and said, 'We need a seventh here among us!'

176

Then as all seemed subsumed in the effort of helping Thyme, all hunched over her, Spindle said, 'But there's only five of us Tryfan, five.'

'Six with Thyme: these two guardmoles, you and I, Pennywort and Thyme. Six moles making, yet seven are now needed.'

Dark had that burrow become, desperate, and Thyme was slipping from them, weakening as even Marram joined in the touching and said gruffly, 'Can't you help the lass? She's dying under our very paws!'

'Seven,' said Tryfan weakly. 'Seven needed.'

Unnoticed, silent, staring, puzzled, alarmed, that seventh came. Behind them she came, advancing forward from where she had crept, at first to spy. Angry at first, then wondering, then she came near them in awe, though fighting it as if it was not allowed.

Sleekit: grike, sideem, dark mole. Of all moles, the Stone sent her.

Then Tryfan sensed her presence, turned and called out, 'Touch her now and heal her. Ours is her sickness, ours is her healing!'

Then the others saw her, and were not afraid.

'Touch her!' others shouted, even Alder, even Marram, both fearless now.

Yet Sleekit only stared. Caught in some moment of change that her years of harsh sideem training had never prepared her for. Caught and commanded.

'Make the seventh!' called out Spindle, barely knowing what he meant.

And Sleekit raised a paw, and reached forward and held it above Thyme's weak and shivering flank, as Pennywort cried out, 'Touch her, complete us, help us now!'

Sleekit stared, fear on them all.

Then Thyme, with one last effort, turned her head and looked at Sleekit and whispered, 'For love once given you, once long ago, do it now for me who you know not.'

Then Sleekit, with a sigh and a cry remembered love once given, and reached down and touched Thyme, and

177

there was a sigh among them as of a storm that passes.

'This,' whispered Tryfan, as Thyme lay suddenly peaceful beneath them, 'this is the first Seven Stancing. Here, now, with us. Whatever moles we are, whatever mole we were, whatever moles we may still be, here the healing of moledom begins. We made it, each to come here to this burrow, seven moles come, each with trouble, each with faith, each with hope: seven moles come. Yes. This is the first Seven Stancing.'

For a moment there was silence, and then a fading. Then, most strange of all, it was as if the Stancing had not been, for the moles slipped back from one another, guardmole with guardmole, Pennywort with the now sleeping Thyme, Tryfan with Spindle, and alone, powerful, forbidding, accusing, Sideem Sleekit, dangerous mole indeed.

'You!' she said sharply, staring at her taloned paw as if scarcely believing that a moment before she had touched another with it in a caring way. 'You!'

'Yes?' said Tryfan.

'Whatmole are you?'

'A healer,' he said.

'Of which system?' she asked, as if choosing to forget the extraordinary moments that had just passed between them all.

'East of Fyfield,' said Tryfan. 'I told your guardmole that when we first arrived.'

'You did,' said Sleekit, 'but I liked not the way you did it. What do you know of the Stone?'

'Very little,' said Tryfan.

'Would you forswear it?'

'I think I have many times,' he said.

Sleekit gazed at him coldly.

'Would you forswear it?' she repeated.

Tryfan sighed as if whatever subtle evasion he had been practising was no longer desirable.

'Not consciously,' he said.

'You are of the Stone?'

178

'I am, as you are, as all moles are.'

Sleekit smiled slightly, and her eyes lightened, as a mole's does when faced by a challenge she, or he, might enjoy.

'And the Word?' she whispered.

'What of it?' said Tryfan sharply.

'Indeed,' said Sleekit, her eyes narrowing. '*What* of it?'

'I know it not,' said Tryfan.

'It is merciful,' said Sleekit. 'To allmole. You may be initiate. And your friend. Indeed . . . anymole may be.'

'Well,' said Tryfan, 'and if I was, would I still be of the Stone?'

'Of course not!' said Sleekit.

'Are you sure?' said Tryfan, suddenly menacing in spirit.

'The two conflict,' said Sleekit. 'You would forswear the Stone?'

'I might,' said Tryfan, 'but I fear the Stone would not forswear me or anymole. Not even thee, Sleekit.'

Sleekit was suddenly angry, though it would be hard to say quite why everymole in that chamber knew it for she appeared quite expressionless.

'Your true name, mole?'

'Tryfan,' he replied. 'Of Duncton born.' And Sleekit sighed as if she had been expecting such a response, and was relieved now to hear it.

'I have met others like you, Tryfan, obdurate. That one you saw punished in the chamber was one such. Tomorrow you will meet Eldrene Fescue, and she may or may not listen to you. I doubt that she will. But if she does I suggest you speak more carefully, more meekly, than you have to me.'

'And you,' she added, meaning Marram and Alder. The two of them, Marram especially, looked utterly abject and frightened, as if sure that what they had allowed to take place earlier meant a snouting for them. But Sleekit seemed not to be much concerned with it, and all she said was, 'Make sure these moles are here tomorrow or else. . . .'

'We shall,' said Marram hastily.

Sleekit glanced at the six of them, shook her head with distaste, stared once more in puzzlement at her paw, and said, rather weakly, 'Do nothing against the Word and it will be merciful. Blessed is the Word!' And with that she left.

'Well!' said Spindle.

'You heard what she said,' began Marram aggressively. 'No wandering, no escaping; in fact, no talking.'

'Any sleeping?' said Tryfan mildly. With which he settled down, rested his head along his paws, and peacefully closed his eyes as the guardmoles went back to their stances.

For a time Spindle and the others watched him, restless and worried by Sleekit's visit. Finally Spindle went close to him and whispered, 'Tryfan? Tryfan!' And when Tryfan opened his eyes he said urgently, 'What are we going to do?'

'Sleep, I hope.'

'But tomorrow. . . .'

'Tomorrow the Stone will protect us,' he said. Then he closed his eyes again, and the others, flank to flank, seemed to sigh and relax around him as night came: Pennywort with Thyme, Tryfan and Spindle, Marram and Alder.

'I'll take the watch!' said Marram, trying to sound stern.

But he spoke to moles who were one by one slipping into sleep, good sleep, peaceful sleep, and his voice echoed around a burrow that, though ill-kempt and dirty, now carried a kind of hope.

Then sleep came into that burrow, where moledom's first Seven Stancing had taken place, and sleep took him too. So that, watcher though he was, he did not notice Sleekit return and pause for a long time at the burrow entrance, staring at the moles there, and most of all at Tryfan. Nor did Marram hear her when, much later, she crept away, as if to disturb that peace was blasphemy, but against something greater by far than that in which until that day she had been trained to believe, which was the Word, whose name was blessed. As if, perhaps, she had heard the sound of a Silence that day and she crept from it with a fear and awe the Word could not help her with.

Chapter Eleven

Tryfan woke suddenly to find the half-light of dawn coming in at the surface entrance. The others were mostly deep asleep, their bodies as dull and featureless as molehills on a misty morning, but Marram, the guard-mole, was half-awake, quietly grooming himself.

Pennywort was curled into a corner, while Spindle was stretched out with his paws angled against Thyme, whose head rested against his flank.

Tryfan stared peaceably at them for a few moments thinking it was good to be with other moles, and to see Spindle in company, for the cleric had suffered terrible loneliness in the long years he had hidden in the Holy Burrows.

As for himself, Tryfan knew – or thought he knew – that because he was a scribemole and a leader, his could not be the way of ordinary mole – to mate and attach himself as . . . as . . . as Spindle might do with somemole one day. Thyme turned and moaned a little in her sleep, settling her head more comfortably into Spindle's flank while he brought a paw protectively over her shoulder and sighed.

Tryfan felt a sudden, unexpected and unwanted pang of loneliness and, understanding something of the true isolation of a scribemole, he shivered. Then he looked around uncomfortably, hoping it might be just the chill of dawn and not something more, much more. But he remembered Boswell explaining that scribemoles are no more isolated than other moles – for all moles are isolated before the Stone – but they may seem to be because they have stripped away other diversions and truly faced the isolation of the way they go.

He knew the life he was embarking on was his own choice, and he recalled how one day long ago in Duncton

Wood, as the other youngsters played about him, he sensed he was a youngster no more and he had left the system, crossing the pastures to live in temporary burrows for a time and listen to the sounds of the night and watch the days go by. His peers had been surprised because he had been liked and needed; then he was gone, with no word nor explanation.

When he had returned moleyears later, the youngsters he remembered had long since grown up and dispersed, and he had found his way to Duncton's Stone and there had met Boswell for the first time. Then, he had felt, his life had begun.

Crouched now, in the dim light of that Buckland burrow, with slumbering moles about him, it struck him that a mole's life alternated between times of security and times of risk. Each was a mole's own choice but for the first, which was the birth in the home burrow.

How strange, thought Tryfan to himself, that a moment ago I should have remembered my meeting with Boswell as the time when my life began! Did it not begin at my birth? Is it not beginning again now as I realise that my long journey with Boswell is over, quite finished, and his teaching done? Now I have begun something new, and though I have Spindle for a companion yet I am alone. Perhaps the fear of taking risks is but the fear of being alone which is where change and newness puts a mole.

Tryfan looked across at Thyme and Spindle once again, thinking that now they were locked most gracefully together, and he remembered their conversation about females and mates, and wondered at his own choice, which seemed implicit in his life as a scribemole, to have no mate at all. A choice with which Spindle was in tacit agreement. Yet he . . . Tryfan smiled, though somewhat wanly, and reflected ruefully that it was one life for a scribemole, and another for everymole else. So he sighed, and felt alone, but an aloneness that went far deeper than the yearning for a mate inspires. An aloneness that even a mate cannot overcome, for it is the isolation a mole feels when he turns at last to face the Stone's Silence and chooses not to run from it.

Well, whispered Tryfan to himself then. Well, and could I not meet another who might stand beside me in that place where the Stone rises and the Silence begins? Could not the Stone grant me that comfort, to know another, one other – and not just Boswell! – who knows that isolation too? One to comfort the other? Could it not? Surely, if a scribemole was to find such another as he, but female, would the Stone stop them loving each other and mating?

The vows he had taken that night on Uffington Hill before Boswell did not mention celibacy as an absolute prerequisite of a scribemole's life, though others – including Boswell himself – seemed to accept such a restraint. Tryfan pondered this yearning some more, and felt better for concluding that if ever such a female came along, well . . . he could behave as other moles did. But she would have to be . . . And Tryfan laughed to himself. Making conditions! Ordaining what only the Stone could ordain! He would trust the Stone to do what was right, and 'she' – if she existed at all which he doubted – would be what she would be, and meanwhile . . . he must get on with the tasks each day presented and order them to take Spindle and himself onward, towards that strange quest whose direction and object he knew not, but whose purpose was a preparing for Silence among allmole.

As for beginnings, and starting a new life, well Boswell taught that that happened at each moment of the day. But the real beginning, to *him*, that went further back than anything, before he could remember, when, in a dark burrow, he had been safe and Rebecca had encircled him. When he looked at a mole as he had looked at Alder, and as he looked at Spindle now, he felt as if his shadow was not his own but Rebecca's, and Bracken's, who had made him, and they were there and always would be and so was the great love they had given him. They were there to show him how to see, through him and he of them, and behind all of them was the Stone where each one of them began, and which each one sought, in his different way, to return to. As for Boswell, who was old, so old, a White Mole, whose paws had touched his, and whose teaching was in his heart, why, Tryfan sometimes thought he went back further even than the Stone itself to the love which was before the Stone, and would be after it.

'May you be protected Boswell,' whispered Tryfan, 'and may you return home safeguarded.'

The dawn light spread, the guardmole Alder stretched, and Tryfan called softly to Spindle, a call that Spindle immediately responded to, disengaging himself with some difficulty (and not a little surprise and embarrassment) from his entwinings with Thyme.

'What's wrong?' he said, looking about warily.

'Nothing,' said Tryfan. 'We must be alert today, and ready to move on.'

'Yes,' said Spindle, 'except that mole Sleekit has told the eldrenes everything about us by now. You shouldn't have told her your name or admitted to the Stone even if – ' Spindle's brow creased as he tried to remember exactly what had happened the night before.

'Even if she was part of the Seven Stancing?' said Tryfan. 'Well Spindle, followers of the Stone will get nowhere if they lie about who they are.'

'H'm,' said Spindle doubtfully, for though he was a truthful mole his time among the scribemoles had taught him that, at times, there was nothing wrong before the Stone in *discretion*. On the other paw. . . 'You're the scribemole, Tryfan, so you should know what can be admitted,' he conceded.

'It seemed to be the Stone's will to say my name,' said Tryfan a little defensively, for in the cold light of dawn it did seem that he may have been a little too open. 'At least I didn't say I was a scribemole, which is as Boswell wished!' he added.

'You told that Sleekit everything but,' scolded Spindle. Thyme awoke, stretched, and as Spindle shifted away

185

from her and pretended to groom himself, Pennywort eyed her in wonderment.

'You're better,' he said.

'Yes,' she said, yawning. 'Feel *much* better. Feel good! Feel hungry!'

So the burrow awoke as sunlight began to filter in and the moles groomed and readied themselves for the coming hours. And though nomole mentioned the events of the night before, yet all were quiet and subdued as if reluctant to break up whatever it was that had happened to them. Even the guardmoles moved little, and did not object when Spindle burrowed around to find some fresh food to start the day with. Of all the moles there, it was around Tryfan that the others seemed to centre, for there was something about him, as Spindle was often to remark, that brought moles together, and made them feel as one. And what had been a miserable burrow of separate moles when Tryfan had arrived was now cheerful, and positive, and purposeful.

But a short time later, when a shaft of sunlight had broken down into the burrow and the distant rustle and thump above them on the surface indicated that a herd of cows was on the move their way, two guardmoles busily appeared, large and aggressive. They were grikes, menacing, with strong squat bodies. One said nothing at all, the other everything. He was one of the ones who had threatened them when they had stopped in the system's main communal burrow.

'Word be wi' thee!' he said to Alder.

'And thee!' said Alder automatically.

'All well?'

'Is well!'

'And?'

'And the Word not forsworn,' added Alder hastily, looking sheepish. He had forgotten to say the full greeting.

'Smarten up you two!' said the guardmole. 'Now . . . which are the newcomers?'

Alder led him over to Tryfan and Spindle.

'Which one's Tryfan?' asked the grike.

'I am,' said Tryfan.

'Right, Eldrene Fescue is going to give you instruction so you and your so-called assistant are to shut up and follow me. Can't expect her to come to you here, can you?'

'We weren't,' said Tryfan.

The guardmole looked around the burrow and then, as if to assert himself said, 'Bloody shambles this place. You two better get it sorted out before the day's end.'

With that he turned back to Tryfan and Spindle.

'Met you before,' said the guardmole. 'Didn't like the snooty look of you then. Don't now. Follow me.'

They were only able to say the briefest of goodbyes to Thyme and Pennywort before they were harried out of the burrow and marched rapidly down the tunnel, back the way they had originally come. Before they left Alder whispered, 'Act stupid, say little and agree to everything,' while Thyme touched them briefly in turn, her paw lingering on Spindle's who looked at once confused and pleased until he was pushed on by the second guardmole with a painful talon-thrust.

They soon found themselves back in the system's communal burrow, which was now nearly deserted of mole. At the far end, however, in the area near where the tree roots descended, they saw Eldrene Fescue and Sideem Sleekit. At the sides of the burrow, posted at the entrances, were guardmoles whose presence and appearance was threatening. They openly scowled at Tryfan and Spindle, sucking and picking malevolently at their teeth with their talons, as if their meal had been interrupted by Tryfan and Spindle's arrival.

'Move it,' said the guardmole leading them, and the one behind pushed them roughly forward until they were a few feet from Eldrene Fescue, who looked down on them, as Sleekit did, from the slightly raised stance they had taken.

'Are these the ones?' asked the eldrene.

'Sleekit nodded. 'Yes, we have reason to believe they are. This one' – she indicated Tryfan – 'is Tryfan of Duncton whom we have been seeking since Boswell's capture. He claims to be a herbalist – the latter fact may well be true by the accounts I have had. The other mole is called Spindle and is from Uffington way. They are confessed Stone followers, for I have talked with them.'

'Do you confess it?' asked the eldrene. Tryfan gazed at her steadily but Spindle could hardly bear to for her face was a deep displeasure to look upon. She had tiny grey eyes flecked with yellow, and the meanest, thinnest, bitterest, most wizened looking snout Tryfan had ever seen.

'Well?'

Her voice was mean as well, and hard, pitiless as a stoat's.

Tryfan looked at her, then briefly at Sleekit, then back again. He hesitated, wondering if he might be able to gain information about Boswell. The guardmoles at either side of him and Spindle began to grow restless. Sleekit stared, her eyes small.

'Answer the eldrene, mole,' one of the guardmoles began, but Fescue raised her talons to silence him and Spindle noticed they were translucent and cracked, the talons of a sterile mole.

'I was with Boswell in Uffington,' said Tryfan finally, 'but this mole Spindle is barely known to me and has accepted the Word.'

'Has he now?' said Fescue maliciously. 'Ask him!'

Before either of them understood her command the larger of the guardmoles, who towered over Spindle, drove his talons viciously into Spindle's flanks, drawing blood. Spindle half fell against Tryfan who put out a paw to support him and turned on the guardmole to attack in return. But he was rapidly restrained by guardmoles from behind and powerless to stop a second strike at Spindle, who gasped out in pain.

'I am of the Stone,' said Spindle bravely, 'and I always shall be.'

'Brave mole!' said Fescue heavily, turning indifferently from him, and back to Tryfan.

'So this is the power of your Word, to torture and hurt defenceless moles!' said Tryfan.

'We have no wish or desire to hurt another,' said the eldrene, 'but we must combat the evil of the Stone with strength and, if necessary, force. You are, evidently, Stone believers.'

Tryfan smiled grimly.

'And you have seen what happens to such moles?'

'We have seen the evil that the Word does, yes,' said Tryfan.

'Well now, as a friend of Boswell you might well have information that will be useful to us,' said Fescue, 'but I rather doubt, even from the little I have seen of you, that you will freely confess it, even if that were desirable. Nor do I think either of you will yield to reason before you accept Atonement and the power of the Word. So . . . there are other ways.'

Fescue looked round briefly at Sleekit, and the two seemed to reach some tacit agreement about what to do with them. But then Fescue seemed to have a sudden thought. She relaxed and smiled a little – if smile it was that lighted those evil eyes – and Tryfan was on his guard.

'I can see you are a mole of intelligence, Tryfan, however misguided you may be,' said the eldrene. 'Now tell me, for what purpose did Boswell travel from Duncton Wood to Uffington?'

'Has he not told you?' asked Tryfan carefully.

'He has freely told us much,' said Fescue, 'but we like to be sure.'

'What has he told you?' Tryfan said, feeling relieved as the eldrene's answer indicated that they did not know, or were not sure, of the existence of the Stillstone. It also suggested that Boswell had resisted attempts to convert him to the Word; but best of all what she said suggested that Boswell was still alive.

'Why did he travel to Uffington? Answer the question,

mole, or it will be worse for your friend,' said Eldrene
Fescue, her mask of civility slipping. She nodded at the
guardmole who gave Spindle another quick talon-thrust.

'Don't worry about me!' gasped Spindle.

'Oh but he does and how much!' said the eldrene
peering closer at Tryfan. 'Very noble. Very stupid. I have
seen such concern before on the faces of Stone followers.'

'Boswell travelled to Uffington,' said Tryfan heavily,
his paw outstretched to Spindle whose breathing was
heavy and laboured from the thrusts he had received,
'because it was his home burrow. He desired to die at the
place of his birth, as all moles do.'

'Nothing more?'

'He told me nothing more. What might there be?'

'A Stillstone, for example,' said the eldrene, her eyes
suddenly greedy. Sleekit moved a little nearer, her black
eyes searching Tryfan's face.

'A Stillstone?' repeated Tryfan.

'Taking one to Uffington,' said the sideem.

'If anymole would have known, it would have been me,'
said Tryfan. 'And I saw no Stillstone on all that long
journey.' Which was true enough.

There was silence as they contemplated his answer.

The eldrene turned and whispered to Sleekit and then
looked around at them again.

'Well now,' said the eldrene, 'we are inclined to believe
you. Tell us this. Does a Stillstone exist? You Stone
followers seem to believe so much in them.'

'I believe they do.'

' "They". . .?'

'There are said to be seven.'

'And would you know where they are?' The eldrene's
eyes were still as a frosty night.

'No,' said Tryfan, which was also true, for he did not
know their precise location.

To his relief the eldrene did not press him further on
this, but asked him instead which was the most important
Stillstone.

'All moles know that,' he replied. 'It is the Stillstone of Silence.' As he said this last word his gaze shifted from Eldrene Fescue to Sleekit and he gazed deep on her, and she looked away.

Fescue shifted her talons and seemed in pain as, suddenly, she lost interest.

'It is well. He will say more later,' she said tersely. 'Take them to the burrow-cells and feed them ill. We will talk again, but a time of discomfort may help you both understand that the Stone does not help its own.' Then, turning to the guards, she said, 'Take them the public way that others might see and know them, and express their feelings on Stone followers who desecrate one of our systems with their presence.'

* * * * * * *

Now began the dark and desolate period of Tryfan and Spindle's time at Buckland which scribes, retelling those historic events, have usually passed only briefly over, perhaps because the two moles themselves later had other, and more difficult, matters to attend to. But an account does exist, and it was truly scribed by the one mole who was witness to those terrible weeks that Tryfan and good Spindle suffered in the burrow-cells. His name . . . but let his name be told in due time, as it became known to each of them.

They were taken from their first interview with Eldrene Fescue by a long route deliberately chosen to expose them to the scorn and talon-thrusts of those guardmoles who happened to meet them on their way. So that by the time they arrived at the burrow-cells, which lay then at the damp south end of Buckland, they were half unconscious and bleeding from the many buffets and wounds they had received.

The cells were hewn in the interstices of soil between flints and rocks in which, centuries before, twofoots had lain underground. They were narrow, barely big enough for a mole to crouch in comfort, and they were deep, down in sterile subsoil that dripped moisture and chill, even in those summer months. Several guardmoles were there watching the tunnels outside the burrow-cells, and the prisoners were separated so that none easily knew how near or how far others might be.

There was about the place the smell of blood, and excrement, and hopelessness; and others were there unseen but often heard. For there was evil in that place of interminable darkness followed by dim light, followed by darkness once more. Screams of pain, the laughter of grikes . . . all melded into one as the days (or were they weeks?) passed by. At intervals, but not regularly, Tryfan was dragged out and interviewed, sometimes by grike guardmoles, sometimes by the eldrene Fescue, and sometimes by the Sideem Sleekit. He saw nothing of Spindle and, apart from a last whispered word of reassurance and blessing, had been able to say nothing to him since their appearance before the eldrene.

They were brought food erratically – and never wholesome worms. Instead they found such fare as maggots, or rotting rat, or the entrails of sheep infested with vile worms. At first Tryfan refused to eat, but when he realised he was beginning to weaken he made himself eat the foul stuff and ignore the guardmoles who peered in at him saying nothing. At least it gave him strength to resist their questionings, or at least give little enough away. There were fleas, too, glinting in the gloom, and for water Tryfan was told to lick the slime that dripped and trickled down the flints that formed two walls of his cell.

Escape there was none: the subsoil was too hard for burrowing, the guardmoles too many to fight, even had his strength been good. But he knew he was weakening for lack of air and exercise and yet his resolve to survive, and to resist the ministrations of the eldrene about the Word, did not fade. Rather it grew stronger, and from clues they gave – small impatiences – he surmised that Spindle was alive and resisting as well, inhabiting a cell somewhere nearby.

He knew, too, that others were there, for he heard the

guardmoles shouting at them, he heard punishment, and twice he heard screams after struggles to the surface which, he guessed, was the dread sound of a snouting.

Some guardmoles were less aggressive and uncommunicative than others, and gradually as the days wore into weeks he learnt a good deal about Buckland, and the grikes. For one thing, he learnt that there would have been more snoutings but for the imminence of Longest Day and the intention of Henbane to visit the system then and conduct a ritual snouting of Stone followers.

It was confirmed, too, that the system was to be a centre for guardmole training and activity and that it was being prepared for this. More than that, he learnt that the Slopeside, which formed the northern part of the system, was presently still being cleared of plague corpses – a dangerous and perilous task, for most of the moles doing that work died eventually of disease, and a disease whose name was whispered in disgust and loathing: scalpskin. Though what this was, or what it looked like, Tryfan did not know since in all his induction into healing he had never once heard of the complaint.

'How are these clearers directed, and by which moles?' he had asked one of the more friendly guardmoles.

'Zealots of one Longest Night,' was the reply. 'Young moles willing to lay down their lives in the cause of the Word. Strong must they be, and believers. If they survive their term they are given a good command, and if not, well, glory will they have.'

'What glory?' Tryfan had asked.

'Names scribed on the Rock in Whern where the Word be spelt. This is a glory Word followers strive for, to have their name so scribed. Names that will live for ever more. Aye, and that's an honour.'

But what Rock this was, and where the Word might 'be spelt', Tryfan did not know, but it was one of the things he vowed to find out if the Stone spared him. And he had no doubt that Spindle, a more curious and persistent mole than he for facts, would, should *he* survive, make it his business to find out.

Of the other moles who were incarcerated with him in the burrow-cells he knew little, but for the sounds of suffering they made. Talking was not allowed between cells, and nor was one mole allowed out at the same time as another. Yet by peering out from his cell Tryfan occasionally caught a glimpse of some other poor mole taken off for questioning and sometimes, he knew, such mole did not return. His time would come. If not through weakness and death here, then at Midsummer when, he had little doubt, this Henbane would make him one of her snoutings to the Word. And thinking of that, Tryfan knew fear.

One murky and gloomy day, but with light enough for him to see something of what went on, he heard guard-moles' jeers and laughter as they harried a mole along by the cells. It happened that they stopped within sight of Tryfan's cell, but were too absorbed with the mole they were tormenting to notice Tryfan watching.

'Oh yeah?' one of them was saying. 'Scribe can you? And write your name in rock no doubt. Ha, ha, ha! Very clever.'

'He's a clever one he is, clever at lying!'

With some difficulty Tryfan made out a mole who, even by that light, he could see was broken in body. His back and flanks were so gaunt that the line of his vertebrae and ribs could be seen through them, and his fur was patchy and torn from ill-treatment. His snout was low and he moved, when he moved at all, with pain and difficulty.

His voice was the barest whisper and what it said, continually, was, 'I am, yes, yes, yes. I am. That I am.' A final, desperate, affirmation of the self he had nearly lost in this place of torture. At first Tryfan found it hard to make out the mole's words, but when he did he noticed immediately that he spoke in the same precise manner as Boswell did and, hearing him, Tryfan was deathly still, and whispered a prayer of help to the Stone.

'What are you, mole? A scribemole or a liar, or both?' mocked a guardmole.

'No, no. Yes, yes, yes. I am, I *am*!' whispered the mole.

'Then scribe on rock for us, mole. Go on, scribe my name. Burr's my name. Can you scribe that, so my name lives for ever?'

'Nomole can scribe on rock,' said the mole.

At that they hit him viciously saying, 'The Word-Speaker can scribe on the Rock of the Word and may one day scribe *our* names!'

And they pushed the mole against the walls of the tunnel and forced him to raise a paw to the black flint.

'Now scribe, mole!' they said, laughing. And they forced his talons pathetically over the flint's shining surface.

Tryfan, watching, saw that even as they did this the mole not only continued his refrain of, 'I am, I *am*!' but contrived to move his other front paw on the floor, to scratch it . . . or. . . .

He is scribing! said Tryfan to himself, scarcely believing his eyes. But what it was Tryfan could not make out in the half-light.

The grike guardmoles lost interest in their game and drove the mole on, and all Tryfan could do was stare at the spot where he had been, and at the weak scribing left on the chalky floor.

The next time Tryfan was taken from his cell he contrived to pause at the point where the mole he had seen had been, and he ran his talons over the meagre marks the mole had striven to make in the hard chalky subsoil of the tunnel floor.

'I am, I am,' the mole had whispered again and again, and there in the floor, even as the guardmoles had mocked his failure to scribe on flint, he had scribed who he was, and Tryfan touched it, and knew it, and gasped. For the name the mole had scribed was BREVIS, the scribemole who had been Spindle's master, and who had escaped Uffington before the massacre there by the grikes. The scribemole who had reported on the Buckland system, and whose home system this was. Brevis was alive.

And there in the few moments he had, pretending weakness and confusion, Tryfan scribed something in return, that Brevis might find it and be heartened.

For days after that Tryfan waited until one evening, as night fell, the mole was led down the tunnel again. Tryfan saw that he was weaker now, his paws hardly able to drag his frail body along. He passed over the point where Tryfan had scribed and, as Tryfan breathlessly watched, his paw ran across the scribing he had made, seeming not to recognise it. Indeed he slowly carried on until, a moment later, he seemed to hesitate and pause and reach back as if, from a great distance, the words Tryfan had scribed had been heard by him.

'Come on, old mole,' said the guardmole who was one of the kinder ones. 'No dallying.'

'But I . . . but there's . . .' Brevis whispered, wanting to reach back to Tryfan's scribing and yet, perhaps, not quite daring to, and he was pushed on.

But Tryfan knew – or hoped – that Brevis would return that way later, and watched on. Until at last, seeming even slower now and dreadfully weak, he was dragged past by the guardmole.

'Rest,' whispered Brevis as he reached the spot again. 'Rest a moment . . .' And so he contrived to pause at Tryfan's scribing.

'Just for a moment then,' muttered the guardmole.

Tryfan saw Brevis run his talons over Tryfan's scribing, not once, or twice, but three times, the guardmole suspicious but not interfering, for he would not recognise scribing himself. Brevis was still and seemed wondering, and then, from his cell, Tryfan softly spoke out the words he had scribed. Ancient words they are, and magical, the words of greeting one scribemole makes to another, words Tryfan had never spoken as a scribemole before, nor ever, perhaps, imagined that he would have the chance.

'Steyn reine in thine herte,' he said.

Then Brevis turned to the darkness from where Tryfan's voice came and spoke out the proscribed response, using the same old language, his voice full of awe:

'Staye thee hol and soint.'

'Me desire wot I none,' replied Tryfan, wondering if the guardmole would intervene. But he seemed bemused by the language the two moles were speaking, and stilled perhaps by the peace between them. More than that he was taken aback by the evident strength that, so suddenly, seemed to infuse the body of the old mole who moments before had seemed near death. For his snout was up now, and his body alert, and he spoke out the last line of the greeting firmly, and with a love that silenced any protest the guardmole might have wished to make, and which also brought tears to Tryfan's eyes:

'Blessed be thou and ful of blisse,' said Brevis, adding for good measure, in a voice full of joy: 'Blessed be thou, mole, whatever thy name!'

It took some moments more for the guardmole to find his senses, so suffused did the tunnel seem with light and strength.

'Eh now, what's this?' he said. 'No talking, you know the rules.'

'He's a friend,' said Tryfan from the darkness, the Stone giving his voice the power of command and persuasion. 'Just for a moment. . . .'

'Well, then . . .' said the guardmole doubtfully, retreating a little and letting the two moles talk.

'Whatmole art thou?' said Brevis, his voice full of wonder.

'A friend of Boswell, Tryfan my name.'

'Boswell! Does that mole live still?'

'He lives as the Stone lives,' said Tryfan.

'And your name is Tryfan?'

'Tryfan of Duncton. And one you know is alive, and here in these cells. His name is. . . .'

'Good Spindle!' said Brevis joyfully, though scarcely

197

able to keep his stance now, so weak was he and affected by Tryfan's words. 'I thought I heard, I *knew* I heard his voice. Tryfan of Duncton, I have prayed for such a moment. But art thou . . .?' He pointed a talon back at the scribing on the floor but did not speak the word 'scribemole'.

'By Boswell made at Uffington.'

'Then blessed is this moment, blest be this day! I thought I was the last!'

'And I!' said Tryfan, tears coming to his eyes again. 'And I.'

Then the sound of other guardmoles approaching could be heard and Tryfan whispered urgently, 'Be of faith. We will have need of thee, Brevis, for this is your home system and you know its tunnels. Have faith!'

'I have faith I'll be snouted at Midsummer,' said Brevis. 'It's what they're keeping me for.'

'Well, then, we must set you free of this place. And in any case there are other tasks, more important tasks, and you will be needed now, for there are few of us.'

'Do they know what you are, Tryfan?' whispered Brevis, even as the guardmole roughly took his shoulder to pull him away. The other guardmoles were near at paw.

Tryfan shook his head.

'Boswell wished it so,' he said. Then he said to the guardmole with a voice of authority, 'Treat him well lest one day you answer for not doing so!' And there was something about Tryfan that was to be obeyed, and, with a final exchange of blessings, the two scribemoles were parted. Then Tryfan turned back into his cell, and, drained of strength, thanked the Stone for the coming of this hour.

Chapter Twelve

For the next few days Tryfan remained buoyed up in a state of hope and confidence at the discovery that Brevis was alive. But no more meetings proved possible, for Brevis was not brought past his cell again, and despite questioning of the more friendly guardmoles he could get no news of him, nor of Spindle either.

The guardmoles left him alone, and he was not taken for further questioning – interludes, he now realised, he had enjoyed as a respite from the lonely darkness of the cell. Despite the dampness he could tell that the summer was advancing, for the air grew a little warmer, and he became even more plagued by fleas.

It was then, at the time of despair and anticlimax that arose in the weeks after seeing Brevis, and greater physical discomfort and weakness, that Eldrene Fescue and Sideem Sleekit resumed their interrogation. To them Tryfan would be taken by bullying guardmoles and forced to suffer their questionings. That much he remembered subsequently, and that for answer to any questions they asked about Boswell or the scribemoles of the Holy Burrows, and others about Stillstones and the Book of the Word, the original copy of which they seemed to be seeking, Tryfan chose to talk about something quite different, which was Silence and the place he told them it might be found, which was in Duncton Wood. He remembered that this seemed to infuriate them, and that Sleekit, despite her involvement in the Seven Stancing was as ruthless as Fescue in ordering the guardmoles to hurt him.

But there came a time when their beatings and talonings had no more effect, and he retreated from them into a world of his own in which they could not reach him. So that then, when they told him Spindle was dead, their words had no effect on him, for he was able to evoke the memory of his friends so vividly that the Spindle he knew, like Bracken, and Boswell, and Rebecca, and good Comfrey, were alive and in his cell.

'No, no,' he would call out. 'Spindle isn't dead! He can't be, he's here, look! Spindle, talk to them!' When he started talking like that the eldrene seemed to go away and not come back, and Sideem Sleekit stared at him and then was gone, quite gone.

So Tryfan survived. But then there was a period of doubt, and uncertainty, and one he survived by prayer to the Stone and by practising his scribing on the dusty floor across whose narrow length, for two short periods each day, a dull grey light from some distant entrance cast itself. Here he wrote the names he loved – Boswell, Comfrey, Rebecca, Bracken, Spindle . . . and places he dreamed of visiting again – Uffington, the Holy Burrows, and . . . Duncton Wood. And he knew those moles were not in his cell at all. All gone. Even Spindle, too, it seemed. And Tryfan wept and did not touch the food the guardmole left.

Then, too, he strove to meditate on the teachings Boswell had given him, doing his best to use that time of enforced solitude well, as he felt Boswell himself would have done. He had often heard Boswell talk of his time in the silent burrows of Uffington, where moles sometimes chose to live isolated from all others for moleyears at a time, and some, even, until death took them to the Stone. He remembered that they ate little, but that they did eat, and drink, especially drink. So he did the same, licking the foul walls of his cell, eating the filthy food they left. Surviving.

It was then that Tryfan of Duncton, already disciplined by his years with Boswell, found a yet sterner discipline, and through the practice of meditation kept some measure of balance and harmony between his mind and his tortured body.

200

Throughout that dark night of his life Tryfan always thought of Spindle, not believing he was dead, but praying that the Stone might give the cleric strength to survive. And at darker moments still, Tryfan permitted himself the indulgence of reverie, remembering again the warmth and light of his puphood, when the beech trees on the high part of his beloved Duncton Wood had caught the light, and the leaves, first young and bright green and then bigger and duller, but yet magnificent, had fluttered in the breezes high above him as he explored the system in which he had been born.

'I will go back there when we are free of Buckland, go back there and find companionship and help, go back . . .' And though he did not know it he began to speak such thoughts aloud, mumbling the words in his weakness, his mind reaching the limit of its endurance and beginning to drift now. . . 'Yes I will, and Comfrey will come to greet me, and I'll find Boswell once more and show Spindle, yes Spindle, that was his name, a mole I knew long ago, Spindle. . . .'

It seemed that he heard moles calling sometimes, and that sometimes it was night when it should be day, and that light across the floor of his cell was so dark, yes, yes it was, and those creatures there not meant for eating, unless they be there to eat him up! A blessed relief! Yes, yes, and he could laugh, and did, silently, and brought his mind back to things that made sense, names he remembered, like B – Bos . . . yes, yes, and R – Re . . . What was her name? Spindle, *that* was a name and a mole too. Ha, ha!

'Spindle!' he mumbled. 'Spindle . . .' And Tryfan called out to the blinding light that seemed to come into his cell, and felt tears on his face fur. 'Spindle. . . .'

'Tryfan! Tryfan! Can you hear me? Tryfan!'

It was Spindle, talking to him from somewhere among the trees near Duncton's great Stone, calling to him. . . . '*Tryfan!!*'

It *was* Spindle. But here, really here, in the sudden light at his cell entrance, which the guardmoles had unblocked.

'Spindle?'

'Yes, Tryfan. Me. Spindle. Your friend.'

An old-seeming Spindle, even thinner than before, his flanks gaunt and hurt with half-healed scars, his talons broken and blunted, his fur ragged and patchy . . . not the Spindle he had known. . . .

'Tryfan . . . They're taking us out of here! – and not, I think, to snout us.'

Tryfan's paws seemed slow to move, and his body ached, and the guardmole had to come in to help him towards the entrance of the cell before he was able to whisper, 'Spindle? You?' And he reached out and touched him as if he doubted his ears and eyes. And they wept and praised the Stone that brought them together again.

'Yes, it's me.'

'But you look so old,' protested Tryfan, suddenly bad-tempered. 'You're a fraud!'

A weak smile came to Spindle's face.

'No more than you,' he said. 'Come, we're to leave here now! Come Tryfan.' And Tryfan permitted himself to be helped out of the foul cell that had been his world too long.

As he went he tried to remember something, something he had to remember, *must* remember to tell Spindle, if this was really him. Something scribed.

'Brevis!' said Tryfan suddenly. 'I saw him. He's here, Spindle.'

'Yes, I know,' said Spindle. 'These last few moleweeks I have been better cared for, as he has too, and I have been in a communal cell with him. I'm afraid I did not have your strength for isolation, Tryfan, but I am better now. Much have I learnt of Buckland that may be useful.'

'Good, good,' said Tryfan, stopping, so that the guardmoles cursed him. Ahead, across the tunnel, fell a shaft of sunlight, and it was this that Tryfan had stopped to stare at. And the sound that seemed to come from it: of birdsong out on the surface above, high and beautiful, and life busy and good.

'We survived,' whispered Tryfan. 'We did, Spindle.

And by this confinement the grikes have made us stronger. It is the Stone's will.' To Spindle's astonishment he seemed to have found something of his old strength and purpose, for he asked boldly, even if he did totter against the tunnel wall as he did so, 'Now tell me, where are we going and why?'

They soon found out, for after making a journey down tunnels in which guardmoles jeered and buffeted them, they were pushed before Eldrene Fescue in that same communal chamber they had good reason to fear, filled once more with a mob of moles, talking and eating excitedly, as they seemed to like to do before an Atonement or a punishing.

How loud and big and strange so many moles seemed to Tryfan, who had known only solitariness for so long.

Fescue crouched with Sleekit at her side, both looking smug. Tryfan looked to see if he could find the slightest trace of pity or concern in the eyes of Sleekit, for he could not comprehend how she had shared the Seven Stancing and yet be so cold ever since. Unless she had been afraid of that Silence she had heard. Yes, thought Tryfan, a mole might be afraid of that and need much help towards it.

'Well, well!' said Fescue coming close to Tryfan, her talons poking painfully at his shoulders and ribs, lingering there a little too long. 'I see your Stone has not protected you. See!' she cried out, her harsh voice silencing the rabble of guardmoles who turned to listen, sadistic smiles on their faces. 'Here we have two Stone followers. Won't listen to the Word. Don't want to know the Word. I and Sideem Sleekit have questioned them and got the most we can expect to get. This one here even knew one of the Uffington scribemoles, a White Mole no less! Now I'm wondering. . . .'

Her voice dropped to a whisper as she paused for effect. 'I'm wondering what to do with them. . . .'

Tryfan and Spindle instinctively moved closer together, as if each might protect the other from the hostility about them.

'Snout the bastards!' shouted a guardmole.

'Aye, snout them slow!' cried another.

A guardmole came up to them, breaking past the ones who had brought them there, and thrust his yellow evil-smelling teeth towards each in turn.

'Thought you were scum, said you were scum, now you are scum,' he snarled. He was the grike who had first accosted them in the burrow, and who had ordered them to call him 'Sir'.

'Snout the scum,' he shouted suddenly, turning towards his friends.

Fear is a numbing thing when there is no recourse to hope or escape, and Tryfan and Spindle began to feel that now as the grikes shouted all around, calling for their death.

'Stone protect us, Spindle, that cell I have been in seems a sanctuary compared to this.'

Spindle, whose thin flanks were shaking, said, 'I don't like this Tryfan! I mean what can the Stone *do*?'

What *could* the Stone do? Tryfan had to struggle to shake the numbing tide of fear in him before he was able to adopt a stance of stillness, feeling his four paws on the chamber's floor, and fixing his gaze a little over the heads of the rabble of grikes and beyond to the silverine and russet roots of birch that came down into the tunnel beyond the eldrene's place. The Stone, he was thinking, would do something as it could only ever do something – through another mole; yes, through mole. A mole *here*; there must be one to help them, as he himself had been here before to bring hope to the heart of that nameless mole they had seen killed in this chamber. Tryfan's fear was suddenly replaced by calm and certainty: even in the face of these rabbling calls for their death he was certain now they would not die. Not yet. Not here. More to do, so much more. He stretched out a paw and even as the shouting reached a climax about them and the grikes turned back towards Eldrene Fescue for her verdict, Spindle felt his calm and was calm too.

'The Stone will save us,' whispered Tryfan. 'Now show them you have no fear.'

But whichmole would do the Stone's work? Which one here. . .?

Tryfan began to look about the chamber, but all he saw was one frenzied guardmole after another, eyeing them with hatred and triumph, looking for their death. One after another he stared at them, their shouts ever louder, and he knew that what he sought was a mole in doubt and fear, one in whom was the light of the Stone's grace, however feeble it might yet be. But nomole that he could see held such a light in his eyes. Beginning to despair he turned to look at Fescue, as the grikes were, and saw only her evil eye, and then looked again at the vertical roots of the birch, which plunged down behind Sleekit, silvery and beautiful, shining, yes, yes, shining on Sleekit's glossy coat, grey light, good light, shining. Tryfan looked on her and into her eyes, and he saw the fear he sought, and the doubt, and he knew that only in thatmole, who had been caught by the Stone at the strange Seven Stancing, lay now the hope of life for Spindle and himself. And as so often with Tryfan, he saw more than the immediate need; he saw also the future way. For if his life lay now in Sleekit's paws – though he could not see how she could do much to save them now – so in the future would the great quest towards Silence on which they had been sent depend always on others. He was but the pointer to the way, others would help him onwards, and others might finally reach the place where that quest ended. He was a scribemole, and nothing: always needing others, as he and Spindle needed Sleekit now. And he understood what Boswell had once said to him: 'We scribemoles are the leaders, and yet we must be led.'

Spindle felt Tryfan's stillness and saw the direction of his gaze, and that Sleekit looked uneasy, her talons stressing the soil before her, her eyes not meeting theirs, or anymole's.

'What are you waiting for, Eldrene? Tell us to snout

them!' shouted the grikes. 'Or mark them! Aye a marking! A marking!'

As guardmoles nearby began to turn and flex their talons, and more than one prodded and poked at Tryfan and Spindle, Tryfan saw Sleekit grow suddenly still, her talons become more certain, her command return.

'Enough!' cried out Fescue suddenly, raising her paw, and everymole fell silent, heaving and breathing and sweating in their bloodlust, spit on their mouth fur, waiting for the eldrene's command.

'Well? All of you have made your feelings of revulsion and dislike of these Stone followers known but one, and that is the esteemed Sideem Sleekit here. And what do you think, my dear?'

The eldrene turned a slitty eye on Sleekit and the excitement in the mob abated a little, for few there liked the sideem, least of all Sideem Sleekit, whose power they were afraid of, and whose authority was mysterious but certainly greater than it seemed – more, perhaps, even than the eldrene's. So yes, yes, yes, what did Sideem Sleekit think? The grikes leaned forward, listening, mouth open, the air rank with their sweat, the burrow shaking with their desire for a snouting.

Sleekit came forward a little, and for a moment so short that very few noticed it she looked in the direction of Tryfan, then she smiled strangely and then her face went hard.

'Snouting,' she began, the word provoking a wide sigh of relief among the moles throughout the chamber. 'Snouting,' she continued, the repetition of the word almost massaging the sigh into a groan, 'is . . . too . . . kind a punishment for these moles.'

There was a shudder of puzzled hope in the chamber, and the moles were silent, listening. Snouting too kind? What then? Has the sideem something even more hurting than that?

'No, not for these moles. Who have caused us trouble, made us search for them, forced us to question them and then given us lies. Yes: not good enough. Easy to snout. Easy to kill that way.'

'So then?' said Eldrene Fescue, who liked snouting and perhaps sensed better than the others that something might be apaw that was going to frustrate them all of having these moles' lives. Fescue's eyes glittered and were cold, and she said, half turning back to the grikes for their support, 'Surely you're not suggesting anything less than an immediate snouting?'

There was a hiss of delight among the grikes, and then the beginnings of a chorus of 'Yes!' and 'Snout them now! The eldrene says it! Yesss'. . . But before it became uncontrollable, and the guardmoles about Tryfan and Spindle turned on them to do what the mob desired, Sleekit raised her paws sharply, turned them strangely, twisted her body hugely, grotesquely, seeming almost to intertwine with the birch roots behind her as her mouth opened into a snarl and her eyes fixed on the two Stone followers with what seemed hatred. The grikes fell darkly silent, some perhaps were even afraid, and across that silence Sleekit whispered a word that made a mole shudder and withdraw.

'Disease,' she whispered.

'Disease,' she shouted.

'Yes! Disease . . .' she implored, and the grikes were still, appalled, for the very way she said it seemed an eating on the flesh, and a corrupting of the fur. 'Yes, that's the best punishment, let them begin to die of disease . . . and where? The Slopeside. Let them go there. Let them be put among the clearers. Let them know the first gnawings of scalpskin . . .' There was a wave of disappointment among the grikes, who wanted gratification now, here, today, this minute, and the blood of these pathetic moles of no account spilled *now*. The sideem was suggesting something slower, not so good, not such fun. . . .

Disappointment gathered and a wave of dissent began rolling towards the sideem, but Sleekit hunched her smooth dark body forward and turned the wave back on itself, saying, 'I say, let them suffer the first touch of scalpskin and then, when Longest Day comes and the WordSpeaker herself is here for the Midsummer ritual, let the clearers be ordered to snout them for us, so their Wordless blood is not on our good talons . . .' And Sleekit's voice rose, suddenly hysterical, 'Let them be snouted by their own kind after they have known disease. Yes? Oh yes?'

There was silence for a few moments, and grike after grike turned their gaze from the risen, shaking rage of Sleekit and looked appalled at Tryfan and Spindle, as if the two moles were already diseased and untouchable, and revulsion had replaced bloodlust.

'Yes!' cried out one of the grikes.

'Yes, yes!' cried out others.

'Slopeside them, disease them, have others snout them when the WordSpeaker herself is here.'

The shouting continued for a few moments more and then subsided. The grikes looked at Eldrene Fescue. She looked briefly and dismissively at Tryfan and Spindle and then back at the grikes.

'Well, you have decided,' she said a shade petulantly. 'Do it. The WordSpeaker may be well pleased that we have restrained ourselves so that she herself may witness the snouting of these two.' Then she turned away and was gone, leaving Sleekit in charge.

Tryfan, whose paw had been on Spindle's throughout, said, 'May the Stone be praised!'

'Praised?' said Spindle astonished, for he was shuddering now at the thought of suffering some terrible wasting disease. 'For what?'

'For showing Sleekit what to do,' said Tryfan. 'She had heard the Silence, she saved our lives, and the day will come when she will be of us.'

'Really?' said Spindle as guardmoles jostled about them, and, looking cautiously over to where Sleekit was supervising a selection of guardmoles who were to accompany them to the Slopeside, added, 'If you say so, Tryfan,

I suppose you must be right. Slopeside. Disease. Snouting. Clearing! That's what we'll have to do! Clear. Corpses by all accounts.'

'I thought you were the great believer, Spindle,' smiled Tryfan as a dispute broke out among the guardmoles over who was to go with them. There seemed a marked reluctance to do so; nomole liked going near the disease-ridden Slopeside.

'I am,' said Spindle. 'But in these circumstances even Boswell himself would have doubts.'

'Have faith,' said Tryfan.

'I've faith the Stone's keeping us alive,' mumbled Spindle, 'but for what? More suffering. More misery. More. . . .'

Then Tryfan smiled, for grumbly though Spindle was there was a firmer note to his speech, and a new confidence – that of a mole who has escaped the shadow of an untoward death and can, at least, begin to hope once more.

Around them the guardmoles continued to grumble.

'Silence!' commanded Sleekit's voice, and silence fell on all moles there. Her smooth form, smaller than the moles' around her yet still commanding, looked here and there.

'I like not guardmoles who decline their duty. You, mole, do you volunteer?'

A guardmole came forward and took his place next to Spindle.

'And you!' ordered Sleekit.

A second came forward.

'One more is needed!' said the sideem, but the guardmoles were looking everywhere but in their direction.

'You,' she said, 'why do you hesitate?'

'Disease,' said the guardmole she had picked on. 'You said it yourself, Sideem Sleekit.'

There was something about the voice that was distantly familiar and Tryfan looked up and saw the guardmole she had picked on. It was Alder, crouched next to Marram, the two who had been in the visitors' burrow when they arrived.

'Well,' said Sleekit harshly, 'you had better go and prove me right. I am placing you in special charge of the mole Tryfan, and if anything happens to him, mole, it will be a snouting for you. Now, go, all of you. *Go!*'

She waved them out of the burrow, and there was a general air of relief among the many others there that had not been chosen. Yet as Alder came towards them, seeming not to recognise them, Tryfan could see a hint of pleasure in his eyes and as he passed Sleekit there was a hint, too, of some acknowledgement of a deed done privily and without others knowing.

'Why,' whispered Tryfan in astonishment, 'it was arranged. Sleekit arranged it. . . .'

'Come on, mole,' said Alder, giving him a buffet. 'On you go. Scum!' And with many others jeering and laughing behind them, and calling ribald remarks after the three guardmoles assigned the unpopular duty, they were taken from the chamber. Alder dawdled a little so the other two guardmoles took the lead with Spindle, while he took position at Tryfan's side and they started on their way.

Here and there, when Tryfan stumbled, for he was very weak from his long confinement, Alder put out a surreptitious paw to support him, and as they progressed through the spartan tunnels of Buckland the little party became spread out, with the other guardmoles at times well in front.

When Alder could talk without being observed he did so, speaking in a hurried but quiet way.

'Do you know about the place you're going?' he asked first.

'Little' said Tryfan, 'but that it is dangerous.'

'You'll die there if you stay too long,' said Alder matter-of-factly, 'so you'll have to escape. Soon, too. Moles die of disease there and none will want to see you after or come near. Plague is rife there and the clearers are a vicious Wordless lot. The surface above the Slopeside is patrolled by former Slopesiders who have done their time and survived, or by grikes afflicted with some disease or other, if not of the body then of the mind. They are an unruly and murderous group, feared by the rest of us, and they show no mercy to escapers. But they have undying loyalty to the Word and the WordSpeaker, and escape by the surface will mean death if you are caught. And a terrible death.'

'Do you know of their dispositon?' asked Tryfan.

'You mean where their patrols are? Only that they end at a stream coming from the slopes above. I have seen it myself but it is uncrossable. Beyond it is the derelict system of Harrowdown, but when we took that we did so by a long trek upstream which is a way close-guarded. Across that stream may be your only chance. Try to reach there quickly, avoid contact with anymole in Slopeside, guard your back, and do it before Midsummer for the WordSpeaker will be here and none will forget that you and Spindle are to be found and snouted.'

'Why do you seek to help us?' whispered Tryfan.

'I know not, mole. Only that I have been much troubled since you left the visitors' burrows, and I would know more of the Stone. . . .'

'What of the others we met?' asked Tryfan.

'Come on, stop dawdling!' cried out Alder, pretending to talon-thrust Tryfan to provide cover for his answer.

'Both well,' he continued in a low voice, 'and both agreed to be initiate, both to Atone at Midsummer, but that was to save their lives until they too can find a way of escape. Thyme taught me a little about the Stone but I crave to know more.'

'Then the Stone will guide you,' said Tryfan, 'for it loves all moles.'

'Whatmole are you?' asked Alder, seeming in awe of him. 'You are surely more than "just a mole". I felt peace come from you in the chamber, and you seemed unafraid, even before such hatred.'

'I am nomole but what others make me. But there is one coming greater than I, and you will know him,' said Tryfan. 'So be of good cheer and worry not for us. Now tell me more of Pennywort and Thyme.'

'They have tasks in a system by the Thames, for they are used to wet ground and the eldrenes are dangerously short of good tunnellers. Different ground down here than the North where our tunnelers come from. But they hope to escape . . . as I do. But I don't know where to go . . . Since that healing of yours in the burrow I – I don't know what to do. . . .'

'You awoke and were blessed, Alder, and blessed shall you remain,' Tryfan said. 'Be of faith, try to talk to Thyme for she is a mole of faith, and worthy. Find others like yourself. Trust in the Stone. And as for us . . . Spindle will see that I survive!' He laughed briefly, and Alder wondered to see him so confident and full of courage, and himself felt stronger.

'What of your friend? He was of the Seven Stancing too. He was chosen by the Stone.'

'Marram? He suspects my Wordlessness yet says nothing. He will not talk of it to me. He may in time be of the Stone. He is a good mole, Tryfan, and strong, well trained in fighting. He likes not the punishments the guardmoles mete out. He is afraid, but he will not betray me.'

They pressed on steadily upslope through tunnels and past burrows which were well ordered. The moles they saw were ordinary enough, healthy and clean, but they looked on Tryfan and Spindle as if they were outcasts, drawing back.

'Moles for the Slopeside!' they called to each other, and they stared. Yet Tryfan could only look at them, and catch glimpses of their good burrows and caches of worms and wonder that such normality could exist at all in a regime of cruelty.

'Are you of the Stone?' one female asked as they passed her by.

212

'Yes, we are!' said Spindle eagerly, but she spat at him, and drew back. 'Blessed be the Word for punishing such evil!' she shouted after them. 'May you die in torment!'

The gradient steepened and the soil changed to the lighter, drier soil of sandstone. The tunnels were lighter and high, and the sound of their talons scraping and scuttering on the floor was about them.

Then suddenly the guardmoles ahead stopped where the tunnel widened out and they saw that another was waiting for them there.

While the other two guardmoles talked with this new one, Alder contrived to stay with Tryfan and Spindle, and in the few moments he had left again urged them to escape as soon as they could, for otherwise death was certain to be theirs. Then impulsively he suggested they might try to escape now, with his help.

'That is not my way,' said Tryfan, 'for surely you will be killed, most likely snouted, and, weak as we are now, we would be easily caught. I think the Stone has better plans for all of us. We will go to this Slopeside, for it sounds as if moles there need our help, and there will be others of the Stone who may, perhaps, give us help and guidance. As for this plague or illness that kills moles there, well, am I not a herbalist? I think we will not die quite yet! As for you, Alder, perhaps you should follow your own advice and escape this system.'

'But where can I go alone?' whispered Alder, 'I am a grike and recognisable.'

Tryfan looked at him and saw his nascent faith shadowed with doubt, and his courage mixed with fear. But he saw too a strong mole and one of purpose and decision, and sensed that Alder was a mole for whom the Stone had a task, perhaps a great one, and that he would find strength to fulfil it.

'Listen now,' said Tryfan urgently, 'and tell others of the Stone you may meet what I tell you. Tell Pennywort and Thyme, if you see them. Tell those you trust. Tell them this: there is a system that is chosen, and in its

213

ancient tunnels dwells the light and the Silence of the Stone. It will always be of the Stone, for love of it dwells always in the hearts of moles whose fur has been touched by the sun and wind in the range of its tunnels.'

'What system is this? Tell me its name, and I will try to get there. Tell me . . .' There was a yearning in Alder's deep voice, a yearning whose origins lay far, far back before he met Tryfan, before even he left his beloved Northern system. A yearning for love, and light and harmony that deep down a mole feels, however hurt or angry or corrupted he seems to be. 'Tell me its name,' whispered Alder.

'Its name is Duncton Wood, and there a great Stone stands, ancient and good. Tell other followers of it, Alder, tell them to seek it out. And when you yourself reach Duncton, ask for a mole called Comfrey. He is my half-brother and nomole is truer, or braver, or has more trust and faith than he. Find him, tell him what you know, and he will teach you to hear the Silence of the Stone.'

He spoke softly with Spindle supporting him on one side, yet his voice was certain and strong.

'And if,' he continued, his voice still more quiet, and faltering a little now, 'if you find that we are not there and do not come, if you find that, tell Comfrey that I thought often of him, and I loved him, and tell him to touch the great Duncton Stone for me. For there my parents lie and such a touching and thanksgiving I would have done myself.'

He stared at them both, Alder and Spindle in turn, and they could at first find no words to say.

'Duncton Wood!' repeated Alder at last. 'I have heard of it. It is not yet taken by grikes.'

'Nor will it be; or if it is its spirit for the Stone will never die, and will remain a light for other followers who seek the Stone, and a star that one day all of moledom will see once more. So now, Alder, will you tell Comfrey what I have said if you should be there and we should not? Wilt thou do this?' asked Tryfan in the old way.

'You will do it before me,' whispered Alder.

'And if I do not . . . if I do not, tell Comfrey his name was the last I spoke before we entered this dread place called the Slopeside,' said Tryfan.

'I know not how to pray to your Stone, but I will try, and my prayer will be for thee and thy companion Spindle.'

At which the other guardmoles came up, and drove Spindle and Tryfan upslope, into the dark and narrow tunnel from which a foul air came, and an odorous threat, and they were gone from Alder's sight.

Chapter Thirteen

The tunnel twisted and turned and at times the air was so foul that they might have tried to go back, but behind them was the sound of the guardmoles, heavy of talon and paw.

But before long the tunnel turned sharply into a deep, dark chamber with a single shaft up towards the surface which cast grey light, across which from time to time moved the shadow of a mole: one of the surface patrols which Alder had warned them of. At the far end of the chamber was a blocking stone in front of which a mole squatted, scabby and malevolent, his face ravaged by some disease that made his eyes seem large and staring and pulled back his mouth in a rigor of pain. He said nothing, but seeing them, came forward and peered at them and grunted to himself with some kind of twisted satisfaction.

He then turned from them a little upslope and called up the shaft. Immediately two more grikes came down, huge and fearsome, their grimy talons worn and stubby.

'New clearers,' muttered the scabby mole.

'Two,' said the first grike.

'Yeah,' said the second. 'Males more's the pity. Nice welcome you'll get, scum.'

Tryfan and Spindle did nothing and said nothing.

'Right,' said the scabby one, indicating the blocking stone. 'When we roll it, you go in. Don't go in, you're dead. Got it?'

Tryfan nodded.

'Your pal got it?' said the second grike. 'Okay? Don't go in and you're dead as a crapped fly.'

Spindle nodded, eyes wide, flanks shaking.

'Right, roll 'er,' said the second grike.

They did so, and as they did the tunnel ahead revealed

itself. A musty gust of air came into the chamber, hot and dankly vile like the breath of a dying stoat.

'Ready? In you go!'

One of the grikes grabbed Tryfan's shoulder and pushed him forward and the other took Spindle and shoved him along behind so that, however deep the instinct of both moles was not to enter the tunnel, whose very air was like disease itself, they were forced forward, tumbling against each other, and before they knew anything more the blocking stone behind them had been rolled back into place, and a murky darkness was on them, and a crawling fear. All about them was a stench, enough to make a mole retch, and a sense of darkness and death.

What is evil when it is unseen, and dread when it is invisible, and apprehension when tunnels give no immediate cause for it? Fear.

Fear that eats at a mole's insides and has him cowering at himself as if a low snout is the best protection. Fear that drives from a mole's heart consciousness of the things which he loves and for which he might, at another time, have thought he lived: the warm light of a good day, the comfort of friends, the dreams and desires that come with spring. . . .

Spindle felt such fear now.

Tryfan, too, was touched by it.

But after a few moments crouched still they mastered themselves and became aware that a little ahead was the dim light and echoing sound that heralded a chamber of some kind. They started forward and, silhouetted there briefly, saw the form of mole. Then it was gone.

Tryfan instinctively moved in front of Spindle, though he himself was weak, and crouched still watching, ready to fight if need be. Fighting might not be a scribemole's way, but Tryfan had learnt much on his journey with Boswell and knew that the best way to guard oneself is to look confident.

Ahead, the murk did not lighten; and nor did the stench in the tunnel improve. There was something sharp to the thick air that made a mole's eyes water, and it was hard to make out if that shape they had seen – *if* they had seen one! – was moving once more. Wait! Spindle's paws gripped Tryfan's flank. They heard a stealthy sliding followed by a scamper of talons across a floor.

'He's watching us,' whispered Spindle.

After a moment more of this waiting and holding breath, Tryfan stepped forward and said, 'If you're there, show your snout and give us some guidance where to go.'

Appraising silence greeted this, and the peering of a mole from one shadow or another.

'Come on, Spindle,' said Tryfan losing patience. 'If the mole ahead can't speak or come to us, we'll go to him.'

'Oh bold, very bold, bold indeed,' said a voice from the murk, and a good way to the left of the spot where Tryfan had been looking. Thin it was, male, young, rather whining, anxious to please. Yet quick and clever in a way.

'Show your snout, mole,' said Tryfan more fiercely.

'Very, very bold now! Positively plucky!' said the voice with a sudden laugh. It seemed to have changed location and was now to the right side of the chamber ahead. 'Not craven, cowardly or timid, no. Not those. So . . . welcome, oh yes, most welcome, brave Sirs, here, right here to the Slopeside.'

Then more softly, 'Don't be afraid!'

The mole ahead moved a little, a slinking touch of a move, and a thin paw came into view and beckoned them.

'Yes, yes, yes, this way,' said the mole.

'Come, Spindle,' said Tryfan, 'we will die if we stay here, for surely there is no more wormless tunnel than this. This mole ahead is – '

'Yes?' said the mole ahead. 'Worthy, honourable and utterly brave, Sir. What is he?'

'Harmless,' said Tryfan.

The mole ahead was silent. Thinking. Then he whispered, 'Harmless? Harmless! How very amazing. I have been called everything but that, everything, oh wise Sir. Never harmless. I will think about it and let you know.

218

Meanwhile, I repeat, good Sirs, that most welcoming word: come!'

But as they approached the mole retreated, slinking back in the shadows, reluctant to let what dim light there was fall across his face. So, moving ahead of them in the very crevices of the tunnel that went on beyond the chamber, the mole led them on, keeping up his unctuous chatter as they went.

'Not so bad this place, once you know it, Sirs. No, not so bad. Got you some food, always do that, least I can do. Burrow-cells was it? Nasty. Long, lonely solitary confinement, I know, I know. I have heard others, dear Sirs, who have known it. Well, we'll look after you here – if you let us, we will, and your strength will return phenomenally and most brilliantly. Yes. . . .'

There was about his voice, as there was about what little of his stance they could see, a quality of both eager and pathetic, as if, like some guilty creature that has lost its parents and found them again, he wanted to run forward and show himself but dared not for fear of punishment or rejection.

'Pause, stare, snout, look, and eat, Sirs, I am privileged to know and serve,' he said suddenly. And there on the tunnel floor before them they saw some food.

'Eat, crunch, chew, relish and swallow,' said the mole gaily. Which they did.

When they had eaten the little there, the mole said, 'Please to be kind and generous enough to follow me, yes, as quick as you are able to; yes, please to follow.' And with that the mole turned and led them into another tunnel, his meagre shape scurrying ahead of them, but pausing sometimes, a snout peering round, as if he doubted they were following him. Yet still they could not quite see him.

The tunnels were old and ruined, patched here, half blocked there, sealed off elsewhere. The atmosphere was poor, the air currents weak and confused, and the smell fetid and filled with decay: a sweet, sick smell of death and putrescence.

219

Ahead there were sounds of mole, but not the cheerful sound of talk and chatter, or the run of paws of busy mole, or the song of a female whose work is done: rather the forlorn dragging of tired mole, mole of sickness and lost hope, abandoned mole driven by fear and the desire mixed with the one hope that all moles cling to until the end: that change will come, that life is better finally than death. Such dragging, moaning, suffering sounds came to them from tunnels or burrows ahead, but living moles they did not yet see.

They had drawn a little closer to their guide, but still he contrived to keep his face and most of his body in the shadows, and some natural sense of propriety prevented them coming closer. He paused suddenly and they saw that a few yards ahead the tunnel they were travelling crossed a much bigger one, from which most of the sounds of other-mole they had heard so far came. The mole crouched down and politely asked that they did the same.

Now they heard nearer sounds, of a mole coming. A female, for they could hear her voice moaning or humming in a bereft kind of way as she approached. She was panting, too, with effort and fatigue, her breathing raspy and difficult. Then they could see her passing from right to left down the big tunnel. A terrible sight. No fur, just grey-pink skin, all hanging and worn. She was old, and sometime in the past had pupped for her teats hung sacky and low, dragging on the floor, and one of them was no more than a suppurating sore. She seemed to have an affliction of the neck, because every other step or so she flicked her head nervously back, as if to lick or dislodge some irritation which she could never quite reach. Her paws were cracked and her talons broken. The strangest – and most frightening – thing about her was that she carried in her mouth, its teeth pointing up the wrong way, the upper jawbone of a mole, all white-yellow. It was as if, moleyears before, a mole had attacked her and they had locked jaws and he had died, leaving this final relic of his

220

assault. Where her mouth clenched round this terrible thing she dribbled and sucked occasionally.

'Who is she?' whispered Tryfan.

'Kind Sir, caring Sir, there is no need to whisper,' said their guide rather loudly. '*She cannot hear you!*' he added, shouting it in her direction. Yet she paused for a moment as if hearing some distant thing that she yearned and she snouted around, the bone still in her mouth. As she did so they saw her eyes were red raw flesh, but before they could say or do more, she moved on down the tunnel and was gone.

'Apologies and commiserations, splendid moles, for this brutal sight of ambulating sickness,' said the mole. 'Yes it is shocking, and yes it is terrible, and yes it would be nice to do something about it. No cure here, no hope, no chance of anything much but lasting longer than they expect you to. I know, oh yes, very much I know *that*! So, now, that promising word: come!'

But Tryfan did not move. Instead, as the mole started off once more, Tryfan called out, 'Mole, what is thy name?'

'Oh! Kind it is, thoughtful, most meaningful to ask,' said the mole, half turning. 'Thee, thy, thine: 'I've heard of it but never heard it used. Very pretty, very ancient. You must be a learned mole. Yet you are right, learned brainy Sir, yes: even a mole as humble and unimportant as I has a name, yes, he has. Do you want to hear it? It's a good name and it *is* mine.'

'Yes, mole, we do,' said Tryfan, 'so that we may thank you for the food you gave us and the guidance you are giving us.'

'Oh!' said the mole again, stopping quite still and sounding pleased. 'Wish to thank me, they do these good Sirs, these excellent kind moles. Why now, that is something to remember, something to think about, something to be *thankful* for!'

As he talked like this, half to himself, it seemed, they caught up with him, though he still kept his back to them, and huddled his frail body in the deepest shadow he could find.

'Thy name?' said Tryfan gently.

'My *name?* Yes, my name. Well it's not much, not really . . . I . . .' And he sounded timid, and afraid.

'Show us thy face, mole,' whispered Tryfan.

'I . . . well . . . you don't want. . . .'

'Be not afraid of us, mole, we will never harm thee.'

Then as they waited, with the terrible sounds of sick and defeated moles about them, the mole timidly turned round, his body and face still in shadow, so that they caught only the glimpse of eyes in the light, humble and wary, and teeth, yellow and bent, and talons, thin and worn as if the mole was old.

'Show us thy face,' said Tryfan again.

But the mole shook his head and retreated into the shadow again, snout low.

'You are afraid, mole,' said Tryfan.

'Yes,' the mole said.

'Of what?' said Spindle.

'That's my secret, special and strange. My own, nomole knows. Indulge me, Sirs, just for now.'

Tryfan stared at him, or at his shape, and said softly. 'I think I know thy secret.'

'Yes? Really? Incredible Sir, most extraordinary intellectual Sir to deduce such a thing, what is it? Most interested am I since I barely know it myself.'

'Do you greet all newcomers to the Slopeside?' asked Tryfan.

'My privilege to do it, my great pleasure.'

'And because they have not met you before they have no opinion of you.'

'Clever, Sir, most alarmingly clever.' The eagerness had gone from the mole's voice, and he sounded tired.

'Then you want to keep your name from us, and the sight of your body from us, to preserve for as long as you can your sense of our good opinion of you,' said Tryfan calmly.

222

'I . . . Good Sir . . . I – ' and the mole was stuck for words.

'Is that your "secret", mole?' asked Tryfan.

They heard him come forward fractionally again.

'Well, Sir – ' he began.

'Is it?'

'Yes, Sir,' said the mole simply.

For a long time there was silence between them as some sense of trouble or emotion seemed to afflict the mole until at last Tryfan said once more, and so gently it might have been a May wind across a field of buttercups: 'Thy name?'

Then the mole came forward, and he looked at them as if he was ashamed of his very being and he held his snout low and was unable to face their gaze longer.

As he crouched down, in the light before them they saw that his face was bare of fur, and that his sides were hollowed and pock-marked, and his paws scabbed as the grike guards' had been. His flanks were red raw as the female's eyes were, though not diseased. Like wounds that had never healed.

If ever a mole was ashamed of himself it was the mole they saw before them now: but not ashamed of an act he had done, but rather of his whole self, inside and out. And yet there had been in his voice, before he allowed them to see him, some other sense of self that was confident and intelligent as if, behind that absurd and flowery use of words, which was so obviously a front, there *was* a mole of confidence, though he did not seem to be before them now.

'Why mole – ' began Tryfan, shocked, and instinctively going forward to touch him.

But the mole retreated immediately and said, 'You mustn't touch me. No, no, no, you must not. You don't want *this*,' and his right paw waved with utter resignation over his flanks and furless skin.

'Thy name,' said Tryfan firmly.

'They called me Mayweed long ago,' said the mole, 'and that's my name forever.'

223

He cowered away from them even more but Tryfan would have none of it, and reached forward and touched him.

As he did so Mayweed looked down at Tryfan's talons and uttered a soft 'Oh!' in wonder and then 'Oh!' again, and he looked up at Tryfan and then at Spindle.

'Not good to touch me, kind Sir,' he said. 'No, not good.'

'Who called you Mayweed?' asked Tryfan.

'I – I don't know. I don't remember now. . . I – '

'Who gave you your name? whispered Tryfan, his paw on Mayweed's shoulder.

'I . . . she . . . he . . . *they*, Sir, but it's a long time ago and I don't want to remember. Not that. Don't touch me like that, Sir, it puts me near my tears.'

'You're a mole, aren't you?' said Tryfan.

'Oh, very good that, "You're a mole aren't you?" Very good!' said Mayweed, recovering something of his former confidence. 'There's moles and moles, aren't there?' Well, Mayweed is a mole of sorts, he supposes, but moles don't usually touch him, in fact never do, except to hit and that's not the same thing as a touch is it, Sir?'

'No,' agreed Tryfan. 'Then why do they hit you?'

'Because I'm Mayweed of course!'

They stared at each other in silence and then he turned away, rather sadly, as if thinking that soon they too would treat him as others did, they would *know*; and yet, as he went on down the tunnel, Spindle noticed that there was a little more vigour and confidence to his gait, as if, only for a moment in his life, that brief touch of Tryfan's had given him the sense of what it might be to be accepted.

Perhaps this thought occurred to Mayweed too, for he stopped suddenly, turned and said quickly, 'Good to be touched it is, Sir, kind and generous and brave, Sir, good and very good! Mayweed will not forget. Mayweed never forgets.'

Then all three progressed on down the tunnel until they came to another chamber, more substantial than the one they had started in.

'Tell them he's a tunneller!' said Mayweed urgently, indicating Spindle. 'Tell them that or he'll not last long.' Then before they could say anything more he was gone down a side tunnel, and out of sight.

Facing them in the chamber were two grikes, a male and a female, both young and strong looking, and both with the humourless clean looks of zealots who know they are right and everymole who does not agree with them must be wrong. They saw that the male had small sores on his flanks, and the female was losing the fur from her face. The Slopeside must be foul indeed that such moles as these became diseased.

'Word be with thee!' said the female.

'And thee!' said Spindle hastily, covering for Tryfan.

The female looked at them appraisingly. 'Mayweed led you here, did he?'

They nodded.

'Don't trust him,' she said. 'A snivelling oily little mole, that one.'

'You're to be with Skint at the North End,' said the male curtly.

'My friend here,' said Tryfan with as much conviction as he could muster and doing his best despite his weakened state to look as if he had authority, 'is a tunneller by birth and training. He – '

'Shut up,' snapped the male. 'Mayweed told you to say that. We're putting you with Skint, who'll soon find out what your friend is or isn't.'

'Skint?' said Tryfan.

'Yes. That way.' And they were dismissed northwards up a wide communal tunnel. 'And don't talk or dawdle on the way,' the female shouted after them. 'Carry on and you'll find Skint, or he'll find you.'

But no sooner were they round a corner and out of sight of the chamber than a familiar voice said out of the shadows ahead, 'Psst! Me, marvellous Sirs. Mayweed your friend and intrepid guide. Follow me and I'll lead you there, right to Skint himself! Yes I will, for nothing too!'

Mayweed was as good as his word, though only after a long trek through tunnels of decay and past moles of misery. Yet to the North End they finally came, to find themselves before a mole who had all his fur, even if it was short, wiry and flecked with grey. There was no spare flesh on his body, yet he looked strong, and of all the moles they had so far seen in the Slopeside he looked the healthiest.

'Well?' he said, taking a confident stance in the burrow where they found him.

'Two new subordinates for you kind Skint, Sir, to make your life easier! Intelligent moles they are, easy to train, kind too. . . .'

'Be quiet, Mayweed, and leave.' Skint's voice was low and commanding, and Mayweed did what he was told.

'And what,' said Tryfan, by now weary with the travelling, 'are we to be trained for?'

'Clearing,' said Skint.

'Clearing?' repeated Spindle, who had said little since they had arrived on the Slopeside. 'Do you really think we need training for that?'

'Moles need training for everything,' said Skint uncompromisingly, 'especially southern moles. Soft lot the southerners.'

'Really?' said Spindle.

Skint gave him a withering look.

'Now, you'll not make much of a job of clearing in your present state. So, you can have some food and sleep and we'll start you slow.'

He led them some way off to some unused burrows which, though dusty and draughty, were serviceable enough.

They were immediately joined by Mayweed coming, as usual, from the direction they least expected.

'Food for them? Nice food?' he said.

'Half a worm at most,' said Skint, scowling.

'Yes Sir, half a worm, Sir, immediately, Sir,' said

Mayweed, dipping his snout low and generally making obeisance to Skint.

He came back a moment later carrying a fresh worm in his mouth which he was about to bite into two for them when Skint said, 'Not half a worm each, half a worm between them.'

'Sorry Sir, silly me, utterly ridiculous me, half a worm *between* them Sir, that's generous even magnanimous.'

'It is so,' said Skint shortly, crouching down and looking at the two of them as they shared their tiny ration. 'Give moles as weak as this too much and they sicken and die. You can leave Mayweed; *now!*'

'Thank you Skint, Sir!' With a brief unctuous smile in their direction Mayweed left.

'You probably made the mistake of being nice to him,' said Skint, 'so he'll be back. If he is don't fraternise with him, don't encourage him, don't have anything to do with him. He's a scrounger and a nuisance and he's trouble, and probably an informer to Eldrene Fescue.'

'Does that matter?' said Spindle, whose general annoyance and anger with all they had witnessed had made him bold. 'If she's of the Word you'll wish her to be informed. Aren't you the same?'

'Was once. But now? Word, Stone: when you've been a clearer as long as I have, and seen the things I've seen, it all amounts to the same. Get a job done and move on, that's the clearers' motto. Mayweed's useful because he learns things and can't keep his trap shut. He also knows his way round this place better than anymole else. Useful that. Now get some rest. If you work hard and don't try and escape you'll be as well treated here as anywhere. There's not more than a few months work left before we move on again, and I daresay the next pitch will be healthier than this place.' With that small hope Skint left them.

No sooner had he gone than Mayweed reappeared, popping his head around from some unexpected quarter and peering inquisitively at them.

'Warned you off me did he, splendidly unkempt Sirs?

Said I was a bad lot. Well I admit I look a bad lot, but what can a mole do on the Slopeside? Not what you call wholesome, is it? Not exactly a place a mole chooses to go if he wants to be smart, would you say?'

He was entirely in the burrow now and when Spindle saw him close to, with his bald skin and smelling sores and over-familiar laugh he instinctively drew away in disgust and might have told him to clear out but for a sign from Tryfan.

Tryfan looked at Mayweed with neither dread nor fear, but, rather, some interest. Mayweed stared back at him and the silence lasted some time.

'You're a sly one, Sir, I can see that. Most clever. You know how to make a mole talk, you do, yes,' he said, his former timidity now apparently quite gone and thrusting his snout to within inches of Tryfan's. 'Haven't you heard you'll die in days if you so much as touch a mole with scalpskin, Sir?'

'Scalpskin? What's that?' asked Tryfan.

'What I've got. This!' and he pointed a talon at his bare head. 'And this is what it smells like when you've got it so bad you're bound to die . . .' And he turned his flank to Tryfan and showed him the suppurating sores on his flank.

'How long have you been here?' asked Tryfan, not reacting to Mayweed's sudden exposing of his sores.

'Longer'n any of them,' said Mayweed, suddenly sulky. 'Longer than eternity.'

'Well then,' said Tryfan, 'if you're not dead, there's no reason why we should die just yet, is there?'

'Oh clever, once-again-brainy Sir, very, very cunningly clever. Clever as a fox, very neat. You'll die presently, healthy Sir, through madness, through snouting, through scalpskin, through wasting, through seizure, you'll die. Sooner than later, Sir, kind though you are.'

Tryfan regarded him impassively.

'You haven't,' he said.

'I have a reason to live!'

'What's that?' asked Tryfan.

'Wouldn't you like to know? Not telling. Never told nomole. Never will. Got a reason.'

'Well we've got a reason to live, too,' said Tryfan with a smile.

'Clever again! Tell Mayweed, Mayweed won't tell anyone. Tell him now!' He seemed eager as a pup to know.

'No,' said Tryfan. 'And now if you don't mind I'm going to sleep.'

'Not fair – tempting a mole and then going to sleep. Not fair. Won't get worms for you. Won't help you, not never again.'

But Tryfan had closed his eyes and before long had fallen into a deep, untroubled sleep.

Mayweed disappeared back down a tunnel, and Spindle tried to sleep as well, but was restless and fitful, and unable to settle.

'Hiss! Psst!'

'Yes?' said Spindle.

'What's his name?'

'Tryfan,' said Spindle.

'And yours, Sir?'

'Spindle.'

'What's his reason, Sir, you can tell me. Won't tell a single soul, just want to know.'

'I expect he'll tell you,' said Spindle, rather less afraid of the mole and his condition than he had been before, though quite why he did not know. It was to do with Tryfan not being afraid. And this reason! Well, presumably that was the Stone.

'There's a worm for him, Sir,' said Mayweed, impulsively producing a worm from his tunnel. 'Don't tell Skint.'

'Thank you!' said Spindle.

'What's his name? Tryfan, is it?'

Spindle nodded wearily.

'Where's he from then?'

'Duncton Wood,' said Spindle, being careful not to give anything else away.

229

'Big system, is it?'

'One of the Seven.'

'He's a Stone follower then.'

'Yes, he is.'

'Tryfan's a good name. Funny name though. Tryfan!'

'Ssh!' whispered Spindle. 'Don't wake him.'

'He wasn't afraid of my scalpskin.'

'There aren't many things Tryfan is afraid of.'

'Last lot were afraid. Afraid of everything, they were. Went mad, chewing corpse bones and all sorts. Tried to get away and were caught and snouted although I warned them, yes. Still hanging up there. But Tryfan wasn't afraid.'

'Why should he be?' said Spindle gently.

'Cos it's catching.'

Tryfan stirred and opened his eyes.

'Fear's catching,' he said.

'Ha, ha, ha! laughed Mayweed with genuine delight. 'Clever that! "Fear's catching!" Too right, brilliant Sir!'

Spindle was tired now and his eyes closed, and Tryfan seemed to have fallen asleep again.

Mayweed looked at them in some wonder, and then gone was the smile, gone the cunning, gone the effort to please. And he looked suddenly very young, and very afraid.

'Won't mind if I sleep near, kind Sirs? Not mind, will you? Just near, where I can see you. Like the company. Don't like being alone and asleep. I like you, Sir. You're good, Sir, yes you are. You touched me you did and that was. . . .'

Whatever it was he did not say for he settled down, his snout along his front paws, contemplating Tryfan and his eyes closing as if, after a long time, he had found a measure of safety and wanted to enjoy it.

Much later, when the burrow was in deep silence, Tryfan awoke and saw him there and was pleased. There were moles around him who were lost, and who suffered; others who knew not where to go; others who waited to find something they did not know they sought. And others, like Mayweed, who were good, deeply good. And such moles a scribemole could love, whatever else they might be.

Through others, he was beginning to see, if he was only able to survive, he would find his task, if only the Stone would grant him strength and wisdom to fulfil it. He touched the strange lost mole Mayweed, where his sores were, and where his fur had withered and he whispered invocations of the Stone that this mole might know no fear, and might be blessed and find healing.

For a moment Mayweed stirred, his eyes looking up at Tryfan in apprehension, but Tryfan's voice was as gentle as his touch, and the mole settled again, dreaming perhaps that a mole protected him, touched him, watched over him, a great mole, a mole beyond his dreams, an ancient mole, kind like Tryfan; and Mayweed found good sleep for a time.

Chapter Fourteen

Tryfan and Spindle quickly discovered that the fear Alder had had for their safety was founded on the grim and frightening reality that the Slopeside was no more nor less than an extensive and complex system of tunnels, separated from all others, into which a mole, once confined, must work until he died. Or, if he survived, until he was moved on to clear another system. Few survived two such terms, none three.

The first impressions they had, of moles engaged in hard and dangerous tasks in poor conditions, and under threat of instant punishment and snouting, was correct. But there was more to the Slopeside than that, more that was subtle and unseen, more that was evil; and something that was doomed, something that allmole scents in time where there is no hope, purpose or faith. But *that* it took the two moles a little while longer to find.

The day following their arrival, and after Skint had berated Mayweed for insinuating his way into their burrows, he began to instruct them. Skint looked rather less friendly in the light of the new day than he had seemed the evening before, but he was obviously a mole to respect. He peered at them from small dark eyes set deep in a sturdy face. His fur was healthy and his manner brisk. He had a wrinkled snout and was lithe and muscular, and rather smaller than they had at first thought. His eyes affected lines of meanness and distrust, as if he felt he should suspect all moles of cheating and robbing him, and yet there was a certain twinkle to them, and grace to his movements, that made a mole think he might not be quite as ill-tempered and untrusting as he made out. His voice was thin and accented similar to Alder's and he spoke in quick, sharp bursts, as if used to being in charge.

'The last lot Eldrene Fescue sent were useless as legless fleas so I don't have much hope for you,' he began. '*I* get little thanks for training you, so don't expect much of my time. Words cost effort, and effort requires food, and food is scarce so listen well because I'm not in the habit of saying things twice.'

They nodded their heads and settled down to listen.

'First some history. The Slopeside is the worst clearing job we've ever had, and the biggest. The original moles must have died like flies here because their bodies are packed three or four high in some seal-ups. Hundreds of corpses, and only the surface to put them on. They died of buble-plague, infectious plague, malodorous murrain, self-cannibalism and swelling starvation. The moles downslope must have been a nice bunch: they abandoned them and sealed them all in and they killed a lot more who tried to break out. They forced others up here who came in panic from other systems, so that today we are left with burrow after burrow of unappealing death. Not nice.

'We came here from Rollright in January, which is a fair while to be clearing one system, but the WordSpeaker herself has decreed that this is to be the central system of the whole of the south so a lot of accommodation is needed – though not as much as we've got here I would have thought. But there you are. Orders! It's taken longer than we expected because this place generates virulent scalp-skin and –'

'What exactly is scalpskin?' asked Tryfan.

'It's what that mole Mayweed's got. Most seem to get it in the end. First there's the itching over the scalp. A mole can't think of anything else for a while: drives some mad. Then where they itch the fur goes, the skin dries and sores develop. Then sores develop down the neck and along the belly, sometimes even when a mole doesn't itch. But itching speeds things up. Once those sores turn bad and smelly, that's the end. No cure. Mind you, a lot linger on: moles don't like losing their life, but they go in the end. The end is not nice and not pretty, worse than the plague itself. Eyes go, snout ulcifies, terrible aches. We put such moles out of their misery unless they've taken themselves up on to the surface and the guardmoles kill them.'

'*You* haven't caught it.'

'No,' said Skint, smiling grimly. 'Lucky that way. Had itching, but didn't give into it. Not once. Got discipline. The itch went and no sores, yet. Most get it quickly, a few don't. Tell you one thing: those zealot grikes who are meant to be in charge of us get it quicker than anymole. Don't ask me why – unless it's because they want to die quick for the glory of having their name on the Rock of the Word.

'Now, back to business: our task. Get rid of the corpses and remake the tunnels by Midsummer, which gives us little more than a few weeks. The worst is over. It was bad here in the first months, very bad; not many survivors from that, I can tell you. I'm one, Smithills, who you'll meet in time, curse him, is another though he's got it starting, Munro has done well, no sign of scalpskin at all; Willow's got it bad, but she's a mole and a half, she is, and if we can get her out of here she might survive.' Tryfan noted his voice had softened a little at the mention of this mole's name; and his eyes stayed soft beneath the scowling expression as he added a last name: 'Oh, aye, and that Mayweed. He's survived, but his scalpskin's getting worse. Don't give *him* long.'

'Now, I'll let you into a secret. Eldrene Fescue made a promise to Smithills back in Rollright after he did her a favour that when this job was finished he was to be allowed to travel back to his home system. And I'm to be set free after Uffington.'

'Uffington?' said Tryfan sharply.

'Not many corpses there now,' said Spindle, regretting immediately he had said it. But Skint did not pick him up on it, saying instead, 'We won't be *clearing* there.'

'What then?' asked Tryfan.

'Ruining more like. As long as there's Holy Burrows, Stone followers will have a place to yearn for, won't they?

That's the theory. They don't ask idiots like me, of course. If they did I'd say they were daft: you don't kill a belief by killing a tunnel, do you?'

'No,' agreed Tryfan. 'You kill it by showing there's a better one.'

'That may be,' muttered Skint. 'Yes, that may be. Now, to continue with this briefing. We've got to make a final push to finish up here before Midsummer so that the eldrenes and the rest can move in and establish a guardmole stronghold here. Henbane was going to make Rollright the centre but the Word told her different; the Word said this was to be the one. When our work's done and the guardmoles can move up here in safety, the sideem will come from the north and make the lower tunnels and burrows worthy of being a stronghold for the Word. From here all southern moles will be taught and the good times will come.'

'Why don't they just leave this system sealed up and start another one?' asked Tryfan. 'Wouldn't it be safer?'

'Ours is not to reason,' said Skint darkly. 'The Word-Speaker says it must be for 'tis written in the Word that moles will dig and delve that all might know the Word. Moles dug this place, moles must save it. And all signs of the plague must be driven out forever.'

Tryfan noted that as he reached this part of his 'instruction' he spoke, for the first time, with little conviction.

'You'll be with me for several days,' Skint continued, 'while I show you how to clear corpses economically, as the eldrenes put it. There's ways and means to shift a corpse, some for speed, some to avoid contamination. I'll show you how. As for you, Spindle mole, you'll have your chance of tunnelling and if you prove yourself the zealots'll use you.

'Now listen. I'm boss. I'm in charge of worms. You eat no worms in these quarters without my permission. Did Mayweed come and give you more food?'

'Yes' said Tryfan, deciding honesty was the best policy.

'Thought he might. Nuisance that one. Well, when you have your own beat you'll have your own worms. Eat them then as fast as you like and more fool you. Food gets scarce and the indulgent die. Moles eat too much anyway. Meanwhile, while you're with me, there's to be one at waking, three at rest, two at sleeping: that's all a mole needs.

'Which brings us to . . . cleanliness. Dirtiness is death. Cleanliness is life. My life is clean, my fur is good. Other moles are dirty, their fur is bad. Look at Mayweed. Dirty. Look at Smithills when you meet him, dirty. Always has been, and I've known him since a pup. Now he's got scalpskin and I haven't. Draw your own conclusions and act on them. Too many moles here don't take into their brains what their eyes see. Idiots!

'So . . . rules of cleanliness. Groom before and after each and every corpse removal, with especial attention to talons. Do not eat maggots. Avoid fleas. Eat no dead worms. Clear out your burrow once every four days. Defecate on the surface – the guardmoles won't hurt you – or do it in separate tunnels. Sort out airflow in your home burrow. Avoid physical contact with dirty moles. Have no sex with female clearers. Any questions? No? Right! Get moving then and I'll take you to an easy enough section where you'll not find it too hard if you do as I say.'

He led them busily off down a tunnel until they arrived at a burrow whose seal had been only roughly broken so that they had to clamber over debris to get inside. What they saw there was grim and pathetic.

'A mass seal-up,' said Skint. 'The moles here were probably prevented from burrowing out by healthy moles in the tunnels and on the surface, and held captive until they were too weak to do more than climb desperately on top of each other.' He eyed the mound of corpses impassively, letting Tryfan and Spindle take in the sight in their own way. Spindle's snout lowered in misery at what he saw, but Tryfan, though shocked, still stared numbly around the burrow and took it in.

Despite the poor light, they could see it was large and crudely dug, the walls rough and dusty. The centre and one side of the burrow were entirely taken up by a confused tangle of mole corpses. There were few there that were not dried and desiccated beyond facial recognition. Most were skeletal but with skeins of fur and skin hanging from them and entangling with other moles. A large skeleton lay across the top of several beneath, its left paw dangling loosely down and into the skull of a juvenile, whose head consequently looked as if it was being taloned to the ground. Another, smaller, and probably a female, had somehow become inverted and her talons curled upwards in a gesture of submission. Beyond her two corpses seemed obscenely meshed together in an act of skeletal mating, the pale skull of the male caught in the act of biting the central vertebrae of the female beneath him. All were packed tight, and covered by a light brown dust from the roof above. The more he looked about him, the more Tryfan came to understand the reality of the plague years, which had come to his own home system of Duncton moleyears before he was born, and nearly destroyed it. Indeed, the lower slopes of Duncton Wood had been abandoned by survivors in favour of the higher Ancient System, the opposite to what had happened here at Buckland.

'For reasons we don't fully understand,' Skint went on, 'the last survivors generally climbed up the ones below – my guess is they were trying to get to the best air. Sometimes you'll find evidence that individuals have survived long after the others have died; sometimes, if the season was spring, there is evidence of females giving birth in the final moments of their life. The pups did not last long for talon worms got them and they had no milk to suck.' His voice was bitter and cold, his eyes expressionless.

'Sometimes you find survivors, though they're usually demented and best put out of their misery. Survived on cannibalism, could have got out eventually but didn't dare

237

for fear of the moles they thought were still outside the seal-up waiting to kill them. That mole Mayweed . . . that mole . . .' He shook his head and for a moment that impassivity changed to a look of disbelief.

'What about him?' asked Spindle, ever curious.

'Survived. Here. In the Slopeside. Strange story.'

'Tell us,' said Tryfan in his most persuasive way. Skint looked at him curiously, as if acknowledging that he was a mole of more authority than some, and settled down to tell him.

'When we first came to the Slopeside, there were persistent rumours among the clearers that there was a mole already living up here: one who avoided contact with others, yet never left the Slopeside tunnels. The first real evidence was when one of the clearers got injured and then confused by foul air and lost. Some days later he reappeared, saying a young mole had appeared out of the darkness, a most strange and talkative mole, who led him to a fresher chamber, brought food to him, waited until he had recovered and finally led him back to tunnels he knew.

'The grike patrols got to hear of it and naturally they could not tolerate a mole running free, even if he chose as his freedom tunnels that other moles were beginning to see as a sentence to death. By then we all knew that a particularly virulent form of scalpskin prevailed in the Slopeside because we had lost several good mates to it.

'Well we laid a trap for him. A mole pretended to be lost. Sure enough the mole we now know as Mayweed showed up and was nabbed. Hello, said we, and what are you doing here?

'The only mole he'd talk to was Willow, bless her. Cried like a pup when he saw her. Reminded him of his mother, you see. She worked out what must have happened. Must have been an autumn mole, and they're meant to be the lucky ones! He might even have been pupped inside a seal-up, though Word knows how his mother suckled him to weaning, or what she lived on – or what he did. Don't like to think of it. But some others must have survived

238

because he could talk when we found him, and a polite lot they must have been judging from the expressions he uses, calling everymole "Sir" or "Madam", and praising them. He must have been told not to leave by the last survivors because he'd be killed by the plague-free moles and he never did, until we found him.

'At first he never stopped talking and drove us mad. But he knew the tunnels and knew the food supplies and he could run rings round the patrols and back again. We think he even knows ways down off the Slopeside but he won't show us. Never known a better route-finder in my life, and I've known a few. It's like he was born with a snout which always knows the best way to go.'

Skint paused, admiration in his voice. 'You'll never get him out of the Slopeside, that's for certain, so Word knows what'll happen to him when we finish up here, which isn't long off now. For the time being he's attached himself to us at the North End, and when's he's not off on his secret travels he's here with me or over on Willow's beat.'

Skint said no more but got up and wandered around the chamber with an appraising eye to work out the best way of clearing it.

From above, through the roof, trailed the pale green roots of living plants, which seemed to have sought out these bodies of seasons past and, grotesquely finding sustenance there, had crept and crawled their way among the bone and sinew, and in places grown downward through skin and fur.

'This looks like a twenty-burrow to me,' said Skint coolly, talking of the corpses as if they were merely things. 'An experienced clearer should be able to deal with this lot in four days, but it'll probably take the two of you longer than that. Still you've got to start somewhere.'

'Why not just re-seal the burrow and leave them in peace?' muttered Spindle, his voice hard and a little hysterical, for he felt an angry helplessness as he looked about the burrow.

'Because it's quicker to clear than make new burrows and tunnels,' said Skint, 'especially if you've got a mole to do it for you who you don't mind wasting; and because Henbane the WordSpeaker says so, and because it's your job for the Word.

'Now before I show you what to do, a few general observations,' he went on. 'The roots are the real problem, because if you try and remove a corpse too quickly attached roots may create a roof-fall which will make for work later. So watch them carefully, and bite them through where necessary. Next, always try and work from above when removing a corpse from a pile, otherwise they've a habit of shifting about and trapping you. These ones look clean enough – no putrescence, which is the real danger to health. It's normally the bottom ones which are the problem – life stays on them longest and the air doesn't get to them. Putrescence and pestilence linger there and can be dangerous. Munro's brother Larch shifted corpses badly, didn't he? Got trapped and half suffocated. When they found him he was still alive, but talon worms had got to his flanks and back and once in never out. He was paralysed in three days. Munro himself put him out of his misery. That was February, so be warned.'

Skint fell suddenly silent, concentrating on the base of the pile of corpses. He darted forward and stared into what seemed dark shadow. He snouted and sniffed, whispering, 'Yes, I thought so. We're in luck.' He backed away and stared at the pile of skin and bones above him. He signalled Tryfan and Spindle to come to him and pointed into the shadows near his front paws.

'I was talking about talon worms. Look down there.'

They looked. It was a mole's skull, yellow-white. There were dried, dark red worms on it, thin and short. And a curious smell as of crushed nettles.

'Talon worms. Dead. Nothing left to feed on. Died where they were, the little buggers. Note the smell and keep your wits about you when you come across it. If you *ever* smell crushed nettles again you move fast, especially if you're wounded or sore-ridden. They'll not normally attack a healthy mole, but they smell blood and go for it, and an open ulcer is an open invitation. Not seen any for a while, though, so maybe they've cleared out of here. They like fresh, suffering life.'

'What are they exactly?' asked Spindle nervously.

'Red-black, shiny, carnivorous, fast. Luckily they hurt so you know they're on you. Kill them quick.'

He moved round the pile and took up a dead mole's paws in his own. 'Never drag a corpse by the paws,' he said. 'They break off and leave you with a pawful of nothing much. Shoulders and pelvis, preferably shoulders. Don't be squeamish . . . ' He thrust his right paw between the mole's shoulder blades and vertebrae and half lifted the entire body up. 'There you are, easy. Not too fast and not too slow – a half drag is best. Try and keep them in one piece.' He expertly pulled the corpse across the burrow.

'Two's better than one getting them out on to the surface. One to heave and one to shove. If they're rotten never get below – nasties fall on you. One way or another you've got to get corpses out on the surface as quick as you can. But don't linger up there – rooks like a mortuary site, so do owls, and the patrols have been known to kill an idle mole just for the sake of it.' He looked up at the glimmer of light that came from an old exit and briefly across his face went that look of a mole who for too long has been underground and wishes to know once more the feel of sun and wind in his fur for as long as he likes, rather than just hurriedly while he disposes of a corpse and must go below once more. All three were silent, thinking such thoughts together, for Tryfan and Spindle had not been on the surface at all for molemonths on end and longed to wander as they had been used to doing in the days, which seemed so distant now, when they had been free to do so.

'Any other questions?' asked Skint.

They stared dumbly at him.

'Right. Now you can stay together for the time being.

You've to clear four between you for this session so get on with it. Two days like that then you'll be working as a team but then you have to clear six a session. Remember you get less worms if you shift too few.

'One last thing. I repeat: don't go wandering off. Guardmoles are on the surface and in the peripheral tunnels and don't give clearers many chances.'

With that Skint left them to it and went off to direct other moles' work, and occasionally they heard his muffled voice from nearby tunnels.

The work was slow, tiring and depressing but they did it well enough together, taking corpse after corpse on to the surface. Occasionally a mole would go by, but none stopped to talk. All had sores on their backs and flanks. An unpleasant-looking mole came and watched them for a time and then was gone: a grike probably. On the surface a large male watched them as they cleared, and shouted at Spindle to 'get below, scum' when he paused briefly to enjoy the fresh air. But in a way he was glad to, for the surface was scrubby and unkempt, and littered with dried skin and bones of cleared moles, and there was the dark threat of rook to the west. Perhaps it was hardly surprising that the patrols were irritable. . . .

Night came and with it an exhaustion of body and mind. The initial shock of the work gave way to a numb distaste for it, and the knowledge, certain it seemed, that they could not last long doing it.

They finished that first night three corpses short of their target, and yet were so tired they hardly ate the reduced rations they received in consequence. The second day, the third day . . . and by the morning of the fifth the burrow was cleared and made good. Then on to another. . . .

It was on the sixth evening, when for the first time neither felt too tired to talk, that there was a commotion near the chamber where they were eating a night meal with Skint. A large mole appeared at the entrance.

He was ragged in appearance but, by the standards of the Slopeside, seemed well fed, for his stomach had a

242

pleasing roundness and his face was cheerful. His paws, too, seemed well made, even if, like some of his flank fur, they were muddy and ungroomed. On one side he had a sore, and the fur near it was sparse and the skin beneath flaky and raw: the signs of incipient scalpskin.

'Eating as usual, you mean bugger!' declared the newcomer, looking at Skint. 'These poor idiots your new apprentices?'

Skint barely looked up but Tryfan acknowledged the mole.

'My name's Tryfan,' he said, 'and this is Spindle.'

'Yes, so I hear. Smithills, that's me. Working the east part of the North End of this forsaken place. Area of putrescence. Nasty. Nearly done. Last job, then I'm going home. Eh, Skint? You too tight even to say hello, Skint?'

'He's a scrounger,' muttered Skint with a malevolent sideways glance at Smithills, 'and he'll have your worms off you quick as light.'

'Scrounger?' said Smithills furiously. '*Scrounger?* Nothing to scrounge round you, Skint. Never met a meaner mole in my life.' Smithills let out a chuckle and settled himself down, watching Skint pleasurably as if hoping to get a rise from him.

'None of that now!' said Skint sharply. 'Not one word of that or you can get right out of our burrow!'

'Well you disprove it then and give me a worm or two.'

'You're filthy, Smithills. Clean yourself up!'

'You're so tight with worms it's a wonder you're still alive,' retorted Smithills . . . And so the two moles, whom Tryfan could see were old friends, carried on for a time at each other until Smithills was given a worm, and Skint, in a moment of sudden generosity, announced that the two of them had not done badly for newcomers over the last few days and deserved an extra worm apiece.

'Mayweed!' he called out. '*Mayweed*! Get us some more worms.'

But Mayweed, who never seemed far away, must have

243

had some ready for he immediately appeared with food and said, 'Wonderful moles, deserving of more than sustenance, I, Mayweed, bring it to you feeling privileged and honoured to do so, paltry and pathetic though I am and always will be.'

'I'll have the big one,' said Smithills with a grin.

'A great and goodly pleasure to see *you* again, Smithills Sir!' said Mayweed.

'At least one mole here's welcoming then!' said Smithills, starting on the worm Mayweed offered him.

Skint scowled. Then, rather grudgingly, he said, 'Well now you're here you might as well tell us what news you've got, if any.'

'Oh I've got news all right,' said Smithills, pausing for effect.

'Yes?' said Skint eventually.

'He's glad to talk to me now, you see,' Smithills said mischievously to the others, 'now he knows there might be something in it for him. Always been like that, has Skint, haven't you, you old miser? Just as well I've got a generous forgiving spirit.'

'You've got a generous forgiving stomach more like,' muttered Skint.

In a far shadowy corner Mayweed, who had taken a stance there hoping nomole would turf him out, laughed and said, half to himself, 'Oh funny that, witty and droll, the worthy and quick-minded Skint making a comparison between heart and stomach, yes: most excellently done. Very – '

'Shut up, Mayweed!' said Skint impatiently. 'I want to hear Smithills' news.'

'Yes Sir, please Sir, I will Sir, only complimenting you Sir.'

'Give over, Mayweed,' said Smithills in a kindly way. 'There's a good mole.'

'Wonderful!' said Mayweed ambiguously, and shut up.

For a time they all chewed contentedly, enjoying that pleasant silence and settling down that precede a good evening gossip such as all moles love. But still Smithills' news remained unshared.

'Well?' said Skint, getting increasingly frustrated.

Smithills looked meaningfully at Tryfan and Spindle, as if to say that he would prefer to know more about them, to see whether they were trustworthy before revealing whatever secrets he had.

'Well, mole,' he said to Tryfan, 'now we're fed and comfortable you can tell us how you came to be here.'

'It's a long story,' said Tryfan, disinclined to tell it but becoming aware that these two experienced clearers were assessing them. When violence, snouting and death came to the Slopeside at Midsummer then perhaps he and Spindle should be allied with strong moles like these.

'All the better to start it now, then!' said Skint cheerfully, easing his paws forward, and somehow making Tryfan understand that he had best humour Smithills. Smithills too settled again, while Mayweed sighed a little, clearly delighted to be allowed to stay though finding it hard to remain silent. His eyes darted here and there, from mole to mole, until they settled expectantly on Tryfan and waited for him to begin.

Tryfan told his story, omitting only an account of how he himself was ordained a scribemole, that he and Spindle were travelling in service of the Stone and he made no mention of the Stillstone. But other things he told of – of Boswell, of the destruction at the Holy Burrows, and of Brevis and his present captivity in Buckland.

The two clearers listened attentively, particularly to what he had to say about belief in the Stone, for they had not met so articulate and knowledgeable a Stone follower before, and Tryfan sensed that they were dubious of the Word, and knew that a mole in doubt often had an open heart.

Of his own deeds in protecting Boswell he was modest, but he said enough to make it clear that he was a mole who could account for himself. Finally he spoke briefly of Spindle's exploits, enough to make Smithills realise that there might be more to the cleric than there seemed.

'Interesting and well told,' declared Skint at the end.

'Agreed,' said Smithills.

'Worthy Sir, you have fascinated us with – '

'Shut up, Mayweed,' said Skint automatically. Mayweed shut up and contented himself with a ghastly grin of approval.

'I don't suppose it matters if these two newcomers hear what I've got to say, Skint. I've got a feeling healthy and resourceful moles are going to be needed in the days and weeks ahead . . . My news is that Henbane of Whern is on her way to Buckland and will be here in the week, and that after that we better get a move on and clear up this place or snouts are going to suffer. My news also is that something's apaw with some of the patrols because they're being increased, and certain of them have been put on peripheral duties and certain have not, which I seem to remember happened at Rollright before those goings on I don't like to think about. . . . '

Skint looked suddenly serious.

'When did you learn this?'

'Today,' said Smithills, also serious now. 'We've got decisions to make, Skint. We got to be on our guard once more. We must plan.'

Neither mole explained what decisions they had to make, who the 'we' included, against what they must be 'on guard' or what 'plan' they might make. Instead Skint just crouched, thinking. Smithills respected his silence and chewed his food. Tryfan and Spindle decided to say nothing.

Eventually Skint said, 'How are the others?'

'Willow's confused, Munro's fit as a thistle, never better. What about these two?' Smithills nodded in the direction of Tryfan and Spindle. 'Can they be trusted?'

'Not sure. Too soon to tell yet. Only been here six days. But we need support.'

Tryfan listened to their rapid talk. He and Spindle were still being assessed. Trouble was coming and it had to do with Henbane and the future of the clearers. Would

246

Fescue and Sleekit remember their promise to snout him and Spindle at Midsummer? They had to escape before then. The burrow, formerly relaxed, was suddenly tense as if things needed to be discussed and the two older clearers might wish to do it alone.

'We better go,' said Tryfan to Spindle.

'Stay,' ordered Smithills. 'What I've got to talk to Skint about can wait some days yet. He knows that. And maybe we could use a mole like you.' He looked meaningfully at Tryfan and then, rather dismissively, at Spindle, who was tired after the days of clearing and had taken a fatigued kind of stance and was fastidiously cleaning the crevices between his pale talons.

'He's with me,' said Tryfan aggressively, to make clear that he and Spindle travelled together.

Smithills nodded quickly, 'Yes, of course he is, I wasn't suggesting. . . .'

But when Tryfan was alone again with Spindle he wasted no time in saying that, since dangerous times were ahead, they had best keep their ears and eyes open, and be ready for action. There was something doom-laden and final about the atmosphere in the Slopeside.

'We stay together, Spindle, and we gather what news we can. Skint and Smithills seem to be moles worth knowing.'

'They're not of the Stone,' said Spindle.

'And yet they don't seem very much of the Word either' added Tryfan, 'but we'll see. One thing is certain: when this mole Henbane arrives, we're in trouble, and we had best have our plans made and our purpose clear if we are to survive.'

That evening with Smithills proved to be the first of many such that the moles were to share during their time of service under Skint – evenings at which they met other clearers, and began to realise that they had been lucky to be seconded to Skint, for he was respected by others, and though he pretended to be bad tempered and mean it was only a defence against the impossible and dangerous life he had led for years.

His story, and that of Smithills, came out soon enough. The two had been born in the system of Grassington, which lay, they explained, in the very shadow of Whern. Far from being a dark and worm-poor place, as Tryfan and Spindle imagined all systems to the north of the Dark Peak to be, it was, according to their description, as goodly a home system as any, though very different from southern systems, having greater rainfall, racing rivers and streams all about, and different rock and vegetation.

They grew up in adjacent burrows and, like many youngsters of their generation, saw the grikes of Whern marching south in the service of the Word, whose good news was preached in every system they passed through. When the time came to leave their home burrows in the summer, Skint and Smithills joined the southward march and were soon promoted to guardmole duty. Both showed a talent for fighting –Smithills in paw-to-paw combat, and Skint in a more strategic way: and they worked together very well and were accepted as a team.

But the Grassington moles are naturally independent, and used to better than the sparse life of Whern, and neither Skint nor Smithills took kindly to the rigid imposition of the Rule of the Word, nor to the need to impose it cruelly. But they did well enough and rose steadily to middle-ranking positions.

After various escapades, including one in which they attempted to return to the north but were caught, they were demoted to the ranks once more; and at Rollright, where the battle for supremacy over Stone followers was a hard one and there was some mutiny, they offended Eldrene Fescue, who was appointed by Henbane to impose order on the rebels, and were made clearers. Skint, not used to long subterranean confinement nor proximity to death, had immediately become ill and another mole, an old female called Willow who came from a system near his own, had cared for him and seen him better. Since then the two had always protected her, though she was independent by nature and preferred to live some way off in her own burrows. But they took care of her, and counted her as one of their group. A fourth mole who was 'with' them was Munro, a sturdy mole who, though not very intelligent, was strong, reliable, loyal and could fight when he had to, and he too they had met at Rollright. There had been others, but in recent moleyears they had died of disease, been snouted, or gone off to other parts and the group had been reduced to the original four from Rollright who, one way and another, watched out for each other, tacitly accepting Skint as their leader.

Since coming to the Slopeside of Buckland the mole Mayweed had attached himself to them and, despite their verbal abuse of him, he seemed to like to be around them.

Smithills and Skint said there had been a massacre of clearers at Rollright when the job there was finished, only the healthier moles being allowed to leave on the trek to Buckland. Now the rumour was that the patrols were being strengthened here, preparatory to another massacre before the trek to the next job. Of Skint's little group, Willow would certainly be killed, and possibly Smithills too now that his scalpskin was marked. Tryfan and Spindle were healthy but might survive only to be snouted. As for Mayweed, he would surely be killed in any fight with guardmoles.

In the privacy of the beat they were given a few days later, once their apprenticeship with Skint was over, Tryfan and Spindle agreed that they had best be watchful, and stay close to Skint, for the more they met of other moles on the Slopeside, the more they realised that the Stone had served them well to put them in his care.

Chapter Fifteen

Tryfan and Spindle's period as trainee clearers came to an abrupt end when the angry-looking zealot they had briefly met on their arrival appeared out of the murk one day and said curtly to Spindle, 'You! Here! Now!'

The grike was flanked by two large scabby-looking patrollers, only one of whom had they seen regularly in the North End. The other was a new face, and healthier. Both looked ready for a fight and all three behaved as if they were expecting trouble.

Tryfan, who was nearby, turned and came forward too, if only to give Spindle moral support, for the three moles looked murderous and aggressive indeed.

'Not you!' the zealot said. 'The Word does not summon you yet.' Tryfan fell back but stayed watching, and though he got some unpleasant looks he was not told to leave.

'True or false,' said the zealot, 'you being a tunneller?'

Spindle hesitated, only dimly remembering that this had been a claim Tryfan had made for him at Mayweed's suggestion.

'It's what your friend said when you came. You don't look like a tunneller, but you southern moles don't look like anything much, Word help us. Could have been what that Mayweed told you to say, it could have been the truth. We'll soon find out!'

The guardmoles at his side grinned unpleasantly and looked at each other. The consequences of 'finding out' that Spindle was not a tunneller if he claimed to be one were clear enough.

'Now, mole. Are you a tunneller or not? If you're not and you say so now you can just stay here and continue with clearing duties. If you say you are and we find you're not you'll be punished by the Word. Well?'

250

Spindle peered round nervously in Tryfan's direction and then back at the zealot.

'Actually,' he said, using his best Holy Burrows voice to disguise any trace of the lie he was telling and perhaps to give himself confidence as well. 'I am. Well trained and willing, for I begin to see the might of the Word, and the wisdom of its ways.'

The zealot's face softened marginally at this piece of nonsense and said, 'Well then, come with us. Job to do. Needs a healthy mole, which for the time being you appear to be.'

'Sir,' said Spindle pleasantly, 'I wonder if you would be kind enough to allow my friend to come too?'

'Is he a tunneller?'

For the briefest of moments Spindle hesitated again, but much as he wanted Tryfan to come with him now he did not wish to risk both their lives with the discovery that they were not tunnellers; but more than that, some instinct told him that this was a task he had best undertake alone.

So Spindle laughed, doing his best to sound both superior and derisory, which was not easy since neither attitude was natural to his vague and preoccupied nature.

'That mole a tunneller?' he said. 'Hasn't got the intelligence!' Then he looked hard at the guardmoles and said more confidentially to the zealot, as one equal to another, 'Some moles have brawn, Sir, and some have brains. My training was in the strategy and planning of tunnels and quite frankly, if I may say so, these tunnels of the Slopeside, and some that I have seen that have since been made, are made with more brawn than brain. You could do with some proper planning.'

The zealot allowed himself a brief smile.

'Come with us then, mole, and I hope your "planning" is as impressive as your tongue, or else you will not live long. As for your friend . . . ' he turned and whispered to the North End guardmole and then turned back to Tryfan. 'Report later for instructions as to which beat to take. Meanwhile carry on with what you were doing!'

251

With that, Tryfan's good companion of the past few months was suddenly gone, and he was left alone to whisper a prayer of protection after him, and hope that the bluff would work.

Skint was not pleased with the way things had gone and neither he nor Smithills held out much hope for Spindle's survival. Other moles had tried the same trick over the years, for tunnellers got preferential treatment and a much wider run of the tunnels where they worked, but few had ever been seen alive again. All moles can dig and delve, but planning tunnels is an ancient skill, and one passed down from parent to pup, each system having but a few families who know the secrets of air, soil, water and light, which are the key elements of a tunnel system.

'He's a mole of surprising knowledge,' Tryfan told Skint and Smithills, 'and though he will not have tunnelled as such in the Holy Burrows, he will have studied what he saw there, and certainly learnt something of Buckland's tunnels from Brevis, who was his master.'

'Aye, well, we'll hope then,' said Skint. 'If it works he'll find out a lot that even Mayweed can't discover, for Mayweed's listening is cowardly and surreptitious whereas a tunneller must know what's going on and be in the thick of things. Mind you, I don't know what they want tunnellers for since most of that work has already been done. He's a braver mole than he looks, that one, but . . .' and Skint shook his head, 'I'm sorry, Tryfan, but you'd best not hope for too much. Now, if you don't mind, Smithills and I want to talk alone.'

Tryfan was disappointed but not surprised. He knew that neither of the two clearers trusted him yet, nor had reason to, and if there was going to be trouble in the Slopeside, they would want to keep their group, which already included Willow and Munro as well, as small as possible.

So he felt very alone now, and for several days after was restless and irritable. The guardmole had soon returned and moved him to his new beat, which lay some distance from Skint and on the way to Smithills' patch, and was one of the last pockets of burrows needing clearing. Here he established himself in a burrow he made clean and good, found wormful soil and began to eat well and rest as much as he could, for he felt it likely that if he was going to have to survive alone he would need to recover his health from the long ordeal in the burrow-cell. So he was careful to observe all of Skint's advice on cleanliness.

* * * * * * * *

One evening, after he had done two hard sessions of work and was doing his best to meditate, there was a scurry nearby and Mayweed appeared.

'I know you're sad, I imagine you're worried sick, clever Tryfan, Sir, about splendid Spindle.'

'I am,' said Tryfan, glad to see the strange mole.

'Don't be,' said Mayweed, with commendable brevity.

'Have you seen him?' asked Tryfan eagerly.

'Dead, Sir? No, Sir! So he must be living, Sir! Muddling along I should say because he isn't a tunneller is he, devoted Sir? You can't fool Mayweed. But he's something more than that, like yours truly here, Mayweed is: a survivor, living not dying, thinking all the time *that* mole, very clever and intimidating to a humble, ignorant mole like me, merely Mayweed. So don't worry, Sir. I have not seen his corpse yet and don't expect to! Mayweed did not recommend your good self to tell them that the inestimable Spindle, your friend, was a tunneller for nothing. Mayweed sees a mole, and Mayweed knows. Spindle looked to Mayweed, when this pathetic mole first saw him, as if he had an eye for the veins of a system. We'll find out soon enough good Sir.'

With that, Mayweed made to go, but Tryfan called him back.

'You'll watch out for him won't you, Mayweed?'

'Kind Sir, you have been good to me, I am good to you. I have done nothing but watch out for him these long days past, Sir, but . . . things are happening. Dark musterings of moles Mayweed likes not. Mayweed's weak and not a

253

fighter with talon and tooth. Mayweed's scared, Sir, and frightened now. Harder for Mayweed to get information. Tunnels chock-a-block with moles who could kill him with one talon-thrust, so Mayweed's somewhat restricted which he doesn't like, not at all. Doing his best, but currently his best is somewhat roundabout, to say the least, ha! Troubled times now.'

'Skint will look after you if you let him. He likes you!'

Mayweed scratched himself and shook his head as if trying to avoid the embarrassment that was attaching itself to him.

'No, no, no, Tryfan, Sir, *you* will look after me if I let you!' He grinned and then smiled toothily, and added, 'Conundrum that! Mayweed likes such! Mayweed will get news of Spindle for you!' and with that, and a too-loud laugh, Mayweed was gone, leaving Tryfan feeling hopeful for the first time in days. Then Tryfan smiled to himself and settled down. If Mayweed was to be the first follower that he and Spindle gathered to themselves, their followers could only get better! Then he scolded himself for thinking such a thing, for all moles are equal, however pathetic some might seem. But then, he thought, Mayweed was not nearly so pathetic or weak as other moles seemed to think. He might be a worthy and respected follower indeed on the long march towards the Silence of the Stone!

A few days after this, as Tryfan returned from taking a corpse to the surface, he was surprised to find an elderly female shivering and miserable in some corner near peripheral tunnels where she should not have been. She was confused and seemed to have been trying to escape but did not quite know where to go. He guessed who she was and gently said, 'Where are you going, Willow?'

But this only confused her more, and she seemed to think she was back in her home system and that she knew him well.

'Oh aye, it's you again, you come to fetch me now! Wind good outside, is it? Shall you take me there?' And she giggled, her voice weak and old and yet contriving somehow to make her sound young and happy, as once she must have been, long, long before the dark days that had overtaken her, and now were killing her.

'You can't go outside here, Willow. There's moles about won't like it,' he said, taking her shoulder to guide her back down to safer tunnels, and perhaps over to Skint's burrow, for that mole would look after her. But she would not go with Tryfan, and protested when he tried to make her. He was frightened that the commotion she was beginning to make would attract a patrol above, so he crouched down in a leisurely way, hoping to calm her, and was relieved when she did the same.

'You weren't going off and leaving your friend Skint behind?' he said. She thought about this a little and then snouted about and seemed to understand where she was once more.

'To Wharfedale was I bound, my dear. Yes, just there for a while for 'tis dark here and getting darker with each day that passes.'

'To Wharfedale with its river you're not going!' said Tryfan with mock authority. 'Not today anyway, too far!'

'Then tell me,' she whispered, 'tell me, my dear, for you're from there, you are, yes I know I've seen you. Tell me of Wharfedale, and how it has been these troubled years.'

There was such longing and need in her old voice that Tryfan quite forgot his own problems and moved closer to her, saying softly, 'Why, now in our Wharfedale 'tis summer and the larks they sing high over the moor, and the wind burrs in the heather above us on the slopes. Down here the water runs and the food is sweet and the roots of tormentil and toadflax make the tunnels fresh as morning air. Can you snout them out, Willow? I'm sure you can . . . ' He paused and she screwed up her eyes and pointed her snout here and there as if sniffing at the balmiest, sweetest, freshest of summer winds, rather than at the heavy filthy stench of the Slopeside.

'Aye, I can that,' she said eventually, 'and I can hear the patter of the sheep's hooves, soft as rain; can you hear that too?'

'I can . . .' said Tryfan, pausing again, for how does a mole evoke in another the memory of a system he has never been to? Well, such words come if a mole is loving enough and ready to let the Stone use him. From some deep good place they come, like clear water from a sunny hillside or the words of reassurance a father knows who has never had need to speak them before; yes, they come, and they came for Tryfan then, drawing perhaps on things that Skint and Smithills had mentioned of Grassington, or stories Boswell had told him of the northern systems.

However it was, Tryfan spoke such words then to lost Willow . . . ' 'Tis good is our system and the tunnels so rich, and the young learn to sing those old songs . . . no system in the whole of moledom is like our system by Wharfedale . . . ' and Tryfan felt the strangest of longings, to travel north and see those systems that were to him but places of stories and legends.

'Aye, my dear,' Willow said, 'you'll take me there; nay, go there now, just for a moment, for 'tis so dark here I feel bereft of the tunnels I once knew.'

'Not yet, Willow, you stay safe here with me and sing a song. . . . '

'Not of Word or Stone, not them. The songs before that, aye which I learnt, I did, I know I did,' she said.

'You sing one now then, Willow, one of Wharfedale . . . ' and his voice soothed her into a cracked old song that once a young female learned before the plagues came, and before what the plagues brought came, and before the shadow of the Sideem and the Word came across moledom and took moles from their homes who never went back. She sang of a home system she had loved, and when she had finished she said, 'Will you take me back to my burrow before you return to Wharfedale?' and Tryfan did, leading her slowly down the tunnels to safety, and letting

256

her lead him the last part for he had not been that way before.

'So, now you can leave me,' she said when she reached the entrance to an untidy ill-made burrow, barely more than a scraping, 'this is my home now.' She looked at it briefly and then at him and seemed suddenly ashamed of it and herself and said, 'I had a burrow once, the prettiest you ever saw. *You* remember . . . ' and she sounded so tired.

'Yes,' he said, 'I remember.' And he went forward to her, and laid his paw on her flanks, where the sores were, and then across her aged, furless face, and he whispered, 'May the Stone be with thee, and may you know content once more.'

'Don't,' she whispered, 'don't,' but she did not move away as he touched her. 'I'm so tired,' she said.

'Then sleep now, and you'll feel better when you wake.'

'Yes,' she said, and turned into the darkness of the only place she had left that she could call her own.

Tryfan watched after her, and then turned away and back down the tunnel she had brought him to, not seeing in the shadows the mole that had watched them, and followed them, and heard all that had passed between them.

That mole went quietly down to Willow's place after Tryfan left and looked in on her and her voice came sleepily out of the darkness, 'Whatmole is it there? Is it Skint? Eh? Skint?' And then, 'I was going to Wharfedale but a mole stopped me. Young he was and I knew him well, met him once, but I couldn't remember his name. Did you see him, Skint?'

'Aye, I did. His name's Tryfan.'

'Tryfan?' repeated Willow shaking her head. 'No, that wasn't his name. He touched me, Skint, here he touched me, and here. He touched me like . . . like my . . . it was like I was a pup again. Like that. Like my . . . What was his name?'

'Tryfan,' said Skint again. 'Now you sleep, Willow, we

257

want you rested. Might have to journey. Might have to make a run for it soon and you'll be coming.'

'Who is he, that mole?' said Willow, mumbling to herself and beginning to breathe slow and deep. 'Because I remember being touched like that, yes I do, before, when . . . I should have asked his name.'

As she fell asleep Skint looked up the tunnel the way Tryfan had gone and there was puzzlement and awed curiosity on his face as he whispered to himself, 'That mole? I don't rightly know . . . not sure who he is! But . . . I don't know.'

If this incident made Skint feel that Tryfan might well be a mole to trust, then another, which occurred a day or two later, made him think he was a mole to respect as well.

It started in a trivial way, after some ominous doings out on the surface when the moles of the North End heard the patrols catching and punishing an escaper. Skint had gone to make sure that Willow was secure, and on the way had met up with Tryfan. The trouble had seemed to pass and both moles went back to their tasks.

But a short time later, when Skint had reason to be briefly and legitimately out on the surface, a strange guardmole confronted him.

'Hello, scum,' said the mole, coming close to Skint.

Skint, ever a mole to respect, took a solid stance and said nothing.

'Yes, Sir, I'm scum, Sir,' said the guardmole laughing. 'Say that, scum.'

Skint did not feel inclined to. He had outfaced guard-moles before. But now a second appeared, and then a third, and then a fourth. The last two had bloodied talons, and that wildness to their eyes and heaving to their breath that follows a killing.

'This scum won't say he's scum and needs to be made to,' said the first.

'This scum needs punishing by the Word!' said the third.

'Bugger the Word,' said the fourth. '*This* scum needs

258

punishing by *us*!' He laughed and Skint suddenly knew fear, and knew he was facing death. These guardmoles were corrupted, and maddened in some way by the punishment they had inflicted earlier. To flee would mean chasing, and chasing incensed such moles; to stay meant he would have to find something to say, something quick and clever, something. . . .

Too late. The third mole came forward and thrust a talon under Skint's snout.

'I don't like you,' he said. He was grinning.

'*None* of us likes you, scum,' said the first.

'You're coming with us,' said the fourth, hunching his shoulders and moving round the back of Skint and pushing him forward through the grass.

'We've got something to show you,' said the third unpleasantly, and Skint knew it had to do with the blood the mole had on his talons. Smithills, I need you, was Skint's last thought before he was led away.

A mole running, a scabious frightened mole, running through those North End tunnels, panting and desperate, running to find not Smithills but Tryfan.

'Sir! Now, Sir!'

'What is it, Mayweed?' said Tryfan, who was working.

'They're going to kill, Sir. Kill Skint, Sir. Please, please now, *now* sir.'

Mayweed never forgot the way Tryfan responded to his plea. Mayweed, who had heard and seen the patrol take Skint, for he had already heard and seen that same patrol kill another clearer and, seeing them head in the direction of the North End, had followed secretly and unobserved. Then Skint had been caught, and then taken back towards where that other mole, that mole that wasn't a mole now, that. . . .

'Where is he?' said Tryfan softly. Enormous he was, his coat dark and his talons purposeful. No, Mayweed never ever forgot that, nor doubted that, of all moles he had seen and would ever see, Tryfan was the one who would know what to do, and how to do it when resolve and decisive action was needed.

259

'Follow me, Sir, now, Sir, strong Sir, follow!'

Mayweed ran fast, this way and that, all under the surface, across the North End and then beyond it to places strange, the twists and turns, and roots and stones in those tunnels seeming to fly past Tryfan as if he was dreaming them.

'Is it much further?' he called out.

'It's here, Sir, ssh, Sir!' said Mayweed almost skidding to a halt and pointing forward and upward. 'Just ahead . . . ' The tunnel was really now no more than a dried crack in the ground which somemole (Mayweed! realised Tryfan) had made a little bigger. The light came in clearly and ahead a fence post, the cause of the crack, thrust down. Wire whined in the breeze from it, and there was the low murmur of thuggish voices nearby.

'Scum, that's all you are, and that's why – ' a voice was saying.

Tryfan did not hesitate. He pushed past Mayweed and then straight up on to the surface, the soil and grass seeming to burst open as he came through it. So fast and unexpected was his arrival that the guardmoles all fell back in alarm, and the one who had already raised his talons to strike Skint simply stared in alarm.

Tryfan advanced straight on them, thrust his snout towards the largest and fiercest, and said in a voice of extraordinary power and command, 'And what do you all think you're doing?'

Before a single one of them had gathered himself together to find an explanation, Tryfan taloned the biggest on the shoulder and said, 'Is this where you're *meant* to be patrolling? No. I thought not. Have you any idea whatmole this is you're just about to kill? *No? Then get back to your posts or by the power of the Word itself you'll suffer for it!*'

The four guardmoles stared at him some more, and even if a couple of them had seen him before they would not have recognised him. For Tryfan seemed huge and menacing, darker in effect, terrifying in appearance, and his talons seemed black and shining.

'This mole is named Skint, and scum though he is he happens to have more knowledge of these bloody tunnels than any other mole alive, so we *need* him. Now get out of here before you go on report. . . .'

The guardmoles looked at each other doubtfully, but none had the nerve to ask who this strange mole was. He seemed important, and he was certainly threatening. Tryfan glared at them and they at him, and for a long moment it seemed that his bluff might be called, and he would be challenged. But no, one of the guardmoles stepped back and muttered that he was off, and then another, until all of them left.

Even after they had gone Tryfan loomed, and afterwards Skint reported that if he had been frightened before he was frightened even more as Tryfan turned and stared at him, his eyes cold and black, his talons fierce.

Then the moment was gone and Tryfan was himself once more, and he hurried Skint away from that place, where that other mole, less fortunate, lay, limp and bloody where he had been killed.

From that day on Tryfan was part of Skint and Smithills' councils, and privy to their intent to escape from the Slopeside when the right moment came, or the violence that seemed to be brewing in the tunnels erupted. They had decided to take the only route out that seemed feasible, and the one that Alder had mentioned to Tryfan – over the northern stream.

'We'll get you over that!' said Smithills confidently. 'Northern moles like us are used to streams and rivers, floods and spates. There's ways to get across troubled water if you keep your wits about you, and know what to do.'

Skint did not trouble Willow with their plans, though she came to their evenings together more frequently now, but Munro, the other of the Rollright clearers, was briefed, and Tryfan was glad to meet him. He was, as Smithills had hinted, short of a sensible word. But he was cheerful enough, and generous with his food, and would laugh and thump his paws to the tunes that Smithills liked to hum.

'Food and song – that's what you like, isn't it Munro?' Smithills would say, and Munro, beaming, would grin his agreement, easing his large form into a more comfortable position and accidently knocking poor Willow from her stance.

'Sorry, didn't mean to,' he'd say, helping her back.

' 'Tis all right, dear,' Willow would whisper.

'You never "mean to" but you do!' Smithills would scold him.

'Sorry,' said Munro.

Tryfan had never seen him angry but there were stories that he could be, and once a threatening guardmole had retreated in fear of him, and he'd saved a mole or two from snouting without really doing much at all.

'Useful mole, that one,' Smithill's would say, 'eh Skint?'

'Munro? Aye,' Skint would reply shortly.

Then, quite unexpectedly one morning, when Tryfan was hard at work and had just been visited by a guardmole, Mayweed popped his head round an unpredictable corner and said, 'Surprised Sir, it is I, humble Mayweed, tired from a journey, and one I have not undertaken alone! No, no, no, no! Not alone at all!'

But before he could go on, somemole pushed past him muttering and, to Tryfan's delight and relief, Spindle appeared. He looked healthy and had put on some weight, returning him to his normal thin self rather than the skeletal form he had had when he left to be a tunneller.

His greeting was so hurried and perfunctory that it froze Tryfan's before it began.

'Yes. Greetings. No time. Not meant to be here. Trouble coming now, very soon. You know the season?'

'Summer,' said Tryfan.

'Midsummer, nearly,' said Spindle. 'Henbane of Whern has come to Buckland. Guardmoles are massing,

262

the patrols are strengthening and massacre is apaw. Massacre, Tryfan!' His brow furrowed and his eyes were troubled. 'This *will* be,' he said. 'Now listen. . . .'

It seemed that new tunnellers had come from Rollright and were directing the clearing of tunnels and burrow debris from a point just below the Slopeside, in the hope of avoiding becoming diseased themselves. It was as one of several go-betweens that Spindle had been taken on. He had managed to convince the grikes that he knew what he was about, but others who had tried the same thing had failed, and died. He had no illusions about his own future. Go-betweens like him would be killed once their task was finished, and it nearly was. Hard for an individual to say exactly when the task was done, but the night before one of the tunnellers had disappeared and he himself might well be the next.

So he had come while he still could. He had had limited access outside the Slopeside into Buckland. He learned that the clearers were to be moved, mainly by surface, before the tunnellers came in to finally clean up the system.

'By the surface? So many?' said Tryfan, surprised and suspicious. He knew that overland mass movements of moles was dangerous, making them prey to owls and corvids.

'I think the "move" is really an excuse to get them out into the open and kill them. Have you seen strange guardmoles up on the surface? Are the patrols strengthening?'

Tryfan nodded.

'Yes, I thought so. Listen. I was able to talk briefly with Alder, who reported that Thyme and Pennywort are safe and well, though partially guarded, working down near the riverside tunnels. Alder has talked to the mole Marram and he is inclined now to be sympathetic to the Stone. But more than that I was unable to discover.

'But something more serious is that they're expecting trouble from the clearers and have moved many guardmoles up to peripheral Slopeside tunnels and round on the surface to stop any of the clearers trying to escape. It may be too late for Skint's plans. Now – Brevis. I haven't heard anything definite about Brevis, but I came across one of the guardmoles who was there when we were and he said there's hardly any moles left in the burrow-cells at all. They've either been snouted or sent on up here. He thought Brevis would be kept there until Midsummer because there are definite orders that he's to be snouted as part of the rituals . . . I must go now, otherwise . . . Mayweed will bring news, and when he does, act swiftly Tryfan. My life will depend on it and so will that of Brevis. Swiftly . . . ' and Spindle was gone, and Mayweed with him to direct him back through the complex way he had come.

Never had Tryfan felt the ominous frustration he felt then. To see his friend go back into the very midst of danger, to be unable to follow him, and to have to wait and wait, night after night, day by day, starting at every sound, uncertain of every shadow, yet ready at every moment . . . imagining his friend and companion, whom he had grown to love, dying unloved, unknown, unfulfilled.

He told Skint what Spindle had said, and Skint readied the others. If any of them discovered anything, or saw any sign of killing, they must summon the others immediately. Willow, protesting, was brought to Skint's burrow and made to sleep there, for her own miserable place was too far off to be safe. Munro moved closer, too. The nights were dark, the days long, and sleep when it came was restless and shadowed, full of starts and distant rolling darkness which flared sometimes as a roaring owl's eyes flare across the sky; but red not yellow, red as the blood that drips from a feeding owl's beak. Those nights were nights of fearful sleep. Fearful and . . .

'Psst! Wake up! *Sir*!'

Tryfan rolled over and took immediate stance, his talons ready to kill.

'Only me, Sir, Mayweed. Ssh, Sir! Follow me.'

'Where to?'

'Spindle says to come with me, Sir. The time's here now and there's no time.'

But Tryfan would not go.

'Must, Sir, please, Sir, Spindle said, Sir. Now, now, now, now. It's Brevis. Getting him we are, taking him we are, away, away. Tonight's the only chance, the last chance.'

'I will come,' said Tryfan rapidly, 'but first I must warn Skint.'

'No time, Sir,' moaned Mayweed, half sobbing. 'None.'

'Well I'm going to, Mayweed, right now, and then I'll come.'

'Skint'll stop you, and he'll hit me.'

But Tryfan did not argue any more and ran quickly through the dark, still tunnels to Skint, whom he found was awake, already sensing something was wrong.

'It's trouble, isn't it?'

'It's death for moles on the Slopeside before long,' replied Tryfan, his voice purposeful. He rapidly told him about Spindle's summons to make an attempt to rescue Brevis and said that they intended to bring him back to the Slopeside, which would certainly bring up grikes in force if they were not already there. . . .

'Now listen: gather Smithills and the others and get them to my burrow quickly, very quickly.'

Skint did not argue with the younger mole; he had saved his life once, and he was willing to let him do so again! He, Skint, might know about clearing, but there was more to this mole Tryfan than met the eye, and Skint trusted his judgement.

'You get Munro, I'll bring the other two,' said Skint.

And they did it, silently, urgently, urging the protesting Smithills and the sleepy Willow along the tunnels to Tryfan's beat, where Mayweed was now in an agony of waiting.

'*Please* Sir, now. Now *please*, decisive Sir!'

'Shut up, Mayweed,' Tryfan found himself saying. 'Now listen and trust me,' he continued, addressing the others, 'I do not know what is going to happen, or when, but I know it will be soon and it will be fatal. Mayweed has brought a warning from Spindle and it is best you are somewhere hidden and safe. Nomole knows this system better than Mayweed and he will be our guide. We will find a place on the way to Spindle where we can leave you in safety while I travel on with him and get Brevis in whatever way Spindle has organised.'

'But we'll come with you,' said Skint. 'You'll need a few extra paws.'

Tryfan shook his head. 'It is best you all stay together at a place that is secret and safe. You can then leave, when confusion reigns in the Slopeside, as we agreed. Before then, with luck, Spindle, Mayweed and myself will have brought Brevis back and we can all escape together. If we don't come, then you must go, Skint, and take the others to safety.' Skint nodded grimly.

Their plans made, Tryfan turned to Mayweed who, by now, was almost dancing about the tunnel in fear and trembling at delaying so long.

'Good Sirs, fair Madam, follow this menial mole mutely, right *now*!' he said, and was off.

Tryfan had never been taken on such a confusing route in his life. It was generally south-eastward, which is to say in the direction of the run of the Slopeside tunnels down into Buckland, but in detail the route was anything but direct. Down murky ill-kempt tunnels, through concealed burrows which had not been cleared and where the corpses of moles glinted palely in moonlight from collapsed entrances. Then to a place where an isolated tree rose above pasture, whose surface roots were gnarled and useful. There, where the moonlight shone, Mayweed stopped them and suggested it was easy to defend, easy to escape from, and easy to remember, and there Tryfan insisted the others stayed.

'Be silent, be patient, and do not wait for us too long once trouble starts,' said Tryfan.

'Where is this scribemole that you are rescuing?' asked Skint.

'In the burrow-cells just below the Slopeside,' said Tryfan. 'But worry not of that. Remember, when dawn comes, and the light is easy for escape, you leave whether or not we are here; and leave sooner if the trouble threatens you. And if you don't see us at all, and we do not find you later, then remember that you will find sanctuary in Duncton Wood, which lies far to the east. Remember that!'

With these words Tryfan turned to Mayweed and signalled for him to guide him on, and the others shrunk into whatever shadows they could find, to wait for a dawn that might decide the lives of all of them; and more.

Chapter Sixteen

A tawny owl, roosting in the branches of the tree whose roots had been their haven, rasped its claws and called sharply as Mayweed and Tryfan left, and the night seemed dark and dangerous.

'Surface now, Sir, just a bit. Owls don't strike under their own trees, Sir, Mayweed knows . . . ' and on they raced once more.

Across dew-wet grass, then suddenly down, down between deep stones, sharp and strange, and on into narrowness that pressed a mole's belly from below and his shoulders from above until he felt he was going to be crushed, *was* being crushed. Then out into a huge space that echoed with their pawsteps. An ancient, forgotten twofoot place of bones and glinting things all redolent with death.

'That's it, Sir, don't dawdle. Almost there! Mayweed knows the way.'

And then into a small tunnel leaving their echoes far behind, and up again they were, among surface roots where the wind played and a moon shone above, and a mole darted out at them from shadows: Spindle!

'Tryfan! No time now, not for greeting or pausing.'

'But – '

'*No* time. At dawn the guardmoles will start moving to all the peripheral tunnels and one by one the clearers will be ordered up to the surface. One by one. They will be killed as they emerge. One by one. None shall know, none suspect. Owls will take them. The grikes have done this before.'

'How do you know?'

'I know. A tunneller hears. You were right to get me this task Mayweed, unpleasant though it has been. We are going to get Brevis and bring him back by the tunnels we first came up but we must do it before dawn. By then most of the guardmoles will be up on the surface and it should be possible to make our way more easily up through the Slopeside and beyond by tunnels Mayweed knows to the northern periphery of the system.'

'Mayweed knows, knows it's dangerous, but will do it, Sir. Won't come with you afterwards because Mayweed's scared, isn't he? Yes, he is. Very. Mayweed will stay where he knows, where he's safe. But he's your servant until then!'

Tryfan explained briefly that Skint and the others had been left in a place of safety, and that they had agreed to try to get back to them with Brevis by dawn and then travel on together. Above them the night was still dark, but the moon had sunk lower and somewhere or other an occasional bird stirred, as if preparing for the dawn yet to come.

'We must go,' said Spindle. 'Mayweed knows a way, and I have arranged with Alder that he will be one of the guardmoles at the burrow-cells – that was easy enough because most of the others want to be in on the killings.' With a shudder he turned, and, signalling to Mayweed to start again, they disappeared silently into the tunnels once more, moving swiftly.

Occasionally they heard the low murmur of guard-moles' voices, or felt the vibration of a stolid grike treading upslope in the tunnels through which they slunk. But Mayweed's route was clever and took ways and passages guardmoles would not normally bother with, for they would have assumed they led to dead ends. Mayweed had made many false seals and blocks of his own so that several times they arrived at what seemed a blank wall and were able to pass through it by the quick removal of a stone or innocent looking roof-fall, all of which Mayweed quickly and expertly replaced after they were through.

'Mayweed knows, Sir, Mayweed remembers. Nomole else knows or cares, and Mayweed hears, too. At dawn,

Sir, blood Sir, the tunnels will be red with it. But not mine, Sir!'

He ran on, down and down a narrow tunnel, until he stopped and indicated that they should be very quiet. For a time they crept silently along and when Tryfan heard the regular stomp of mole paws beyond the wall to his right he realised that they were running parallel to a major tunnel.

'Nearly there!' whispered Mayweed, grinning with pride. 'Took time, did this one, nearly caught often.'

'You *made* this tunnel?' said Tryfan, amazed.

'With my own humble, pathetic and diseased paws, Sir,' said Mayweed. 'Clever or no?'

'Clever – very,' said Tryfan, meaning it.

'Best seals are light gravel and earth, Sir, can't be seen but not easy to fix. Mayweed worked out a way, didn't he? Sited especially in shadow. Now, now, now, now . . .' his talons ran along the wall, which was of a gravelly soil at this section, and he nodded with satisfaction. 'Now we wait for silence.'

Silence did not come quickly, indeed the traffic in the adjacent tunnel suddenly increased for a time, and the three moles had to crouch still, fearful that the slightest noise would alert the grikes to their presence.

Even when silence did come at last, giving them an opportunity to break the seal and slip through, Tryfan was uneasy and concerned, cautioning Mayweed who went first to take it slowly.

It was as well that he did. No sooner had he done so than they heard a sound ahead and froze in the shadows where the seal opening emerged, whispering urgently to the others to stay where they were as more moles were coming.

At first all they heard was slight vibration of pawsteps and then voices, low and authoritative. Not the shouts and curses of guardmoles, but quiet, almost leisurely conversation.

'Yes,' a voice was saying as it approached, 'Yes, quite so. The Slopeside starts a little further on and we will surface soon.'

270

The voice was hard and used to command, and yet its sound slid round the tunnel walls like the roots of bittersweet, the scent of whose purple and yellow flowers is poisonous to mole. Tryfan knew the voice but could not place it.

Then, as the sense came on all of them that moles of grim power were approaching, the mole who had spoken came into view. Male, strong but not big, a snout that twisted to the left, eyes that missed nothing to left and right, but for the shadow that was all Mayweed seemed to be.

Tryfan looked round at Spindle in alarm but needed to say nothing, even had he dared. The mole they saw was Weed himself, left-paw mole of Henbane. Yes. . . .

Then their hearts seemed to stop and their paws to tremble and their flanks to sweat and shake. A second mole followed on, larger than Weed, darker, huge in that tunnel which barely seemed able to contain her, so powerful her presence and evil her aura.

Henbane of Whern. There, a few moleyards from them, there! Her coat was glossy and dark, her form quite beautiful, the sensual line of her body turning elegantly on itself so that when she moved she seemed not to move at all.

Even as Mayweed involuntarily started back, Tryfan put out a paw to still him, and tightened his talons on Mayweed's flank. But even this fractional movement seemed to attract her attention because she turned her head and looked, as it seemed, straight at them. Her eyes were red, or if not red then black and red, yet alight and alluring, most beautiful and frightening, stilling a mole into obedience. And Mayweed gasped, panicking, as Tryfan's talons dug sharply into his side, pain to conquer fear.

She paused, loomed a little towards them, her eyes watchful now, and then Weed called out ahead of her to direct her attention to a route to the surface. Still she stared, uncertain, her body massing for attack. The tunnel

271

was silent as the darkest, stillest night. All seemed transfixed. Still Henbane stared and those she seemed to see could not believe they were not seen. For Mayweed there was only fear, total and complete. For Spindle fear as well, but a feeling mixed with dislike and suspicion. But for Tryfan there was in that first sight of Henbane something more, something which went beyond the power and beauty he saw in the mole who had so changed the history of moledom. He saw a terrible pitilessness which no words, no thoughts, no feelings might affect. And yet, as, mercifully, she turned away, with Weed calling her once more and a guardmole coming up behind, there was the glimmer of another feeling, very different, very disturbing. And it was this that made him distracted and impatient as the other two, the moment Henbane and her entourage had passed by, stared and sweated and talked nearly hysterically about how lucky they had been not to have been seen. But Tryfan stayed silent. There was something behind those eyes, something that he needed to know. But what it was he could not guess, and he shook his head as if to rid himself of a puzzle he knew he could not easily solve.

'The burrow-cells are not far downslope from here,' said Spindle, recovering himself, 'and there'll be two guardmoles on duty as well as Alder. We'll need to be swift.' He suddenly looked nervous, for he was not a natural fighter, and nor was Mayweed. Of the three of them only Tryfan had the size and bearing to confront a guardmole, and though he had eaten better lately, he was still not fully recovered from the privations he had suffered.

Nevertheless Tryfan now took over, advancing quietly down the tunnel but not slowly, for time was passing, dawn must be coming, and they had much to do. If Henbane and Weed and moles of their ilk were about, then something of moment would happen soon enough.

Spindle was right about their position, for soon the short, square tunnel leading to the burrow-cells came into view, and Tryfan felt a tightening of fear coming on him as he remembered the grim time Spindle and he had spent there.

They could hear guardmole talk, and, hoping that Alder was near to help them, and that surprise would give him the chance to disable at least one of the two other guardmoles, Tryfan signalled Spindle and Mayweed to stay hidden while he advanced down the burrow-cell tunnel.

Here the tunnels were light with distant dawn, and birdsong outside was mounting. He went forward, turned a corner, and there were the guardmoles, all three. The Stone was protecting them for Alder was furthest into the tunnels and talking to the others, whose backs were to Tryfan. He saw Tryfan and gave him the briefest of nods, which Tryfan took to mean he should continue to advance.

He did so resolutely and slowly, weighing up the indentations and burrow entrances on either side of the tunnel in case he should need them for fighting advantage. He knew he had much to learn in the art of fighting, for his father Bracken had taught him only a little and told him to find a mole to teach him as he had been taught. 'Your time to learn will come one day,' he had said, but it never had, and he suspected that he might be at a disadvantage with one trained guardmole, let alone two.

'Behind you! Danger!' shouted Alder suddenly, rearing up and looking at him. For a moment Tryfan was taken by surprise, but as the two turned and one lunged at him he saw Alder bring his talons down with appalling force on the guardmole nearest him, who, taken unawares, collapsed dying at their paws even as the other's talons came down towards Tryfan.

Tryfan parried him powerfully, sidestepped and thrust towards him. But his blow was easily warded off, and another was sent at him which got through his guard to hit his shoulder.

But he stepped forward again and thrust hard and

powerfully, and even as he did so Alder behind, whom the guardmole still did not realise was an enemy, talon-thrust him. The guardmole stopped fighting, his paws raised, unsure which way to turn, and Tryfan took him swiftly and ruthlessly, deep in the belly and Alder finished him off. The guardmole died, a look of surprise and puzzlement on his face.

For a moment they crouched bloodied and heaving over their two victims before Alder said, 'I'll fetch Brevis and then you must leave swiftly.'

He returned moments later with a bewildered Brevis, and the two scribemoles greeted each other formally before Tryfan swiftly explained the situation.

'Well I've been fattened up for the kill,' said Brevis lightly, 'so I'm fitter than I was. I'll not be able to travel fast, but with the Stone's grace and thy direction, Tryfan, we will get to safety soon enough.'

'Come then,' said Tryfan, 'we must go.'

'Not me,' said Alder, 'I am going to get Thyme and Pennywort out.'

'But if you stay and they find you they may know you have helped us,' said Tryfan urgently.

Alder came closer to him. 'I put up resistance, didn't I? I got wounded, didn't I? . . . Strike me, Tryfan. Strike me!'

It was a moment before Tryfan understood what he meant and then, when he did, and only after he had tried to persuade Alder more, he struck him suddenly, hard enough to draw blood but only in the flank, where injuries are not serious unless they are deep. But at least he looked as if he had been attacked.

'Now go,' said Alder, his teeth clenched in pain. 'Go!' And Tryfan did so, as Alder lay down on the ground near the two dead guardmoles, using their blood to make his own wound look worse, and pretending to be hurt and dazed.

'May the Stone grant that we see you again!' said Tryfan, and then, pushing Brevis ahead of him, he left.

Mayweed and Spindle were nervously waiting for them, and with hardly a pause Tryfan urged them back the way they had come, pausing only moments to ascertain there were no moles in the main upslope tunnel before turning north into it and setting off.

They hoped that if mole came from north or south before they reached the tiny shadowed entrance into the secret way Mayweed had brought them through they might hide in some burrow or cul-de-sac.

But it was not to be. They heard sounds of alarm and discovery behind them, and they hastened forward, urging Brevis on as fast as he could manage, until they saw guardmoles ahead, examining the wall at the point where they had breached it and, perhaps unwisely, had left it unsealed to permit them to make a quick retreat through Mayweed's tunnel.

Two guardmoles were near the wall and a third watching in the wrong direction. But he heard them, turned round, warned the others and suddenly Tryfan's party was facing three large and determined guardmoles, while behind them more seemed to be in pursuit.

Mayweed began shivering with fear, grinning stupidly in some hope that this might charm somemole into helping him out of a situation that seemed impossible to escape from.

'Please Sir,' he began. 'Mayweed's not happy, Sir, Mayweed didn't mean . . .' but whatmole he was addressing it would be hard to say.

Tryfan raised a paw. Took stance, gathered the others about him, and with but seconds before the guardmoles reached them muttered, 'Look abject and defeated, and listen. And shut up, Mayweed. By the Stone and for the Stone are we protected. Now follow me and do not stop, nor falter, nor hesitate a single time. Spindle you take the rear, Brevis you in the centre, Mayweed you come with me.'

'No, Sir, *please*, *Sir*, I'll do anything, Sir, don't like this, sharp talons and and, and . . . ' whined Mayweed.

But pushing him first Tryfan suddenly charged forward, just as the guardmoles were relaxing in the belief that the little party they had stumbled on were submitting, and shouted, 'Disease! This mole is accursed, this mole has the plague, beware, beware . . . !' As the guardmoles looked at one another and then at the pathetic Mayweed, with his bald head and foul-smelling sores and yellow teeth, Tryfan surged powerfully past and caught the first mole a great blow on his face, and the second a strong enough strike to unbalance him and make him wrong-paw back on to the third. Then he pulled Brevis through the melee, thrust Spindle along after him and ordered them and Mayweed to run. He turned round and, with mighty thrusts, caught the third of the guardmoles across the flank.

Then, as the others raced on upslope, Tryfan cried out, 'Traitors, miscreants, here, here!' The pursuers from the burrow-cells, who must have found Brevis missing and his guardmoles dead or 'wounded', were closing in and he hoped to confuse them by setting one group against the other for long enough to get himself clear.

Then he began chasing after the other three, turning from time to time and seeing the guardmoles gather themselves, sort out their confusion, and then come in pursuit.

If they could reach the main entrance to the Slopeside, which was narrow and easily defended, if they could only get there . . . but the guardmoles were getting ever nearer and he could hear their angry shouts and heaving breath as they closed the gap, twenty yards, fifteen, ten. . . .

Ahead he saw Spindle pause and turn, and Brevis and Mayweed disappear into what must be the chamber before the Slopeside tunnel. He saw the look on Spindle's face as he registered that they had almost got Tryfan, were almost touching him, reaching forward with powerful talons, as he ran and ran up the steep slope.

Tryfan stopped, turned, and talon-thrust blindly back at his pursuers. But their speed was too great and he felt himself falling upslope, talons on him, and his strength leaving as he sought to right himself and take stance in the narrowing tunnel. Guardmole on guardmole slowed and ranked before him and he knew he was moments from capture and death now, with no hope of escape.

'Take him,' said one to another. 'Then after that the others before they get into the Slopeside. *Take him!*' And as two of them lunged forward at him, and Tryfan raised his talons to try his best to ward them off, he felt his balance suddenly go as talons from behind grabbed him, and a voice, slow and familiar, said, 'Go on Tryfan, back now and leave them to us!' He staggered back and the great solid form of Munro took his place, with Skint on one side, and Smithills on the other.

'It's a fight you want, is it?' he heard Skint say.

'We're ready for you!' Smithills cried out with glee.

And the guardmoles found they faced moles long used to surviving and using their strength in narrow places, as Tryfan withdrew behind the solid wall of talons and muscle his friends had made, and ran after Spindle and the others into the tunnel leading into the Slopeside. Methodically behind him, the three clearers fought off the guardmoles, beating an orderly retreat until, one by one, with the guardmoles cursing in frustration and pain at the great parries Munro was making, they retreated into the Slopeside tunnel.

Once there they seemed to know what to do. For Munro bodily pushed them all further in as Smithills and Skint burrowed rapidly at the walls and ceiling above the tunnel, and with a crash of dust and debris the whole lot collapsed down, sealing the Slopeside off from the advancing guardmoles.

'That's just for starters!' roared Smithills through the debris at the muffled shouts and voices of the guardmoles. 'Come through here and you'll be diseased for life!'

'Welcome to the Slopeside, scribemole!' said Skint, addressing Brevis and shaking the dust off his fur. 'I can't say I'm a Stone follower, but you can't be worse than the moles of the Word after what we have witnessed this day!'

'But I said . . .' began Tryfan.

'You said to wait, but clearers protect their kind, and you are a clearer, Tryfan, and ever shall be one in our eyes. Come, the others are safe enough. The guardmoles are out on the surface killing those they can get their talons on, including the zealots, and we will make our escape with Mayweed's help.'

'Yes, Skint Sir. Can I have worms when we've done?'

'As many as you like!' said Skint, 'Now take us back to where you first left us.'

'This way . . . ' began Mayweed.

'*That* way?' questioned Skint and the others.

'Safe way, good way, quick way, Mayweed knows, none will find us. I know the best ways, Sir.'

'Go on Mayweed, we'll follow,' said Tryfan with a laugh, for he felt exhilarated by the chase and escape and knew that the Stone was with them, and would see them safely through that day.

One by one they followed Mayweed up into the strange tunnels he knew, by root and by post, by lost chamber and by false seal; by dark and by light, as on the surface overhead to north and south, to east and west, all across the Slopeside, a massacre as bloody and notorious as any in the history of moledom began.

Chapter Seventeen

'They must not be allowed to escape! It will be worse for all of us if they do! Henbane the WordSpeaker is here, and Weed. All of them! I have never seen Eldrene Fescue so enraged.'

The panic-striken voices of grike guardmoles played back and forth across the Slopeside as patrols searched desperately for Brevis and the moles who had made his escape possible. Now near, now far, Tryfan and the others heard their paws going this way and that as they tried to snout them out, not quite knowing how many moles they were looking for.

Dawn was long past, and the massacre of the clearers all but over, its dreadful sounds fading but never to be forgotten by the moles in the narrow tunnels beneath the tree that had been their refuge, the same spot where Tryfan and Mayweed had originally left them.

It was from there that Skint had led the others after Tryfan and Mayweed had left, rightly believing that they might be needed, and risking leaving Willow alone while they did so. She had not wandered, except a few yards about to collect food against their return. Nor, once Brevis was safe into the Slopeside, had they been pursued, for the tunnel block had held, and, in any case, the chasing grikes were not eager to enter the diseased tunnels into which the clearers had fled.

So they had successfully got Brevis back to their original hiding place, but further they could not go, partly because they were all too tired, but also because the Slopeside surface was busy with moles, and they would not have got far.

No sooner had they regained their refuge than the first light of dawn had come, and all about them, in a silence broken at first only by the uncomfortable flutter of corvid wings and the thump of grike paws, clearers had emerged thinking they were to travel now to a better place, their job well done. Many were diseased, many blinded by a light they were not used to, most weak and unable to resist. At first the slaughter had been easy enough, and the grikes had methodically got on with their work, killing the clearers one by one as they came out, the panting of the righteous bloodlust audible even where Tryfan and the others crouched hidden underground.

Then fitter, more cautious clearers must have sensed the carnage going on and had begun to resist. Some tried to flee, and a very few had stayed to fight. But the grikes were well prepared, sending down zealots to herd them out or kill them in the tunnels where they crouched.

Now only a very few remained as the tunnels were checked and the last few taken out and brutally killed. Until the final and most ruthless act of all – organised it seemed by Eldrene Fescue, as mole historians of those times have established she organised the similar killing at Rollright – for those zealots who had gone into the Slopeside, and the guardmoles whose task it had been to patrol the surface since before this cynical and cruel operation, now found that they themselves were victims. Each of them was killed in turn, as if Henbane and her associates feared contamination from anymole who had been in the Slopeside.

Now even that phase was over, and still the mole Brevis had not been found, nor his helpers, and now the last energies and anger of the grikes that day was being spent on finding them as they crouched in their hideout in silence, terrible silence, waiting and wondering what to do.

On the surface above them sun shone, and a black mob of corvids had descended to feed on the fodder that the clearers had become. It was a scene such as nomole who saw it would ever forget, and one by one, quite silently, Tryfan allowed them all to creep to a surface entrance and stare across that pitiful ground which the Slopeside above Buckland had become. Just the fallen blood-sodden bodies of moles, and the shining, turning, beaks and wings of predators and above them, wheeling sometimes, the white wings of a gull, sensing food but driven from it by the mass of rooks already there. That was the sight Tryfan and his companions saw that day; they were the witnesses, theirs would one day be the testimony.

What made it seem a worse sight was that, for corvids at least, mole is not a favourite food. So they pecked disdainfully at the dead and dying moles – for some were still living, a few still able to call out in despair – pecked and discarded and pecked again at anything that moved, completing Fescue's foul work.

And Henbane? Not seen. Watching no doubt, but not getting her black talons wet in those shameful hours. Let others do the dirty work, for that is the way of the Word!

At midday the rooks suddenly all clamoured more loudly, and then the hiding moles heard the flapping of a thousand wings and a great shadow darkened the tunnels, circled, faded, darkened it once more and then was gone. The rooks had flocked, and left.

Silence fell on the surface except for one lone surviving mole, calling out in despair off to the west, weaker and then heard no more. Silence, but for the occasional shifting of their tree in the slight gathering breeze, as down some of the more ancient roots came the sinister churl of roosting owl, and the wither and flap of a wing in a dark recess. Patient still. He would not discard the fodder round his tree. He would swoop and take it when night came, and pull it to pieces at his roost, and if, even after that, it lived still, he would relish it, to death.

With afternoon came the frightening stomp of the guard-moles in the Slopeside tunnels, and the voice of Eldrene Fescue in a rage, directing a search for . . . themselves. A search which still brought out a few last survivors, cleverer moles who had suspected something was amiss and had taken refuge in some corner or burrow they thought might go unnoticed. Sometimes one was found, and was dragged screaming to a surface entrance, beyond any help that Tryfan and his huddled band could give against such numbers, and there murdered with a talon-thrust.

'No prisoners, no witnesses, for these are traitors to the Word and blasphemers, and deserve to die!' So under the evil Fescue, the willing grikes performed the noble work of the Word.

The guardmoles were thorough and occasionally came near to the escapers' high and obscure hideaway, and all huddled still as death lest the smallest sound should give them away. Until, by mid-afternoon, all the tunnels seemed to have been explored, and the last clearers found and killed.

'I know they are here somewhere near, for the place is surrounded and they would have been seen getting away!' Fescue cried, ordering the search to continue, even to the most unlikely places. 'I will have them found.'

' 'Tis that Henbane she's afraid of,' whispered Spindle, 'for I've heard she's displeased with this and that at Buckland, and it is said some think the Slopeside moles should have been killed weeks ago.'

'But the clearers have only just finished clearing the main part of it, and on time for Midsummer too,' Skint protested. Even now he took a pride in a job well done.

'They didn't want to *use* the tunnels, not for guard-moles, not for living, Sir,' smiled Mayweed. 'Never wanted that. Oh no . . . not for *using*.'

'What do you mean?' growled Smithills.

'Nothing, Sir, and no harm please,' said Mayweed.

'He means,' said Spindle heavily, 'that the Slopeside has been a way of keeping the clearers in one place and under control until Henbane was confident there was no further use for them; at least, that's what I heard. It was a useful way of getting rid of unwanted moles as well, like Stone followers – like us. She never had any intention of using it, did she, Mayweed? A few were going to be kept for snouting at Longest Day, including Brevis here, of course. . . .'

'Yes, Sir, correct very much so, very exactly so,' agreed Mayweed.

Skint and Smithills were appalled.

'Why didn't you *say*?' they said together.

'Mayweed wasn't sure, Sir, couldn't be certain, didn't want to tell no lie nor partial truth, he didn't. No, no, no, no. Mayweed only guessed too late, only knew too late again. Mayweed's sorry, Sirs and Madam. Mayweed's frightened, too.' His voice had become a whimper.

But as they talked a strange silence seemed to have fallen in the Slopeside tunnels, and there was a sense of change and chill, as if the sun had gone in on a warm day, and a northern wind sprung up.

'Don't like it,' whispered Skint. 'It's time we thought of leaving, Tryfan.'

But as Tryfan started to reply he was cut short by the beginnings of a thumping, at first quiet and then louder, of the kind they had heard when Weed and his guardmoles had been chasing them at Uffington. The tunnels vibrated with the frightening sound, and occasional deep shouts and orders; then absolute silence, then thumping again.

The moles looked at each other with fear in their eyes, except for Tryfan, who gathered them near to him.

'I think another mole is in charge. Weed, perhaps. Or . . .' and the same thought occurred to all of them: 'Henbane!'

'Aye, 'tis likely she's taken charge,' said Smithills. They looked around uneasily. Outside on the surface the sun was beginning to set on the long, warm day, inside their burrow the urge to run out and try and escape was strong. The thumping was so ominous a mole could hardly bear to crouch still.

'We'll not move yet,' said Tryfan firmly. 'That's probably what they want. It's what such a mole as she *would* do: frighten us out to the surface. Then she's got us. No doubt guardmoles are ready higher up, or lower down if we went that way, to get us. So we'll crouch it out and wait till dusk. Easier to get clear then, less danger, too, of gull and rook and possible, perhaps, for us to creep unnoticed out on to the pastures.'

He looked around at their party, studying each in turn for signs of panic or weakness. Skint was crouched low and relaxing, experienced at crises; Smithills was scratching himself and looking here and there. Munro was grinning, frightened of nothing – too foolish, perhaps. Willow had stayed closed to Skint, half asleep and looking old and ill. Sometimes she snouted about a little but Skint would still her and she seemed content with that. Brevis was meditating, his snout a little to one side, but a muscle in his left flank twitching. He looked thin and grey, older than his years. Spindle had taken stance near him, and his eyes were open and his face upset. The massacre had shocked him deeply: he was the only one who had gone up to near the surface more than once to see what was going on. The last was Mayweed, who grinned nervously all the time. One of his scabs was weeping and he gnawed at the raw flesh of a sore just above the talons of his right paw. Nomole looked more nervous than he. Yet all kept silence.

As for himself, Tryfan was calm and resolute, determined to keep the spirits of his friends high, but knowing that they could not stop here for long and that he must time their departure well. There would be no second chance. He was pleased with the positive way most of them had taken stance, not realising that it was his own confidence and purpose that gave them hope. Skint and Munro could be relied on as fighters, along with himself; Smithills was tired now, but loyal and dependable; Spindle would hold his own and had shown cunning and courage in equal measure these past weeks. Willow was weak and confused, and Brevis very tired, but both could be got away with help and encouragement. Which, with Mayweed, made eight of them, an awkward number which could not safely be split up.

'Please, Sir,' said Mayweed, interrupting his thoughts

284

and seeming to read them, 'Mayweed doesn't want to go where you're going. Mayweed is safer here, which is his home. Mayweed won't ever be caught here by guardmoles . . . but if Mayweed leaves he will be caught and if he's caught he will be hurt and if he's hurt he doesn't know what he'll do.'

'Or say,' muttered Skint. The others shifted uneasily at Mayweed's outburst.

'It's best you come,' said Tryfan quietly.

'But, Sir . . .' whined Mayweed.

'But nothing,' said Tryfan. 'Falter and I will not hesitate to kill you, Mayweed. If you are caught your end will be painful and I do not doubt you would tell them what you know of us first.'

'Know, kind Sir? Mayweed knows nothing. *Nothing.* Not your name, not your sex, not your intention, not your destination, no nothing! At all, at all!'

'Now remember, we will move swiftly as one, hoping there will be better cover by the stream across the slopes above. Do you know how far it is, Mayweed?' he asked.

'Honoured to be asked, privileged to reveal: two flaps of an owl's wings, two hundred of a pigeon's, confident Sir, name of Tryfan.'

'What's that in moleyards?' growled Smithills.

'Can't do it in one run, wise Smithills, might do it in two if you didn't have a mole as venerable as Willow with you and another as weak (through no fault of his noble self) as Brevis. Yes. About that.'

'The guardmoles won't be expecting us to go that way, and might not even see us,' said Tryfan, talking to Skint more than anymole else. 'But if they do they will hesitate to follow singly, for fear of owl, and we will gain some time.'

He looked at them all and instinctively they became more alert. He had made a decision. The time to leave was nearly on them.

'Skint and Smithills: you will take the front flanks; Brevis, Willow, Spindle and Mayweed: you will be in the

285

centre. Munro and I will take the rear, and if we have to we will talon you forward. . . .'

'Sir – ' began Mayweed.

Sudden sound, nearer, and a single look from Tryfan shut Mayweed up.

'We're going to have to surface it,' whispered Tryfan, starting to brief them for their attempt at escape. The others looked at him in surprise, except for Skint and Smithills who had made escapes of their own. They nodded approvingly. On the surface an escaping mole could run fast, was less easily trapped, and had the advantage of surprise.

The steady thumping mounted again . . . and faded. Guardmoles hurried this way and that, sometimes unpleasantly near, and harsh shouts sounded, but Tryfan kept them all calm and resisted the impulse to flee too soon. Yet how slowly the sun seemed to sink, how slow the light was to fade. But fade it did, the colour draining from the roots and walls about them, and the trunk above turning pink and then dulling down as the sun set to the west. To the northwest, which was the direction they were going, the sky now steadily darkened, giving them the promise of better cover.

Thump, thump, thump . . . 'Try higher up, *this* tunnel has not been checked yet . . .' and they knew the guardmoles were near now, and heard a new voice in charge, and one that was strong and full of authority.

'Weed!' whispered Spindle. 'And they seem to have found the tunnel here.'

Silently Tryfan looked around at each of them in turn, nodding purposefully, giving encouraging touches, and letting Skint and Smithills past him, as they would lead them out. From the tunnel behind them they heard talon scrapings and heavy pawsteps.

'Still want to stay behind, Mayweed?' asked Skint grinning.

'Mayweed's changed his mind, Sir, Mayweed'll go with you, Mayweed wants to go *now*,' whimpered Mayweed. '*Please!*'

With a nod from Tryfan they took their positions. Skint breathed deeply, thrust a front paw up on to the nearby surface, heaved himself up and, after a quick look above, whispered back down, 'All clear for now, come on!' And then they did, rapidly, and as soon as they were assembled in the dusk beneath the old tree they turned, snouted the quickest way towards the stream whose running dampness they could sense clearly, and set off. . . .

Today story-tellers make much of that desperate journey across the fields of carnage which the Slopeside had become. One after another they ran, with the stronger helping the weaker, and with each playing his own part. Of the owls that swooped they tell, and how Munro warded them off: of the guardmole patrol that reared out of the gloom, the very same four who had abducted and nearly killed Skint . . . and how Tryfan and Smithills took them on, and Munro too, brave Munro, who in that skirmish for other moles' lives took the blow that was so soon to lose him his own. Of how they lost their way after the guardmoles fled, turning too soon to the west and hesitating as other moles came up behind. Yes, lost! Then Mayweed, strange Mayweed, suddenly ran to the fore and said, 'Please, Sirs, please Madam, please to follow me for Mayweed has a snout that finds out ways that others never know! Follow!' And despite Skint and Tryfan's curses, for surely the mole was going the wrong way, he led them, led them in those crucial minutes back on the path they needed, then below ground, and out, suddenly, on to the bank of the raging stream.

Then, of all moles there, it was Willow who went forward, saying she liked a stream, especially a rushing one, and this must be the Wharfe itself to be so fine! (Though it looked dark and dangerous indeed to the southern moles.)

So forth she went, and Skint with her, then Smithills, the other northern mole, took a stance midstream, and helped the others, pulling poor Mayweed, who was terrified of the water, and bodily got him across.

But Munro did not cross that stream alive. As the others began their passage over he heard more guardmoles coming, and bravely went back and led them another way. But he was weakened by wounds, and when he reached the stream, far lower down, the grikes off-scent now, all he could do was hurl himself into the water and it took him, and turned him, and drowned him dead. The first mole to die on Tryfan's long and terrible march towards the Silence of the Stone.

But Munro's life saved the others, for they were not seen to cross, and the grikes went no further, hesitating on the bank of the stream for a time as the remaining seven huddled and hid unseen in the grass on the far side.

Later Tryfan and Smithills went in search of Munro, and they found him, washed up on the bank of the stream and slumped there, touching but never knowing the land beyond that stream. Some say that Tryfan made a prayer for him, others that they crouched in silence for a time; but the best source of all, the cleric Spindle, has this to say of the last journey of Munro: 'My master Tryfan and Smithills of Grassington pushed his body back out into that stream, and watched it float away, and Tryfan uttered a prayer that Munro's body might not be taken by owl, but might join the great Thames itself, and journey down that river to reach the place that one day they would try to go to, which is called the Wen, and take there, ahead of them, his good spirit of courage and companionship.'

However it was, Tryfan returned with Smithills and rallied them all, giving them the courage and strength to press on there and then, not downslope, as would have been easier, but upslope to that isolated copse of trees which moles call Harrowdown.

They reached that place deep in the night, and crouched in silence staring out over the darkness of the vales north and east of Buckland, where only the occasional light of a roaring owl showed.

Down they stared at the darkest part of all, which was

the Thames, and Tryfan said a prayer, that all of them repeated, in memory of Munro and in thanksgiving for their lives.

'Here we'll stay awhile, for the place has a Stone, I'm told, and is protected. It will give us a haven for a time, and when we have strength, and the grikes have given up searching for us in the vales below, we'll head north to the river, and then find a crossing place and then. . . .'

'Yes, Tryfan?' said Spindle.

'To Duncton we will go. For there will be sanctuary and support, and there the Stone will give us guidance. But for now, sleep,' whispered Tryfan wearily. 'Yes, sleep.'

'But we must not tarry long,' advised Spindle. 'Not for too many days.'

'No, no, Spindle, not for long. . . .'

Then Tryfan slept, and Willow and Mayweed too, and Brevis.

But Spindle watched over his friend, nervously looking back in the direction of Buckland while Smithills and Skint took up watch positions, and the night deepened yet further over Harrowdown.

Chapter Eighteen

Again and again in the chronicles of moledom, chance and circumstance combine to bring the full weight of a great moment of history upon a system unknown before, but whose name is not forgotten afterwards.

Such a place, that June, was Harrowdown, though it is unlikely that the small group of moles gathered there then knew or even sensed the importance of the change of which they were the essential part. Unless it was Spindle, whose early training in the Holy Burrows and subsequent attachment to Tryfan of Duncton, uniquely placed him to observe and wish to record all that he saw and experienced in those brave and dangerous times. Perhaps it was at Harrowdown, in the quiet days that followed their arrival there and which preceded the celebration of Midsummer, that Spindle first felt the desire to learn scribing.

Today, when all moles of intelligence and common sense can scribe, it is hard to imagine the great change in thinking that the expression of such a desire in a mole like Spindle demanded. But Spindle was trained only as a cleric and assistant, taught from his earliest moments that scribemoles were apart and special, and that scribing as such was a mystery and skill that only scribemoles learnt or could learn.

Yet even as that long journey from the protection of the Blowing Stone on the morning of their departure from Uffington started, Spindle began to believe that what he was witness to should be recorded, and that he might be the mole to do it.

These radical possibilities he did not communicate to Tryfan, not from any shame or wish to keep his desire secret, but rather out of modesty, and the sense that Tryfan, who was the living embodiment of the historic change that was apaw, but which might yet come to nothing, should not be bothered with records, chronicles, accounts or history. Yet Spindle was concerned, for he saw what nomole before him had seen, unless it was Boswell himself, that the time for scribing to be secret and hidden, and concerned only with rolls and records of the often arid kind that the isolates of the Holy Burrows had kept, was over. Moledom was changing, the plagues had done more than the Word or the Stone to see to that, and if the truth was to be known then records of it must be kept.

It is part of Spindle's greatness that even before he learnt the art of scribing, he saw that the 'truth' was not a constant thing, and nor was it something a single mole could hope to record. It was for others to judge long after the chroniclers were dead. All a mole who was so minded could do was to be curious, to observe, to record, and to preserve. So it was that Boswell, White Mole, had chosen Tryfan's companion wisely: for few could have been better suited to be such a scribemole's companion than one who not only had faith and loyalty to the central core of Tryfan's quest, which was Silence, but who had been trained as a cleric by a mole like Brevis, and had the imagination to see that the destruction of the Holy Burrows was not an end of scribemoles but a new beginning for them, and one in which all moles might play a part. It was at Harrowdown that Spindle first began to see that records of Tryfan's quest must be kept.

Perhaps in times long past the name 'Harrowdown' applied to more than the copse that stands there still, isolated today as it was then, windswept and off any regular track known to mole. Twofoots knew it well enough, for they had ploughed the fields all about and for reasons of their own had barbed it round and left it to the wind and the creatures that called it home.

But anymole visiting that place knows well enough why twofoots let it be. For there, not large but large enough for mole, rises a Stone, caught among the stunted trees, and

291

twofoots touch not Stones. So, the copse was small and poor in worms, and all else too, for it was set high, and exposed to winds whose steady assault had bent the young ash and oak trees that were established there. Badgers there were, living over on the north side which reached down to the distant river. A fox too, judging by the droppings, though they never saw him. There was evidence still of the moles who had lived there until the grikes came, but as far as tunnels went there were only poor burrowings and the simplest of runs.

On the southern side, the remnants of snouted moles hung on the barbs, pathetic and soggy with decay, placed there by the grikes. Most were skeletal: remnants of a meagre life that ended terribly. When the wind blew from the north those bodies could be scented still and a living mole might feel sick in the stomach as well as sick in the heart.

On the first full day they were there, Brevis led Tryfan and Spindle to that side of the copse to make a prayer and commendation in memory of the snouted moles, some of whom he had known, and they crouched in respectful silence in the summer sun. Skint and Smithills, though they were not of the Stone, came along too, and crouched respectfully enough, but Willow stayed away, for such things were not her way, while Mayweed watched uneasily from a distance, screwing his face up against the holy words Brevis spoke, and looking over his shoulder unhappily at the Stone that rose quietly among the trees.

'Mayweed doesn't have to touch it does he, Sir?' he had asked Brevis. Brevis had simply shaken his head, a mole of few words.

A few days later Skint and Smithills had gone and removed the bodies, dragging them out among the green wheat of the field and leaving them there. It was a distasteful job and left them feeling angry and dejected.

'Your Stone did not protect them Brevis, did it?' Skint said bluntly afterwards. 'No more than the Word did much to protect those moles in the Slopeside. No offence,

292

of course, but to practical moles like Smithills here and me, the Word and the Stone are as bad as each other!'

'The Stone cannot prevent suffering,' said Brevis.

'Not much point in it, is there then?' said Skint.

'Clever Skint Sir, clever and astute!' said Mayweed suddenly, delighted. 'Mayweed, suffering as he does from fear, disease, humbleness, and a general awareness of his complete and abject inferiority, has often and frequently thought the same! "Not much point in it" are words he has often muttered to himself, yes, yes. Mayweed awaits the brilliant Brevis's answer and riposte, he does.'

'Brevis has no "brilliant" anything,' said Brevis wearily. 'Brevis knows that life is difficult and that moles who do not accept that fact are likely to waste time trying to put things right that can't be put right. Whether or not there is the Stone or the Word, moles will still die, some terribly by snouting as the harmless Harrowdown moles did, some by talon, but most from disease and decay. Life is difficult.'

'H'm,' growled Smithills. 'Then Munro's well out of it, isn't he? Doesn't leave much for us to look forward to, being told "Life is difficult"!'

'Agreed, agreement and concord with your friend Mayweed, sanguine Smithills,' said Mayweed. 'And what does Tryfan say?'

Tryfan had said very little those past days, and had spent much time alone, crouched before the Stone, meditating. The others had left him alone, except for Spindle, who was rarely far away, and Brevis, who talked with him. But all there respected Tryfan's silence, and knew that he was in some way preparing himself for the journey ahead.

'We need to be peaceful, to rest, to find our health again, and then we shall be ready to go. Just rest, and thank the Stone, or the Word, or whatever you chose to believe, that we are safe. When the time is right we will leave.'

He spoke these days with a new authority, one that was

partly physical, for he had survived the rigors of the burrow-cells and the horrors of the Slopeside better than most, and of them all was the strongest and healthiest looking. And these few days past a peace and acceptance had come to his eyes, and growth in purpose, and the space and silence the others had given him was as much out of respect for some inner and indomitable will as of liking for him. Indeed, there was – as Spindle later recorded – a distance or aloofness in Tryfan that made it hard for other moles to get close to him, and it was already showing itself then. Although none but Spindle and Boswell knew that Tryfan had been ordained, yet those who knew him then, and many subsequently who did not suspect the truth, instinctively understood that he was a mole apart, with a mission different from the norm and one which might demand that sometimes he seemed distant and unreachable.

'You could find time to talk with them,' said Spindle one day. 'We are all a bit afraid for the future, and uncomfortable staying here in case the grikes come.'

'Too tired to move yet,' said Tryfan.

'You could talk to them, to Smithills, Willow and Mayweed. His sores especially are worse. . . .'

'Mayweed's well enough,' said Tryfan, sharply.

But a little later he did at least take time to talk to all of them together, making them feel he was of them utterly, and his words were theirs alone, special; the words of a loving mole, and one who cared. And so believers and doubters alike, the young and innocent and the old like Willow, came closer and listened. Such a moment came in June shortly before Midsummer when Mayweed asked him if he agreed with Brevis's dictum that life is difficult. . . .

Perhaps Tryfan still had much to learn, for he missed the special appeal in Mayweed's voice, and a new look of pain and suffering in his eyes. But though Tryfan's answer was a general one, it was memorable all the same, though he still felt more comfortable quoting his old master. . . .

'Boswell used to say that the problem for mole is to decide *which* life: the real one they experience, or the one they try to make despite experience. Living *is* difficult, for unless a mole stays in his tunnels he is beset by danger and difficulty on all sides. Even in his tunnels, and alone, he will face difficulties, some would say far greater ones than he would ever face outside. Yes, life is difficult and finally it is mortal, for all moles die. If their life is merely protecting themselves from death, then their life is more than difficult – it is impossible, for they have set themselves a task at which they can never succeed; and they have made themselves afraid of life itself. So accepting that life is difficult is the first step to freedom from fear. It *is* difficult, as Brevis rightly says.'

He fell silent and Mayweed twisted his snout this way and that, as if trying to find some complex route through something simple; then grinned, and then stopped grinning.

'Mayweed hears, Mayweed learns, Mayweed waits for more,' he said, and sighed, moving to shadows as he had when Tryfan and Spindle had first met him.

'Well then, Mayweed, know this. With fear there is no Silence, no great light: only noise and darkness, and tunnels without end and without escape. Tunnels in which a mole will finally lose himself, however good his route-finding might be.' Mayweed shifted about very uneasily, for it was his nightmare that he would be lost beyond recall in tunnels without end.

'For some of us the way towards light and Silence is the way of the Stone. We make that choice and we follow it as best we can. For a few, like Brevis here, who is a scribemole, the way they go is hard indeed, and disciplined; for others it may be easier, but the end may finally be further away. So my friend Boswell told me.'

'So this Stone of yours does not demand to be followed, or have rules and rituals a mole must see to?' asked Skint.

Tryfan shrugged. 'Rules for scribemoles, perhaps, rituals for allmole as well, such as we have at Midsummer and on Longest Night. But if you mean *must* we do them, as a Word follower must or risk punishment, then no, that is not the way of the Stone. But I think acceptance of the difficulty of life means that a mole must have some discipline, and perhaps rituals help him with it at times of doubt or special darkness.'

'That's right is it, Brevis?' asked Skint, turning from Tryfan as if he did not quite respect his word enough.

Brevis smiled briefly and then nodded. 'Yes, Tryfan is right, he speaks well.'

'Mayweed has a question and a query he has, Sir and Sirs. A question difficult and doubtful, and a question he longs to ask.'

'Yes?' said Tryfan.

Mayweed grinned and then looked slyly about and then smiled (as he thought) winningly.

'If it is better for a mole of the Stone to be a scribemole to reach the Silence and the light, then Mayweed wonders what hope there is for humble and pathetic bodies such as he, Mayweed, me, myself? Or is Sir saying, magnanimous Sir, and very wise too, that a diseased mole such as Mayweed, born in the darkness of Slopeside and forcibly taken from it with the best of intentions by Tryfan himself, might aspire to scribemoledom?'

It was a strange moment and in the way that Spindle understood, a historic one. Tryfan sensed it too and paused, and looked about and then took a few paces northwards to have a better view of the north and eastern vales, and then beyond, further than mole could see, to the northward expanse of moledom itself.

'There is nothing of the Stone that prevents a mole learning scribing,' he said, 'nothing at all. He need only find a scribemole and ask.'

'Well, Sir! Incredible! Wonderful!' declared Mayweed.

Tryfan laughed but Brevis did not.

'And what would you scribe?' asked Tryfan. There was sufficient seriousness to his voice that the others did not laugh.

Mayweed wrinkled his brow and for once seemed short of words. Then, in a way that was touchingly humble, he looked at his talons and his diseased flanks.

'Mayweed would scribe his name, that's what he'd do. Then he'd show it to other moles to prove that he was a mole worth knowing because he could scribe his name from its beginning to its end.'

Tryfan spoke softly to Spindle and was gone, leaving Mayweed to ask what he had said.

'Something good, something bad, sublime Spindle?'

'He said you are a mole worth knowing already. You don't need to scribe your name for a mole to know that.'

'Oh!' said Mayweed, very surprised. 'Did he?'

'Yes he did and he meant it,' said Spindle.

'Oh!' said Mayweed. 'Oh!'

The moles had soon made some comfortable burrows and established a basic system of tunnels such that they might get warning of mole approach, and have routes of escape. Skint and Smithills did part of the tunnelling to the north and west, solid worthy tunnels in the northern style. Spindle worked part of the east and south, making less straight tunnels that made idiosyncratic use of the few flints and stones in the soil, and had an air of pleasing vagueness with fits and starts and niches of great comfort. While Tryfan's, the first he had made for many a month, were of the Duncton style, tunnels of a powerful mole, with room to breathe, a sense of purpose, and well made for entrances and exits. These Mayweed liked best, and took up his own quarters near Tryfan, who soon gave up trying to control Mayweed's wanderings, realising that he had his own way of making his space, and there was never a mole who knew better how to find out strange routes and hiding places.

Spindle made a burrow for his former master Brevis between his own and Tryfan's at a place that faced south and caught the sun all day, for Brevis was weakened by imprisonment and the stress of the escape and needed long days of rest.

On the ninth day at Harrowdown, Skint announced that he and Smithills intended to sing a few songs the following evening because it marked Midsummer, and whatever moles of the Stone might do, moles where he came from had a good laugh then. And a song helped.

'And a story!' said Smithills.

'Each can make his own ritual, and all can share,' said Tryfan. And so the moles went their separate ways, to prepare something for the morrow and share it. From Skint and Smithills came singing and laughter, from Willow a tuneless humming as she practised a Wharfedale tune; from Brevis the mutterings of some invocation from the Holy Burrows. Spindle practised a story and Tryfan crouched silently, enjoying the warmth of that month and the sound of life about him. Only Mayweed look troubled, his brow furrowing and his talons fretting, and he went off by himself, route-finding and wandering, staring at the stars as if he had lost something but he did not know what it was, or where he might find it. And the morning of Midsummer he stayed in his burrow and said nothing at all.

Midsummer began with as beautiful a dawn as ever was, the sun rose slowly at Harrowdown. Each mole readied himself for the evening to come, and none went near the Stone for they knew that whatever it was each would do, all would end up near the Stone as night came, and that Brevis or Tryfan perhaps would say a prayer or two, and they could listen even if they did not join in.

So a day of lazy leisure passed, and evening came; and far below in the vales the sun caught the surface of the Thames which turned this way and that among the trees and fields far below; then, too, twofoot lights twinkled and the eyes of a roaring owl stared briefly and turned away, and as another came dusk travelled into Harrowdown.

'Where's Mayweed?' asked Tryfan softly, for all but he had gathered, and were waiting now.

'Haven't seen him all day,' said Smithills.

'He looked unhappy yesterday,' said Spindle.

'In his burrow this morning, gone now,' said Skint.

Tryfan looked worried and said, 'Well, he'll come soon enough so we'll wait.' But he did not come, not even when night fell and the new moon rose, and not even when the others went calling for him.

'We had best begin. He'll come,' said Tryfan looking beyond the circle of their cheerful faces to the shadows where another hid, wanting to join them but not knowing how to. 'He'll come,' said Tryfan gently.

So they began, singing and joking and telling stories, making up their own celebration of Longest Day to mark Midsummer as they went and watching the moon rise beyond the trees. What a song Smithills sung, what a tune Willow remembered, and what fine prayers for the future old Brevis spoke. As for Spindle, well, he told them of this and that he had heard about Brevis's younger days at the Holy Burrows and that made them laugh. Then Tryfan smiled, and looked beyond the circle again, and said loudly enough that somemole might hear who was not near, 'I *wish* Mayweed was here, I miss him!'

'Hear! Hear!' said the others.

But still Mayweed did not join them, and the shadows in the wood turned, and whatever Tryfan had seen earlier was gone.

Then Tryfan told them about Duncton Wood and the moles who had lived there before the plagues. Dramatic stories, those! Good to remember the past! Then, as night deepened, some food and some more singing, and the moles gathered closer to the Stone, talking and laughing that good night away. So much so that they did not notice Tryfan creep away, or if they did they thought it was for just a moment.

But it was more than that, for he looked concerned, and went to the western edge of the copse, which is in the direction of the Slopeside. He snouted the ground, looked ahead, and then went swiftly downslope, snouting now and then as if following a scent until he reached the banks of the stream. The water was lower now, but very dangerous still.

'Mayweed!' he called out softly in the dark. 'Mayweed, I know you're there!'

But no answer came. So Tryfan went down the bank to the edge of the stream and, very worried now, snouted here and snouted there, calling softly and quartering back and forth up and then downstream.

'Mayweed!'

He found the mole, though more by luck than judgement, for Mayweed was huddled and hiding by a rotten branch that had been brought down by winter thaws. He was wet, and shivering, and muddy, and his snout was as low as a mole's could be. And he had been crying.

'Mayweed,' said Tryfan, and the care and concern in his voice made Mayweed cry some more.

Tryfan let him, his paw gently on his shoulder, until he was ready to speak.

'Mayweed's very . . . bedraggled,' said Mayweed at last. 'Very, very bedraggled.'

'What were you trying to do?' said Tryfan, who only half guessed.

'Trying to go home, humble though it is, and diseased, and dangerous; Mayweed was trying to go home. Mayweed wanted to go home.'

'But *why*?' asked Tryfan.

'Mayweed was sad,' was all Mayweed could manage to say before he wept again, terribly, and then, 'Very, very sad.'

'But why didn't you say something?'

'Couldn't. Didn't dare Tryfan, Sir. Frightened.'

'What of?'

'Being sent away. Mayweed thought he'd go before he was sent.'

'But what have you done that would ever make us do that? You saved our lives when we escaped, you were the only mole who knew the way. You are one of us, Mayweed.' Which only made Mayweed cry the more.

300

Then, finally, he said, 'Mayweed wanted to join in but Mayweed couldn't. Skint and Smithills had their song, and Willow had her tune, and Brevis had his prayer, and Spindle had his stories and you, Sir, good Tryfan, had Duncton Wood to tell of. But Mayweed had nothing to give, Sir, Mayweed *has* nothing, no memory but darkness and tunnels and nothing.'

Then Tryfan was silent and ashamed, for he felt he should have seen this suffering of a mole in his care. But then he was still, for there was something more, something worse.

'What else is it, Mayweed?' he asked.

'That, and something else. I . . . I'm frightened, very. My – my – ' But he could not speak. Never in his life had Tryfan known a mole so broken as Mayweed was then. Wet from his abortive and dangerous attempt to swim the stream, ashamed of himself because he felt he had nothing to give, and now something more, something that frightened him.

'Tell me,' whispered Tryfan.

'It hurts now, Sir. My scalpskin hurts, it hurts and hurts and hurts Mayweed, it does, it does . . .' and he stared at Tryfan, and everything was gone from his eyes but fear and hopelessness. 'Mayweed's dying,' he said. And over them the moon was strong, its light fierce and white, and it shone on Mayweed's flanks where his sores were, and Tryfan saw they were raw and black and bad. And that when Mayweed said it hurt him, he meant it, and he talked of mortal, fearful pain.

'Wanted to drown, Sir, not go home, wanted to die. Life was *too* difficult for Mayweed, Sir,' he said finally.

'Well then,' said Tryfan, not sure what to say. 'Well then! I think your hurting had better stop.'

'Yes Sir, sensible Sir, but *how*? Mayweed knows, Mayweed has seen death. Mayweed didn't know it hurt so much.'

'Come on Mayweed, you come with me.'

'Can't Sir, won't Sir, you'll take him to that Stone where

301

the others are and Mayweed's nothing to give. He smells now, he's dying now, he wants to die . . .' Then Mayweed made a terrible lunge for the stream and Tryfan grabbed him, which in a way was worse for he must have caught his sores and maybe caused some internal damage too, for Mayweed screamed and shuddered and wept, and as Tryfan felt him, he knew how ill he was. Not with a disease as Thyme had been, but with a sickness through and through, deep and dark inside him, and one he had fought until now with a terrible courage and told nomole about.

'You should have said something,' whispered Tryfan holding him.

'I would have been sent away, back to being alone.'

'Come,' whispered Tryfan, 'you are not alone any more. I have something I want you to hear, something that will help you.'

'But I have nothing to give,' cried out poor Mayweed.

'Yes you have, as all moles have.'

'What?' Mayweed asked, trembling.

'The Stone will show you, trust it. So come now.'

Then Mayweed let himself be taken back upslope, slowly, step by painful step, leaning against strong Tryfan, the thin light of the solstice moon throwing their shadows before them as they went back to Harrowdown.

They were met halfway there, first by Spindle who had become concerned, and then by the others, even old Willow, and each of them touched Mayweed in their way when they knew what was wrong. And somehow in their touch it was as if Mayweed's sickness got worse not better, and the more he saw they were not going to send him away, the more he allowed his pain to feel. So that when they reached the Stone he could not place one paw before another without suffering, and they saw that the mole they had come to know was racked and hurt beyond imagining, and his eyes were full of fear, and he was young, so young, and so alone and hurt.

Tryfan took him to the very base of the Stone while the

others fell back like guardians around a place of holy rite. They saw Mayweed leaning against Tryfan, and they saw Tryfan raise himself to stare at the Stone.

'Guide me,' he whispered up to its heights. 'Help those who suffer on this special night for it is the Longest Day, the shortest night, and yours is the power to help a mole who is hurting and adowned.'

Then was Tryfan silent, waiting for guidance, letting his mind free as Boswell had taught him, trusting the Stone. Nomole knows how long that Silence was, not even Spindle who was there and part of it. But in it peace came slowly and settled on Harrowdown and Tryfan lay Mayweed down and turned to the others.

'Tonight we are none of us at our home system, yet all of us think of it, and the good rituals we were taught when we were pups. In Grassington, in Wharfedale, at Seven Barrows, yes, at Buckland before the plagues; and at Duncton Wood. Yet there is one mole here who had no home system that a mole could truly call such and has been alone. Born in the autumn, born in darkness, lost until the clearers found him. And this has been his first Midsummer, this is its night.

'In days gone by, for generations now, in my own home system of Duncton Wood, this was the night when moles who had not seen the Stone before were shown it. For them was an invocation made, and it was one my father learnt of Hulver, an elder once of Duncton and as good and brave a mole as ever was. My father taught it me as he taught it to my brother Comfrey that we might teach it to others in our time.

'This night my brother will be saying it at Duncton, as I say it now for you, and especially for Mayweed who is of us, and with us, and trusted by us. And I ask him to say it now, as I say it, that his spirit may find truth in it, and his body rest, and his heart know love. . . .'

Then Tryfan turned to Mayweed, and put his paws on Mayweed's hurting flanks and back, the moon's light striking them white and black, and said, 'These are the words my father taught me for this night. . . .'

While far across the vales beyond Harrowdown, far to the east, that same moon's light fell on a different Stone, a taller Stone, the great Stone of Duncton Wood. And it fell on a mole there, an untidy vague-seeming sort of mole, but one with a face full of concern, and paws that might touch another with healing and with love.

Why Comfrey had come back up to the Stone he did not know, for the rituals of that night were over, and all was joking and jollity underground. Yet up he had come, called out he knew not why, except that somemole he knew called him, somemole he missed, somemole he loved.

But which or why he knew not at first, except that he was of the Stone and calling, and that he and his needed him.

So old Comfrey had come and crouched by the Stone and, as was his stuttering way, whispered this and that to it, and had touched it, and been patient.

But now he knew what he must do and he spoke those words Bracken had taught him and which he had said once already that night when the youngsters were gathered about. But he said them again willingly, for somewhere was another, and one who had not heard them yet, and before he spoke them he said, 'Oh St-Stone, if it's T-Tryfan that's calling me, t-t-tell him I know, t-tell him I'm here, yes tell him that. Now l-let me see. I think I know them, always think I'll f-forget but I d-don't. Don't d-dare! Now. . . .'

Then Comfrey raised a paw to the Stone, and instinctively turned west, for that's where the call was from, and he began to say the words allmole should say that special night of nights:

> '*By the shadow of the Stone,*
> *In the shade of the night,*
> *As they leave their burrows;*
> *On your Midsummer Night . . .*'

'Well,' muttered Comfrey interrupting himself, 'I kn-know perfectly well they left their burrows long ago and are now asleep as their elders and betters get on with some song, b-but I have to say it aright!'

> *'We the moles of Duncton Stone*
> *See our young with blessing sown . . .'*

And there was ardour in Comfrey's voice now and no more hesitation and he turned from the Stone and spoke the words to the west, to where, he felt sure, a mole needed the help the words gave. . . .

> *'We bathe their paws in showers of dew,*
> *We free their fur with wind from the west,*
> *We bring them choice soil,*
> *Sunlight in life.*
> *We ask they be blessed*
> *With a sevenfold blessing.*
>
> *'The grace of form*
> *The grace of goodness*
> *The grace of . . .'*

Then, as Tryfan whispered the words far, far away his half brother Comfrey spoke them too and Mayweed began to find the strength to repeat them, and more than repeat them, to say them, stronger and stronger so that Tryfan's voice fell away and the other moles there watched and listened in wonder as at the Stone in Harrowdown Mayweed gave to them something they would not forget. He gave them a blessing out of darkness, a blessing out of pain, and from doubt he spoke in faith. . . .

> *'The grace of suffering*
> *The grace of wisdom*
> *The grace of true words*
> *The grace of trust*
> *The grace of whole-souled loveliness.*

> *'We bathe their paws in showers of light,*
> *We free their souls with talons of love,*
> *We ask that they hear the silent Stone.'*

So is it chronicled that Mayweed spoke, though from where he found the words, or the strength, or the Silence to so speak nomole knows. But to the east he turned, and the light was on his face and though suffering was there, there was knowledge too, and hope, and his loneliness was gone. For a moment he had heard Silence and in that moment he was healed, and the darkness of his puphood was gone from him, and he could love and trust.

Then all the moles at Harrowdown were silent, and many others across Moledom too, including good Comfrey, who watched that short night through, until when dawn came Mayweed was helped to his burrow and then the others went silently to theirs, to sleep and let a new sun shine.

Which, when it did, brought discovery of healing at Harrowdown, of Mayweed, whose hurt was gone and whose sores would dry and heal; of Smithills, whose scalpskin began to clear; and of old Willow, who found in the days that remained to her a peace that gladdened the hearts of everymole there.

Chapter Nineteen

So Midsummer passed at Harrowdown and each one of them there, even Mayweed now, was quiet and peaceful, content to wait two or three weeks longer until Tryfan decreed that it was time for them to move on from the environs of Buckland.

'But we better not wait too long,' warned Skint, 'because I know the moles of the Word – nomole better than I. They'll see our desertion as blasphemy and will not stint to find us. We'll be outcast, which means that no system can harbour us without fear of punishment and snoutings. So we best get away before they send out orders.'

But Tryfan was cautious, arguing that the grikes had not pursued Spindle and himself very rigorously after they left Uffington, and probably the last place they would think to look now was at a little system like Harrowdown, so close to the Slopeside.

In any case, there were no signs at all of searching guardmoles or patrols and their hiding place had gone undiscovered this long, and the grikes had other things to occupy themselves with now.

Of the events by the Stone, and the healings, Tryfan said nothing and the others little, and though few of them yet knew he was a scribemole all instinctively felt his authority and accepted it. For Skint and Smithills and the others it was enough that they were free of clearing and the Slopeside, and able to make each day their own for a time.

After a day or two of rest following the healing of Mayweed, Tryfan went to Brevis and said formally, 'Much have thou to teach me and there is little time.'

'What can I teach thee?' said Brevis, respectful of the

younger mole, 'for thou art a scribemole beyond need of my knowledge.'

'Of scribing itself canst thou teach me, for there I have yet much to learn that Boswell did not teach me.'

Which Brevis did, in that high wild place called Harrowdown, teaching all he knew to Tryfan as if there was indeed little time left and too much to learn. Long days of quiet instruction in the ancient texts of the Holy Burrows, such as Brevis was able to remember, summarise and pass on, so that the sound of talons on bark and soil filled their burrows.

It was then that Spindle persuaded Tryfan and Brevis to begin to teaching him scribing, a skill that Mayweed was allowed to learn as well; but more than that, he suggested that Tryfan should consider developing new texts which would be very different from the spiritual and academic studies that had been traditional in the Holy Burrows, and which were all that Brevis knew, important though they were.

So it was that, for a time that late June and early July, Harrowdown became the centre for rediscovering an old kind of record-keeping, one that recorded the memories and experiences of ordinary moles. It was then that Brevis himself made his *Memoranda of Grikes in Buckland* taking down in their own words the stories of Skint, Smithills and Willow, and instructing Tryfan and Spindle in the making of such accounts, and showing how a scribemole must listen to another mole, and let him or her speak their own words true without prompting or alteration.

It was then that the mole Willow dictated to Spindle, that he might practise his new skill, her *Songs and Rhymes of Wharfedale*, the finest collection of such material gathered from a single source, and a Book (for such it be) which preserves for ever the name of Willow of Wharfe.

Tryfan made several Memoranda and Briefs of his own in that rich period of scribing, the most important of which was the seminal *Teachings of Boswell, White Mole*. But there were other texts too, including the extraordinary

Escape from a Seal-up, The Tale of Mayweed of Buckland
which is scribed by Tryfan to Mayweed's dictation, and
Tryfan's first *Annals of Duncton Wood*.

Spindle was much concerned with the preservation of
these texts, for he argued that they would not be able to
take them safely with them when they left Harrowdown,
and accordingly he showed Smithills and Skint how to
create a small deep burrow for their preservation, until
such time as it might be possible for them to be recovered
and taken to a place worthy of them.

It was a time of extraordinary activity at Harrowdown,
for each mole sensed that their time there was short and
there was much to do. Each helped each other, all but
Willow took their turn to watch out for danger, while
Mayweed, pleased to have a role to play, began to explore
the northern environs which were the slopes leading down
to the Thames, in an attempt to find a quick route of
escape away from the area of Buckland.

Sometime then, too, Skint and Smithills came to the
two scribemoles and Skint said, 'Well now, if we're to go
with you when you leave this place, it might be a good idea
if you told us something of this Stone of yours, as we've
told you what we know of the Word. Not saying we want
to be believers in the Stone, but we'd be better off
knowing something of it, eh Smithills?' Smithills nodded
his agreement.

So it was that Tryfan made his first formal teaching of
the Stone, though unwillingly, for he felt himself to be
unworthy. But both Brevis and Spindle urged him to talk
with Skint and Smithills, and he did so by morning and by
sunlight, by evening and by dusk, and the others listened
– Willow, quiet and peaceful now she was clear of the
Slopeside, and Mayweed, too, staying as always a little to
one side, listening from a tunnel of his own, or from some
shadowed nook where he felt comfortable to be unseen.

So time passed until there came a night when the air was
warm and the sky was covered in stars, and somewhere
beneath them Tryfan sensed the great flowing of the

Thames, and knew that their days at Harrowdown were nearly at an end. Troubled he was, for the sky that evening had been deep blood-red, and the Harrowdown Stone had been cold to the touch. That night it was that he called them near and warned them that their time there was done. That night too, perhaps, moles crept unseen over the stream on the eastern boundary of the Slopeside, sly and sneaking moles, curious and suspicious, and finding tracks that led up towards Harrowdown.

'Searched there?' said one grike to another.

'Think not,' said a second.

'Mmm,' mused the one in charge.

But of this the moles at Harrowdown were unaware, and they felt safe enough for there were always watches out, and Mayweed had found ways they could escape if an attack ever came.

But that evening all were gathered to hear, and no watches were kept, for what Tryfan had to say was important.

Skint said, 'You have told us much of the Stone, and of its rituals and powers. What shall we remember?'

For a long time, beneath that dark, starry sky, Tryfan was silent, and then he breathed deep, and talked with them, giving then the sayings that are known as the Three Tenets of the Stone.

'First,' he said, 'a follower must find discipline, for without it he or she will never solve the problems that arise from the simple truth that a mole's life is difficult. Many avoid such problems and so they never truly live, for living is in the solving; restlessness is in the avoiding.

'Discipline is in dwelling on what is, rather than living in a self-made dream of what is not; it is in accepting that there is risk in the way ahead, yet taking it; it is in telling truth whatever the loss may be; it is in learning to live in the darkness while always seeking the light.

'Second a follower must give love, which means he must know it. Love is not desire for oneself. Such a thing is lust, or greed, or fear. Love is the desire to lead another on the way of the Stone, selflessly. It is to put the other before oneself. And yet it is to put oneself first as well. A mystery! A follower must have a sense of humour! A mole learns love at puphood, but if he learns it not then, and many do not, he learns it later from others who know it; or from the Stone itself.

'Thirdly, a follower must live, conscious of himself as he is conscious of others. The Stone helps him, the Stone helps her, and knowledge of the Stone deepens with knowledge of other moles: with them, by them, through them, away from them. Living is in all of that. Remember that its nature is open, and free, and full of light; it is not secret, nor imprisoned, nor in dark. Trust before you condemn.

'So a follower will yearn for discipline, will yearn to love, will yearn for life; as hunger yearns for satisfaction. Not easy! Never easy!'

Tryfan's voice was warm, his final words a shout, and the final sound he made in that teaching a laugh, for a follower, as he said, must have a sense of humour.

Yet there was a shiver in the air, and an uneasiness, and Tryfan said, 'We will leave tomorrow, yes tomorrow!' But all there felt uncomfortable as the darkness beyond the wood that night seemed ascurry and fractious, though there was no sound in the warning tunnels or out on the surface where Smithills and Skint, for safety's sake, made a patrol.

'Don't like it,' were Skint's last words that night.

'We leave on the morrow,' said Tryfan.

Spindle set off for his burrow but on his way turned west, scurried on to the surface, and then down again by a fallen branch, seeking out a tunnel so well hid that though he had been there many times he always had to search for it. It was the deep chamber Smithills and Skint had built to preserve the scribings they had made in the weeks past. He began to seal it up, then stopped. Re-emerged, went to Brevis's burrow, and, despite Brevis's protests that the text was only half complete, he took a book the old scribe had been working on. Then back to the secret chamber he went, carefully put the last text in, and, backing out, sealed the place up, not once, not twice but thrice. Nomole would find that place without being told exactly where it was. Then he went back to his own burrow and, tired out, slept.

Meanwhile, Tryfan, restless still but satisfied that all were now aburrow, took stance out in the open above the northern vales and for a moment it seemed that the whole of moledom turned round the heights of Harrowdown, and the Thames far beneath seemed briefly to catch alight, its meanders shining as if caught by stars. He shivered again and went aground, wondering if he should have led them away that night, but feeling tired and believing that the morrow would do.

That night, while they were asleep and unwatching, moles of darkness came, moles of death. So that when dawn came with the grey flap of a heron's wings the grikes were there too, unseen and creeping. Moles nameless, approaching. Moles so quiet that evil guided their talons. Moles led by Weed.

A mole hard to see in light, was Weed; impossible at dawn, for his coat held that special grey which is the twilight of insinuation.

But he was there.

So were others whose names in time would be known, as if massing about Harrowdown were the moles who in the long struggle to come of Word and Stone would meet again, and again, fortunes changing and volatile.

So filthy Smaile was there, and Pewle his friend, and Fescue, eldrene notorious.

A single signalling thump, then the silent, creeping, secret expedition to surround Harrowdown was ready and alert. Two others were there who can be named. One was Sleekit, sideem and trusted, but to be trusted ever by whom? The other was Henbane, sensing a light beyond the light of stars and seeking now to put it out.

Yes, she was there, not directing but present and essential, as fear is the essence of a frightened group, or darkness is the essence of night. That mole was there, choosing a stance apart to watch and feel and know, awaiting her time. Oh yes, she was there that dawn on Harrowdown.

As sunrise came they closed finally in, expertly seeking out the entrances the hiding moles had made and waiting there. Careful not to go too close and to stay windside, lest scent or air current warn the sleeping moles.

Yet Tryfan stirred uneasily in his burrow, and as he did he was wakened by a sharp and urgent whisper.

'Wake up! Tryfan! Wake.'

It was Skint, crouched down alert, his head on one side. Smithills was by his side.

Tryfan was suddenly alert and listening, snouting into the air for movement or scent.

'Nothing,' he said, but stayed absolutely alert.

'Something,' said Skint.

'Yes, something,' agreed Smithills.

'Spindle and the others, get them,' said Tryfan. And silently they left to muster the group together.

By a dawning light they assembled, the last coming being Mayweed. 'Danger Sir, I smell it, I heard it, I feel it: grikes, Sir. But Mayweed's not afraid, he knows a route away.'

'If they come, they'll come quick and violent and resistance won't be much use,' said Skint. 'I knew we should have gone. . . .'

It was true. The tunnels were built for hiding not fighting, for there was not much seven moles could do in such a location against resolute guardmoles.

They looked at Tryfan.

'We should have left before. But now that is past, so listen. I trust Skint's judgement, and Mayweed's. I cannot hear or sense danger, but they can and that is enough for me. If we stay here we cannot fight because there is no

313

room, nor have we any chance of escape. If we attempt to escape together we shall certainly be heard. The best is to confuse, and that means dispersal.'

Skint and Smithills nodded at this.

'Each go silently by his own tunnels which he will know best. Stay underground. Surface and meet on the north side of the wood where the day will still be darkest. Brevis will come with me.'

'But . . . ' began Spindle, for he had no wish to be separated from either of them.

'Do it now, fast and silently. It would need many moles to guard all our exits, even if they could find them. Get to the north side.'

'Mayweed knows a way by badger route and fox path. Down, down, down it goes for he has done it, Sirs and Madam. Follow it and trust it and you will be at the Thames's side itself. Mayweed advises and hopes you'll listen.'

But no sooner had he said this than there was a rushing in the tunnels, distant at first, but all around. Dangerous now, very.

They said no more. Above ground they heard a rustle, and the gentlest of thumping signals, but audible enough for all of them to know that danger was near. Skint's instincts had been right.

Then they turned and left, and the burrow where they had been was suddenly empty, echoing only with retreating pawsteps, each going his way, with Skint taking Willow at his side.

Tryfan, directing Brevis to stay right behind him, crept away along the tunnels he himself had made, the surface above creeping now with menace. He was angry with himself for having delayed at Harrowdown too long, angry . . . but now it was too late, and moles were going to suffer.

It was not long before, from the tunnels behind, he heard commotion and fighting and it was all he could do not to turn round and help. But dispersal and flight is

314

often the best for a small group which believes itself surrounded, and guardmoles will tend to take prisoners of single moles, but kill several together, so this way survival was more likely.

Brevis and he ran on, the commotion continuing north of them on the surface. Skint or Smithills must have been taken. Then pattering above, crouching still, and any sense of what was happening elsewhere in the system was gone as the tunnel ahead was filled with a huge guardmole, and the roof behind collapsed as two more tunnelled down.

'Resist and you'll be taloned but not killed,' said the guardmole ahead of them.

'Resist and you'll be maimed,' said the ones who had come behind.

'Resistance is folly,' said another above, whose voice Tryfan knew, for he had heard it giving orders on Uffington Hill.

He surfaced, and Brevis with him, and they found themselves surrounded by moles, and Tryfan was looking into the face of the one he had last met at Uffington.

'Well, well, well,' said Weed, with a grim smile. 'I wondered when we'd meet again. I knew we would. Outcasts do not escape the discipline of the Word. You did well to survive this long. And you as well,' he added, looking at Brevis with menace. 'How nice.'

· He came nearer, his twisted snout giving the curious impression that he was circling them though in fact he came straight to them. He peered at Tryfan.

'Tryfan of Duncton, which means the mole Spindle will be nearby, and Brevis, late of our burrow-cells.'

Tryfan nodded.

'How many of you are there here?' asked Weed, unblinking.

He doesn't know, thought Tryfan. Or if he does he wants to catch me out. It doesn't matter. . . .

'Four,' lied Tryfan, taking a gamble. It was the least he could say: Brevis and himself, and the one they had heard

315

the fighting about, and another one nearby . . . must be four.

'Four? We shall see. Bring them,' Weed ordered the guardmoles, who were not slow to use talons if either of them lingered for one second.

They took them by surface to the south side of the wood where others had been gathered. Skint was protesting loudly when Tryfan arrived: 'Take your dirty talons off me, lad, or you know what'll happen. You'll get plague. . . .'

Tryfan smiled to himself. Trust Skint to resist. Then Smithills was brought in fighting hugely, and it needed four guardmoles to subdue him. At a word from Tryfan he was still.

Willow was there, wounded, though not badly. And then they brought in Spindle who must have been talking too much because as they arrived with him one of the guardmoles was saying, 'If you say another bloody word you'll get a talon-thrust you'll not forget.'

'I was only. . . . '

'Spindle!' and Spindle was silent at Tryfan's command.

They were herded together by the barbs of the fence at which the original Harrowdowners had been snouted.

'All in?' asked Weed, his quiet, hard voice bringing an instant silence to the crowd of moles.

Nomole said a word. All looked around. Each of them saw that one only had not been found, and that was Mayweed. Everymole was silent.

'No more there?' said Weed.

'Not a one, not half of one,' said a guardmole. 'Plenty of tunnels there, and we searched them; strange daft affairs where you couldn't hide a flea. But nomole.'

'Strange,' said Weed sarcastically to Tryfan, 'strange how you followers of the Stone call six moles "four". Maybe this will help you count more accurately!' And with that he raised his talons and brought them crushingly down on Brevis, who gasped in pain and staggered bloodily from the blow.

Tryfan immediately attempted to strike back, but the guardmoles held him, as they held the others who protested.

Brevis righted himself, attempted to stem the flow of blood from his shoulder, and said in a shaking voice, ' 'Tis nothing, Tryfan, nothing that the Stone can't heal.'

'Any more, old mole?' said Weed.

'More?' whispered Brevis.

'More of you,' he said, raising his talons threateningly.

'No more,' lied Brevis.

The talons crashed down, Brevis staggered and fell, the others groaned.

'There *are* no more,' said Brevis bravely.

Weed looked malevolently about them all, his healthy grey fur and strong body a contrast to Brevis, whom he towered over.

'Are we to believe him or not?' Nomole, including the guardmoles, were sure at whom this question was directed. All the captives were silent, praying that Mayweed would stay hidden and not give himself away and reveal Brevis's denial as a lie.

'Only six of you then?' said Weed, gloweringly.

'Seven's a number they like to travel in,' said a cracked voice of a female. They turned and saw the vicious eyes of Eldrene Fescue. 'It's lucky they say,' she added.

Weed smiled. 'Lucky is it? Well, well. Guardmoles, search their burrows and tunnels again for I would like to change their luck, and if others are found then as many will we snout, and if none are found then we'll snout some anyway.'

Never have the minutes of an hour dragged by so slowly for Tryfan, for that is how long it took the guardmoles to search the tunnels again. Brevis was not allowed to crouch low to ease his pain, nor was Willow. Skint never took his eyes off her, angry with the guardmoles who did not let her rest or give comfort or help. The time went slowly by and the sun rose on a summer's day, but all of it was lost to Tryfan for it seemed certain that at any moment Mayweed must be found. Over them hung fear.

Weed waited patiently, crouched low and comfortable. The guardmoles were disciplined and silent. Then as the time went by, Tryfan began to sense that there was another mole there, one he could not see, for it seemed a darkling chill had come over Harrowdown, though what its source he could not tell.

Brevis, too, seemed to sense it for he looked uneasy and restless and began, suddenly, to whisper an invocation against the eyes of evil.

'You can shut that right up,' said a guardmole immediately. 'Now!' And he taloned Brevis's haunch. Brevis fell silent, his breathing hurt and laboured.

Then, one by one, the guardmoles who had been searching drifted back. Nothing to report. The tunnels were empty. It seemed there were only six after all.

'Strange,' said Fescue, 'there are seven burrows. Well, we'll find the truth out, no doubt.'

Then a sudden silence fell on the guardmoles, indefinable but infinitely deeper than before, as if fear was settling on them, and awe. As one they seemed to look towards the south and step back a pace or two as if their fate itself was approaching. Fescue moved her thin and raddled body near to Weed. Weed smiled.

Then around the edge of a great oak tree, whose roots rose higher than where they were gathered, fell a shadow and then a shape. It moved slowly and with purpose and at first it was hard to make out, though it was clearly mole. But there was dark light there, sinister light, strangely blinding at first, for its colour was grey black and its fur shone with the light of the sky in it, but it held a beauty that was of pure dark. It was mole, but huge seeming, powerful seeming, frightening.

Tryfan was struck still, as were the other moles there, and the only movement was Weed's, for his paws kneaded the ground in expectation, and his eyes smiled and his face seemed to lighten as he looked up to where the mole came. While Smaile made obeisance, and dared not look at where that dread female came; and Fescue smiled in sickening humility.

Turning, her body; powerful, her presence; ominous, her stance, as if she held moledom itself within the sharp compass of her talons. Henbane of Whern was there, studying them, and in her presence a mole felt she had only to move a talon and he would be dead.

She gazed at each of the captured moles in turn with eyes so dark they swallowed a mole whole, and Tryfan felt the world go silent about him as their gaze fixed upon him alone.

'So,' she said appraisingly, 'So you are Tryfan.' And she stared into him, her dark spirit in him, and he was struck still and in awe.

'My name is Henbane,' said the mole softly, and her voice was a wind of allurement, and Tryfan felt himself beginning to be caught in bonds he could not fight against. She looked hurt, as if Tryfan and the rest of them were guilty of wounding her in some way and she could not understand why they should do such a thing.

'And you are dear Boswell's friend?' she said.

'I am,' said Tryfan, his voice seeming far from him as if coming from a great height.

'Then I have news of him for thee,' said Henbane, her body seeming massive and a thing of treacherous beauty, her talons black and sharp, her eyes upon him as if she could see into his very soul.

'I wish for news,' faltered Tryfan, trying to fight the terrible feeling that he liked her, wished to serve her, was guilty in some way. 'What . . . what is thy news?' he managed to say.

She smiled, and it seemed that in that smile was a terrible suffocation and a death that a mole might like, might yearn for, might almost plead to be given.

She reached forward and caressed him on shoulder and face, and her touch, her touch was sensual and deep and he wanted it more, he wanted, he desired . . . and trembling, struggling, fighting her gaze, he whispered again, 'What is thy news?'

319

'Oh, nothing much.' she said lightly. 'Boswell, the last scribemole, White Mole, greatest mole of Uffington, Boswell is dead,' she said.

And even as the world thundered and broke in Tryfan's ears, and he staggered and seemed to suffocate, her touch turned to pain as she tightened her grip on him, her talons digging into him, her face contorted into evil and malevolence, and she turned from him, raking his cheek hard and drawing blood, as she pointed at Brevis and Willow and said in a voice that was darkness itself, for it lacked all pity and care, 'Snout them.'

Chapter Twenty

Henbane of Whern's stark command was no sooner given than several of the guardmoles obeyed it with ruthless routine. Before Tryfan and the others' horrified gaze, first Brevis and then Willow were taken on either side by a guardmole, and a third came forward and plunged his talons one after another into each of their shoulders.

Protest, cries, shouts of rage and fear, horror, struggling . . . It was no use, and force was met with worse force. Brevis and Willow went into an initial state of limp shock as, without a single word, the guardmoles got on with their task. Above them, in the stunted trees of Harrowdown, a wood pigeon flapped and called to the blue July sky beyond, as if nothing in the world was wrong. And sun slanted through the wood, catching the white flowers of helleborine there, flower of mourning, flower of death.

They took the two moles over beside the loop of barbed wire that hung down lowest to the ground between the old fence posts that edged the wood. Above it bent a branch of a blackthorn, its gnarled and vicious branches stabbing in the soft breeze.

Brevis was now half conscious from the talon-thrusts he had had, and Willow was half mad with pain, crying in her cracked old voice and calling out to Skint to help her. While Skint and Smithills, fought desperately to go to her and, failing, bent their snouts low in distress.

All the time the guardmoles were silent and efficient, indifferent to the nature of their task. 'Move him along a bit, that's right, there, just there. . . .'

'You're not helping, old bird,' said another to Willow. 'The quieter you are the sooner it will be over.' Both moles tried feebly to resist, sensing perhaps the awfulness so

321

soon to come, but the taloning of their shoulders had disabled their front paws, which hung at their sides, and dripped blood into the ground.

When they were ready the guardmoles looked to Weed for the signal to continue, but Tryfan called out, 'In the name of love of allmole, Henbane of Whern, stop this cruelty. And if you will not, let me take their place for I am their leader and responsible.'

Henbane raised her talons and the guardmoles held their victims fast, the barbed wire ready above their snouts, and waited for a signal to begin.

'But of course Tryfan, of course! I understand. Discipline and right punishment is always distressing. You need only Atone and they shall live.'

'What is this Atoning?' said Tryfan.

'Oh nothing much. Just a confession of sin, an admission of the Word, and a rejection of the Stone.'

'I –'

'No!' cried out Brevis even from his agony. 'Thou canst not.'

'As a mark of my special favour,' continued Henbane, coming closer once more, 'and because I think these two moles are too frightened to make the right decisions by the Word, you can Atone for them all.' She paused and watched Tryfan closely.

'Just a word,' she said. 'Just a nod,' she whispered. 'Just. . . .'

'You're accursed,' hissed Willow suddenly, 'and neither he nor any mole speaks for me.'

'Well, Tryfan?' purred Henbane, her talons caressing him.

'I – I – If I atone, can they and the others go free?' he asked.

She smiled. 'I will do what is right,' she said.

'Will they go free?'

'That may be possible.'

'*Free?*' insisted Tryfan.

A momentary anger crossed Henbane's face. She did not, it seemed, like to be questioned.

'The Word is merciful,' she said.

'Eldrene Fescue promised me freedom,' cried out Smithills, 'and I am not free.'

Henbane ignored this, but the moment of danger seemed to be passing, the guardmoles were getting restless, and strength, of a kind, seemed to be returning to the captors.

Henbane moved swiftly to recover the initiative.

'Well, Tryfan? Will you Atone for these moles and yourself?'

Never was a mole more troubled and more suffering, never was a mole so bereft of life as Tryfan seemed then. His world was dark, and the darker for the knowledge that Henbane had said that Boswell was dead.

'For myself, Henbane, I can speak, but for others I cannot. Brevis has said he does not wish to Atone, and Willow, than whom a more harmless mole there could not be and whose snouting proves your Word as merciless and cruel, has said you are accursed. But for myself. . . .'

'Yes?' whispered Henbane.

'I will Atone if you swear by the Word itself to set all these moles free.'

For a moment Henbane looked at him, angry and intense.

'Clever, but not possible. Enough of discussion. I like not this mole. There is something about him. *I like him not.*' She was suddenly enraged, her mouth ensnarled, her eyes narrowed, her presence huge and dark.

Then to Weed she said indifferently, 'Give the order on these two, then snout them all.' Then her voice rose to a scream that nomole could ever forget: 'For the Word, and by the Word, and to the Word shall they be punished. They shall not Atone, nor be forgiven, and as their screams die so shall they be forgotten. And it will be made known that Tryfan of Duncton was coward enough and unbeliever enough in the Stone that he offered to Atone!'

323

And Skint and Tryfan shouted, 'Take us in their place, have mercy on them.'

But Brevis and Willow turned one final time and looked at their friends and there was love in their eyes and no fear, and Willow spoke for the scribemole too as she whispered softly to Skint, 'Nay lad, I am ready to die and I'll be glad to go. But thee, why, thou have strength yet to go to Wharfedale for me and go thou shalt, whatever this wickedness of a mole may do or say. Say you'll go home now.'

And bleakly Skint nodded his thin snout, tears of pity for Willow on his face.

'*Snout them!*' cried out Henbane.

Then Willow and Brevis were raised up, their snouts above the metal barbs, and suddenly, dreadfully, swiftly, they were pulled down on to the points, their snouts bursting blood and their mouths opening into an agony of pain.

Then they were let go, hanging unsupported there, their crippled paws trying for a brief moment to rise up and break themselves free, their bodies shaking into the rigor of pain, their eyes open in the fear that precedes the knowledge there is nothing left but to die.

Yet as they began to scream Tryfan rose up despite the guardmoles that held him and cried out, 'Stone, take them and show thy mercy. Let them know thy Silence now.'

At which it seemed a sigh came from each of them, first Brevis and then Willow, peaceful and strange, and Silence was theirs, and death. Where their bodies hung their spirits were no more.

At this the guardmoles seemed amazed, and one of them went near to Brevis's body and talon-thrust at it and another pushed him away saying, 'Can't you see he's dead? Now leave the poor bugger be.'

Then was Tryfan powerful, his shoulders huge, his talons fierce. 'And this is what the Word says you must do?' He waved his talons at the pathetic bodies hanging from the barbs. 'Such a Word will never speak to me!'

324

The guardmoles holding him seemed afraid at his strength and might, and not one moved to stop him as he turned on Henbane and cried, 'Thou art accursed by Stone, and thy Word is false. Thou shalt die and thy Word will die.'

It seemed that his anger and contempt crossed the sky above Harrowdown itself, for there were great black clouds there, and for a moment the sun was gone, and the winds were bitter for a summer's day.

Henbane seemed suddenly affected for she stepped back, staring at him as if, in his strength and purpose and defiance, she saw something like her own. She reared up to strike him, meeting defiance with murderous revenge, but in that moment what Tryfan had lost the evening before, by not acting on instinct and leaving Harrowdown then, he regained now in the sheer power and surprise of what he did.

For instead of doing Henbane's will and meeting her talon to talon, which is what the others there expected, he turned away from her and with one mighty strike killed the guardmole on his right, and with another struck dead the guardmole on his left, and with a third the other just in front. Then with more thrusting, and pushing, he was past them all, and over at Skint's side.

'Now,' he cried out to all of them, '*Now*! The power of the Stone is with thee, use it for thy lives!'

Then as Skint talon-thrust to his right and left, so too did Smithills and Spindle, so that together they made chaos all around them and all four fled back into the wood as guardmoles turned to each other in confusion.

'Kill them!' cried out Weed taking the lead, sensing now that this had been more than an ordinary mole before him, and he himself led the charge on Tryfan and the others. Like a great tide of darkness were the guardmoles then rising up and surging after the four moles.

'Follow me!' shouted Tryfan, instinctively choosing a direction towards the sun which would make them hard to follow, 'and Smithills you take up the rear. . . .'

325

'Catch them,' ordered Henbane calmly. 'Bring them here!'

But they had got a good start, and whatever route Tryfan led them on it was a subtle one, one only an experienced woodmole might have made, by root and leaf mould, by rotting branch and uprooted tree, and always back into the light of the sun when the pursuit got closer, doubling back on itself and clever. So that the grikes had to look right and left to check where their colleagues were, unable to follow a straight route or to locate Tryfan and the others by sound because of the noise their own moles were making.

Until when, at last, Weed was forced to call them to a halt, and all was still, they heard Tryfan not south at all, but far off to the north, near to the wood's edge where it contoured round the hillside that fell by ploughed field and pasture to the distant Thames.

'Follow them!' and the trees of Harrowdown seemed to shake with Henbane's angry voice as she came through the wood, sensing that the guardmoles were failing.

Then the four at the wood's edge broke cover as Tryfan found what he had been looking for, which was the badger run Mayweed had mentioned, which would take them down across the field and overslope to the distant Thames.

'Follow!' they heard Henbane shout, but the guard-moles were at first unwilling, for they could not find any run, but rather assumed the Stone followers had picked a route at random.

But such was Henbane's power and Weed's fury that together they organised the guardmoles to follow them and set off in rapid pursuit. And the sounds of moles running were loud across the slopes below Harrowdown.

Tired were Spindle and Skint, tired was Smithills but Tryfan seemed inexhaustible as he urged and drove them on, and made each encourage the other.

'Not far, not catching me, won't get us, keep *going*,' they said, one to another.

326

'Keep going if it's the last thing you do,' ordered Tryfan.

But the guardmoles were fit and remorseless, and Henbane and Weed were at their head, and the gap over that difficult ground began to narrow. And then the guardmoles found the badger run they had taken, and their pursuit became faster and they began to catch up.

Then Tryfan led them off the run and round to the east saying, 'I can snout a stream ahead, it will give us protection.'

In moments they reached it and guessed it was another of the streams that ran down towards the Thames and, though wider than the one they had crossed with such difficulty when escaping from the Slopeside, it was shallower. Its waters rushed and tumbled before them, seeming impassable.

'Have faith!' said Tryfan.

'Stupidity more like,' grumbled Smithills.

'Madness!' cried out Spindle.

'Courage,' shouted Skint.

'Now!' shouted Tryfan, and they plunged in, one beside the other, Smithills watching over them all for he was the strongest in water.

Then as the guardmoles surged behind them, they struggled and swam across the stream, its flow going over them, its bottom eluding their desperate grasp, and water tumbling them over and getting into their snouts and thundering in their ears, talons to wet rock and reaching up to air they could not reach, struggling and beginning to gasp and gulp in death, cold, cold, cold the water and thump! Gasp! Desperate scrabbling, back paws on nothing, nothing, something . . . and with last desperate pushes they were up the far side, Spindle the last out with Smithills' talons roughly helping him.

'Smithills and Skint, over the bank and out of sight. Spindle lie down and look half drowned, I shall do the same!' So swiftly ordered Tryfan, and it was done, so that when the guardmoles breasted the near bank all they saw on the far side were two moles, wet and shivering, exhausted beyond escaping.

'Cross and hold them,' commanded Weed, his eyes narrowing. 'But beware. Feigning tiredness is an old trick.'

Two of the guardmoles immediately went into the water and began to cross a little upstream so drifting, as Tryfan and the others had done, down to where Spindle and Tryfan puffed and heaved. Two more went upsteam before going in and also began to come across. Then Tryfan watched them apathetically, feigning fear, and seemed to turn and try to escape up the bank, but his injuries were bad. . . .

Henbane came to the crest and Weed was at her side.

'Only two left,' he said, 'the others have escaped. The Word will punish them.'

'Do not kill either of them. Bring them here. I shall punish them myself.'

On the far bank Spindle groaned and glanced accusingly at Tryfan. If looks could kill, Tryfan would have been dead.

But then Tryfan turned and faced the oncoming moles, watching their progress carefully. As the first two landed and began to make slow progress towards him, obviously tired from the chase and river plunge, and the others began to scramble ashore nearby he rose to his paws at first unsteadily, and then suddenly charged them with speed and power that put awe into those watching on the far bank. As he charged he called to Skint and Smithills to come and help, and to Spindle too, and then he was on the first of the two moles advancing on him. Two thrusts was all it took to push him back in the stream, and the water was filled with a racing turbulence of blood and a dying mole. Then he despatched the other, as Smithills bore down on the other two and stopped them sufficiently for Skint to charge in and strike one down. There was little more struggle as the fourth and last guardmole turned tail and plunged back into the stream which carried him down into its depths, and surged him along past them all as he reached out a taloned paw for the bank and was engulfed and taken out of their sight.

Already more were coming across, but now Tryfan was dominant and with the others at his side they were able to pick them off as they tried desperately to climb up the bank, or go back again. Four more died as Henbane and Weed looked on. Then she commanded them to stop.

'It seems this mole is not going to die today, that much is plain enough. It is the Word punishing the failure of the guardmoles. Punishment is wreaked in many ways.'

There was silence then as Tryfan, Skint and the others, blood on their talons, waited for more to come, and Henbane and the remaining guardmoles stared at him across the stream.

Henbane looked more curious than angry and observant moles, as Spindle was, recorded that Weed looked at her, his eyes narrowed and surprised, as if he saw something he did not wish to see on the face of his mistress. Which was, so Spindle later said, respect, and even pleasure to find after so long an opponent worthy of her, and one she could relish defeating when the time came.

Tryfan stared back at her, and for the first time seemed to see her clearly. The light of the sun was on her flanks, and dark were her eyes and shining her talons and her shoulders large. The sky seemed a fitting frame for such a mole. Between them, over that stream, was a grim respect.

'What moles are you?' she said across the gulf between them.

'Of the Seven Systems am I,' said Tryfan, hardly knowing what he said for it seemed he spoke from Silence, 'and to them am I bound.'

'Your purpose?'

'To honour the Stone and fulfil a quest that will bring Silence on the Word. To avenge the life of Boswell, not with force of talon but with force of love.'

'Ah yes,' she said, 'Boswell. A worthy mole.'

329

Then Tryfan knew without need of words from her that Boswell was still alive. And his heart rejoiced.

'He is dead to you, Tryfan, and where nomole of the Stone can reach him.'

Her ambiguity did not fool him. Boswell was not dead. Must *not* be dead. Tryfan said nothing but stared at her expressionlessly. She had no power over him.

'Where does your strength come from, mole?' asked Henbane. Her voice was soft and genuinely curious. Weed shifted at her side uncomfortably.

'Of the Stone am I ordained,' replied Tryfan.

'You're a scribemole?' said Weed.

Tryfan nodded, and the moles at his side came closer as if, now that what they suspected was confirmed, they had even more reason to protect Tryfan, and follow him.

'When I see thee again, mole, I will make sure you die,' she said softly. 'Until then anymole that talks to thee, or succours thee, or follows thee, will be snouted in the name of the Word. Thou art cast out and reviled by allmole, thy life is gone from this time on. Atoning will never be thine, nor communion of others.'

Tryfan raised his talons and said softly, 'May the Stone have pity on thee and thy Word; and may Boswell know its Silence.'

'I want not thy pity,' screamed Henbane rearing up as if burned by a light too powerful for her. 'I want not thy Stone or thy Silence!' Behind her the distant trees of Harrowdown were bent and old and wasted with the winds.

'So one day will you be,' whispered Tryfan.

'Will be what?' snarled Weed. 'What, mole?' For a grike does not like mystery or silence.

But Tryfan said no more, and with Spindle at his side and the others following, climbed up the bank, and never once did he look back, though he and his pursuers knew that by leaving so he had given ground, and might have been easily chased and caught. Yet Henbane gave no orders other than to turn back to Buckland. She was last to

330

go, and she stayed and watched Tryfan until he could be seen no more.

'Whatmole are thou, Tryfan of Duncton?' she whispered, and in her gaze there was strange loss and trouble. 'And what words are these: "So one day will you be"?' She turned away, and looked upslope, and saw, as Tryfan had seen, the silhouettes of the trees of Harrowdown. Black they were and bent, and at their edge hung moles she had killed. Withered was that place, and seeming lost, and so, and so. 'And so one day will I be?' she whispered. *No. . . .*

She moved upslope and Eldrene Fescue was there, old herself, yellow-toothed, past her prime and usefulness.

'Your fault!' said Henbane, and she raised her talons and struck them hard into Fescue's balding chest, and killed her.

'All your fault!' she screamed, and blood was on the ground where her paws went and the guardmoles trembled and dared not look at her.

Except for Weed, choosing his moment, eyes smiling, snout turning.

'That mole will go to Duncton Wood,' he said, 'for nowhere else will he find safety once your outcasting of him is known. Perhaps we have been mistaken believing the reports that it had been destroyed by plague and fire and allmole in it dispersed.'

'Yes,' agreed Henbane. 'If that system can still produce such moles as this Tryfan, then to it we will send a crusade, and raze it, and root out each one of its Stone followers, and kill them. This is the command of Henbane; this is of the Word!'

Then she said to the guardmoles around her, 'None will speak of these moles as escaping the Word, or defeating our intent. That is not the truth. The scribemole Brevis was snouted and that is a triumph; the other was better dead in any case. But as for the others, know only this on pain of death: the Word has spared them for it must have a use for them. Knowing this I let them run free.'

'None will speak . . .' yet somemole did. Of Tryfan and

331

how he escaped a snouting and killed ten or eleven moles; no, more, many more. Yes, hundreds perhaps . . . Of how Henbane of Whern herself was bested, and forced to retreat empty-pawed. Of the death of the hated Fescue . . . Of it all rumour spread, though secretly, for Henbane was feared and her talon-thrust long.

'His name is Tryfan. . . .'

'He can kill at a single thrust. . . .'

'He is huge and fierce. . . .'

'With a name like that he'll be a Siabod mole.'

'Siabod!'

'Aye, that's the system of wild moles, and one which has defied all incursions of the Word.' Which was true, for Siabod had never been conquered by the grikes, and was a source of rumour and doubt among them. That Tryfan had a Siabod name, and that he had defied Henbane added to Siabod's fame, as the association with Siabod added to his own.

'Of the Stone is this Tryfan . . . and he has many who follow him. . . .'

'Catch him and bring him alive to the Wordspeaker and you'll have a worm-rich burrow the rest of your days. . . .'

'Catch him and you'll be dead. . . .'

'Tryfan eh? Must be quite a mole . . . From Duncton some say, others Siabod. . . .'

So rumour spread, and would become the festering talon-thrust in the flank of the grikes. And yet . . . and yet Henbane was not angry. But rather she seemed pleased, whispering of the Word at night and saying that at last it had sent her an adversary worthy of her, and his killing would, in time, be a death blow to followers of the Stone.

While from her whispers, and those of cunning Weed, other, slower, darker rumours spread: of how a mole called Tryfan, who claimed he was of the Stone, was a coward and let a brave old mole called Brevis, and a harmless female called Willow die in his place . . . Weed smiled, rumour to counter rumour, it is the best of ways.

Rumour. The Stone and the Word; the light and the

dark; a mole is caught between them and needs a steady paw and a faithful heart to know which path to tread.

As Tryfan and the others ran, the ground below Harrowdown stream became progressively wetter and more difficult to travel. The air was heavy with the moisture of the nearby Thames, but its great width they could not yet see. The ditches they now had to start traversing were filled with sedge and reeds which rose high, and whose base was not yet dry with high summer. They swayed softly in the sky above them.

The sounds were strange to them, though less so to the northern moles who had travelled much and already crossed the great Thames, though by a roaring owl way. But here, in wide damp fields, the wind in the high reeds, the sound of coot scuttling in the sedge, and the croak of unseen frog, made them all uneasy. The scents, too, were heavy and threatening, of water vole and fox, and above them wheeled blackheaded seagull and once a heron darkened the sky.

They fell into silence as evening came slowly on them, each thinking grim thoughts of the escape they had had and the deaths they had been witness to. They stopped by a ditch, borrowed the abandoned tunnels of a weasel, and rested. Thin mist hung a few feet over the grass and caught the light of the setting sun, mysterious and quiet.

Then Tryfan spoke.

'I cannot think I did well as your leader,' he said, voice and snout low. 'Brevis and Willow are dead and Mayweed is lost and probably in great danger, if not already discovered and snouted. May the Stone protect him and forgive me.

'No doubt guardmoles will have stayed to watch over the wood they found us in, especially as Weed never seemed quite certain they had found us all. When Mayweed emerges he will be found and I cannot leave him up there alone, and I will not. Yet I cannot ask you to accompany me back. . . .'

'No use going back, Tryfan,' said Skint firmly. 'That Mayweed's more of a survivor than any of us.'

'No' said Tryfan, 'I must go . . .' and for a time Smithills had to restrain Tryfan from leaving them to climb the long way back to Harrowdown. But eventually he saw sense and said, 'If he *has* escaped, then the problem is knowing what Mayweed might do and where he might go.'

'Beats me how he avoided being found,' said Smithills, shaking his head in wonder and admiration. 'I've never been so nervous as I was when they were looking for him.' The others nodded their heads.

'That mole has more to him than mole might think,' said Tryfan, aware only now of how, in such a short space of time, he had grown fond of Mayweed, as of them all. 'Now, if I had been him . . .' Tryfan fell silent.

'*He* would go to the river eventually, I think,' suggested Spindle, 'because that's what he told us to do, and what he'll expect us to do.'

Tryfan agreed. 'We might wait for him or at least leave a sign we have been this way, as we agreed . . . But it's probably best to rest until the morning and see if he comes by, and if he does not then we must move on. Now you others rest a little, I'm going to watch and think,' said Tryfan, going out a little into the open.

He turned over in his mind what Mayweed might do if he had survived: come to the river, that seemed certain. But where would he go from there? Downstream to the east, towards Duncton Wood, presumably. Mayweed knew that was where Tryfan had already decided to go. That being so, and Mayweed being a sensible kind of mole when it came to routes, he would head downstream to a point where a passing mole could easily be observed: a way over the river, perhaps. Yes. . . .

As Tryfan thought like this he began to feel more hopeful. There was something about that mole Mayweed that seemed like life itself. No, no . . . But Tryfan's thoughts were brought to a stop by a beam of yellow-orange light which arced into the sky from the east, was still and then disappeared. He focussed his senses in that direction, and heard the soft rumble of roaring owl, now louder, now softer. And lights, roaring owl lights; then suddenly arcing again over the valley and going out. A crossing place. *The* place which Mayweed would find. Yes. . . .

Tryfan rejoined the others, some of whom were already asleep.

'We're leaving,' said Tryfan urgently. 'We're leaving now.' He rapidly explained his belief that they would do well to stop near a crossing place for roaring owls because it was as clear a spot as any for Mayweed to seek out. That's where he would go when he escaped and Tryfan would go there too.

'Grubby places, roaring owl haunts,' grumbled Skint. 'But maybe you're right. How far off is it do you think, and how long will we have to wait?'

'It's not far, but we may have to wait days. We must give him every chance.'

'And if he doesn't come? If he hasn't survived?'

Tryfan's face went serious.

'We will decide that when it happens. He is a worthy mole.'

They regrouped and set off immediately, approaching the river cautiously where, to their surprise, they found an easy surface route well shielded by grass. Here and there they left markings of their passing in the hope that Mayweed might find them and follow on.

There was much life about – badger by the smell, and rustling hedgehog, but nothing ominous. There was also mole, for they came upon more than one hill, fresh dug as well. They decided to pass these by, making their pawfalls heavier to disguise the fact to those below that they were moles. After what Henbane had said, the fewer who knew they were about the better.

As they progressed the lights of the roaring owls got brighter, and their turning across the landscape gave the grass and trees above them a lurid magnificence which disturbed Tryfan and Spindle more than it did the others, who had seen it before.

'Just don't look into the eyes of roaring owls,' warned Skint, 'because they mesmerise you, and keep as shielded as you can when they pass close by for the vibration is so great they can leave a mole senseless for a moment or two, and vulnerable to attack.'

The noise got louder, and the route yet closer to the river, which flowed dark and deep beneath them and on ahead, catching the great yellow lights that hung above the roaring owl way where it crossed over a stone bridge.

'Where shall we go from here?' asked Skint. 'There's no more sign of mole.' The ground was flat and grubby, covered by soggy grass which smelt unpleasantly of dogs and twofoots. They kept to the peripheral shadows and Tryfan led them round towards the base of the bridge.

'I think this is the place to which Mayweed will come: the first clear mark on the river downstream of where we were. Let's explore first and then find a suitable place to wait.'

Above them the bridge rose high and noisy, twofoots came and went, roaring owls turned and lit up, and left their heavy smell. Skint looked about uneasily.

'Never did like this kind of thing. Never got used to it. Hard for mole to live here.'

'Well, we'll have to wait here a day or two at least,' began Tryfan. Then he paused and stopped, and snouted.

'Mole!' he said. 'Look!'

Ahead, on the worn and dirty grass, was a fresh hill.

'Solitary,' said Skint, 'and just begun. Shall I explore?' But it took only a moment.

'This is not a real hill. Just the semblance of one. . . .'

It was an old mole trick to attract a mole to where he could be seen, and then attack him. Even as Skint and Tryfan turned from the hill a voice said from the shadows: 'Don't move!'

'Who . . .?' began Tryfan rearing up to fight.

336

'We are not your enemies. Go to the bridge. Do it. Now.' There was something authoritative and sympathetic in the voice and they obeyed, not looking back.

The bridge loomed nearer and its base was in deep shadow and beyond it the river was a moving blackness. As they reached the buttress of the bridge, the air became dank and cold and the ground was wet. Then it became hard and unburrowable: concrete. Nomole likes that.

'Further in, out of the light,' the voice behind said.

Above them, where the bridge arched high, there was a sudden echo of the pattern of their pawsteps on the ground.

Tryfan stopped. Ahead of them there was the shifting of paws and then a shining of snouts. Moles. Friendly it seemed.

'Right, this is as far as any of us goes until we know who you are and what your purpose with us is,' said Tryfan, bunching instinctively with the others lest they were attacked.

'Good,' said the mole, 'very good. You are welcome.'

As Tryfan's eyes adjusted to the light he saw that the mole looked familiar, though it was hard to say quite how. But even as he thought this, one of the moles ahead came forward and said, 'Hello, Sir! Pleased to see you, Sir, most welcome and glad I am and you are. Surprise for you, pleasing it will be!' and he laughed.

An appealing voice. An unctuous voice. A most beloved voice!

'Why, it's Mayweed!' cried out Tryfan going forward with pleasure and surprise.

'It's more than Mayweed, Sir' said Mayweed, 'and not just me!'

'But how . . . what . . .?' the others asked in admiration.

'Mayweed hid, Sir, and then Mayweed ran when the searching started. Mayweed ran fast as a hare, didn't he? All the way over to the stream, nasty and wet *that* was, and on to the Slopeside and there Mayweed stopped and had a think and ate a red worm. Mayweed said to himself, Tryfan won't die, not meant to. Tryfan will go down to the river by the badger runs, and over the tumbling stream, oh yes, Mayweed knows, no need to say! It was so?'

Tryfan nodded with a smile.

'Then Mayweed thought: no time at all to lose, none whatever. Get going while Henbane and the others are away. So Mayweed went off down the tunnel to the Slopeside and Mayweed remembered moles you talked of and moles you liked named, if he remembered right, Pennywort, Thyme and a guardmole you trusted named Alder and Mayweed got those moles, didn't he? All by himself he got them!'

Tryfan's heart leapt! Thyme! Alder! Pennywort! Mayweed had brought them?

'They're here?' he asked.

'Yes, Sir, tired but free.'

Out into the light they came, timid Pennywort, then Thyme, and then Ragwort, the mole who had been deputed to guide them to the visitors' burrows.

Then from behind them the mole who had commanded them to come under the bridge, and who Tryfan had half recognised, came forward. It was. . . .

'Alder?' asked Tryfan, uncertain.

'Aye Sir, me Sir. Doing my best and nervous, but Mayweed here said you would see us right, Sir.'

Tryfan looked at them all, welcomed them, and then Alder, reading his thoughts said, 'My friend Marram wouldn't come, though we tried hard to persuade him. But he won't report us, Sir.'

Tryfan was dumbstruck. All these moles safe, all followers now, all depending on him, looking to him to lead them.

'We are well met,' he said, 'and our cause is right. Now for the moment I would like to collect my thoughts alone, and then we can discuss what we shall do . . .' and he went to the river's edge and looked into its dark flowing depths and thanked the Stone that so many were safe.

Thyme went close to Spindle.

'Well!' she said. 'I thought I would not see you again!'

'Er, no,' faltered Spindle, embarrassed by her direct gaze, and surprised at the transformation in her since they had first seen her. She had fattened out and was comely.

'Um . . . you've changed,' was all he could say.

She laughed. 'And you're even thinner, if that's possible. Spindle's a good name for you!'

'Yes,' sighed poor Spindle, who had always found it hard speaking to females. They took his breath away, especially ones like Thyme. 'I suppose I am. Not the best of diets in the Slopeside, and up on Harrowdown.'

'I hoped I might see you again,' said Thyme softly.

'Well here I am then!' said Spindle looking this way and that.

At which Thyme laughed.

'Better see if Tryfan's all right,' muttered Spindle turning from her. Then he went off awkwardly and she watched after him, smiling.

It seemed an age that Tryfan stared into the darkness of the great river. Above them the roaring owls quietened, and fewer showed their shining eyes into the night. Then the great yellow lights over the bridge suddenly faltered and went out. Occasionally the voices of twofoots sounded for a moment or two, and one came down to the shadows of the bridge to leave its spoor there, and show what its territory might be.

Its breathing was heavy, its step clumsy and heavy, and the moles shrank and backed away into deeper shadow sickened by its smell. Then it was gone, a roaring owl roared and shone, and went away into the night. And all was silent.

Tryfan turned and faced them, and they came to him, staring at him in the dim light of stars and masked moon.

'Outcasts are we now,' said Tryfan, speaking slowly and deliberately, 'with little strength but that we make for ourselves as one. But I believe that if we trust each other, and have faith in the Stone, then what was started today at

Harrowdown will be known in time throughout moledom, and will begin the ending of the Word.

'But long will the struggle be, and much suffering will we have to bear.' He paused and looked at them one by one, to see if they faltered or were irresolute. He saw only trust and faith.

'Now listen,' he said boldly. 'To Duncton Wood will I lead you, by ways known only to scribemoles, which Boswell taught me. And there we will gather others and make an army of Stone followers whose purpose will be to put the Word to rout.

'But that will only be the beginning. For we followers will prepare ourselves for the coming of one who will help us hear the Silence of the Stone. For it is ours to hear if we have strength, and courage and good purpose. The mole that will come in our time will be great and good, and for him must we be ready.'

'What is his name?' asked Thyme.

'In the old books and prophecies of Uffington he is called the Stone Mole, but his name nomole knows, nor will they know it until he is among us.'

'What is he?' asked Pennywort her brother.

'One more than all of us. One who has Silence and can forgive. Wisdom is his and love; purpose and kindness. By him will the burden of the grikes be lifted, with him will the last snouting be; his coming is the Stone's blessing on mole, our time is the age that has been chosen.'

They stared at him, wondering. He spoke powerfully and his words echoed in the bridged space above them.

Then one by one Tryfan touched and blessed each mole there, as a scribemole should, and he spoke their names. 'Bless thee, Alder . . . and thee, Thyme . . . bless. . . .'

'He's not just a mole,' whispered Thyme to Pennywort, 'that's for sure.'

'N – no, I don't think he is,' replied Pennywort.

While in the darkness there Thyme let her flank touch Spindle's, and Spindle did not draw away.

'Are you scared?' she asked him.

'No,' he said simply. And she looked at his talons and gaunt flanks and felt strangely touched.

'Spindle!' she said, her voice a little more commanding.

He turned to her in the dim light. And she to him.

'Then why are you shaking?' she said.

He grinned a little sheepishly.

'Not used to being touched,' he said.

'It doesn't hurt,' she whispered.

'No,' he said settling his flank to hers, 'it doesn't *seem* to.'

'So when do we leave?' called out Skint above the chatter.

'Now!' said Tryfan. 'Now we leave!'

At which he turned out from under the bridge, climbed up the bank at its side, and, passing silently over its wide reach, started to lead the followers on their long trek east to Duncton Wood.

PART III

Duncton Wood

Chapter Twenty-One

Duncton Wood is the most easterly of the seven Ancient Systems of moledom, and today, as ever since the events with which the Duncton Chronicles are concerned, it is the most beloved.

Yet even now it remains one of the more mysterious of the seven and certainly the least visited, for it is cut off from other systems, being surrounded on three sides by the great sweep of the Thames and its associated marshes; while on the fourth it is bounded by an enormous way for roaring owls which travelling moles are disinclined to cross. Yet passing under it is difficult for the only route is by a huge and echoing concrete cross-under, used by cows, in which a mole feels much exposed.

The ancient Wood itself, which is beech and ash in its highest parts and oak lower down, is on a hill which rises majestically from the clay vales of those parts, and the river and way are sufficiently distant that the moles of Duncton rarely hear the roaring owls and never visit the river. To the west are the Pastures, wherein live the Pasture moles, who are no friend of Duncton though they share its isolated site.

When Tryfan's parents, Bracken and Rebecca, were young, the active system was for the main part located on the northern lower slopes of the hill. Indeed the Stone for which Duncton had been famous, and whose holy powers had made it one of the seven, stood neglected among the great beech trees at the top of the hill, guarding the deserted tunnels of the lost and forgotten Ancient System.

It was to those tunnels that young Bracken turned and found inspiration to lead his system back to its beginnings; and later, with Rebecca, to lead the moles of Duncton through the period of their trouble of which, perhaps, their neglect of the Stone was a precursor. But whatmole can tell? It is enough that Duncton was torn by feuding and strife and two moles emerged for a time as the evil leaders of the system: Mandrake of Siabod, Rebecca's father, was one; Rune the other, known now to be of Whern and a Master of Dark Sound. Evil was he, and enemy to Bracken, lusting after Rebecca and might have had her had not Bracken protected his own. So Rune and the sideem, of which he was the spiritual leader, had reason to respect Duncton . . . and reason to wish it destroyed and the moles there forever dishonoured. Their rule was ended only by the coming of the plagues, and the fire which destroyed many trees on the Wood's lower slopes.

So that by the time Tryfan was born, Rune and his doings seemed little more than a bad memory, and the survivors of the troubles were content to follow Bracken and Rebecca up into the Ancient System and there, under their guidance and following the example of their love, established an order that venerated the Stone with simplicity and faith; and celebrated the festivals with merriment and story-telling, especially those of Midsummer's Day in June and the greatest of them all, Longest Night, which comes in December and marks the seasons' great turn from darkness to light.

So it was into a bruised but hopeful system that Tryfan had been born, and a once-venerable one; and one whose Stone gave him a sense of purpose and love, and whose parentage gave him strength and courage.

When the seventh Stillstone was found beneath the great Stone of Duncton, and rescued by Boswell, it was natural that Tryfan, the born leader of his generation, should accompany old Boswell back to Uffington.

Natural too that Tryfan's half-brother Comfrey, born of Rue and Bracken but nurtured and raised by Rebecca, should take over the mantle of healer and leader, timid though he seemed then and unsure of himself. But what he lacked in outward strength he made up for with an inner

346

peace and love, and trust – he it was who had given
Rebecca the faith to leave Duncton in search of her
beloved Bracken when he most needed her, and it was
Comfrey who led the Duncton moles in her absence, and
gave them hope in the long years following her final
departure with Bracken to the Silence of the Stone. Much
was the timid-seeming Comfrey respected, and much
loved.

When his younger half-brother Tryfan had left with
Boswell, Comfrey's last words to them as they left were
but a whisper, and a stuttered one, for his birth had left
him with that defect: 'M – m – may they return home
safeguarded,' and he had laughed, which was a rare thing
for him, for he had trust that the Stone would protect them
on their perilous journey. And one day, perhaps, one day,
the brother he most loved would come back at last. . . .

It was November, and from over the Pastures came the
kind of blustering cold wind Comfrey liked, driving the
odd remaining leaves on the trees before it, and reminding
a mole that if he has not got his winter tunnels ready he had
better do so, for the rains and the cold were coming, and
snow too perhaps before another moleyear was out, and
the time of keeping down and out of sight was on paw.

'Tum, tee, t-t-tum,' hummed Comfrey to himself as he
bustled around his burrow near the Stone, wrinkling his
snout as he looked about and indulged in his favourite
pastime, which was to jumble up his pile of herbs and
seeds into a new and even more sweet-scented untidiness.

Then overhead a mole stumped and, entering down one
of his burrow's entrances, called out, 'Comfrey, are you
there?'

Which of course he was, he always was when he was
needed, for that is the healer's first art, taught him by Rose
and then Rebecca: to be there when needed. Sometimes
moles came visiting just for the sake of it, for they liked the
comfort of his tunnels, and the sense of harmonious
disorder.

347

'C-c-come down!' called out Comfrey, continuing his task and muttering to himself as he did so: 'Now where . . . w-w-*where* are those wre–wretched . . . no, not here. There. yes. Oh no, not there. I know, or I think I know . . .' How Duncton moles would laugh with pleasure at his absent-mindedness, not knowing it was his way of making them feel at ease, and relaxing them so they might find healing in just being. For he knew well that healing is not in the herb, but in the manner of the paw that gives the herb, and the heart that receives it.

'Cold wind, Comfrey,' said his visitor.

'Is it? C-c-cold, Maundy?' He was glad to see her for of all Duncton moles he felt most content with her, and knew that she had least need of healing or advice or anything much else.

'I think so,' said Maundy.

'Oh!' said Comfrey, vaguely puzzled. He didn't remember it being cold when he was out on the surface a little while before. He just remembered it ruffling his worn fur pleasantly, and bending the trees and shaking their branches above his head. He remembered thinking the season didn't matter much to a mole of the Stone.

'Those autumn youngsters are doing well,' said Maundy, who had a burrow on the Eastside, and often came to talk to Comfrey and bring him the system's news. Neither had a mate, nor seemed to wish for one now, though she had had one once and pupped, but it was enough they were friends who remembered the old days and enjoyed a chat. Their fur was tatty now, their snouts wrinkled, and they laughed at memories others had forgotten or were too young to know.

'D-d-doing well, are they? I'm glad, really I am. The system needs youngsters.'

'Needs more'n youngsters, Comfrey; needs life,' said Maundy darkly.

'T-t-takes time to recover from plague. A generation or t-t-two, and the Ancient System is not so worm-rich as the lower slopes were.'

348

'One day, maybe . . .' started Maundy, and stated her opinion, often expressed, that it might be a good idea for somemole or other to start exploring the lower slopes again.

'The St-Stone will tell us. Not till then.'

The female shrugged.

'You know best, Comfrey, everymole knows that.'

'The St-Stone knows best,' said Comfrey gently, repeating something he often said, 'n-not me. I just listen to its Silence and say what comes from there. Anymole may do that.'

'Not so well as you!' declared Maundy. 'You had Bracken and Rebecca to teach you!'

'Yes,' said Comfrey, 'I did.'

She saw a look of nostalgia and a little sadness come over his face, and she knew she was one of the few in Duncton allowed to see that.

'Do you miss them?' she asked, coming closer so he might feel her care for him. A leader and healer is often alone, and needs love as much as other moles.

'S-s-sometimes I do,' said Comfrey. 'I miss Rebecca in the spring, when the anemones come out. She used to love them, and danced among them, even when she was old. I miss Bracken at moments when I know I must be strong of will, because he was. B-b-but. . . .'

'Yes, Comfrey?' and her voice might almost have been Rebecca's in its sympathy for him.

'Well, I miss . . . I miss T-Tryfan. He was my half-brother and I liked him. He was stronger than me. Do *you* remember him?'

'We all remember him, who were alive at the time he and Boswell left for Uffington. Never seen a more handsome mole than him.'

'D-do you really think so?' said Comfrey.

' 'Course I do. And he loved you like he loved Bracken.'

'How do you know that?'

'I could tell.'

'Oh,' said Comfrey. 'Well, I miss him in the autumn

because that's when he left. And I go up to the Stone and pray for him. In fact I did it today.'

'And what did the Stone tell you?'

Comfrey was silent, snout lowered, his talons teasing at the stem of dried thyme that lay along one wall of the burrow. Maundy eyed him, much concerned, for though she was allowed to see him like this yet he was rarely so troubled. And she was not entirely surprised, for something had drawn her over to his burrow that day, something that told her she was needed.

'It did tell you something?' she said encouragingly.

'Yes it d-d-did' said Comfrey at last, 'and n-n-not for the first time! At Midsummer's Night I went up to the Stone, after everymole was below ground. Tryfan needed my help and I gave it him.'

Comfrey said this as if it was the most natural of things, and Maundy had no doubt that it was the truth. She believed in the power of the Stone, and knew very well how much Comfrey missed his brother and how often he thought of him.

'So what happened today?' she asked.

'As I prayed for Tryfan I saw tunnels deserted, and they were Duncton tunnels. And I saw blood. I saw evil. The Stone's Silence was gone and there was noise and hurt. Something's going to happen here and I d-d-don't know what it is.'

'Did you learn anything of Tryfan?'

'N-not sure. Unclear.' Comfrey was silent again.

'Shall I say a prayer to the Stone for you?' said Maundy, because sometimes she did and she knew he appreciated it.

'Well I st-stopped today because I was afraid! Not perfect, am I? But now you're here I feel better and we could g-g-go back to the St-St-Stone and say *something*,' he said.

Out on the surface the wind was still blustery enough to part a mole's fur this way and that, and to send leaves, which were soggy from overnight rain, helter-skelter among the surface roots and back again.

They traversed the rising ground between Comfrey's highest tunnel entrance and the Stone clearing, and approached reverently the Stone itself, which rose massively above them, the branches of the beech trees behind it swaying against its passive immobility, their bark a shining grey in the dull November light.

In Bracken and Rebecca's day an additional beech tree had stood adjacent to the Stone, tipping it over to one side, until, on a day much like this, it had fallen mightily, its roots heaving and shifting out of the soil around the Stone which instead of itself falling had been shaken and then shifted back into an upright position. Twofoots, who rarely troubled Duncton Wood, had come and taken the fallen tree away and levelled the area around the Stone, and since then left it in peace, so that now the disturbed chalk soil had flattened and two seasons of beech leaves had drifted across it, and the Stone stood proudly alone.

Comfrey's prayers and invocations were special to him, for he had become healer by accident and circumstance. But then Rebecca herself had been wayward in the art of invocation, and so had Rose, who had lived out on the Pastures and was not traditional in any way at all. Perhaps healers are always so. In any case, Comfrey had a poor memory for words, and little feeling for rhythm, preferring to talk to the Stone as if it were a mole just like himself.

'Well,' he began, 'we thought we'd say a pr-prayer for T-Tryfan, who is a worthy mole.'

'Yes,' agreed Maundy, staring up to the distant heights of the Stone and then all the way down again and feeling small as a pup.

'I wasn't happy before about things,' continued Comfrey, 'th-things going to happen, and I'm not now. And I hope Tryfan is protected and if we need him that'll he'll come back soon.'

He snouted about here and there as if he smelt a scent but could not quite make out its nature or direction. He gazed up at the Stone. It seemed almost to be moving against the stirring branches and drifting grey cloud beyond it. Tilting westwards . . . So, taking the hint, he turned round and headed to where the clearing abuts the Pastures on the western side of the wood, which is not many moleyards from the Stone itself. Maundy followed him, asking what was apaw, but he ignored her, snouting the air instead as if, as if. . . .

'It is T-Tryfan,' he said.

'What about him?' said Maundy. '*What* about him?'

'He's coming,' said Comfrey matter of factly, 'but he's in trouble, he's not happy. Yes. Th-that's it.'

He looked round seriously at Maundy and said with a quiet certainty mixed with surprise, 'Tryfan's coming home. He is!'

'But that's good, Comfrey!' said Maundy.

'No . . . it's n-not good,' said Comfrey firmly. 'There's trouble.'

'When's he coming?' asked Maundy.

'Soon,' said Comfrey, snouting about a bit more and sniffing a few times, and then crouching down with his snout facing over the Pastures to the west. 'Well,' he added, 'soonish.'

But when other moles in Duncton heard the prediction that Tryfan was returning, 'soonish' seemed an irritably long time coming.

Within hours of Comfrey's announcement the whole system was abuzz with the news: Comfrey had prophesied Tryfan's homecoming, and therefore it would be. Soon, too. Tryfan, the young mole who had honoured the system by being guardmole to old Boswell. Tryfan coming home!

Some moles immediately set about cleaning out their burrows, others wondered whether (and if not why not?) he had found a mate and if so what young they had had. On the other paw (observed others) he might have become a scribemole and *they're* celibate. But then, if he was coming home he could not be a scribemole, and as he had

352

wanted to be something must have gone wrong. Yes, something was wrong. So euphoria gave way to doubt, doubt to unease, and unease to more surmise so that every possibility under the sun and many under the moon was discussed and assessed.

The practical problem was *when* was he coming? – for the moles who expected him within hours of Comfrey's announcement were soon disappointed.

Only one thing was agreed by everymole: Tryfan should be greeted, and greeted properly. Which meant somemole or moles better go and meet him.

Maundy herself was the main force for this idea and gained Comfrey's support for it except that, as he pointed out, Tryfan might come from almost any direction.

'You were snouting towards the west when you said you felt he was coming,' observed Maundy.

'Oh dear. Was I? Well that's probably right. That's where Uffington is, sort of. I sup-sup-suppose he'll be coming from there.'

Then other moles remembered that the only way into and out of Duncton Wood was by the cow cross-under which went beneath the roaring owl way to the south east, and so a couple of moles were sent off across the Pastures and round to the way itself, and there they waited patiently. For a day. For two. . . .

Until they were replaced and others went and doubts set in about Comfrey's prediction. And anyway, the grumblers began to suggest, nomole wants strangers in a system and one mole means more moles, so Tryfan's coming might not be such a good idea after all.

But Comfrey remained quietly certain. He could feel the fact of Tryfan's approach but not the when of it. Then November gave way to December and the cheerful prospect of Longest Night, and most moles' thoughts were on other things than the prophecy of Tryfan's return.

Naturally some hoped he would come back especially for that holy night, but most said, 'Don't you count on it, it's been a moleyear and a half since Comfrey's prophecy and not a snout in sight, and hardly a mole these days who'll go and do the greeter's duty! Not me! I've done it twice already!'

Which was true enough, for most had put up with travelling down to the roaring owl way and waited vainly in the cold for Tryfan's return. Of course it would be an honour to be the mole who was there . . . but a mole's got better things to do with Longest Night coming and preparations to be made, and youngsters to be reminded of the songs and rituals.

So Longest Night came and with it all the excitement of the season. The rituals began early in the afternoon, as the light began to fail, and one by one, or in twos and occasional threes, the moles made their way by tunnel and surface to the Stone. Some whispered their own prayers, others stared at the Stone as darkness fell which made it seem even more massive than it already was.

Many came to meet old friends whom they might not have seen for many a moleyear, for moles like peace and quiet if they can find it, and nomole disturbs a known solitary.

So there was chatter and quiet laughter, and the celebrants came and went, each one remembering to whisper the name Linden, for she was the first White Mole, and her story is always remembered and repeated on Longest Night.

The clouds thinned above and the moon began to show – misty, perhaps, but visible enough to mole, a good sign for the cycle of seasons ahead. A mole likes to see the moon show on Longest Night.

Comfrey made his own visit to the Stone, barely noticed at first, but when he was moles let him be for all knew he liked to say his prayers undisturbed. When he had done, Maundy wished him a happy Longest Night, a little shyly perhaps, and they nudged each other in a friendly way which others liked to see, for if ever two moles should have mated it was those two.

'So is Tryfan coming tonight then?' somemole said out

of the dark, daring to ask the question all wanted an answer to. For all hoped he would, though few dared admit it, for there was an air of incompletion and waiting over *this* Longest Night.

'He's very near,' said Comfrey. 'I th-think he'll come.'

'Is he very fierce?' asked a youngster, for Tryfan was famous among them and many tales had been told of him.

'He's strong,' said Comfrey.

'But is he fierce?'

'I don't th-think so,' said Comfrey smiling. 'Except with enemies.'

'He's clever, isn't he?'

'Yes,' said Comfrey.

'And ever so good-looking,' giggled a young female, born the previous spring and not yet mated.

Comfrey didn't answer that.

'Shall we wait for him then?' asked somemole else.

'N-n-no. Waiting slows things down,' said Comfrey. 'We'll have some good food down in the communal chamber and tell some tales. And maybe a mole or two can stay on the surface to greet him.'

But nomole wanted to do that on such a night, and Comfrey himself could not as he was needed to lead the festivities. 'Well,' he said, reluctantly allowing himself to be dragged down to the chamber, 'it would be b-b-better . . .' But one mole quietly left them and made her way to the surface, for she could see Comfrey was unhappy not to have somemole there to greet Tryfan should he come.

'Where's M-M-Maundy?' asked Comfrey later, noting her absence and feeling sad, for he liked to have his old friend nearby on such a night as this. But nomole knew.

Out on the surface, by the Stone, Maundy watched the night deepen and listened for a time to the muffled chatter and laughter of the celebrating moles.

She sighed and said a whispered prayer or two, thinking that there could be no better gift for Comfrey, who had given so much to Duncton Wood so selflessly, than the arrival of Tryfan. And yet . . . the night deepened, and the revellers were getting quieter and some, no doubt, especially the youngsters, were beginning to grow tired and think that a snooze would be a good thing for a mole to do before trekking back from the communal burrow to their own burrows to east and west and north.

Old Maundy sighed, wished her wish again, and, thinking that it was as fine a night as any could desire on Longest Night, she set off out of the wood on to the Pastures, down to the way itself, as if by doing so, she might bring Tryfan nearer sooner, if he was ever going to come at all.

Then, when she reached a point near the cow cross-under through which she expected visitors to come, and with the way's sides rising steeply above her into the night, she settled down to wait, watching the high passage of the roaring owls, whose eyes gazed on the edges of the way above, but whose fumes, mercifully, a mole rarely smelt down below. Back and forth they went, in ones and twos, the ones going south on the far side of the way. Strange things, thought Maundy, roaring and shaking and gazing so far.

If you're on the way, Tryfan of Duncton, please hurry up! she said to herself, staring ahead at the tunnel beneath the way that moles travelling from the west would need to use. Then she smiled, for it was a good night on which to spend a little time alone, to think of the past seasons, and those new ones about to come.

'Mole! It's mole! It *is* mole!'

Poor Maundy had fallen asleep and now woke very frightened, for a huge male was looming over her, quite close.

Beyond him were the daunting rising heights of concrete that formed the pillars leading to where the roaring owls ran. Before her was the fearsome wall that girded the pillars, and beneath it the tunnel that led (so it was said) under the way. Not that she had ever tried it, she had never been further afield than this, and never wanted to.

Now, from so close she could hardly focus on him, a mole said, 'Mole!' and sounded very fierce.

'Hello!' she said into the darkness, as brightly as she could.

'It *is* mole,' said a different voice. 'Beware!'

And then, before she could so much as gulp, Maundy felt a talon at her right flank, and another at her left, and saw a third mole stancing off ahead as two more came out of the cross-under tunnel.

'Whatmole though? Of the Word? Of the Stone? Vagrant? Diseased?' They chattered among themselves in deep voices and then gently but firmly pulled her into the light that was cast down on the ground from the roaring owl way above.

'Well, I was . . .' she began. Then, fully awake, and feeling suddenly annoyed, Maundy shook herself, peered around at these threatening moles and said proudly, 'Of Duncton am I! And that means you can take your talons right out of my flanks *now*, young mole!'

There was a deep laugh at her side.

'*Young* mole eh, Smithills?' said Skint. 'She thinks I'm young!'

'And what if she does?' said Smithills, politely going to the front of this fierce old female. 'That makes me young too!' He grinned in as friendly a way as he could manage to show he meant her no harm.

'Who are you?' said Maundy, her voice a little shaky. 'And why threaten a harmless mole like me?'

'Begging your pardon,' said Smithills, 'but we were just checking you out.'

'Checking me out?' repeated Maundy angrily. 'Check *me* out? I live here. I'm here to check *you* out!'

'These are dangerous times, and cross-unders like these can be traps for the unwary. Why aren't you snug in a burrow with your friends celebrating Longest Night?' asked the one called Skint.

'I *was* until I came down here,' said Maundy. 'I . . .' But she stopped, for through the tunnel came more moles until she seemed surrounded by them. 'I came down to greet a mole, not to be insulted and threatened by strangers!'

A mole, still in the shadows, moved forward a little and Skint turned to him.

'She says she's of Duncton,' said Skint, 'and I'm ready to believe her.'

The new mole laughed, deep and happy, and there was something about him, warm and reassuring, that put old Maundy, who was perfectly willing to defend herself against a hundred moles if need be, quite at her ease.

'Well!' she said. 'And who are you?'

He came out fully into the light and stared at her, and she stared back, uncertain, half recognising him, but not quite sure. . . .

'Don't you know me, Maundy? After all this time have I been quite forgotten?'

'Well!' she replied, excited and suddenly breathless. 'But you're – ' and then she reached out and touched him in the most natural and friendly way as if to see that he was really there.

'I *am* real,' he said, laughing again.

'And so I should hope, Tryfan of Duncton. You're late!' she said.

'Late?' echoed Tryfan.

'*Late?*' said Skint.

'Late?' said the others, amazed.

'That's what I said, and that's what I meant! Duncton moles don't gallivant around the countryside on Longest Night, they pay their respect to the Stone, they eat a bit, they sing a bit, they stay in one place and they tell stories. And . . .' she added, advancing threateningly on Skint and Smithills, 'they don't go scaring old moles like me! You're late, Tryfan, and you'd better come along because by the time we get there they'll all be asleep.'

She turned to lead him back up towards the Wood, but

then she suddenly stopped and turned back to him, her seeming anger gone. She touched Tryfan again with that same warmth his friends recognised as being like his own, and she said, 'Nomole will be more welcome on this night or any other. Welcome home, Tryfan. Has your journey been long?'

'Longer than a mole's life,' he said. 'Is Comfrey – ?'

'Comfrey is well and awaits you. He will greet you with joy.'

'Did he guess I was coming?'

'The Stone told him in November for sure, but I think he knew at Midsummer. We've been waiting, Tryfan, and we have need of thee.'

'As I of Comfrey and of you all,' he replied. Then he smiled around at his friends.

'Did I not say Comfrey would know?' he said to them.

'You did!' said Spindle.

'Comfrey knew,' said Maundy. 'Now follow me and feel welcome, for there's food and song awaiting Tryfan, and any who are his friends, in the tunnels of Duncton Wood!'

So it was that old Maundy led Tryfan and the other followers on the final stage of the journey into Duncton, at that most holy of hours, just after midnight on Longest Night, when moledom knows that a new cycle of seasons is beginning.

Some say that even as they reached the edge of the Pastures Comfrey knew Tryfan had returned, for he stopped in mid-song, snouted up at the surface, and said quietly, 'I th-think you can waken the youngsters again, and c-come with me, for T-Tryfan my brother is come back.'

Then up to the surface he went, and the moles of Duncton followed him, gathering at the Stone as from over the Pastures they heard the coming of moles, and at their head was Maundy, proud and sure as any mole could be, and tears wetted her fur for the happiness she knew she brought that night to Comfrey by the Stone.

'T-T-Tryfan?' said Comfrey as his brother came out of the dark of his long journey. 'It *is* Tryfan!'

And whatmole was there who did not share their tears as the two brothers, separated for so many moleyears, greeted each other with affectionate pats and friendly snouts and words of love and pleasure.

'You've got a few more lines in your face, you have!' said Tryfan.

'And s-so have you!' replied Comfrey.

And they all laughed, and joked, and praised the Stone for the blessing of reunion it had wrought.

Then when the greetings were done, Tryfan introduced his companions.

'This is Spindle of Seven Barrows, who has been a friend and counsellor on all my long journey from Uffington; and this Skint, who –' and one by one they were introduced: all safe, all well, all close and trusting of one another. Except for one, who had made himself scarce.

Then there was another round of introductions as Comfrey made Tryfan's friends known to those of the system who were there, concluding, 'And, last but not least, in f-f-fact most of all, my dear friend Maundy who greeted you and led you home! Yes!' said Comfrey, glad to have Maundy at his side. 'Yes!' And if each touched the other, and laughed and seemed like mates why this *was* Longest Night, and a mole had best enjoy himself, and herself, and all.

'When you've quite done,' declared Skint, 'and not wishing to be impolite, and with the compliments of the season and all that, *is there any food?*'

Food! There was that! And song! There would be that as well! And stories, many of those to tell! And more food! Much, much, more of that!

'Below, everymole below!' cried Comfrey, 'And we'll have a Longest N-N-Night that nomole will forget!'

But when they got below one mole was already there, crouched in the most comfortable stance, chewing the

juiciest worm, surrounded by the most admiring youngsters.

'A pleasure it is, and a pleasure will be, Sir!' said the
mole, with a wide and winning smile. 'Got tired up there
and came down here, thought it best to do so soon, Sir, I
did! Yes. And no better burrow, no better youngsters,
rarely better worms has this humble mole seen, or (Sir)
eaten on Longest Night, not ever before!'

'Who is this?' said Comfrey, amazed at this mole who
stopped everymole in his tracks with this long speech of
. . . well . . . of greeting, he supposed.

'Mayweed is my name and I am most welcome!' said
Mayweed, looking guiltily at Tryfan.

And then they laughed, and told Mayweed to stay in the
comfortable place he was, adding that since he had eaten
the first worm of all of them it would be only fitting if he
told the first story, which Mayweed did not want to do at
all, but if they insisted, he supposed he might try, if it
pleased them, and he would, yes, he would!

So as the moles of Duncton and the followers of Tryfan
found a place in that warm, friendly and crowded
chamber, it was Mayweed the outcast, Mayweed the
survivor, who began the story-telling saying, in the
traditional way (well nearly), 'From my heart, Sirs and
Madams, to yours, I'll speak and tell of how a humble
mole, skinny once but fatter now, diseased once but
healthier now, lonely once but befriended now, of how
that mole, born in the Slopeside of distant Buckland, came
by routes diverse and difficult, secret and strange, Sirs and
Madams, all the long way to a system mysterious where
now he is and you are, which is here and called Duncton;
that's what I'll tell in my own simple way, if you'll
listen. . . .'

'Yes! Yes! We will!' laughed the many, some eating,
some sighing, some snuggling close to others that they
liked, and Comfrey smiling at Tryfan, and Maundy
smiling at them both.

'Well then, Sirs (and not forgetting Madams), I'll

begin . . .' and Mayweed did, beginning a story-telling such as few systems in moledom that night can have witnessed, and none could ever have forgotten.

Chapter Twenty-Two

Yet when the story-telling was done, and Longest Night past, and the excitement of Tryfan's return with his followers was over, Comfrey soon learned that his instinct had been right: Tryfan's coming heralded trouble for the system and perhaps the shedding of blood.

'I do not know if this danger would be on you if I had not come back here,' Tryfan said one day, 'for I and those with me are outcast by Henbane, and her guardmoles will continue to seek us until they find us, for our very being is an affront to their Word. Defiance is not part of their sterile canon. But, in any case, I am certain they will come here because Henbane not only knows this is my home system, but that it is one of the two remaining seven Ancient Systems outside the orbit of the Word; the other is dread Siabod.

'For this reason, as well as my own need to see Duncton again, I have come to warn you to prepare for a dark future.'

January had come, and with it the winter blizzards, and they were snugly crouched in Comfrey's burrow surrounded by the sweet summery smell of herbs as the harsh wind rattled and cursed at the entrances. Comfrey listened to Tryfan now as he had listened to the grim tales told on Longest Night of their fugitive journey, yet it all seemed hard to believe, for the kind of evil and change that these 'grikes' brought was beyond his experience. It was true that rumours of the Word and the grikes had reached Duncton Wood, but for the most part the Duncton moles had kept themselves isolated and out of touch with the spread of the Word.

Now, to convince him that drastic action might be

needed if Duncton's peaceful way of life, centred on the Stone, was to survive, Tryfan reported in more detail some of the things he had seen, or heard from witnesses.

In Fyfield, to the west, the grikes had come the previous spring and sequestered an entire generation of pups and juveniles on the pretext that the adults in the system – and there were not many after the plagues – would learn thereby the meaning of Atonement. The youngsters were reared to the Word by eldrenes and sideem, and encouraged to report on their parents' 'wrongdoings' and 'blasphemies'. Many were the deaths that followed from this and that system now was fanatically devoted to the Word.

In Frilford, a system on sandy heights above the Thames, the grikes judged each mole there for their willingness to learn the Word and be faithful to it. Again, the youngsters were encouraged to adhere to its harsh codes and disciplines, and again the parents and the elders were effectively destroyed. Only a few escaped and these were the witnesses Tryfan was able to speak with.

'We heard that the moles who failed the grike-inspired inquisition were taken out on to the flood plains of the Thames and forced to burrow into waterlogged soil, on pain of snouting. Many were so killed, or snouted. The moles who accepted the Word and Atoned satisfactorily were encouraged to watch this torture, and to mock the victims as being not of the Word. A few poor moles had been granted their Atonement by pushing others on to the flood plains to their doom. Of these most are now maddened and cast down, and are serving out their blighted lives as clearers.'

In Bladon, Tryfan reported, there had been similar campaigns against the older moles by the younger, aided and abetted by grikes, and it seemed reasonable to assume that it was in this way that throughout moledom the followers of the Stone were suppressed, and belief in the Word established.

'Yet in each of the few systems we have seen there have

been protesters and rebels, for there will always be moles who are not easily subjugated,' said Tryfan. 'In each system we visited, or of which we heard, there were one or two such. Some wanted to join us, but we were not ready. What I did say was that when Henbane and the others march on Duncton, then as such moles hear of it they should take their courage in their paws, and make for Duncton as speedily as they can, to inform us of what is apaw, and join with us. I believe that by this means we will have good warning of the approach on our system of the grikes, and will gather here only those moles who have true courage and fortitude. For those will be the ones we need in the future, and in their brave paws will the future lie. Let Duncton be their sanctuary and their inspiration.'

Comfrey nodded but said nothing. The world he knew was quieter and more peaceable than this, and he could see that the Duncton of the future would need a different mole than he to lead it.

'What of the few followers you have brought with you?' he asked. 'They seem a varied lot!'

Tryfan laughed. 'The Stone has its ways, and I have been blessed to find moles worthy of the great quest that Boswell sent me on. Over the long moleyears of our journey here I have grown to trust each of these moles, as much as I would you yourself, Comfrey. Each is loyal, and each has different qualities and skills.

'Skint, for example, whose history I have told you, has become an expert at roaring owl ways, and leads us across in safety in places other moles would die; Mayweed is as good an underground route-finder as ever there will be, and he has courage and loyalty. Thyme and Pennywort bring good humour and quiet faith to us all, especially Thyme who has that quality a few moles possess of making a burrow where she is a warm place, a comfortable place, and one that calms the moles about her. Smithills uses his great strength to protect the faithful, while Alder seems to understand how to deploy moles to best advantage, and at Frilford certainly saved all our lives by clever generalship.

He is trained as a guardmole, and understands grike ways of fighting.'

'And Spindle?' asked Comfrey.

Tryfan's eyes softened. 'Nomole, *nomole*, has been truer to me than he. Boswell gave him the task of seeing that I kept my faith and purpose and he could not have chosen better.'

For a time they were silent and then Tryfan said, 'And what of this mole Maundy? She seems fond of you, Comfrey.'

'Wh-what of her?' said Comfrey mildly.

'Well,' said Tryfan. 'Have you not mated with her? She seems always near. . . .'

'Never enough time, Tryfan, so much to do. Too old now for that sort of thing! No *time*.'

Tryfan laughed and then fell serious.

'Time is running out, brother,' he said, 'and you had best do as the Stone desires.'

'Perhaps,' said Comfrey with a sigh, nervously pushing a pile of thyme-leaved toadflax one way then another. 'M-m-maybe I will!'

Then he looked at Tryfan, and touched him affectionately, and said, 'What about you, Tryfan? Have you not found a mole to love?'

Tryfan grew more silent, and just a little distant. But at last he said, 'Well, when I was ordained by Boswell I took upon myself a vow of celibacy. Not that Boswell asked it of me, and indeed it is more traditional than mandatory in the Holy Burrows. But, well, there is much to do, many places to go, and I must care for the followers of the Stone, as you have cared for the moles of Duncton Wood. No time, Comfrey! No time!'

Comfrey shook his head doubtfully.

'Doesn't seem right to me for you to be celibate. I'm different, always have been, but you, Tryfan, well, you're a mole to love and be loved. Don't you ever – ?'

'Yes, I do! And as January passes and February comes I shall think of it more, but celibate I shall stay. Perhaps one day, if peace should come, and the Stone is worshipped once more, then I can take a mate. But for now I shall not.' He frowned and looked irritable and Comfrey changed the subject hastily. At times Tryfan could be intimidating, even to him.

'Now, Tryfan, there was one thing you did not mention on Longest Night, and have never mentioned since: the Stillstone? Tell me of that.'

Which he was about to do when, with a stamp and a shake and a brrr! Maundy joined them, snow melting on her fur:''Tis wet and cold and mucky outside,' she declared, 'but here I am!'

Tryfan watched with pleasure as Comfrey welcomed her and made her comfortable in his simple way, bringing her food and talking amiably of this and that for a time.

Then he turned back to Tryfan saying, 'Maundy can be trusted, she kn-knows the secrets of the system far better than I do! So tell us of the Stillstone.'

Looking at them both then, crouched flank to flank and as trusting as a loving pair could ever be, was a moment Tryfan ever afterwards remembered, because it was then that he understood that though a mole can only ever hear the Silence of the Stone alone, yet it is unlikely that he will ever hear it if he has not known the true love of another mole. In that, he afterwards would say, he first began to suspect the nature of the quest that Boswell had sent him on. Perhaps, too, it was in that moment, that his yearning for a mole like Maundy at his side deepened and became a longing whose frustration might be the greatest sorrow in his life, and whose satisfaction might be the the greatest joy.

So then, asked about the Stillstone, Tryfan settled down, and told Comfrey and Maundy what had happened at Uffington and how Spindle had led Boswell and himself to the stone field near Seven Barrows, and how he had himself hurled that Stillstone out into the night to fall anonymous among a hundred thousand other stones; and there to wait until a mole came who would take it, and the

367

other Stillstones, seven in all, back to their final resting place.

'And then . . .?' asked Comfrey.

'And then, I think, the work that so many moles have done, and which old Boswell oversees like the White Mole he is, will be done, and well done. But more than that I cannot say!'

'And what d-do you say t-to that?' Comfrey asked of Maundy.

' 'Tis a story and a half, and I say that at the end of it all Tryfan should have a mate!' said Maundy bluntly. 'As for the Stillstones, they'll sort themselves out well enough I should think.'

'Humph!' said Comfrey, and left them, a little tetchily, to peer out on to the surface, and burrow a route up to the snow, where he could crouch and say some prayers.

When he was gone Maundy said, 'Tryfan, I have heard those followers of yours talking: Skint and Smithills, Ragwort, Alder and that Mayweed.'

Tryfan nodded absently, his mind on the Stillstones yet.

'They talk of evacuating the system, they talk of finding a safer place than this, they talk. . . .'

Tryfan raised a paw to stop her, but she quietly continued.

'I do not doubt that what you will do is right, but when it comes to leaving Duncton, well, we can't all go, the system must never be deserted of all Duncton mole, and a mole or two should be left behind. If you're wondering who, leave *me* behind, I can cope alone and look after myself down in the secret places in the Marsh End, which was occupied in your father's day.'

'I could not leave you to the cruelty of the grikes,' said Tryfan, 'you don't know – '

'Take Comfrey, but not me,' she whispered. 'If one of us must stay, just one. . . .'

But Tryfan only shook his head.

Later, when Maundy had gone and Comfrey had

returned, and they had eaten, Comfrey said, 'Er, Tr-Tryfan. Something I just wanted to say, while we're alone. N-no need to mention it to anymole else. . . .'

Tryfan, his eyes warm, listened to his half-brother affectionately.

'Well,' said Comfrey, 'when – and I know you're going to have to, only sensible thing to do really – so wh-wh-when you lead the moles to somewhere safe you don't want me slowing you down. I'll stay behind. Must have one Duncton mole here, you know. Plenty of places to hide I remember as a pup: Marsh End, Westside . . . I'll find somewhere. But of course, you're to take Maundy, can't have her risking her snout. You'll see to that w-w-won't you?'

'We'll be guided by the Stone,' said Tryfan carefully, but thinking that there were times when the Stone was use to neither mole nor beast.

January is not a time for travel, nor February either, especially when the weather is as bitter as that long winter's was. Wise moles stay underground when the ground is frozen and turn their thoughts inward to matters of the mind and heart.

But when, finally, the first stirrings of spring started underground, when the frosts were still hard but the worms and pupae began to stir again in the soil, and root-tendrils to quiver and begin their silent white-green quests, then a few paw-picked moles poked their snouts out into the cold air, and heaved themselves abroad.

These moles had been trained by Alder as watchers, and had volunteered to risk going out beyond the roaring owl way, to watch for signs of grikes, and arrange for other friendly moles to watch out as well. The lessons of Harrowdown had been learnt, and Tryfan and Skint intended never to let themselves be taken by surprise again.

Meanwhile, the Duncton moles, and a few of the followers, chose to get on with what all sensible moles do

369

as spring comes close, which is to find a mate and ready themselves for young. So that pair by pair, responding to the season, began to busy themselves about their tunnels in an exclusive kind of way, and spend time together talking about nothing in particular except the fact that they would prefer not to be disturbed by anymole else (except each other) if you *don't* mind.

All this being so, in the preceding weeks Thyme had found reason aplenty to talk with Spindle, who, while not overtly encouraging her advances, yet somehow found his way to her tunnels on one pretext or another when the gap between their 'chance' meetings seemed too long. But pairing, even *mating*? Spindle denied any intention of such a thing, looking most embarrassed and saying he had task enough being companion and help to Tryfan than to think of *that*.

'Well, Sir, if you don't mind Mayweed observing this fact, Sir, it's the sort of thing a mole *does* at this time of the year and nomole would be surprised if you and lovely Thyme, most good-looking Thyme, did, and would be disappointed and surprised if you did not,' said Mayweed, speaking for many a mole who hoped to see the shy Spindle pair.

'Did not what?' asked Spindle, eyes innocent.

'Most cunning, most clever, most unconvincing denial, Sir, Spindle, Tryfan's friend, clever mole,' said Mayweed with a wide smile. 'Secret meetings, that's what; mating, that's the thing; love they call it, yes, yes, *yes*!' said Mayweed, who for some reason laughed.

'It's not funny, and it's not your business,' said Spindle. 'So go away. I suggest you stop talking about it and go and find yourself a mate yourself. That'll keep you busy!'

At this, Mayweed looked hurt and sad. Then he smiled, but a brave hurt smile, and said, 'Cured I may be, denying Sir, but allmole can see that my puny and pathetic body has been ravaged by disease and that my face is bald and my fur patchy. Nomole would have Mayweed, not now nor ever, and your friend Mayweed is to be alone and unloved all his life, such of it as yet he may have. In that respect, Spindle Sir, and only in that disadvantageous respect, am I like Tryfan. Both celibate, both unloved by female mole. Sad is Mayweed, miserable and physically bedraggled to think of it, and therefore uncomprehending why one such as your splendid and revered self should turn his back on love, *especially* with one so desirable to the discerning mole as Thyme.'

'Well, yes,' said Spindle rather contritely, regretting that he had hurt Mayweed. 'Anyway, I doubt that Thyme is interested in that sort of thing and certainly not with me!' Mayweed did not miss the query in Spindle's voice.

'Doubt it do you, Sir? Splendid and predictable. When love is so uncertain, love is on the way! Yes, Sir, good luck, Sir, the system wishes it to be so, Sir, and will be disappointed if it is not.'

'*Go away*, Mayweed.'

'Sorry, Sir!' And he was gone, and Spindle was in a bad mood all day after, and avoided Thyme's company until the evening, when she found him, and they ate together with barely a word between them, and each wishing they could find a word to say.

Mayweed's effusiveness about Thyme was not out of place. She had changed a great deal since Tryfan and Spindle had first come across her in Buckland when she had been so ill. Then her face had been gaunt and her eyes rather lost, and her illness had sapped her of energy and life. But the summer of travel and good company had brought a gloss to her coat, and a pride to her face that made her a worthy mole in any company, and a cheerful mole to have about the place. She was liked by the Duncton moles and soon accepted by them, respected for the travelling she had done and the way in which she made a good burrow, and kept visiting moles content, well-fed and cheerful.

More than that, she believed in the Stone, and prayed to it, and though there were plenty of males who cast their eye upon her and pointed their snout in her direction – the more so as February came and the essential femaleness of her seemed indefinably to grow. Yet she was not interested: too few seemed true followers of the Stone.

'I want a mate who not only says he believes in the Stone, but who lives by it and for it, and whose life is in it,' she confided one day to Maundy, with whom she got on very well and near whom she had occupied tunnels and created a charming burrow or two for herself.

'Well now,' said Maundy wisely, 'is there not a particular male you have in mind? February is advancing and you can't dilly-dally the weeks away.'

'Well,' began Thyme, looking shy, 'I do have dreams, yes.'

'Dreams?' repeated Maundy. 'You mean longings?'

Thyme pondered the word 'longings' and conceded that yes, possibly, that was what they were.

'Have you ever mated?' she asked Maundy, to avoid the issue.

'And littered, *and* raised. But not for a time or two now. 'And Comfrey needs me, you know, and I think he's got his mind on other things.'

Thyme laughed. 'You mean better things?'

Maundy smiled and said nothing.

'You love him, don't you?' said Thyme.

'Yes,' said Maundy simply. 'I believe I do.'

They were silent for a time, and at peace.

'So?' said Maundy. 'Whatmole's it to be?'

'You know perfectly well,' said Thyme shortly, looking irritated.

'But does he?' laughed Maundy, adding, 'That's a mole who may need encouragement.'

Meanwhile, poor Spindle was in a growing agony as the days went by and the others about him seemed intent on talking only to the opposite sex. Alder had long since disappeared over to the Eastside, and now even Skint and Smithills, who he had thought were too old for 'that sort of thing' as he put it, had gone 'exploring'. He knew what *that* meant: females.

372

Instead, Spindle busied himself preparing a chamber off a tunnel deep in a little known part of the Ancient System where books and texts might be stored as Tryfan scribed them. For Spindle too had a dream, as yet shared with nomole in its fullest glory, which was that one day there should be at Duncton a library such as moledom had never seen before outside the Holy Burrows, one to which the texts he himself had begun to preserve, first at Seven Barrows, then at Harrowdown, and now here at Duncton could be brought. Tryfan had already begun to scribe certain texts of his own, while Spindle and Mayweed, in their lesser ways perhaps, made scribings to chronicle the events of those times that moles of the future might know the truth of them. Those winter months had been the perfect time for Tryfan to continue the instruction he had started at Harrowdown, and both Spindle and Mayweed had learnt much. So Spindle the Cleric had constructed a library in a location discovered by Mayweed and then developed by him in such a way that to find it was hard indeed. In fact, when Tryfan had visited it he had gone right past the small tunnel that led down to it, not once but twice, and would not have found it had he not been shown. For the time being those three were the only moles allowed down to it, and Spindle was busy indeed down there. His instinct told him that the day might soon come when the system might be partly or wholly taken by the grikes, and then it was essential that the embryonic library was not found.

It was these concerns, and the labours they gave rise to, that had been disturbed by the mating season, and those curious unspoken longings which drove a mole to look at females and be with them.

So Spindle had sought out Thyme, and that coming to nothing yet, sought consolation in Tryfan's company by telling him that he felt decidedly 'strange'.

'Strange?' said Tryfan yawning, for he was growing tired of Spindle's indecision on the obvious fact that he and Thyme should be together doing what moles at the end of February always do if they have opportunity and sense.

'Well, peculiar,' said Spindle. 'Odd. Uneasy. Unfamiliar. *Strange*.'

'I wouldn't know,' said Tryfan, 'I'm vowed to celibacy.'

'Really?' said Spindle. 'I didn't hear any vows about that when Boswell made you a scribemole.'

'It's how it is,' said Tryfan, and it seemed he accepted the fact now, and certainly felt no inclination as the other males did to pursue females.

'Of course I like Thyme a lot,' said Spindle, adding, as if it was a thought that had taken him by surprise and had nothing to do with feeling 'strange', 'she's very nice.'

'Nice!' said Tryfan. 'If that's all you think her then I wouldn't blame her if she found somemole else.'

'Why, is she thinking of it?' said Spindle in alarm.

Tryfan had the sense to stay silent and let Spindle suffer this thought to whirl about in his mind.

'Well,' he said finally, 'I mean more than "nice". She's – well – she's, um, sort of . . . well, you *know*.'

'What ?' said Tryfan.

'Well, um, beautiful.'

Spindle darted his eyes this way and that and lowered his voice as if to utter the word was a terrible admission.

'When are you going to ask her then?'

'Tomorrow,' said Spindle immediately and with dubious conviction. 'Or the next day. When I've practised the words. Yes, definitely the next day.'

'Definitely?'

'Almost certainly,' said Spindle uneasily.

Tryfan laughed.

The day after, it happened that Maundy met Tryfan near the Stone.

'Will they or won't they?' she asked.

'I hope they do,' said Tryfan, 'but Spindle won't get on with it.'

'Maybe they need help. That's what Comfrey says.'

'Help?' Tryfan gazed at her, perplexed.

'You're a wise mole, Tryfan,' said Maundy, 'but there are some things you don't know anything about yet.

'Lots of things I should think,' said Tryfan ruefully. Sometimes he felt so young – and his return to Duncton had increased the feeling.

'Maybe,' said Maundy after some thought, 'you would take us on a tour of the lower slopes. Choose a nice sunny day when the tunnels will be light and the surface safe and show us Duncton Wood as it was.'

'Us?' repeated Tryfan.

'Spindle, Thyme, and me.'

'Why?' asked Tryfan artlessly.

'Nice things happen on such tours of systems, moles get to know each other, opportunities arise.'

So it was to be, for a day or two later – and Spindle still hesitating – the rendezvous was made and all four, under Tryfan's guidance, headed off down the slopes. The day was cold but crystal clear, the leaf mould on the surface beautiful with hoar frost which, even as they travelled, melted magically underpaw into drops of water that caught the sun like crystals scattered on their path.

For some reason Spindle kept clear of Thyme, and on the one occasion when the configuration of the surface caused their flanks to touch, he seemed almost to jump out of his skin, and Thyme did not know where to look.

So it was Maundy and Tryfan who made the conversation: 'And what's this place?' she asked, knowing the answer anyway and ignoring the silence between Thyme and Spindle.

'This is what used to be called the Westside,' said Tryfan, taking them to an edge of the wood adjacent to the Pastures. 'My father Bracken was born here but he did not stay after May because he was the weakest of his litter and was driven out.'

'I thought he was a powerful mole,' said Thyme, for lack of something better to say.

'He was,' said Maundy, 'but he only became that with time.'

'Not this "Thyme"!' said Spindle, making a bad joke and laughing in a strange high-pitched way.

Tryfan and Maundy looked at each other and laughed. Thyme did not.

Spindle looked about the places they went with a complete lack of curiosity. That day, with Thyme so near and him not knowing what to say, and him thinking such strange thoughts, and him a mole in love and with unfamiliar desires and not knowing what to do about it, *that* day, a tree might have toppled over in front of him and him not notice it.

'They say it was a worm-rich place before the fires,' said Tryfan.

'It was,' said Maundy, 'but I never came here. Very high quality moles the Westsiders, and rather exclusive.'

'Where were you from, Maundy?' asked Thyme.

'Near Barrow Vale,' she said vaguely, snouting over towards the east.

Many of the trees about them still carried evidence of the fire that followed the plague, being dead or burnt up one side: the wind that had driven the fire through the wood had been from the north, driving over the marshes into Marsh End, and then upslope almost to the Stone itself. Up there the great beeches had withstood it, for they were spaced apart and had too little undergrowth beneath them for the fire to take effective hold.

But down here, where the four wandered that day, the wood was derelict, though many of the trees still had life in them and were beginning to burgeon and shoot again. While between them, taking advantage of the extra light that the thinner canopy allowed, shoots and saplings of birch and ash were already pointing up their stiff stems, while around them wild flowers were starting, though few were yet in bloom.

Anemone and bluebells, and wild daffodils where none had been before; and the shoots of rosebay willowherb

376

which would, once summer came, rise into their full red-pink glory and sway as tall as the foxgloves midsummer through. But not yet: for now just the snowdrops glistened here and there, and yellow aconite.

But insects were astir and ants beginning to scurry as Tryfan led them on through the wood, telling them with Maundy's help, of its recent past, which now seemed like an age gone by.

'Mandrake had his burrows here somewhere, in easy reach of Barrow Vale itself because in those days that was the centre of the system where everymole met and had a gossip – except in the breeding season, when things always go a bit quiet.' Thyme looked shyly hopeful; Spindle affected gawky indifference.

'Let's find Barrow Vale!' declared Maundy, 'I think it's this way,' she added, going in the wrong direction.

'I don't think it is,' said Tryfan, surprised. She rested a paw on his and turned to Spindle and said, 'Tryfan may be right . . . you take Thyme that way and see if it's down there.'

'But I – ' began Spindle.

'I'd really rather stay with – ' continued Thyme.

But Maundy had turned and gone, dragging Tryfan with her, and the reluctant Spindle was left alone with the uncertain Thyme as the wood around them filled with winter sun, and every surface, every tiny shoot, seemed alight with it; while on the trees the lichen was green with life, and even last year's leaves were full of richness and colour beneath their paws. Somewhere near a wren flew and stopped, darted and peered, whirring away only when a female blackbird scuttled among some dead bracken searching for a twig or stalk for the nest she was beginning to build.

'Well, I don't know why they went off like that,' said Spindle grumpily.

Thyme was silent, looking at her talons. Then she looked up, her head jerking with nervousness.

'I feel very strange,' she said.

Spindle did not know where to look, but crouched with his head on one side as if thinking very hard and in fact thinking of nothing at all except that he ought to say something but could not think what.

'Really?' he said eventually.

'Yes,' she said with sudden certainty and feeling a lot better for saying so, 'I do.'

Spindle said, 'I feel a bit strange too. Um . . . um.'

Um. The word hung between them and Thyme suddenly looked a little irritable.

'Well, Spindle?'

'Um.' He said again, daring to look at her this time. She returned his gaze.

'Er . . .' he said, his paws all awkward, 'I suppose . . . we had better . . . go . . .' His voice slowed breathlessly as they continued to look at each other and Spindle discovered that it was nice doing so and not going anywhere.

' . . . We had . . . er . . . better go . . .' he suggested again.

They came fractionally closer.

Spindle said, 'I'm not very good at this.'

Thyme stared at him.

'I don't think you are,' she said. But she didn't look away and Spindle was so close he was almost touching her. 'I don't think I'm much better,' she added helpfully.

'No I don't think you are,' said Spindle. 'I mean, you're not much *help*.'

They were now so close that if either had moved one hair's breadth closer . . . if either . . . and both did.

'Mmm,' breathed Thyme.

Spindle's view of the trees and roots and sky were obscured and fuzzed by Thyme's fur, and his senses overtaken by the warmth of her body.

'Mmm!' he said as well, since it seemed as good a thing to say as anything else.

'Thyme?' he said.

'Mmm . . . mmm?' she whispered, her flank blissfully

378

firming against his, all warm and delicious and like nothing he had ever felt.

They crouched closer, though two moles trying to crouch and not lose touch with the caress that had started with such difficulty is a clumsy thing and the crouch was more a tumble, and the tumble turned the caress more into a friendly buffeting embrace – such that there were sighs from Thyme and groans from Spindle and there was nothing in the whole of moledom at that moment apart from what they were feeling for the other.

'Ooooh!' sighed Thyme.

'Yes!' said Spindle with more confidence.

There was silence and the sun shone around them and their eyes were closed. And they touched each other in many ways, one to the other, in many, many ways, for a very long time until their sighs were more than sighs, and that sunlight in the wood was an ecstatic thing, golden about them, and bright too, shining, carrying their sighs into the very skies.

Until, when they had done that, and done that some more, and the light had faded back to normal and they found the easy grace that moles have once they have been lovers, Spindle observed profoundly: 'Love is a strange thing.'

'Yes, it is,' replied Thyme eventually, and that was the full weight and extent of their conversation for a long time after. For more confident now, he reached out a paw and pulled her to him and she, resisting slightly, made him pull all the harder. Then she came to him, and he to her, and whatever they did moles had done a million times before, and as long as loving moles live it will be as good for them as it was then to Spindle and Thyme, for they were moles who have taken their courage in their paws and reached out and touched each other.

Much later their conversation resumed.

'Spindle?'

'Mmm?'

'What were we doing?'

379

'When?'

'Before.'

'Finding Barrow Vale.'

'Shall we do it now?'

Spindle got up and stretched. Thyme snuffled. Spindle snuffled back. Both felt replete but had not eaten a single thing.

'What was I doing?' asked Spindle.

'Stretching,' said Thyme.

'So I was,' he said lazily. And so, in a leisurely way, they got up and, with no difficulty at all, they found Barrow Vale.

In the middle of which, surrounded by trees, snout stretched in the sun, Tryfan lay dozing.

'Hello!' he said, alert before they even showed. He smiled to see Thyme coming ahead, and Spindle behind, a little sheepish and a little proud, certainly very different than he had been before.

'Where's Maundy?' asked Thyme.

'Gone upslope,' said Tryfan. 'You've certainly taken your time.'

They spoke no words, but their gentle looks to each other told Tryfan that they had done what had seemed inevitable to everymole that knew them.

'Well, then, this is Barrow Vale,' said Tryfan, and he took them about it and told them of the days of the elder meetings when Hulver had been alive and Mandrake; and Rune had come. Good moles and evil, all gone now, leaving behind them a derelict system. Then he led them down to the Marsh End, mysterious and gloomy.

'Can't we go down into the tunnels?' said Spindle.

'Better not,' said Tryfan. 'Comfrey made a rule about it – to leave the tunnels in peace for two generations.'

'Haven't they ever been cleared then?' asked Spindle.

Tryfan shook his head.

'Well, they've got some real live clearers in the system now so perhaps they should use us! You and me, Skint and Smithills – we could clear the tunnels in no time!'

380

Tryfan said nothing. It wasn't the time for that, there were other things before then. The system here was not ready for life again yet, as if it had to lie fallow for a while, its tunnels gathering dust, its burrows collapsing, the life that plague and fire had robbed it of slowly returning.

The afternoon came as they explored here and there, and with it a slight chill to the air.

'I'm glad you brought us here,' said Thyme, 'because I feel as if I'm being introduced to a system that will be important to – to us . . .' She reached out a paw for Spindle, and Tryfan was glad to see their love beginning to be open.

'Well,' he said, 'it's time to go. I'm heading back . . . you can find your way back, can't you?' And with that he left them, and set off in a circuit of the Marsh End and the Eastside. Somewhere on the way he hoped he might find something of the burrow that Rebecca had once occupied, and which she herself had shown him, to which Mekkins, the greatest of the Marsh-Enders and a much loved mole, had brought Comfrey as a pup, that she might have one to love after she had lost her first litter.

He felt a little lost and alone, the more so because of Spindle's happiness, and thought this visit to a place near where his mother had been would give him strength. So he turned and left them, and was gone, a rather lonely figure, into the winter-bare wood.

The sun began to set, its light fading over the Marsh End as slowly, forever stopping and touching, Spindle and his Thyme went back the way they had come and found themselves, as the bare, battered tree trunks about them caught the pale pink of the dying sun, in Barrow Vale once more.

There for a short time they crouched until Thyme said, 'I would like to go down into the tunnels for a moment, just to see.'

'Tryfan said . . .' began Spindle uncertainly. 'I mean, there won't be much to see.'

'Spindle, can't you feel it, something special here? Something here for us?'

381

'I don't think so . . .' he said, hesitating. 'I can't, I . . .'
But above them the pale evening sky held its first white
points of stars though the sun was still just up, and the
daytime noise of the wood had faded to near silence. Then
deep Silence and there was peace in Barrow Vale.

'Yes,' he said with confidence, 'I can feel it.'

So they crouched together in awe, flank to flank, and
about them the light seemed shining and white and they
knew the Stone was with them and of them.

One or the other must have gone first, but after neither
remembered which: rustling among the undergrowth in
search of an entrance until, turning round upon themselves they saw an entrance, clear as daylight, as if it had
always been there, and around it a light of welcome and
the hushed whispering of a breeze that said, 'For now this
is your place and your presence honours it. Come, come to
me . . .' and they entered in that strange entrance and
found themselves in the great and famous communal
barrow of Barrow Vale, dust thick on the ground yet still
each pawstep echoing. Around them the ancient roots of
trees that had burnt away still twisted and turned, cracked
now in death; tunnels went this way and that out of the
burrow. But the air was sweet and warm and good.

'Thyme . . .' and Thyme turned to him as he to her and
his talons were on her back, not nervous now or unsure as
they made love and life together, their own sighs of ecstasy
echoing and rushing around them. Until when they had
finished it seemed that Barrow Vale was theirs and always
would be now; their place, yes, theirs and all their kin.

'Spindle,' whispered Thyme. 'Can you hear it?'

'Yes,' he said in awe. 'It is the Silence of the Stone.'

'Here in Barrow Vale it will be, the end and the
beginning, for the Stone is the symbol not the place, its
place is everywhere. Oh here, here,' she sighed, 'I can feel
it coming from a long way in the future. And we are of it,
Spindle, strangers here, strangers still to each other,
unknown and nomole knowing that we came.'

'I don't know, I'm not really sure,' said Spindle,

'but . . .' But he stopped speaking because around them was the light of Silence, white and clear, and from its deepest place the mewings and callings of young came, and beyond them the chatter of growing pups, and beyond that the run and play of siblings and other young, and far, far beyond that, no more than a whisper, the calling of one saying a name neither could quite hear, to which there was a reply that seemed all around them in the light, a reply of warmth that filled their eyes with tears and made them clasp each other.

'Spindle, I'm frightened,' whispered Thyme, for she had heard the life inside her and its generations yet to be.

'Thyme,' said Spindle, his thin form proud and sure, 'may the blessings of the Stone be on us and our young.'

'My love,' she whispered, 'if ever we are separate, whatever may still be, let this place be our place, the place to which we come.'

'Barrow Vale of Duncton,' whispered Spindle. 'Yes. . . .'

'Our place,' she sighed. 'Our sanctuary.'

'To here we shall return,' said Spindle, 'from wherever we go and whatever we may be. We will tell our young, and they will tell theirs.'

'Oh yes,' she said, 'whatever we may be, and wherever the Stone may send us *this* is our place.'

Then they turned back from the burrow, and found the entrance they had come in by and went back to the surface where dusk had settled and the colours gone.

'We must go back upslope now,' said Spindle, as the first owl called.

'Yes,' said Thyme vaguely, for she was looking about Barrow Vale trying to find something. She came close to Spindle for comfort and said, 'Where is that entrance we went down? It isn't there.' And nor was it, for it had gone as if it had never been.

'We must leave now,' said Spindle, and so they did. But as they reached the edge of the circle of trees that surrounds Barrow Vale, Thyme paused. Spindle put a

paw out to her and both were suddenly still, for ahead of
them on stem and leaf and branch and twig was a light that
came from behind, from where they had been.

'Don't look back,' whispered Thyme, 'my own love,
don't look back.' And nor did Spindle do so, but rather
crouched low and humble for a time and then, that light
shining still before them, they journeyed on.

While behind them, where the entrance into the burrow
had been, an old mole, a White Mole, watched after them,
and he reached out his talons to them, through the wood
he reached as if he was everywhere, guiding them this way
and that so that without knowing it they found the safest
route back to the top of Duncton Wood: free of owl and
free of fox.

Then that same ancient mole, White Mole, beloved
mole, reached out to touch another with his blessing:
Tryfan, scribemole, brave mole, leader, and for now
alone.

Tryfan, who had found Rebecca's old burrow, gone
down into it, and there for a brief moment had lain down
where once Rebecca had suckled Comfrey and whispered,
'Help me.'

He felt low and alone, and knew now that he could not
stay forever in Duncton, but had come here to gain
strength, and allow the others with him to breathe
something of the good air of a system still blessed by the
Stone and free of the Word.

'Guide me, for I feel comfortless and lost in darkness.'

Then the night breeze stirred in the wood above, and
whispered, 'You are much loved Tryfan, much cared for,'
and Tryfan heard its voice and knew that the Stone was
with him and felt the touch of its love gentle on his flanks.
Then Tryfan went out on to the surface, and saw a light
about him and felt the presence of an old mole, a mole he
loved and knew, and wept that he missed him, that he
knew him, that he loved him, and that he trusted he was
safe.

Then Tryfan began his solitary trek back to the great Stone, in deep Silence and quite unafraid to thank it for its guidance.

Chapter Twenty-Three

It was at the end of March, after a final burst of bitter winter weather and when the surface was thaw-wet with melting ice and snow and the sun so bright that a mole had to screw up his eyes on first sight of the surface, that a frightened male, weary and half-starved, arrived at Duncton Wood.

He was escorted up from the roaring owl way by Ragwort, who had become one of the watchers Alder had sent out in February, and had come from a system near Buckland itself by way of Fyfield, where he had very nearly been caught and made to serve as a clearer.

He had come, he said, because he had heard of a mole called Tryfan, who had defeated Henbane of Whern and killed twenty of her guardmoles single-pawed. A mole who was just and believed in the Stone. A mole who would right wrongs, and lead those who supported him to freedom, a mole, a mole. . . .

And Tryfan, listening to the distraught young male, who had witnessed the snouting of all three of his siblings, and the crippling of his mother, and had only been saved by the courage of his father before he too had been snouted . . . Tryfan guessed that this might be but the first of the many who in the molemonths, or the years, ahead would come forward to be led. Some from faith, some from fear, some from greed for a better life, some to serve dark ends another way. As he gazed on that eager, willing male, Tryfan felt that the burden of the task Boswell had given him was heavy.

He prayed silently: 'Help me, O Stone, to be true to thy Silence, and guide these moles forward with justice for justice, with peace for peace, with truth for truth. Help me.' For he guessed, as he listened to that first vagrant refugee, that it was one thing to lead a small group of moles on an escape from Buckland to Duncton, but another, and far harder, to lead a group of vagrants and refugees from grike systems to . . . to where?

'Help me avoid making the cause of the Stone no different from the cause of the Word. Help me towards light, and towards Silence. Help me guide these moles to thy peace.'

'Where is this Tryfan?' asked the young male. 'Take me to him so that I may pay my respects and pledge my loyalty to him.'

And the scribes say that Tryfan replied, 'The Tryfan of whom you've heard, and you have described, does not exist.'

The mole bewildered, said, 'But this is Duncton Wood. Is he not here?'

Tryfan said, 'He is but a mole like you, and if you will be led by him then let *him* make obeisance to thee and all thy kind, and obey him only in one thing, first and last.'

'I shall!' said the mole at once, but was still puzzled.

'Then pledge your loyalty to the Stone and not to him, except so far as he is of the Stone. And serve him by letting him serve thee. If you do this, mole, than you are truly a follower.'

'I'll try!' said the mole, 'I will! Let me tell him so myself.'

Tryfan smiled and said, 'Thou hast done so,' and he lowered his snout before the mole, and asked that he touch his right shoulder in acknowledgement of the importance of what he had said and to emphasise for all to see that among the followers of the Stone it is the leaders who are privileged and who should make obeisance to the led.

As April came others arrived at Duncton in ones and twos, telling as the first one did bleak stories of atrocities and takeovers by the grikes; each arrival had known the shadows of horror and loss on the way behind them.

It was Spindle who suggested that as these moles arrived

387

accounts of how they came to leave their home systems and make their way to Duncton should be scribed down, work begun by Tryfan and continued by Spindle aided by Mayweed. From these scribings not only was Tryfan able to build up a record of the strength and disposition of the grikes, but Spindle was able to start those records which today are known as the Rolls of the Refugees, and chart the scourge of the Word as well as setting down as much oral history of each system, its rhymes and traditions, as the ever-curious Spindle was able to gather.

From all this information, Tryfan and the other senior moles were left in no doubt that as spring advanced towards summer the grikes were massing in the systems around Duncton, and an attack on a large and probably unstoppable scale was going to come, and before long.

From some of the more discerning arrivals there came another and more sinister report. It was that the methods of the grikes had changed since last Longest Day and brutality and snoutings had given way to subtler methods of the kind Tryfan himself had already observed in Frilford and Bladon. As young moles were born, so their minds were twisted with the Word, and the Stone was mocked and reviled to them. A process helped, it seemed, by the fact that grike males seemed more fecund than southern plague-touched males, and females preferred them when the mating season came, so that many of the youngsters being born were half-grike, and the more easily influenced.

'I tell you, Tryfan, this may be a greater danger than it seems,' warned Spindle, 'for we may be fighting no vicious newcomers but a way of life accepted by increasing numbers of moles.'

'But a way of life without a centre,' replied Tryfan. 'Without the Silence of the Stone. One that will finally fail unless it finds a centre that can sustain a mole's inner life, or change it for the better.'

Spindle shrugged.

'What ordinary mole knows of such Silence, or "inner

life," or cares for it? If they have order, and health, worms, and a warm burrow, and can pup in peace and fight once in a while well. . . .'

'Then why do refugees seek out Duncton?' asked Tryfan.

'I am just warning you of what moles say,' said Spindle.

Tryfan smiled, and then looked serious.

'Stay close to me, Spindle, whatever I may say or do. The burden of leading these moles is heavy and will be heavier yet, and I sometimes desire to be alone. There is no time . . . Stay close, warn me if I grow distant, remind me that I am but ordinary mole for I will always listen to you.'

'I will, Tryfan,' said Spindle, 'even if the day comes when you do not wish it!'

'That will never come,' said Tryfan,

Spindle made no comment, but left soon afterwards when Skint and Smithills came to talk over the need to prepare for the coming of the grikes as quickly as they could.

It was in this atmosphere of preparation and change that the youngsters of that spring were born, and those few who survived ever afterwards remembered the excitement of those times. The adults seemed constantly busy, many of the males and the unpupped females were trained as watchers under the overall command of Alder and Smithills, and involved in making defences on the south east side of the system where only the roaring owl way protected it.

As for the pupping females, the fact was that fertility was not high. Many of the females had aborted, and the relatively few who gave birth managed litters of only one or two with just a very few of three. The females themselves knew the cause well enough: disease. Ever since the plagues fertility had been low, and it did not go unnoticed that where a female was clean and a male diseased, even if his disease was now healed and gone, pups were aborted or born deformed. In those few cases where such females did give birth, their burrows were dark indeed, for the young had to be killed lest the moles forthcoming, poor deformed things, should survive and shame their parents.

That this was so was generally unknown to the males for males were not present at birth, nor allowed by other females near birth burrows, and what male could argue when a mother reported the young dead?

Yet Tryfan knew that 'dead' meant 'killed', and his source was Smithills.

Smithills' mate, an Eastside female, had borne young and he had been told they had been born dead.

'I thought 'twas to be expected, Tryfan,' he explained sadly. 'Anymole who knows anything about scalpskin knows that a mole that has had it, whether male or female, does not make healthy pups. Pregnant she may become, with pup may he make her, but if one or other has had the sores then those pups will not be born at all, or if they are they're as good as dead.'

'But your scalpskin was cured,' said Tryfan, who had done it himself.

'Begging your pardon, Tryfan, but you didn't cure me, you healed the sores, and that's a different thing. I'm not saying I'm not grateful, just that I know 'tis too late for me to have young now.'

'Did you tell your mate that?' asked Tryfan.

'Course I did – for it wouldn't be fair otherwise. But you know what females are: if they think there's a chance of a pup and there's no other male around they'll have even a rough old mole like me, and I'll not stop 'em.'

Tryfan chuckled but, uncharacteristically, Smithills did not and Tryfan saw he had more to say.

'Fact is, that there was young born alive of my mate's litter, but they were killed.'

'Who did that?' asked Tryfan appalled.

'Other females. 'Tis the way. They stay in the birth burrow and watch over, and if the young aren't right why, they kill them.'

'By who's authority?' asked Tryfan.

'By tradition's,' said Smithills. 'I asked my mate and she said that 'twas the desire of the Stone. "And what was wrong with the mites?" I asked. "Three paws upfront, and no snout," she said. "No shame to kill them, but shame for male to know." '

Smithills lowered his great snout.

'They say it has been bad that way since the plagues, some say even before. And now it's worse, Tryfan, and surviving young are few.'

'And the more precious to us,' said Tryfan.

Of all of this Tryfan later questioned Maundy in Comfrey's burrow.

'Smithills is right, 'tis females' lore,' she said. 'Seems cruel, I know, but it's for the best. A female can't be trusted to do it for herself, though some are willing enough. But we try to have another there to help.'

'To murder you mean,' said Tryfan angrily.

'Such young are better dead,' said Maundy matter of factly.

'But Boswell himself was such a one, wouldst thou have killed him?'

Maundy stared at Tryfan and said, 'Aye, in this system such a mole would not have lived.'

'It's not right, Maundy. The Stone is life itself and desires not that its young be killed however hurt they may seem to be.'

'Then may the Stone itself grant that you never witness some of the births I have seen since the plague,' said Maundy, 'or have to decide what pups of a bad litter must live and what must die.'

When she had gone Tryfan asked Comfrey, 'Did you know of this?'

'N-not many males know, but I d-did, T-Tryfan. Yes I d-d-did.'

Later, when he was calmer, Tryfan asked Maundy, 'Have any scalpskinned moles ever parented successful young?'

391

'Never have to my knowledge, never shall is my belief, not ones with sores. Nor moles touched by plagues, nor murrain, nor any such. There's many a mole in moledom would have young if they could, but their body's been tainted with disease, and the Stone won't permit them young. But there you go.'

Tryfan saw there were tears in Maundy's eyes, and sadness, for a mole likes to make her own young, and teach pups what she knows.

Learning this, Tryfan was not surprised to hear that Thyme, too, had difficulty pupping after she and Spindle had mated. Spindle had not caught scalpskin in the Slopeside and seemed clean enough, but Thyme had been ill when they first met her, and was ill again during her pregnancy. So ill, indeed, that both Comfrey and Maundy tended her and Maundy herself stayed to watch over her when she pupped.

That was a long and dangerous thing and the young when it was born, for there was only one, was weak. But not so weak as Thyme herself, who seemed to suffer a recurrence of the illness she had suffered in Buckland and was quite incapable of tending to her pup. More than that her bleeding would not stop, and no amount of care from Maundy or herbs from Comfrey could prevent it stopping either. So for a time after the birth the youngster was left to mew alone, unsuckled and alone while Thyme fought for her life. But then the moment came when Thyme seemed to accept that her weakness would not improve, and she bravely asked Maundy to find another, stronger mother for the little thing.

'Ask Spindle himself to take him, he'll find a female will have want of him,' she said.

'It's better I do it,' said Maundy. 'Female won't take it from a male.'

'No, no, let Spindle take him,' whispered Thyme. 'He'll know where to go.'

So it was that Spindle was summoned to Thyme's birth burrow and there he saw his love so weakened by the birth she could barely reach for him; and at her dry and wasted teats he saw their male pup, tiny and striving.

'Take him,' whispered Thyme. 'While there's time take him, my love.'

'But I didn't know you were so . . .' said poor Spindle, shocked to see Thyme so ill and thin with the effort of birth and the ravaging of her illness.

'Surely he'll be all right if only – '

But Thyme shook her head.

'Don't delay, Spindle, take him now. Find a female who will care for him. Go now, please go. . . .'

'I don't know where,' said Spindle.

Then Thyme reached for his paw and, touching it, said, 'There is a place you know, a place we said we'd always meet, the place where we first found our love; take him there, my dear, but hurry now.'

So Spindle took his pup up by the skin behind his neck, awkwardly, for a male is not so good at such a thing, and Thyme smiled and said, 'Bring him to me.'

Which Spindle did and laid him before her. Thyme looked at her one and only ever pup and said, 'My father's name was Bailey, let that be his.' Then she spoke as best she could to Bailey, and caressed him, saying again and again, as if those words she spoke then were all the words that pup would ever hear from its own mother, and they must say everything, 'You are much loved.'

Again and again and again, but weaker and weaker, her voice fading in that dark burrow.

Then Maundy nodded to Spindle, who took up Bailey once more, and turned away and did not hear as Thyme whispered after him, 'And you, Spindle, never forget you too are loved, so much.'

Then Spindle was gone, down the long slopes of Duncton Hill to the north, knowing where he must go, which was Barrow Vale, where he and Thyme had known their love and sworn to meet again one day, or tell their kin to do so.

Of that long journey Spindle left no account, nor of

what happened when he got to Barrow Vale. But another mole did, one other mole knew, and she remembered and repeated what she knew.

There in the dark of Barrow Vale, where the roots of dead trees were, and dust of the past, Spindle brought Bailey and found a female waiting. Gaunt she was, but her teats were full and her longings were great.

'Whatmole are you?' asked Spindle when he saw her and placed Bailey before her.

'Prayed to the Stone,' whispered the female, very afraid. 'Said to come here. Said . . .' But she stopped there and bent to tend the pup, licking him, caressing him, and curling her body to his that he might suck.

'What is your name?' asked Spindle.

'He's a lovely thing, what's his?'

'Bailey,' said Spindle.

'A good name,' said the female, trying to suckle the pup.

'Have you young?' asked Spindle, puzzled.

'Aye,' said the female. 'Two good, one bad. The bad was killed. Bailey'll replace him.'

Spindle wanted to say, 'Tell him he was of Thyme and Spindle,' but instead he told her, 'Tell him that when in doubt in days to come he's to trust the Stone and come to Barrow Vale where you found him. Will you do that?'

Then the female looked up at him, her eyes filled with the joy of a mother who has found her young, and said, 'As sure as the Stone is good to me, I will. That in times of doubt then Barrow Vale is the place where he must go. I'll tell him.' And she turned back to tiny Bailey, and nudged him close as close can ever be.

'I must go,' said Spindle, fearful for Thyme, eager now to get back.

'Aye, aye,' said the female vaguely, and she did not look up as Spindle left the dusty tunnels of Barrow Vale.

Yet he left the whisper, 'You are much loved . . .' and he wanted to turn back for a terrible fear was in him to hear those words Thyme had said, and repeated so strangely.

Then again, 'You are much loved.' So he ran from Barrow Vale, and up the long way of the slopes, but even before he reached his mate's burrow once more, Maundy was coming to meet him and he knew, from her face and her gait he knew it, that his Thyme was no more.

Some say he ran then to the Stone; others that he was mad with grief and attacked Tryfan himself. But one knew the truth, and told it. Spindle of Seven Barrows went back down to Barrow Vale to find Bailey again, and take him back, but when he got there the female was gone, and Bailey with her, and he stayed alone at Barrow Vale, mourning his loss, and angry with the Stone.

Now, as spring advanced, everymole in Duncton sensed urgency, and the tunnels were imbued with tension and purpose, as each there knew a time of trial was approaching, and that many among them might die.

Already a Council of Elders had been formed, with Comfrey as its senior member and Tryfan as its natural leader. Skint was on it, and Maundy, Spindle too and Smithills.

Alder should have been, but some in Duncton still did not quite trust a mole who had been a guardmole so recently, but they were content that he should remain in charge of new arrivals, many of whom became trained watchers as they were taught discipline and made fit for the long struggle to come.

As for Mayweed, he reported only to Tryfan or Skint, but followed his own rules, disappearing nomole knew where, exploring tunnels and routes nomole else could fathom, thinking his thoughts; confiding in Tryfan of this and that secret he knew, or secret way he had found.

Everymole in the system knew that with each day of warmer weather the chances of grike attack increased. The watchers beyond the system had been increased, yet the only reports they had were of a certain restlessness which always comes to moledom in the spring. If the grikes were coming they were biding their time, making their plans, massing their forces. But where, and when . . .?

Meanwhile, Tryfan and the Council made plans of their own, though only after much discussion, and some dissension. War was not natural to Duncton moles, and nor could they really believe the cruelty that might come. The Pasture moles, to the west, when asked if they would fight alongside the Duncton moles, simply laughed.

Tryfan's experience in Buckland had taught him that there were advantages in the kind of organisation and planning the grikes evidently used, and they had better use it themselves if they were to survive.

Skint had been deputed to check the defences of Duncton, and it had taken him three days to travel its circumference in the company of Smithills and Mayweed, following the course of the Thames which largely encircled it, and then the route of the way itself, under which he and the others had first come, using the narrow cow cross-under, twofoot made. Not nice for moles, but efficient so long as the weather was dry. They found drainage conduits under the way, buried in gravel and hard to reach, and memorised their locations, making sure to hide their entrances and exits.

'But the fact is,' reported Skint to the Council on his return, 'if grikes come from the south east, which is the only way they can, we will be unable to escape without having to fight through their ranks because there's no way of getting over the river, and they can cover the other ways out.'

'Then the first thing we must do is to establish positions beyond the way, which will divert attack and leave exits which will be safe,' said Tryfan.

'We really must l-l-leave Duncton then?' said Comfrey unhappily.

'There will be no way to defend it, or the moles in it, against prolonged attack by superior numbers,' said Tryfan. 'Yes, I think we shall have to leave – for a time. I believe that Henbane would wish to massacre us here, as proof of the Word's power, and as a lesson to anymole remaining who harbours hopes of being loyal to the Stone. So an evacuation is not a failure so much as a frustration of her objectives, and allows us to fight when we are in a better position to do so.'

'So why not get out now while the going's good?' said Smithills, not needing to add that had they left Harrowdown earlier Brevis and Willow might still be alive. Tryfan was discovering, as his father had before him, that leading moles is not easy, and demands a balancing of one option against another, for which there are few rules, and where instinct is one strength, and purposefulness another.

'Skint and I have already discussed that,' replied Tryfan, 'and we feel that an evacuation now is premature. For one thing we cannot be sure where the grikes are, and therefore might make the mistake of fleeing towards them in country we do not know and which we cannot defend as well as our own system. But certainly they are not very near because otherwise our watchers would have seen evidence of them. Secondly, each day that passes a few more refugees come and swell our ranks. Although their number has now declined, we might still miss some who would have joined us.'

The Council heard what he said and reluctantly approved it. All there wished to protect the pups that had recently been born, for they would be vulnerable in attack, but they recognised that the longer they stayed the stronger the pups would be when they left, and the more would survive.

But Tryfan had another point to make. 'And finally,' he added, 'we must prepare Duncton for the time after our evacuation.'

'After?' queried Maundy.

Tryfan and Skint nodded.

'We are too few to defeat Henbane's forces outright, and to do so may – will – take many moleyears. But until now moles of the Word have had little trouble from the systems they have overtaken. Not only have such systems been severely weakened by plague, but for decades past, perhaps even centuries, moles of the Stone have lived peaceably, and there has rarely been inter-system fighting. So the grikes have never faced serious resistance. They have offered order and security to moles demoralised by plague and weakening belief, and what little resistance there has been they have crushed with threats, cruelty and punishment.

'But now, here in Duncton, there *is* resistance, and there are moles willing to fight to the death for what they believe.'

The Council moles nodded – there was not one there who would not die for the Stone. And increasingly it was being said (though Tryfan discouraged such ideas) there was not one who would not die for Tryfan himself.

'We were taught by the grikes themselves,' said Skint, 'though unintentionally, that it is possible to resist them from *inside* a system, by the use of secret tunnels, surprise, and a strategy of withdrawal. This is not the traditional mole way, but then nor is snouting and the injustice of the Word. So far we are small in number, and we must find ways of making what strength we have be felt a hundred times. The day may come when Henbane and Weed will regret the creation of punishment tunnels like the Slopeside, for it taught us that we can survive in conditions not thought fit for moles, and from out of those conditions successfully fight, demoralise and escape. We have three moles among the followers – Skint and Smithills here, and Mayweed – who survived the Slopeside, as you did yourself, Tryfan, and Spindle here. . . .'

'Yes, yes,' said Tryfan, 'but what is your plan Skint?'

'Seems to me now that we should create secret tunnels in Duncton, ones to which we can return after an evacuation and from which we can cause trouble for the grikes if they stay here. Some of us can remain and hide after the rest of you have gone, to harass Henbane's guardmoles, or learn things they do not wish us to know.'

'Aye,' said Smithills, 'that's work I'd willingly do, and others too if I'm not mistaken.'

'M-m-may the Stone guide us, and k-keep us safe until we are ready for the c-coming fight,' said Comfrey at the end of the meeting, and doing his best to sound inspiring, though fighting was never his way.

Yet, perhaps the Stone was listening, or at least guided the moles of Duncton in those dangerous days. It certainly seemed to have guided one mole, and that was Mayweed, who came searching out Tryfan one day as excited and eager as he had ever been.

Mayweed had changed a great deal in his time at Duncton Wood, as had many of the moles. He had become fuller, more cheerful, and more winningly enthusiastic about what he did. He had also, in a strange way, become more mysterious and secretive, and was much liked by the youngsters, many of whom he knew and with whom he was relaxed, and who loved him to tell his long-winded stories.

But on the day he sought out Tryfan he was anything but leisurely.

'Bold Sir, come quick come now, come eagerly! Mayweed has something astonishing and amazing to show you!'

'Which is what, Mayweed?'

'Not tell – show, Sir. Spoil the surprise telling, and tunnels have ears and Mayweed thinks this is something nomole should know but splendid Tryfan himself. Ssh, Sir! He tells it not.'

Tryfan sighed, for he was busy and Mayweed's 'secrets' had a habit of taking a long time in the showing, since they invariably involved journeys to the strangest of places.

'I'm very busy, Mayweed, moles to see, moles to direct. Can you at least give me a clue?'

Mayweed smiled his wide and ingratiating smile.

'One word tells it, Sir. One word only. Ssh, Sir, I whisper it . . . Escape.'

'Escape?' repeated Tryfan.

'From Duncton, Sir!' said Mayweed, delighted with himself.

'Who?'

'*All*, Sir. All down to the oldest and smallest. Everymole.'

Tryfan stared at him and Mayweed stared back.

'Pleased, Sir?' said Mayweed.

'Show me,' said Tryfan, 'now! But we'll go by Skint's burrows as he should see what you've found.'

'If we must, Sir, we shall do so, and secure scheming Skint's approval, Sir.'

Tryfan smiled. Mayweed and Skint had a strange respectful relationship which hid under a continual irritability from Skint and veiled sarcasm from Mayweed. Skint would pretend not to be interested, but he would come.

Which was how it happened, for Skint had to be persuaded to make the trek down to the Marsh End where Mayweed explained they had a mole to meet, who would guide them to what it was he wanted to show them.

So down the tunnels they went, this way and that as was Mayweed's fashion, until they came to the moist Marsh End, and into a tunnel where a mole waited who was as dirty as a mole could be. His fur was caked with mud, his talons grimy beyond grooming, his snout snuffly with filth. But his eyes were wide and innocent, and he was a young mole by the look of him, but most unprepossessing.

'And this is the mole who's going to guide us is it, Mayweed?' said Skint dubiously.

'Holm, Sir, that's his name. But he won't speak much, though he *can* and does, but not often, no, *no*, Sir, not very much, do you, Holm?' said Mayweed proudly, patting his friend on the back as he introduced him.

'Where are you from, Holm?' asked Skint, naturally suspicious these days.

Holm said nothing, but stared at them, very shy, rather small, weaselly of expression, so far as any expression could be seen beneath the dirt. He looked at Mayweed to speak for him.

'Where's he from you want to know, Sir? From where? Where to, more like, that's the better question!' Mayweed grinned winningly. 'I found him, Sir, where nomole but him could be. Up a tree wasn't he? Lurking like a bat or owl in a tunnel he made all by his mysterious self. Not *far* up, but high enough for me to say to myself that this was a mole worth cultivating, as it were, Sir. *Up a tree!*'

'What were *you* doing there?' asked Tryfan, smiling. He liked Mayweed, and trusted him.

'Exploring. And there was scent of mole, there was scribble-scrabble of mole; there was Holm. Scared me – didn't you, Holm?'

Holm nodded, and he snouted about the place they were in restlessly, as if he did not like being in one place too long.

'Where is this tree?' asked Skint, still suspicious.

'And where was Holm going?' added Tryfan.

Mayweed grinned hugely, his teeth showing with pleasure, his head on one side, his quick eyes darting from one to another, appraising them as he considered what to reveal.

'The tree was in the Marsh, Sir, dead as dead can be. And Holm here was going up it, Sir, to see if it would serve him when the floods come.'

'What floods?' asked Skint.

'Next year, year after that, sometime, Sir. Holm is a mole of the future, Sir, makes his plans well. That's why he's living, Sir, and others are very dead indeed. Now bold Tryfan and smart Skint, a tunnel I have to show you, very special, very good. Holm found it, I explored it, we finished it. Very good and very clever, Tryfan Sir and Skint Sir; you will be pleased. Won't they, Holm?'

Holm nodded his weaselly head vigorously, and, looking to Mayweed for support, managed a sickly smile.

'Then take us, for Stone's sake,' said Skint impatiently.

'Immediately, Sir. Why did I not think of that before?

401

Silly me! Ridiculous us, Holm! Hee, hee, hee.' And, laughing nervously, or pretend-nervously, Mayweed led them north by tunnels that led out of the roots of the wood and into the Marsh itself.

He travelled so rapidly that it was hard enough just keeping up with him let alone complain, which was what Skint would have liked to do since moles don't go journeying in marshes if they can help it, and the ground was soggy wet so that their coats picked up wet earth and slime the moment they touched a tunnel wall.

On two occasions Holm stopped, signalled, and they back-tracked, and then they travelled rapidly on, always generally northwards. Then Mayweed came to a sudden stop and said, 'We're nearly at its start, Sirs both! This is very good, very pleasing, a great honour indeed! . . . and you are both naturally completely lost, clever though you are, but that was our intention was it not, happy Holm?' Holm nodded, and both Tryfan and Skint had to concede that they had little idea where they were relative to anything at all before Mayweed would take them onwards.

Except that the soil was dark and dank, and had the slithy feel underpaw of soil that was near water.

'We're north of the Marsh End, aren't we, Mayweed?' said Tryfan.

' "North" is correct and very precise, oh yes, Sir; north, north, north and almost too north! No, worry not but follow gladly, Sirs, but carefully, tread warily. Holm goes last so you don't get lost. Mayweed myself goes first. Nasty it is, nasty it will be, but very, very good when you reach the end, which for Duncton moles will be a new beginning. How poetic Mayweed gets, how carried away in his excitement! That's the good thing!'

Skint looked wearily at Tryfan, whose patience with Mayweed he did not share, and they turned to follow him. Almost immediately Mayweed stopped.

'Dark it gets, Sirs, dark as night.'

'Black mostly,' said Holm suddenly behind them, which was the only thing he said that day.

'Stay close. Holm will see you do.'

The tunnel suddenly dipped down and turned cold, bitterly cold, and its sides were waterlogged and made a mole uneasy. A tiny stream ran along on the right side of the tunnel disappearing ahead of them into darkness, and though they tried to avoid it, from time to time their paws sloshed into it, sending spatterings of muddy water on to the mole ahead, or back to the mole behind.

'Are you sure you know this goes somewhere?' asked Skint, as they progressed downslope and the tunnel got darker and darker as the overhead entrances, such as they were, got further apart until they disappeared altogether so that the gloom ahead was lit only by the fast fading light behind.

'I'm sure, Sir, but unfortunately you're not. You will be eventually!'

Mayweed's voice echoed about them, broken strangely by the ominous drippings of water at their side, and sometimes from directly above. And it became even colder. The light finally dimmed into total darkness.

The streamlet at their paws seemed to be growing deeper and spreading wider so that soon they were wading through it, and in darkness so thick that their progress slowed as they snouted their way ahead, Mayweed first, Tryfan second, Skint next and Holm at the rear, evidently taloning Skint in the haunch occasionally to keep him in touch with the two ahead.

Soon Tryfan had lost all sense of where he was and in what direction he was going, his position defined entirely by Mayweed ahead and a grumbling Skint pushing into him from behind.

'Where are – ?'

'Ssh, Sir.' Mayweed's voice echoed back to him. 'Best to be silent it is down here. Listen!'

And Mayweed stopped, and they all bunched together, paw to paw and flank to chilled, wet flank, and the silence about them was broken only by the hissing and rippling of water ahead.

'Not far to the beginning of the end, one and all!' said Mayweed from out of the darkness. 'But the sound is confusing so stay near to the left-paw wall, near enough to touch it, but don't touch it too much: wet it is and muddy. Unstable, nasty, not nice to be, eh?' Mayweed sounded annoyingly cheerful. Tryfan muttered, 'All right,' Skint grunted and behind them all Holm said absolutely nothing.

They progressed slowly on until, without pausing, Mayweed whispered back to them, 'We'll swim the next few feet. Feels longer but it's not.'

Then they were up to their bellies in water and with 'Brr!' and 'For Stone's sake!' and other grumblings from Skint they were into water thick with silt for what felt like a long time, with pitch blackness all about and only the sound of Mayweed ahead to guide them on.

Then, to Tryfan's relief, he felt the bottom again, and stumbled up out of the water and found his paws were on better ground than they had been travelling before.

'Gravel and sand now, Sir,' said Mayweed ahead, 'and not far to go.' They plodded on until, indefinably, light came slowly back, and Tryfan saw once more, though still very dimly, the form of mole ahead. He turned round and was able to see Skint rather more clearly. The tunnel steepened upward, the ground, as Mayweed had said, was gravelly but the sides were still very wet, and Tryfan felt cold, but relieved. He had never been in so deep and wet a place before and had not liked it. He doubted if other moles would like it much either.

They felt cold air currents at their snouts, and then saw surface entrances above, and the welcome sight and scent of worm and life, and in the roof the first tendrils of fresh roots appeared.

They progressed on now in silence for a few minutes more, the air getting warmer by the second, the light brightening to the point where they could see each other clearly, and the sounds on the surface returning once more. Yet not the sound of Duncton Wood, nor even the danker sounds of the Marsh End.

They heard the click of coot, and the quack of mallard, and the surging sway of wind through mat-rush, whose roots were solid in the alluvial soil about them. And another sound, of roaring owls, near and powerful. Where were they?

'Now Sirs, we can go to the surface,' said Mayweed with triumph in his voice. 'Follow!' and they did so, emerging into a sunshine that had not been there when they went underground, and on to ground that might as well have been another world from the one they had left. And four more muddy-looking explorers never appeared on the surface before, for each looked at the other and saw their fur was bedraggled with slime and wet, and their talons caked with sand and mud.

Mayweed led them past a bed of mat-rush on to pasture grass and they saw the great river itself, flowing peaceably along.

'But . . .' began Skint astonished.

'. . . it's flowing to our left!' finished Tryfan, amazed.

'But, but, but, but, yes, yes, yes, yes, brave Sirs!' grinned Mayweed.

Tryfan snouted the direction of the sun, looked again at the flowing of the great river, and said, 'You've brought us under the Thames!'

'Correct, Sir, agrees Mayweed modestly,' said Mayweed.

'But how did you find such a tunnel? And how can such a tunnel exist?'

'Good question, simple answer, you brace of pleased moles,' said Mayweed. 'I snouted about down by the Marsh End and came across Holm here, as I've accurately described, up a tree or rather up the inside of a tree, or part of it, and noticed (when he came down) that he was muddy, Sir. Very. He's a Marsh mole, Sir, capable of going into small wet places and coming out again. His forebears were Marsh-Enders, Sir, who ventured out on to the dangerous marshes and survived, Sir, muddily.

'When the plagues came the Marsh moles were affected

like everymole else and Holm here, like me, was left alone, Sir, and did not learn much about the art of talking and what he did learn he did not like.'

Holm crouched up, nodded vigorously at this and then shook his head and crouched down again. Unlike the others, who were grooming themselves as they spoke, Holm was basking contentedly, his snout pointed towards the river, his eyes half-closed, and the mud on his fur drying and cracking in the sun.

'But he talked to me, didn't you, heroic Holm, full of knowledge Mayweed wanted, full of ways your good friend Mayweed desired to know? Yes you did. And he said he had heard of this tunnel and so we set out to find it. Blocked up, dark, gaseous, dangerous, not the work for a mole working alone. Likely to go mad, Sirs, both, and die in darkness.'

Holm groaned to himself.

'You can imagine, intelligent Sirs, one and both, Mayweed's delight and surprise when he emerged some days ago as you just have, here on the wrong side of the Thames, and being the first mole within living memory to have trans-tunnelled this great river from one side to another. Mayweed is not an idiot, Sir, and Mayweed said to himself, This is the way the Duncton Wood moles will evacuate the system and not leave a trace behind! That's what Mayweed thought and thinks and seeing your faces, Skint Sir, and Tryfan, fine mole and leader, he knows you agree with him.'

'But – '

'But how do we get a lot of moles through the pitch blackness, Sir? Mayweed's moment of glory, Sir. Mayweed will lead them, Holm will follow along behind and others of courage, purpose, resolution and without faint hearts will take up the middle positions while a few with large talons and bullying natures will take up the rear and we'll harry them through, Sir! Mayweed humbly suggests, Sirs, that you tell nomole, not until they're here and then make them do it. Democracy, Mayweed boldly

406

avers, on this occasion is not appropriate because anymole
with the slightest trace of intelligence would refuse point
blank and absolutely to go through the trans-tunnel,
brilliant though it is. But fun and excitement it will be for
us, Sir, and helpful Holm can't wait, Sir.'

'Does anymole else know?' asked Skint.

Mayweed looked hurt.

'Mayweed is very well aware, both Sirs, that there are
untrustworthy moles about. He repeats: he suggests you
keep it in the dark, Sirs . . . Hee, hee, hee.' Mayweed
thought this remark very funny and his thin sides went in
and out in a grotesque way and he wheezed laughter.
Holm followed suit but in complete silence.

Skint glowered.

'The tunnel. Keep it in the dark. That's Mayweed's
little joke, Sir,' said Mayweed in explanation. Skint
frowned and scowled and glowered. Mayweed said,
'Sorry, Sir, not funny, extremely unfunny, Sir, Skint dead
right, Sir, nothing to laugh about. Shut up, Holm *now*.'
But Holm thought Mayweed's pun so amusing that he
continued to laugh in such complete silence that the effort
of it had him toppling over on his side and curling up as if
he was dying. Then as suddenly as he had begun he
stopped, crouched up, fell obediently still and lowered his
snout.

'Holm is back in control now,' said Mayweed.

'And where,' asked Skint, 'does this go?' He waved a
talon along the river bank towards a rising front of dense
willows which grew out of a ditch that ran down into the
river.

'Redeem yourself by showing them, Holm,' said
Mayweed.

Holm led them quickly along the river bank, which
curved off to their right, and then over a wooden plank
that crossed the ditch. They saw, rising high above them
and curving away, the concrete columns of the roaring owl
way and high above them the purr and the roar and the
screech of the owls, though no stench, for the only scent

they had was that of the river, and the drying mud and sand on their fur.

'Is there a way under it?' asked Tryfan.

Holm nodded.

'Then I think, Skint, and I believe, that Mayweed and this Marsh mole Holm here may have found a way for us to escape from the grikes without the need to fight, and with maximum mystery and confusion for Henbane. I think Mayweed deserves congratulations.'

'Reserve it until he's got us back under the river alive, if you don't mind, and don't over-praise him because he's going to be even more insufferable,' said Skint, eyes narrowing as they came back to Mayweed, who was now enjoying some food.

'Welcome, Sirs and Holm. . . .'

Skint raised a paw.

'Just say nothing and get us back safely, Mayweed,' he said.

'Indeed, Sir, Mayweed shall. Now!' Which wetly, darkly, and muddily he did.

Chapter Twenty-Four

As Maytime came to Duncton Wood, the final preparations for the coming of the grikes were made amidst growing tension and secrecy. Alder's watchers had reported a slow massing of grikes at Fyfield, and there were rumours that among the refugees that had come to Duncton were members of the sideem, or Henbane's spies.

Nomole knew then or ever discovered if it was true, but Tryfan decided to take no chances, and the rest of the preparations were swift and secret. Tryfan himself travelled down again to the Marsh End with Mayweed and went through the tunnel under the river to explore for two days the routes beyond, and be certain that a swift passage east towards the Wen would be possible if they went that way.

As soon as that possibility was confirmed, Skint was deputed to seal off the Marsh End, so that nomole might suspect what plans were apaw there, while Maundy oversaw the evacuation of recent mothers and their now growing and rebellious youngsters from the vulnerable Eastside to the central slopes.

Meanwhile Alder completed his training of the watchers by dividing them into groups of four, which was deemed the most manageable fighting and defensive unit, and put them into the recently vacated Eastside burrows to develop communication tunnels and retreats designed to enable a small number of moles to put up a protracted defence.

Other units were sent out on the exposed south-eastern slopes beyond the wood, which faced the roaring owl way, to prepare successive lines of defence at two levels, a system which Alder and Skint pioneered and which was to mark them as the greatest strategists of their time.

Meanwhile, in complete secrecy, a few selected moles, whose names even to this day are not known for they are not among the records kept by Spindle (except that it is known they were led by Tryfan himself under the guidance and inspiration of Mayweed and the ever monosyllabic Holm), created tunnels and false cul-de-sacs in the rank and grubby corners of the eastern Marsh End where, it was hoped, a small covert group of brave moles could stay on after the main body of the Duncton moles had gone, to harass and intimidate the invaders.

The only other elder who knew of this work, not excepting even Comfrey himself, was Skint, who, with Tryfan, shared the overall knowledge of what the plans for the whole system were.

Night after night Tryfan and his few companions crept down to the Marsh End, now guarded by watchers, and there they delved and dug those strange chambers and secret ways which, in time, would be known to all moles as the Marsh End Defence. At four levels they worked, secret sometimes even from each other, developing entrances and exits of such subtlety and cleverness that it was said that more than once a mole exited from the depths at which he had been working to take fresh air only to find he could not find his way in again.

The only mole, apart from Skint and Tryfan (and Mayweed, whose wanderings could never be controlled), who moved freely was Spindle, who spent those final days in Duncton Wood talking to the old moles and collecting from them what he had collected from the refugees – the rhymes and rituals and traditions of the system, and chronicling them. If a mistake had been made in all these preparations it was that the secret library he had created was located in the south, and therefore where the conflict with the grikes would most likely be. So Spindle worked day and night scribing what moles told him, helped occasionally by Mayweed who added his own scribings of this and that he'd heard, and also the patterns of the

410

tunnels he had found, the first time any system was ever recorded that way.

'What is it?' Spindle would ask as he worked at this strange scribing.

'It's routes and ways, scholastic Sir,' said Mayweed, 'to help moles to find where they are.' But where the Marsh End Defence was he left a blank on the bark, lest his scribing might be found and interpreted by alien moles.

Sometimes then, though always briefly, Spindle would go up to the surface of the Ancient System and look about its empty glades and wish that Thyme was with him still. Thyme he had loved and lost. Then he would wonder about his son Bailey, and fret for his safety and well-being, and hope that he was safe and well. He had heard nothing of him, though he had travelled more widely in the system than most, but then youngsters are kept near their burrows at that time of year, and a male might easily never see them. Then back down would Spindle go, to lose himself and mask his sense of loss once more in his self-appointed tasks.

Meanwhile, on the surface and in happy contrast to these grim and feverish preparations, the sweet tide of May passed through the wood, and brought to it a beauty which, though few in those stressed days stopped to ponder it, all there were to remember after as a dream which left them always yearning to return.

Up on the Ancient System, at the highest part of the wood, the great beeches turned from bud to frail green leaf, and then from that same frailty, as if at a single breath of the scented May breeze, the leaves matured to form a majesty that rose in high green sinewy chambers of light above the brown leaf-strewn floor; high above the great Stone itself rose those great branches of green light, and put into a passing mole the thought that to be a mole, and to be in Duncton, is to be alive and to be forever in the way of summer.

While on the southern and eastern slopes, where Alder's watchers strove to make defences underground, the dry surface of beech leaves and scrub was broken by the rising curl of green bracken shoots, whose stems seem filled with sunlight, and whose leaves unfurled with each passing day from weakness to strength, rising higher and higher, and side by side, stiff and sure in the breeze.

While among them, startling here and there, grey squirrel ran, and green woodpecker flitted, and sometimes the snapped frond of bracken, and the skein of its thwarted sap, showed a place where a fox had gone, pausing, marking, lightly breaking, and then scampering on from the eastern scarp over to the wide hunting space of the Pastures.

Yet most simple and most beautiful of all was that flush of bluebells that spread down over the lower slopes budding as April ended, and flowering now in May, replacing the white layer of anemone, and flooding with blue those quiet places where, with the first warmth of spring, yellow primrose had come. While more darkly, where the fires of earlier years had not made their way, the green dog's mercury rose, giving cover to mole and blackbird alike. Sometimes then the sun shone deeply down, lighting up some open secret place between the damp boles of trees where a purple orchid peeped, or a wood mouse paused, hesitating, nervous, brow furrowed and wondering if the moles, the masters of the wood, would ever return here, to this lovely place, where once, before the plagues, they had held sway. Until such time then he, like the other creatures, would go but nervously about, for all creatures know the balance of a wood, and wish to see the ancient order restored; and to know that the troubled years are past. In Duncton that would one day mean that moles were masters once again.

The tranquil busy-ness of May travelled on, then, to the moist depths of the Marsh End scrub where once only the lowliest Duncton moles went free and now only the most secret crept.

Yet there too came beauty, for a stand of ramsons brought a delving mole out to see the stars of its flowers, seeming bright in that damp place, while along the very edge of the wood itself, where it fronts onto the inhospitable Marshes beneath which Mayweed had found them a way of escape, the pink flowers of lady's smock caught the gentle wind. Then from floret to floret, on an early summer's day, an orange-tip butterfly dipped and fluttered, landed and was still, its wings gently rising and falling as it fed, before it rose above the pink flowers once more and the breeze caught it, and it gaily travelled out over the sedges towards the great Thames itself, but suddenly nervous, as if it sensed that the moles, whose spirit it knew as the greatest of all the creatures in the wood, were nervous too.

So might a breeze have blown, so might an orange-tip have fluttered, and so, too briefly, might a mole have paused and wondered at the beauty of the Stone-protected wood before, with a sigh he, or she, turned, and listened, and prepared: for movement was apaw, and mole knew what it was, and that it was dark, and approaching from the west.

Then on a day when the sun was summer-hot for the first time, and the air heavy with an evening storm, Alder himself came up from the south-eastern slopes accompanied by not one but two travel-worn watchers.

''Tis starting,' he said in his deep voice. 'The grikes are on their way. Tell Tryfan what you have told me.'

They had come back to the system quite independently of each other. One from Fyfield and the other from Bladon, both to report movement of grikes Dunctonward. Steady it was and slow, for the routes were not known to the grikes and they made some false turns. The watchers, who had travelled night and day, estimated that they were at least two days ahead, but not more than four.

'Other watchers will start coming in now, Tryfan,' said Alder, 'and we'll know more accurately what the strength and disposition of the grikes really is. But allow yourself two days and you'll be safe enough.'

413

Although Alder knew that Tryfan had several options for an evacuation from the system, he did not know the details and nor did he yet wish to know. He went on, 'We'll keep you informed of what we hear so that when the time comes you can make your decisions. The watchers are with you to a mole.'

'Aye, and will fight for Duncton to the death,' said one of the watchers fervently, tired though he was.

It was the moment Tryfan had waited for, and for which he and the others had planned. And that evening he summoned as many moles as he could into the great chamber near the Stone where Longest Night had been celebrated when they had first come back to the system. Then all of them had managed to get in, but now, their numbers swollen by refugees and pupped youngsters, not all could, so some crammed the tunnels leading to the chamber, and others craned their necks to peer in from surface entrances to listen to their leader speak.

'Your time in Duncton is nearly over, for all here know we cannot fight the grikes with talons, for they are stronger than us, and more numerous,' Tryfan began. 'So we will leave. . . .'

But mole looked at mole as a ripple of anxiety ran over them, for most had thought the building of defences meant that they would stay for a time at least.

'But we will leave in an order and by a route that your elected elders have prescribed, and the organisation of it will be in the paws of Maundy and her helpers, who have been trained for such work. There will be no alarm and no panic, not among moles young or old. All will be calm, and all protected as is the Stone's will. I cannot pretend there is no danger, for there is. And some here may be asked to show courage beyond what they believe they have. But history will remember this time, and history will say that those moles of Duncton, whatever mole they were, showed courage and purpose and resource.

'You will each have your orders and your task and we will leave this great system, which has been haven to

414

followers of the Stone for centuries; and will be again – '

'Aye, 'twill be so! Aye!' shouted somemole.

'For the Stone will protect us and give us the strength we will need in the days, and the months, and the years that are coming. All of you here are followers, as I am, and you believe in the Stone, and in its great Silence.'

'Yes we do! Praise be the Stone!' many shouted.

'Well now, moles of Duncton, and those others of you who were born in other systems and yet honour us by making this your refuge, and us your friends, the Stone has given you a great task whose true beginning is now and in the days ahead. For you are the first of the followers who turn against the grikes of dread Henbane and say, "No more! You can maim, and instruct and torture, and snout, and chase to death itself, but our spirit and our purpose you cannot kill!"'

'Aye, 'tis true every word! That's what we think!' yelled out one of Alder's most trusted watchers, who was not normally given to many words, and his cry was taken up and repeated loudly by others so that the chamber shook with support for Tryfan.

'Well, the Stone will give you strength if you hear its Silence, which is what my father Bracken knew and it is what Boswell himself has showed me. . . .'

'Blessed be his memory!' cried out an old female.

'Tell us what we must do!' called out another, 'and we shall do it, Tryfan. Tell us where you will lead us to!'

'Then listen and I will tell you. Grikes are ruthless, well organised and purposeful. Their guardmoles are well trained to kill and to fight. But we have made our plans, some of which you know, others of which we felt it best to keep silent about until they are effected. Some of you here will be taking your places down on the south east side, where soon I will join you. You will delay the grikes as long as you can, and you will retreat only slowly, as Alder has instructed, and this will give the best time to escape.

'Others among you have been instructed in how to lead the youngsters to safety, though the route we finally use has not yet been decided. The longer we delay using it, the more certain will it be that the grikes believe we are all here. Then more of the guardmoles will be sent to Duncton leaving us less likely to be attacked once we are clear. . . Others have their own instructions, of which I have no need to talk.'

'But where shall we go and where find refuge?' asked one mole for the many, and they were silent then, and concerned, for it is one thing to retreat, another to arrive again in a place of safety. Then also, for the first time, it was coming into the hearts of many that soon, very soon, they would leave their beloved system; and among them were some who might never return.

'We shall go – ' began Tryfan, looking around the packed and silent chamber. 'We shall go – ' But he stopped and lowered his snout and was silent for a time, his mouth moving in some evocation to the Stone, and Spindle on one side and old Comfrey on the other waited in silence as the others did for him to speak.

Finally he looked up and said, 'What I have to say now is most especially for the youngest of the system, and the mothers that made them, and to those who have seen but one Longest Night through, for these are our future, and to these will I speak. So let them come forward, let them by.' And one by one the youngsters, and some late ones who were barely more than pups, and many such who, for reason of their smallness and lowly status had been pushed to the back or the tunnels outside the chamber, were found space as the older moles gave way to them, and encouraged them to go as near as they could to Tryfan and the other elders. While at Tryfan's side, Spindle stared at this throng of moles and sought to see if there was one there who might be Bailey, whom he had a wish to see, if only once.

'I have been asked where we are to go in moledom, which seems forsaken of the Stone and overtaken or harassed by the grikes. Well, I will tell you the truth: I know not where we will be tomorrow, or the day after that.

416

Nor next week nor next month, I know not. But only this: where you of Duncton now carry a memory of Duncton Wood, of a system beloved by many moles and trusted by many more who have never been here, where *you* carry your memory to, there will *we* always be. When you remember where it was that you were pups and loved, and where your spirit first grew within sight of the great Stone, there will we be. And there, in that memory, a part of which each one of you holds as a most precious thing, there will we all wait. As the leaves of the great beeches will wither and die in the autumn so will we leave this system now. But as the buds return once more, and then the leaves, and then the great glory of the trees in summer, so one day will some of us return. Distant that day perhaps, unknown yet, but in the good sweet earth of your memories will our system survive as seeds that time and love and faith will nurture, scattered though you may become, until a dawn breaks when you, or your pups, or your grand-pups, turn your snouts to the good air and say, "Now, now is Duncton ready once more, to Duncton we will go." Then you, or your pups, or your grand-pups will come, and in the shadow of the Stone in which your faith dwells, there you or yours will know that where you have been was never far away, never away at all.'

Then Tryfan's voice dropped low, and the youngsters seemed to reach nearer to him as he continued. 'Remember this, you who have many Longest Nights to come, and wonder why we collect here, and why we are worried, and why we talk low: there will be a time when I shall have gone, and Comfrey whom you love, and Spindle here my friend; then you may recall something dimly, something distant, a memory of May. When moles who cared for you and saw you threatened, and knew that their future lay in your hearts and paws and not their own, did their best to see you safeguarded.

'In all the long history of Duncton there has been no time like this, though there have been troubles enough. But not a time as now, when we must leave, taking with us something which now we share, but which with the passage of time will be broken and separate, a dim thing, half seen, half felt, yet sweet and lovely and remembered as a pup remembers the contentment of its home burrow.

'You who listen now, and are still young, look around at our faces this day here in the heart of Duncton, and know that you are loved, and remember that you were loved in the shadow and the Silence of one of the great Stones of moledom.

'And how will you know when to return? It will be hard to know that, and perhaps it will need as much courage for some to come back as it takes us to leave. How then will you know?'

Tryfan paused, and looked around at Spindle, and Spindle smiled and touched his friend as if to say what all there were thinking: that Tryfan was their leader, and they would follow him, and trust his words.

'Oh yes,' continued Tryfan then, his voice stronger now, 'yes you'll know. For one is coming who will bring the troubles of these years to an end, and he will be the Stone Mole.

'He will come, and I believe that we in Duncton, and you who have not yet even seen one Longest Night through, will aid his coming, and give it meaning and purpose; I believe that the name of Duncton will ring out to all of moledom, as the sound of a talon on true flint rings out and is heard.

'The Stone Mole will come and the Silence of the Stone will be allmole's and then the truest coming of all will be. When those fragments of memory of a system that was – for fragments are all they will be by then – turn and reverberate in your hearts, or your pup's hearts, and tell of a place that was and is, where once moles were loved, and will be once more. Not only loved but *much* loved, and safe, and belonging.

'Not much different, perhaps, this system than another, not special or different or chosen but as any other might be. But its moles never turned from the Stone. For

418

this will the Stone Mole be sent, to give back what we lost of ourselves, and to show how moles may live true wherever they may be.

'One day across moledom, moles will say, "Duncton? They were true moles, they helped, they had courage, they had faith in the Stone, they were never, not once, of the dark Word. Not once."

'Then those who follow us will feel pride. Then will those memories that you yourself made stir anew. Then will there be a yearning to return once more. Then will the few who remain dare to come back and start again.

'So listen now: go up into your wood, go among the trees, go down into your tunnels, touch their walls, go even to the Chamber of Roots that surrounds the Stone, go into the sunlight alone and together, look, touch and remember. And then, when you have each done that, return one last time to touch your Stone.

'For there is our beginning and ending and in its shadows will be our beginning again. It sends us on a journey soon, but one day it will guide our kin back home, safeguarded.'

Tryfan stopped and reached to touch the nearest moles, who reached to touch and bless others near by, so that the moles of Duncton knew themselves and showed their love for one another. Then, when that had been, and in silence, they went up on to the surface of the wood, or down loved and familiar tunnels, and did as Tryfan had bid them do, which was to go out into their system and know it one last time, and remember it for always.

Some saw the bracken that grew, and the great beeches that rose, and some the bluebells that spread across the lower slopes: others paused and touched and talked, and took the scent of the worm-rich ways of their system; a few danced while others sang, and all made a memory that would see them through the troubles that lay ahead.

'No Starling, we're not allowed to! Starling!'
'He said we could go anywhere! Anyway, Lorren,

419

you're always so *pathetic* and *we* want to go down there and see.'

The voices were those of youngsters, both females. That of Lorren was uncertain and fearful; that of Starling utterly bold. She spoke with the authority of the pup who rules the others and will have no truck with questioning or doubt. There was no fear in her voice, only impatience and curiosity, mixed with delighted excitement.

The place was Barrow Vale, and the mole listening to their argument about whether or not to go into the tunnels was Spindle. He had come down after Tryfan's address to the assembled moles, making his way through the lovely trees of the slopes, to return one last time to the place that he and Thyme had so gently and sweetly taken hold of their love and made it. He had come as Tryfan had suggested to make a memory, but also to say farewell, for he knew his task was ever with Tryfan now, to follow and advise him, and be close when he was most needed. Yet he had come, too, for something more than that, as if answering that need Thyme had made in him, that at times of trouble and doubt they and theirs might go to Barrow Vale, and there find help and comfort.

So he had ventured down once more into the tunnels where first they had loved, and then brought his pup, and now he was there a third and last time, to find peace with his memory, and strength for what was to come.

But just as he thought he should venture out once more and go up to the Stone as Tryfan had wisely suggested they might all finally do, there had been a patter and a scurry of mole above, first one, and then two more. Then the voices and the argument, and Spindle stayed in the shadows and listened.

'Well, what do you think? Do you agree with Lorren or with me? It *was* your idea?'

It was Starling's voice again, seeming to ask a question but really giving a command. Spindle smiled in sympathy with the third mole and waited for the reply.

When it came it was too soft for Spindle to hear but its

content was clear enough, for immediately Starling shouted in triumph, 'There you are, Lorren, you'll have to come with us now or be left all alone, and we won't care.'

'It's not fair!' said Lorren plaintively.

But her protest was in vain, for the other two scrabbled at the surface, found an entrance near where Spindle had come down, and poked their snouts in and peered about.

'Spooky!' said a voice.

'Dusty,' said Starling's. 'Come on!' And with that, and Lorren following, they helter-skeltered down into the hallowed chamber of Barrow Vale.

For a moment Spindle watched them in silence as their eyes adjusted to the dark and they snouted this way and that. Two female youngsters and a male. It was obvious which was Starling, for she was bigger than the others, and had that appealing eagerness of a mole in love with life, and impatient to get on with it. While Lorren was smaller and uncertain, though like Starling a good-looking mole of glossy coat and clean paws. The third, the male, was of solid build and well contained, and took a serious stance and looked about him appraisingly but with considerable concern.

'Hello!' said Spindle in as friendly a way as he could.

The three youngsters were as startled and surprised as squirrels. Starling immediately said, 'Come on!' and half laughing, half shrieking sought to lead the others away. Lorren followed willingly, shrieking too. But the male stayed still, staring, and unafraid.

'What's your name?' he asked, as a mole asks who trusts the world, for he has never been hurt and never expects to be.

'Spindle,' said Spindle.

'I've heard of you!' Behind him, peering round a tunnel entrance, the two females whispered and watched, and then Lorren giggled and Starling shushed her to listen.

'I'm not going to hurt you,' said Spindle.

'If you did Starling would come and protect me,' said the youngster with complete assurance.

421

'And your name?' asked Spindle. Then he frowned and said, 'Though I think I do know what it is.' For he did, or felt he did, as well as he knew his own.

'What is it?' asked the mole.

'You're Bailey,' said Spindle softly.

'Yes,' said Bailey, quite unsurprised.

The two came a little closer together and the females stayed in the background, as if sensing that this was something not to interrupt.

'Why did you come here?' asked Spindle.

'Don't know,' said Bailey. 'I wanted to see Barrow Vale and Starling said today I could see what I wanted. *She* wanted to see the Marsh End. But she said she'd come with me, and Lorren had to come too. We go everywhere together. They're like sisters to me and Starling is my best friend.'

'You're lucky then. A mole needs friends.'

'Why did you come here?' asked Bailey.

'To meet you, I think,' said Spindle, tears in his eyes.

'Why?' asked Bailey.

'So you'd remember Spindle, all your life. And hear him tell you that you, like those other two giggling over there, are much loved.'

Bailey looked very serious.

'Are you going to take us back to the Stone now we've seen Barrow Vale?' he said. 'Is that why you came?'

'I think so, Bailey, yes. That's probably why I came.'

Then Bailey turned and sought out Starling and Lorren and said, 'He's going to take us to the Stone. He's a very important mole. His name's Spindle.'

'Hello!' each of them said, rather shyly.

'Will you tell us some things on the way?' asked Starling.

'What about?' asked Spindle, leading them back to the surface.

'Anything interesting,' said Lorren.

'Something utterly fascinating nomole else would tell us,' said Starling.

Spindle turned to Bailey, who had taken a position just short of his right flank.

'What would you like me to tell you?' he asked.

'Well, I don't know really,' said Bailey. 'Anything, I s'pose, but don't go too fast!' And Spindle slowed, and let his son come close to him, very close.

'Then I'll tell you about a mole called Thyme,' said Spindle.

'Is it a story?' said Lorren.

'I bet it's about love!' said Starling.

'Will it make me nervous?' asked Bailey.

'Yes and yes and no,' said Spindle, and no happier mole than he made trek to the Stone that afternoon, with his own at his side, close as a mole could be. And of all the moles that made memories that day, as Tryfan had commanded they should, none made happier nor more durable memories than Starling, and Lorren, and Spindle, and his pup by Thyme called Bailey.

Nor were there any four more comforted by each other's presence as, later, by the Stone, Tryfan and Comfrey said a prayer and blessing for all the moles there, and wished them well, and told them to return to Duncton Wood one day safeguarded, never afraid of the grikes, ever faithful to their home system and the Stone.

Nor did any other four take such pleasure in having so briefly met, as that evening, as dusk fell, they went their ways back to their burrows, to prepare for the morrow, and the coming of the grikes.

Chapter Twenty-Five

It was two days later, at that grey time before true dawn when a watching mole may not be fully alert, and the light makes the simplest thing ambiguous and doubtful, that the grikes came to Duncton Wood.

Suddenly, powerfully, and bloodily.

Over the top of the roaring owl way they came, which was the least likely route they might have taken, down a sluice and then silently across to the flank of one of Alder's defence outposts, avoiding the moles guarding the cow cross-under.

'Hey! Mole! Which way from here?' Some guardmole or other called, his voice pretending weariness.

'Where do you come from, mate? A new arrival? The watchers send you . . .?' and whatever mole that was spoke no more, for the full thrust of guardmole talons was in his screaming mouth and throat, and as pain took his body into death another crashed on by, huge and menacing, and took the second watcher there, and then the third, and blood was in that tunnel, and it was Duncton's.

So, turning the defences over by surprise and resolution, the guardmoles came, and for a time it seemed that it was all the Duncton moles could do to contain the first onslaught, let alone get a message up to the main system that the grikes had come.

But then Alder arrived, took command of the attacked section, and killed two of the three first entrants with his own talons, urging others to take the now empty places in the defensive burrow, and running down the hidden tunnels the watchers had prepared to the cross-under itself, where the main attack would soon begin.

Despite the initial losses, Alder was too experienced a

fighter to be disheartened or even surprised by what had happened. The damage would have been much greater if Duncton Wood had not been surrounded on three sides by the Thames, and so protected against attack. As it was, the fourth, the south-eastern side, was well defined by the roaring owl way which rose above the slopes blocking off that side too, and very effectively. Only in a few places – like the main cross-under, the route which the bulk of the grikes would have ultimately to take, and some drainage pipes – was the way breached, and these places were well defended. But no defence could protect against attackers coming over the way at any point along its length, except that they would have to cross the drainage dyke that ran along the bottom of the way. This was crossed by tiny bridges, pipes and sluices of one kind and another, and were less easily defended. Alder's belief was that because to get into the Duncton system via them attackers would have to cross the way, these were unlikely to be major threats. The more so because such attacks were only possible during the night and early morning when the roaring owls were not travelling in numbers.

So an attack at dawn, by one of the sluices, was no real surprise, though it was hard to trace precisely where the point of entry was. Pausing only to send a messenger warning Tryfan that the grikes had come, Alder himself went to see what was apaw.

'There! *That's* where they're coming from!' He cried out after investigating the area south of the cross-under. He stationed moles at the foot of the sluice and for a time grikes and watchers fought to keep control of the sluice way. It was hard, and it was fatal for some, but Alder's watchers contained the attack and drove the remaining grikes back up the sluice with shouts of rage from both sides, and the first awareness of how violent such fighting might be.

So, with bloodied talons and pain, with swift death to either side, the attack on Duncton began as a dawn sun rose across the vales below Duncton Hill, and on its highest part the great Stone was flushed with a light as red as blood.

The attack settled into a prolonged battle, and the plans that Tryfan and Skint had prepared began to go into smooth action.

Sleepy youngsters were woken, mothers alerted, males who were to be travellers rather than fighters took their places in the tunnels they had been directed to, and the first stage of the evacuation of Duncton began. No time left to say farewell to the places or friends who were loved, those times were past. Now all were silent in the tunnels, and obedient, trusting the elders and Maundy's helpers, and following their orders as they cared for the young who were frightened by the sudden change, and for the oldest ones who were confused.

Their places and positions had long been established, but a few still had to travel the tunnels to take them up, mainly adults who had had tasks away from their families. These now went urgently through the tunnels which echoed with the solid patter of purposeful paws.

Others went more leisurely, among them Maundy, checking that the groups were in their appointed places and settling them for the wait to come – for nomole would travel until the order was given and none, indeed, knew where they would be bound, for that secret was well kept.

Once or twice a mole got lost, and had to be guided. A youngster from a large family who always got lost found himself suddenly among a group of watchers, grimly talking, their flanks seeming huge and threatening, and he began to cry, eyes wide in sudden insecurity, until a calming paw of one of the adults settled on his shoulder and a deep voice said, 'Here now, it'll be no good if you cry! You won't be able to help us fight off the grikes if you do that! Now why don't you tell me your name and tunnel?' And the youngster's sobs ceased, and he allowed himself to be led away, rejoining his family with an important watcher at his side, the sobs all gone, and the cheerful expression on his face of one who was lost, is back safely, and has an adventure to report once the scolding is over.

While elsewhere, on the upper slopes, Maundy found an old male wandering, very confused, and saying he was off to find some food because he always did at this time of day.

'Come on, old thing, come with me. You know me, I'm Maundy.'

'Aye, Comfrey's lass. . . .'

And Maundy smiled to be so called, and took the elderly male back down to the safety of the tunnels, and into the care of the watcher in charge of his group.

Meanwhile, in the elders' chamber by the Stone, Skint, Comfrey, Smithills and the others were listening, at a meeting presided over by Tryfan, to the reports of the fighting and evacuation as they came in.

They had known this time would come, and had prepared several routes up from the Eastside through which messengers would have a clear run. Neither Tryfan nor Skint had had any illusions that the grikes would be kept back forever. It was more a question of an orderly retreat from one defensive position to the next, and it seemed now that after the initial surprise of the attack, which had been ably dealt with by Alder himself, the fighting had stabilised at the cross-under.

'Alder's watchers are covering the flanks, are they?' Smithills was asking.

'Yes, yes, the other potential routes in are well covered, and reserves are ready to go to them when attacks come there as surely they will,' replied Tryfan. 'If their spies have not already told them of those ways in, they will find them soon enough.'

'I'm not of a mind to stay up here talking for much longer,' said Smithills restlessly, flexing his talons and pacing around the burrow. 'I mean, 'tis a fine thing to plan but I want to get my talons at the bastards.'

'There isn't one of us who doesn't want to be down

there,' said Tryfan, 'and your time will come, Smithills, but it's better to have waited here and hear the reports as they come in and make sure that the evacuation is under way. Anyway, Alder must be given full command down there to gain his own confidence and that of his watchers, but I shall be going down there shortly myself and you, Smithills, will come with me. You'll have your chance.' Smithills nodded, satisfied, and crouched down again silently.

Tryfan turned to Skint, who had taken a stance close to Comfrey and was tense and serious.

'Skint will stay here as we arranged,' Tryfan told them, 'for he knows the defensive planning and the details of the evacuation.'

'Have you d-d-decided which routes you're taking, or will we have to wait until we see which way the f-fighting goes?' asked Comfrey. In recent weeks he had given up the running of the system to Tryfan, and had approved the decision that the only moles with full knowledge of the plans were Tryfan and Skint.

'Yes, we have decided on a route out,' confided Tryfan, 'but even now we will keep silent about it . . . It is essential that the grikes never know what route we use.' He paused, for there was a commotion down the tunnel as Maundy arrived.

She was calm, but breathless, and with a warm glance at all of them said, 'I'm not as young as I was, but that's not going to stop me! Now I can tell you that the groups are all in place, there is great calm, and they wait only our instructions. Rushe is continuing to check and double-check, and will send reports.' Maundy took her usual place next to Comfrey, who reached over and touched her gently, as he always did.

'Good, you have done well!' said Tryfan. 'Now, one or other of us must always be here to decide when the evacuation will start. But we need to draw as many of Henbane's forces to the centre of the fighting to be sure that the ways from the system itself are as clear as they can be.

'Remember all of you, if for any reason both Skint and I are lost then listen to Mayweed: he knows, and he will guide you.' The others looked at each other: 'lost' meant killed. They all faced unknown risks now, and whatmole knew what Tryfan might find when he went down to the front near the cross-under? One reason why Smithills was going with him was to be protection for him.

Tryfan looked round at them all confidently, and they felt his calm purpose.

'Now,' he said, 'where's Spindle?'

'Yes, where the Stone *is* Spindle?' said Skint.

'I saw him a short time ago,' said Maundy immediately, 'near the Chamber of Roots, carrying some records and saying he wouldn't be long and you're not to worry.'

Tryfan smiled. 'He's hiding the records for future generations, just as he hid certain things in Seven Barrows, and at Harrowdown.'

'Well, there's better things to be doing,' grumbled Smithills.

Tryfan raised a paw to stop him.

'Each to his own. Don't you want future generations in Duncton to know what part *you* played in these historic days?'

'Me? Knackered old Smithills scribed about? 'T'would be a fine thing that!' said Smithills chuckling.

'Whatmole knows what records Spindle's keeping?' said Tryfan. 'I certainly don't! Now I think we had better go down to the Eastside, Smithills.'

'What of Spindle?'

'He'll care for himself well enough,' said Tryfan, 'and he'll show his snout in the right place when the time comes, have no fear of that!'

The two moles said a quick farewell to the others, and took the fastest route downslope, just as the early morning sun was beginning to slant in at the surface entrances, bringing colour to the lighter soils on the Eastside of Duncton Hill. They could tell there was a light wind from the south east, for it carried the first steady sound of the roaring owls, which always took their course on the way as morning came. In winter they formed a line of staring eyes at this time of the morning, in summer just a sound and the stench that sickened a mole.

'If they were kept out of that sluice, then there'll be no more across the way until nightfall, when the roaring owls slow down,' said Tryfan as they hurried along. But Smithills was silent still, his face serious: he had dreamed of getting his talons on a grike for many a moleyear, and now his time was coming.

They surfaced at the highest of the defence burrows and found the moles there tense but calm.

'You are welcome, Tryfan,' said their team leader, 'and in time to wish us luck, for we're going down shortly when others who have taken their turn come here to rest.'

Tryfan said a word of encouragement to each, adding that not only would he and Smithills wish them luck but they'd come along as well, for they wanted to see the defence of the cross-under for themselves. The moles' tension seemed to lift, and their spirits to rise yet higher, for to go into the fighting with Tryfan himself, why that was an honour, and surely good luck. . . .

One mole, a young male, was silent and a little apart from the others. He seemed to be whispering to himself as Tryfan went to him.

'Well?' said Tryfan easily. 'Are you as nervous as me, mole?'

'Are *you* nervous, Sir?' said the mole in surprise.

'Oh yes,' said Tryfan, 'but don't tell the others!'

'I thought it was just me,' said the mole.

'I doubt that!' said Tryfan. 'Now, what were you whispering about?'

'Just a prayer, Sir, to the Stone. Just something I was taught in my home burrow. . . .'

'Well then, mole,' said Tryfan, raising his voice a little, 'I think you could repeat it for all of us.' And the others, hearing this, nodded and fell silent, as the young mole made a petition for the Stone's guidance, and protection.

As the prayer finished, and they each uttered their own endings, there was a scamper and a clamour in the tunnel leading upslope to them and two very weary moles tumbled in, followed by another, limping and bleeding from a long cut to the shoulder. A fourth was encouraging him from behind.

'It's Ramsey wounded!' said one of the waiting reserves. Ramsey was known to Tryfan as one of Alder's ablest and most aggressive stalwarts, and not a mole to trifle with.

'Guardmole bastards,' muttered Ramsey, 'but I got two of them. They're not so powerful as all that, once you get your talons into them.'

Then as a mole tended to his wound he cursed and swore and finally conceded it would be better if he crouched down, and rested for a bit, Tryfan nodded to Smithills and the reserves and left on the final part of the journey. They surfaced near the cross-under itself, and as the four they travelled with were directed to the right side of the cross-under, whose entrance rose darkly above, Alder came forward to greet them.

'Tryfan! You are welcome! What was the last message you had?'

'That the cross-under is held stable, and the sluice safe now that the roaring owls have started their morning run.'

'Aye, 'tis true,' said Alder.

Tryfan looked at him. His fur was bedabbled with grime, and on his right paw and shoulder were flecks of blood and gore. He looked tired but alert. From time to time, moles came up to him and he gave his orders to them clearly and with confidence. The moles were well disposed to protect the cross-under, and Tryfan knew that in making Alder commander of the watchers, he had chosen well.

'Thing is, Tryfan, the guardmoles don't learn. They're coming as we expected them to, though the initial attack down the sluice surprised us. Probably Weed's work with the help of a spy.'

'Any sign of Weed or Henbane?'

431

Alder shook his head. 'But don't worry, they'll be near here somewhere. I'll give them that, they're not cowards.'

Tryfan told him briefly that all was well in the system itself, and all the preparations made, and that he could tell the watchers that their kin and friends would be well protected.

'The longer we can hold them here, the more resources they are forced to bring and the safer will the evacuation be.'

'Have you decided a route yet?'

'Perhaps,' said Tryfan obscurely. He was keeping the river tunnel secret to the last, even from trusted moles like Alder.

'How are the watchers faring, Alder?'

'Well. Very well. They'll do so the better to see you here, so come and show yourself as we talk.'

Alder took him on a tour of the back tunnels of the cross-under, Tryfan being careful to show his snout to as many of the watchers as he could, and to speak encouragingly to them, and tell them that the youngsters – for many had young up in the system – were being well cared for and were out of harm's way.

'It's a quiet period at the moment while the grikes prepare another tactic. We've watchers on all the likely openings, and back-ups on the slopes.'

Tryfan nodded his agreement.

'There'll be a problem tonight at the sluices, for the way will be crossable for mole again as the roaring owls ease off,' he said. 'But if we can hold them till then – better still until the morning – before giving up the cross-under and retreating to the next line then we will have done better than we hoped, and shown these moles that the followers have purpose and strength.'

Tryfan stopped speaking as Alder raised his paw to indicate that they had almost reached the most advanced point of the Duncton moles' defence line in the cross-under itself. They moved silently down a concrete drainage run built by twofoots but blocked off by mole.

'This takes us to the most vulnerable part of the cross-under route,' whispered Alder, and they emerged on to the surface with the cross-under roof high above them. The air was colder here, the sun cut off by rising concrete buttresses, and the place echoed to an ominous mix of sound made up of distant roaring owl, water dripping, and the sinister drumming of guardmole paws.

A watcher platoon waited in the surface burrow to one side of the tunnel's exit, another was spread out on the surface nearby and a third, with Smithills among them, crouched a little forward, by a high litter of grey stone blocks. The ground was wet and puddled, and off to the far side lay two guardmoles, dead, blood from their sodden bodies staining the water around them.

'There were more,' said Alder tersely, 'but we tipped them down into the sluices.' He indicated the low wall that edged the entrance to the cross-under, beyond which, Tryfan knew, the ground dropped vertically to a deep sluice.

'How the Stone did Smithills get out there?' grumbled Alder. 'What's he doing? We're perfectly capable of – '

But suddenly there was a rush out of the murk ahead and three guardmoles came running, straight at the forward group. With a roar Smithills rose to them, the others at his side, and he smote one hard to the flank and then moved forward to meet the other two, the shouting and screaming echoing around them all in the cavernous cross-under, drowning out all other sound. . . .

Tryfan moved automatically forward but Alder put a restraining paw on his shoulder.

' "We will win this war by an orderly planned retreat when the grikes come, not by a show of bravery and pointless courage . . ." Your words, Tryfan. I think Smithills and the others can deal with this assault.'

So it seemed, for the guardmoles, though joined for a time by three more, soon broke up and retreated. Smithills grunted and swore after them, as one of the watchers, wounded, was helped back to them and another immediately replaced him.

433

'You see they can't make headway except in a large group and when they tried that we were able to hide in the surface burrows and emerge for quick strikes which broke them up and confused them. They don't know what to do,' said Alder. 'They're just not used to persistent opposition.'

'Don't worry, they'll learn soon enough,' said Tryfan grimly. 'But perhaps not so soon that we have not gained the valuable time we need to make good our escape.'

Smithills shook his talons aggressively down the cross-under one last time and came back to the defence burrow.

'And that,' he said, 'was worth waiting a lifetime for. I didn't kill the bugger but I wounded him and gave him a message to take back to his friends.'

'And what was that?' asked Tryfan.

' "Tell them there's plenty more like Smithills waiting for them in Duncton Wood!" That did it! That's what I told him.'

Tryfan laughed. 'Come on then, come and do a Smithills somewhere else, for we're going to visit the other routes under the way.'

'I'll stay here awhile,' said Alder. 'You'll probably find Ramsey's gone back down that way again over by the sluice, preparing some defences for the evening. Maybe you can persuade him to take a rest – I can't!' It was good to see the loyalty that Alder inspired.

So they moved on and found Ramsey weary, still limping from his wounded shoulder, but triumphant for the early morning's success. Only from Tryfan himself would he take the order to retreat upslope to rest again. Even that was difficult, for he said that Tryfan should not be out with only Smithills to protect him.

'What the Stone do you mean "only Smithills"?' said Smithills with mock outrage.

'Go on, Ramsey, off upslope with you,' said Tryfan. 'The Stone will protect me, and if it doesn't I'm sure Smithills here will do his best. It's all I can do to stop him setting off to wage war all by himself on the guardmoles, so Stone help any guardmoles who reach us here.'

434

Yet they did have their moments of danger later in the morning. For having followed the defensive tunnels north east to the river they retraced their steps south west, and trekked the long way down to the Marshes themselves. The ditches all along were generally impassable except where they had been crossed by a plank or fallen tree, and at these points defences had been made and watchers waited. It was down that way that escape routes had been planned, but Tryfan had little doubt now that they would be unworkable with the grikes in force on the far side of the way. The order to evacuate by the tunnel under the river would have to go out, but not too soon . . . the timing of that, Tryfan knew, was now the most important decision he must make.

Having checked that these crossings were secure, and the moles there informed of what was apaw and how essential it was they stayed in place, Tryfan and Smithills were returning to the cross-under when they came upon a skirmish at one of the wider dykes. Here the guardmoles had built up strength and the stand of the watchers was beginning to break down such that they had retreated, and were still doing so when Tryfan and Smithills came.

'Seven dead, Sir, replacements running short, can't hold much longer,' said one of the watchers as he came off the line and saw Smithills. Even as he spoke the mole line ahead broke up as a charge of guardmoles came fiercely through.

Tryfan, quickly ascertaining that the defence tunnels were still defended, stepped forward with Smithills at his side and found himself face to face at last with attacking guardmoles. Spindle's chronicle suggests that even then he might have not become involved in the fighting personally, because it had been agreed that he should not, lest he got wounded, or worse.

Nor would he have done but for the chance that he saw, among the watcher dead, a mole he knew and, in a way, had come to love. Not a mole many remember now, for his part in the history of those times is small, unless a mole

435

accepts, as Spindle himself did, that history could not be made without the moles none ever hear of. So Pennywort, brother of Thyme, one of the original Seven Stancing at Buckland. Since Thyme's death he had been lost to himself, and had become a watcher, though only for defence for he was never strong or of fighting stock. Yet here, at this weak point, he must have played his vital part, as so many brave moles did that day, for now he lay where Tryfan saw him, killed by the grikes while protecting a system that was not even his.

Seeing which made Tryfan angry and dangerously purposeful, and he did not hesitate. With Smithills at his side, he stepped forward and went straight for the largest and most fierce looking of the guardmoles, a huge male whose flanks and shoulders were massive and threatening. He thrust hard straight at him, and followed it up with a brutal lunge at the mole's haunches, as beside him Smithills did the same to another grike. The forward charge was arrested but the guardmoles swiftly regrouped to surround the two Duncton moles. It seemed for a moment that they would be deluged and lost, but then Smithills raised his talons with a mighty shout and Tryfan charged and at the sight of their leader's courage, the watchers rallied, turned, and with cries for the Stone forced a passage through the guardmoles to reform at Tryfan's side.

For a time all was noise and confusion, but then suddenly the guardmoles broke formation, one fell, another turned, and the Duncton moles were on them, chasing them, forcing them into yet more disorder until they ran back along the pipe crossing the dyke and Tryfan was without further target for his thrusts.

Smithills chased after them yelling, 'You're evil and you're losers!' He caught up with the last of them, had fastened his talons on him and spun him round to strike him dead, when Tryfan called, 'Let him be!'

The guardmole was frightened and wounded, but defiant.

'You are accursed of the Word!' he was shouting hysterically, blood pouring from a wound on his back. 'Accursed!'

From the far side of the dyke the others turned and watched.

'Shall I kill him?' said Smithills coldly, his talons raised to do so.

Tryfan looked at the mole and shook his head.

'Leave us,' he said. Smithills was reluctant to allow Tryfan to be exposed in the open with a guardmole, even a wounded one, but Tryfan again ordered him to do so. And Smithills obeyed, for the grikes showed no sign of coming to the rescue of their comrade.

When Smithills had retreated Tryfan looked at the guardmole, who in his turn seemed terrified, as if he knew his last moment had come. Perhaps, in any case, it had for his wound was deep and a steady flow of dark red blood was coming from it.

'Do what you like, mole of Duncton,' said the guardmole. 'Kill me. Your own days are numbered!'

'I would not have you die quite yet,' said Tryfan with a grim smile. 'You can take a message to Henbane. Tell her this is not her system to conquer and never shall be, for there are moles behind us and yet more behind them waiting to get their talons into you! Tell her that the Stone protects us, and that even though she may gain access to our system by force of numbers, yet the Stone will make us invisible and she will not find us, or kill us. Tell her, as you will tell others you speak to, that if you would find us then listen for the Silence. . . .'

'The Silence?' whispered the stricken guardmole, puzzled that this great and powerful mole above him was speaking gently, and assuming his survival.

'Aye,' said Tryfan softly, 'you may find us in the Silence which is for allmoles to know. To there shall we go, and none of Henbane's forces shall find us!'

'There are many of you,' said the guardmole, weakening from loss of blood, 'but not so many that we

437

cannot take your system. Then will we find you. . . .'

Tryfan shook his head and it seemed to him, and to the guardmole he spoke to, that the battle all about them had ceased, and a peace had come.

'Tell Henbane when she wonders where we have gone, that we went into the Silence, tell her that.'

He reached a paw forward and the guardmole shrunk away in fear.

'Be not afraid,' said Tryfan, and with his left paw, he touched the mole where his wound was and felt, as he had before with Thyme at Buckland, and Mayweed at Harrowdown, that the power of the Stone was with him. He felt its wonder, and its goodness and knew that in some strange way he was near Boswell now, or that Boswell was near him.

'We wish you no harm at Duncton,' he said, 'but we must defend our own. But now, fear not. By the power of the Stone you will be healed.'

For a moment the mole stared at Tryfan in astonishment, then he looked round at his wound and the flow of blood there had stopped and he was able to move his front paws. 'But I – but – ' he whispered.

'Tell no other mole of this. Now go back to your own, mole, and remember that though we may be "accursed" as you have been told, yet we are moles as well as you, no different and with the same fears and desires. Now go.'

Then the mole found he had strength to turn, and strength to walk. There was a look of awe in his eyes as he said to Tryfan, 'What is your name? I would know that.'

'My name is Tryfan, of Duncton born. To this place, which is my home, I would have all moles come in peace and all moles be safe. I would seek to heal all as I have healed you, I would wish it as a sanctuary beyond the power of the Word, beyond the power of the Stone as well if ever it was to be corrupted.'

The injured mole looked at him, and saw a mole of strength and certainty.

'My name is Thrift,' he said uncertainly.

'Yes, Thrift?' said Tryfan, his gaze powerful on him.

'If I can do anything, I mean, if ever. . . .'

'That day may come, Thrift, for mole needs mole and always will.'

Then Thrift raised his eyes to the slopes that rose behind Tryfan, and on past them to the trees and woods themselves, on which the morning sun now shone with great beauty. 'And I will not forget you desire that Duncton should be a place of peace, and a place of safety. I will not forget. We didn't want – '

'Go in peace,' said Tryfan interrupting him. 'Go now . . .' for grikes were advancing across the pipe once more, and watchers were coming forward. The mole Thrift went, looking back but once as he was lost among his own kind, looking at Tryfan with wonder and strange comfort.

Then Tryfan turned back to his own, and joined them without a further word of what had happened.

Afternoon came and Tryfan left Smithills at the front line of the fighting to relieve Alder, while he himself went upslope with two watchers appointed to guard him, to return to the main system to see how the moles waiting there were faring. Yet as he went he found his paws dragging, and he felt the need to go out on to the surface, and snout back downslope towards the now distant roaring owl way and beyond it to the fields in whose shadows the New Moles lay hidden.

'Smithills said not to let you go on the surface again alone, Sir,' said one of the watchers.

Tryfan smiled. 'Smithills would,' he said, 'but I'll only be a moment or two.' The watchers did not argue, sensing their leader needed privacy. So, in the sunshine of a May afternoon, when the future of Duncton, and perhaps of moledom, itself lay in his paws, Tryfan paused and stared.

He thought of Comfrey and Maundy, of Alder and Smithills at whose flanks he had fought, of Mayweed whom he cared for and who must be down at the Marsh

End now, and of Spindle whom he loved, and who would find him before the day was out. He knew that many of the valiant moles fighting against the grikes that day would not live to see Duncton Wood free again. Many among the guardmoles would not survive either.

At such a time a leader may feel alone, and so then did Tryfan, and he could only pray that the Stone would watch over these moles, as it watched over all of moledom, and its followers would heed its calling.

'Tryfan, Sir!' called out one of the watchers worriedly, 'Please, Sir! You *must* come now!'

Tryfan waved a paw at them in acknowledgement and then, with one last look down the slope towards where the watchers fought, he turned to the upslope tunnel and back to the task of saving the moles of the system he most loved.

Chapter Twenty-Six

The grikes finally took the cross-under and broke through to Alder's second line of defence late the following night, after a protracted and clever assault at three points – the main cross-under, the sluice and the lesser dyke that Tryfan and Smithills had themselves played an important part in defending the previous day.

But long before then and without any major mishap or panic, the different groups of moles awaiting evacuation had been led down towards the Marsh End. They had entered tunnels deserted since the early days of Bracken's leadership, when the plagues had come and the old quarters had been deserted.

Now moles returned, and Barrow Vale, once the heart of the system, echoed again to the sound of youngsters playing, and adults admonishing gently, and talking. But the voices were low, the adult moles subdued, and the tunnels dusty and in places blocked with vegetation and roof falls. Yet here they waited as night came, looking at each other questioningly as messengers went up to the elders' burrow near the Stone, and news of the battle filtered back down to them.

Youngsters slept, adults watched, night deepened on the surface, and darkness came to the tunnels. Several trusted moles, Maundy leading them, went here and there, comforting, encouraging and reassuring the youngsters and their friends, and their parents too; for all feared they would lose loved ones in the battle.

Sometime before midnight, when the wind had grown stronger and the tunnels were filled with the strange draughts and air currents that beset decayed tunnels and which disturb moles' liking for harmony and order, even the most deeply sleeping of the youngsters were woken by the sudden crash of thunder that cracked across the wood, and the flashes of lightning that sporadically lit up the tunnel entrances, and cast into brief, lurid light the huddles of restless, waiting moles that silently lined the tunnels.

Then heavy rain fell, and after it more thunder and lightening, then the pounding of yet more rain as here and there the tunnels began to drip and moles had to move themselves to avoid the leaking of water from the surface.

It was late in the night, when the rain had settled to a persistent downpour, that a single mole hurried along the surface of the wood from beyond the Marsh End. He knew his way, moving rapidly by clever and cunning routes that gave him protection against owl, which were known to strike creatures unwary enough to think the rain might give them cover.

Down briefly into Barrow Vale itself he dropped, past the wondering snouts of the evacuees who pulled a little away from him when they saw what he was, for his looks were strange, his stare intense, his smile off-putting to a mole who did not know it.

'Excuse me, thank you, very kind, wonderfully thoughtful of you, yes, yes, yes, no, you are not in my humble way . . .' said Mayweed as he squeezed by the crush of waiting moles and then hurried on, only pausing sometimes to listen to the rain with a worried frown.

Meanwhile, from the line of defensive surface burrows on the Eastside, where the campaign to keep back the grikes was now being hard fought in darkness and rain, messenger after messenger was bringing news to Alder, who had taken a central position a little upslope. The news from the various points where battles were being fought and incursions made was that the retreat, though orderly, had not slowed. What was more, Duncton casualties were rising, and Alder was beginning to have to pull in reserves from outlying points where they had been used as watchers in case the grikes tried to get into the system by outflanking the main defence lines.

442

Tryfan had given strict instructions that the moment those reserves had to be called in he must be informed, for then the evacuation would have to start. They could not risk an incursion of grikes into the system itself, for all the fighters were at the front, and death and confusion and a disorderly evacuation would result. Worse, the tunnel of departure might be discovered, and the point of the surprise and mystery of the 'disappearance' of the Duncton moles would be lost.

The grikes now not only controlled the cow cross-under, but had begun a systematic advance on the flanks of the defensive burrows. There was no sign at all yet that they were sending parties further afield, but Alder was taking no chances and as dawn approached, and the rain that had come over Duncton Wood with the storm had eased into drizzle, the order went out for further retreat.

This still left a group of Duncton moles hidden in deep tunnels right in the midst of the advancing grikes and these, led by Ramsey, would make one final confusing assault to slow the advance before they retreated by tunnels too deep for the grikes quickly to find them. But the end was coming, and Alder, now tired, and with two superficial wounds to his face and a deeper talon-thrust to his shoulder which was giving him pain, sent out the freshest of his messenger moles to warn Tryfan that the time of final retreat was coming.

'Tell Tryfan we will await his command to leave, though if I hear nothing before the sun rises over the way itself I will take the initiative and conduct a retreat then,' Alder told the messenger and, as he left, he turned wearily back to the defence burrow, to check and recheck the reports coming in. He wished in any case to stay a little longer where they now were to give Ramsey the cover he might need to get back with the rest of them, though the deep tunnels ought to provide a hiding place if all else failed. His last instructions to Ramsey had been that he should leave by mid-morning at the latest.

At the Stone itself dawn light was late coming because the cloud cover was so thick, and when it did it showed a surface that was bedraggled and dripping wet with trees lifeless after the storm and rain.

In the elder burrow there, Tryfan had been waiting with a few others for news of the fighting, and had nearly gone down to see for himself once more when Mayweed arrived after his trek from the Marsh End.

'Begging your pardon and not wishing to worry any-mole here,' he said, interrupting their deliberations, 'but I think, Sirs one and all, I think, consider and believe that you better get a move on. The river tunnel's beginning to flood with the rain. Yes, Sir, sorry, Sir,' said Mayweed.

It had, of course, rained before in the past weeks and Mayweed had had a chance to see what the effects were. The worry was not so much that it would flood right through – it seemed never to do that – but that the ground would become dangerously muddy and the passage of so many moles would not only be slowed, and nomole could guess what the effect of the vibrations of their pawsteps and scrabbling alongside already sodden walls might be.

Even as Mayweed was recovering from his rapid ascent to the elder burrow, and the others were absorbing his news, and being briefed at last by Tryfan and Skint about the tunnel escape route, Alder's messenger from the Eastside arrived: the retreat had not slowed, the system's flanks were beginning to be exposed, the time had come to leave.

Rapidly Tryfan gave out his final orders. Comfrey, Maundy, Skint and Mayweed were to go straight back to Barrow Vale, where they would lead the evacuees down through the Marsh End – Comfrey and Maundy's presence being judged essential to inspire trust and confidence. The Marsh End was much feared as being a place of dankness, disease, and haunting, the ground beyond it was regarded as impassable. But if Comfrey was there then moles would follow him.

'And what of Spindle?' asked Comfrey.

'He will come when the time is right,' Tryfan reassured him . . . which meant then at that moment, for the cleric appeared frowning at the chamber's entrance, peered at them all, and said, 'Do I presume we are leaving now?'

'We are,' said Tryfan.

'Well,' sighed Spindle, 'a cleric's work is never done! But I have done the best I could, and if Henbane's moles find the library Mayweed and myself have hidden, the Stone is not as friendly as I thought it was!'

He looked tired, which was not surprising since he had chosen to spend much of the past two dangerous days making final records of what he had seen, as if to remember for a future generation a time which would come to be seen as a crisis of change, though the leaders like Tryfan and Skint and Alder were too busy to take stock of it.

'I think I will come along with you, if you don't mind,' he said, on learning that Tryfan was going down to see the retreat. 'I might as well see the end of it all and anyway, I have a snout for where the main action is, and I have a feeling . . .' but he stopped, his thin face on one side, his pale talons fretting at each other.

'You come with me then,' said Tryfan, more pleased than he knew, for he liked to have Spindle near, as if in his friend's seeming weakness he felt his own strength.

Tryfan, with Spindle, would therefore join the others later, probably during the passage through the tunnel, but not before he had made sure that the retreat from the Eastside was complete, and the moles who were to occupy the Marsh End labyrinth had made good their escape to it, or at least were in a position to do so.

For Comfrey of all moles, and for Maundy too, it was a terrible moment, for it was likely that they might never see the Duncton Stone again. But the policy had been agreed, and the plans made, and there were many among the moles of Duncton who would not leave if they did not see their most beloved elder leaving as well.

Comfrey had himself told them that Duncton Wood

must now be left in the care of younger paws, and it was for moles like himself to set an example of courage and patience in retreat, and to pass on, as best they might, the stories and traditions of Duncton to moles who, one day, might find the strength and the opportunity to return.

So then, for one last time together, the elders went out to the Stone clearing, and there in the rain they said their last prayers, and old Comfrey went finally to the Stone he loved and touched it, making a blessing on the moles whom it protected.

He said finally, 'And if others c-c-come, let them hear thy Silence, Stone, and know thy love. Let this be but a dark passage on the way to the time when peace comes once more to Duncton, and moles may be free here, to live without fear, to think what they might, and to heal each other with the love that comes from the sound of thy gr-gr-great Silence.'

The others watched as Comfrey turned to Maundy, and reached out to touch her paw as he continued, 'We two are old and have seen m-many things, and now, for the first time, when the end of our two lives is near, we are to t-t-travel on. Well, 'tis thy will, Stone, and we trust it.'

'We do,' whispered Maundy, coming nearer so that her grey and wrinkled flank touched Comfrey's. So they crouched, and the others with them, with the Stone rising high above them to where the great beech branches still dripped sporadically with rain, and the high wood was a chamber of dull morning light.

'Come on, my dear,' said Maundy softly, 'we must leave now.' Then, as if performing a rite of farewell for Comfrey, who seemed too moved by the moment to do such a thing himself, Maundy went to each in turn and touched them, and whispered their name, and wished that each one of them might one day return home safeguarded.

Then the two old moles led the others away, leaving Tryfan and Spindle alone by the Stone.

'Well!' said Tryfan. 'Time to go . . . and I feel nervous, very.'

'I know you do,' said Spindle with a smile. 'Why do you think I'm here with you? You've found it hard being a leader, haven't you?'

Tryfan nodded.

'It *is* hard. Moles do not want to see doubt or weakness though I feel them often. And the fighting, Spindle, there must be a better way than that. The last messenger told me that our casualties have gone up. There are females down in the Marsh End who will never see their mates again, and youngsters who will not hear their father's voice but as a memory. What am I to say to them? And there will be others who will die, and many who will never return to the home they loved. And all because I lead them! Who is to say that they would not be better off staying here? How can we be sure that Henbane would not show some mercy to them?'

'She never has by all reports.'

Tryfan sighed. 'Well, one day there will be a better way. One day . . .'

'And when will that be, Tryfan?' wondered Spindle.

'When the Stone Mole comes. That will be the day. May the Stone preserve me to see it!'

'And I!' said Spindle.

'Now,' said Tryfan, 'now we'll go one last time to see Alder, and ensure the final retreat is orderly.' They took a surface route out of the Stone clearing, and Tryfan's step was suddenly light, as if all the decisions had been made and there was nothing left now but to see them through to the end.

'Come on, Spindle!' he said, moving more quickly as they reached the edge of the wood and the Eastside slope dropped before them.

Neither mole looked back to the Stone clearing they had just left, as the Stone itself began to be lost among the trees behind; nor did they see the sudden shaft of light that came down out of the clouds and caught its wet sides, and glistened and shone where they had been.

They found Alder still holding on to the central burrow of the last main defence line on the south-eastern slopes, but only just. The tunnels were filled now with weary moles, many too tired and injured to look up as Tryfan and Spindle passed by.

What was worse, only a few minutes before Tryfan's arrival, two watchers, one injured, had been isolated on the surface and caught by guardmoles, and even now voices could be heard raised and angry as the grikes discussed what to do with them.

Tired though they were, there was not a mole in the tunnels who would not have gone out to attempt to rescue them, but that, as Alder had firmly made clear, was what the guardmoles wanted and he was not allowing it.

Tryfan could easily see why. The ground beyond the surface burrow was undulating and several guardmoles had taken stance there; while further on, past a barbed wire fence, the ground fell to hidden ground and Stone knows what guardmole lay in wait there.

'They're trying to get us out by keeping the two prisoners in our sight,' said Alder, 'but whatever we may feel, I will not allow anymole to go.' He glared balefully around the tunnels. Like the others he looked tired, and his fur was matted with mud, sweat and blood. The blood of his wounds had coagulated, yet some still seeped through down his face; but others were far worse off than he.

'Can't they be reached by tunnels?' asked Tryfan, watching in horror from the vantage of the surface burrow as the two watchers were paraded near the fence and talons were raised brutally against them. But he already knew the answer to that: there were no tunnels to that point.

'What news of Ramsey and his group?' asked Tryfan urgently. He knew they lay concealed further down the slope, quite surrounded by mole but for the tunnels back to where Alder and the others had refuge.

'None,' said Alder, 'but the deep tunnel to his position is still clear and we think it has not been found. I do not know if Ramsey has made an attack or not, but it seems likely. He has not returned, but we must retreat, Tryfan, if we are not to be overrun and taken. I – '

At that moment the raised voices of the guardmoles stopped, there was a sudden cry of protest followed by a sickening and dreadful scream, and the Duncton moles heard the sound of one of their injured colleagues being snouted on the barbs of the wire fence.

Anger, impotence, rage . . . the surface burrow was dark with hatred of the grikes.

'We must do something, Alder,' said several moles at once, 'we must. . . .'

As they spoke the taunting voice of a guardmole came to them: 'One up and another to go!' it cried. 'Unless you lot want to give yourselves up. Well? You've not got long to make up your minds . . .' They saw the hapless uninjured watcher struggling as three guardmoles grabbed him and held him ready by the wire to hang him on a barb adjacent to the one where, so terribly, the body of his friend still shook with the rigor of pain that a snouting means, blood gushing from his snout, spilling from his mouth and bubbling as his last screams were lost in a drowning too terrible to imagine.

'We're going to go, Alder, even if you won't lead us,' said one of the moles. 'We can't just let them do it to Wilden. He's my *friend*.' Wilden was the second of the captured moles.

As he spoke another couple of guardmoles appeared, one of them rather larger than the other. This mole stared over towards where the defence burrow was and Alder stiffened in surprise.

'But that mole there . . . that one! Aye. That's Marram, Tryfan, that's who that is.' It was the mole who had been Alder's colleague at Buckland.

They stared at him and he looked impassively back, and as he did so Tryfan suddenly moved forward and took command.

'You will not go out on to the surface, any of you,' he

449

said in a voice chilly with authority. 'Now tell me quickly, if I take a surface route, where *exactly* will I find an entrance to the deep tunnels in which Ramsey still lies hidden?'

The direction was pointed out to him.

'Now listen, and listen well. I shall go out alone. I shall seem to wish to parley with them. They will hesitate for they will be surprised to see a single mole. I will take my moment and lead – what is his name? Wilden? – I will lead him on downslope. There will be confusion.

'Take that moment to evacuate as many injured upslope as you can. Maintain a guard here for I will attempt to return, with Ramsey and any others I may find through the deep tunnels. Send other messengers along the line and order an immediate and final retreat. Once that mole is safe, and Ramsey's group is securely back, we will retreat altogether. . . .'

The taunting voice of the guardmole came upslope to them again.

'Well, Duncton moles, your friend is beginning to sweat and shake. Is it cowards he fought alongside? Or have you the courage and common sense to surrender and save his life?'

At that Tryfan left them, and stepped up and out on to the surface. His sudden appearance brought all movement to a halt. Those holding Wilden crouched, tensely watching, as in the drab and drizzly silence that seemed to have descended on that part of the Eastside, Tryfan moved slowly and with authority towards them.

As he did so he said clearly and with an intent that was very obvious to the watchers behind him, 'I come in peace and with the good will of the Stone for all moles. If there is any among you who has pity, or has ever thought he might desire the Silence of the Stone, let him come forward now and make peace with us!' As Tryfan spoke his eyes were on Marram, who laughed and said to the others, 'Some hope he's got, mates, to find a mole of the Stone here!'

'Aye, you'll have to do better than that!' said another.

But the watchers noticed that Marram dropped back behind the others, and then moved away downslope and, for the moment, out of sight.

Meanwhile, on either side, hidden in grass or thistles, guardmoles had taken advance positions and they watched with narrowed eyes and ready talons as Tryfan approached among them. His heart hammered in his breast, he had eyes only for the terror that he could now see was in Wilden's eyes the closer he got. Moledom seemed almost silent about him. Almost but not quite, for there was a panting and a pattering behind him and he slowed, unsure if this was an attack but determined to show no fear.

'I really think you could have *waited* you know,' said a scholarly voice. 'I mean . . .' It was Spindle, running to catch him up, with anxiety on his face combined with a studied innocence.

'What the Stone. . .?' began Tryfan through clenched teeth as he tried to maintain his pose of unconcern and purpose so that the guardmoles, who stared at him surprised and uncertain now, might stay irresolute long enough for him to reach Wilden and make his move. But with Spindle. . . .

'Well, I mean,' continued Spindle who, having now caught him up, dared to move ahead at a slightly more rapid pace as he talked loudly about . . . what? 'I mean that it isn't reasonable to have the pleasure, if not the privilege, of surrendering to these splendid moles who have come all this way just to – '

'Spindle!' said Tryfan, trying to stop him, and now only moleyards from the fence and Wilden just beyond it.

' – to, er, rescue moles from that dreadful fallacy, for that's the only word for it, which is called, I believe, the Stone.'

As Spindle said the words, smiling as he did so, with Tryfan furious at his side and the guardmoles looking at each other and wondering quite who these two moles were who were wandering so nonchalantly into their very midst talking about the Stone, the two reached the wire itself. The snouted mole hung bloodily before them, his paws arced up in a death agony. The slope dipped down more steeply beyond the fence, and the morning sound of the roaring owls came over the Pasture from out of the humid air.

Across the slopes below were several other moles, perhaps ten or more, and at Tryfan's appearance, which must have been a surprise to them, they reared up and stared.

'I think,' began Tryfan, taking his cue from Spindle and sounding utterly calm, moving under the wire and even dipping his snout so that he was vulnerable to attack, and with Spindle following suit, so they were within feet of Wilden . . . 'I think we had better introduce ourselves.'

The guardmoles began to stiffen into aggressive stances, their grip on Wilden tightened, they moved in closer from all sides.

Tryfan turned to the one who seemed their leader.

'The mole you have captured is Wilden . . .' and Tryfan's voice speeded up as he spoke with sudden compelling authority, though as quietly as before. 'And if we are to talk sensibly I suggest you let him free. He is not about to escape you know.' As the guardmoles let him go, Tryfan added, 'And this is my good friend Spindle, of Seven Barrows born, and my name is Tryfan.'

There was a moment more of silence. One or other of the guardmoles seemed to find his voice and even open his mouth to speak as others closed in on Tryfan, but before they could do so he said, 'And *now*, Wilden, I think the time has come – ' Then as Tryfan thrust violently forward at one of the four guardmoles near Wilden, Wilden himself felled another who tumbled down the slope behind them. Tryfan had not counted on Spindle but he, not to be outdone, took full advantage of the moment of surprise and confusion and dug his talons sharply into a third guardmole's side as Tryfan reached forward, warded off the remaining guardmole near Wilden, and cried out to

452

them all to run downslope into the very midst of the astonished guardmoles below.

'*Now!*' he cried out, and they paused for a moment and then ran down and down the slope, Tryfan guided by a faith stronger than he had ever known that they would be safe if they acted with complete assurance.

'Stop them! After them! Kill them!'

Then, even as the guardmoles behind turned in pursuit and the ones ahead seemed to come out of the trance into which the Duncton moles' unexpected appearance had put them, it was not Tryfan who saw that their way of escape was there on the Pasture before them, solid and sure, but Spindle. For with a gasped 'Follow me!' he took the lead in the rapid downhill chase and headed straight for the largest and most powerful-looking guardmole on the slope: Marram. There was nothing that Tryfan and Wilden could do but follow him, closing up to fend off the grikes that lunged in from right and left.

'This way!' cried Spindle and he led them downslope at greater and greater speed towards the guardmole who reared up threateningly, his talons huge.

'But,' gasped Wilden, 'you're running towards the biggest of them all!'

'Correct!' said Spindle, 'I think he's with us. And if he's not then none of us has long to live.'

But Marram was with them, though whether it was from Tryfan's words of the Stone, or some decision he had made earlier they did not know or care. As they reached him, he stepped to one side to let them through and then turned back upslope and smote to death the first guard-mole that came, which stopped the guardmole attack dead in its tracks.

Then all was confusion as Tryfan led his party on, confident now, and certain, contouring the slope, eyes running across the surface for the entrance to the deep burrow where Ramsey lay but which was well hidden.

Then suddenly Ramsey was there, thrusting out of a disguised entrance to one side of them, alerted by the shouts and running of paws. He came out on to the surface, followed by two or three others, and they surged past Tryfan and took their places at Marram's side as Tryfan's group, now nearing exhaustion, were directed underground. Wilden went down first, followed by Spindle, and then a watcher almost bodily pushed Tryfan down after them.

'Come on!' he said, 'the grikes seem to be waking up!'

Then he and the others followed Tryfan down as Ramsey and Marram remained to fight off the last of their confused and routed pursuers, and from below Tryfan cried out so the grikes might hear, 'To the main cross-under, to there we will go, not upslope to safety quite yet!'

Then down Ramsey went, and Marram, and the moles on the surface circled and snouted and struck at the ground crying out, 'They're heading by tunnel for the cross-under. Warn Henbane and Weed. Somemole get down there! . . . all moles go downslope! Down the slope to the cow cross-under. It's a counterattack, Word knows how many there are below!'

Some tried to enter the deep tunnel but received vicious talon-thrusts on the snout and they soon gave up and left, and the Duncton moles breathed a sigh of relief.

'We are well met, Marram,' Tryfan said. 'Well met, indeed. Now moles, let us make good our escape!'

With that, they took the deep tunnel back upslope, far away from the attentions of the guardmoles, until they reached the surface burrow where they had left Alder.

Alder had done his work well, for the defence was now very nearly deserted, the injured having been evacuated, leaving him with just two of the fittest watchers waiting in the hope that Tryfan would return in safety.

'A friend to greet you!' said Tryfan as Marram emerged. Then Alder, who had been in complete command of himself as he had of the watchers for two days, was struck dumb with amazement and then delight. He buffeted his old colleague, and they laughed deeply together.

Agreeing that they would have much to say to each

454

other later, Alder said, 'We had best take advantage of the grikes' confusion and make our final retreat.' But as he left he had time to turn to Marram once again and say, 'Old friend, I have a job for you you're going to enjoy!' Then, with a laugh and a shout, the last of the watchers left the south-eastern slopes, for the grikes to take at their leisure.

Upslope they all paused to look back.

'They'll take their time,' confirmed Marram. 'Always do. They'll check every tunnel and surface burrow on the way up to the main system, and I would not be surprised if there are serious flanking incursions going on – grikes do things by the Word, which is cautious when it comes to invading new systems.'

'We've given them something to think about anyway,' said Alder.

'They were very surprised when they met resistance here yesterday because they're not used to it. But they learn fast so you won't get a second chance!'

'Well, then,' said Tryfan, 'we had better get going.'

Then he turned towards Duncton Wood, and led the moles north across the Ancient System and then down-slope towards the distant Marsh End, leaving behind him a system entirely empty of moles but for the last watchers to the east who, like him, were retreating now, for the north, and beyond.

Chapter Twenty-Seven

By the time Tryfan and the others reached Barrow Vale the main group of moles, under Comfrey's leadership, had already made their way down to the Marsh End, and then in groups to the very entrance of the river tunnel itself, leaving behind a single watcher to tell Tryfan what had been done and to give directions to any other watchers still coming in from the defensive positions on the south-eastern slopes.

Only when they were satisfied that the system was cleared and all moles accounted for did Tryfan and Spindle go on down to join the others. Then, after ensuring that the evacuation under the direction of Mayweed and Comfrey was proceeding smoothly, the two of them went with Skint to join the team of watchers who were to hide in the special tunnels in the north east of the Marsh End. Alder and Marram, much interested, went as well, while Smithills stayed at his post on the Duncton side of the river tunnel to give Comfrey support should he need it.

The farewell between Skint and Smithills, who had never been apart since they left Grassington so many moleyears before, was brief and touching. They grumbled a bit at each other, talking of other things, but then fell into a clumsy embrace, the big Smithills nearly lifting the smaller Skint off his paws as they wished each other luck, and looked forward to the time they would meet again, and do what they had long promised each other, which was to travel north at last, back to their home system.

'Aye, and not forgetting Wharfedale, where we've a prayer to say in memory of old Willow, bless her!' said Smithills.

456

'That'll be a happy day, and the happier if you're at my side, you unkempt and grubby old rascal!'

'Well then, you'd better make sure you survive, hadn't you Skint? Don't be so mean with the worms, fatten yourself up a bit, otherwise I'll be there without you!'

The watchers who had already established residence at the Marsh End Defence, had seen to a final camouflaging of entrances, and were establishing some food caches when Skint and the others arrived.

Skint and Tryfan had discussed at length the campaign against the invaders that Skint would conduct – a secret warfare for which, so far as either knew, there was certainly neither moleword nor precedent. The idea was to use attacks on individual moles to harass and confuse the grikes, to make them perpetually uncomfortable and demoralised.

The secret group consisted of seven moles – enough to be able to operate in two places at once, but not so many that leadership would be a problem. Skint was in overall control with Ramsey, still recovering from his efforts against the grikes, as second in command. One of the original seven had been killed in the fighting and his place was to be taken by the watcher who had waited for them at Barrow Vale, a mole called Tundry.

Tryfan looked around the dark burrow where the group crouched quietly – a tough-looking lot who might, in the course of the next few months, learn a great deal about the grikes; or, on the other hand, might all die.

Apart from Tryfan, Spindle and Mayweed, and now Alder and Marram, nomole knew they were staying behind, and when asked by others Tryfan intended to be vague about where they were and what they were doing. He made a final inspection of the tunnels he, Mayweed and Holm had developed but which he had not seen for some weeks. The entrances were well disguised, the Marsh End soil being dank and dark and covered in thick unwholesome vegetation which had the virtue of being nearly impenetrable. The entrances led into shallow tunnels which had been constructed to look as if they had been deserted. There were roof falls and accumulations of vegetation, and any root growth that might normally have been cleared had been carefully left in place.

This made the entrances from these tunnels into the deeper ones easier to disguise, and also made it possible for holes and passages to be open to permit the deeper penetration of light, which would be needed if the health of the moles was to be maintained.

But this secondary complex of tunnels was itself a disguise for a third and yet deeper level, which in many places was in total darkness: narrow, devious miserable affairs which Mayweed had intended to develop as permanent living quarters, the real base of the covert operations Skint and the others would mount.

But it was not all darkness. Mayweed had centred this complex on an old lightning-burnt tree whose dead roots radiated round and down into the soil, and which had a hollow, burnt out trunk. Originally this had been filled with the debris of rotten wood, humus and the putrified remains of rodent carcasses caught by the owl that used the top of the trunk as a roosting point and who, occasionally, dropped prey down which he was unable to retrieve.

Mayweed and Holm had burrowed up into this, cleared it out, and so provided a safe source of light, and even sun as well as rain for the moles who might, at times, have to stay hidden for weeks. But certainly the area around such an obviously owl-bound tree was one any invaders would avoid, and so they would never suspect that beneath it, using the opening to the sky it gave, moles might live and survive.

Looking up from the chamber Mayweed had built under the tree the light was strange – green and grey, pink in places from the colour of the wood, and here and there where branches had broken off or woodpeckers had worked, there were holes which let in more light so that the passage of the sun and clouds, the whole lighted movement of the sky, seemed to play inside the trunk and be reflected down on to the floor of the chamber in a marvellous changing mutation of tones.

It was in the chamber on the third level that Tryfan and the others settled for a last briefing, and to say their farewells. One reason why Marram had come was to tell Skint what he knew of the command and disposition of the grikes, and this he now did. Information which was later to save the lives of more than one of those watchers.

Just as important for the future was the need both Tryfan and Skint felt to establish a basis on which they might communicate in the future. It was Tryfan's view that the operation should not continue indefinitely. Nomole doubted that it would be hard, dangerous and tedious, and that if the moles were to keep their spirits high they must know that their time in those tunnels would be limited. On the other paw, nomole could tell what would happen, or where Tryfan and the others moles would go, and it was hard to make a definite plan.

The problem had taxed the elders considerably, and it had been decided that contact would be made the following Longest Night, a good time for meeting since moles tend to travel to their home systems at that season and strangers are not so noticed, and discipline is more lax.

But where? They had chosen Rollright as the meeting point, for though that system was controlled by grikes, its tunnels were very well known to Skint and Smithills, who had cleared them, and the system itself was diffuse and hard for guardmoles to monitor. It was, in any case, one of the Ancient Systems, and its Stones were powerful indeed. They all favoured it as a location, for it lay not far north of Duncton and yet was reachable from the Wen to the east as well. And being north it was on the way, if only a small part of it, to the North, and ultimately Whern, to where, Tryfan suspected, Boswell had been taken and he himself would one day have to go.

But, they all agreed, such a plan was tenuous, and many things could undermine it.

'We cannot know now, nor will we for several mole-years, how our struggle will develop,' said Tryfan. 'We will each of us be concerned to prepare the ground for the coming of the Stone Mole, by heartening those who have faith in the Stone, and by preparing those who will do battle for it. Where, or when, or how that may be we cannot know.

'For myself, and for Spindle here, our task and direction has been set for us by Boswell. To the east we will go, to the very centre of the Wen itself, for he told us we will find inspiration and guidance in the journey itself, and at its ending. Others will go where they will, or the Stone directs. They will for a time be lost to Duncton, and to each other. Each will pursue his own quest for the Silence of the Stone, and I believe that some will find it, or come near to it, but that it will only be with the coming of the Stone Mole himself that the true Silence will be known.'

'What of those like me who have doubts of the Stone, and of the Word, and of any such beliefs?' asked Skint bluntly. 'Same goes for Smithills.'

'And me!' said Marram. But Alder said nothing, for he was of the Stone.

'There are many doubters such as yourselves,' replied Tryfan philosophically, 'and though I would have you be believers, well, nomole has the right to tell another what to think or do. It is enough that you support us, enough that you recognise the corruption and evil of the Word. But I would say only this: do not bear false witness of the Stone. Be as open with each other as Skint has always been with me, discuss your doubts, and honour those who, though they do not share your faith, yet speak from their hearts with truth and dignity. It is not the mole you attack but the idea, and the Stone embraces allmole whatever he may be.

'If in time you find faith, then I shall be pleased. But I would prefer to have one doubting truthful mole at my side than a hundred moles who profess to the Stone yet feel they do not carry its truth in their hearts and paws.

460

'One last thing about our future meeting,' Tryfan continued. 'It may be that circumstances will militate against us reaching Rollright next Longest Night. Much has yet to happen. So remember this: in the long moleyears of struggle that I think is yet to come, the Stones of the seven Ancient Systems will always be there to guide moles who trust them. I know that at Longest Night or Midsummer, moles of the Stone will always strive to be at a Stone, whether it be of the Seven or not. So if you are lost and isolate, and know not where you are or where you should go, listen to the Stones, be guided by them, and they will see you right.

'I know that in time it will be necessary for the followers' leaders, whoever they may then be, to summon a convention, to discuss our strategy against the moles of the Word. A way will be found so that you know when it is. It *must* be found!'

The moles nodded to each other and talked some more until the time came when those moles leaving Duncton had to join the others at the entrance to the tunnel under the Thames. Throughout this Marram had been quiet, but he came forward at the end and said, 'I know not if it matters to the future, but I can tell you that you're not the only moles resisting Henbane.

'There have always been one or two in places difficult to attack, but you'll know of them . . . But lately I've heard the Siabod moles have begun to fight back. We all knew that the attack on Duncton would have come much sooner if Wrekin had not had to deploy some of his forces back to Siabod, and not to much avail I'm told! Well, I thought it might cheer you to know that you're not alone in moledom in offering resistance to the Word!'

'I'm sure Tryfan's glad,' said Spindle, 'for he's named of Siabod.'

Which several there not knowing, Spindle quickly explained, for Tryfan's mother had been to Siabod and pupped there, though not of Bracken's mating. Yet when Tryfan was born, Bracken named him after Tryfan's

461

snowy heights, for there stand two Stones, unreachable by mole. Few moles have even seen them, but Bracken did and ever remembered it, and when he first saw his pups he said it seemed he was reminded of the form of that mountain in the way one of the male pups moved, and so named him Tryfan.

'It's true enough,' said Tryfan, 'and it's heartening. The Siabod moles are like no other, and I have kin there of my mother, and would one day be there, or at least know them.' He thought in silence for a while, but said no more of it.

Then, after last words of parting to the watchers Skint led Tryfan and the others back to the surface. His last words were for his friends: 'You watch over Smithills for me, Tryfan. You've got to keep the old fool going until I can join you again, so I can lead him back up north! He'll never make it by himself. He'll get in some scrap or other and get himself killed!'

Then to Spindle he said, 'And *you* . . . you look after Tryfan for all of us, for I've a feeling you're the only one he listens to, though Stone knows why!'

'Yes, I will, or I will certainly try!' said Spindle.

At which, with a laugh and a final touch, Skint disappeared into the undergrowth and was gone back down to his companions, and the wood was silent, and the great dead tree rising, as if nomole lived there, and never had.

'That Skint's as brave a mole as I'll ever meet,' said Marram with admiration. 'And not even a Stone believer!'

'He's closer to the Stone than most,' said Tryfan. 'It's what a mole does, not what he says that brings him to the Silence.'

'Well, may he be kept safe to see a Longest Night or two through yet,' said Alder, who had grown to respect Skint greatly. 'And at my flank as well!'

'We'll all agree with that!' said Tryfan.

Under Comfrey's leadership, the evacuees had already

made their way down to the far edge of Marsh End, and then in groups to the very entrance of the deep tunnel itself. By the time Tryfan and Spindle arrived, two groups had already gone through and the third was setting off, under the guidance of Holm.

It was a vulnerable time, for there was too little space underground to accommodate all the waiting moles, and they had been dispersed on the surface, not far apart but in an encirclement of positions, with outlying watchers to guard the approaches in case of attack. Indeed, Tryfan and Spindle themselves had been stopped in the murky light of the afternoon by a watcher, a fact by which Spindle was impressed and Tryfan reassured.

But his news had been grave.

'Tryfan, Sir, the grikes are into the system at the high south end, and making their way steadily in on the Eastside. Two of us delayed to watch them come in, and a third joined us after watching their southern entry. I know not how long they'll take to come north down here, but if they're swift they could just catch us!'

'Well, mole, you have done well to wait . . . Now come with us lest you're left alone.' And so, with the grikes already into Duncton, Tryfan reached the area near the river tunnel.

Below ground, at the tunnel entrance itself, the air was cold and wet. Although the rain had long since stopped on the surface it was still seeping down, and the moles waiting there stared uneasily at the dank and dripping walls.

Reception burrows on the far side had been prepared in the weeks before to accommodate the evacuees and to avoid the problem of surface exposure which, because there was little vegetation on the far side, meant danger from owl attack.

As Tryfan waited, staring down into the tunnel, a voice came up at them out of it, accompanied by the sloshing of wet pawsteps.

'Sirs, welcome; welcome, Sirs. It is a relief and a privilege to see you in this dark and dirty place, most certainly it is; and all so successfully done, so expertly accomplished, so brilliantly conceived, awesome Sirs!'

At first they could see nothing coming towards them, then hardly anything, then a mole who was the same colour as the mud and wet of the walls around him, but for the pink, glistening point of a thin and weedled snout. But the voice and the words told them who it was: Mayweed!

'The third party is proceeding through nobly, valiantly led by my good friend Holm,' continued Mayweed, as he approached them. 'I passed them in the middle of the tunnel. But, and it is an ominous inauspicious but: I have to say, Sirs, that we had better get on with it since the walls are getting wetter and more unstable by the second; yes, it is so, unfortunately it is!'

'Tell us what has happened so far. Is Comfrey on the other side?'

'To answer your concerned query: Comfrey and Maundy are already through and taking good care of things over there. It has all gone well according to your noble and grand strategy, Sir,' said Mayweed, his muddy face breaking into one of his earnest smiles, and his teeth, whose normal appearance was yellow, appearing for once nearly white in contrast to the filth on his face.

As the next party assembled, he told them both, as quickly as he was able, and with as few 'Sirs' as he could manage, what had happened earlier. . . .

Conditions were worsening so rapidly that he had advised Comfrey not to wait for Tryfan's arrival before the old mole gave his authority for him to lead the first group through. He had made sure that the youngsters among them were well placed between adults, and that silence was strictly kept so that instructions could be heard clearly in the black, dripping and echoing tunnel.

The first group got through easily, but in the second an elderly mole lost touch with the party and, dreadfully, drowned in the mire. Mayweed and Holm had the grim task of finding and removing her body, for it was unthinkable that they could continue with it there, lest more panic ensued should it surface from the water.

Mayweed was careful to make sure that those still on the Duncton side did not know what had happened, for a general panic would certainly have slowed proceedings down, and perhaps made the continuance of the evacuation impossible. Holm had taken the group on through the tunnel and in pitch-black Mayweed had buried the body in a wall and been rejoined by Holm to return for the third party from whose crossing Mayweed had just returned, having left them at the halfway point to save time.

About the death, Mayweed, normally voluble, was nearly monosyllabic.

'Hard, Sir, not nice. Nomole knows but Holm and self, Sir, nomole . . .' he said. 'Must move on quickly, Sir, tunnel soft, tunnel dangerous, more water each time at the lowest point, more mud. Hard for youngsters, so hard for them . . . I know how they feel, Sir, was young myself once.'

Mayweed smiled, a real smile; but it was sad, and wan, and a little haunted. Tryfan noticed that Mayweed stayed near the most nervous of the youngsters, encouraging them, joking with them, and telling them that on the other side the tunnels were lined with golden sunlight, which some of them half believed.

While for their part the youngsters, who clearly knew and trusted Mayweed, clustered around him.

'Really, Mayweed?' he heard one young female say. 'I mean, if we get through will it be sunshine?'

'Weil, Madam young thing, this mole would say it *was* sunshine but others might say different. Yes, yes, but if *you* think it will be then it *will* be in the end, always and ever. Yes. Don't be scared. . . .'

'I want to go with you Mayweed, Sir!' said a voice that Spindle recognised.

'Me? Sir? No, no, no, not worthy of that! That's for Tryfan here and Spindle. What's your name and where are your parents and siblings?'

'Lorren's me and my sort of brother's Bailey and my sister's Starling. Don't like her.'

'But she's your sister,' said Mayweed.

'She's mean, wouldn't share a worm and let us play. My father's fighting with Alder. My mother's somewhere around, but I want to come with you, please, Mayweed. You're nice.'

Mayweed smiled in an embarrassed way at Spindle who was looking for his son Bailey and Starling. At first the crush was so great that he could not see them, but then a paw tugged at his side, and from a drier spot, which she had carefully won for herself and Bailey, Starling smiled.

'Hello!' she said. 'Bailey wants to say hello.'

'Hello!' said Bailey in a small and serious voice.

It was not hard to see why he sounded serious, for having greeted Spindle, his gaze had moved to Tryfan, whose size and strength seemed to fill him with awe, and before whom all the youngsters fell silent.

'Well now,' said Tryfan, looking down at Bailey. 'And who's this Spindle?'

But Spindle's expression of concern and unfamiliar parent love was enough to tell Tryfan exactly who Bailey was. He knew that the youngster had been given out to a pupped female on Thyme's death, and that Spindle had only seen him once since.

'Well, mole, you look calm enough to calm the rest of us!' said Tryfan, reaching out a paw to touch Bailey's head.

'Thank you, Sir!' said Bailey, eyes wide.

'My name's Starling,' said Starling, pushing forward. 'I bet I look calm too.'

'Very calm,' said Tryfan with a smile, and turned away to see to other things. But it was Spindle's touch that Bailey afterwards most remembered, for though it was nervous, and hasty, and that of a mole not used to being a father, yet it was caring and accompanied by a whispered message that was for Bailey alone, and which not even Starling heard.

'You're much loved, Bailey, never ever forget that,' said Spindle, and turned then from his son to accompany Tryfan on his rounds.

'What did he say?' demanded Starling.

'It's a secret!' said Bailey.

'Tell me and you can come through the tunnel with Lorren and me,' said Starling.

'No,' said Bailey, 'I won't!'

'All right then,' said Starling. 'Come on, Lorren!' And in her most haughty and commanding way, and without another look at Bailey, Starling went up to Mayweed and said, 'We're coming with you.'

'But beauteous Madams, I'm not a mole to go with, not humble Mayweed who goes here and there and everywhere. You'd get lost with me.'

'Well, that's not good enough!' said Starling. 'You'll just have to make sure we don't get lost because Lorren gets very nervous, don't you Lorren.'

'Yes!' said Lorren.

Mayweed sighed, and grinned, and nodded, and told them that they'd be in the group after next and they were to watch out for him and he'd see them through.

'And Bailey,' said Starling. 'He's with us too.'

'I thought you said he couldn't be,' said Lorren.

'That was just to teach him. 'Course he's coming with us, he's *with* us.'

But Bailey was not there. He had thought Starling was serious, but, quite unperturbed, he had turned to follow after Spindle. Yet somehow in the darkness and the crush of moles, some going this way, and some going that, he had lost sight of Spindle, and of Tryfan, and could not seem to find anymole he knew.

Not that he panicked, but, rather, started to search for somemole who would look after him, as Starling, for all her superior ways, *always* finally did.

Anyway, he said to himself, if nomole else does look after me she'll come and find me, and that will be all right.

Meanwhile, Mayweed had begun to lead the fourth

467

group down into the mud-filled tunnel, hurrying them along and allowing none to pause, reassuring them as they sunk into the wet and slimy darkness, where a mole could lose direction and never know he had done so. Tryfan had taken a place in the middle and Spindle and some other adults brought up the rear, but it was Mayweed who directed them all.

'Keep touching the one in front . . . yes, yes, move on . . . now *don't* start panicking because it'll be all right. I'm right in front of you. . . .'

'Where's Mayweed. *Mayweed*!' A youngster called out pitifully, his voice rising towards hysteria.

'Here I am, good Sir! Ahead in the pitch-blackness and enjoying myself very much, thank you!' Mayweed's voice came back to them, cheerful and comforting, as their paws sloshed into the increasingly mud-filled water, and they did their best to keep to the higher left-paw side.

Going through for the first time in several days, Tryfan noticed that the hishing roar of the river overhead was louder than it had been before, and that here and there water tumbled down from the ceiling onto his face. The sound of wet pawsteps, nervous effortful breathing and the occasional reassuring voice – sometimes for a youngster, but there was one older male at the back who seemed to be being got through by one of his offspring – was all he could hear.

Then light at last, and the climb up the more gravelly higher part of the tunnel until they were beyond the river and there were moles there to welcome them, and help the youngsters groom themselves clean again.

Tryfan felt relieved to have crossed, but knew he would have to go back again. He felt more and more respect for Mayweed and the silent Holm, who had done the terrible journey several times already.

Indeed, almost the moment they had seen the new arrivals to safety, Mayweed was turning back to go through once more.

'Must go, Sir, not many now. Tired, Sir, you are, very.

Mayweed can go on, Sir, you stay here with good Spindle.'

Tryfan laughed. 'I may look tired, Mayweed, but you look awful. I'm coming with you for this last journey through the tunnel. We'll take the remaining moles through as one party.'

'Indomitable you are, Sir, I can see it even now written on your face: hero, moledom's finest son!'

'Let's go, Mayweed,' said Tryfan shortly, as moles around them grinned at Mayweed's flowery words.

'What I was saying, intelligent Sir.'

The reason for Mayweed's haste was clear enough: although they could see little at first, and nothing after a while, it was apparent from the sound of water running and dripping, and the slurry that had already surged across their path in places, that the tunnel was near collapse. There was an air of imminent crushing, drowning, muddy slump to the place, and when they reached the lowest central point, where before they had only had to swim a few feet, it was now necessary to swim several moleyards. Tryfan himself would have become completely confused but for Mayweed's special skills. . . .

'Here, Sir, here! Come to the sound of my voice . . . Here, Sir!' said Mayweed, and Tryfan did so in the blackness, reaching forward in the water so that his paw went up into air even as his back paws found muddy ground again. He reached out carefully, felt about and his paw touched the soft, wet face-fur of Mayweed.

'How do you do it, Mayweed?' said Tryfan.

'I was born in blackness and I survived in it,' said Mayweed, his voice low and without the normal false sing-song. 'I do it by sound and vibration. I do it because I learnt to do it.'

His voice was suddenly strong and certain, as if in this blackness, where he could not be seen, he could be himself: a strong mole, a mole who had conquered fear and learned to survive alone.

There was something so direct and clear in Mayweed's

answer to his question that Tryfan found himself saying, 'I'm nervous down here, Mayweed. Very nervous.'

'I know you are, Tryfan,' said Mayweed using his name without qualification, honorific or adjective for the first time ever, and then more softly, and with a touching reassurance, 'I *know*.' And Tryfan knew that he did, because he had been nervous once, nervous to the point of dying of fear, nervous for molemonths, perhaps years on end, in tunnels black, tunnels filled with plague-dead moles. Abandoned as a pup to what must have seemed eternal darkness and forever obeying his mother's last command: 'Don't go out or they'll kill you. Stay here, stay . . .' And Mayweed had survived, and was here, and in the blackness where none could see his scarred thin body he was himself and truly strong, as he was in spirit.

'I know,' he said again and Tryfan knew that Mayweed understood his fear.

'Come on now, Tryfan,' said Mayweed. 'We have not so far to go.'

They advanced up the tunnel, Mayweed going ahead, and Tryfan almost did not want the light to come as it did, for he could see the old Mayweed returning, the unctuous body, the turning laugh, and the strong and certain mole, the mole whose voice had been reassuring and confident down there in the blackness, was being replaced before his very eyes by the one who advanced into the light, turned and said, 'Very good, Sir, we're through, Sir, we have done very, very well, haven't we, Sir?'

'Mayweed – ' began Tryfan hoping to bring back the Mayweed he had briefly 'seen' in the tunnel, but with the slightest shake of his head Mayweed refused to acknowledge Tryfan's attempt to reach through the facade he presented to other moles.

For a moment Tryfan paused, and watched the hunched, thin mole that seemed to be Mayweed, but which was not Mayweed, and he whispered a prayer to the Stone that if ever the time came that Mayweed could be helped to be . . . himself . . . to be that mole that had courage to get others through the darkness Tryfan would like the chance to take it.

'Please, good, kind Sir, come now. The last groups of moles are waiting and, as you rightly suggested, we'll take the remaining moles through together because time is so very terribly, awfully short, Sir.'

'It's Mayweed! He said he'd come. For us, for me!'

It was Starling, the only mole in the cluster of nervously waiting moles who seemed to have any energy left, and near her Lorren watched her every move.

'Well, well, well, young molethings!' said Mayweed. 'And whatmole did not forget you?'

'You didn't!' said Starling.

'You look very confident, young Madam,' said Mayweed.

'I am, she's not,' said Starling, pointing dismissively at Lorren. 'But I can't go because I've lost Bailey. He must be somewhere, silly Bailey!'

Which he was, right at the back, past many moles, having found Rushe, the mole he had learned to call his mother, and decided that, after all, he preferred her reassuring presence. Starling was all right but there were times you wanted somemole big at your side.

Having found Bailey, Mayweed offered him the chance of coming forward again to be with Starling.

'Not going with *her*,' said Bailey, and crouched firmly next to Rushe.

'Then you'll go last, young and excellent Sir!' said Mayweed.

'I don't mind, but don't tell Starling you found me then she'll be scared.'

'Not nice, not generous and not right at *all*,' said Mayweed scoldingly. 'I most certainly will tell Starling, young Sir, *and* that you told me not to! I'll tell Spindle, too, because I think he'll want to know where you are.'

'Okay,' said Bailey with the world-weariness of a youngster who knows that moledom is full of adults who will not do his will, and whose way he must accept.

Mayweed and Rushe exchanged nods and smiles, glad of the youngsters to relieve the tension, and with Ragwort and other watchers taking up the rear, and Tryfan, Marram and Alder in the middle, Mayweed reached the front, Smithills with him, and set off for the final time.

'Dear Sirs, splendid Madams,' called out Mayweed, as they reached the real beginning of the noisome tunnel, 'we will go now, and go fast. Follow the mole in front, do not talk because I need silence to find the way, and be prepared to swim a little when you reach the centre of the tunnel.'

'But I can't – ' began a timid mole.

'But you *can*, good Sir, mature Sir, strong-looking mole, and those in front and behind will help you . . . nothing to it! Ha! Easy as getting muddy, easier! Close, quick, nomole left behind? We leave!' Then, before they had time for discussion or for discovering more doubts, they were gone for the final time into the depths as, up on the surface, the afternoon darkened and more storm clouds blew over the heights of Duncton Wood.

The only noise, apart from the squelch of pawsteps in the murk, was the chatter of Starling and Lorren whom Mayweed had made the mistake of telling to be completely obedient during the trip underground.

'Well *I* will be!' said Starling brightly.

'You're not usually,' said Lorren, 'and I don't expect you will be now. I think – '

'Shut up,' said some unidentified mole from out of the dark. A mole of few but sensible words.

'Shut up yourself,' returned Lorren.

Then a grim silence fell on the moles as they went down deeper and deeper into the dreadful tunnel and the going got darker and muddier. The distant roar of water had deepened, and here and there, the further they went, Tryfan noticed that what had been merely dripping water before had been replaced by ominous oozings of mud. Then they were into darkness, and the sound, dreadful and frightening, of sucking and slumping in the tunnel around them, and moles whispering nervously and asking how much further it was.

Instinctively Mayweed went more slowly, whispering orders behind him that everymole must tread warily and avoid touching the wall to their left if they could.

Despite this, the only serious hold-up was at the central pool, as Mayweed had predicted, and he and Smithills having crossed it easily, they had to talk over the moles one by one until Tryfan himself was through.

'Lead them on, Tryfan,' said Mayweed urgently in the dark, for around them the tunnel seemed to move and quake, and the ground beneath to be sinking.

'Come on then,' said Tryfan, but though Lorren was willing to go on she did not want to when Starling insisted on staying with Mayweed.

'You must go!' said Starling peremptorily, ordering her on. 'I'm just going to wait for Bailey who can be very silly at times and Rushe may be wanting to be rid of him.'

Mayweed sighed, made sure where she was and told her to hold on to him, and then called to the next mole to cross the water, the tunnel trembling now, and even his cheerful voice beginning to show signs of tension.

'Come *on*, young Sir, *please* hurry now. . . .'

Meanwhile, Tryfan led the others on and at last the tunnel head lightened, and began to rise a little as they reached the harder gravelly bottom that heralded safety on the far side.

'Hurry now,' Tryfan called, 'hurry!' and he stood to one side as he helped Lorren and the others past him, towards the moles up there waiting to welcome the newcomers, and bring them cheer and comfort. How slowly they came, tired and mud-covered, their fur a wetness of yellow-brown silt, their talons lost in clinging ooze . . . with little Lorren looking back fearfully to see if her sister, Starling, was safe, and Bailey too.

'She'll be here soon enough,' said a female, as Tryfan signalled her to hurry the first batch of them away, for the tunnel was changing now, and the ground unpleasant, and overhead the roof was sinking, wetting, lines of clear water running along it.

Tryfan went back down into the tunnel, his paws reaching out and pulling the youngsters and others through more quickly, but many were tired, and there were so many more yet to come, and they were pausing and talking and telling each other they were safe. . . .

Tryfan called out down into the darkness, 'Mayweed, hurry now, *hurry*. . .!'

But his words were lost in a sudden rumble and rush. A strange bellowing of movement in the air, and the smash of water or of mud and a cry from inside the tunnel of Mayweed's voice, almost echoing Tryfan's . . . 'Hurry now Starling, run now, *run*! And you others. . . .'

But that was all Tryfan heard, for then the roaring became louder and as Tryfan stared back into the gloom, and a couple more figures came desperately out of it, he saw behind them, surging and huge, dreadful walls of mud and water, yellow and terrible. Bearing massively down, coming faster and faster with what seemed an ululation of cries, overtaking them, turning them over, driving them towards him, higher and higher up the tunnel . . . and he too was taken by the wall of mud, turned over, choking, reaching desperately for something, anything to hold on to, turning, turning, and no idea where the floor was or the ceiling, and mud at his mouth, forcing its way into his snout, his orientation quite gone and desperate for air as his lungs pained and then tightened and he wanted to breathe, he must breathe, and the mud was in his mouth and. . . .

Somemole grabbed him and pulled him clear, and he found himself gasping and retching and staring down into a sea of mud where the tunnel had been.

'Are they. . .?' he began, taking up stance and looking around. But nomole answered, not even the one who had grasped him, for they too were mud-covered and wet and behind him and around him he saw the horror of shock and drowned death. The mud before him bubbled, and shook, and stirred with dying moles.

Then before others could stop him, and with a shout of '*No*!' he dived into the mud-water and dived again and again until suddenly, and with a struggle and heave, he pulled a spluttering, gasping Mayweed clear.

'Sir, Sir, I had Starling . . . she's there, Sir, *please* Sir . . .' and as willing paws pulled Mayweed clear Tryfan dived again down into the mud-water, seeking for a body with outstretched paws until, giving up, he turned for the surface even as a weak, desperate scrabble of talons touched his leg.

Down he went a third time, and grasped hold of a limp form which, dragged out, was a female: Starling.

'Take her, Mayweed, *take* her . . .' and as he did so, pulling the half-drowned body of Starling clear, Tryfan turned and went under once more, though only half so this time, floundering here and there until, exhausted, he returned to high ground. Others tried too, but no more moles were found, dead or alive.

The tragedy was worse than it had first seemed. For not only had most of the moles in the tunnel been lost, but the surge forward of mud and water had taken many of those who already thought they were safe, sheltering in the burrows so carefully prepared for them. In one of the burrows all the moles were drowned where they crouched. In another a third had been sucked out and pulled back down into the tunnel. While all of those who had been between the burrows and the tunnel as Tryfan had been, had survived. It was most strange, most terrible, and the tunnels were filled with the sobbing of moles, from shock and from loss.

When a count was taken more than half of all those escaping had been lost: more than half! And all the moles could do was comfort each other, and do as the few leaders surviving told them, which was to groom themselves clear of the cold mud and try to get warm.

Tryfan and Spindle and Mayweed were safe, and so was

Smithills, who had personally saved several moles, and Marram and Alder. Comfrey was alive but in shock, for so many of his friends had been drowned.

Several, including Tryfan, watched over the terrible mud, but no life came from it, only the occasional rolling flank of a drowned mole, and then another. But they were left where they were, for what was the point of bringing them out, only to lie them down with the many other dead in that place?

Lorren found her sister Starling, and the two huddled together crying terribly for Bailey, who, with their mother, must surely be lost, and staying close to Mayweed as if they would die if he left them. Ragwort, of course, was lost as well, and others who had been in the deepest part of the tunnel. But grief brings its own terrible fatigues, and with night came fitful sleep, with Starling and Lorren flank by flank with Mayweed, his paws around them as he stared with lost eyes over the chamber.

'You're looking after us now,' said Starling, waking suddenly, 'aren't you Mayweed?'

'Yes,' he whispered, 'yes I shall. Now settle down, young Madam, please. . . .'

Perhaps nothing else but their need for him could have kept poor Mayweed sane that night. His eyes were haunted with guilt and loss, for had it not been he who had first found the tunnel?

'They would have suffered a worse fate than that!' said Tryfan bitterly.

'But they'd still be alive, Sir,' said Mayweed.

'Perhaps.'

That long night Mayweed never slept. He kept his paws on his young wards, comforting them, and long afterwards Spindle, who was there, chronicled that sometime at dawn the look of a lost pup, which had always been with Mayweed, left his eyes forever. In its place came the look of an adult, angry perhaps, and forlorn, yet it had a will and purpose and would see life through. And as Starling fretted and stirred, Mayweed whispered hour after hour, 'Mayweed won't ever leave you, young Madam, not he.'

So the surviving moles slept, the restless sleep of the troubled and lost, who have only death behind them and danger ahead.

Morning came, and with it grim awakening. Tryfan wandered among the stricken moles with Spindle at his side, both disconsolate. Tryfan for all the moles who had suffered losses, Spindle for the fear that Bailey, his only pup, was lost to him forever, and not even Starling's urgent clinging to the belief that Bailey *must* have survived could take the anguish from his thin face.

Only Comfrey seemed to have recovered, as if, in his old age, he could bear his losses in a different and silent way.

'We b-better have an elder meeting here, T-Tryfan,' he said slowly, 'where all may hear us.'

Smithills came, and others grouped around.

But there seemed little to say. Barely one among them had not lost a friend or relative in the fighting or drowning, and their numbers seemed small. There was hope that some might have survived the drowning and been pushed by the water underground to the other side, but it was faint indeed. They knew that even had moles survived, the grikes would get them.

As for Skint and Tundry and . . . 'Well, where are they, Tryfan? They weren't in that last party coming over.'

But even then Tryfan could not tell the full truth lest, in one way or another, it got back to the grikes.

'They are safe enough, and some of your mates as well,' he said rather weakly, for he felt he had nothing to say that could cheer them. Anger suddenly mounted among the survivors.

'It would have been better to stay. . . .'

'Aye, and I'd have a brother still,' said another.

'Only your word that the grikes are that bad. Can't be worse than death. . . .'

Tryfan and the other elders stared at them uncertainly, tired from the weeks past, shocked by the events of the day before.

'Aye it's your fault Tryfan! Without you. . . .'

'You'll have to say something more forceful to us all,' whispered Spindle to Tryfan. 'They don't want a bunch of elders looking miserable, they want to be led . . . so lead them. Tell them you're taking them eastwards for safety, and that you trust in the Stone to protect those remaining in Duncton Wood. Tell them.'

A hush fell. It was as if all there sensed that a moment of change had come. They looked at Tryfan and, troubled, he looked at them. The chill call of coot came down into the chamber, then the shrilking of geese, and a flapping woosh as they took off across the nearby river.

Tryfan sensed that they must move on, and take up the challenge the Stone had given them.

He raised a paw and said softly, 'What I have to say I will say on the surface within sight of our great system.'

'Once-great, you mean!' said an angry mole.

'And will be again!' cried out Tryfan. 'Aye, and *will* be again.'

Then by the sheer force of his presence he led them up on to the surface, in the wide and exposed area near the river, beyond which, dimly, they could see the slow rising of the trees up Duncton Hill. The weather had cleared since the day before though the sky was still cloudy. But the air was good and here and there pockets of sun rode across the ground and lightened the trees of the wood, then the tall swaying sedges of the river, and then themselves.

Tryfan turned instinctively eastwards, for that was where they were bound. There he might lose them in groups in other systems and there they would stay, biding their time until one distant day the Stone followers would return, with the coming of the Stone Mole, and those of Duncton Wood might find their way home.

Some of them might even go as far as the Wen and even

on into it, and in time, too, bring back their stories, and enrich the canon of their system's history. Some would never return.

Duncton was once, Duncton was future. But for now they were vagrants, travellers, lost moles, and each must find courage in memory, in hope, in faith, and in the trust of each other.

Silent were they then around Tryfan, for they saw he was lost in some wonder, and that his tiredness and defeat were leaving him, and he was turning to them strong now, and seeming as if the very light of the Stone itself was in him, which it was. For had he not been to the Holy Burrows themselves, had he not been taught by Boswell, had he not . . .? And they hushed as he began to speak.

'We are the future,' said Tryfan quietly, 'each one of us here, yes and any that survive still in our great system. Today the river divides us, loss divides us, fear breaks us, hopelessness defeats us, uncertainty weakens us, and yet . . .' He leaned forwards towards them, 'We will survive, for the Stone is with us and in us and will be our guide. It will take us eastwards, even to the Wen itself, even into it.'

Many moles' eyes were wide with wonder at this, and trepidation too.

'For how long will our troubles last?' asked an old male, who had known many who had died.

Tryfan smiled softly at such faith. The Stone was with him, the question could be answered.

'Until the Stone Mole comes,' he said. 'Then will your time begin, then will the returning be. Until then I can promise you nothing but the rewards that will come with this great journey of the Duncton moles, rewards of companionship and faith, rewards of learning and courage, rewards that lead to the Stone's great Silence. I can make no false promises or offer false hopes. Many of you will not come back, but your young may, or their young after them. So you here now must carry the story of these days to the future, and tell it where you go to moles

479

you can trust, pass it on, and tell of a place that one day can be returned to, and whose name is Duncton Wood.

'Tell too of the declining that has been on the system, as it has on all systems of the Stone; tell of how the followers lost their way and the moles of the Word came offering something new and clearer, finding a way not by their strength but by our weakness. Tell your young of this, and of how you had to learn to replace weakness with strength and made a journey to discover it.

'We will start our journey now, but not as a crusade which others join. We will be the silent ones, and as we journey on, some will go one way some another, each to find out their niche for waiting, and for sharing what they know. One distant day we will come together again, but for now I lead you to nowhere but towards your-selves. . . .'

He finished, and Comfrey broke the silence that followed with whispered blessings on them, and asked that one day, distant though it might be, the Stone would grant that the moles of Duncton return home again, safeguarded.

Then Comfrey turned to his half-brother Tryfan and said, 'Lead us, T-Tryfan, take us from here. Guide us for the b-beginning of our journey until we have strength to go our own ways, for we trust you and we trust the St-Stone. Give us faith that one day the Stone Mole will come, and in his coming will some of us be blessed to f-find our way back to Duncton Wood again.'

'Then come,' said Tryfan finally, 'come! For now our time here is over and our journeys into Silence must begin.'

Then one by one the others followed them by the route established already by Tryfan and Mayweed which began nearby. Some stared briefly to their right over the river, many did not, for their days at Duncton were over for now, and they must turn their gaze to what was to come. One by one they turned eastward, entered a tunnel once more, and were gone, leaving the place where they had been with just the tall sedge swaying and the deep water of the Thames flowing black and silent, forsaken of mole.

While beyond it the trees of Duncton caught the day's changing summer light, sometimes dark, and sometimes in the sun.

Today, moles like to speak of the escape of the Duncton moles as a triumph, a turning point in moledom's history, a success. But Tryfan never saw it as a success, and those close to him, who were aware of the trials and the stresses he suffered in the pursuit of his tasks for the Stone, knew that no event took greater toll of him than the terrible escape through the river tunnel, when so many moles were lost. Some say that he ever wished to be punished for it, as if in punishing he could assuage the pain those deaths caused. Others believe that Tryfan of Duncton was punished, terribly punished, in the moleyears that followed. But perhaps it is not for mole to judge the Silence that others, of their own free will, enter into; nor even to guess if it is punishment, or bliss.

Chapter Twenty-Eight

Henbane of Whern was ready to kill. Wrekin, the head of all her guardmoles knew it. Sideem Sleekit knew it. Smaile, servant to all of them, doer of evil and unpleasant things, knew it.

But most of all, Weed, adviser to the WordSpeaker, was quite certain of it.

Never in all his long acquaintance with Henbane – 'acquaintance' was exactly the right word since neither mole ever liked the other much, or could have been said to have been a friend – had Weed known her more dangerously angry. It would need but a slip from any one of them for her to turn, thrust, and kill.

Her anger had been mounting ever since entering into this Word-forsaken place the locals revered and called Duncton Wood, when they had discovered that there was not a mole in the system. Not one. Not a half one. None at all on whom Henbane might have vented her annoyance at the Duncton moles' protracted defence. So annoyance changed to anger and now, by the look of it, anger was turning to murderous rage.

So the atmosphere about the great Stone as they crouched there a few days later having a 'conference' was tense, and as explosive as the seed pods of rosebay willowherb on a hot September day. . . .

From the first, the coming of Henbane and the moles of the Word to Duncton had been curiously ominous, and cast a shadow over what she had already been claiming as the end of her long campaign to conquer southern moledom, and annihilate the Stone followers.

For two days the Duncton moles had fought with unexpected courage and resolution, sustaining fewer losses than they inflicted, and causing the first real setback

Henbane ever suffered, unless a mole included the irritation of Siabod, which resisted the Word still but which Henbane herself had dismissed as of no great consequence. But Duncton was different, more central, and demoralising to moles who had been nowhere near ever losing a battle.

Indeed, but for Weed's military leadership, and Henbane's determined purpose that brooked no failure, and the guardmoles' fighting strength, the defence might easily have been even more successful.

Eventually the Duncton moles had weakened and retreated, first from the cow cross-under that witnessed so many grike deaths, and then upslope by as clever a line of defences as Weed and Wrekin had ever seen. From there they had held out another half day, even mounting an effective counter-assault downslope, which slowed the guardmoles yet more for a time.

Then suddenly they were gone, gone on all fronts. Surface burrows deserted, defence tunnels empty, quite gone.

Few guardmoles who were there then forgot – or allowed others they told to forget – their first eerie entry into the Duncton system. The slow advance upslope expecting ambush at any time, the entry into the wood itself and the graceful ancient tunnels they found there, deserted but for the strange rootsound of the high trees which made a moor mole nervous and jumpy. So much so that there were at least two incidents of grikes believing they had seen an attack coming and assaulting their own moles. Unheard of.

But there was no doubt about it, the place was deserted, from south to north, from west to east, quite empty, the moles gone. Not a trace, and, to make it worse, the tunnels were left tidy and the burrows clean, so there had been no panic or disruption; and, as more than one grike whispered nervously looking over his shoulder, 'as if they are going to come back.'

While looming over it all, threatening to moles of the

Word, was the great Stone of Duncton, silent, always silent; a silence that was an intimidation every moment of the day and into the far reaches of the night. A silence that made a mole want to scream.

Then there was the curious report of the guardmole Thrift, who claimed to have spoken with the leader of Duncton, Tryfan, during the battle. Incredible. Wrekin did not believe a word of it, but Weed did, and got as much of the truth from the mole as he was ever likely to. Enough to bring Thrift privately before Henbane herself and have him repeat what he had been told to say by this Tryfan, which was that if Henbane would find the moles of Duncton let her 'listen to the Silence' of the Stone. It was when she heard that, that Weed observed Henbane's annoyance first shift towards anger, and stay there, and he wondered if Thrift would be the victim of her anger for bringing such a message. But no, stranger still, she asked him to describe this Tryfan again and again, and she listened to the guardmole's faltering and limited words ('big', 'strong', 'powerful gaze', 'seemed kind' – kind!) with evident fascination. Henbane had always liked moles who stood up to her, even if she killed them or had them killed in the end.

Whatever that message about listening to Silence meant, (Weed was careful not to have Thrift repeat the nonsense about a healing. In battle? By one foe to another? Ridiculous!) it was one more dark portent that the takeover of the system which had most significance for Stone followers, because of its ancient connection with the Stone, was not as happy as it might be for moles of the Word. Never had a takeover been so marred, for there seemed no satisfaction in conquering moles who were not there or pleasure in a system whose very tunnels seemed to make guardmoles disgruntled and uneasy.

But if their initial unease was caused merely by ill-temper mixed with superstition, they soon had something more real to go on. Within a day of their arrival, a group of guardmoles exploring the Ancient System made their way down to the great vertical lines of the roots of the trees that formed a protective circle round the buried part of the Stone. They were hoping to find a way to the Stone's base, but the roots barred their way. In truth they had none of them seen anything quite like it: strange twistings and torsions of tree roots, some old and grey, others young and palely moist, all quivering and vibrating and sounding to the movement of the trees they fed and supported.

Among them they went, trying to seek a way through, a little unnerved by the way the roots hummed and shifted, making them lose their orientation, coming close to them, touching them, pushing them, catching them, and suddenly loud in their noise and vibration as great gusts of wind seemed to catch the trees above ground and turned the chamber of roots into a crushing, grinding, twisting place of horror. One after another the guardmoles saw each other caught and turned, pinioned and wrought, and then crushed; eyes bulging, veins breaking, mouths gaping, jaws cracking, stomachs bursting, the others' screams the last thing they heard as the roots took them into painful death.

Six died that way, and word went about that that was six for each of the Stone followers' seven Ancient Systems. Would have been seven if Siabod had been taken, aye and there would be a seventh killed if it ever was. . . .

What was subtly worse was that Henbane and Weed were within earshot of those terrible deaths and came running and could do nothing but helplessly watch their own moles die. Afterwards not a guardmole dared go among the roots to get the bodies, which hung twisted and broken before them, the roots quivering like living things. So a few tree roots showed that Henbane was not infallible, and some tiny part of her credibility died with those moles.

Then, two days later, two guardmoles were found, dead, in quite different parts of the system. Talon-thrust to death in public communal places where others should have seen; but there was never a sign nor sound of othermole. Then a third guardmole simply disappeared, sent on some errand or other and gone: no sound, no trace. Then yet another! Panic and unease, patrols only willing to go out in twos and threes. Henbane was formally approached by guardmoles through Wrekin himself and asked to speak the Word and protect them from further 'assault' from the ghosts of dead Stone followers.

Which she refused to do, dismissing the guardmoles' superstitious fears, and ordering instead a systematic search of the system to find the moles perpetrating the attacks, who must be hidden somewhere or another. Which Wrekin had done from the high wood down to the very Marsh itself. Nothing, no trace of mole. She ordered that the routes in and out, which in this system were well defined, be guarded, lest these moles were creeping in, killing and creeping out again. For a week guardmoles kept to their stations and nothing more happened and confidence began to be restored. Then suddenly another mole was killed inside the system, the ninth so far, and the two others who had vanished. His body was found at night after the strangest and eeriest of sounds, a calling, a haunting, a frightening.

So the guardmoles had been sent out to search the system yet again, and Henbane had summoned the moles she relied on to the Stone to hear Wrekin's report. But the search had once more drawn a blank and not a living mole had been found. Henbane, now crouched staring, had become more frustrated and enraged. For a time she had stared malevolently at the great Stone, seeming to see more in it than Weed could. To him it was just a . . . Stone. He had seen them before, most impressively at Avebury. High rising things that caught the light strangely.

So she had stared, and then she had muttered, 'Silence? What Silence? *What* Silence? How does a mole hide in Silence, let alone a whole system of moles?'

Then her eyes shifted this way and that, staring at each of them, looking, Weed knew well, for weakness. She found it soon enough, in Smaile of course. But he was not going to be killed. Moles who carry out orders as well as he, moles who keep their traps shut, moles whose highest ambition is to do unpleasant things for others are rare indeed, and Henbane too clever to kill them. Her anger was not yet that mad.

Wrekin would not weaken before her gaze, and nor would Weed himself; Weed knew *that*. But Sideem Sleekit? Mmm . . . Weed eyed her. Promoted above the heads of all the sideem currently serving in the south, picked out at Buckland soon after the death of Eldrene Fescue.

Weed knew the type, he had *trained* that type of sideem in the days when he was in Whern with Henbane, coaching her for Rune. Yes, Sleekit was the type all right: clever, cold, secretive of speech, utterly cynical, organised. And yet: *something*. Weed knew not what. *Something*. Something about her that made him think she was not quite right; had been once, was not now. *Something*. So he had Henbane promote her so that he himself, sideem too of course, very special sideem, could watch her the better.

Until here, today, this fretful afternoon, with Henbane malevolent, Weed had had a clue, and at first dismissed it as unthinkable. Impossible. And yet there it was, in her eyes, nearly all of it disguised. But he was a trainer, an expert, and not passionate like Henbane, so he could see that tiny part the sideem could not hide. Awe before the Stone. It was not that she was afraid of it, what grike wasn't? Unless he was stupid. No, not afraid, but in awe, yet more than awe. Love. That was the bit she could not hide. Love. Tiny, fractional, distant, but there. A sideem in love with the Stone. Quite unthinkable. And of course unstoppable. She probably did not even yet know it herself. He must think of a way of using it. Most original. Don't tell Henbane. Don't let Sideem Sleekit know I know, thought Weed. Yes, yes, *use* a sideem who is in awe of the Stone. *Use* her to reach this Tryfan. Mmm. . . .

Weed turned his attention back to Henbane, his face inscrutable. She was going to speak. About time too.

'And where, Wrekin, do you imagine they've gone?' said Henbane. She was well aware that Wrekin, like Weed, was one of the very few moles who had no fear of her. 'And where do these invisible moles who kill your guardmoles appear from? What of the Pasture moles to the west?'

'We have sealed their system off and have guards at all entrances.'

'Are there *no* other signs of mole at all?'

Wrekin was prepared for this and had his little surprise, perhaps kept back to deflect Henbane from the matter in paw. Anyway, Weed listened. . . .

'No signs that are fresh. But we know, or think we know, how they escaped. To the north are marshes, beyond them the River Thames. We found tunnels to its edge, and temporary chambers there filled with mud.'

'Moles never escape through mud!' said Henbane impatiently.

'There is more than mud there, WordSpeaker. There are bodies as well. Many of them. Drowned moles. We think that they made a hasty tunnel under the river, that they tried to escape through it, and that some of them drowned when the tunnel collapsed.'

A tunnel under the river? Henbane mused on it and relaxed. Such a tunnel *was* a sign of panic and disarray. Such a futile attempt pleased her, made her feel less affronted. The Duncton moles were not so clever after all.

'Are there no survivors?' Her voice was cold and she asked in the hope of retribution on those surviving, not out of charity or care.

'None that we have seen. But naturally, it is possible, and unfortunately the Marsh End of the wood is not only foul and filthy, but riddled with tunnels of a kind. We are searching them thoroughly, and if moles did survive then we will find them in due course. But the idea that such moles are causing these other deaths seems to me far-fetched. Moles who survive such a thing as a water-collapsed tunnel do not usually mount covert attacks.'

Then Wrekin added thoughtfully, 'If that *was* the means of escape, rather than some twofoot crossing we have so far missed, it shows these moles to be resourceful and bold. I say that merely to warn you that it is easy to underestimate one's enemy after as long a series of successes as we have had. Needless to say, many of the guardmoles are attributing magical powers to the Duncton moles for escaping, but of course there will be a rational explanation and I now think the tunnel is it.'

Henbane stared at the stolid fighter and, had she not been in such a grim mood, she might have smiled darkly. Wrekin won systems by logic and reason, and in the moleyears he had campaigned for her he had developed a nearly infallible approach to taking over systems. One after the other had fallen to his guardmole forces.

But here, at Duncton Wood, something different had happened than ever before and Wrekin seemed not to appreciate the fact. As far as he was concerned, all that mattered was that victory over another system had been achieved: these later deaths and troubles seemed to him relatively unimportant compared to that.

'We'll find out, WordSpeaker, rest assured of that. I left enough guardmoles in adjacent systems to pick up information about any escapers, and that news will come in soon enough now. They've orders to take prisoners and get what information they can from them in whatever way seems best.'

His mouth hardened and his eyes went cold. Wrekin was a fighting mole, not a torturer, but his instincts told him that these Duncton moles were more insanely fervent than other Stone followers they had defeated, and he feared that the job of getting information from them might have to be given over to the sideem. Which meant that Weed would have a paw in it.

Wrekin said no more and Weed, who had been crouched nearby, shook his head in exaggerated disbelief.

'And that's it, is it?'

'What more is there to say?' asked the fighter coldly. 'They put up a good defence, they weakened, and we won. Now they have gone leaving a few residual problems. But they fought well, and I respect them.'

'*Respect* them? Hasn't it occurred to you, Wrekin, that what has happened here in Duncton Wood is strange and ominous?'

'You see shadows in the brightest sunlight, Weed. You always have, you always will. We *won*, Weed. We defeated them. What more do you want?'

As Weed opened his mouth to argue further, Henbane raised a talon to stop him, turned to Wrekin, complimented him on all he had done, and told him to go and rest. But when news came in she wanted to know about it.

As Sleekit made to go after Wrekin, Henbane motioned her to stay, saying, 'You should hear all things, sideem, everything. Did not the Master tell you that?' Henbane's voice was soft as a willow's bud, and frightening. Sleekit smiled, glanced at Weed and settled down.

'Well?' said Henbane, turning abruptly to Weed. 'And did we not defeat them?'

Weed stirred, got up restlessly and stared up at the Stone, peered about the sinewy rising branches of the beech trees, and snouted at some moist leaf litter at his paws.

'I don't like Duncton Wood,' he said, his snout twisting round as he glanced again briefly at the Stone. 'Not a place for us to stay long. Strange the empty tunnels, and the trees on a hill. Never did like that. Vales are where trees should be, hills are for treeless moorland.'

He darted a glance at Henbane to see what the effect of his reminding her of moorland was. She had been raised to moorland and he knew that she missed it. As the campaign in the south had gone on these last few moleyears, she had begun to lose interest and to want to return north for a time. And, too, to see Rune again. Yes, she wanted that.

But she was silent, waiting.

Sleekit had sidled into shadow, and was still as death.

'What Wrekin is missing is the fact that there was resistance here at all,' continued Weed. 'In all the long years of our progress over southern moledom, I cannot remember a better defence than the one we faced here. Nor can I remember a better retreat: total. All gone. Some drowned but many survived to plan and fight another day.'

Henbane nodded, unusually quiet. Weed was a mole she listened to, for though he did not have Wrekin's ability to lead the guardmoles he was capable of seeing the subtler – and the more ominous – possibilities of things. He was useful to her as a listener, a sounding wall.

'This Tryfan, he seems to be a cleverer mole than any we've come across in many a year,' said Weed. 'And judging from the way he evacuated the moles here, he must be something of a leader too.'

Henbane shrugged.

'There have been other "leaders",' she said, 'all dead now. He might be dead.' She stared over at the Stone, then indifferently at Sleekit, then at nothing much, a moment's memory in her eyes. Weed knew of what well enough. Of moles, of males, of 'leaders' she had known, known very well briefly, and then, having used them, made them die.

'Mmm,' muttered Henbane suddenly. 'Yes. Rebels have their uses. They give the guardmoles something to do, somemole to vent their frustration on. I am not the only mole to wish to return to Whern,' she said unexpectedly.

She knows my thoughts too well, thought Weed – some of them.

'What worries me about this place is the sickly smell of faith it has' he continued, 'and the unfamiliar notion it puts in moles of the Word that, for once, the nature of things is against them.'

'Tell me more, Weed,' commanded Henbane, turning to face him full on, and listening to every word he said.

'Sleekit knows,' said Weed quite suddenly, turning on the sideem and lunging close. 'You know don't you?'

The question was almost violent and for a brief moment Sleekit looked shocked, and once again she glanced at the Stone, and then away.

She smiled coldly at Weed.

'I know much that you have taught me, much that I have learnt. Duncton is not a good place for moles of the Word and I am sure that the WordSpeaker is thinking of ways in which it can be destroyed such that moles will never return here.'

It was a good enough reply, thought Weed.

He turned back to Henbane and said, 'Without even realising it, we've lost the initiative over the Stone followers. They have made us all look powerless, and we have no prisoners to interrogate.'

'Then find some! Find some, *find* them,' she said violently. 'I want them found.'

'We will do so,' said Weed, wondering who 'they' would turn out to be. If there was one thing Henbane did not like it was to be ignored, and though this mole Tryfan could not have known it, by evacuating the system he had delivered to Henbane an insult she would not forget, or allow to go unpunished.

'See they are found, Weed, find them for me, find anymole of Duncton that I may . . .' she said, her voice now curiously weak, weak as only Weed was allowed to hear it.

'I will,' he whispered soothingly.

'Do so, Weed. But if they find Tryfan I want him alive, very much alive.'

Weed's eyes smiled and his yellow teeth showed and his tongue flicked pinkly and was gone.

'But before then, find me a Duncton mole, any Duncton mole, for I would talk with him.' Her eyes were suddenly angry and bitter, her talons flexing at the humus, her mouth open. Weed decided he had better find a dispensable mole, for the first of Duncton Henbane saw would be dead from the moment she saw him.

'Leave me now,' said Henbane waving them both away.

492

When they had gone Henbane turned peremptorily from the Stone, and a look of astonishing sadness went over her face, and then weariness. She crouched down.

'How long?' she whispered. 'Rune, how long?'

Silently, as a tear coursed down her face, she whispered, 'Rune, I am weary now, longing for Whern. And you, do you wait my return?' She sighed, deeply, almost like a pup in distress. She stilled, eyes everywhere, face hardening. Mole watching? Mole to see her like this would be mole to die. She relaxed again, and stared round balefully at the Stone.

Yet as she did so, a mole watched. Weed. From shadows to the south. It was his job and he was good at it.

She seemed about to whisper again when noise came from beyond the circle of trees round the Stone: surreptitious, timid, nervous, weak. She stared, eyes narrowing, talons tensing, shoulders huge and black.

Behind her, unseen, Weed tensed too. Mole *was* coming. Word help the mole that disturbed Henbane's privacy. Weed relaxed. He was about to see a mole die.

Henbane seemed to disappear into the shadows about the Stone, and yet she did not move.

The intruder from the north poked a small pink snout out of vegetation, stared up at the Stone and, still staring, came out into the open before it.

He said in a small male voice, 'I knew I could get here by myself.' He looked tearful, and very nervous.

'Well done,' said Henbane heavily from the shadows, except that suddenly she was not in shadows at all, but there, seeming almost bigger than the great Stone and certainly awesome.

'Oh!' said the mole.

'Whatmole might you be?' said Henbane sweetly. A mole might well tremble before the threat in that voice.

'Of Duncton born,' said the young mole.

'You're dirty, you're frightened, you're in the wrong place and I'd like very much to know how you got here, past my guardmoles.'

493

'I avoided them,' said the youngster. 'It wasn't easy, but I did.'

Henbane smiled, the mole relaxed, and, unseen behind them both, Weed tensed. She would kill for sure.

'What is your name?' asked Henbane, most reasonably, her talons flexing ready for a thrust.

The youngster turned to her, eyes wide and trusting now, and went to her.

'I'm Bailey,' he said.

* * * * * * *

From the moment Tryfan left them to join the evacuation from the system, Skint's command of his small group of moles was tight and disciplined. Silence was the principle rule, obedience the next. And Skint knew that if they were to survive, then mutual trust would be needed.

After Tryfan and Spindle had left, he had set them to completing the deeper burrows that they felt they would need, using the precious time left before the grikes infiltrated the system.

Skint sent out two trusted moles as watchers, to report the moment sight or sound of the grikes was established, deputing Yarrow, an older male who had proved himself in the fighting earlier and was uninjured, and Tundry, who had been a watcher over near the river throughout the battle and had kept a cool head. The two were told that when they returned they were to try to do so silently, to test out the sounding systems in the hidden tunnels and burrows.

Meanwhile those staying behind checked they had food enough, double-checked the disguised exits and entrances, adjusted some of the sounding stones and roots in the tunnels above which would be useful indicators of the presence of alien moles, and as mid-afternoon wore on settled down and waited for the return of Yarrow and Tundry.

The sounding systems worked well: Yarrow was heard early on, and Tundry picked up only a little later, coming from a different direction. They reported they had heard and seen the arrival of moles near the Ancient Systems and after making some assessment of their numbers, and checking the Eastside out to confirm there were more there, they left well alone and returned to the Marsh End.

'Right now, we may hear nothing for hours, for days even,' said Skint, 'but we will hear something eventually. As we can't just sit here and rot we'll investigate, and bit by bit we'll learn what the grikes are up to. We know they're well ordered and they like regularity, so there'll be guards, patrols, and all the rest, and the main thing will be to find out what their positions and routines are without ever once giving away that we are in the system. Any questions?'

'What if one of us gets caught?' asked Fidler, a young watcher who had shown he was resourceful and capable of working by himself. He had been one of Skint's recommendations.

'Get caught and you're on your own. Don't expect to be rescued. Say nothing. It won't be nice, so *don't* get caught.'

They looked at each other grimly. Getting caught probably meant death.

It was a full twenty-four hours before they first heard mole sounds, up on the surface. Quite loud, very confident. Two moles . . . no, one lingering, the other going.

Tundry went up to investigate and was soon back.

'Male, large, dim-looking,' he whispered. 'Came to within a few feet of the east entrance but saw nothing.'

'Any sign of the other we heard?' asked Skint.

'Only tracks. Another male. Heading south.'

They heard the alien mole wander off.

The following dawn Fidler and Yarrow went out on patrol. They came back two hours later looking sheepish.

'We discovered a single male,' said Yarrow. 'Had to kill him. He saw us.'

Skint was not pleased.

'A killed mole means there's living moles to do the deed, and that means investigation. We're going to have to think about that . . . but it will at least cause consternation – and no doubt make them increase their efforts to find living moles in the system. Covert means secret and it means discreet,' said Skint. 'It means unknown, it means *very* silent. We are going to be the most unknown moles in moledom. *Got it?*'

The others nodded, grim-faced, as tough a lot of Stone followers as had ever been assembled at Duncton.

'Now we've had a few days of this, and we're going to have a whole lot more. So from now on we do *nothing* without planning, and without thought. I'm not saying that what we've done so far is a disaster, but it's not been controlled enough. You know what our objective is? Eh?'

Skint looked around them all morosely.

'Fear,' he said. 'Yes, fear. Grikes have terrorised moledom for as long as I can remember, and they've done it two ways. First they've done it by brutality, second they've done it by fear of the Word. Well, now. Well . . .' Skint thought for a bit.

'We're going to make them so afraid of Duncton that they won't want to stay here very long. We're going to take grikes out, one by one. We're going to kill one or two savagely. Or make it look savage. If you've got to kill do it quick and painlessly, we're not doing *that* any other way. But make it look savage afterwards. A few grikes are going to disappear because that's what makes their friends worried. I know. That's what happened on the Slopeside. And you know what else we're going to do. . .'

* * * * * * *

'Bailey?' repeated Henbane, her eyes narrow, her talons lusting for the feel of his innocent flesh.

'Yes,' said Bailey. 'And my sister Starling and my other sister Lorren and. . . .'

'And?' purred Henbane.

'You haven't said your name,' said Bailey coming even nearer.

In the shadows Weed blinked. The mole was not dead.

Henbane's talons had retracted somewhat. The mole was unpleasantly close to her. And then the mole. . . .

'*Never* do that again!' said Henbane, rearing up.

'I only touched you,' said Bailey. 'Your fur's funny.'

There was a long silence. Weed blinked again. He was sweating now, though the day was not overwarm. The tedious youngster was *still* alive.

And then Henbane laughed. Laughed as if she had never laughed, laughed so much that the guardmole who had failed to apprehend Bailey came running, and stared. Henbane laughed almost hysterically.

'What's funny?' said Bailey.

She stopped as fast as she had started. She had seen the guardmole.

She said to Bailey, 'Stay here and don't move.'

She went over to the guardmole.

'Did you see this young mole pass by?'

'No, WordSpeaker. I . . .,' he hesitated. Henbane killed him. And Bailey stared, wide-eyed, just stared. He stared at the blood on her talons. He stared at the guardmole slumped before her. He stared at a second guardmole, who had come running and was now grey of snout and shaking with fear until he was killed too.

Then Bailey said, 'I don't like you.'

At which Henbane turned on him, angry now, that anger she had started with redoubled, trebled, quad-rupling as she seemed to ripple with it and Bailey backed away from her as she slowly advanced on him, until his back was against the Stone, which rose high above him.

Watching, Weed gulped.

'Also,' said Bailey, 'I don't think the Stone likes you, it doesn't like you at all, and it will never like you and if Starling was here I know what she'd say, I know exactly what she'd say, she'd say, she'd say . . .' As he spoke these last words his voice had begun to waver, and his eyes to fill with tears, and he looked from Henbane to the dead guardmoles and back again.

Then to watching Weed's astonishment Bailey,

trembling yet determined, came out from the shadow of the great Stone of Duncton right up to her, as if he was not in the slightest bit afraid, and he said, 'Starling would tell you to go away and never, ever, ever come back. *Go away!*' He screamed it out, and began to cry.

At which, to Weed's yet greater astonishment, Henbane, conqueror of moledom, daughter of Rune, WordSpeaker, Henbane of Whern stared at the youngster mole aghast, her eyes wide, and her mouth working, and she reached forward a paw and pushed or, more accurately, half lifted Bailey aside, and then turned and waved him to be still, not unkindly, but in some way that told them both it was better that he shut up now, he had said enough because *because* – and she raised her talons and crashed them down where Bailey had been, and stared at the humus and leaf all ripped and churned. Then she raised her talons again and brought them down, but gently, so gently, as a mother might, where Bailey had been and she lowered her snout and she too began to cry.

Nomole, *nomole* must see her. No one but must die. Weed acted quickly. He came out of the shadows and Henbane did not respond as normally she might: with anger at his sneakings. She ignored him, her sobs as passionate as her anger or her hatred, terrible to hear; the sobs of a pup never once allowed to cry, who cries at last.

Weed allowed no others near, but this wretched, idiotic Bailey. He stayed whimpering. Nomole else.

Then when she had stopped Weed said, 'You had better rest, WordSpeaker,' his voice respectful but authoritative.

She nodded, not looking at him.

'He's coming,' she said, meaning Bailey.

'I'm not,' said Bailey.

Weed grabbed his shoulder and hissed, 'You are, youngster, yes you are,' and Bailey, very frightened suddenly because this mole's snout twisted and made him think he was going dizzy, said, 'Yes!' And as if they were two pups, Weed herded the most powerful mole in moledom, and, until a few moments before, the weakest, down into the Duncton tunnels, to a chamber well out of sight.

* * * * * * *

Henbane was not seen again by grike for days. Not by Sleekit, nor even by Wrekin, though Wrekin soon had things to report. She was not seen for days, but laughter was heard, and a youngster was seen, Bailey by name.

But then another grike disappeared, and another died. Henbane must be told. Weed said he would, perhaps he did, but Henbane did not appear. Just that laughter, like pups playing down there, and a warning that if Bailey was found, eating up on the surface, he was not to be touched or harmed.

Grumblings then, and Wrekin enraged. What was the WordSpeaker up to? Demands to see her. Weed smiled.

'Does she know what's happening? Does she know that there are still killings going on in this miserable system? Does she know the Duncton moles who escaped have been sighted And she *plays*?'

'She knows,' said Weed.

It was more than two moleweeks before Henbane appeared, and when she did that Bailey mole was at her side. Nomole dared say a thing. She summoned Wrekin, and Sleekit, and several others.

She stared at them and seemed to be thinking, though what she had to say suggested she had thought a lot already. Bailey said, 'Come on, 'cos I'm going to show you the Eastside where my burrow was.'

Whispers. A Duncton mole. More whispers. Henbane smiled.

'I'll come, Bailey, soon now. Leave us for a time. *Leave* us.' It was said kindly, in a voice none of them had ever heard. A voice that made her seem almost *mole*. Bailey left for the surface.

She turned to Sleekit and said, 'Tell me, where is scalpskin still prevalent nearby?'

'Avebury had it,' said Sleekit promptly, for it was her

499

job to know such things. 'But nearby, well . . . East Bladon, Frilford and some at Wytham. And – '

'Yes?' Henbane's voice was terse and efficient.

'I said Avebury had it, and that's true, but it seems to have been replaced there by something worse. Eats a mole, churns a mole's skin, terrible . . . Some say that this disease will replace scalpskin. It is not pleasant.'

'Good. Now listen all of you. I am aware that moles are hiding in Duncton. I have heard of the new killings from Weed. I do not think we will easily find the moles responsible, and nor do I think we should bother. Such a covert campaign is not easily defeated, if ever. Nor is a system such as this ever easily destroyed. Was Whernside ever destroyed after Scirpus went there, despite all the efforts of the scribemoles of the Stone over the centuries? No it was not. But I have had a thought . . .' Her eyes narrowed, her voice lowered and slowed.

'I want arrangements made that moles afflicted by scalpskin and any other scourge – the more catching the better – are brought to Duncton. In fact, are summoned to Duncton. If the Duncton moles wish to desert the place then let us find moles who will not. Moles who have nowhere else to go. See that every diseased, idiot and crippled mole in those systems is brought here, all of them, Weed, *every one*.'

'I will,' said Weed, pleased to see that Henbane's spirits and cruel guile were recovering.

She turned to Wrekin.

'Your surmise about a tunnel was right. The charming young Bailey has confirmed it. The Duncton moles used a tunnel, and though some died many escaped. Perhaps too many.

'So . . . your guardmoles have a task, Wrekin. The moles Tryfan, Spindle, Comfrey, Alder, Mayweed and Marram are to be found, and brought to me, wherever I am. Alive. These names Bailey has given me. Any other mole of Duncton, whoever they are, wherever they are, however long it takes, is to be found and killed. I repeat: found and killed.'

'We have already had reports that a group of them are moving east,' interrupted Wrekin.

'Good.'

'We have sent out a force after them.'

'Good indeed. But others may escape. Use any means you like to find out where they have gone to. If Tryfan is the mole I think he is, he will disperse his moles. Fine. *Find* them. Kill them. We are going to destroy this place by making it a system of shame, of disease, and an affront to the Stone that rises over it. Nomole will ever wish to be associated with it again in any way. We will also destroy forever the moles who once lived here and those who call themselves Pasture moles. From this moment Duncton is no more.'

A ripple of excitement ran through the moles heeding her. This was Henbane as once she had been. Powerful and determined. Clever. Cruel. Thinking.

'One other thing, Wrekin, and any other mole who has to do with finding Duncton moles. If *ever* a mole called Starling is found, or one called Lorren, I wish to know of it. On pain of death, at my talons personally, is the mole Bailey *not* to be told. Never. Or at least – ' and she smiled terribly. 'Not until after I have had my way with them. So . . . remember their names: Starling, Lorren.'

'Are they to be killed?' asked somemole.

'Oh no, not by their finders, no. I want them alive as well. Indeed, I would have those moles almost as much as I would have Tryfan before me. Those moles I have named will one day wish that they had never lived. And one day each of them will forswear the Stone, and forswear their very selves. They will forswear their kith and kin, and even, I suspect, their siblings. Find them. Bring them.'

'Yes, WordSpeaker. . . .'

'And Wrekin,' she said. 'I wish to speak to you of Siabod.'

501

He nodded, in awe. This *was* Henbane. This was the mole he liked to serve.

'It irritates me, Wrekin,' she said simply. 'Take it.'

'I will,' said Wrekin.

After all but Weed had gone, Henbane said, 'Well, Weed, you did not expect that!'

'I think I did,' said Weed.

Henbane laughed, laughed as she did when Bailey was with her.

'I have a wish to go home to Whern for a time. I have a wish to show Bailey to Rune. There is something about that mole that will please him.'

'What is that?' asked Weed, genuinely curious.

'Innocence,' said Henbane. 'And a faith in the Stone and in his sister Starling so unshakeable that it will amuse the Master in his old age to find a way to break it.'

Weed smiled, and understood, and felt pleased. He too wanted to go home. For a time at least. Yes.

'When shall we leave?' he asked.

'When I am satisfied that Duncton is re-settled with the diseased and deformed moles you will find.'

'What moles will be its command?' asked Weed.

'I am surprised you ask, Weed. You're getting old. Guardmoles, of course, the stupider and crueller the better. And then, when they are all here, let them have no support from us, none. This Duncton will become a place nomole will ever wish to visit. And if, as I suspect, there are covert moles here who hope to scare us, then they, my dear Weed, will be the ones who will soon most wish to leave! But of course Wrekin will see that the cross-under is garrisoned. For once a mole comes to the new Duncton Wood he or she will never leave alive.'

Then she went to an exit and looked up into the light.

'So . . .' she sighed, 'see to it, Weed. And now I must find Bailey. I think he wishes to "play". Now that's a word, Weed, I never once heard my dear mother Charlock use. "Play". Quite charming. Well one day, one day . . . that mole will play indeed. And his sister Starling will be

502

there. Poor thing. Poor vile thing. Oh yes, Bailey will play. And Rune will be well pleased.'

Then she laughed bitterly and with jealousy, and then almost savagely. 'That Tryfan,' she said softly before she left, 'would have had me listen to Silence to find him. There is no Silence, Weed. None. Not ever.'

'Are you coming?' called Bailey from the surface.

'Yes, Bailey, I am.'

Weed's curled snout seemed to glisten in the deserted chamber, and circled with his thoughts, his brow furrowed. Was it good or was it bad, this cruelly playful Henbane? Hard to say. For the first time in his life it was beyond his experience. What did it mean? It meant that, yes, it was time, perhaps, for her to return to Whern, time for Rune to be seen to assume control.

Chapter Twenty-Nine

For the first few days following the Duncton moles' tragic departure from their system, Tryfan was determined that they should move as far east as they could, and as fast as possible. He had little doubt that the grikes would soon be sent in pursuit, and, although they would have to find a river crossing and their way would be circuitous, they would travel at speed – much faster than Tryfan's group could.

Several trustworthy moles, led once more by Alder, whose stature among them all had increased enormously following his success in defending the system, were deputed to watch for danger. The bulk of the moles travelled in three groups, the first consisting of young adults led by Tryfan himself, in the second went older moles and youngsters under Comfrey and Maundy, and in the last, led by Smithills, travelled the watchers and good fighters. Some moles like Mayweed, Holm and Marram suited themselves where they went, while Spindle made it his job to mix with all the groups, and was the eyes and ears of Tryfan for what moles were thinking.

Tryfan had real worries. He had expected some deaths from the stresses of the journey, and the first came two moleweeks into it. One day an old male died and a day later a female wandered secretly off, in the way that old moles do sometimes, not wishing to cause trouble, nor to be found, for a mole has a right to die as he or she will.

These deaths, of respected moles, had their effect. The group was already beginning to travel more slowly, and Spindle reported a decline in morale as the full horror surrounding their departure sank in, the losses of friends and relatives was felt, and the initial impulse to escape was replaced by uncertainty about the future.

It was then that Tryfan and Alder, recognising the problems of defending so large and vulnerable a group, decided that the sooner the moles could be dispersed the better. It would be relatively easy to do such a thing in those eastern parts since such systems as there might be would not have been taken over by grikes. Hopefully, and with the support of indigenous moles, the Duncton moles could quietly infiltrate in smaller groups and, for a time at least, be 'lost'. Even if grikes subsequently took over their new system, Duncton moles could disguise their origins, and submit to the grikes, and wait for their time to come again.

The problem was when they might begin such dispersal. They were still within the great vale from which Duncton Wood rises, and did not feel far enough away yet to be clear of danger. They had crossed the treacherous Otmoor and travelled on over the heights of Brill, and then on via the system of Thame, which is known to scribemole though of little account. But it did not yet feel far enough.

Beyond Thame they noticed that sometimes at night, when the atmosphere was moist and misty, the sky to the east seemed to glow, as if the ground beneath it was filled with the gazes of roaring owls and twofoots. This, Tryfan realised, must be the beginning of the Wen, and as the ground rose steadily to the east he guessed that the Wen itself lay in an enormous vale such as the one they were climbing out of, and that their best point of dispersal might be when they reached the escarpment that must divide one great vale from the next.

The moles travelled mainly at dusk and early morning, avoiding the depth of night and the heat of day, and as most soon guessed that a dispersal was coming, they were silent and thinking, as if preparing themselves for the separations to come.

Few intended to travel alone, and so moles began to split and group in twos and threes, some in old associations of family and friendship, others with moles they had only met since the evacuation.

But a few moles already had very specific places to go, none more certain and distant than Alder and Marram. Quite when it was decided, neither they nor Tryfan ever knew – and Spindle's chronicle is not clear on the subject – but decide it they did: that those two strong moles, both grike-trained and proven in strategy, would finally turn back west and make that trek which so few moles have ever done, the long journey to Siabod. If Marram's information was correct, Siabod must be the only one of the seven Ancient Systems not yet fallen to grike forces, and there seemed to be no doubt that Henbane would wish to change that now Duncton was taken. If she did, then Siabod might welcome two such moles as Alder and Marram, and wish to know of the plight and experience of the Duncton moles.

'I would come with you myself,' said Tryfan with real regret, 'but I know my own journey must be eastwards into the Wen. But nomole would be more suited to such a venture than you, Alder, who has travelled far with me, and knows our ways, and can brave the fastnesses of Siabod to make contact with the moles there, and enlist their support against the grikes.'

'Aye, and I shall go with your spirit with me, and your good will, and the more willingly that Marram can accompany me,' said Alder. Then Tryfan told the two all he could remember of what his parents had said of Siabod and its moles.

But they agreed not to leave until they had accompanied Tryfan and the others to the dispersal point, for their special strength and courage might yet be needed if the Duncton moles met trouble before they reached the far edge of the escarpment ahead.

Others made their decisions, too – Smithills, for example, decided to travel north a little, and be within striking distance of Rollright so that he could be there to meet Skint at Longest Night if Tryfan and his party did not return in time from the Wen. Smithills already missed Skint greatly, and had no stomach to travel too far from Duncton.

Tryfan had given much thought to the moles who might accompany him, thinking at first that he might travel with several, perhaps seven in all, and one of those he had assumed would be Smithills. But Smithills' decision changed that and he thought perhaps he should travel with just Spindle and one other.

But who? It was clear that Comfrey was too old now, and in any case Maundy would want to go with him and they themselves agreed that they would be a liability on such a venture as a journey into the Wen. Indeed, Comfrey was already giving Tryfan cause for concern, for he grew tired easily and was unable to travel fast, or even very far, without frequent stops.

Tryfan considered taking one of Alder's watchers, for he would be disciplined and well trained, and would be reliable and loyal in the event of difficulties. And difficulties were what Tryfan expected.

But Tryfan of Duncton hesitated, for he was aware that whatever mole he chose would be involved in a venture such as few moles ever embark on, and that he would need more than courage, endurance, and intelligence. He needed a mole able to stand alone, a mole able to survive.

Survive! One mole, more than any other he had met since his parting from Boswell, who could survive, and would do so, was Mayweed. Strange Mayweed, a mole he had grown to respect and like, and one whose strange nature, though it made some impatient, made Tryfan laugh and gave him pleasure.

Since the collapse of the tunnel Mayweed had been much changed. Withdrawn, silent, sombre, his old chirpiness quite gone. He was, these days, never out of the company of Starling and Lorren. Since that fatal night when they had lost their brother Bailey, when their mother Rushe had been lost as well, they had clung on to Mayweed as if he was their father. Not once, not for a moment, had he let them down. They travelled with him, and they all seemed to support each other in some curious way. Holm, too, was of their group, and so far as there were any preferences, Holm cared for Lorren, and Mayweed for Starling.

There were times when Mayweed and Holm had to go off alone, for Mayweed was recognised as the best route-finder among them all and liked to explore ahead and around the flanks. Starling complained bitterly that she was not allowed to travel on these explorations with him, but she was too young, as was Lorren, and Mayweed put the two of them under the care of Smithills who, typically, gave them fighting lessons.

'You'll need to fight when you're bigger,' he said jovially, 'so you might as well learn to enjoy it.' Starling complained about that too, but she soon discovered it was worth learning because the other youngsters started obeying her commands and she did for them what Maundy tended to do with older moles, which was to be the mole they trusted and tended to group around.

'She's a natural leader,' observed Tryfan to Spindle and Comfrey one day. 'With moles like that for the future our system will survive. But . . . well, she's attached now to Mayweed for a few months yet, as her sister is, which means that, desirable though it might have been, we can't take Mayweed into the Wen with us. Can't take a gaggle of youngsters too!' Yet Tryfan watched Mayweed, and was pleased to see Starling gain in confidence each day, and he wondered, after all, if these were the moles he might make his great journey with.

So, ever watchful for danger, making plans for the molemonths and years to come, and awed by the lurid night sky of the Wen which was brighter with each mile of the journey, they travelled on. Day by day, week by week, as May gave way to June, and mid-June came.

Then, grike was spotted. Not by the watchers or by Mayweed, but by monosyllabic Holm, who, on the outskirts of the Thame tunnels, crept, crawled, slunk, and heard.

'Grikes. Two. Talked. Coming. More, more, more,' he said, the long statement such an effort that he leaned over to a tunnel wall and stared blankly about.

'When?' said Spindle.

'Two days,' said Holm. 'Not one, not three, but two. Lots of them, army of them, oh no.'

'Oh yes! Helpful Holm, yes *yes*!' declared Mayweed excitedly, clearly delighted that his protégé had managed such a feat of reconnaissance all by himself and perking up from his recent customary gloom. 'Brilliant Holm, *clever* Holm, is not he so, triumphant Tryfan?'

Two days behind. But had they seen the Duncton moles? It seemed so. The female who had gone to die had been found – alive. She had talked to somemole who spoke to another. News travels; grikes knew. Yes, they knew well enough.

For Tryfan and the stronger moles the problem now was to get the other slower ones to keep up a steady pace. Some, like Comfrey, offered to step aside and be left behind, so as not to hold the others up. But not a younger mole there would have allowed that.

If Holm's information was right, then two days behind might perhaps give travelling moles five or six days' grace before they were actually overtaken. Tryfan believed that they would reach the highest part of the rise they were on well before then, and there they would know what to do, and how best to disperse.

Strangely their spirits lifted, for after several days' climbing they had got above the clays on to chalk country. The tunnels they found were old and good and soils were light and airy, so all of them but Holm, who liked marshy soil, felt safer. None was happier than Spindle, who had been brought up on such ground and knew its special ways, and the flowers that grew there.

'Look!' he called out to Tryfan early one morning. 'Look!' And there, rising in the grass ahead, with the first light of dawn catching at the shiny wings of waking rook and the glistening leaves on the beech trees about, rose two harebells, the delicate pale blue heads nodding against the sky above. He paused and said quietly, 'That's what I remember when I was a youngster, flowers such as these among the great Stones that rise about Seven Barrows.'

'You're not so old now, Spindle,' said Tryfan.

'Older,' said Spindle. 'Like you, like Mayweed even. We had best all of us do what we have to do while we can!'

'I think we shall now,' said Tryfan, breathing the air deeply. 'These are good parts, and they feel safe, too, for there are Stones about here . . . not far now, not so far. . . .'

A feeling Comfrey later confirmed, for Tryfan fell back to join him on part of the way and he said, 'D-d-do you sense it, Tryfan? D-d-do you?'

'A Stone?'

'Maundy doesn't but I d-do.'

'He's always sensing Stones is Comfrey,' said Maundy at his side. 'Says there's a Stone round every corner for the mole that knows how to look.'

'There is!' said Comfrey, sounding rather like a pup. Tryfan noticed that he went unsteadily now, and had aged these last weeks, quite terribly. His eyes were paler, and he seemed to stare here and there as if lost.

'I want to die by a Stone,' said Comfrey, more to himself than the others.

'You'll not be dying yet, Comfrey!' said Maundy with a quiver to her voice and a look to Tryfan of helplessness.

'I'll see my m-moles to safety first,' said Comfrey. Then, as if to prove that he would, he found a little extra energy and went on ahead of them both, and Tryfan watched his brother, and saw that his fur was grey and thin, and his flanks hollow, and his pawstep frail. He saw, too, youngsters go to him, strong young things, their fur good and their spirits high, and how they instinctively gathered around Comfrey and talked with him, helping him along with their growing strength.

At Tryfan's side, Maundy's eyes warmed with pleasure to see it.

'You should have had young with him, Maundy,' he said.

'Oh, we did, Tryfan, we did . . . you can see them

510

there, and here . . .' And she reached out a paw to touch a youngster nearby. 'There's more to having young than breeding them, much more. Comfrey was the best father the system could have had when you left with Boswell after the plagues, and there's not a single member of the system who'll forget him, or the things he taught them of the Stone.'

'None will forget *you* Maundy.'

'Well, maybe not. Maybe not,' she sighed. Then she suddenly stumbled and fell against Tryfan's strong flank and he stopped and helped her as, for a moment, she seemed dizzy and weak.

'What is it?' he asked, much concerned.

'Don't tell him,' she whispered, 'don't fret him with me. . . .'

It seemed to Tryfan as if all the world he loved and that was familiar to him was breaking, or stumbling as Maundy had, and it was leaving him and he, despite the effort and discussion and plans they made, was to lose them all. He stopped the group then and insisted they all rested, feeling that whatever darkness was behind and uncertainty in front a mole must try to be still sometimes, and at peace.

It was a hot day, a day to be still, and the youngsters gathered around old Comfrey, and he told them a tale, a legend he said, about a mole who lived long, long ago whose name was Rebecca, and whom he loved more than anymole he ever knew but one.

'Who was that?' asked Lorren.

'He won't *tell*, silly,' said Starling, 'but we could guess!' Which, being Starling, she did, and correctly, looking across the burrow they were in to where an old female dozed, her breathing a little troubled, but a look of contentment and peace on her lined face.

'Maundy?' whispered Lorren. 'He meant Maundy?'

'Yes,' nodded Starling, 'I *think* so.'

When Comfrey had finished his tale, and packed off the youngsters to the deep corners of the temporary burrow to sleep the day through, Tryfan watched as he came over to

Maundy and tenderly snouted her, caressed her back, and lovingly fetched her some food, though she seemed able to eat little of it. Then Tryfan saw Comfrey settle down by her, and the two old moles rest their snouts along their paws side by side, with youngsters all about, and sleep.

Tryfan stopped the trek short again that evening, after setting off only an hour or two before and in spite of the dangers of delay, for Maundy was much weaker, as were two other elderly moles. A little later Maundy asked that she might be helped out on to the surface, with just Comfrey for company and Tryfan to watch over them.

A clear dusk came and to the east the Wen gazes were great across the sky; while where the sun set, to the west, they saw, or felt they saw, rising beyond the deeps of Otmoor, Duncton Wood itself.

'I feel so tired my dear,' Maundy said softly to Comfrey, and he, with no words to say, came closer still. 'You look tired, too,' she added, nudging him, 'but you'll see them all to safety, won't you?' And as he nodded she rested herself against him, staring back in the distance to the system they had loved. Then, gently, she fell into sleep. Then, slowly, into something more than sleep. Comfrey looked helplessly over to Tryfan with tears in his old eyes, and Tryfan came and looked at Maundy and touched her gently. Though she stirred she did not waken, but rather seemed to nestle closer to Comfrey, ever closer, and Tryfan saw tears on his brother's face.

Then Tryfan left them, and saw that nomole disturbed them as through the next few hours of the night, Maundy's flank grew cold to Comfrey's, and he knew she was no more. Leaving her beloved Duncton had been her ending, but she had done it to be at Comfrey's side, and had wished to be with him as long as she was able, and among their own.

It was there they left her as dawn came and the sun rose in the east. But Comfrey judged he should leave her facing west, back towards Duncton, for that would have been her wish, to see the sun's light rise one last time on those beloved slopes and trees. So Comfrey watched, with Tryfan at his side, and then they turned away and headed east.

Comfrey said, 'There's a St-Stone ahead. Not far. A day or t-two. I want to get there, T-Tryfan.'

'You'll get there, Comfrey, and much further than that.'

'The St-Stone is as far as a mole ever needs to get,' replied Comfrey.

A day and a half later, on a pleasant afternoon, with the wind fair and the white clouds high in a blue sky, and all the sounds of June about them, a watcher came in, accompanied by Alder. They came through the high dry grass of the chalk, and the air was good and sharp. They might all have been a million molemiles from nowhere. But at night now the eastern skies were bright and garish and the air was beginning to stress frighteningly with the sense of twofoots and roaring owls. But for now they might have been isolated, as Alder came with bad news.

'Grikes?' said Tryfan.

The watcher and Alder nodded.

'Half a day behind, maybe less,' said the watcher. 'From Thame way.'

'Many?'

'Too many,' said Alder.

'Then we must hurry,' said Tryfan. 'There is a Stone ahead, not far. Hours only. Beyond it I think that these heights fall away at last, and down there we shall disperse, as we have already arranged.'

'There's many too tired to rush,' said Alder.

'They'll die if they don't,' said Tryfan. 'Bring your watchers in now Alder, bring your own group up fast and I will tell the rest.'

Down the lines and among the moles it went: hurry now, grikes coming fast, here by nightfall. Dangerous. Hurry and we might escape. Tryfan says. . . .

Bless them all, if there was one mole who got the others going for those last few miles to safety it was old Comfrey:

calm, never panicking, never complaining, but finally stolid and determined to get ahead, and inspiring other moles, young and old, by his indomitable will to overcome their fatigue and fear and go on, up the final miles, through the grass and over the sheep pasture, past hawthorn and under fences. Until the ground began to level, and progress was even faster, and ahead now they could feel, each of them according to their ability, the presence of a Stone. Oh yes, and Comfrey was so tired, but the Stone was there, not far now, and his moles around him: the Stone towards which he had journeyed all his life.

'Why, my M-Maundy's there ahead of m-me!' he whispered, as the evening sun shone all about and seemed to make his eyes shine bright with joy and love.

'She *is*, Tryfan, there ahead in that Silence around the St-Stone. She is!'

The others fell back as Tryfan helped Comfrey forward those last few yards towards a solitary stone which rose at the very edge of that great rise they had been steadily climbing for days. The fading light was warm upon it and it seemed to offer hope to everymole that saw it.

The surviving moles of Duncton Wood had reached the heights of the Chilterns and stared eastwards towards the advancing night. As darkness came the sky lightened strangely ahead, high diffused light, orange and yellow . . . and the vale ahead, where the Wen started, why, it twinkled with a thousand twofoot eyes, perhaps even a million, far, far, far into the distance, light here and there, lights strange and mysterious, the gazes of roaring owls and twofoots, the lights of danger. . . .

'And yet, from here,' whispered Comfrey as he and Tryfan settled by the Stone, 'it looks beautiful, not dangerous. Why I almost wish I was c-coming with you myself.'

'But Comfrey. . . .'

But Comfrey lay a paw on Tryfan's flank, as if he would be supported, and the paw was frail and shook with age, as if age was overtaking him ever faster, and tiredness too, and he had no strength to argue more with Tryfan over what the Stone desired, which he knew, because he could hear it, and it was clear as the air tonight, and beautiful like those lights, if a mole knew how to look and hear. There was light more beautiful than those that stretched away in the distance beyond them to the rising sound of Silence.

'Tell the youngsters,' whispered Comfrey, for he seemed unable to speak above a whisper now, and his flank shivered against Tryfan's strength as his brother came yet closer to him to warm him for he seemed so cold . . . 'Tell them to be brave, and to remember all they can of the system they've known, because one day, one day. . . .'

'Yes, Comfrey?'

'Will you t-tell them?'

'I think you're telling them, Comfrey,' said Tryfan gently, for the youngsters had come softly forward in the night and gathered around the two of them, with the old Stone rising above them, and the sky so strangely lit ahead.

'Yes. Well. Yes . . . just to remember, the thing to remember is what Rebecca told us. *You* remember . . . that a mole must be much loved, yes much loved, and what we in Duncton, tried to do, was to teach a mole that; and we did it through stories and touching and so many ways, but most of all we did it through the Stone, for that is where love can be, there, to touch if a mole has courage and has been shown. It isn't hard, Tr-Tryfan and Rebecca showed m-me how. She loved me. And when I was old, Maundy loved me too. You know, maybe you don't, yes you do because you're Tryfan aren't you? . . . You know Rebecca wasn't my mother, Rue was, but she let Rebecca have me and Mekkins . . . oh yes, tell them that. Tell them to go back one day because that's where they started, and a mole must never forget where he started or he forgets something important of himself; but if they can't go back let them tell their pups, tell them to weave stories

515

about a system they once knew, to which their pups can return and proudly be, and touch the Stone I loved, and Bracken my father loved. I miss him, Tryfan, and I miss Rebecca, but most of all I miss Maundy. Is she waiting for me Tryfan, waiting just beyond the beginning of the Silence so I can join her and we can start that journey together? Is she? Tell them that they won't do much good going round in circles, tell them to go forward, oh so many things, but they'll have to learn, won't they? . . . You'll show them, Tryfan, as we were shown. You will.'

'Yes, I'll try,' whispered Tryfan . . . and there was Silence then, and great light across the sky, and darkness behind where Duncton had been, and many came to touch old Comfrey and he looked into the eyes of each of them with love. Then Lorren came. And last of all the youngsters came Starling.

'You're much loved, Starling,' whispered Comfrey.

'And Bailey, say it for him, please,' she said.

'Yes,' whispered Comfrey, for he could not manage more, 'Yes . . . B-B- '

'Bailey,' said Starling.

'Mmm,' said Comfrey. Then the night came deep, and Tryfan knew they would be safe for a time longer yet as the youngsters about them went to sleep, and the adults watched over them.

Cold, stiff, dawn just distant, Tryfan stirred.

At his side, warm, thin, Comfrey sighed and said, 'Let me watch you go now, Tryfan, for you will be safe down there, let me see you all go to safety . . . and leave me here.' His eyes allowed no argument.

Then quietly the moles stirred and got up and one by one led by Smithills and Mayweed they left that Stone and set off down the steep slope to gather one last time together far below where they would disperse as they had planned.

Old Comfrey saw them go. Until just Tryfan was left, and Comfrey stirred wearily and said, 'G-g-go on, Tryfan, they need you now, and they will love you as we were loved.'

Then Tryfan touched his brother one last time and turned and followed the others down into the dawn not seeing where his pawsteps went for the tears he shed for the passing of so much he had known. He looked ahead into the far distance to the Wen, where nomole had been for centuries. And he was afraid.

Yet as he went on down he knew at last with certainty what moles would travel on with him and how it must be. Only three others. Spindle for one, Mayweed for two, to guide them, and help them, and make them laugh. And last would be Starling, bright youngster, the future. Mayweed would not go without her anyway, but with her, why, she was the brightest of her generation and the Stone would protect her into the Wen and out of it! Yes, they were the ones.

Later, far downslope where the vale levelled off, Tryfan found himself surrounded by the moles one last time. All were ready to go now, many north, many south and just the four of them eastwards into the Wen.

A youngster asked, 'Please, Sir, what was that Stone where we left Comfrey?'

'That was Comfrey's Stone, the only Stone in the whole of moledom that is named after a particular mole,' said Tryfan. So simply was that place named.

'Why?' asked Starling.

'So he won't be forgotten.'

'Well, I won't forget him,' said Starling, 'and nor will Lorren neither.' Then she thought some more and added, 'And Bailey won't when I tell him!'

'You're sure he's alive, aren't you Starling?'

'Bailey's my brother so he must be,' said Starling.

' "Comfrey's Stone",' whispered a youngster, looking up at the great height they had climbed down so quickly.

'Yes,' said Tryfan. 'Remember that place, for I think that one day, a long way off perhaps, something that moledom will never forget will happen there. Remember that Stone! Tell your kin of it!'

As they stared upwards they saw the light of the rising sun touch the great scarp face, and at its top, where the Stone stood, the sun seemed to cast a point of light so bright that it took a mole's breath away.

'Did we climb down all that way?' asked Lorren in awe.

'Of course we did,' said Starling.

'You see,' whispered Tryfan, 'that is Comfrey's Stone, and a mole that can reach it, and touch it, will surely one day find his way home . . . Now, go as we have planned. Go secretly, carefully, this way and that way, go with moles you know and trust, go now. . . .'

Then they did so, quietly, some touching their farewells, others saying them, to north they went and south, Lorren with Holm, for she was older now and could say farewell to her sister Starling, for there comes a time for sibling goodbyes. Then Alder was gone with Marram, strong into the day. And good Smithills, reluctant to leave his friends and saying how they would meet soon enough, up in Rollright, and Skint would tell them all his news. . . .

Until only Tryfan was left, with Spindle, much moved by the partings, and Starling tearful but brave, and Mayweed, near her, four moles to go east.

'Come then!' said Tryfan.

'Tryfan, Sir, and splendid Spindle, and bold Madam Miss, Mayweed is honoured, Mayweed is thrilled, Mayweed will not let you get lost!' said Mayweed.

'Come!' repeated Tryfan; and Spindle smiled, and Starling's heart raced with the excitement of it all as she tried to look adult and nearly succeeded.

While running behind the three of them, Mayweed looked this way and that, as was his habit, for a mole had best remember where he has come from if he is to find his way back. Then, one by one, they were gone, among the trees, towards the heart of the Wen.

While watching over all the moles of Duncton as they lost themselves in the vales far below, by Comfrey's Stone, was a wise and loving mole, still now, so still; and a light greater than the sun's was on him.

Much later, at mid-morning, grike guardmoles came huffing and puffing up the long chalk slope and found not the many moles they were hoping for, but just one, lying still and cold by a great Stone.

'Move him,' their leader said harshly. 'Hang him up for others to see.'

But the sun was in the east, bright and blinding, and its rays touched the Stone massively, shining and fierce, and the grikes backed away, and there was not one there, not a single one, who dared go near the old mole where he lay under the protection of the Stone, and touch him.

So their leader himself, a tough grike, a seasoned campaigner, approached the mole, the light of the sun so bright that he could barely see, but when he touched the mole – why, he was unable to move him for sound seemed to go and a terrifying Silence was on him.

He backed off with a curse, said it didn't matter, said they would rest. They would find living moles. Yes, they would and when they did they would do as Henbane had bid them, which was to kill them. Let none survive, but those she had named.

'Aye!' shouted the grikes to raise their faltering spirits. But their shouts seemed lost and weak against the bright sky into which that Stone rose, protecting its own.

Chapter Thirty

The moleyears of that summer were busy ones at Duncton Wood, full of decisive comings and goings, as the grikes, led by Henbane of Whern, used it as the temporary centre of their operations.

Henbane had never felt better, and nor had Weed ever seen her so, as if final victory over the moles of the Stone, which the invasion of Duncton had come to symbolise, had seemed to revive in her a spirit and energy which she had had when she had first left Whern and Rune so many moleyears before, but which she had lost along the way of southern advance and imposition of the Word.

Once the initial anger and affront that had accompanied the entry into Duncton Wood had quite gone, she acted once more with purpose and resolution, bringing to a triumphant close her long campaign as she gave out order after order for the final subjugation and transformation of moledom to the way of the Word. The operation against the retreating Duncton moles had been as successful as a mole could expect. They had been tracked to a Stone to the west of the Wen and from there a good number had been chased and caught as they tried to flee to north and south. All those caught had been killed after they had been made to talk.

The mole Tryfan and a few others of no importance had travelled on eastwards and Wrekin's moles had not found him. But that was now of no great consequence, for Wrekin, showing an unusual cunning for so straightforward a mole, had let the word go out that Tryfan *had* been found, and had exchanged his life for information about the whereabouts of the Duncton moles. In short, Wrekin's guardmoles told all moles they met that the great Tryfan had betrayed his system and his followers to save his own life.

Wrekin was not so foolish as to suggest Tryfan had been killed, for there was always the possibility that he would reappear, though it seemed unlikely since he had gone towards the heart of the Wen, and the grikes who had tried to follow him reported that the going had become so difficult for them that it seemed unlikely that moles would have got much further and survived. Roaring owls, twofoot gazes, fumes, vibration, concrete, tunnels that flooded, rats . . . the grikes barely got out alive. Nomole could survive in the Wen for long they said.

Wrekin was not so sure. Tempted though he was to spread the rumour that Tryfan was dead he resisted it, and sowed the seed of betrayal instead. He knew that not all the Duncton moles would have been caught and that those who had not would hear these stories, and be cast down by them.

If they gave themselves up, and were willing to Atone, the grikes said, then they might be allowed to live. Another lie. A few did give themselves up, hoping, perhaps, that they could find a peaceful integration in grike-run systems, with the possibility that in the mole-years to come there would be change, and Duncton would be accessible to them again. But they were vain hopes indeed: for each of those moles was interrogated, and killed. But of *that* the grikes kept silent.

So, according to Wrekin's assessment, the Duncton moles were destroyed as a viable force by late August, and their leadership discredited, and Henbane was well pleased with Wrekin when he came back from that campaign.

'I could have wished that you had found Tryfan, and those others I named, but despite that your guardmoles seem to have done well.'

Wrekin smiled grimly.

'It pleases me,' said Henbane.

'I had thought you would have left Duncton by now, WordSpeaker,' he replied, 'for surely your wisdom and the guidance of the Word is needed at Buckland.'

'Perhaps,' sighed Henbane, enjoying Wrekin's respect and seeming to need his advice and support. It was a way she had, to make moles relaxed and feel she needed them. It was hard to resist, but Wrekin had not survived so long by being fully taken in by Henbane. His eyes stayed respectful but cold.

'We have missed you,' lied Henbane. 'Much has been decided and done for the future, and the position of Buckland as the centre of southern moledom is now secure.'

'What eldrene is in charge there now?' asked Wrekin, his voice betraying the distaste he felt for the eldrenes. Henbane smiled. It was a clever thing to have eldrenes in charge of systems but guardmole armies separately controlled by moles like Wrekin, with she herself in charge of both. She liked it best when eldrenes and guardmole leaders disliked each other. And she liked it most when they combined to dislike the sideem. In such an atmosphere of dislike and distrust it was, as Rune himself had once suggested to her, easiest for a WordSpeaker to maintain control, and keep absolute power.

'Eldrene Beake rules Buckland and she does it well.'

'Beake? She's young,' said Wrekin.

'I was young, Wrekin. You were young. Youth may have the ruthlessness such an eldrene needs. Beake will do. She supplies you with guardmoles enough I think?'

'She does,' agreed Wrekin; guardmoles and spies. Sideem too, probably, though of them, she most likely does not know. Wrekin had his way of spotting spies and informers and though he had never said a word, such moles, placed no doubt by the eldrenes at the command of Henbane, had a way of having accidents under Wrekin's command. Henbane knew it, Wrekin knew it, Weed knew it, the eldrenes suspected it. It was a game played between them, never once acknowledging its rules. 'Oh yes,' said Wrekin, 'there are guardmoles enough, though not of the old grike school we knew first. We need more of those and must make do with grike half-castes bred of

522

grike stock in southern wombs. Good, strong enough, well moulded by the eldrenes, loyal to the Word, dismissers of the Stone.' Then he added with an unusual display of nostalgia, 'Yet not of the old grike school of Whern, WordSpeaker.'

Henbane smiled. She liked a mole to talk.

'Well, we all miss the north, Wrekin, each one of us.'

'I am glad to have Siabod to fight for, WordSpeaker, it is good to be able to offer guardmoles more than guard duties. Many ask to go and it is easier to keep them in order that way. We will take Siabod before long now.'

'Yes, so I have heard. It is well. I would like to have had that settled before we . . .' But she stopped herself saying more.

'Before?' queried Wrekin, easing his squat and stolid body at its stance. These days his face was lined, and he frowned permanently from an old scar that coursed his face.

'Before,' repeated Weed from the shadows. 'Before this and before that.'

'Ah!' said Wrekin, realising he had asked too much and Henbane had made a rare slip. He did his best to remain impassive. He had not even known Weed was there.

'So, all is well. All in order. All settled,' Henbane said.

Wrekin was suddenly uneasy and alert. All in order, what in order? All settled, what settled? All's well, *too* well? Yes, he was uneasy.

'You will go to Siabod?' asked Henbane softly.

Should he? Shouldn't he? What did she want? Him away perhaps, but away from what? Yet he felt powerless without the best of his guardmoles and they, the very best of them led by Ginnell, a mole he had trained himself and whom he trusted, were already at Siabod, or on the way there.

'I had hesitated to go, WordSpeaker, until you made your desire known.'

Henbane narrowed her eyes. From his corner Weed watched impassively. Wrekin waited, watching and listening. He was uneasy.

'My advice rather than my desire, Wrekin, is that you go. Siabod may be harder to take than we think. It may need your experience. But go back to Buckland when you are done.'

'You will be there by then?'

Henbane shrugged.

'If I am I will wish to speak to you. If I am not then I would wish to have a mole I trust at Buckland.'

'And Beake?'

'Beake will not be there.'

'Ah!' said Wrekin noncommittally. 'To Siabod I shall go then. And return to Buckland.'

'Fast, Wrekin. Fast and furious. I like not such a system's defiance. Siabod is the last of the seven, the very last. When you have taken it and subdued it, send news to Whern. Whern would know. Whern *must* know.'

Ah. So. Henbane is to go to Whern, thought Wrekin. It was likely to be so. Yes, then I had best be in Siabod with good guardmoles behind me. Yes.

'So do it,' whispered Henbane, sighing again. 'Now, I am tired. . . .'

Wrekin left, with a parting glance at Weed. Henbane turned to Weed.

'I would hear from Rune, Weed, I would know.'

'Soon now, Henbane, soon I am sure. He has been sent word.'

'Good. Good. Siabod is the last decision. Wrekin will do it well. Yet do you trust Wrekin? The mole that desires rest and dreams of home needs replacing. I would leave before September ends. I made a promise that we would.'

Then she left, and Weed was alone. He did not move. He thought.

"I made a promise that we would." Weed smiled grimly. Oh yes, he had sent word to Rune, but it was not a request. It was a suggestion. 'Order her back,' it had said. 'The time is come.' For Weed knew that Henbane's good spirits were not only to do with the fact that she had sought to conceal from Wrekin, which was that she would be returning to Whern soon, and certainly long before he ever came back from distant Siabod.

No, it was not only the prospect of that that cheered her. But also the presence of a mole every grike in Duncton had grown to dislike, including even Weed himself, whose habit it was not to dislike or to like, but as Rune had taught him, to evaluate. The pathetic Bailey had cheered her! And his evaluation of the mole Bailey was that he was trouble, for he had released in Henbane something that not even Rune had guessed was there. Something the Word had no name for, something unruly. All the moleyears of summer since the youngster had come had Weed pondered it, concluding that only Rune would know best what to do, though he, Weed, had now come to a conclusion, and would offer his advice. So Weed had sent that suggestion urgently: order her back. And he would be glad, too, to see its positive response. Like Henbane, like Wrekin, *he* too wanted to go home.

* * * * * * *

Bailey smirked at Henbane's side, secure in her patronage, the grike guardmoles disguising their hatred of him behind blank stares. Henbane was angry. Chubby Bailey smirked.

Since his first coming to the Ancient System he had been happily adopted by Henbane. Others had seen it before with young male moles, but Weed, who knew her better than anymole but Rune himself, saw there was a special quality to her interest in Bailey. It was something to do with Bailey's innocence and misguided faith in her, as if, having lost his older sister, he had elected Henbane, most evil of moles, to this trusted post. Not only that, but he assumed an access and right to her attention such as a younger brother may assume, or even a son, for there were elements of mothering in Henbane's attitude to this innocent male. He accepted willingly enough that at times he was not welcome. But however much she rebuffed him, which she could do with savagery, he came back, secure in some mysterious certainty of his own that she must receive him.

Weed knew this because Weed had eyes to spy with, and ears to eavesdrop by; Weed was silent and secret and knew ways of learning the most secret of things, most shameful of things . . . and now most extraordinary of things.

For what he knew, and nomole else did, was that in private, where nomole was allowed access, deep in the burrows she had requisitioned as her own, Henbane changed. With this mole Bailey, Rune's daughter, the most feared of all moles, the most cruel, who maimed her lovers when she had used them and then had them killed . . . this same Henbane became a pup again – with a pup's rages, a pup's sulks and . . . often, a pup's laughter. . . .

'Where *were* you Bailey?'

'Don't know.'

'You must have been somewhere!'

'Was, but it's my business.'

'I know you know where you were! I hate you, Bailey, and I'm not talking to you.'

(And *this* was Henbane. No wonder that Weed sent word to Rune.)

Silence.

'What were you doing? I *asked*, "*What were you doing?*" '

Silence.

'*Bailey!*' she screamed, her elegant beautiful flanks fluffing up with rage, her face fur swollen with anger, her eyes suddenly pig-like: her shining talons hooked and dangerous.

And Bailey, still smaller than her though he had grown much since he had come, and still vulnerable-looking, stared at her unmoved.

'Won't tell if you're not nice,' he said. 'Won't *play* with you! I was hungry, Henbane, I wanted to eat, I had to eat and I found some food and I ate it.'

'You'll get fat!' said Henbane, ruler of moledom.

'That's what Starling used to say.'

'I don't care what Starling used to say,' said Henbane. 'I

don't like you talking about her. You've got me now. I thought you had forgotten her.'

'Yes,' said Bailey quietly, 'yes . . .' Low voices then. Tickles? Silence. Laughter. *Laughter*! Then . . . 'I *still* don't like you saying her name, Bailey.'

'No,' said Bailey.

Weed heard the hurt in his voice and the loss, and knew, though Henbane did not seem to sense it, Bailey remembered more of his past than he claimed. Much more. The youngster might look innocent, but he knew enough to play the game of seeming to like Henbane to the exclusion of his past, and Weed did not doubt that he remembered more than he ever mentioned.

Why at Midsummer's Night Weed had found the youngster crying by the Stone. . . .

'What are you doing?' Weed had asked, snout turning, for he disliked the Stone. 'Worshipping, yes?'

'N-no,' sniffed Bailey. 'But Duncton moles come here on Midsummer's Night. Starling would have made me come, so I came.' He stared at the Stone and whispered gibberish as if by this southern magic he might invoke some prayers or song he felt he had forgotten.

'You came to do what?' asked Weed.

'Don't know,' said Bailey. 'Can't remember.'

'The last such night was before you were born, so we wouldn't expect you to, would we Bailey?'

'N-no,' said Bailey.

'Well best to run along then, the WordSpeaker will be missing you,' said Weed.

'Do I have to?'

Weed laughed.

'Don't have to, but best to,' he said.

'All right,' said Bailey. . . .

Though the molemonths had passed and it was nearly September now, Weed did not doubt that Bailey still remembered things that Henbane would have preferred him to forget.

527

'Didn't you think about me waiting? We were going on the surface down to Barrow Vale,' said Henbane shrilly, continuing the argument. 'I'm angry with you,' she concluded, mock petulantly.

Bailey grinned.

'I could find you some food, if you like; then you won't be angry.'

'Well. . . .'

'I can! I'll get it now.'

And Weed, in the shadows, round a corner, listening and spying, watched Bailey patter by before he peered round and down the chamber and saw Henbane soften and look, for a moment, defenceless, almost molelike. And he, who knew her better than anymole, saw what none had ever seen, or perhaps ever would: Henbane of Whern, happy with herself, playful, affectionate, curled in a corner like a young female pup at play with others.

So Bailey found favour, and the leaner, harder, bigger grike guardmoles could not understand the attentions Henbane showed him nor have guessed correctly what it was that the two did deep in the privacy of Henbane's quarters.

'Is he . . .?' they wondered.

'Has he . . .?' they asked.

'No,' said Weed. Henbane showed no interest in *that* with Bailey.

But sometimes her anger with him was real enough, and expressed in a violent way. Once she struck him in front of Weed, drawing blood on his shoulder. Another time (and, although nomole saw it, plenty heard it and assumed he would be dead by the time she finished with him) she hurled him from a chamber in a moment of pique whose origins none knew and then, so much later, went to find him and cosseted him till it made a mole sick to hear it.

And Bailey dared to smirk. A face, however innocent, can change unpleasantly if it is brought up wrong. Bailey's had changed. But anyway, more than that, a youngster's face will always change as autumn comes and blood runs

528

faster, and strength comes to a body whose mind is not yet used to it, and feelings run riot for a time until they settle down. So Bailey now.

He had shown interest, very timid interest, in a female, the youngster of one of the guardmoles – an interest about which the guardmole had complained verbally, having been inclined to thump Bailey but deciding, wisely, not to risk it.

Henbane knew the female, by sight. A silly young thing who had, it seemed, encouraged the liaison and even boasted about it to her friends. So . . . Henbane was loudly angry with Bailey whose initial smirks had been replaced now by embarrassed hurt and anger, since he had never had such feelings before and they seemed harmless enough to him; and Henbane was being a *pain*.

Then he was scared. Scared sick. Henbane had gone cold, which she had never done on him since their first meeting by the Stone, and he felt that cold as if it was a winter freeze, all around him, robbing him of life. And he knew that what he had done, harmless enough though he thought it, would make her do something now. He did not know the words 'revenge' and 'retribution', but he suddenly sensed the consequences of them, as a mole might know the cold grasp of an owl's claws even as he gazes into its looming eyes.

Unjust retribution came that day, and with it the shadows closed a little on Bailey and darkened him.

Scurryings, arrestings, ordering, comings, summonings.

'She wants you,' said a guardmole, insolent. His eyes hated him.

He came. The youngster he had known had a mother, the mother was there. Just a mole, a guardmole's mate. An imported female from Buckland way.

Henbane was there, powerful and dark. The female was still as death, her fur wilted-wet with fear.

'Watch this,' said Henbane when he came. She looked triumphant, *she* smirked, and her eyes joined all the others that hated him too.

'Please don't,' he said.

Henbane talon-thrust the female to death. It took only a moment, which made it all the worse. Then, before Bailey could even begin to speak, her daughter, the mole Bailey had so briefly known, was brought in. She was laughing. A guardmole had gone for her and told her there was a pleasant surprise for her. . . .

Her mother dead. Those shadows reared and closed on Bailey as he heard her shouted cries.

'It was your mother or this Duncton mole to die, one or the other,' said Henbane, 'and I thought you would want the Duncton mole you like alive.' She spoke to the youngster, but looked at Bailey.

The youngster was so shocked and distressed that she seemed almost to stop breathing. Then she looked at Bailey and he saw for the first time the desire in another's eyes that *he* was dead. Henbane purred her pleasure at this cruel scene.

'*Get out!*' she shouted, and they all got out, dragging the body too. All of them but Bailey.

'*You stay,*' she screamed.

Silence then. Heavy, heavy silence.

'I had to do it,' said Henbane, again and again. 'I am sorry to distress you, Bailey, but your actions made me do it. I am fond of you but you must not dishonour that fondness, no?' As she wiped the blood from her talons she wept real tears, which made Bailey cry as well. 'Did you have to make me do it?' she said, again and again until it was Bailey saying sorry, and the darkness all about.

For days Bailey barely slept, tossing in nightmares in which a mole, female, stared at him, hated him, rejected him, and that mole was Starling his sister, lost to him for ever; and Bailey cried.

'What is it, my sweet?' whispered Henbane in the dark privacy of his burrow. 'Don't be sad.' She whispered words and ways of saying them she learnt from her dread mother Charlock, who taught her as she was teaching Bailey, and Bailey cried and accepted her comfort, confused and distressed for she was the cause of his hurt, and he felt he hated *her*, and yet it was she who was there comforting him.

'I hate Starling, she left me,' he muttered, and Henbane smiled and said, 'Yes, she did,' and turned that lost mole's dark feelings on his sister Starling.

And yet, a mole that is loved in infancy, truly loved, never quite loses the light of love from his eyes; and one not only loved of mole, but brought up near the Silence of the Stone, may hear that Silence, though he knows it not and the world has deafened him.

So Bailey.

One day, driven by a madness of despair, he escaped the watching guardmoles and even Weed himself, and made his way to Barrow Vale. He vaguely remembered that when he was a pup he was to go there if he needed to, and *that* was something Henbane did not know. None of them knew. Not *that*. So he went.

He crouched, he cried, and, filled with darkness and guilt, he finally whispered one single awesome word: 'Stone.'

No answer. Nothing at all. Just the drag of a breeze above on the surface. Nothing to ease his distress, whose nature he could not understand, nor take away the fear and the love and the dependence on Henbane that pulled his heart this way and that.

In agony he ran out on to the surface.

'Mole! Be still!'

Bailey stopped. He was on his way back, fearing to be seen, never wanting another to know where he had been and here was a mole, barely visible finding him.

'Mole!'

'Whatmole is it?' he asked, frightened.

'Sideem Sleekit.'

He relaxed. Nomole trusted her, but she did not scare him physically as most of the others did.

'I've been looking for food,' he lied.

'You have been praying to the Stone,' she said.

531

'I haven't!' he almost shouted. And then more quietly, almost pleadingly, his plump sides going in and out breathlessly, 'I haven't.'

The sideem came out of the shadows. She stared at him. He saw no hatred. Nothing much at all.

'When the Duncton moles were here – '

'Yes?' he whispered.

' – did they ever talk of Silence?'

He dared say nothing, but he nodded.

'What is it?' she asked. 'This Silence?' Her eyes were wide, and he recognised something he knew because he had felt it before and felt it now, perhaps. He saw fear and doubt and searching.

'Don't know,' he said.

'Can't you remember?'

'It's where a mole's safe, it's hard to get to.'

'Where is it?'

'Near the Stone,' he whispered.

'What is it?' she asked again.

It was as if his heart opened and cried out; it was as if Starling was there to run to; it was as if, once again, he was safe, going as once he had up these slopes to the Stone, beside a male called Spindle who was special and told them all about a mole called Thyme. It was as if Thyme was there to go to and he wanted to, he needed to. It was as if the Stone had heard him and would let him hurt it, shout at it, threaten it, *hate* it and still be there for him to feel safe by.

So Bailey cried. Before Sideem Sleekit he lowered his snout with shame and loss too terrible for him to bear, and he cried his heart out. No words, just tears and sobs. But he knew she would not tell, would never, ever tell. He knew he had a friend. He knew more than that: he knew he had made a friend and that something in him was still good, something was there of what he was. He knew that. So he looked at her in wonder and then he left her knowing something good had been.

When he was gone Sleekit stayed quite still. Nothing in

all her life, with all her training, with all the power of the Word had prepared her for this. It had started with Tryfan in Buckland when she had been part of a Seven Stancing. For the moleyears since then it had troubled her. It had worsened before the Stone of Duncton, to which, when she first came, she knew instinctively her life had been directed. Now, here, quite unexpectedly, it had found its blossoming with the tears of a mole for whom not one in that subjugated system had anything but contempt. Yet he had cried before her, and given an answer she had sought so long, to a question she had hardly dare ask: 'What is it, the Silence?'

But not with words had he answered. There between them had been the Silence, where no words were. And Sideem Sleekit was joyful and wanted nothing more then than to go upslope and give thanks before the Stone. And as she went she knew that Henbane must not know, nor Weed; and that it was more important now than it had been in the moleyears before. *They must not know.* If they did they would not understand, but they would destroy her to find out from some dark instinct they had for what was dangerous to them.

That mole Tryfan had told the guardmole Thrift that the Duncton moles might be found in the Silence. For a time it had maddened Henbane, who liked not riddles except of her own making. Then she seemed to have forgotten it, though Sleekit doubted that she had. Henbane forgot nothing.

But Sleekit understood now why Tryfan might have said it. Of course. For a mole seriously to seek anything in the Silence was to know something of the Silence; and knowing that, a mole might well find Tryfan, but if he, or she, did so, then knowledge of the Silence could only make them wish to join him, not to kill him.

Sleekit laughed, and ran. And she saw beauty among the trees of Duncton and could guess how much a mole who loved this place might miss it. Yet the Duncton moles had gone. Then she saw how dark the Word must be to drive out such moles. And she had a wish to join them by searching for the Silence. Oh yes! Sleekit, a sideem, felt humble. A mole had opened his heart to her, and trusted her, and given her an answer whose meaning was great indeed.

'Help him!' she whispered.

But she knew it was for another mole than Bailey that she prayed. A mole who was female; a mole who was a sideem; the mole who was herself. A mole endangered now.

'Help me!' she said.

* * * * * * *

With September the moles of disease and deformity that Henbane had decreed should be settled in the system began to arrive, and with their arrival most healthy moles there felt the strong urge to leave.

They came in twos and threes, herded along by most reluctant guardmoles, sore-ridden, lame, pathetic. Some seemed struck mute with their disease, others were blind, some worse than blind, for their eyes and snouts were eaten away by that disease for which there was no name, but of which the dread scalpskin had been the precursor.

They were brought into the system by way of the south-eastern cow cross-under, but then hurried, on pain of death (though few seemed able to put up much resistance), along the Eastside, and thence down to the filthy Marsh End.

It was a natural choice for the grikes to make, for, so far as they had formed any notion of where the hidden moles might be who attacked them from time to time, it was at that northern end of the wood where the air was damp and the vegetation foul. So . . . discard fearsome moles in a feared place.

'What would they have us do here?' the diseased moles asked.

'They want us to stop here,' said the deformed.

Their fear turned to silence, and their silence to

534

laughter when they were told they were to do nothing but live, and die.

'Live?' said one, out of a body so stricken that it was his torment minute by minute.

'Here?' whispered another, who could not see much of the sky above, nor ever again hear the birds sing. But the grike she could see, keeping well clear, signing her to go where she wanted.

So through September they came, the new inhabitants of Duncton Wood, summoned by Henbane's order: and such moles as these would send a shudder through moledom when it was known they lived in one place, making their own rules, making their own maddened laws, electing their own elders, governed by only one simple grike rule: they must never leave. Here they had come, here they must stay, making whatever hell they liked of a system that had once been venerated and loved.

So little by little, trickle by plague-touched trickle, as all the diseased, disabled, maladjusted, discontented, belligerent, psychotic misfits and miscreants, dissenting, lawless and ailing, queer, wasting, palsied and cancered moles that the grikes could find in adjacent systems were brought to fabled Duncton Wood and set free.

Henbane was well pleased, and Weed and Smaile, who had overseen the settlement, were impressed. Murders were already starting. Gangs forming. Disease spreading.

'Snoutings have had their day, Weed. The punishment by banishment to this new Duncton is a worse thing, and more fearful thing, and will be judged to be so across the whole of moledom once word of it spreads. A banishing to Duncton will be worse than snouting. It will be a living death.'

'How will the word spread?'

Henbane shrugged.

'It will, it always does. But I have sent for Eldrene Beake to make the final arrangements. She will order the sealing off of the system, and appoint guardmoles to patrol. In time patrols will not be needed, except perhaps

535

occasionally if the new Duncton moles become over-confident in their filth and seek to spread forth. Then they will be dealt with. But I believe that here in Duncton will develop a system so foul, so unkempt, so undisciplined that nomole will ever come here, or wish to, but those we choose to punish by sending here.

'And what will moledom say? It will say that the Stone, of which the Duncton Stone is such a great emblem, did not protect its own. It will laugh and it will mock. But most of all it will desire that those moles who are strange, or misfits, or disobedient, or diseased, or sick, or unpleasantly individual . . . why, it will ask they be sent to Duncton. Yes?'

Weed smiled. Clever, very.

'Rune will be well pleased,' he said.

'Rune . . .' she sighed. 'He will send word soon?'

'He will,' said Weed. He hoped. It seemed so long since he sent word north . . . and nothing back, nothing at all. Except a false alarm when a mole arrived who proved to be Beake. She was displeased at her new command, but nomole could deny Henbane.

But at last Rune's messenger came. Up through the cross-under with an entourage of grikes. Original grikes. Dark, strong, expressionless. It would have done Wrekin's heart good to see them.

'Take me to the WordSpeaker,' their leader said curtly. He had a voice a mole obeyed. Weed, hearing, smiled. He knew him. He had last seen him as a vicious pup. Rune had chosen Henbane's successor wisely. He hurried to find her.

'They have come,' he said.

'You have spoken to them?' asked Henbane.

'Seen them, heard them, know *him*,' said Weed.

'What mole has Rune sent?'

'He will tell you his own name, Henbane. He will be loyal. He will do as you say and what you order. Rune has chosen wisely for it will need a mole of much ruthlessness and small imagination to succeed you in the south.'

Henbane smiled.

'We will keep him waiting,' she said, impatient though she was to see this mole. The hours passed. She played with Bailey. Laughter was heard. The mole who had travelled so far was furious. Night. Sleep. Restlessness throughout the system.

Morning came.

'Summon him,' said Henbane.

He came, strong, younger than Wrekin, but with talons not yet so astute.

Henbane regarded him silently.

'WordSpeaker,' he intoned, as if he was speaking to a deity. Henbane purred.

'Your name?'

'Wyre,' he said.

'You have a message?'

'Rune would have you home to Whern. Soon. He is well pleased.'

'And you, Wyre, what are you to do?'

'To take your place in the south.'

'Then you will do so.'

Privately – except that Weed was there and Sleekit – Henbane told him what he must know. It took a time, and they ate. He told her of his journey. Moledom was subdued. Plenty of rumours. Recently of Duncton, and how it was outcast and not a place for mole. Tryfan taken, moles knew of that.

'Not so, but good,' said Henbane. 'Very good.'

A day later Henbane and her party prepared to leave, to travel north. Beake, reluctant, was to stay at Duncton and see it sealed and guarded. Wyre was to go on west to Buckland.

'I would speak privately with you, Wyre,' Henbane said before they left.

On the surface she did it, in the open, nomole near.

'Weed listens otherwise,' she said by way of explanation.

'His job,' said Wyre.

Henbane smiled, then her eyes went cold.

'How is Rune?' she asked.

'Tired,' said Wyre. 'Desiring your return. I will fulfil your expectations, WordSpeaker. It is an honour.'

She waved him to silence. He looked at her.

'You would have me do anything else?' he asked.

She nodded.

'When Wrekin returns to Buckland, Siabod will be subdued. Moledom will be entirely ours. So – '

'Yes, WordSpeaker? My will is yours.' Wyre's dark eyes glinted. He had the eager stupidity of the earnest young to make their mark. But Henbane had no doubt that he would do so. A good choice for the time being.

'So Wyre . . . when Wrekin returns, kill him.'

Then Henbane of Whern turned from him, and with Weed nearby and Bailey in her party, and Sleekit too, she and a few select guardmoles made their way down to the cross-under and passed under it. A few deformities of moles were pulled into the shadows by the guardmoles who were bringing them. Their bereft eyes travelled from the awesome female passing by on to the hill before them, and the wood that covered most of it.

'Be happy in your new home, scum,' said one of Henbane's guardmoles with a laugh, relieved to be leaving.

Henbane passed on by, and then, without one glance back at the system she had destroyed, she turned northward, to start the long trek home to Whern.

PART IV

Journeys into Silence

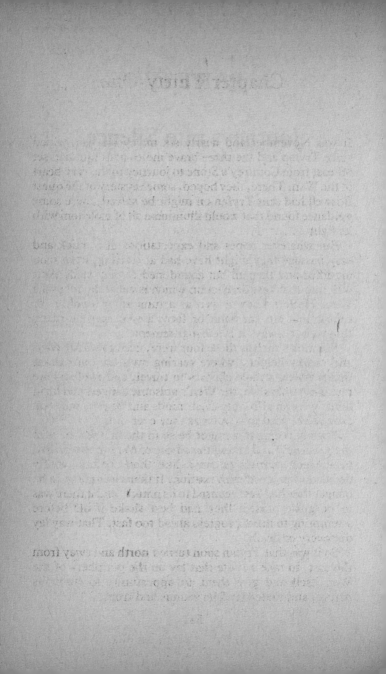

Chapter Thirty-One

It was November and nearly six moleyears had passed since Tryfan and the three brave moles with him had set off east from Comfrey's Stone to journey to the very heart of the Wen. There, they hoped, some mystery of the quest Boswell had sent Tryfan on might be solved, there some guidance found that would illuminate all of moledom with its light . . . .

But whatever hopes and expectations of a quick and easy passage they might have had at starting, were soon modified and then all but abandoned as they made their way into that vast dereliction which is called by mole the Wen. Healers know a wen as a tumour or a goitre, or cancer that sits on flank or face; a wen may be many things, but always it is a disfigurement.

For moles such as those four were, used to woody ways and chalky heights, where roaring owls are but distant things unless a mole chooses to travel, and twofoots are rare if not unknown, the Wen's noisome dangers and lurid lights were an affront to their minds and bodies, and took time to get used to – so far as they ever did.

Tryfan, seeing this might be so in the first few days of their journey, and taking the advice of Mayweed who had never seen tunnels or ways like those before, wisely decided to proceed with caution. If there was going to be danger they had best get used to its nature, and if there was to be grike pursuit they had best shake if off before attempting to make progress ahead too fast. That way lay discovery or death.

So it was that Tryfan soon turned north and away from the east, to take a route that lay on the periphery of the Wen itself and give them an opportunity to study its nature, and understand its sounds and traps.

More than that, it was a chance for the four to learn to travel as one, for Tryfan had no doubt that in the moleyears ahead times would come when they would need to know each other's thoughts without speaking, if they were to survive.

So as June passed into July, and July into August, they had travelled here and there, using concrete tunnels such as the Wen is riddled with, finding new sources of food in places they never knew existed, and teaching each other what they could.

Tryfan taught them much of Duncton's history, and the legends of old mole, beguiling the rest times with his stories and memories of what he had been told. From Mayweed came knowledge of route-finding which, Tryfan was quite sure, would in time help each of them. From Spindle came a curiosity to know what the world about a mole could teach him or her, for there was much of mystery where the Wen was concerned. Perhaps nomoles ever were so close to twofoots for so long, unseen of course, for the twofoots are blind at ground level and rarely see a mole; unscented too, for the twofoots have no snouts though they odour well enough. But dangerous, yes, for they are clumsy and crush whatever may be in their way.

Of that other mystery to mole, roaring owls, they found things out as well. Very dangerous to mole when not asleep, yet when asleep the only creature known to moles that makes no noise at all. Silent as death. Then roar! Bang! Hoot! Howl! – and roaring owl wakes. No stretching, no thinking on the day to come as sensible mole must do, but roar and off! Oh yes, dangerous to mole. But for all their clumsiness twofoots seem to understand the roaring owls and live with them amicably enough, though whether one fed on the other from time to time Spindle was never sure.

The fourth of their party, Starling, reminded rather than taught them. She reminded them of life and growth, and her good spirits and young laughter brought a smile to each of them at times; and her absolute confidence that all would be well was a strength that kept each going.

Yet, by October, when the weather was worsening and a mole thinks of planning to deepen his tunnels and make his winter quarters, a new excitement had settled on Tryfan's group. They had seen, they had learnt, and now they were eager to get on. Most significantly, and mainly with Mayweed's guidance and Spindle's deductions, they had made sense of the new tunnels they had found. Some, like those smaller ones that ran beneath the roaring owl way near Duncton Wood were for drainage of rain, and though they scared a mole at first, once the run of them was understood and the weather known, a mole was safe enough in them. Others were for drainage too, but were much bigger, deeper, and awash. Here a mole might have to swim, and here too a mole had best be careful, for other creatures use them, especially voles and rats.

A third group of tunnels were deeper still, and evil of nature, for they carried filth and effluent, and the spoor of twofoots, and disease.

Each one of them, in the initial period of their journey had been struck down by illness if not quite disease. Runny snouts, painful eyes, bowels uncontrolled, no appetite, and dizziness. Spindle and Starling had been most hard hit by this. Tryfan had been ill for a time, but not badly, while Mayweed, though he never suffered the fever and runs the others did, cut himself in dirty water and the cut had festered. Starling cleared it by biting and cleaning, brutal, but it worked. After that the moles were careful of wounds, and very careful in the filthels, as they called them.

These tunnels, the filthels, which were bigger than any they had ever seen, were difficult to navigate at first because their sounding qualities were so different from the earth and chalk tunnels they were used to. They echoed, they were filled with strange noises of falling water, metal on stone, distant roaring owl hoots and even what they took to be twofoot shouts. The air currents were confusing

543

too, and often, in the bigger ones, were much stronger than any they had ever known, driving them backwards and tugging their fur almost off their backs and making them shout to be heard. The light was different, and cold, for such places were always wet and much of the light was reflected. Its sources were high above a mole's head, from apertures that went up into day, or from other tunnels at the side.

Most strangely, at night the light did not go away but changed, being often brighter and from different places so that a tunnel by day might be very different at night. Mayweed explored these things, teaching them to be still in a strange tunnel and use their paws and snouts and erect tails where the walls or ceiling were reachable, to first feel the tunnel, then scent the air, listen for a sound ahead as guidance across great chambers whose sides disappeared in the murk, and, difficult though it was at first, he made them all learn to use wind direction. Mayweed was careful, too, to teach them to memorise the route they were taking so that they could find their way back if they had to retreat.

Moles generally live in one place and forget how they learn their routes, even more so when they have delved the tunnels themselves. It was Mayweed's great art to develop a way of learning new tunnels, and to do what few moles ever needed to: to relate one part of a tunnel system to another and guess how he might make passage in between without becoming disorientated.

All these skills they taught each other slowly through that summer, finding more familiar places of fields and trees and using them as a base from which to venture into Wen tunnels and learn to survive in them.

Food was plentiful, though the worms were thin, red and sparse of taste. But there were plenty of them, and a cache of thicker lobworms was sometimes found and, as summer advanced, an aging beetle or two turned up to add variety. To find such food, though, they had to turn up the strange objects they found in those tunnels, objects for which Spindle furnished the names from a medieval text he had had the fortune to hear discussed by Brevis once, entitled *Journaye Forbode* and scribed anonymously by a mole travelling near Alban, an ancient and long abandoned system, who had ventured beneath the twofoot ways.

He described obstacles he had to negotiate made of material nomole had ever seen before, and since then had only found on ploughed fields and by roaring owl ways: pieces of wood but with straight edges and right angles; fractures of what in that old text is called glas, which is sharp and dangerous and what Mayweed cut himself on. Yet glas was also the material from which round objects were made which were usually bigger than moles with a hole in at one end, inside which earth collected where moles could sometimes see worms but not reach them. Then there was what Spindle thought must be 'clathe', soft coloured stuff, usually wet and stinking, made in strange shapes that stretched here and spread there, and sometimes had round shining objects attached to it.

There was also much metaille, hard sharp material, often rusting, which mole found from time to time everywhere, though never so hard and shining as they found in the Weñ. Strangest of all, and quite unfamiliar, was what they called thinbark, which was nearly as thin as silver birch bark, usually white or black, and waterproof. Yet easily punctured.

Starling knew *that* well enough, for one object like it she found, white and curving above her and unstable, which she talon-thrust, and water poured out and nearly drowned her. But 'thinbark' came to mean anything to the moles that was waterproof, smooth, and had no odour at all but that which other substances gave it.

Sometimes they found these materials in bits no bigger than a mole's paw, sometimes as objects far bigger than a mole could contemplate. Their uses they could only guess at, and hope that in time, as their journey proceeded, such things might make sense.

As for predators, there were so far very few. Rats they scented but never had to confront; bank and water voles there were aplenty. Weasels and stoats they came across, but not many.

Foxes were plentiful, but for mole always easy to escape by burrowing. In any case, fox do not like mole's flesh and the danger was being harried rather than killed. Worse were the dogs, of which the Wen was full, and cats which only Tryfan had ever seen before. Dangerous indeed.

But these were cautious times, and such dangers as they came upon they were able to watch from a distance to learn about, in preparation for the time when Tryfan decided they must turn south and then east once more, and start their journey in earnest . . . .

Spindle has left an account of what Tryfan was like at this historic moment when the moles finally headed on into the heart of the Wen.

He worries for us all, fretting when one of us is absent, concerned when another is uncomfortable, determined when one of us weakens. He has kept us from the Wen until now, using one excuse or the other, but mainly I believe for fear that we were not ready. But now, even if we are, he will worry still.

Tryfan has been much silent of late, and taken time to be by himself on or near the surface. I watch close by him, and sometimes, if there is sound of predator or doubt, I will disturb him. At such times of prayer and meditation he seems to notice nothing, and sighs when I approach him, and is ever good to me, asking me to spend less time with him and more with the others, lest they feel isolated. I assure him they do not. We all of us know how much Tryfan has suffered from the departure from Duncton Wood, the sense of failure he has that so many moles died, and he was much affected by the deaths of Maundy and his half-brother Comfrey. Starling's continuing faith that Bailey is alive gives him

546

comfort, and makes him believe also that some of those we parted from at Comfrey's Stone will survive.

Sometimes we ask him to tell us of the Stone but he says he knows little of it yet, pleading that he is too young, too inexperienced, too . . . he says his time will come to talk. Boswell told him to spend time thinking, meditating, and this is what he is doing. Yet though he says he is young Tryfan has aged this summer. His face is lined now, his body strong but leaner, his eyes concerned. He begins to look as the celibate scribe-moles look – strong yet needing to be touched more than they ever were. Yet he is a touching mole, and the four of us are often close. A mole meeting us might think we were all moles in love! I hope that the Stone may grant Tryfan of Duncton the love of a female he desires, though I doubt that he would wish me to make such a prayer! Well I, who knew such love with Thyme, desire it for him. I cannot but think that it brings a mole closer to the Silence.

Yet sometimes, for a little he will speak, as once he did on Harrowdown when he healed Smithills and Mayweed, and Brevis knew that this was a scribemole whose memory would live. . . .

There are other things in Spindle's famous account of Tryfan's life, among them his sense that the scribemole was beginning to suffer then that sense of being alone which plagued him through his life, a shadow that few other moles were able to see but Spindle, for they saw only their own need to be led and supported, not the needs of the scribemole who leads them.

Two days after Spindle wrote that part of his account and buried it, they were back near their original point of arrival at the Wen and Tryfan decided the time had come for the entry into the centre of the Wen.

The tunnels where they had taken shelter when Tryfan told them of his decision continuously shook and shuddered with the great way which rose to the east of it. It was a massive thing that rose on great grey legs from the ground and ran through the air far beyond a mole's sight, and where at night lights raced and shone violently. While at ground level there was a maze of impassable conduits and walls which stank with the smell of rat and rubbish and dogs, and where twofoots went, heavy and quick.

The sound there was strange, echoing and confused, roarings and shakes, screeches and lulls. But by the water course that Mayweed soon lighted on as the best way under the way, the air was still, the sounds muted, and above them the walls rose high so that the sky seemed shaped into a thin line as when a juvenile's tunnel breaks the surface and reveals the sun. It felt dangerous because nomole likes a route that is overlooked, where a predator can wait above unseen and attack when he will.

So quickly along this route they went, moving forward in stages between safe stances such as they could find. Some stances were drainage pipes from the wall towards the water, others less reliable – a wooden square beneath which was the stench of dog spoor, a white shapeless heap of rubbish where rats had gnawed and left their greasy stench upon the ground; weak metaille, rusty metal, so thin it caught the vibrations of the roaring owls above.

To each of these points the moles travelled in turn, one waiting for another and then the first leading on. Few words were spoken as they made fluid progress, as each covered for the other, listening and feeling out for threat and sound. By shadows they moved, by dark surfaces, that they might the less easily be seen.

To their right, over a wall that prevented view, they could smell the water flowing eastwards, deep and dark, in a tunnel carrying the vile stench of twofoots. It was a filthel.

Above them the concrete columns to the way rose high, and strange winds blew grubby paper and thinbark round corners and eddied it into piles at wind-dead places. They pressed on, disciplined and determined, until they passed under first one way and then another and then a third and ahead there were no more. Just tunnels, and apologies for grass, and filth, and as dusk fell, the roaring of owls and the shaking of them all about, and lights most strange and dazzling.

'Twofoot!'

The warning came down the line from Mayweed, and each took stance and froze. Then a high irregular sound as the twofoot came by, the ground too hard and stable to carry much vibration, but the sweet sick smell clear enough. A great grey thing bigger than a mole came down on the wet dust near Starling, who snuffled at the impression it left soon after the twofoot had gone.

'Its paw,' said Spindle.

'Didn't see us!' said Starling.

'Don't. Blind. Stupid,' said Spindle with unusual passion. He had been near enough to twofoots this past few weeks to know they must be blind, for sometimes his cover had been thin indeed and they had passed him by undisturbed. Mayweed was even more contemptuous of them, saying they were too high up to see low down. Not like cats, especially Wen cats, which could see through stone and against which a mole had little protection except to make a tunnel that was too deep and small for cat's paw to reach. Rats and weasels were different again.

When the twofoot had gone Tryfan said, 'Well, we are in the Wen. Every day we spend here is another day of danger. So we will travel fast with our minds and bodies always alert.'

'What are we looking for?' asked Mayweed.

'Where are we going?' asked Starling.

'We are looking for mole, or sign of mole. I believe we will find it. We have got here without trying too hard – but with initiative and courage. Others may well have have done the same in years past. The question is how far they had got, and, should any still be alive, what they may tell us if we can contact them.

'As for where to . . . well, I believe there will be Stone guidance here. I cannot feel it because the Wen is too confusing for a mole easily to feel a Stone's guidance. But I believe we will find help, for the Stone is everywhere, and so it will be in the Wen. And where it is then there will the moles we seek be. We must each of us try to find peace and stillness.'

'In this place!' said Spindle as the tunnel they were hiding in shook with roaring owl.

'In this place,' said Tryfan.

They travelled on then, each watching for the other as they had practised so often, a tight, close group that kept to shadows and shelter, and avoided open places. Seagulls swooped from the concrete heights above them sometimes; once they smelt fox; occasionally they found a run of grass, though always filthy with dog spoor. Once they found a tree, but its surface roots smelt of twofoot and they passed on by.

They travelled as quickly as they could in four-hour bursts, breaking off to rest when Tryfan told them to, maintaining a good speed. Mayweed did all the initial route-finding and, apart from one diversion south, by a concrete tunnel he preferred, they were able to head eastward most of the time. They travelled by night as well as day, four hours on, a few hours off, on and on, aware that with each step they took the Wen seemed to hem them in more and more, and the open countryside they knew to seem further and further away, as if they were in deep water, swimming they knew not where, and solid land might never be reached again.

It was in the early afternoon of the fifth such day when they were beginning to despair of ever finding mole, that they first saw the signs of tunnelling. Nothing much, just a surface run and a heap at one end where the mole had gained depth. The tunnels were old and empty, corrupted by vole and scrabbled at by dog, but it was a sign.

Mayweed was for pressing on but Tryfan said, 'We'll make temporary burrows as quickly as we can and rest. Tomorrow perhaps we may find them . . . ' There was an air of excitement about the group, as if all the journeying might finally bear fruit.

An hour later, as dusk was falling, Tryfan asked where Mayweed was. The coming of dusk meant that in the concrete desolation they were in, yellow lights were beginning to spring into the air and shining at sharp angles and across corrugations to where the moles had taken refuge. But the sky was still light, if vivid Wen violet was ever to be called a daylight sky.

'Exploring,' said Starling. 'He went off to see what he could find.'

'Well I wish he had waited,' said Tryfan. 'This is uneasy territory.'

But no sooner had he said that than there was a scampering out of the darkness ahead, a scurrying, and then Mayweed's voice.

'Come!' it said, but not to any of them: 'Come *on*, nervous Sir, timid and doubtful mole. Come and meet the friends of humble me!'

But whatever mole was to come was slow doing it for Mayweed approached them backwards, apparently urging a creature towards them until, eventually, they were astonished to see a thin and wiry mole reluctantly following him.

'Well!' declared Tryfan.

'Most brilliant, most clever, most splendid, am I not?' said Mayweed, coming as near as a mole can to patting himself on the back. 'This worthy mole found me!' he declared.

The mole stared at them.

'Stainree,' he said, rather loudly, as if they were deaf.

They looked at each other.

'Stainree,' he repeated, yet louder.

'Says only that,' said Mayweed.

'Stainree,' shouted the mole, looking expectantly at each of them in turn.

Then some distant memory, some strange connection, came to life in Tryfan, and as it did something similar came to Spindle, and each of them instinctively went forward as if they knew they had to say something, but knew not quite what.

'*Stainree!*' repeated the mole, shouting so loud that his paws lifted off the ground with the effort of it.

'He's saying . . . he's saying . . . .'

'He's saying "Steyne ree",' said Tryfan, whispering the words which are the start of a scribemole's greeting, and which he had last spoken when greeting Brevis at Buckland.

'Yes,' said Spindle, all fatigue from the day's travel replaced now by fascination. 'He is greeting us formally.'

The mole came nearer to them.

'Stainree,' he said yet again.

'Oh yes,' said Tryfan. 'Yes. Staye the hol and seint . . .' and his voice was deep as he gave the ancient response which, he had thought, only scribemoles knew.

But the mole seemed not to understand and he merely repeated the word, 'Stainree'.

'Staye the . . . *Staithee!*' said Spindle, corrupting the proper response.

Then the mole relaxed, looked at each in turn, and then said, 'Follow!'

'We shall!' said Tryfan.

With no more ado the mole led them out across the open scrub, gave a contemptuous glance at some black-headed seagull that came wheeling and squealing out of the bright-dark sky overhead, and then after taking a way that was all surface, and lasted a good half hour, they dropped into tunnels the like of which none of them had ever seen before.

* * * * * * *

'Rubbish!' said Spindle finally. 'Twofoot and roaring owl rubbish! That's what this is . . .!'

The tunnels were only occasionally of earth, for the rest they were made up of all those materials which the moles had been discovering all summer and autumn past, but squashed and flattened, turned and torn, jumbled and shoved together so that the tunnels were now walled with glas, now with thinbark, and now with long lines of wood to give them astonishing straightness, now with rusting metaille.

The sounds were extraordinary, all loud and vibrating.

The other moles looked at Spindle and he smiled that smile that moles do when they have solved a problem others have only just started formulating.

'I wondered why so many things were in the tunnels, for surely the creatures that had them must want them. But no, they were discarded. Here we have what a mole might call a place of total discard: rubbish, in short, such as a mole might dispose of outside his burrows when spring comes.'

They had paused briefly while the mole guiding them had gone on ahead. Now he came back, and, shouting above the noise all about them, said, 'Come on and meet Corm!'

On they went, round a corner, and there in a chamber defined by angled metaille mesh, with a ceiling high above them, was a fat and dirty mole. His mouth was full when they arrived and his right talon clogged with the food he was eating, much of which was on the floor before him. It looked like oval orange beetles without legs covered in a thick orange juice. It smelt sweet.

He looked up at them from piggy eyes and grinned, his teeth orange with whatever it was he ate.

'Stainree!' he shouted in a friendly way, spitting globs of orange muck on Tryfan and Spindle's fur.

'Staithee!' said Tryfan, as Spindle fastidiously groomed his fur clean.

'And welcome you are. Damn me, we haven't seen stranger moles in . . . how long is it, Murr?' he said to the gaunt mole who had led them there.

'Long enough to make it remarkable,' said Murr, 'but not so long that I have forgot! They came by the western pipe bridge.' There were muttered explanations of surprise at this, and Tryfan presumed they were referring to the awkward passage Mayweed had found for them over a waterway that morning, and deduced that Murr must have been watching them for some hours.

'And did they now? Stone me!' said the mole, looking at them with obvious respect. 'Well, my name's Corm, and Murr you've met already . . .' Their voices were so *loud*! Tryfan looked at the others: perhaps they would start talking loudly when they had been long enough surrounded by such continual noise.

Tryfan introduced himself and the rest of them one by one, and gave a guarded explanation, mentioning grikes only in passing as to why they had come. He was never comfortable telling even a half truth, but felt it best, initially at least, to be careful of what he said. These moles might easily be of the Word for all he knew. . . .

'Grikes? We've heard of them, all right!' said Corm. 'Pains in the arse they are, from what little we've heard. Stoneless aren't they?'

Tryfan and the others nodded, relaxing.

'Well, you're safe enough here because they'll not get through without persistence, like you lot seem to have, or with help, and that they'll not get . . . As for us, we don't go westward out of the Wen. Dangerous out there, what with plagues and fires and grikes and all.'

'If you don't go out there, how do you know about it then?' asked Spindle reasonably.

'You're not the only ones daft enough to come avisiting, mate! Especially since the troubles started. There's easier routes than the one you took. When you leave tomorrow, Murr here'll show you. Myself, I don't travel much, and nor do most moles round here.' He patted his ample stomach and grinned.

'We're . . . er . . . not leaving tomorrow,' said Tryfan. 'At least, not back westwards. We're going on.'

'Here we go again, Murr. I told we was about due for some more intrepid explorers.' He raised his eyes with resignation, tucked into some more of his food and then let out a loud and smelly belch. He patted his stomach again,

554

as if to push it into a more comfortable position and made a smaller, softer belch, a gentle echo of the first. Then when he was quite comfortable, and Spindle, a prim mole about such things, had shifted about uneasily, he said, 'Don't tell me, just . . . don't . . . tell . . . me. You're searching for the very heart of the Wen. You're hoping to find moles there who will guide you on to something or other.'

'You know a lot,' said Tryfan.

'I know bugger all, chum,' said Corm, pushing Murr's paw away from what little remained of the food he had been eating and muttering, 'I haven't finished yet.' He nibbled a bit more, as if to establish his right to the whole lot if he wanted it, turned away, waved magnanimously for Murr to eat what he liked and said, 'What I *do* know is that you'll not find whatever it is you're looking for. You'll get yourself killed, and you'll get these moles killed, and nomole will be any the wiser. Waste of everymole's time.'

'You've tried it?' asked Tryfan.

'Me? Come off it! Only thing I've ever taken any risks over is food, but round here . . . well, you'd be daft not to. Very interesting this place for a mole who likes food.'

'Is it where the twofoots of the Wen bring all their rubbish?' asked Spindle.

'Oh clever, very clever. Took me a *long* time to work that out. But no, it's not. This place is just *one* of the places, there's dozens of them, hundreds of them, maybe thousands. The Wen is big, big, which means bloody ginormous. That's one good reason why you'll never get to the heart of it. There isn't one.

'You are looking at a mole who was once thin. This mole you are looking at decided to take a risk and set off as you have for the heart of the Wen. He got here and started eating. He has not stopped eating since. He has travelled no further. He has found happiness.'

'Fat and obese Sir, mole of amplitude, Mayweed, a humble mole but one with curiosity will ask you a question, no?'

Corm's eyes nearly popped out of his head as Mayweed

555

suddenly spoke. He raised his paw and turned to Tryfan and said, 'What's he on about?'

Tryfan grinned and shrugged.

'Rotund vagrant,' said Mayweed, coming closer and peering into Corm's eyes, 'have you travelled east of here?'

'No,' said Corm, 'but I know a mole who has.'

'Magnificent Murr?' asked Mayweed turning to Murr with a wonderful and engaging smile.

'Give over,' said Murr. 'I never go east if I can help it. Nasty things happen east.'

'Then who, tubby and ample Corm, is the mole who has travelled east?'

'Comes here to feed up a bit and then goes back again.' Corm yawned. Talking was an effort, and his eyes flicked this way and that as if his mind was beginning to drift back to the subject that occupied most of his waking thoughts: food.

'Yes, comely Corm?' said Mayweed, obviously enjoying himself. Starling was giggling, but only because Corm seemed fascinated by Mayweed's adjectives and was muttering some of them to himself as his eyes half closed with sleep . . . 'Comely . . . Obese . . . what else?'

'Rotund,' repeated Mayweed.

'Mmm,' said Corm patting himself again and smiling. 'Yes, rotund.'

'Well, hungry Sir?' nagged Mayweed.

'Don't say I didn't warn you, but there is a mole a few miles on, and I mean miles, who has ventured further than any other I know into the Wen and lived to tell the tale. The poor idiot's name is Rowan.'

'Why . . .?' began Spindle.

Corm waved a paw impatiently.

'He'll tell you, tell you everything and be glad too. Ask him. He'll warn you off, but as I can see you'll not listen to anything a mole will say I can only suggest that you go and chat to him. Goodbye and good luck. Don't say I didn't tell you.'

'We'll wait until morning if you don't mind,' said Tryfan.

556

'Not if you're going east, you won't. I don't mind, but you will. Go in the morning and the dogs'll eat you alive, go now and you'll avoid them. They come out in the morning. Very nasty. Murr, show 'em!'

'But I never go east. Hate it.'

'Murr!' warned Corm.

'Oh, well, all right, I suppose so. Regret finding you but will take you there.'

'Words of advice,' said Corm as they left. 'One: watch out for cats. Give them a good talon-thrust on the nose and tunnel away. They don't kill with one bite like a dog does. Two: ignore Rowan's tears and tell him you're in a hurry or otherwise you'll be crouched there till Longest Night listening to him.'

'Longer,' muttered Murr.

'Three: if you find out anything interesting and survive to tell the tale I'll be glad to hear of it, very interested in fact.'

'Where will we find you?' asked Tryfan politely.

'I don't move much,' said Corm.

* * * * * * *

It took them all night to travel to where Murr wanted to take them, but they might have been quicker had not Mayweed stopped him from time to time to check out directions, for the route was through complex tunnels and surface ways and Mayweed liked to remember such things.

So it was dawn before they arrived, though nomole was immediately in sight.

'He'll come,' said Murr, looking about uneasily. 'I'll leave you here.' As he went he tapped Mayweed on the shoulder and said, 'See you later, Mayweed mate!'

' "Mayweed mate," ' repeated Mayweed with great delight. 'Very droll, very jokey, and Mayweed likes that! He says in reply, "See *you* later, chum Murr!" ' And Mayweed laughed himself silly as Murr left them.

'Shut up, Mayweed,' said Tryfan, irritable with tiredness.

Dawn came, and then dogs. Yapping, barking, spooring, sniffing, sniffling, pulling twofoots with them. The place was grass and concrete, and there were great concrete walls near and far, all very high. But Tryfan's group were well hidden in tunnels, and nearby, flowing in a channel in the ground, very wide and grubby, was a stream which went to the northern edge of the grass and then under a huge arch and into deepening darkness, where it boomed and sounded frightening.

It was a dull day. The dogs and the twofoots went, and roaring owls sounded all about but quite unseen. Then a snuffle, and a shake, and from out of a crack in the concrete, near where they had taken refuge a mole appeared and made straight for them. He rushed into their tunnel, puffing heavily, and stared at each of them in turn.

'Greetings wanderers, greetings one and all. Rowan, that's me. And you are . . .?' They told him their names in turn and he muttered words like 'Good!' 'Yes!', 'Well then!' and 'Splendid!'

Though his voice was young and his looks eager, he was an old mole, wrinkled and grey. Like Corm, he did not look short of food, but he was unfit rather than obese. From the first he had stationed himself near the entrance to the burrow from where he could see right down to the archway into which the stream disappeared. He looked that way very frequently, as if he was expecting a mole to come any moment. His attention was taken up so much by this archway that Tryfan asked him, before they said anything more, if he *was* expecting anymole.

'Any moment, minute by minute,' said Rowan, frowning and worried. 'Yes, any moment now they'll come. Or I *think* they will.'

'Who?' asked Spindle.

'Moles I once knew,' said Rowan, but in such a way that the word 'once' was suggestive of a very long time ago indeed.

'Where have they gone?' asked Tryfan.

'Where I once went,' said Rowan. 'Oh, I did! Once. Long time ago.'

There was a terrible sadness in his voice, and a longing, as of a mole who has lost most of his life down a high arched tunnel, and is waiting for it to return.

'What were their names?' asked Starling softly. She went close to him and for a moment he turned to her, interested in a way he had not been before as if this mole among them all would understand what he had to tell them.

'Haize was my sister, Heath was a friend. Shall I tell you?'

He looked away from them, back towards the archway. His voice was diffident, as if he had no real hope that they would wish to hear.

Tryfan remembered Corm's warning and looked around at the other three. He saw in each of their eyes sympathy for this old mole, and kindness, and curiosity too. He saw no impatience, no condescension. He saw the eyes of moles he had learned to trust and respect, he saw three moles that he had learned to love. He knew that he could find no other three with whom he would be more willing and confident to travel into the depths of the Wen, through the archway and down the tunnel at which Rowan gazed so longingly.

'I think we'd all like you to tell us,' said Tryfan with a smile.

'Really?' said Rowan, rather surprised.

'Please,' said Starling.

'Yearning Sir,' said Mayweed, 'it would be this mole's privilege to hear you.'

'I'm sure we all would like it,' said Spindle.

'Well then!' said Rowan, 'I shall.' And he turned from his eternal watching, settled down, and told them of how he came to be where he was that day and every day and would be for evermore until that special day came – and he knew it would! – when the moles he waited for came back out of the Wen.

Chapter Thirty-Two

It was during that same wet and windy month of November, as Tryfan and his moles were finally poised to enter the most dangerous part of the Wen, and when moles look irritably for shelter and despair that good weather will ever return, that Alder and Marram first came near the last stages of the journey to dread Siabod.

They knew little of Siabod but what Tryfan had been able to tell them of his parents' own account of the place, and what they had picked up from other moles on the final stages of their journey.

They had travelled steadily and well, not using their own names, and the fact that they were grikes counted in their favour, for most of the systems they passed through were entirely grike-controlled and guardmoles were inclined to trust their own kind. All knew that a final assault on Siabod had been planned for many months and, though the main forces had gone on ahead, Alder and Marram were able to convince guardmoles they met that they had special skills and duties that might be needed in Siabod and had been sent up from Buckland to provide them. So they had no trouble getting help towards their destination along the way.

A few eldrenes had been suspicious, a few grikes unhelpful, but on the whole their passage was easy and they were glad, as autumn gave way to winter, that they had travelled fast and before the snows had come, for Siabod is not a place to be out in when ice and snow are about, let alone the blizzards that rage there when December comes.

'By Longest Night we'll make it and have billets as comfortable as a home burrow in summer,' Alder had been saying cheerfully all the journey long. Marram was less certain and by himself might not have had the persistence that Alder showed. He was a mole like many who, given a lead, will perform great things, but without leadership may do nothing.

It is hard to say now whether already in the back of Alder's mind were some of the possibilities for battles and campaigns which he would one day plan and seek to execute, as one of the great mole commanders of his time, if not the greatest. Some would suggest that the journey he took to Siabod was a deliberate way of gathering information about the state of moledom which was later to stand him in such good stead.

However that might have been, the fact was that on their long journey he was indeed able to learn a great deal about moledom in general, and some systems in particular, which he was later able to use successfully to the advantage of the moles of the Stone.

For now, it was enough that he saw how powerfully entrenched the grikes had become, and how wise Tryfan had been to retreat and disperse to await such time as conditions were ripe for the Stone followers to re-emerge into light. System after system that Alder passed near or actually went through was well organised for the Word, with powerful and effective eldrenes, obedient moles, and no evidence of much interest in the Stone. Such as there was was negative, for moles did as the sideem had planned they should, which was to blame the Stone for the plague years, and to see Henbane and the grikes as their saviours; and, most alarming of all, to dismiss the period of snoutings and massacres and outcastings as a necessary time of countering the evil of the Stone believers' indulgence and superstition with the Atoning redemptive might of the Word.

News of Duncton's defeat had gone ahead of Alder and Marram, along with stories of cowardice and treachery by the Duncton moles themselves. Since Alder and Marram knew these to be false, they were well able to disbelieve the more ominous story they also heard, of Tryfan's capture

561

and his betrayal of his fellow moles. Yet such stories naturally concerned them, and might in moles of lesser faith have bred doubt and disaffection. But Alder's reaction to such false rumours was to make him all the more determined to establish contact with other moles of the Stone and organise resistance.

But Alder and Marram did more on that journey than observe the state of different systems. They also had the opportunity to learn something of what moledom had been before the decline of faith in the Stone. Coming as they had from systems of the Word and with a faith in the Stone that was so far untutored, they had none of the experience of rituals and traditions which moles from Stone systems had.

But they had curiosity, and for that reason, on the way to Siabod, Alder and Marram began to deviate from a direct route here and there to investigate those places which Tryfan had told them were once strong of the Stone, and still must have their Stones where a few brave followers might still be. No doubt they realised that such moles, if they still existed, would in future moleyears be needed and not only for the power of their talons. In fact they met few moles at such sites until later in their journey, and instead the visits were a time of wonder and contemplation as they stared, in simple awe, at the great deserted Stones and wondered where their power came from.

Alder remembered always the strange interlude with Tryfan out on the surface of Buckland, when by some power that Tryfan had drawn on he was made to see plain the wrongs of the Word as if he could see them all the way across moledom. He remembered too the peace he had felt afterwards, and something of its Silence, and matter of fact though he was by nature, that memory had left such a mark on him that he desired to meet moles who had faith, that he might learn from them, and know more of the Silence he had so briefly been made to hear.

In a strange way Marram understood this, as if Alder

emanated some light from the memory he had and Marram could see it, and seek to follow it as well. Indeed, quite often, while Alder was busy assessing the systems they went through for their strengths and weaknesses Marram, dour though he might seem at times, was able to discover places of the Stone and lead Alder to them as if to say: There you are, it's nothing much to do with me, but I thought you might like to see this Stone. . . .

So it was that on the way to Siabod they visited many obscure Stone sites and found that while most of these places were quite deserted, some still had fresh tunnels and signs of mole habitation, though nomole came out of hiding to greet the two travellers.

'I get the feeling at the Stones that we're often being watched,' said Alder.

'More than likely, but it's no good chasing after shadows because these moles, if they're here, will be used to hiding and evasion.'

'Aye, that's right, they'd have to be to have survived a grike invasion this long.'

It occurred to Alder only after several such Stone visits that perhaps there was something they could do to make contact with moles of the Stone.

'If I was really educated to the Stone like Tryfan or Spindle,' said Alder one day, 'and I was watching moles like us visit such a place, what would I want to see? I'll tell you Marram: I'd want evidence that the visiting moles believed in the Stone. So from now on, whatever Stone sites we go to, we touch the Stone and generally make it look as if we are experienced followers. Right?'

Which is what they did for the rest of their journey, touching each Stone they found, crouching by it so long as they were reasonably certain that grikes weren't about, and generally acting as they imagined followers would act.

'And the strange thing is, Marram,' Alder said one day in November as they were reaching the higher ground of the Welsh Marches and beginning to sense that they would soon reach Siabod, 'I enjoy touching the Stones, I feel better for it! Maybe they do have the powers Tryfan believes they have after all!'

'Maybe!' said Marram.

But for all his unwillingness to admit such a thing Marram still insisted on touching each Stone as well, and would look round at them with longing as they left such sites, the more so if he thought Alder was not looking.

'Well, we'll be at Caer Caradoc tomorrow, and *that's* one of the seven Ancient Systems, though not lived in for generations according to Tryfan. But if any Stones have an effect on us those at Caradoc should,' said Marram. And they did.

They reached Caer Caradoc as the first snow of the season came, light and powdery and making those higher parts look cleaner and more clear after the drudgey look of autumn when bracken wilts and the leaves of trees have begun to disintegrate across the ways moles go and make them difficult to pass.

So they came to Caradoc, and hurried among the Stones that rise there to find shelter from the biting wind.

They stared about, snouted here and there for enemy, found none, and then, ever mindful that they might be watched by Stone followers, chose the finest Stone of several there and, shivering a little and keeping their snouts from the wind, touched it and made obeisance.

It was as they were doing this that they both, simultaneously, sensed mole nearby, watching mole, and they stiffened ready for attack.

With the slightest of gestures Alder indicated that they would stay still until provoked: he had the feeling that in the shadow of the Stone a mole of faith does not attack another first.

So they waited, and the movement nearby increased and then stopped as a mole watched from somewhere behind, uncertain and, perhaps, afraid. After what seemed a long wait they heard a slight movement again and a voice said, 'Welcome, moles, to Caer Caradoc!'

Alder swung round as Marram stepped back to take a covering stance.

The mole was two cycles of seasons old, and unkempt, as if he had been in a strong cold wind, and his voice was thin and accented. He crouched before them openly but with a diffidence approaching fear, and said, 'I was expecting you! You're the moles who – '

'Expecting us?' asked Alder.

'Word gets about, especially of moles who make a point of visiting Stones as you have done. But whether you were grike spies or followers, we did not know.'

'Do you know now?' asked Alder.

The mole laughed nervously.

'Followers, I think and hope! But if you are spies we'll know soon enough from what you say, and you'll not leave these parts alive.'

'And you, mole?' said Alder, speaking in the way of natural authority that had come to him by then: 'Your name?'

'You may call me Caradoc. I watch over these good Stones, and have done since my father died. I am the last mole of this system, or the first when the good day comes.'

'The good day?' said Alder.

'The great good day, when the Stone Mole comes. That day Caradoc will be re-born.'

'He's coming here?' said Alder, looking about the desolate place with surprise. 'Aren't there better places for the Stone Mole to go to?'

'Better places, yes, and I've no doubt he'll go there first. But this is one of the Ancient Seven and he'll come here one day. My father said it, his father said it, his father said it, and his father before *him*; and I? I believe it. Well, I'm the last until I have some young and one of them will believe it as I do, and one after that if need be. But I hope I see the Stone Mole myself.'

There was silence then and the wind blew and though the mole looked cold and his snout was blue he seemed not to feel it much.

'Whither are you bound, moles, and why?' he asked. 'I know what you have said in systems you've visited, for I've been told, but it can't be the reason.'

'What did we say?' asked Marram.

'That you are on a special mission and on the way to Siabod. You're not grike spies, are you?'

'No we're not,' said Alder simply, and he knew he was believed. Knew, too, that before the Stone a mole does not easily lie and this mole Caradoc knew it as well, for his eyes had not left Alder's once.

'I see you speak the truth,' he said.

'We come from a long way off to the east, a very long way. And we go to Siabod because we've heard it is resisting the grikes and we will join the moles there, and help them if they'll let us.'

'Where are you from then?' asked Caradoc.

'I thought you knew everything about us!' said Alder with a smile.

'Not everything, no. Only heard of you in August and you haven't been saying anything of where you came from.'

'From Duncton Wood,' said Alder.

The mole heard him but, if he looked anything at all, it was doubtful.

'Your accent is northern,' said the mole. 'Duncton's southern.'

'He didn't say we were born there, he said we came *from* there,' said Marram.

'You're not pulling my paw are you?' said Caradoc, his eyes suddenly excited and hopeful.

'No,' said Alder, 'we're not.'

'We're too bloody tired to go round pulling moles' paws,' said Marram.

'But –?' began Caradoc, evidently too full of questions and excitement to know how to continue.

'You trusted us, mole, we'll trust you and tell you who we are and what we wish to do,' said Alder. 'Perhaps you can help us. We were sent to Siabod from Duncton by a mole called Tryfan.'

566

'Tryfan!' exclaimed Caradoc. 'Well bless me!'

'Aye, Tryfan sent us,' continued Marram. 'We're going to Siabod and. . . .'

'And we have much news for the Siabod moles, and much to ask them. They stand alone now against the grikes, and we've heard they stand bold. But the grikes are getting stronger. We know of fighting, and we know of grikes, and we know much that might help them. From Tryfan we bring messages of hope and purpose and greetings of the Stone. Tryfan is our leader and we his emissaries.'

'What message do you bring?' asked Caradoc.

Alder looked up at the Stones about them, and on to the snow-touched hills beyond, and said, 'That though night has now come to moledom and the grikes rule wide and strong, yet light will return and with it a different sound than that which dark talons make will be heard by allmole.'

'And what sound would that be?' whispered Caradoc.

'The sound of Silence,' said Alder.

Caradoc's eyes filled with tears as he stared at Alder and heard his words. The wind blew cold about them and yet not one of them felt it.

'Though we come from Tryfan, we know little of the Stone ourselves,' said Alder. 'We desire to know more. We've been visiting Stone sites all along our journey, and we've felt other moles watching, but you're the first who has come to talk to us. So tell us, mole.'

'The most a mole can do is reveal something of himself,' said Caradoc, 'and that's not easy. But I'll tell you how I came to be here, and why I came out into the open to ask you who you were. . . .

'Moleyears ago two moles came here as you have done. It was before I was born, before you were born, I think. Their names . . . aye, I see you know their names. Their names were Bracken and Boswell, one of Duncton and one of Uffington. They came here at Longest Night and they prayed by the Stones and a mole watched them as I watched you. That mole watching them was my father.

'He was timid, was my father, and yet he had faith. That's why for so many Longest Nights he came up to this abandoned place and said the rituals as he had been taught. That night he came up and found those moles here before him and he was very frightened, for he feared they might hurt him. He had been too long alone in his faith, you see.

'So he watched, and he heard what that mole Boswell said as he prayed to the Stone, and he told me it was like nothing he had ever heard before: it was beautiful, he said. Then he knew they were not moles to fear. . . .'

'So did he greet them?' asked Alder.

Caradoc shook his head and lowered his snout, as if ashamed of his father.

'Felt he wasn't worthy, you see. Felt he was nothing. Felt ashamed for his system. He sensed that the mole Boswell was special, very special. Not much of a mole to look at – he had a withered paw as a matter of fact and limped – but my father was frightened of him.

'Later, when they had gone, he heard who they were. How they went to Siabod, how another called Rebecca came, heard all of that. Moles hereabouts know that story well. Aye, many said that it was the beginning of the Stone Mole's coming. Most believe that.

'Well now, my father changed after that Longest Night. Come the spring he found a mate, which wasn't easy for a nervous mole like him. That was my mother. Out of the three pups born I was the one he put his faith in because he said I was the most timid of the three, as he had been!' Caradoc laughed affectionately at this memory. 'Aye, well . . . I was the one to carry on. He told me all he knew. He used to say he had only one regret and that was that he did not have the courage to speak to Boswell and ask for his blessing. He said to me, "Look lad, when moles come up here you'll be afraid, but don't do as I did and hide. You trust the Stone and say hello. Promise?" So I promised!'

'So when we came today you did as you had promised him,' said Alder.

'I did,' said Caradoc, 'and I'm glad I did though I'll tell you this: when two great moles like you, with strong talons and fierce expressions suddenly appear, it's a bit of a shock to a mole. Not that you're as big as some of the Siabod moles, but you'll do!

'Now, you'll need help to get to Siabod, for the grikes are entrenched around its accessible eastern and northern parts now. Even if you got to its tunnels you'd not easily find the moles you need to find.'

'Will you help?' asked Alder.

'I will!' said Caradoc excitedly. 'I'll take you to Capel Garmon which is as near as you can get to Siabod without needing guides. There I know moles who'll take you on to where you need to go. I know the Stone sent you, I do know that!'

'How do you know?' asked Alder.

'Because moles like you are needed now. You know why I came up to the Stones today? I came to pray. I came to ask for help.'

'Why now?' asked Marram.

'Because Siabod is nearly Siabod no more. The Siabod moles are tired and dispirited and nearly beaten. Many have fled, many have gone over to the grikes. They're bold, yes. They're fighters, yes. But moles can only go on so long alone and they've been alone too many years. All the moles hereabouts know that, but there's not much we can do against the grikes. But the Stone . . . well, I thought if I came. . . .'

'So long as there's one mole prepared to take stance and fight then the grikes can still be defeated,' said Alder.

'Then come with me, Alder and Marram, come now, for there's moles who need to hear you say that, and be shown how to take stance. They're not moles you'll ever be ashamed of to have at your side.'

'Then take us to them!' said Alder, and northwest towards Siabod they went.

★ ★ ★ ★ ★ ★ ★

The final part of their journey to the edge of Siabod was

into high, rough country and took them some moleweeks.

'It would have been quicker to go by the river valleys Bracken and Boswell followed when they came to Siabod, but now those parts are grike-controlled and even if you could bluff your way through some of them it's not worth the risk,' explained Caradoc. 'Also it may be best if your coming is not suspected by the grikes or even some of the Siabod moles.'

Alder must have looked surprised at this for Caradoc added cryptically, 'Traitors and cowardice. I understand that the grike siege has broken the spirit of many Siabod moles and they are willing to inform on their system in return for a promise of safety. So far the grikes have not accepted that.'

'They wouldn't,' said Alder shortly. 'It is their way to engender so much fear in a system that when they do finally enter it the moles give up without a struggle and fall over themselves to inform on their fellows and serve the Word.'

'Well, that's how it is at Siabod now, and I'm told the communal tunnels are heavy with suspicion. Nomole trusts another. But we of the Stone have our ways of knowing others who are true, and if I can get you to Garmon then I can put you into the paws of moles you can trust.'

But perhaps 'if' was the more important word for now. The weather had worsened, which in North Wales means that it had gone from bad to very bad. The powdery snow that had made the landscape seem chilly but tranquil at Caradoc had given way to bitter winds that carried hail and sleet, and drove into the eyes and snout of an advancing mole to make his vision blurred and his spirit low. They had hoped to catch an early sight of Siabod itself but were disappointed.

'Are we near Siabod yet?' they asked Caradoc from time to time.

'Not far,' said Caradoc. 'You may be eager to see it but it's a sight to shrivel a mole's hopes. Not a place for normal mole.'

'So when were you last there?' asked Marram.

'Me, mole? I've never been there. Never will. Warned off it by my father.'

'What did he know of it?'

'My father? Nothing! He had been warned off it by *his* father.'

Alder laughed deeply.

'It must be frightening indeed that moles who live so near never dare venture there!'

'It is,' said Caradoc. 'And the moles who live there, traitors though some may be, *they're* frightening too. It's the place, see. Shapes a mole strangely. Makes him serious, makes him watchful, makes him wary and quick to take offence. Siabod moles need pawdling.'

'Pawdling?'

'Like a touchy mother, needs careful pawdling.'

'Well, it's no bad thing to be quick tempered and touchy. They may be just the qualities needed to resist grikes. But whether they're what's needed to defeat them, that's a different matter. Now, is it true they don't speak mole?'

'Speak Siabod, don't they? But don't you worry, they can speak mole if they want to, or most can but a very few who choose to hide away in the hills and are never seen.'

They had begun to go downslope across sheep pastures, taking routes that Caradoc seemed to know which made use of the dry stone walls that deface those slopes and confuse a mole who does not know them. But to one who did, like Caradoc, the walls gave safe and lengthy runs.

There was little life about but for rooks and a few raven squabbling over sheep carrion. Occasionally juvenile herring gulls swooped down to give a dash of white-brown colour to the scene. But as the winds got stronger, even this life stilled as the birds huddled at some low, sheltered promontory, their excrement bold white and purple about them.

'The purple's bilberries,' said Caradoc. 'Useful to mole on worm-poor ground. Carrion's useful too if you care to

571

risk the rooks. Burrow from below if you have to. Nerve-racking.'

Alder looked round at Marram and grinned. Survival in these parts was difficult, and a mole did well to listen to what locals said.

The skies were still low and grey as they turned across a grubby field and came to as sorry a collection of Stones as Alder and Marram had ever seen on their long journey.

'Capel Garmon,' said Caradoc shortly. 'One of nature's natural derelictions, though Stones are here so moles must have been in the past. None in residence now, but we vagrant moles of the Stone use it as a safe meeting place.'

They looked about, huddled against the cold, and stared at the Stones, and then found shelter in a large empty burrow Caradoc seemed to know.

'I sometimes think a wrong was done in this place and the spirit of the Stone deserted it. Perhaps moles died of plague here alone and forsaken. Whatmole can say? Even the grikes have ignored it since their initial reconnaissance. A few Siabod moles know of it and come here if they want to make contact with the outside world.'

'Then Siabod's near?' said Alder, looking westward past the battered and wan-looking Stones to the cloud and mist that obscured all view.

'Five days or so. Now, I'll have to get a message out and that'll take a day or two. And then a mole or moles will come to take you on. That could take a day or two more, so you've a bit of a stay. Don't stray while I'm gone!'

'You're joking, mate,' said Marram. 'We'll be glad of the rest.'

It was five days before Caradoc returned and when he did he had a good few moles with him and all but one as thin and ragged looking as he was. Indeed, they looked as if they had all got cold at birth and never warmed up since. The exception was a large and silent mole who glowered from the back and said nothing.

'A Siabod mole is coming as soon as he can to guide you

on,' said Caradoc, 'but meanwhile . . .' He seemed apologetic. 'These moles wanted sight of you. Tell them what you told me.' Then Caradoc added in a whisper, 'Don't worry about the big one at the back. His name's Troedfach and I'll tell you of him later.'

'Can they be trusted?' asked Alder doubtfully, for they were a sorry, unprepossessing bunch.

'They'll swear to that!' said Caradoc with feeling. 'There's not one here who'll not touch the Stone!' With that he nodded to the circle of moles who were staring silently at Alder and Marram, and then one by one they went to the nearest Stone, put a paw to it, and, looking at the rest said, 'May this paw wither and this heart die on the day I forswear the Stone. I wait for the coming of the Stone Mole with longing, aye!'

One by one they said it, and as they spoke, however abject and pitiful they seemed – and it was clear that some had little food to live on and led a vagrant hunted life – they somehow came alive as they spoke, and their eyes lit up not just with faith but pride and passion too. Their final 'Aye!' was chorused by the others, so that the swearings became rhythmic and the 'Ayes' ever stronger. Then they looked at Alder and Marram expectantly, and Caradoc whispered, 'You must do it now, and they'll know you're true!'

So both of them did, staring around at the followers and threatening themselves with withered paws and dying hearts, and invoking the name of the Stone Mole.

When that was done Alder spoke to them, telling them the recent history of Duncton and its evacuation under the leadership of Tryfan. Many asked questions, and wanted to know of the grikes and Henbane, and a few of Whern. But mostly they wanted to know what Tryfan had said of the Stone Mole.

'Will he come soon?' asked more than one, with longing in their eyes.

'To kill the grikes?' asked another. 'And lead us back to the vales where once we lived?'

573

'Before a full cycle of seasons has passed?' asked a third.

Alder replied, 'I know not when or how or where the Stone Mole may come. I think perhaps all moles of the Stone seek him now and that Tryfan will find guidance in the great Wen to which he has gone and of which I have told you what I know. But allmole is on a quest for him and he will come when the time is right. Meanwhile we must have faith, and courage. I do not think it is the end for Siabod. I know the grikes can be held for I was there at Duncton when *we* held them, for a time at least. I believe they can be defeated and that first great defeat will be here at Siabod. And you moles of courage, who have fled the vales and hold true to the Stone, your hour will come. Stay close, listen, be patient, trust the future as you trust each other and trust Marram and myself whom you hardly know. Our long winter is here, but if we have not strength to survive it and faith to live it through then why should the Stone Mole help us? This is our time of great testing. He will come to moles worthy of him, and to systems where, however faintly, moles still call out that they might one day hear the Silence that is the Stone's great gift. This is Tryfan of Duncton's message to you.'

After that the moles spoke far into the night to Alder and Marram, telling them of their hopes and fears, and pledging their support for Tryfan and the cause that he was leading. Mole after mole said that though they had little strength or skill for fighting yet they would give their very lives if Tryfan or Alder asked it of them, because they knew that one day – Aye! One day! – the Stone Mole would come.

This meeting is known now as the Conclave of Capel Garmon and moles speak of it with respect and reverence, and are glad to claim kinship to those brave beleaguered moles who were there with Alder and Marram then. So let us scribe a roll of their names that they are ever known: Caradoc, Clun, Mynydd, Cwmifor, Manod, Stitt of Ratlinghope, Wentnor of Mynd and the Pentre siblings, Gaelri and Lymore; last were three moles from the southern Marches, Blaen-cwm, Dowre and Troedfach of Tyn-y-Bedw.

Of these twelve moles one alone would later journey on with Alder. This was Troedfach of Tyn-y-Bedw whom Alder had noticed when the moles first joined them at Garmon and who loomed as an oak at sunset rises among lesser trees. They noticed that the others deferred to him, though not in any humble way but rather as if he had some strength or purpose beyond even theirs.

'He trekked from the distant south to come to Siabod,' explained Caradoc, 'and though he says little I know that none more than he waits with longing for the coming of the Stone Mole. He speaks seldom, but others like him and trust him and he has saved more than one life against the grikes.'

Of all the moles there he was the only one who spoke his avowal of the Stone in a language other than mole: deep and guttural and strange, and he snouted close to the Stone as if he could see little but feel much.

It was he too who took the lead as they parted by speaking for the others, saying, 'Your coming has been awaited for many months and we will await your return from Siabod. There is not one here who would not go with you to that place, but 'tis better that only you two go first. We will be ready when your call comes, aye we will!' And the others joined in his shout.

With that meeting the great army of moles that Alder dreamed he might one day lead found its birth. Each would play his part, each find and inspire others to play theirs. Each would have patience to live the winter of the Stone through to its bitter end, and have faith that when the last storm broke and light returned to moledom once again they would have strength to fight for it, aye! That was the hopeful shout from Garmon then, as grey dawn came, and those fugitive few went silently away to wait the call that Alder would one day send out.

A few hours later a solid looking mole with a craggy snout and eyes that seemed permanently screwed up against the wind, even when he was safe aburrow, arrived.

His name, he said, was Cwm, and he was sorry to keep them waiting but he had insisted on coming himself when he heard they were from Duncton Wood. He was sorry again but would they mind swearing on the Stone as he looked them up and down to see if they weren't traitorous. Which they did willingly enough.

'And you now,' said Alder firmly when they had finished.

Which Cwm also did, swearing his oath in a sing-song way and crying out his 'Aye!' as if it was both a curse on the grikes and a celebration of a better world to come.

'Now you listen, and listen well. I've heard your story already from others including some I met on the way this morning and who spent the night up here. Troedfach himself said I could trust you, and that's good enough for me. I'm taking you now up into Siabod and I'll warn you it's a hard journey.'

'Is it far?' asked Marram.

'Not as the eye looks on a day not cursed by cloud, no. But as the paws go, as courage goes, as faith goes, it's too far for most. We'll see, won't we? It takes five days normally but we'll have to do it in three if we're to avoid the freeze that's on its way.' He spoke in a terse quick way and eyed them appraisingly as if he doubted they had it in them to make the journey.

'We're ready!' said Alder.

'The route I'll take you on goes right through the ranks of the grikes and once I say not to talk, I mean it, see? Not a word. But that's the easy part. Later we'll be going high and it'll be cold and you'll get hungry. I don't want to know, see? You'll eat at the end – not a lot, but you'll eat.'

With that they said brief farewells to Caradoc who told them that when they needed him he would be ready, waiting either at Garmon or Caer Caradoc for however long it took.

'The Stone be with you, mole!' said Alder.

'And with you!' said Caradoc powerfully. The uncertain and timid mole they had met only days before stood

576

proud now and purposeful. Such was Alder's effect on moles he met and spoke to; such is a great leader's way.

★ ★ ★ ★ ★ ★ ★

Terse and taciturn though Cwm was, they learnt much of Siabod's recent history from him over the next three days of journeying.

The grikes had first come nearly a full cycle of seasons before, advancing up the valleys steadily. The first mistake the Siabod moles made was to ignore them completely, so they were able to entrench positions in adjacent valley systems where, apart from an occasional skirmish, they quietly got on with subverting the faith of the indigenous moles, and brutalising those few who resisted them.

It was only when a few brave vagrants appealed to Siabod for help that those moles came out of the high fastness of their tunnels and attacked the grikes. But it was piecemeal and without co-ordination and though some individual triumphs occurred, no progress was made in dislodging the aliens. Indeed, when summer came and the Siabod moles moved into their high tunnels and left their lower tunnels and the routes to the wormful valley of the Nantgwryd unattended, the grikes methodically took them over. It was this mistake which had now weakened the Siabod moles, for as winter came they had been unable to move back down to wormful soils and were stuck in the worm-poor high tunnels.

Even then the Siabod moles might have successfully fought back, for the grikes were spread thin and needed reinforcements. But once again, though the attacks were bold, they were sporadic and without co-ordination, so the moment was lost.

Cwm did not dwell on the disaffection and disarray that followed. Apart from the fact that many young, strong Siabod moles had died in the fighting, old moles died too from undernourishment, while others fled south to grimy Ffestiniog, a place of slate and gloom that saps a mole's vitality and turns him in upon himself to wither and die young.

'So the stories we heard in the south of Siabod's bold resistance were not quite true,' said Alder. 'It was more that the grikes did not then have enough moles to risk striking to the very heart of Siabod and its fabled Stones?'

Cwm agreed that it was so. The summer had given them a brief respite, for they were able to take their young to the higher ground and at least recover some of their strength.

'But now the winter's come again and the grikes are even stronger in our lower tunnels than before. Reinforcements have come and food is scarce and many moles among us feel the best course is to yield to the grikes and hope that a time may come when we can recover our pride and strength.'

'And you, Cwm, what do you feel?'

'I'll fight the bastards to the death, see, and beyond that if I have to.'

'Are there many like you?'

'Enough.'

'Who is your leader?'

'I thought Caradoc would have told you that,' said Cwm. 'His name is Glyder*. Don't you know who he is, moles?'

Alder and Marram shook their heads, and Cwm seemed surprised.

'But I thought. . . .'

'Yes?' said Alder.

'Let him tell you for himself then!'

On the third day they dropped down into the valley to their left and crossed the Nantgwryd by a twofoot bridge. Every field they saw held evidence of grike occupation, but they were not observed as they ran silently behind Cwm through the lines of the grikes. To their right the ground rose sharply and Cwm explained that the Siabod mass lay that way.

'Even if the clouds lifted you'd not see it from here because the valley side rises so steep it obscures it. The

---

*Pronounced 'Glidder'.

main Siabod tunnels start above here, but as they're occupied by grikes we'll travel west along the river and take an unfamiliar route at the north end of the main system.'

The weather was still bad, the clouds persistently low, and the wind sharp and sleet-laced. Yet once they crossed the river and started climbing they were warm enough provided they kept moving, and though the ground was wet, Cwm knew it well and found good temporary burrows for them.

'It'll get cold the moment we're clear of the valley,' said Cwm, 'so rest well tonight and eat well too, for there'll be little enough to find from here on.'

They resumed their climb at dawn to a grey landscape and a distinctly colder wind, while the sky had that chilling luminescence that heralds snow. Below them the river they had crossed snaked blackly eastward among trees. Northward the cloud was lifting and they saw, for the first time, the heights that separate Siabod from the sea. Grey with the first snows, huge flanks of rock, wind-swept moorland of a kind neither had seen before. A place that is death to mole.

Here and there a peak rose higher than the rest.

'They are the Carneddau,' said Cwm, 'unlived in by mole.'

Alder and Marram stared at those heights as the clouds drifted fast across them, revealing a sheer face here, a scree fall there and impassable ridges beyond.

'You think they're frightening? You've not seen Siabod yet!' said Cwm with a laugh, and he turned to lead them out of the valley and on to the northern slopes of the system he was willing to die for.

It was the wind that hit them first, sweeping down from the mist-driven slopes above, and then the cold. But then, beyond all that, a sense of awesome imminence, a darkness to the mist as if it was solid and hard and rising to unseen rocky heights that made a mole peer up expectantly, and then up again.

They travelled through pine woodland, the soil dead and acid, and running with freezing stained water between tussocks of grass and roots. Above their heads the trees shifted in the wind uneasily. It was a place to make a mole shiver and move on. Soon they climbed out of that and went on a way that had the woodland to their left-paw side and a rushing stream to their right. Then the trees seemed to wither and fail and they pressed on upslope over desolate moor.

'It's a wormless place for mole,' said Alder, as Marram looked about uncomfortably.

'There's food if you know where to go, and tunnels higher up, the like of which you'll not have seen before.'

'We said we'd not argue with you, and we won't. But where's this Glyder, and the other Siabod moles?'

'He'll find us, will Glyder, never you worry about that!'

Above them the mist thickened and lowered more. To their right, beyond the stream, the ground dropped away and up it came a swirling mist-filled wind. The light was grey and the brightest thing about them was the bracken, golden brown but dead.

On they went, higher and higher, the wind ever more changeable and carrying flurries of hail or hard snow, though the ground was snowless yet.

'I'm not happy with this,' muttered Marram, looking about him in the knowledge that they could be attacked from any quarter and not know it until their attacker was upon them.

'Nor am I,' said Alder, 'but we've no choice. Stay close and trust that the Stone leads us true.'

'Look!' cried out Marram suddenly, pointing a talon ahead as if he had seen something vast. 'I thought . . . it was dark, Alder, huge . . .' But it was gone, hidden by mist.

They pressed on, getting colder and more tired by the minute, but neither complained of that.

Then Cwm stopped, though why neither could have said, for there was no sign of way or tunnel or anything at all.

'The mist will clear shortly,' he said.

'Looks as if its thickening to me,' grumbled Marram. Their fur was wet with particles of mist and hail.

'You get to know the run of the mist in these parts or you die young,' said Cwm grimly. 'It'll clear northward first.' They turned to look downslope.

Then, slowly, almost imperceptibly, it did. Not near to them – the driven mist from the valley below still swirled up just below their line of sight – but far across the valley they sensed but could not see, over the mist that lay in its depths, there was a sudden lightening and then it cleared to reveal an astonishing sight.

For the sun was shining in the far distance, and lighting on the peaks that rose there, or at least on all but one that lay a little beyond them, its lower half hidden. But two nearer peaks were clear, and a third that lay off to the right, further even than the shrouded one.

'What are their names?' asked Alder.

'The furthest is still in the Carneddau, and that is Carnedd Dafydd, or Dafydd for short. The two nearer ones are Glyder Fawr on the left and Glyder Fach on the right,'

'Glyder!' repeated Alder, for that was the name of the Siabod leader.

'The one in cloud, that's . . .' began Cwm.

But he was interrupted by Marram, who had turned to look behind them and had been so awestruck by what he saw that he instinctively touched Alder's flank, as if to speak would have brought a wrath of rock down upon them.

For the mist had nearly all gone and there rose bleak Siabod, towering above them, awesome and majestic, its faces sheer and dark and quite unreachable. Cloud played at its highest part, drifting across its face and hiding from time to time its uttermost peak.

'Aye, that's Siabod,' said Cwm with reverence. They stared at it for a long time before Alder turned back to look once again at the mountains Cwm had been naming. Mist still came up from the valley but it was thinning, swirling, now deep, now light, playing on the ground before them. There were shapes in it, dark and fearsome, like sheep, like mole. None of them spoke, the wind seemed wild, beyond it all and across the valley, the four peaks rose, the same one still shrouded in mist.

Cwm was silent, staring ahead, while Marram had come closer to Alder, and both had taken stance, for the shapes in the mist were coming nearer and were moving, steadily moving upslope towards them, huge and menacing, three of them; moles.

Then the mist was swept clear and three huge moles crouched before them, two to the left side, and one off to the right, and they had taken stance as if in echo of the mountains that rose so mightily in the distance behind each of them, with a gap where that shrouded mountain rose.

Then, seeing them there, Alder knew their names.

'These are the moles who have trekked from Duncton,' said Cwm, and Alder and Marram lowered their snouts respectfully.

'My name is Dafydd,' said the largest of the moles, the one behind whom Carnedd Dafydd rose in the distance.

'Mine is Fach,' said the second deeply.

'And mine Glyder,' said the last, behind whom Glyder Fawr rose, 'and you are most welcome.' He spoke slowly, with a rich and accented voice of great authority. All three were large, all three greying of fur but very fit, all three strangely similar. Not just to each other, but, as it seemed to Alder, to another mole he knew: big, dark, authoritative, yet younger.

'You know who we are, moles, do you?' said Glyder.

Alder was lost for words. They had come up out of the mist, they were named after the mountains behind them, they seemed so familiar to him, he felt he must *know* who they were.

Then, as he stared at them he saw the clouds shifting from the single peak they had still been clinging to. Dark grey it was, and it seemed almost to rise in the air as the mist about it cleared. But of all the peaks it was the only one that held no sunshine. So darkly it rose, huge and awesome.

Glyder saw where Alder and Marram looked and half turned to look there too.

'That is Tryfan,' he said. 'Tryfan on which the Stones which the moles of Siabod were born to protect stand. Yes, moles, that is Tryfan!'

Then as Alder looked and saw where Tryfan rose, which was in that gap between great Dafydd and Fach, he knew what moles these were; he knew.

For had not Tryfan told him that when his mother came to Siabod she gave birth to a litter of pups, up on these very slopes? And that though born in the open they survived?

'You know what moles we are?' said Glyder. There was longing in his voice and a terrible faith.

'You were of Rebecca born,' said Alder. 'You are the half-brothers of Tryfan of Duncton.'

'We are,' they said.

'But the fourth, there was a fourth,' said Alder softly.

'The Stone took him,' said Fach. 'When we were young it took him. He was greater than all of us, and stronger, but he left his love in us.'

'His name?' whispered Alder.

They looked behind them at where Tryfan rose.

'Our mother named him Y Wyddfa, after the eagles that once flew here. But he died, see, and he did so saving us. Of that we'll tell you soon enough. But when we first heard of Tryfan and his deeds, and where he came from, we knew whatmole he was and what he would do. We knew he was our brother later born.'

'We knew that well enough!' said Dafydd.

'What will he do?' asked Marram.

'He will prepare moledom for the coming that will be! He will carry on his shoulders the very Silence of the Stone, as the great peak after which he is named carries the Stones we three and this system protect. But he'll need help. Nomole alone can do what he will try to do.'

'We hoped – ' And as they spoke it was not clear which was speaking for the wind was strong and their voices deep like a chorus of belief and hope across the mountains. 'We dreamed that he himself would come. But now we know he has sent another in his place, to guide us, to teach us, to show us what we must do!'

'Me?' said Alder in some alarm. It was as if the very mountains themselves were electing him their leader. Then the mountains laughed to see his discomfort.

'You!' said Glyder.

'And where are the other Siabod moles?' asked Alder smiling, for he sensed the rightness of their words, and felt the power of the Stone was all about these parts.

'We'll show you.'

With that they led them upslope some more, until they reached a tunnel as huge as any Alder and Marram had ever seen. An arched twofoot tunnel in the slate.

As the others went ahead, Alder paused at its entrance to look behind him in time to see the clouds swirl, and in the distance he saw first one peak and then the next engulfed. Then, at the last, only Tryfan stood clear, and for a moment sunlight was on it all alone. Then cloud came, and Tryfan was gone, and Alder felt bereft.

'Come on, mole!' shouted a warm voice from the tunnel. 'Siabod waits to welcome you!' Then, with a shudder at the chill winter air outside, he turned from the mist-driven day and went underground.

Chapter Thirty-Three

Tryfan's journey into the final reaches of the Wen with Spindle, Mayweed and Starling, began without them moving a paw at all as they listened to old Rowan's tale of why he waited by that foul tunnel leading eastwards, and whatmole he waited for.

'Three of us came one summer, more than four Longest Nights ago, when I was hardly more than a youngster. We were all reared in Ickenham, which lies west of where fat Corm has his den. It was a proud system once but a roaring owl way was made there by twofoots some years before we were born and the system was all but destroyed.

'That summer had been hot, and my sister Haize and I were persuaded by my friend Heath to explore eastwards. We knew the legends well enough, of moles living there and saviours and all of that, but really we went for fun not enquiry. Heath was stronger than I and more adventurous. Perhaps he just wanted companions for a day or two's exploration.

'Haize went because she liked him, I went out of loyalty because he had saved my life when a roaring owl nearly crushed me. I panicked but Heath did not, pushing me out of the way and nearly getting caught himself. He was not especially big but he had courage, a kind of *mad* courage. There are moles like that, aren't there?'

Tryfan looked around at his group and smiled, murmuring his agreement that indeed there were! Of even madder courage, perhaps.

So, the carefree youngsters had set off, and since they were not threatened by predators or twofoots, and the weather was good and food easily come by, they journeyed on, soon discovering that all the stories of the eastward dangers were exaggerated. Even better, there were some moles about who would pass the time of day and advise on how to proceed a few more miles. So the days ran on and soon they found they had been gone a full molemonth and still not turned back or seen anything *really* worth telling others about.

'We saw dangers it's true, but nothing we could not cope with,' said Rowan, his eyes warm and gentle with the memory, in contrast to the ravage of some terrible event that haunted him still, as a talon-thrust across the face may scar for life. So, though his eyes were gentle, his face was coursed by fear, and a loss to which he was not reconciled.

'As some of the tunnels were complex, Heath devised a way of talon-marking them so that at a junction we would always know which way we had come. He may have been mad but he was thorough, and those markings he made later saved my life.

'The weather had worsened and, as is the way in August, there had been rain and cloud. But we were glad of it, for the dry spell had begun to reduce the worm supply and, worse than that, the warm weather seemed to bring out a danger we had not seen until then: rats.'

When Rowan said that word for the first time, and he said it most reluctantly, he paused in his story as if to let the image from the word take shape in the burrow with them.

'Have you seen a rat?' he asked.

One by one they shook their heads. Snouted, yes. Sensed, yes. Seen, never.

'Rats and rushing water are why nomole will ever reach the centre of the Wen. Nomole!' His voice had dropped to a horrified whisper and those grim lines of care on his face seemed to deepen into ugly shadows as he spoke, and Tryfan knew that whatever event had occurred to change Rowan's life it had to do with rats, and water, and death.

Then he looked back out of the burrow where they sheltered, stared at the arch of the tunnel entrance that seemed to obsess him, then up at the sky; owls roared. Yet suddenly he smiled.

'By then I could see that my sister Haize and Heath were beginning to pair and I was reluctant to stay much longer with them. We had reached this very point where I tell you this story now, and had paused overnight by that tunnel you see there, and I did not want to go further. But Haize and Heath seemed unwilling to be alone, said I was wrong to want to leave them, and told me that we could all turn back after a few more days and head home to Ickenham. So I agreed to go on with them.' He paused again, looked at each of them, and said with a terrible seriousness, 'Let all I tell you now be a warning to you to turn back while you can. Go not one step further. Not a single one. If you enter that tunnel as we did, you enter a world not made for mole, nor made, I think, for any living creature but those whose lives lurk in darkness, and who thrive on killing and the death of others.'

Spindle shifted about uneasily; Mayweed seemed half asleep; Tryfan's stance was firm, his attention total, while Starling stared at Rowan with wide and fascinated eyes, seeming not to believe that what she was hearing, or about to hear, was real at all, and even if it was then she was certain it would never happen to her.

'Go on!' she urged and Spindle nudged her to be quiet: the events Rowan were describing was not a story but were real.

'That archway that I stare at night and day leads after a short way out into a wasteland strange to mole. The filthy river that you hear and scent continues running eastwards making the wasteland's northern boundary.'

So the moles had risked the tunnel, ventured along a ledge that runs its length, and at its end found a great open space, derelict yet alive with creatures, concreted in parts yet abundant with vegetation, surrounded by twofoot structures yet wild at its centre.

At first it had seemed wormful and good, though the pockets of soil were separated from each other by piles of unnatural red rock and poisonous sand, where only scratchy plants like knapweed grew. In some areas between these piles were puddles of water, in others rusting metaille hills and piles – mountains – of dead roaring owls.

At this information Starling let out a little gasp of surprise and horror which expressed how the others felt, for in all their imaginings of the Wen they had never thought it might be so treacherous that it could *kill* a roaring owl.

'At night there was life there, dangerous for us. The smell of fox, though we never saw one live. Dead yes – for we learnt (too late!) that the Wen kills all things – but not alive. There were voles aplenty, and weasels at the edges, and circling above by day and roosting at night black-headed seagulls, kestrel, and owls. But there was plenty of food to eat, and a mole that was cautious seemed safe enough.

'In some places the vegetation was thick and smelt sweet and good with wormwood, and having no name for the place we called it the Wormwood Waste. It was there that for the first time we came upon rats, and we realised that what we were doing was dangerous and that the further we travelled the greater the risks might become.'

The three moles had decided to stay for a time in this food-rich area before venturing to its eastern boundary where, they had agreed, they would probably turn back.

They dallied, and Rowan forgot his earlier reservations about delaying more when balmy September weather came. The days drifted by pleasantly. Then one day, when the three of them were fortunately together, they turned a corner of one of the mounds of waste rock and found themselves face to face with a rat.

'It was huge, had red eyes and it smelt. The ground about that point was greasy with its passage and I began to retch from disgust and fear. But Heath did not lose his courage, for he suddenly darted forward with a shout to us to follow and the rat snarled, flared up and then turned and left, its long tail following like a separate being after it into the two rocks between which it had squeezed and disappeared.'

The moles might have retreated rapidly but the sudden backing off of the rat gave them confidence and they heard, as they paused in the waste ground after it had gone, the sound, coming from underground it seemed, of running turbulent water. A little exploration, in which they were careful to have somewhere to flee to lest they saw more rats, and they found a narrow culvert running north east, whose banks, though once sheer and made of squared rock, was ruinous and accessible to mole. They did not venture down into it, for fear of being trapped there and meeting rats, but followed its edge, their passage being cautious and watchful and therefore slow. Suspecting that the culvert would lead them down to the original stream which had brought them into the wasteland they followed it.

Night came. The sky about them was lurid with light and noise and nearby they heard a cat take a roosting gull and then, in the night light, they saw the white feathers of the gull float by in the water draining down the culvert. Sometime later that same night they were woken by a sickening smell from the culvert, and an acrid steam seemed to rise from it and cause their eyes to stream and their throats to dry. When first light came, the water of the culvert had frothed and made foam up the banks but the smell had faded.

They travelled on, the waste ground narrowing so they were forced to go down the bank and walk alongside the filthy black water. The slimy rock of the bank rose high above them, and they seemed ever more enclosed. At one place they came upon the grease of rats, at another the rotting carcass of a blackbird, all maggoty.

'I think I knew then that the real Wen had started. It seemed to draw us on, to suck us into its filth and death as it sucked the dying life all around us into its subterranean maws. Heath became a mole obsessed, and Haize was under his spell. They wanted to go on, and grew angry with me when I tried to dissuade them from continuing. I wanted to go back but now I dared not venture back alone, and nor did I wish to leave Haize in that place. While deep inside me I was curious – curious! – about what would come next. . . .'

Food became scarce, but they scratched a few worms from beneath rocky rubble and though they were alive yet they tasted putrid.

Then they had nothing but the walls on either side of them, and the muckily flowing water joined a bigger flow and they knew they were once more beside that vile stream whose archway they had first stopped by, and that if any route would lead them directly to the heart of the Wen it would be this one.

Reluctantly, Rowan agreed to go on.

'I remember the dark chill of that tunnel closing in on us as we picked our way down on to its bed, over which the stream of water found its way. Parts were dry and we again smelt rat and felt very nervous. I do not know why we went on. We marked the wall at the tunnel entrance and from then on made our mark regularly, as high as we could, for it was clear from deposits on the wall that sometimes the water rose. The walls were soft and crumbly and took our scrivenings well.

'Light came down from the surface above through distant holes up vertical tunnels in the ceiling. We moved from shadow to shadow and though the smell of the place was sickening at first we got used to it. We heard unidentifiable sounds and slidings all around. We went on quickly, the tunnel turning sometimes, but always sloping a little down and others coming into it. We continued to mark the course lest we could not find our way back again.

'Above us on the surface night came. We found access to a ledge above the bed of the stream, which was beginning to fill with rubbish and slimy filth, and our passage became easier. Night deepened but no real darkness came for the tunnels were lit by lights from the surface. It was in this orange-yellowness that we slept. That night Haize woke me, talons to my mouth. Below us a huge shape came by, brown-black and smooth, and then

590

another. Then a third and fourth. Smooth they went and heavy, snuffling and squeaking. Rats. I could smell them in the murk. I was terrified even though the ledge we were on was too narrow and slippery for such large animals to reach us with effect. But they seemed to have scented us for they ran back and forth, snouting up towards where we crouched. Then they were gone, their shadows running darkly ahead of them. Later we heard rats fighting or mating, hard to say which. Then silence. Long silence. We moved on while it was still night, leaving marks now at every junction, but we were very hungry and resolved to get back to the surface.'

The moles found a smaller tunnel coming down into the river on its far side and scented fresh air riding on the dribble of water that came down it. They were able to cross the stream on rubbish piled in it and to climb up the tunnel.

'It led to the surface and we unexpectedly found dank grass, black sticky soil, and a shrub of a kind. All was grimy, all blighted by the Wen. The only clean thing was birdsong and that was distant. Dawn light struck walls high above us but it was a long time before the sun reached us. We saw we were entirely enclosed. There was a sparrow but no other life. More foetid worms for food, and then we rested.

'We resolved to end our journey there and return the way we had come. As we started back for the entrance to the small tunnel Heath paused on the grass. He sensed tunnels and burrowed and found one. A mole tunnel! Old, blocked by roots, barely passable, but undoubtedly made by mole. We went down it and it went straight for a time and then to a chamber. Just a tunnel and a chamber. Beyond that it was blocked by twofoot work. The other way the same. It was a fragment of a lost system.

'I wish we had not found it. It kindled Heath's interest. But since we all felt better for the rest on the surface, he insisted we continue a little way back down the twofoot tunnels, arguing that perhaps we could find more of the lost system, and even some tunnels to lead us on.' Rowan paused and fell silent.

'Story-telling Sir, Mayweed awaits your next sentence with interest and curiosity, while thinking that headstrong Heath is, or was (you have not said, but Mayweed fears the worst) a mole after his own humble heart; which is to say an explorer, a searcher, a journeyer! So, bereft Sir, speak!'

'Er, yes,' said Rowan scratching himself and puzzled at Mayweed's sudden, and excited outburst. 'We found tunnels all right and not much further down than the point from which we had been able to get to the surface. Lots of tunnels, but quite deserted, all blocked off by concrete walls built by twofoots. The structure even covered them so that these tunnels werre cut off from everything.'

'Was there light?' asked Tryfan.

'Near the entrances, there was twofoot light, but deeper inside no light, no noise. Nothing but . . . nothing but the sounds our talons made if – '

'Yes?' said Spindle.

'Pitch-black, no wind, no sound, nothing. Very old tunnels they felt, and among them a chamber whose walls were rough and yet, if a mole ran his talons down them as Heath did, and then I myself did, why there was sound: extraordinary sound.'

'Dark Sound,' muttered Spindle, remembering the scribings at the Library entrance which he had used to try to frighten Boswell and Tryfan when they had first come to Uffington.

'It was old sound, as of moles singing, deep and ancient. It was not frightening. Their song was an urging or a calling and I was never able to answer it.'

'Answer it?' said Tryfan.

'Yes, it was a calling to go on, and I knew as I heard it, and Heath sounded it again and again, that he would want to follow it. I knew that then. But that was not to be.'

Eventually, the moles went back out into the main twofoot tunnel in which the stream ran, and it was there disaster struck them. From their right three rats attacked, quite suddenly and without warning. They bore down on the three and in the confusion each seemed to run a different way. From then on all was panic and confusion for Rowan. He felt the pain of a bite as instinctively he ran back the way they had so fearfully come, and as he went he heard a mole screaming, though whether it was Heath or his sister he never found out. The rats turned from him back to that scream as a pack and he took the opportunity to flee, making his way, though wounded, back to the place on the narrow ledge on which they had rested two days before, and from where they had first observed the rats.

He reached the ledge as the rats returned and one tried to pull him back down. Somehow he climbed high, just out of its reach. There was no sign of his two companions, but several of the rats had blood around their mouths and claws as they clustered beneath him, scrabbling up the wall to get at him. They were so near he could smell their vile breath. He talon-thrust one in the eye, and he bit the paw of another. One climbed on another's back to reach him and nearly forced him off the ledge, but he was able to pull himself out of its reach.

For two days he lived in a nightmare of fear and growing weakness as the huge rats tried to reach him, replacing each other in an endless relay of snarling and claws. If it had not been for the moisture on the walls, thick, evil-tasting condensation, he might have died, for it was the only nourishment he had. Even so, lack of solid food caused him agonies of hunger until, after two days, passivity and weakness began to overtake him. Yet, somehow, he fought off the rats' attempts to take him, shuffling first this way and then that along the ledge, just out of their reach.

It was sometime in the evening of the third day, when Rowan's world seemed to have reduced itself to feeble pushes at ever more powerful thrusts from rats whose teeth and red eyes and smell was all he knew, that the rats below him suddenly fell away and hunched on the floor below, snuffling at each other and hesitant, and then rearing back on their haunches and snouting the long way up the tunnel westwards, towards the direction in which Rowan and his friends had first come. Two suddenly ran that way and then came skeltering back. Then they all turned, and without a further look at Rowan disappeared down into the subterranean depths of the Wen.

There was a period of silence, then a rush of air down the tunnel from the west, and then an ominous roaring sound and Rowan knew a flood of water was coming. Ahead of it there flowed a sickening enfeebling smell, and even as it attacked his snout and eyes he saw coming towards him a great wave or rush of water, foaming and brown, thick and turbulent, running down the tunnel as high if not higher than the ledge he was on. He had barely time to take stance and find what grip he could upon the slippery ledge before the flood was on him, at him, pulling him, noisy, violent, vile in its suffocating stench, filthy in its touch, slithy in its effect.

The air was full of the racing roaring sound of it and he felt it swirl at his haunches and paws, loosening first one and then the next, lifting him bodily, swirling him, turning him, taking him, throwing him as parts of its brown filth forced their slippy way into his mouth and snout and he felt himself drowning, turning, thrown, thump!

'I was dislodged by it, then nearly drowned by it, and finally hurled by it into some eddy that pushed me back on to the same ledge I had been pulled off, but further down the tunnel. There I clung as near death as a mole can be, until the flood eased and then stopped as quickly as it had started.

'From there I fell, weak and gasping, on to the filthy floor, water flowing round me.' He paused, looked about them with a distaste so palpable upon his face that it seemed almost that he was covered again in the muck and excrement of that filthel's flow. He shook himself with disgust, as if to be free from that memory.

'And what saved me? How did I escape? I heard then, from further down the tunnel, the same call or song that the scribings made in those lost mole tunnels we had found. I looked that way and saw, staring at me, the eyes of a rat, and then another, then a third. Red, bitter, greedy. I saw death in those moments. Yet the soundings went on and I knew it was Haize or Heath signalling they were still alive. I could not know which. Alluring was that call, most beautiful, and those rats, that had hidden in some foul place from the flood and had re-emerged to come for me once more, heard that sound too. First one, then another, then the third turned, their tails slithered in the light, their paws squelched, and they were gone.

'I turned and ran, up that long tunnel, away from that place, leaving whichever mole it was had survived to his or her fate. One by one I found those marks Heath had made and used them to guide myself out. Sometimes I heard pursuit, or thought I did. I did not stop to see but eventually came back to the Wormwood Waste, and then made my way back to here. I had no courage to return, nor have I ever found it since. So I wait here now, hoping that the Stone may forgive me, or that one day a mole will come through that archway who I abandoned long ago.'

There was silence when he had finished and though each one of his listeners sought for words to comfort him none came, for a mole must first forgive himself if he is to truly accept the forgiveness of others.

Eventually he stared at each of them and said, 'Do not venture there. It is not a place for mole and the wrath of the Stone will be upon you if you try.'

It was Mayweed who broke the silence, and by his question affirmed for all of them whatever the warnings old Rowan made they *would* venture on together.

'Stricken Sir,' said Mayweed, 'this humble mole wishes to know for his own interest and pursuit, what mark your friend Heath made upon the walls which guided you back to safety.'

'Mark?' said Rowan in an abstracted voice as if he was

still living the horrors he had described. 'Yes, yes . . . I can make it still.'

With that he reached a worn talon forward and scribed a mark on the tunnel floor into the dirt there. Long it was and curved, and looped at one end.

They stared at it and Tryfan came round to Rowan's side of it and snouted it, and then ran a talon gently along its line.

'Well, well!' he said in some surprise.

Spindle touched it and looked puzzled. Mayweed peered at it one way and then another and said, 'Humble me, Sirs and delightful Miss, has learned a little scribing, but this is just a mark is it not, educated Sirs?' Starling ran a paw over it and looked enquiringly at Tryfan. She had not learnt scribing yet but could see the mark interested Tryfan.

'Tell me Rowan, was there scribing in Ickenham?' he asked.

'I was too young to know that. But scrivening, yes. At Longest Night and Midsummer we said a prayer or two, and made some marks. I never learnt them, but I think perhaps Heath, being the mole he was, did try.'

They all looked at Tryfan, sensing there was something behind his question.

'This "mark" your friend Heath made is not just a mark, it is scribing.'

'But I don't recognise it as such!' said Spindle whose scribing by then was equal to Tryfan's own.

'This mark is ancient, as ancient perhaps as those tunnels you found and sounds you heard. It is medieval mole and is the first scribing a scribemole learnt in the old way, when he was taught by a master as I was taught by Boswell. But more than that,' whispered Tryfan, staring at Rowan's scribing as if he was seeing his own past, 'it is the mark a White Mole makes to show he has passed that way!'

'Does it *mean* anything?' asked Starling in awe.

'Oh yes, it means a very great deal. It means almost

everything. Scribing came first from ideas, and although moles make ideas complex yet all start simply enough. A mole does well to remember that! This scribing represents no more nor less than a worm, and a worm is food. In old mole this scribing represents a word, and that word is "life".

'Your friend Heath could not have found a more potent scribing to mark a way through the tunnels of the Wen. However he learnt it – for I don't think that he guessed it –and whether he knew its meaning, which I doubt, he chose a White Mole's symbol for life itself. It saved your life, Rowan, by guiding you back out of the tunnels. Let us pray to the Stone that it saved Heath or Haize's life by guiding them onwards.'

'But the rats . . .' whispered Rowan.

'Nomole can know, not yet. But when you scribed that word without knowing its meaning on this floor you gave me faith to want to go on. I think the others will come too, and that you, Rowan, will wait on here, but with faith now, and hope, for we will try to return or send you news that may free you of the horror you saw and heard, and from which you never escaped.'

'We certainly shall come!' said Spindle.

'Splendid Sirs, Miss, Mayweed is not filled with delight at the awful prospect but will go all the same.'

'Oh good!' said Starling. 'When?'

★ ★ ★ ★ ★ ★ ★

They left two days later, following the route described by Rowan across the Wormwood Waste. From there they slipped down into the tunnel he had so desperately escaped from, the four of them moving carefully as one, Mayweed in front and Tryfan behind, with Starling and Spindle close by in between.

Almost immediately Mayweed was able to find one of Heath's old marks, though a line of deposit from rising water had partly obscured it. From there they set off down into the sloping wet gloom of the filthel, so used from their summer's wanderings in such places to the strange

597

reflected lights and the echoing sounds that they were able to ignore them and concentrate on the route ahead.

They found the ledge on to which Rowan had struggled to escape the rats, and saw how precarious his position must have been. They stared round the wet walls and the arched roof above, and then along the race of the filthel's stream where it ran among the rubbish and slime, and fancied that they might have found rats anywhere. But there was none, nor scent nor sign of any, and they boldly pressed on.

The filthel's bed became so cluttered that they did as Rowan and his friends had done before them and went along the raised ledge above it. This made the journey easier and Mayweed set a steady pace, rarely needing to pause for the ledge was clear enough. Here and there the tunnel divided, and sometimes others came down into it, or orange gunge spewed out of some pipe set into the curving wall at their side. Occasionally they found another one of Heath's marks and it was strangely comforting, as if the fact that others had been that way meant they were in some way safer. Tryfan especially was struck by this, thinking that perhaps a journey seems hard if not impossible to othermole simply because it has not been made, or *been known to be made* by mole before. But once done, then others can follow with more confidence. Perhaps Alder and Marram's passage to Siabod would be the easier for knowing that Bracken and Boswell had made it safely but a few moleyears before.

Was the journey into Silence no different, then, than this? Made easier by the knowledge that others had gone before? Was that his task, and Spindle's too: to make moles see that they could make such journeys of the heart and soul if only they had faith that they could do so?

As the grim walls of the Wen's loathsome tunnels started to close on him, Tryfan began to see what a triumphant return from this journey might mean to all of moledom; that such a journey could be made and, likewise, that a struggle against the Word could be won.

'Come on!' Tryfan would call out to his companions at such moments of understanding, as if to affirm his own determination to reach the mysterious heart of the Wen, and return from it again.

Night came, at much the same place it had come to Rowan and his friends, and the hideous lights were lit on the surface above them and filtered down into the filthel. Tryfan and the others rested, one or other of them always on guard. There was no sign of life at all, but for the sound of twofoots and the roaring owls above.

Tryfan himself led them on the second day, and they eventually reached the point described by Rowan where a tunnel led out on to the surface. They ignored it, preferring to press on to find the old mole tunnels Rowan had described. Still the earlier moles' marks were evident, Heath clearly being a careful mole however 'mad' Rowan may have thought him, and these made it easy to find the old tunnels.

Mayweed went in first while the others waited outside, but it was not long before he came out again. They were not as extensive as Rowan had said they were, though they were quite as dark, but the chamber was there all right and its scribed walls. Mayweed had been disinclined to sound them, preferring to leave that to Tryfan, and anyway, there was one thing more. In that chamber, slumped beneath the scribing, was the body of a mole. Desiccated, female by its size: Haize, probably. Mayweed, was used to such things from his sojourn on the Slopeside, yet he seemed sombre from what he had found.

They deduced that she had escaped from the rats and hidden in the tunnels, that she had probably been wounded, and she had sounded out the ancient call on those walls which her brother had heard but been unable to answer. When nomole came for her then she, too wounded perhaps to move, had died in those tunnels, alone, forsaken. A chill came over the four moles, made worse by the knowledge that this must mean that Heath must have been the mole Rowan heard screaming and being killed. Each of them had hoped that one or other might have been alive, but it seemed it was not to be.

'I suppose it is possible, good Sirs and cast down Miss, that Heath escaped,' said Mayweed, ever hopeful. But Tryfan and Spindle only shook their heads and said that unless they found more marks soon they must presume he was long dead.

Tryfan and Spindle went back into the old tunnels and, briefly, sounded the walls there. It was a strange and haunting cry and students of Dark Sound have since maintained that those markings were made by Scirpus himself, though probably with the aid of Dunbar which is why they had a quality of light and goodness. Scholars agree that this fragment of system that remains may well mark the point where the dispute between Scirpus and Dunbar flared up, and that here the followers of Dunbar fled with their gentle leader eastward into the Wen. In those far off days, as the disposition of those tunnels suggests, the Wen had not yet grown to what it was later to become, and perhaps Dunbar was able to make his way eastward over the surface. Nomole can be quite certain, but as Tryfan heard that old wall sound he hoped that some good spirit of the Stone had come to the stricken mole who had died there, and brought comfort to her, and let her see the light and hear the Silence even in that dark forgotten place.

Tryfan spoke out an invocation then, and touched Haize's body, and asked for guidance for the others and himself.

A melancholy mood descended on the moles now, and a grim resolution that having started on their journey they would finish it, but be wary and careful and protective of each other. At the same time, as they journeyed on past the furthest point Rowan and his friends had reached, the tunnel itself seemed to deepen, and the surface outlets in its ceiling to rise higher so that they were but points of light far above.

It became a place of cavernous shadows and water noise,

a chill place of rushing, stirring, bubbling, dripping waters, and tunnels that came in on right and left, some dark, some with a glimmer of blue-grey light, each a little different in their scent. A place of wet reflections and glancing echoes. Yet always now the great tunnel pulled them on, ever eastward, a wind from behind seeming to encourage them though its sound and those from the Wen above made them sometimes take stance by some rubbish or concrete promontory, to gain a moment's peace.

They travelled on down this great filthel into another night and then, after a short restless sleep, on into a further day. The only sign of life they saw was dead: a cat, its black and white fur partly awash, its pale mouth gaping in rigor stiffness, its eyes gone soft and white. A predator had gnawed at its stomach, which lay clear of the water, to expose the entrails. Maggots moved there, blanched white, and it was a long time before any of them could eat, especially of the thin worms in the waste that spread into the filthel where pipes ran down from above, which was all the food they could find.

Though Mayweed snouted here and there, peering up each pipe opening they passed, or pausing to note the direction of the air currents and the feel of the scents, there was no question but that their route should follow the main filthel eastwards.

Then, quite suddenly, the filthel swung right and steepened, and there ahead of them the tunnel was barred, literally. Vertical metal bars, which ran from floor to ceiling, made a grille that stopped the rubbish dead but allowed the water to flow on through. Beyond they could hear falling water, and they were able to creep between the bars and follow the water on down.

It now flowed more clearly, over a filthel floor that was all of stone, along whose sides ran several ledges formed in the sides of the concave walls. It was an uncomfortable place for mole as there was no way of escape, and the few pipes were too high up the slippery walls for mole to reach. It was here, for the first time, they scented rat and saw their claw marks on the ledges. Distant and old though the scent was, yet it made them nervous and had them hurrying on.

It was late on that third day, when they were tired and hungry, that the great tunnel they had followed came to an end and joined three others in a chamber higher and wider than any they had ever seen. Here all sound was confusion, and waters flowed into a raging pool too turbulent for them to swim. On the far and darkest side there was another grille and into this the water flowed, or rather seemed to be sucked, hishing and rushing away into a blackness from which only roarings and rumblings came. Evidently no way for mole. Yet which way? Not up any of the four entering tunnels for they sloped to north and south or back westward the way they had come.

Mayweed snouted this way and that and eventually ventured precariously around the pool to the grille itself against which the rushing waters had thrown some debris of wood and thinbark from the other tunnels. Such rubbish kept its place simply from the pressure of the current of the water flowing over and around it.

Mayweed approached the first piece of this rubbish and, leaning his right flank on to the grille itself, put his paws out and stepped over the racing water. Then on to the next piece, and the next, the wood or thinbark he trod on sinking sometimes into the violent flow and throwing a spray upon him, and seeming to seek to clutch at him to dislodge his paws, and suck him between the bars and take him beyond recall. So he progressed, gaining in confidence until he was moving steadily, the noise great about him, and he was in the very centre of where the grille and water met, the race thundering all about him, and rusting bars rising into the gloomy arches high above.

They saw him pause then and peer down into the depths they could not see from where they crouched. A long time he stared, looking this way and that, until, with infinite care he turned back the way he had come, the debris bobbing up and down beneath his paws, and the water rushing over them.

Then he was back, shivering wet, but his eyes cheerful as ever, and that old smile, half pleading, half hopeful, on his face.

'Dry Sirs, elegant-for-now Miss, you've seen me do it, now you can do it yourselves. Mayweed confesses he was nervous, Mayweed agrees it is madness, but Mayweed's instincts tell him this will do, must do, will have to do, if we are to continue with this journey to a place unknown!'

'But is there a way on from the other side?' asked Spindle dubiously. Of them all he was the least good at balancing and heights, being one of those moles before whom even the widest ledge seemed too narrow, making his gawky paws shake, his head swim.

'Mayweed will be frank and to the point, superb Spindle, venturer extraordinary: probably! So now . . . Onward! Forward! Never backward!'

So over they went, Tryfan first, then Spindle, then Starling and finally Mayweed, and if one slipped here, and another nearly fell in there each helped another, all got wet, all found their hearts thumping and all, with a final rush and a relieved jump reached the far side of the sucking grille.

There *was* a way forward, as Mayweed had guessed from his examination of the gloomy depths beyond the grille, for high overflow pipes ran down from where they had reached to where the water raged on the far side of the grille. The pipes were small but accommodated a mole well enough except for one detail Mayweed might have guessed but did not mention: the rounded bottoms of these pipes were slimy and once a mole started down them it was hard to stop himself slithering, and once slithering it was difficult to prevent a slide, and once sliding it was utterly impossible to control it before it became a shooting, heltering, skeltering, tumbling, thumping, headlong fall along and around and down and out of that pipe, splash! Straight into a pool of water at its bottom. And splash again! And twice more before they all emerged wet, filthy, and breathless.

'Wonderful, you astonishing Sirs and dripping Miss! Mayweed salutes you all!'

They looked back up above them and saw the grille they had traversed, and the water shooting through it as a waterfall, and surging down into the pool into which, nearly but not quite, the pipe Mayweed had made them go down had fed them.

There were other pipes there too, from other places above, some gunge, some dry; of them all theirs appeared to be the slimiest, and they spent time grooming themselves clean before saying much at all.

Spindle was the grumpiest, for he liked to keep clean, and clean he was not. Yet his frown changed suddenly as he pointed a talon at the entrance to the pipe they had come down and Starling let out a delighted cry. For there, clear as daylight itself, was a mark: Heath's mark! The mark of life and of living.

'But how . . .?' asked Tryfan for all of them.

'How indeed, ruminative Sir!' said Mayweed and, with one of his old winning smiles, such as he had been more inclined to make before they left Duncton Wood than since, he pointed a talon further down the thundering tunnel to another mark upon the wall, and led them from that on down to a third.

Over the next few days the moles were able to establish that Heath had indeed survived the rat attack and, more than that, had made his way as they had done to these same tunnels. Better still, he seemed from time to time to have retraced his steps as, finding alternative routes to the ones he must initially have taken, and thinking perhaps that one day Rowan might follow him, he had marked his route twice, and on occasion thrice. It was as if he wished to make quite clear to whatever mole followed that there were good ways to go, and bad.

They were able to adduce as well that he had lived somewhere further down those tunnels for some consider-

604

able time, probably moleyears, for the markings developed from the initial single mark to something more, and it was Tryfan who surmised that the additional marks were warning signs: for rats, a kind of hooking mark; for water, a rush of lines; and for something else, though what they could not guess, a smaller mark than the others. More than that, the original mark was sometimes doubled, and the further they went it was trebled, and Tryfan believed this indicated that poor Heath, caught forever in these tunnels of the Wen, and learning to survive dangers only a few of which they had yet met, had seen three Longest Nights through at least.

It took them nearly a molemonth more to venture to the places where the worm mark trebled, which, they believed, meant they were near where Heath must have established himself and might still be. In that time their earlier training on the northern peripheries of the Wen served them well. They began to find surface exits to the tunnel, though very few permitted them to venture outside. Those ways were always finally barred – by slippery concrete slopes or vertical walls, or grilles too fine for mole to creep through, even had they wanted to.

For now they heard no sound of bird at all, and never scented grass or trees. Just roaring owls and the thumping of twofoots day and night.

Food there was of a pallid kind: worms, maggots, moths, muck-filled spiders, and scraps of such a loathsome kind that a mole had better not examine them too close if he is to eat them and not be sick.

Rats they saw from vantage points of higher pipes that Mayweed found, and they guessed they themselves were now so scented from the filthels they had passed through, and inwardly from the food they scavenged, that they emitted only a filthel smell and the rats did not notice them. Perhaps in less noisy tunnels they might have sensed the moles more easily by vibration, but one way or another they avoided them.

Yet they knew the day might come when they would have to fight, and continued to travel as a pack themselves, always ready to defend themselves, and remembering the single lesson they learnt from Rowan's account when Heath had instinctively attacked the single rat they met on the Wormwood Waste, and it had retreated.

A greater daily danger were the surges of water that came down the pipes sometimes, but these they learnt to predict and took stance on ledges above the flow. More serious, and unavoidable, were flows of hot and scalding water which none of them had seen before, filled with fuming effluent which stung their snouts and eyes. Spindle was caught by a surge of this evil water, and its heat caused his back paws to swell and pain him for several days.

The other danger was cuts, which all suffered from, and these healed only slowly, and some not at all, causing pain and ulcers and, in Tryfan's view, a general debilitation of the moles.

They might have tried to venture out on to the surface in one or two places but when they snouted up it was clear that December had set in harshly. The air was cold there now, and in one tunnel, where a grille was set in the roof high above, hail had fallen into the tunnel and formed a circle of white-grey that copied the grille's circular shape. They stared at the hail, and touched it in wonder, for it seemed white and pure, and its light brought back memories that seemed so far distant it was like puphood recalled, when they had been on the surface, among trees and grass, where birds sang and the wind blew free and scented good; a world away from this darkness they were lost in now.

Lost. It was not a word they spoke. Yet but for those marks of Heath that drew them on they might have felt so. Eastward they had travelled, and far eastward they had come, yet Tryfan's scribemole sense of the Stone's way now urged him increasingly to travel up the northern tunnels that came sometimes into the route they went down. And so they might, but that Heath's markings drew them on, as if they might find some guidance from the base he must have made. So Tryfan had Mayweed lead them eastward yet, ignoring the call that got stronger each new December day as Longest Night came near, that they should turn north.

When they finally reached the place where Heath had established himself it was both a surprise and a disappointment. The route he had marked out veered off quite suddenly to the south and took narrow squared conduits for a while, perilously close to roaring owl ways. So close indeed that the conduit reverberated with them as they passed by, and for the first time they were fumed by them, and made to feel ill and nauseous. Water and filthy slush dripped into this long run, and they were conscious of concrete all about them, above and below, and continual noise. The place was wormless and the only life was pigeons which they heard and scented nearby but never saw. Except once, when a pigeon must have sensed them near for its grey-blue beak pecked viciously at a crack above their heads as they went by; down and down it came and then was gone.

Yet they pressed on in the narrow place, pleased to be clear of water for a time, able to cope with the cold and the slush until finally suddenly, blissfully, a mark was at a point where the conduit was cracked, and they squeezed through into something they had not seen for mole-months: soil. Real soil, though compacted, sterile and cold. But Heath's tunnel was real enough and they travelled down it to where the soil was better and found food again.

They called this place Heath's Tunnels but it was clear soon enough that he was not there, nor had been for a long time. The tunnels were dusty and in places collapsed, but they were extensive, and ran under an area of short grassland which they explored in the days ahead. To breathe real air again, to feel wind of a sort, and finally to find water, a great expanse of it, was bliss indeed. It was there they spent Longest Night, recovering themselves from the long journey they had made, thankful that they had survived it, glad to rest.

They knew well that they must travel on soon, and all of them now accepted Tryfan's instinct that they must go north. But they dallied for a while. At night, when they went out on the surface, they found themselves surrounded by sights they never forgot – of lights bright and fierce, of a rising sky that was lit from below, of twofoots wandering, and always round and round and round the place they were, the roaring of roaring owls: never ever ceasing. A place of terrible and fearsome beauty, yet a place of living death for mole.

Here, as they found, Heath must have lived in lonely solitude. Here he had found sanctuary but no rest. Here he made tunnels that started good and true, and ended, as his sojourn there must have ended, strange and eccentric, maddened by his loneliness, desolate. Yet, as Mayweed discovered, the tunnels had a kind of logic, for convoluted and pointless though they seemed, they had an encircling pattern, though what lay at its centre they could not guess since no tunnels ran there, and concrete blocked all subterranean ways.

One night Tryfan and Spindle took a surface passage to this centre and found there a most strange and pathetic thing. A stone yet not a Stone. A stone of concrete. At its base a tunnel and a chamber. Here poor Heath must have come, and at its base he made a place that must have comforted him, for there was dried grass and a cache of long dead worms.

'He must have pretended this was a Stone,' said Tryfan, 'and perhaps come here to seek guidance as to what he must do.'

'Why didn't he just journey on from here?' said Spindle. 'He had done well enough, there must be many ways to continue passage. Why did he continually retrace his steps and mark the passage of the years?'

'I think, for reasons we cannot guess, he lost his courage. Something happened to him. Loneliness can do that to a mole I think.' There was about that little chamber, beneath the concrete post that a mole pretended was a Stone, a terrible desolation and a sense of trial.

'Yet he did leave,' said Spindle.

'Or was taken, or died, or simply was lost in the waters of the main tunnels.'

Yet a few days after they had celebrated their desultory Longest Night, thinking of the meeting they had arranged with Skint and Smithills that they should meet at Rollright, and ruefully understanding how impossible such a meeting would have been, they found the reason for Heath's final loss of courage. And they found it only after they had become careless because, having survived so far, they forgot the real danger they were in.

First, quite suddenly, there was dog, huge and smelling, thrusting its paws and mouth into a tunnel where Starling was, and nearly tunnelling her out. As it was she was bitten on the paw, and in great pain. Then a day or two later, when they were out on the surface at night staring at the sky, rats came. Of that grim fight Spindle has left a full account, and frightening it is. From right and left they came, suddenly, darkly, bloodily. The moles circled together and tried to burrow down: no good, the soil too hard, the nearest entrance controlled by rats. So careless! So then they fought, for their lives they fought, with Tryfan at the front and Starling at the rear, fighting as any creature fights when its life is threatened. From fear at first, and then from anger, and then from mortal fear again, as the enemy prevails and bites, and claws, and teeth and rat-red eyes fill the world, and each moment seems the last. Lurid that great sky above them was then, gashed with red it seemed, thunderous the noise those roaring owls made all about as if triumphantly knowing of the mortal fight between four moles and rats that came and went in the dark. How many rats? It might have been six, and might have been a hundred.

They survived, but only just. All bitten, Tryfan worst of all, his flank torn open and his right paw half ripped apart yet he it was who stayed out on the surface to the last when they finally reached a tunnel entrance and he pushed the others down. Yes they survived, helping each other drag themselves down those tunnels, their confidence gone, their fears made real. Not that they *had* escaped. . . .

The rats came back, circling above, listening for the moles, ripping open roofs, watching, hounding them, attacking at the slightest opportunity, never letting them rest.

So it must have been for Heath. So must he have been hunted, so must he have despaired. So Tryfan and his companions now. But worse than that, sickness struck them all, as if the rat bites were poisonous. Only Mayweed remained half well, seeming better able to withstand the poison that rats put into them.

And Tryfan was beginning to die. He knew it when, for an hour or two, he came out of the delirium he was in, yet felt life leaving him. Which, when it became plain, seemed to urge the others towards a semblance of recovery, and they fretted and worried over what to do.

Still the rats came. Digging down at them, so that the three moles had to drag Tryfan to safety, again and again, ever more desperate, as the tunnels available to them became more restricted, and all creatures on the surface seemed to know the moles were prey. Dogs came, huge and salivating, pawing the ground where they were. Herring gulls pecked. The very roofs of the fragile tunnel seemed to break about with the snarl of rat, the roar of dogs, and the pecking hiss of gull; as if the Wen itself had finally come alive in predation, and its only enemy was mole.

Then Spindle acted. Ill though he still was, he told the others that whatever the dangers he was taking Tryfan out of that once safe-seeming place. Back by the conduit Heath's marks had led them down, and then. . . .

610

'And then, Spindle Sir?' asked Mayweed.

'North!' said Spindle.

'Yes!' joined in Starling. 'Tryfan said for a long time we should go north, and now we must get him away to safety. We must!'

'But, merciful Miss, while Mayweed agrees, Mayweed wants to know where.'

There is often a moment in a mole's life when others who are close see that mole mature; as if all the strands of learning come together, and the puppish ways are spurned, and a mole takes stance and says, 'Now! Now I shall speak as I am and do my best to do what I believe!'

That moment came to Starling then, and in it Mayweed saw a beauty in her he had never seen before, and a concern which she had had once for her siblings, Lorren and Bailey, and would have still if they were there. Now Tryfan was there, only he, and he was their leader and he was stricken near to death, his wounds unhealed, the bites in his flanks inflamed, his fur grey with the fever of illness and the grime of journeying too long.

Then Starling crouched up and she said, 'We'll take him north, and if we believe enough as he did when he was well, we'll find the place we've come to find. We will! You lead us on the best route you can, Mayweed, as if all your life has been for this last part of our journey; you, Spindle, comfort Tryfan, for he loves you and knows you and trusts you; and I will do my best to guard you at the rear as Smithills taught me to. Between us we can get him out of Heath's place. And what is more . . . I think . . . I feel . . . I think I can hear something to the north, something not so far. I think the Stone listens to moles who trust it, as we must now. I think it must help them then. So now I begin to hear something of the Stone, I do Spindle, oh I do, Mayweed!' She reached out her paws to each of them, and then they all touched Tryfan, and he opened his eyes from his illness and looked at them, and they saw he was afraid.

'We are here, Tryfan, all of us, and we're taking you to

safety now,' whispered Spindle, his paws gentle on his friend. And Tryfan shook, sweating and full of nightmare, and he whispered and cried out and mumbled as they led him along those besieged tunnels. Past tooth of rat they led him, past claw of dog, past beak of vicious gull, past fuming of roaring owl, and past the endless mortal thunder of twofoot paws. Away from Heath's tunnels, through the water tunnels north of it, and then not east, on the way they had been going, nor west, back the way they had come, but striking north into older, smaller, rounded, strange tunnels, as Tryfan called out from the illness on him, called out names he knew, events he had witnessed, fears he had. For Boswell he called, for Bracken his father. For his brother Comfrey he cried, the others having to fight to lead him on through the nightmare the Wen had become for him.

Through ancient arches they went, confronting darkness and flood, beset by the steaming waters of pollution, north and north, step by step, each one helping the other on that awful way where rats lived, and brown filth crept, and caverns huge and noisome seemed to swallow them in their vastness: and Tryfan cried out all the things he had known, back and back, until he seemed a pup again, as once he was, lost in the very heart of Duncton Wood, beneath the Stone itself, lost as Boswell was, as his own parents found the very centre of the Stone and a light was on them white and beautiful. To that place he seemed to go as his body bled and his wounds suppurated.

Spindle tried to find words to still him as Tryfan cried out in terror from his dark place, 'Where are you taking me?' For he seemed to think they were taking him into the very darkness of the Wen itself.

'We're taking you to where the Stone will help you, we're taking you to the place Boswell sent you to find so long ago, we're taking you to the secret which the Wen holds true despite itself, for even in the greatest darkness there is light.'

And as the others looked at Tryfan as step by terrible

step he was helped on that infernal way, and poor Spindle wept for him, Tryfan whispered like the pup he had become, 'Then you're taking me to where the Silence will be one day, you're taking me to there.'

'Yes,' they whispered, shushing him, 'yes, yes.' And each one of them prayed that it might be so.

So those four moles dared journey to the dark heart of the Wen, where rat roams and creatures die. Ever more weakly they struggled into its most ancient parts, where even the twofoot tunnels began to die, their walls broken, their waters uncontrolled, earth seeping back to where once it had been removed.

Stricken, weak, all ill, their leader nearly dead, they travelled on until they saw no further ahead of themselves than one paw's pace. Until the day became night became day again, until waking slurred to sleep and sleep slunk into a kind of waking dream. So through darkness they went.

Not seeing the light ahead when finally it came. Nor hearing the sound that was there too. Not noticing they were watched. Not scenting other moles shadowing them now, strange creatures that peered at them from corners of the ancient tunnels they had come to, moles who whispered and conferred, ancient moles of grey-white fur and dried wrinkled skin, moles who were afraid. Moles that whispered in a language none but dying Tryfan knew.

An old language, a language only scribemoles learn, a language all but dead. Strange its sounds, but beautiful, not hard like Siabod, or soft like mole. But strong and sure, its words good, their meaning holy; their spirit of the Stone.

So, unknowing, Tryfan came into that secret heart, sealed off and protected through the centuries by the Wen. Until a mole crouched in the January light of an old tunnel to greet them, saying in a voice cracked with age, and concern: 'Quhateuer mowlitwerpe thou bee, quhateuer syknenesse thou haife, quhateuer quhateuer . . . the Stane ys hir!'

613

Then the eyes of ancient moles watched them, and saw finally they were not enemy but sick, and ill and near to death. Then one by one those strange moles came out into the light and dared to touch them.

If Tryfan's companions had not understood their first words, they certainly understood what those moles said next. For taking them out on to the surface, to a magical place, as it seemed to them then, that was above the roar of owl and the stomp of the twofoot paw those grey-white moles greeted them, touched them, and whispered that word which all moles recognise, whether it be spoken old or spoken new: Welcomyne!

Welcome! And they danced a dance of ritual welcome as stately as an old wood that has come to the very autumn of its years.

Chapter Thirty-Four

'But isn't there a healer here?'

It was Starling's voice, and she sounded angry, frustrated, and impatient, but not a single mole in that strange chamber dared look at her, mumbling to themselves instead, looking shifty, and reluctant to speak.

'Don't you realise he's dying, and all you do is talk, talk, and more talk, and say invocations and. . . .'

'Ancient and crumbling Sirs, withered Mesdames, my friend and fellow traveller the mischievous Miss is upset by Tryfan's illness and concerned, so forgive her . . .' began Mayweed, trying to placate the assembly of moles. But Starling wasn't having it, not any more.

'Well, I bet there is a healer somewhere or other if you only stopped standing on such ceremony and *realised* that Tryfan of Duncton is *dying*,' snapped Starling, for once ignoring Mayweed altogether and making even his determined smile fade. 'So *I* shall go and look if nomole else will!'

With that she stormed out of the chamber and on to the surface and rushed off down a tunnel in a generally westward direction but without having any goal in mind. She only stopped when she heard the patter of paws behind her and one of the more ancient moles breathlessly caught up with her and said, 'Cum fast awaye with me and yow to myn douchter shalle I tak. Cum, let us go thyder togyder!'

'A mole with common sense at last!' she said, and with that she allowed herself to be led away to meet what she assumed from what little she understood of what he had said must be his daughter. Which was good news to her since she had begun to think there was no such thing as a *young* mole in the whole of that place. . . .

They had been initially welcomed and looked after well enough, and for the first few days none of them had stirred from the large and comfortable burrow they were taken to while they recovered from their grim ordeal. Tryfan had been put into a separate burrow.

Tryfan was so ill that he had been put into a smaller burrow, where he would be kept warm and attended to, which had seemed the best thing to do.

How long it was since they had left Heath's Tunnels not one of them knew with certainty, but a molemonth at least had passed, probably more, and they were into January and there was snow on the surface outside.

Only when they began to recover did they learn something of the system they had come to, and it was not until Spindle was fit and well that they were really able to communicate with their hosts, for his training at the Holy Burrows made it easier for him to understand their language. Indeed, it is one of the great good chances of recent mole history that Spindle the Cleric was a member of the party that penetrated through the Wen and reached the moles who had been confined there so long. For he was able to record all that he saw and learn there before it was dispersed and gone forever*.

It is enough now to say that the moles of the system Tryfan's party discovered, or more accurately re-discovered, were the descendants of that small group of moles which had first travelled into the Wen with Dunbar himself centuries ago, following the historic schism and departure of Scirpus and Dunbar from Uffington.

Dunbar, taking the Scirpuscan revolt as the starting of a decline of the Stone in moledom, and believing that only the Stone Mole could reverse this fall from faith and peace, had resolved to preserve the old ways in a system that might not be corrupted by moles of the Word, whom he believed would one day take power in moledom. He

---

*See *On the Extraordinary Discovery and History of the Wen Moles, with an Appendix of Dunbar's Prophecies* scribed by Spindle of Seven Barrows.

established this community of moles near the very heart of the Wen, on a hill that overlooks its central wormless part. Bounded when he first came by the Wen to the south, but with open fields to the north, it had seemed as good a site as any, and better than most.

Before his death, Dunbar had made a number of prophecies of the future, which he had scribed and left as texts to be preserved by his followers.

There were twenty-one separate prophecies, but the three most significant were these: first, that the Holy Burrows of Uffington would fall into decline and the scribemoles be 'disbanded'; second, when the time was right, the Stone Mole (an ancient mole belief in its own right) would come out of the Wen and make himself known to allmole; third, for moledom to be spiritually safe for the future, it would need but one solitary mole to find the courage to hear the full Silence of the Stone. Many might strive for the Silence, and some begin to hear it, but only when one was able to know it full in his heart would all be able to reach into that great light in the Stone.

At some point early on, the vows of celibacy that many of Dunbar's moles had taken had necessarily been allowed to lapse. It may be that some of his followers were only novitiates or clerics rather than ordained scribemoles, and their natural will had prevailed. What had been intended as a male community of scribemoles evolved into a mixed system, and one in which, uniquely in moledom, *all* moles learned scribing, and indeed were required to scribe texts of their own.

By then the system had become cut off, first to the north east, then to the north and finally to the west, except for tunnels leading north to an area of wilderness called Hampstead, to which, for several centuries ensuing, Dunbar moles of both sexes went to find mates. The Dunbar moles must have been strong and fierce in those years, for they preserved their identity well, and the very high standards of order and discipline set by Dunbar himself, and the wise Rule he scribed for the good conduct of his system, were maintained for many decades.

Perhaps, too, because the system was under threat from the Wen itself and all the predatory creatures that it spews forth, the Dunbar moles were alert and their numbers kept at the right level to maintain order and belief in the Stone.

Everymole had to learn scribing, everymole had to make texts, and for two centuries an extraordinary flowering of scribing took place in that system, which all the time was becoming more isolated and unknown. Stories of its doings came out only from the Hampstead system, but as the Hampstead moles were under pressure from the growing canker of the Wen, real knowledge of the Wen moles was finally lost. Yet stories of them passed into myth and legend, which preserved only the simplest fragments of the past: that there were moles in the Wen, ancient moles, and that from among their number one good day the legendary Stone Mole would come.

So, hidden away, all but forgotten, the Dunbar moles lived out their lives, a system unique in moledom in teaching that scribing was a thing all moles could and must do.

This being so, and the Rule being strict, the language and liturgy was preserved as it had been, not evolving as a purely spoken language does by contact with different moles, different languages, and usages. It evolved, however, of itself, which was what made the language especially hard quickly to understand, even for the few moles remaining who, like Tryfan and Spindle, had some textual contact with it.

It is to the credit of the Dunbar moles that in more recent centuries there had been efforts to reach the outside world but these had failed, for no such contact is known. Whatever expeditions set off must have perished in the tunnels of the Wen.

However, more recently, perhaps less than ten generations before Tryfan's coming, an insidious and finally fatal enemy had crept upon the Dunbar system, and one they could no nothing about. Perhaps it was pollution of the Wen's water or poison in worm, perhaps some inherent problem with a population of moles into which new blood was no longer coming: whatever the cause, fertility decreased. Not only did the total number of litters decline, but the number of pups in each litter fell and gradually the population began to age so that the few youngsters who were reared found themselves surrounded by older and often bitter pupless males and females. Strange and sterile attitudes developed which increased the population decline. The Rule was made suddenly stricter so that youngsters were forced to pair with the oldest moles, while jealousies of the few successful pairs became rife. Inevitably internecine feuds developed and a period of shocking violence ensued in which, most dreadfully, the youngsters were pitched against the numerous old and many died.

The system of Dunbar, a system of which its great founder had predicted that one distant day from out of it the Stone Mole would come, had begun to kill itself.

Somehow peace came to the broken system, but then a worse trouble came: plague. The same plagues that had beset the rest of moledom somehow reached the Wen moles. Nomole knows how. Tragically it took more of the younger moles than the old, and left a system desolate and sad and without the possibility of recovery.

But what of its faith in the Stone, and what of its worship? The system had no Stone, only memories passed down by generations. It had a place of worship though, a high point on the hill beneath which the system's pride and glory lay close guarded: its Library.

There the texts of the Wen moles were kept, a Library quite different from Uffington's for it preserved texts known in no other system, and on subjects never known to mole before. For there, hidden, almost lost, seemingly without hope of preservation, was the work of centuries, work which marked the birth, and the flowering, the glory and the great delight, the decline and the sadness: works

619

of spring, of summer and of autumn, great works in forms never developed at the Holy Burrows where scribemoles were secretive and overly religious, and few ever scribed for the pleasure of it. Texts of poetry, of stories, of philosophy, of imagination and even of natural history, for the Wen moles were the first to scribe of the twofoots, and one courageous Wen mole even made a study of roaring owls.

On the surface above the Library where these unique texts were kept, for centuries past, the rituals had been spoken by moles taught to face to the distant west where, as their founding brothers had told them the Holy Burrows of fabled Uffington lay. That way, too, the great Stones of the seven Ancient Systems rose: of Avebury, of Uffington, of Caer Caradoc and of Siabod; of Rollright, of Fyfield and nearest of all, of Duncton Wood. These names, in their ancient forms, were preserved and spoken, and the rituals had engendered a great longing in that system to know those Stones. With that longing went the belief that, one day, the Wen moles would find a leader able to take them back to the good place from which they had first come. That leader might perhaps be the Stone Mole himself, or rise up when the Stone Mole had come.

When Tryfan and his companions arrived the system was but a shadow of its former self. Whole sections had been abandoned and such few moles as survived lived in burrows and tunnels far too extensive for them, as lost and bereft as the last few leaves that cling here and there to the branches of an empty beech tree through the cold months of winter. But in that, the system was no different from many of the plague-desolated systems moles such as Spindle and Tryfan had already seen.

By the time Tryfan and his companions came to the Wen, the final death of the Dunbar moles had almost come. One fecund female alone remained, and she the youngest of all the moles remaining. There were other females it is true, but they were dried and bitter pupless hags, jealous of the younger one, the more so because she

620

herself was the single offspring of the last successful Wen pairing, that between Leine and Paston, the old male who had followed Starling from the chamber and persuaded her to come and meet his 'douchter'.

Bitter the feuds between the ancient males who ogled his 'douchter's' flanks and fur as she matured; bitterness mixed with longing, for few of them had ever mated, perhaps few of them could. But even if they could, were they fertile? Whatmole would know? But that poor young female had had to choose a mate among that aged rabble of bitter males and finally had gone to the Library Hill, and did what she had been taught to do, which was to pray to the Stone and seek guidance.

After which she declared that that guidance said 'wait' and no male mole was bold enough to come forward and insist she abide by the new Rule and choose one of them.

But wait for what? Wait for a lifetime? Wait for a miracle perhaps.

Two seasons she waited, hoping, despairing, and only her father, Paston, to protect her and talk to her. The males wouldn't. The females chose not to. All hated her. Two seasons of waiting with the burden of that system's future on her. Waiting. . . .

It was into this lost and hopeless system that Tryfan's group came, not knowing its history, nor understanding why the aged moles there soon eyed them as they did. Nor why young Starling was touched and harried by grey, aged paws, or why, even before they had recovered, ancient crabbed females smiled and fawned like youngsters over the recovering bodies of bemused and astonished Mayweed, and embarrassed Spindle. Pairing? How could that have crossed their tired minds and beset bodies? As for Tryfan, he was, virtually, ignored. Anymole could see he was dying, nomole had time for him when there were better opportunities to feud for.

So in the days following their arrival, far from showing any genuine interest in the four moles who had arrived, or in moledom beyond the Wen, Dunbar's system had become so closed and inward-looking that all the tunnels hummed with was talk and gossip of who the newcomers might like, and lies and intrigue, until finally Mayweed and Starling had to stand their ground to give Spindle peace to tend as best he could to Tryfan. He, now, was rarely conscious, but lay rank with illness and festering wounds, unable even to move. But by him poor Spindle stayed night and day, watching over him, cleaning him, and asking again and again for herbs or a healer or *help*. Anything but the rabble of old desperate moles trying to paw himself, Mayweed and Starling and offering their crabbed and nauseous favours.

Perhaps by then Spindle had learnt enough to have guessed the truth of the Dunbar moles, for he was able to exercise his knowledge of the rituals of the old systems to summon a council of moles in the chamber adjacent to the Library, invoking some spurious rule or other he made up, with the express purpose of asking them to stop their squabbling and appoint somemole with a knowledge of the surface who could find herbs to heal Tryfan. For without them he would soon be dead.

So, charging Mayweed and Starling with this task of persuasion, for he did not wish to leave Tryfan alone, he had left them to it. But the council had merely talked and talked, suggesting nothing. It was then that Starling had finally lost her temper and stormed off, to be followed by Paston.

She was doubtful of his intentions but, being Starling, and strong, and fed up, and (most of all) willing to try anything to find help for Tryfan, she had gone along with him.

He took her downslope westward, by surface and by tunnel, but having only established that it was his daughter Starling was to meet she had no idea what to expect. Only that she must be old, because he was *decrepit*, but she might be nice.

So on they went, until they reached a humble entrance to a humble tunnel and went down it. Paston called ahead, to warn his daughter of their approach, and then, indicating to Starling to stay where she was, he entered a chamber. Starling noted that the tunnels smelt good and sweet and were dry, simple, and new-made. This female, she decided, must be a mole after her own heart.

Then Paston came out again, ushered Starling forward, and smiling with a touching pride brought her into a chamber where a sweet-looking, gentle-seeming female waited, somewhat apprehensively.

'Myne douchter Feverfew,' he said.

Starling grinned and said a loud, 'Hello!'

Feverfew stared and did not seem to know what to say. To Starling's surprise she *was* quite young looking, and had good fur and a sensible way about her. Her gaze was shy but her eyes intelligent and direct when she had summoned up courage to look at a mole, and she looked fit, as if, unlike the other moles in the system, she spent time in the tunnels and on the surface exploring and keeping herself occupied. She even had some texts in one tidy corner of the burrow and there was evidence of further scribing. A scribemoless!

Starling, a little intimidated by this, said, 'Er, glad to meet you. My name's Starling. Can you understand me?'

Beside Feverfew, Starling felt large and cumbersome, and far too full of good cheer. But she also felt heartily relieved because for the first time in a very long time she was with a female like herself, even if she was older. The others in the system were so old that Starling barely counted them as females at all.

There was a long silence while Feverfew seemed to gather herself together to make a speech, which, finally she did.

'Starling, I recomande me to yow and am in no perell of deth, blessed be the Stane.'

Starling took all this in slowly, but when she had she said, 'Well, that's a relief, I'm glad you're not going to die. Did you think you were then?'

Feverfew shook her head vigorously, looked at her

623

father, nodded, looked at her father again, and said nothing. An uncomfortable silence ensued in which Starling decided this was no time for males to be about. She had to talk frankly to this Feverfew and get her *moving*.

'Look,' said Starling, 'two's company, three's a crowd . . .' She turned to Paston and politely made it clear it would be better if he left, for the time being. No harm would befall his beloved daughter, none at all. Starling smiled at him, a charming and winning smile. This overwhelmed him and he made a long speech full of 'reverents', 'besechementes' and 'hertys desyres' at the end of which Starling shooed him away.

She then turned back to Feverfew who, meanwhile, had relaxed considerably and was smiling shyly. She seemed about to ask a question but instead suddenly darted a paw forward and touched Starling's fur.

'Yonge, soothe and lustie!' she sang, continuing with a song of very good cheer.

'That's very nice,' said Starling, quickly coming to the conclusion that she was going to like Feverfew very much indeed.

Starling settled herself comfortably, realising that this was going to take some time, and she said, slowly and clearly, 'I am very happy to meet you.'

Then, when Feverfew did not understand this, she repeated it, indicating herself for 'I', giggling to indicate the 'happy' and finally touching Feverfew to indicate the 'you'. It took time but when Feverfew at last understood what Starling was so patiently trying to get across she said something similar in old mole, waited for Starling to repeat what she had said, and then, quite unexpectedly her eyes filled with tears and she wept as a mole who had waited for years to weep; but as much with relief and discovery that another mole could like her, as with sadness that for so many years nomole had really done so.

So the two chattered on, learning to understand each other, and discovering the joy, pure and unalloyed, of talking to another female in a world of ailing, dithering or too-familiar males.

When, much later, Starling was able to explain that there was a mole in the system called Tryfan and he needed help and herbs and healing, Feverfew smiled and said in a quiet and gentle way that she would come now, and do what she could.

'Hys nam?' she asked.

'Tryfan,' said Starling.

'Ys hee comely?' asked Feverfew shyly.

'Yes!' said Starling, astonished and laughing, yes Tryfan was! It had not occurred to her for one moment that Tryfan might be the object of any female's interest, but now she came to think of it . . . And with that they both laughed, and passed out of the burrow and ran up to the surface without a word of explanation to Paston who had waited so long and with much puzzlement at the sound of laughter and talk, which, even if he had understood it he would never, however old and wise he became, have *understood* it.

When they reached the burrow where Tryfan had been put they found him now so weak that though his mouth was open his breath hardly seemed to come at all. 'Comely' he may once have been, but not anymore. His right side was swollen and suppurating, and dirty yellow pus leaked from it and congealed on his fur. His flank wounds were an ominous white and grey where the flesh seemed to have began to rot, and smelt of death. His delirium of the journey there had gone now, and he lay still, his eyes half closed. Sometimes he whispered, or tried to, but the words were unintelligible.

Spindle rarely left him, cleaning him as he could, and offering him food which lately he had not touched. Spindle was utterly distressed, trying his best to be calm when he was with Tryfan, but when he allowed himself to be relieved by Mayweed or Starling from that duty, he was restless and unable to sleep or even listen to what another said.

The older moles who plagued him he now utterly ignored, and nomole could comfort him. His friend was dying, and he, Spindle of Seven Barrows, who had been charged by Boswell himself to watch over Tryfan's wellbeing, felt he had failed. His last hope had been that a meeting of these wretched squabbly medieval moles would produce somemole to help, *anymole*; but all Mayweed had come back to tell him was that Starling had shouted at them and gone off by herself looking for a 'healer'. Too much to hope for such a thing *here*.

Now he was up on the surface, Mayweed having relieved him, and was looking this way and that wishing he knew what to do or what to say. It was there that Starling found him, exhausted and muttering to himself in a distressed way, and said firmly, 'Spindle, I want you to say hello to this mole and be very nice to her as she is extremely shy.'

'Not another one come to . . .' Spindle began, until, looking up, he saw Feverfew before him. He stopped his protest: she was younger than the others at least, that was something, and, what was more, she looked intelligent.

'But is she a healer?' he asked.

'I really don't know,' said Starling a little defensively. 'She knows about herbs and I expect if you're nice to her and encourage her she'll do her best.'

Feverfew looked at each of them in turn, not quite sure what they were saying. Spindle managed a weak smile and said rather brusquely, 'Well, thank you. Um, hello! Better come along then, see what you can do.'

'As I am of the blessid Stane, so wyll I doo for youer welbiloved Tryfan,' she said quietly, laying a paw on his and staring into his eyes.

'Well now,' said Spindle, suddenly rather shy, for the only female that had ever touched him closely apart from Thyme was Starling, and *she* was more or less a daughter to them all! But *this* mole's touch, why, there was something almost too direct and intimate about it for Spindle's comfort.

'Er, thank you,' he said again. Then, suddenly feeling better than he had for days, he added unnecessarily, 'Yes! Yes! Good! Let's go then!'

They brought Feverfew down to Tryfan's burrow and she went into its smelly interior without flinching, and was briefly introduced to Mayweed. All she did at first was to indicate to the others to stay back while she examined him.

She crouched down and stared at him, making no sound but for a quite audible and sympathetic sigh and then, as she circled him, snouting closer here and there, she whispered occasionally to herself, and made more sighs, some medieval equivalents of 'Oh!' and 'You poor thing!' and then, as her examination went on she concluded with, 'This is terrible' and finally, 'This will not do!'

Mayweed looked around at the others and nodded vigorously as if to say, 'Spindle Sir and Magical Miss, this mole is impressing me, Mayweed, your humble friend, already! She is!'

Then Feverfew went closer still and, laying a paw on Tryfan's flank, whispered the following gentle prayer:

> Dere Mowlitwerpe
> Wee are nere thee.
> For laik of Symmer with his flouris
> For wintere's nycht with haill and schouris
> Your herte semes dirk and drublie
> Dere Tryfan mowle
> Hav curage now
> Listen! Lyf ys gude
> And thou art welbiloved and frended
> And we to heill are cum to thee.

Perhaps Tryfan stirred at the sound of her lovely voice, perhaps he did not. Certainly story-tellers now, recounting this moment of first meeting between Tryfan of Duncton and Feverfew, a mole who would change his life, and that of all moledom's in time, naturally like to report that Tryfan stirred, and opened his eyes and saw

627

that mole so near to him. Some versions even go so far as to suggest that he spoke to her.

Spindle's account is less romantic than that, but probably the nearest of all to the truth, and it records simply that Feverfew turned from where Tryfan lay with an energy and purpose about her that she had not seemed to have had before, as if the very weakness of Tryfan then was her ensuing strength.

'Conne yew to holpyn hym to heele?' asked Spindle, hoping his attempt at old mole would make sense to Feverfew.

She smiled at his words, and said, 'I know nat yet, but trust hym by the blessid Stane's grace to be clene hole of hys hurttys by sevennyght, by wyche tym we maye truste to have gud tydyngys.'

But now we begin to do as Spindle did and record her speech in mole.

She examined Tryfan further and decreed that he must be moved, and soon, to a place where he would have a better chance of recovery.

'He's too ill to move,' said Spindle.

'The Stone wyl ministere yts beste wen mowlitwerpe ys putte best whay,' said Feverfew.

'Er, which way should an ill mole face?' asked Spindle.

'For word of pawe or word of flanke be weste. For hertis peyne to rysyng sone.'

'Well,' said Spindle doubtfully.

'Stop being so fussy and *old*,' said Starling irritably, 'you're getting as bad as the other moles in this system. It's perfectly obvious that Feverfew knows what she's talking about and the sooner we do exactly what she says the better in my opinion. Don't you agree, Mayweed?'

'Marvellous amazing Miss . . .' began Mayweed.

'Yes or no?' said Starling, cutting him short.

'Yes,' said Mayweed, with enormous difficulty. 'Definitely so.'

'Where shall we move him then?'

'To burowe myn,' said Feverfew, with just a touch of shyness.

Which they did, much to the amazement of the other moles, almost carrying Tryfan through the system and down to the west side of the hill, putting Tryfan in Feverfew's warm and sweet-scented burrow where, gently, she began tending to him, making him lie west-facing, and getting the others to help him to the surface at night, to snout weakly to the west where the great Stones lay, the nearest of which was Duncton Wood.

Lurid the great sky of the Wen, distant the roaring of the owls, muffled the pounding of the twofoots: but sometimes in those clear, cold days of that January when Tryfan lay so near to death, it seemed the moon was so strong that it overcame the lights of the Wen, and made a far-off horizon clear, where a hill rose to a high wood, as if to bring the Stone that stood in the high wood a little nearer. Slowly Tryfan of Duncton settled, and his crisis passed, his pain eased, and there came about him a peace and quietness that comes to a mole who hears something distant which he has waited to hear all his life but has needed another to show him.

So Tryfan began to hear the sound of Silence, and to make a journey through his illness which was harder by far than that long journey which started, so long before, at Uffington. And at his side was a mole he did not know, but whose sweet voice he could sometimes hear out of the chaos about him, and whose touch he could sometimes feel so tender among the pain that was his body; and whose spirit he could sometimes sense was like his own: uncertain and troubled and as yet unfulfilled, but holding on, even in the darkest hour, to its love for the Stone.

* * * * * * *

Tryfan's illness lasted much longer than a 'sevennyght', for January passed and February was nearly done before days began to come when he was fully conscious and beginning to feel at last what it might be to be well once more. He was weak, and nightmares came, and often still he wept, as he had through the worst part of his illness, and images of the past came before him which he thought were real.

He did not speak but to himself, but consciousness must have come because he knew when Feverfew was near and protested weakly when she went away, even for a moment, and gentled into sleep at her touch. So Feverfew stayed near, caring for him, while Spindle was close by, watching over them both and beginning to see that, as he had had his Thyme, and known love forevermore through her, so now Tryfan was beginning to know that love two moles can have if only they will let each other to each other's heart. And Spindle snouted west and thanked the Stone that it had brought Feverfew to Tryfan.

It is clear from Spindle's chronicle that he felt no jealousy of Feverfew as other moles in his position might. He saw only that she gave something to Tryfan no other mole could give, and he understood, better even than Feverfew herself, for he knew Tryfan better, that the agony of body and spirit that Tryfan suffered in those long molemonths were the accumulation of so much that had come from his past.

For in his agonies he had cried out of things that went back to the very beginning of his life, of moments when he endangered his life protecting his siblings, of a time when he grew apart from Bracken and Rebecca and lived alone across the Pastures near Duncton Wood, of those long years when alone he protected Boswell on his journey to Uffington. Years when others saw him as a strong mole, but when he had to deny himself so that other lives were safe.

Then, too, was the distress Spindle now found Tryfan had felt so deeply for the moles who suffered and died in Buckland's Slopeside. And the horror of the escape from Duncton Wood for which he took the blame. Then the final blow that broke him, which was the belief that, having persuaded Spindle and the others to accompany him into the Wen, they would die by the claws and teeth of rats.

By the side of all this was Tryfan's doubt of his worthiness before the Stone, and the terrible loneliness any leader feels and which he had suffered all those years, for a mole needs a mate, and the whole love a mate gives.

Perhaps, too, Tryfan of Duncton needed peace from responsibility, and time to meditate and scribe as his training had prepared him to. So now his illness enforced stillness, and through that stillness he journeyed, not alone in body for his friends were there, but in spirit Spindle knew he was alone, a solitary mole on a way of nightmare agony reaching through illness and pain for some understanding of how a mole might hear Silence.

When those better days came, at the end of February, Tryfan said few words, but would stare out of the westward entrance Feverfew insisted he was placed near, his eyes softer now, his face thinner and older, his nature softer than it had been, as if he understood better other moles' suffering.

One dusktime he turned to Feverfew in that burrow of recovery and said, 'Thy name is Feverfew?'

'Yt ys,' she whispered in reply, 'and you are Tryfan mowle.' It seemed to each of them that they were coming out of a long time in which they had dreamed of the other, and now were meeting in reality at last.

'I want to go to the surface,' he said.

Then, slowly, painfully, he hauled himself what seemed a long way to the surface as she helped him along. When they reached a point that seemed to satisfy him he snouted to the west, where the sun was setting, as to the south, their left, the lights of the Wen were beginning to come on.

But it was the west he wanted to show her and looking at the dying sky Tryfan said, 'Duncton Wood is there, Feverfew, a long way away. I come from there.'

'I ken yt wel,' she said. 'Yte yow hav jorneyied longe and fer fro ther.'

'I want to tell you of it.'

'Then tell me,' she whispered, her flank to his as the first star shone in the eastern sky.

631

'I shall,' he said in the old way, 'from my heart to your heart I shall tell you, of a system that lost its way as moledom lost its way, and of how the Stone did not forsake it, and of a few moles who dreamed of finding Silence, and helping allmole hear its sound.'

'And when you have done that,' said Feverfew, 'I shall tell you from my heart to your heart of how Dunbar has told us that the Stone Mole will come, of how he will help allmole hear that sound of Silence, and of a mole, humble and unknown, who shall be the first to know the full Silence of the Stone and show what all moles may know if they choose.'

Then, to each other, touching each other, those two moles spoke, while the sun set in preparation for a better day, and the stars turned in the night sky far above them towards their great destiny, and that of moledom's too.

Chapter Thirty-Five

It was soon clear to the rest of the moles in the Wen system, as it had been to Spindle from the first, that Tryfan and Feverfew would make a pair and, if the Stone ordained it, would have young. Nor was Spindle surprised when their quiet and almost secret union seemed to have a calming effect on the others there.

Or perhaps it was just that as matings go it was late, and the months of January and February, when mate-questing moles are irritable and easily hurt, had passed, and the other moles had better things to do now that the first signs of spring were showing, than continue their feuds when the fight was so clearly lost.

For Mayweed and Spindle had both made their desire for singleness well known, while Starling, who seemed ever stronger and more full of life with each passing day, so terrified the craven males of Wen that, with the exception of Paston, who treated her as a father, none dared talk to her.

So Tryfan and Feverfew paired, and the system seemed content that it should be so, and that they should have privacy as the excitement of spring took over. For exciting it was, and is, and evermore will be, to even the oldest-seeming mole, or the most insensitive. That first touch of spring sunlight in the dew, that first fresh burst of birdsong in the bush, that always unexpected green of fresh young growth, so long absent but then suddenly returned once more, new and eager. All the more poignant at a system hemmed in by roaring owls ways, concrete structures, twofoot ways and underlain by tunnels, filthy in places and sterile in others.

But already the moles had seen spring underground in the shooting of the white roots of primroses and lady's smock, and the slow turn of waking grubs, while on the surface the first white flowers of snowdrops and purple of crocus came, and the fresh beauty of yellow celandine. Warmer air too, and better light, among which all, slowly at first and then with growing strength, Tryfan went, and Feverfew, talking as moles discovering love *will* talk, of everything and nothing, from day to deepest night.

If Spindle had feared that Tryfan would fight the obvious love he felt, pleading a vow of celibacy, racking his heart from some false sense of honour to a dead scribemole code, he need not have. Tryfan was changed in body as well as mind, and peaceful. He was thinner now, and here and there his fur was grey. But his look was strong and powerful, and about his eyes was a purpose and certainty that had not been there before. His heart had known pain, and lived through it, and his eyes looked at the world with a new simplicity. But though Tryfan's wounds had healed he remained scarred on both paw and flanks so that when the sun caught his sides he looked older. Indeed the scars fell in such a way that he looked as if he was about to spring forward. But close to, a mole could see that the scars ran deep and the skin was bare where the fur had not grown back.

He contrasted with Feverfew who, it happened, was the same age as he. She frowned a little, as if she had been at her texts too long, but when she looked up her face softened and her eyes were warm, and she moved with that same grace and youth Tryfan had once had, but which he had lost in the course of journeying and illness.

Together they seemed one, and quite formidable, as if they were not just a pair together but a whole belief, a whole purpose, and one that could not be forsworn. Never was the union of two moles more clearly of the Stone. Their faith was shared, and their journey each day up to the top of the hill to face west and pray gently re-established the habit of worship on many of the Wen moles.

The strange thing was that neither Tryfan nor Feverfew

seemed aware of the effect they had or that their simplicity in each other, and sense of a shared life that was like a shared smile, brought tears to the eyes of Spindle and Mayweed, and even, as time went on, to some of the more accepting of the Wen moles.

Yet, there was a dark side to the system's response to them, for jealousy was still there, and now there was fear too, for the faith Tryfan had was not routine but daily felt, and the words he used were mole not old mole, and offensive to some ears. Such darker feelings need but an excuse to harden and find expression, and where malevolence exists such excuses are quickly found. But not quite yet. Tryfan and Feverfew had peace to love each other for a while.

But what of Starling? From the moment that it became obvious that Feverfew and Tryfan would pair she, most uncharacteristically, became morose, and uncompanionable. The old females understood well enough, and smiled malevolently to themselves, and slyly too, for they knew how such a female might feel in such a system at such a time. But the males did not, least of all Spindle and Mayweed, who never saw Starling *that* way. So while they took it into their heads to study the contents of the Wen Library, and began to record the histories of the Wen moles much as they had taken data down of the refugees in Duncton Wood, Starling took herself off to the eastside and busied herself making a burrow and tunnels in the Duncton Style: plain, serviceable, and solid.

'We wot nat what the wynche wrocht, nor wherefore!' the old females whispered giving each other meaningful glances, for it looked as if Starling was preparing to mate. But with whom?

One day, when the March sun shone strong, Spindle came over to Starling's new burrows and, with much humming and haaing, told her the good news (as it seemed to him) that Feverfew was with pup. How bright was Starling's reception to this, how overly cheerful her smiles of pleasure at the news, and how good-natured the message she gave Spindle to take back to them. But when he left her burrows he remained puzzled in his clerical way as to why she seemed irritable beyond belief and she had not offered him a single worm in all the time he had been there.

Irritable was an understatement. Furious was more like it: that fury a mole uncharitably feels when another has got what she wants *and can't be blamed for it*! For a day and a half Starling stomped about her tunnels and burrow very angrily indeed. At the end of that time she decided to tell the Stone what she thought of it.

'Look,' she said, taking stance in quite the wrong direction since she was facing towards the Wen, but then what she had to say was so *severe* that whichever way she faced the Stone would hear her. 'I am not a pleased mole. First you make me look after Lorren. Then you foist Bailey on to me, and did I complain? No, I did not! I looked after them until you took them from me (and you'll have a great deal to answer for if they don't turn up again in one piece). As if that wasn't enough, you make me come all this way through quite horrible tunnels, with smelly old rats in them, until I end up in this really awful place with no males around at all. I mean you can't seriously expect me to be thinking of Spindle or Mayweed because if you are that will be the final straw. No, even you couldn't be so idiotic. So what I want you to do is to find me a male who's bigger than me, not decrepit, can speak normal mole, and is capable of fathering the pups that I intend to have *very soon*. Now kindly get on with it as fast as you can as time is running out and you haven't seen me *really* furious yet.'

Having made this clear statement to the Stone, Starling went off and found a lot of food and, basking in the springtime sun and feeling very much better than before, she had a feast all by herself. Then she touched up her burrows a bit and had a good sleep.

The following morning, bright and early, she gave

herself a final groom so that her already full and glossy fur had an extra shine to it, and her talons, never the most delicate, at least looked sparkly clean.

With that she went out on to the surface and said to the Stone, 'Right, I am now ready, please do your bit.'

A day passed, and then two. Starling was studiedly calm. A third day passed. Starling became irritable. A fourth day passed, Starling felt depressed, and wept briefly in renewed rage and frustration. A fifth day came and the sun shone bright and Starling sighed and spent the day resigning herself to puplessness.

That evening Mayweed came visiting.

'Go away,' she said.

The following morning Spindle turned up.

'I hate you all,' said Starling. 'Please leave me alone forever.'

'Er, yes, fine,' said Spindle.

Starling suddenly and unaccountably felt hopeful. She cleaned her talons once more, re-groomed her fur, and sallied forth. Lady's smock were beginning to flower, and some daffodils had bloomed and now caught the sun, but she did not notice them. A peculiar and terrifying purposefulness had come over her. She snouted ahead with as much focussed determination as a fox stalking prey. She seemed to sense something about.

'Male,' she muttered. 'Or sort of male.'

She heard noises in the grass ahead and crouched down into an indifferent and nonchalant stance. She affected not to notice the world about her at all, whereas in fact nomole in the whole of history has ever been so acutely aware of the world about her as Starling was then, in particular of the snuffly sound of an innocent and unaware male enjoying a solitary meal on a fine spring morning, and humming to himself.

Very definitely male, she decided, quietly uncrouching and advancing towards the sound ahead with a heart that suddenly beat twice as fast as usual, but with paws that stayed steady.

637

'Well!' she declared to herself at what she saw as she rounded a corner on the hill, with the Wen stretched out below. Well!

There, in the sun, eating a worm, and definitely male, was a mole. But what a mole! He was not the obvious answer to a female's prayer. He certainly was not young, and he certainly was not large, and he certainly did not have glossy fur or especially clean talons. He was . . . wild. Unkempt, in fact, with fur that seemed to go this way and that in a ragged cheerful way, and a line to his limbs that was easy and muscular, and unconcerned with trivia. A travelling sort of mole who was content with his own company. He ate slowly and with relish, stared out over the Wen thoughtfully as he hummed, ate, and hummed again.

'Hello!' said Starling, suddenly very nervous indeed.

The mole's reaction was total. He dropped the last of the worm, spun round, backed off, took stance with wide eyes and an astonished look on his otherwise cheerful face.

'Stone the crows!' he said. 'You gave me a fright. Don't ever do that again!'

'Sorry,' said Starling with unaccustomed meekness.

'So you should be,' said the mole, and then more calmly, 'so you should be. Dear me! Phew! Gave me a shock that did!' Then he settled down and looked at her.

'You're not very young,' said Starling.

The mole said nothing.

'You're really very ungroomed,' she continued.

The mole retrieved his food in an unconcerned way and stared at her.

'In fact you're a bit of a disappointment,' said Starling.

'Do you know what you are?' said the mole.

'No,' said Starling, preening herself as if some male mole was better than none.

'You're a pain in the arse,' said the mole.

There was a very long silence indeed during which Starling attempted to resolve (but failed to) one of the many paradoxes in mole relationships, namely that when a

638

male mole is direct and seems to be rude but speaks the truth, the female who is the object of his attentions finds him infinitely more attractive.

So Starling then.

'Oh!' was all she could say. 'That's a vile thing to say!'

'Yes, it probably is, but it's not very nice to be told you look like a rat's dinner by a mole you've never met before. It's even worse when the mole concerned is the first mole you've met for so long that you can hardly remember the last time.'

'I know who you are, you're Heath!' said Starling. 'The Stone saved you because of me! That's fantastically romantic, even if you are old.'

'Wait a minute,' said Heath, unaccountably warming to this female who, the more he looked at and listened to her the more he liked her. 'How did you know my name, and anyway what are you doing here?'

'I bet you'd like to know!' said Starling giggling.

'Yes I would as a matter of fact.'

Then Starling, as if not quite believing her good luck, looked earnest and serious and said, 'But friends of mine called Tryfan and Spindle said you had probably gone mad or something because. . . .'

Starling hesitated because Heath was frowning and muttering to himself, 'Mad? *She's* the one who's mad. I don't *need* this!' and beginning to look as if he might wander off.

But Starling was a persistent mole.

'*They* said your tunnels went sort of funny and wandery and you must have well, sort of gone *strange*, you know, being alone so long.'

Heath grinned in a doltish way.

'Do I look strange?'

'Yes,' said Starling, 'very. But I don't mind.'

'As a matter of fact your friends Trindle and Spiffan were right in a way but when a mole's chased by rats for months on end, lost in horrible tunnels, short of water, and has no company for moleyears what do you expect?

However, one day, soon after I left the tunnels you saw, I decided enough was enough. Bugger the rats, I said. Bugger the tunnels. I shall now take a more calm and philosophical view of life. Heath will become happy. So, I crouched down quietly until all my problems seemed to go away, then when they had I moved on and soon after that I arrived here. Naturally when I saw other moles were about I steered well clear of *them*. Moles mean trouble, moles are the equivalent of rats, tunnels and come to that loneliness. Heath had discovered the secret of happiness and was not about to throw it away. Then, today, when I'm hurting no mole, *you* turn up.'

Starling considered this long speech for a time until, sighing in a contented way and utterly ignoring the implications of what Heath had said, declared, 'Don't you think there's something very special in the air today?'

Heath looked about dubiously, snouting here and there before he looked back at her.

'Do you want an honest answer, or the answer you want?' he said.

'Both,' she sighed.

'The air seems perfectly normal to me, and yes, there's something very special about it today. So what happens next?'

Starling looked shy but it didn't last long.

'Love and pups,' she said.

'Not until you've answered some questions,' said Heath, 'the main one of which is "How did you get here?" followed by the second, which is, "How fast can I get out?" '

'Would you like to come to my burrow so I can answer all your questions?' said Starling pleasantly.

'With deep and lasting reluctance,' said Heath. But he followed her, attempting to groom himself into some semblance of kemptness as he went.

* * * * * * *

But in some places Spring, and mating love, had not yet arrived, and one of them was bitter and besieged Siabod.

640

After their meeting with Glyder and the others, Alder and Marram had been led underground to the high and dangerous south-eastern parts of the system. Here the tunnels are twofoot made and cold, running always with torrents of water except when in winter they freeze and the echoing drip of water is replaced by the rasp of cracking ice and the crash of rockfalls in the dark depths of that grim place.

Yet the Siabod moles have, over the generations, made their own strange quarters here, running their tunnels up faults in the slate, taking them through wormless peat, building chambers in the few wormful parts which, often, open out on to sheer drops down to the tunnelled depths below. Dangerous indeed.

So sporadic and scarce is food that a mole must know exactly where to go unless he is to die between one stop and the next, wandering out onto the sterile snowy wastes, his snout so cold, his resistance so low, that he cannot function for long before he ails and his paws freeze to the surface and corvids pick him off.

The Siabods are of two kinds. Those on the lower northern slopes which overlook the Nantgwryd Valley are smaller, thinner, wilier, and are mean with their worms and speech, and look at strangers sideways and drop into their native Siabod and exclude them. They are the watchers, the manipulators, the clever ones, and they often affect to despise the second group of Siabod moles, though they have not guts enough to say so. Yet from this group also come the story-tellers and moles of imagination. Bran, the Siabod mole who first made contact with Bracken on his arrival and later accompanied Rebecca back to Duncton and lived there for a time, was such a lowslope mole.

The second group, of which Glyder and his brothers were members, and from which tragic Mandrake came as well, live on the high slopes. They are bigger, stronger, bolder but uneasy with words, though most speak mole.

These are the true Siabod moles, the moles of Siabod legend, who have since Balagan's time provided the protectors of Siabod's great heritage, the sacred Stones of Tryfan.

Perhaps in all systems there are the moles who talk and those that do; moles of the mind and moles of the heart. In Siabod these groups happen to be very evident, and yet over the generations the system has maintained its integrity, and usually found a leader from one or other group who is accepted by all. But at the time that Alder came to Siabod, the system was in disarray because the lowslope moles, the crafty ones, had, on the whole, begun to yield to the grikes' pressure and compromised their wills and their tunnels in the vain hope of saving their lives.

It was for this reason that the moles summoned by Glyder to meet the southerners and share their knowledge of the grikes, came solely from the moles of high Siabod. Even so Glyder warned Alder that many would not trust outsiders and might need to be won over. Alder smiled at this: he remembered having to win over the Duncton moles, and saw no reason why he should have difficulty in Siabod.

'But let me do it my way, Glyder, as Tryfan would if he were here.'

'I shall trust you as I would trust him,' promised great Glyder.

The moles took several days to gather but when they had they wasted few words on formalities. Nowhere in high Siabod was wormful enough to support so many for long, especially in winter when the cold has set in.

As Glyder introduced Alder and Marram to the others they saw they were a grim-looking lot. Huge and ugly of snout, heavy of shoulder, with talons that seemed to dent the earth where they rested, and with solitary natures that did not mix easily with each other. Cwm was the only lowslope mole there, and though he would have been regarded as an average-sized mole in most systems, he seemed small in that great company.

There was an impressive solemnity about them all, and their deep throated reverence as they followed Glyder in prayer impressed Alder greatly.

They shuffled about a bit after this, and then one of them broke into a chanting song of great beauty, which seemed to carry in its words and driving melody a great and eternal purpose that was of the Stone.

From among these moles great Mandrake himself had come, driven by his own strange desolation away from Siabod, and led by the Stone in its wisdom and fruitfulness to Duncton Wood where he fathered Rebecca, Tryfan's mother. Hearing those moles sing then, and seeing them before him, Alder understood something more about Tryfan, and saw where his physical strength came from and understood how it might be that beneath that strong and sometimes impassive exterior there might be the same passion that rung about the tunnels of Siabod now as the moles sung deeply of their faith.

Yet when they had finished, Alder found any companionable feeling he might have had was driven away by the frank distrust and suspicion of their stares at Marram and himself.

'What have you to say that will be of use to us?' seemed to be what their faces said. 'Aye, and what have you to say for yourselves?'

Alder eyed them back impassively and said nothing. He knew well enough that the stance he took then would set the pattern to a leadership that might have to last moleyears. He was in no hurry to fail.

'Well, mole?' said one of the largest and most menacing moles there, and one who clearly felt himself as much a leader as Glyder, 'We're waiting, see!'

'That's Clogwyn of Y Wyddfa,' whispered Cwm. 'You'll not want to offend him.'

But Alder was not in any mood to be weak.

'For what are you waiting?' he said strongly. 'For advice on how to get yourselves out of the mess you're in?'

There was a ripple of annoyance at this and mutterings in Siabod that soon developed into what sounded to Alder like a full argument between Glyder and the others led by Clogwyn in which nomole seemed on any other mole's side. But what they were saying neither he nor Marram could tell and the two settled down resignedly to let the arguments ring back and forth across the chamber.

Suddenly one contingent of moles seemed to get very angry and the very roof over the top of their heads to shake as voices became louder and talons were raised threateningly. Glyder's brothers ranged at his side and in front of Alder and Marram as if to protect them, as the other group took a threatening stance with Clogwyn at its head. But then yet another group ranged itself; and then a fourth, all shouting, some even buffeting others preparatory to a real fight.

'And all for one remark you made!' whispered Marram.

'*That's* their problem,' said Alder quietly. 'No other. They're as tough a lot of moles I've ever seen in one chamber at one time. If only they could be made to act as one I think no enemy could contain them!'

Then as they listened on, and Glyder and his brothers moved away, some of the moles there turned directly on Alder, shouting at him in Siabod and shaking their talons under his snout so fiercely that Marram took up a defensive stance at his side. But neither flinched, though with such huge aggressive moles it was enough to make most moles quail.

Alder found that his initial instinct about Clogwyn had been right, because as the arguments raged (and it became obvious that there was a lot of feeling about the way the campaigns against the grikes had been run) he in particular seemed most often ranged against Glyder. He was the biggest there, and the loudest, and he had talons to match and looked no fool. Then he even struck Glyder, though lightly, as if half in play, but play that had a serious intent.

What Alder did next was instinctive, and afterwards he

barely remembered the process which made him do it. But moles would ever remember it, and those there that witnessed it would often recount it to their pups.

He thrust aside a couple of moles who were gesticulating and arguing near him and advanced on Clogwyn. He had to buffet another out of the way to reach him clear, and then to move in front of Glyder before he was able to take a calm stance against Clogwyn. The hubbub died down slowly as more and more moles saw what he had done, but Clogwyn himself barely noticed Alder at first. When he did he looked in blank surprise at this sudden threat, but did not take stance especially. He was bigger than Alder, though not perhaps quite so fit, and he was clearly not used to being challenged.

Alder chose his moment well. As the voices around him died down further, but before they had entirely, and, more important, before anymole there would have expected him to make a move, he went forward fast and furious. He talon-thrust hard at the great mole, pushing him back against the wall. Even as he did that, and as dead silence fell on the chamber except for some gasps of surprise, he went forward again and delivered two blows on the mole, the second drawing blood and wheeling Clogwyn round so he stumbled and fell back, not yet having delivered a single blow in return.

Alder moved in a final time and, pinioning the great mole on the ground between wall and floor with his left paw, he raised his right high and said in a cold calm voice, in mole, 'Shall I kill him then?'

The moles recovered themselves, several rushed forward and pulled Alder back and held him so he could not strike a blow, while others held Marram, and all cried out '*No!*' and 'Mole, you've done it now, see!'

At the same time Clogwyn, furious, regained his balance and reared up, his fur bristling with rage and his talons mighty over Alder.

'So,' said Alder quietly but with great authority, 'it *is* possible for you all to act as one and agree on something sensible.' Then he called out lightly over his shoulder, 'There's hope for these Siabod moles yet, Marram!'

There was an uncertain silence as Alder shook himself free and Clogwyn came forward aggressively blood dripping from the light wound Alder had inflicted.

'Mole,' said Alder, 'I apologise. I chose you because of all moles here you seem to me the strongest, and the one most likely to defeat me in a fair fight.' Clogwyn relaxed a little at this and his talons eased. 'But you see,' continued Alder, 'watching you arguing, my good friend Marram and I were beginning to think that there is no easier system for a grike attack to be successful in than one in which everymole argues with each other. Such a system is wide open to surprise attacks. Such a system may find it impossible to mount a concerted defence. Such a system can never act strategically. Against moles as organised and purposeful as the moles of the Word, such a system is doomed however noble its past might be.'

Nomole said a thing until Clogwyn, still shaken by the attack on him and unable, perhaps, to take in as the others had the full implication of what Alder said, growled out threateningly, 'You hurt me, mole.'

Alder smiled disarmingly and lightly stepped forward and touched the lowering Clogwyn's shoulder where the blood ran and, as lightly, touched his bloodied talon to his mouth. Then he turned to the others and said, 'Many a mole must have wondered what Siabod blood tasted like, but *I* know. It's good!'

He grinned again and many there laughed with approval at his stance and black humour.

'The blow still hurts, southern mole,' growled Clogwyn again.

Alder turned sharply back.

'Then strike me mole as I struck you, and let us forget this difference and start planning how we shall defeat the grikes.'

With a terrible roar Clogwyn of Y Wyddfa moved forward and talon-thrust Alder so hard that he fell back

646

against Marram, who was still restrained by other moles.

For a moment Alder seemed dazed, and silence fell again as all the moles waited for Alder's inevitable counterattack and prepared themselves to watch a bloody fight.

But Alder recovered himself, stared at where he had been hit and where blood flowed, touched his talons to his own blood and then to his mouth as he had before and said, a little shaken it is true, 'But I'll tell moles one thing, and in this I speak very true, grike's blood tastes better still!'

With that many there laughed aloud, and more still when, gruffly but with growing good humour, Clogwyn joined in too and he and Alder buffeted each other in a friendly way as Alder said, 'I tell you true, mole, that if you strike like that among friends then by the Stone itself I trust that of all moles I have ever met it will be you at my side on the coming day of victory!'

That moment more than any other marks the beginning of Alder's command over the fighting moles of the Stone. For though on Siabod soil he always took second place to Glyder and acted only as adviser, from that day the Siabod moles accepted Alder's ascendancy against the time when that great system's resistance was taken outside the harsh confines of Siabod itself. Certainly all there were prepared now to listen to what the 'southern mole' had to say, and to understand that the way of victory lay in unity not disarray.

'I cannot say yet how our fight against the grikes will best be conducted, but one thing I do know,' he told them then, 'we cannot fight the grikes on their terms yet, but must create the conditions which favour us. We must make a force of moles that is disciplined and purposeful, and will act for the greater good. I do not think, from what I have seen of the grike siege of Siabod, that anything but disaster will come of seeking to defeat them here and now. You will lose, and lose for good, as Tryfan of Duncton would have lost if he had tried to lead his system against the grikes. Heroic but foolish, as, so far, and with respect, Siabod has been.'

'You're not asking us to retreat then, mole, that's not the Siabod way, see?' said one.

'You want young this coming spring? You want them to survive? You want these tunnels, and those of the lowslope moles, safe and untainted by grike? Or do you want your females mated against their will by grikes, and their half-caste young to be reared in contempt of the Stone. And for once-proud Siabod to be ruined, its language lost and its pride forever destroyed? For that's what'll happen here as it has happened in so much of moledom. It was to avoid that that Tryfan retreated to fight his system's battle, and that of moledom too, another day.'

'Tell us of this Tryfan, and how he gained his name, and what his prowess is,' said Clogwyn.

Which Alder did in no uncertain terms, drawing on what so many moles in Duncton had told him and what Tryfan himself had revealed. Of his journey to legendary Uffington he spoke, and of his struggles against the grikes, first at Buckland and later at Duncton. He spoke of his great task to seek Silence, as ordained by the White Mole Boswell, and he told those moles of Siabod of Tryfan's journey into the heart of the Wen, where nomole had been, or if they had, from which none had returned.

'A brave mole!' said Clogwyn at the conclusion. 'But then he has Siabod blood in his veins!' There was a deep muttering of approval at this.

Glyder said, 'My brothers and I take this mole Tryfan as our brother, sent us by our mother Rebecca to replace Wyddfa whom many of you knew. We trust him, and we trust his purpose in the Stone. We believe he can lead where we of Siabod cannot, for while we know the mountains, and the blizzard life, he knows the south and the ways of twofoots and roaring owls which touch us not. But he fights for more than his system, he fights for all of moledom, and so must we, forgetting our differences, curbing our tempers, remembering our pride in our system and our task for the Stone before ourselves.

'You have heard Alder speak, and seen that he and Marram take bold stance to equal any of us. He comes in Tryfan's place, and as he has Tryfan's trust so he has ours too. We should listen to him, accept his advice, and do as he bids us to as best we can!'

'Aye!' said a good few moles there, but others were still doubtful, unwilling to be so easily persuaded by a stranger that the habits of generations were mistaken. While a few, whose mole was poor and spoke only dialect Siabod had not fully understood all that had been said.

So then a great debate began in the Siabod tongue, ranging to and fro with much passion, some anger and occasional laughter, while Alder and Marram, uncertain what was going on, did their best to maintain a confident stance. Certainly many there looked them over, and some of the old ones came and peered hard at them with furrowed brows and mutterings.

Throughout it all it was clear that Glyder was the advocate for Alder's point of view, and a mole on whom they could rely in the future. Until at last the talking stopped, there was much laughter and some throaty cheering.

'It was the bold stance you took that did it!' whispered Glyder quickly, pleasure in his strong face.

Then great Clogwyn himself came forward and affirmed his acceptance of Alder that all might know and see, and there was great approval among all the Siabod moles at that.

'But you talked of retreat,' said Clogwyn later, 'and to us that means death just the same, but slower, that's all!'

'Not if you do it my way it doesn't,' said Alder. 'For there's a kind of retreat that will do more than preserve your strength, it will give you the chance to build it. There's a retreat that intimidates the enemy, and leaves them extended and vulnerable to raids of a kind and in country which Siabod moles may be most suited to.

'Out of such retreats, which will endanger their moles and sap their morale, will be made the basis for the victories that will come over the grikes. . . .'

So began Alder's direction of the Siabod moles, and from the November in which he arrived through to the following March the plans were made for Siabod's long-term strategy, while in a series of carefully contained raids the grike advance was harried and slowed with nearly no loss of Siabod life.

These successes immediately helped contain disaffection among the lowslope moles, and a few brave moles, under the command of Cwm, were deputed to stay on in the lowslopes to 'collaborate' with the grikes when they started their advance into the Siabod tunnels again, feeding them false information and slowing them.

Meanwhile, traps were set in the higher tunnels to demoralise exploring grikes and increase Siabod's harsh reputation. There were deluding tunnels to fearsome drops, diversions of water, and moles who knew the tunnels who could lead the grikes out into the frozen wastes and lose them there.

But the essence of Alder's plans, like Tryfan's in Duncton Wood, was a long-term strategic retreat which hopefully would leave the grikes thinking that more Siabod moles had died than really had, while those that escaped went north of Siabod to the frozen Carneddau to hide until such time as their return was right.

So, when January had come the Siabod moles started leaving for the north, many pairing as they went, the females giving birth in the dark and secret wastes that lie north of Nantgwryd while the grikes pressed on into the high system, finding little, losing moles, and growing dispirited.

A few others, paw-picked by Alder for their intelligence and ability to work in small numbers, travelled south to make contact with that mole Alder had already marked out as one of great ability: Troedfach of Tyn-y-Bedw. It was hoped that they might train and mobilise moles along the Welsh Marches ready for the distant day when battle against the grikes might be mounted.

As for Alder and Marram, they went up into the Carneddau to continue training and planning for the future. There, in April, they each fathered young, so giving their seed and blood to the Siabod cause, and growing nearer to their hosts as they, building a network of contacts across the northern hills of Wales with moles such as Caradoc, prepared for the day when moles of the Stone could show that they could face the grike, snout to snout, talon to sharp talon.

So it was that by the end of March, the high tunnels of Siabod were empty of mole, and free for grike to travel in, if they were prepared to risk the dangers there. Some did, some died and by April the tunnels were cleared of traps, but sterile, worthless to grike. While the Stones of Tryfan remained in the distance, protected as always by the wormless heights of the Glyders, where few moles had ever been.

It was then, in April, that two moles wearily ascended as high as it was safe to do on Siabod's western flanks and stared about.

'The very edge of the grike domain,' said one, 'and as far as I'll ever want to go. It sends a shiver down a mole's spine and seems too empty to be true.'

'It does!' said the other.

'There was something about the feel of those deserted tunnels we passed through which reminded me of our arrival at Duncton Wood. An orderly retreat! I wonder if the same paw is in this as was there.'

'Alder?' suggested the second.

The first and older and more authoritative turned and stared up at bleak Siabod's black impassive sides, then across the great vale that a mole must cross to reach the distant Glyders and the Stones of Tryfan they guard. Then round north towards the Carneddau.

That mole was Wrekin, commander of all the grike

guardmoles. The other was Ginnell his young second-in-command who had travelled ahead to Siabod a long time before and turned what had been a failure into a slow success. Suddenly, in March, resistance had died and though the retreating moles had left traps, few caused much damage.

'Have we learned nothing from the Siabod moles we've interrogated?'

Wrekin shrugged.

'In all the long years of our campaigns I have never found a system whose moles talk less than they do in Siabod. They seemed proud to be snouted! But I've no stomach for that now. Too many moleyears on the march. . . .'

'But Siabod is the final victory,' said Ginnell.

'Victory? Perhaps, but I doubt it. Were the moles of Whern ever vanquished? No! They held their last fastness until the time was right and a leader was found: Rune. So will the moles of the Stone stay in corners of moledom, waiting. Moles such as those of Siabod, and those of Duncton Wood. Especially Duncton Wood and its Stone. Then, one day, will come a leader, as one came to us.'

Wrekin turned back west to look at Tryfan.

'You know what that peak is called, the high grey one? Tryfan. You know what is said to stand at its summit where nomole has ever been but Balagan himself? The Sacred Stones of Tryfan. Tell me, Ginnell, have you ever heard of a mole they speak of called the Stone Mole?'

'Of course I have. The moles round here will talk of him if you hurt them enough. Threaten you with him they will. "He's coming", they say. And so he may, but do you think your guardmoles cannot defeat him?'

'You've heard of Tryfan of Duncton?'

'Allmole has. Escaped Henbane in Buckland, and then made a fool of us at Duncton. But he's been caught and turned.'

'He hasn't. That was a lie. He has not been caught and nor has he turned, and nor do I believe many followers of

652

the Stone believe he has. In that sense he has not been beaten.'

'He is the leader you're worrying about then?'

'Perhaps, perhaps not. My point is that such leaders are not easily defeated, even though they and the moles who follow them have given all their ground to us. And believe me, they have. Henbane has seen to that! Nomole will return to Duncton Wood, the place is like a living sore with all the diseased scum of moledom in its tunnels, making their malformed young, no doubt, destroying it more effectively than we ever destroyed Uffington.

'Yet still the name of Tryfan lives. That is why I fear that if this Stone Mole comes he will not be easy to destroy. He will be a dream that moles of the Stone follow, as Scirpus made a dream of the Word that others follow. I said the moles of the Stone will wait, as we did, until the time is right. That time will be when the Stone Mole comes.'

'Soon they say!'

'Not soon enough for me!' said Wrekin grimly. 'The battles against the southern moles may now all be won, and no important system remaining that is not of the Word. But I would rest happier knowing that the Stone Mole, whatever he is, has come. Because if we cast him into oblivion as Henbane and Rune have done to another mole who might have been a danger. . . .'

'Boswell?'

'Boswell. If they can do to the Stone Mole as they have to him and preserve order long enough across moledom that the rule of the Word is ascendant and memories of the Stone die, *then* we may have nothing more to fear. Or you may not. I doubt that I shall live that long!'

Wrekin waved aside Ginnell's courteous protest and continued, 'Until then we had best be careful, and watchful. A time of doubt is coming, a time when we will grow slack, a time when the eldrenes will need to take over the ruling of moledom from the guardmoles, which is as it should be. But until that taking over is complete, and this mystery of the Stone Mole is demystified, I warn you that each of us should be careful. For if such a mole should come, Word knows what a force he may unleash. And so long as there are moles about like Tryfan and Alder, that following may be organised and effective against us.'

'So, Wrekin, are you travelling back to Buckland as Henbane bid you do, and sending another to Whern to advise her of this Siabod victory?'

Wrekin laughed grimly.

'I have not lived this long by being so foolish. Buckland is under the command of Wyre now and I have no doubt that Henbane and Weed have commanded him to kill me. No, I shall go north as soon as the snow clears, north to Whern where this long campaign began and take the Siabod news myself. You survive in this world, Ginnell, by being where the power is. Where Henbane is, and Weed, I must be. And to whom shall I talk? Neither of them. No, no. I shall speak only to Rune. He will not have me killed as Henbane might!'

Ginnell looked doubtful.

'I am told he sees nomole,' he said.

'But for young females, and White Moles,' said Wrekin cryptically. 'Meanwhile, I suggest you strengthen our defences to the north.'

'But such Siabod moles as have survived will have gone south.'

'They would, a grike wouldn't. And what is familiar about this place, as it was familiar about the defences of Duncton Wood, was that a mole with grike training commanded the retreat. I believe Alder is hereabouts. I recommend you to be ready for assault from the north. Now, let's leave this Word-forsaken place. The last battles for moledom may seem to have been fought, but I somehow doubt it. When that time comes it will not be at the edges that the victory will be won, but in the centre. Remember that, and beware of this Stone Mole when he comes!'

'For a mole in his moment of final victory you sound sombre indeed.'

'I'm a military mole, not like Weed or Henbane. They have needed me because of the talons I command. Well, I hope they sense as I do that another kind of moledom may be coming, one where battles might be fought not with talons but with hearts, not with shouts of rage but with prayers of love.'

As they spoke, and Wrekin was about to turn back into the dark Siabod tunnels, the sky cleared to the west and the sun shone briefly across the faces of Glyder Fach and Glyder Fawr, and then upon Tryfan itself. Its peak rose snow-white in the sky, but for its steepest part where grey rock rose sheer.

'Impressive,' said Ginnell.

'Beautiful is the right word, Ginnell, but moles like us are not meant to say such things. Imagine a mole that could command such beauty! How would our guardmoles defeat him?'

'The Word is wise and will instruct us against whatever mole endangers it.'

Wrekin laughed deeply and bitterly, and looked at Tryfan's heights as a mole might look who senses that his life's task might seem small against such majesty.

'Anyway,' added Ginnell as an afterthought, 'whatmole could, as you put it, "command" such a thing?'

'Well I don't know, I follow the Word. But it worries me, and I hope it may worry the great Rune himself, that there are moles who even as we snout them call out the name of a mole they believe will command more than talons ever can and whom, they say, *will* come.'

'Well you come now, Wrekin, come north to the lowslopes and tell me how you'd dispose the guardmoles to face an attack from the north. . . .'

With that the two moles turned their backs on Tryfan's peaks and went underground. But long after they had gone the sun shone distantly and bright upon those western peaks, and then it widened north, and touched the secret heights of the Carneddau with colour, and hope.

Chapter Thirty-Six

If the call of Whern had now gone out to Wrekin, as it had long since to Henbane, let nomole be surprised that it was soon heard too in the tunnels of the Dunbar moles, or that it brought with it darkness and dread and the separation of two moles who had found each other and their love but a short time before.

Already by the end of March both Feverfew and Starling had grown heavy with pup; and of the two, Starling rather heavier.

Heath and she had paired well, if eccentrically, for Heath was not a mole to stay in a tunnel for long, especially ones as curious and strange as those he found in the heart of the Wen. He had soon confirmed that he was the maker of what Tryfan and his companions had come to call 'Heath's Tunnels' and that he had vacated them, as they had, under grave and nearly fatal pressure from the rats.

But of his journeys prior to that, and those subsequent, he made light, as if the long moleyears of his travelling had become jumbled into one confused memory which charted a mole's passage into a not unpleasant solitariness in which each new day is accepted as such, without especial regret for the day before, or special concern for the day following.

His attitude to Starling, and to the prospect of pups, reflected this, for he seemed only vaguely bothered about either, as if he had had little to do with them at all. As for the excitement the Wen moles showed over the whole business, it baffled him, as they themselves did, though (to his own surprise) he found their company pleasant enough.

The Wen moles did not know what to make of him at all, nor of his habit of turning up at their burrows and settling down to help himself to their food, ignoring entirely their territorial assumptions and rights, which had grown complex and subtle over the decades.

One or two attempted to challenge him but they were old and less strong than he was, and anyway, he had the habit of continuing to eat whatever worm it was he had purloined, as a mole moaned on, until that moaning mole had nothing left to say. A mole who had successfully survived in the filthels of the Wen for so many moleyears, and who had faced more rats, floods, and near drownings, more twofoots and more roaring owls than most moles could even start imagining, is not liable to be put out by an irritable and aged mole or two.

'All right then?' Heath would conclude another mole's diatribe against him, as if he had had a fit of colic. 'Ready for a chat now, are we?' If the chat soon veered round to the subject of mating, and young, and litters and survival, Heath would say, 'Don't ask me, mate, ask *her*. She'll tell you,' adding with approval, 'Competent mole is Starling, very.'

It should be added that Heath was as little concerned about Rowan, who no doubt was still waiting for his return at the far end of the Wen tunnels, as he was for the niceties of Wen mole territory. Nor even for Haize whom he now only dimly remembered. But, accepted for what he was, which was a passer through, Heath was good company.

Certainly, over the duration of Starling's pregnancy Heath, quite without trying to, won over the moles of the Wen whose females especially, in the tight and prim way elderly moles sometimes accept the cruder, rough young, adopted both of them, and fussed them silly in preparation for Starling's littering. A situation not helped by Heath's magnanimous acceptance on Starling's behalf of any help offered, so that, so far as Starling could tell, just about every female in the system had been promised the job of watching over her when the great day, or night, of pupping came.

But attitudes to Feverfew and Tryfan were not as

657

friendly, and before Feverfew had pupped they were to become downright hostile.

From the first the two moles had stayed in Feverfew's burrows which, being on the far westside of the system, were well away from its centre and near the Library. Tryfan discouraged visitors, but could not prevent all contact nor change the tradition that decreed, as it did in Duncton Wood itself, that a pupping female should be watched over, lest there was a deformity of birth which needed dealing with. Few females had the will to kill their own young.

Squail, the emaciated female deputed to watch over Feverfew, at first seemed harmless enough. Like most of the females in the system she had not pupped and therefore had little to convey to Feverfew of a practical nature. This did not stop her, at every opportunity, from warning Feverfew of the pains and agonies of pupping, and the dangers too, all of which she did with a smug and disapproving I-told-you-so look, as if she took pleasure in Feverfew's discomforts. Feverfew might have borne this well enough, for Tryfan was nearby and able to get Squail out of the way from time to time, but that Squail was a fusser, a fiddler, a meddler in another's burrows, always poking her snout here and lifting some object there. She was a gossip, a peeker, a listener, and neither Tryfan nor Feverfew could stand her company.

Yet they had no choice but to accept her for there was precedence in such matters, and, in any case, so many other females were involved in watching over Starling that none other than Squail seemed willing to do it for Feverfew. As for whether they needed her at all, that was the only matter on which Feverfew and Tryfan disagreed, and Tryfan lost the argument.

Even then, none of this might have mattered but for the terrible fact that not long before her ward was due to pup, Squail discovered, or said she did, signs of disease on Feverfew's flank.

Her mouth pursed, her brow furrowed into hypocritical

anxiety while her eyes looked very pleased, and she said, 'Humph!' in a disapproving way. Then, saying nothing more, went off to the main tunnels to discuss things with her meddlesome and ill-natured friends.

Before Tryfan had discovered what was apaw or able to stop it, those same ill-natured females came and investigated, first demanding that he left Feverfew's burrows, and then after mutterings about 'vystytacyon forfeblit' pronounced that the disease was incipient murrain and Feverfew's pups would inevitably be 'defawtes'.

'Which means what?' asked Tryfan after the old hags had gone and he had got Feverfew to calm down. But Feverfew could not bring herself to say, and it was Spindle who translated the word into mole: deformities.

Now a shadow hung over what had been a happy burrow, and Squail positively fluffed up with the drama and tension of it all, the I-told-you-so look ever more triumphant in her puffy eyes. Yet Feverfew refused to dismiss Squail as if fearful that that would only increase the doubts and hostilities she felt; but then she would cry inconsolably, and Tryfan felt helpless and concerned.

As the final days went by the disease, which looked to Tryfan alarmingly like scalpskin, and one of a very virulent sort, got worse. Dry skin spread across Feverfew's flank in a matter of days, and then cracked and opened bloodily, and her face thinned with worry and she seemed unable to accept comfort from Tryfan as, becoming more tired and strained, she began to settle in the birth burrow where no male must go.

It was about then, when he was at a loose end, that Tryfan one day came across Mayweed on the westside, wandering about and lost in thought. He was, he explained, exploring. . . .

The fact was that none of Tryfan's party had really explored the system at all prior to his recovery at the end of February. They had been too weak, or, when they had got better, too concerned watching over him to go exploring.

Even Mayweed, never a mole to crouch still when a little bit of exploration was possible, had stayed close by until Feverfew's coming and even after that had been reluctant to wander far until Tryfan had recovered.

So it was not until March that Mayweed had started going off once more to explore tunnels long since abandoned by the Wen moles themselves, and set as his objective the task of finding the burrows, if they still existed, of the great Dunbar himself.

The Wen moles put up some token resistance to this enterprise but soon gave up, and some even offered suggestions to him as to where these might be. It was a sign of the system's decline that none had ever bothered to look, and that even when they thought about it, none was much interested. But one thing seemed certain, and all agreed about it, that Dunbar's burrows would be on the westside, facing in the direction of Uffington.

The reason for Mayweed's interest, which soon overtook the earlier enthusiasm he had shown for the texts of the Library, was the haunting memory he had of the sounds – calls and summons, more like – carried by the walls in the ancient tunnels they had found on their way into the Wen, where Rowan's sister Haize had died.

'Mayweed remembers that, Mayweed thinks there might be more of that, Mayweed desires to hear that again!' he had told Spindle.

So off he went into the Wen tunnels to explore and find out what he could. As tunnels went they certainly had a style of their own. They were smaller than the tunnels in more modern systems, and sometimes a mole had to duck low to get into a burrow off a tunnel. They were well made and must once have had remarkable windsound for even now they still carried an echo well and gave a mole a sense of where he was, as good tunnels should. Other mole movements travelled like well-made whispers, clear, distinct yet not intrusive.

They were quite complex, turning here and there, splitting off into high and lower levels, making use of the gravel and flint of that soil in an archaic way, so that a mole felt he had travelled back in time.

The communal tunnels had clearly once been well used and, though dusty and ruinous now, their corners were well polished from the passage of moles' flanks, and the steps from one level to another rounded and worn.

As Mayweed explored he found that the tunnels to the north of the westside were older, and even found some seal-ups which, when broken into, revealed that single moles had been sealed in where they died. With mounting hope he had explored that area and yet had finally found nothing.

It was on such a day of disappointment when Mayweed must have wandered near Feverfew's burrows and that Tryfan and he met for the first time for several days. Tryfan was glad to see him, for he was growing tired of the pupping process, Squail's meddling, and the expectation that he should crouch down and patiently do nothing.

'Paternal Sir, nearly, humble old me can't do much that's useful at the moment either. Overextended Starling has no use for me now, Spindle can't see further than his snout as he learns old mole from Paston, and you and fecund Feverfew are otherwise engaged! So Mayweed wanders and seeks a dream.'

'When you find it, Mayweed, let me know. I would like to see Dunbar's burrows if they exist – which I doubt.'

'Mayweed will, terrific Tryfan, Mayweed will!'

'Feverfew is near to pupping now,' said Tryfan, heavily.

'Mayweed wishes her well,' said Mayweed grandly, 'and hopes pups will be a fitting prelude to your long years with her.'

'Prelude? Bit late for preludes.'

'Mayweed may be single, auspicious Sir, and Mayweed may be humble, but he is not a fool. Mating is a prelude.'

'To what?'

Mayweed shrugged. 'Something better,' he said. 'Mayweed would definitely like to know what, but doesn't. Mayweed is exceedingly ignorant about such things but intends to improve in time.'

'Got your eye on a female then?' said Tryfan with a grin, and feeling better for Mayweed's company.

Mayweed smiled in a confident way.

'Long term is Mayweed's way, like life itself. You put a paw forward on the Slopeside one day and you find yourself in a tunnel in the Wen the next day, as it were. That's long term. Now Mayweed thinks of pairing and tomorrow it may happen. Long term, very. As for your droll question, grand Tryfan, the honest answer is "No!" I have not the precise female in mind as yet. But when I meet her I shall know, and you'll be the second to be told.'

Later that same day, when Tryfan had gone back to Feverfew's burrows to see if he was needed, Heath ambled over to see Mayweed and said, 'I know what you're looking for.'

'So does your humble servant,' replied Mayweed, 'but it doesn't help. Knowing is not quite the same thing as *finding*. Mayweed wishes it were.'

'Well chum, what I'm trying to say is I know where there's some old tunnels. Very old, very comfortable. I know because I lived in them and would be still if I had not been discovered minding my own business and having a quiet worm out on the surface and enjoying the prospect of spring when your friend and mine, Starling, came along.'

'Is the magical Madam near to her big day, wonders Mayweed delicately?' said Mayweed.

'If you mean is she near pupping your guess is as good as mine since I can't get a snout into her tunnels edgeways but that some grinning old female comes up and tells me to get lost.'

'Then take me, hapless Heath, to these old tunnels you found and let's see what humbleness himself can make of them!'

'You're on,' said Heath, turning eastwards.

'Forgive me Sir, twice over, but you're going eastward.'

'That's where the tunnels you want to see are.'

662

'Describe them, hopeful Heath.'

Heath did so, telling Mayweed that they were almost identical in form to the remnant of the other ancient system in the Wen, and that they had chamber after chamber of wall scribings which made strange sounds.

'Er – ahm – Mayweed wishes briefly to thump his head very hard on this tunnel roof, Sir.' Which he did, and then looked ruefully round in a generally westward direction as if to take in at one glance all the myriad of tunnels he had wasted his time exploring. 'Mayweed is now ready, Sir, though if the tunnels you lead him to are definitely the right ones, which they sound to be, he may well be moved to thump his stupid head again.'

They went on a long perambulating sort of route which took in several stops for food and a laze in the sun before plunging below ground on the far eastside and then by various twofoot ducts, culverts and ancient tunnels, to another stretch of grass wasteland overlooking the Wen.

The moment Mayweed went down into its tunnels he saw he was much nearer something very old, and, even better, that the shape and cut of the tunnels was indeed almost identical to those in which they had found Haize's body. But since they were not overlain by a twofoot structure, and since evidently Heath had lived up there for a season or two, the entrances were open and the tunnels lit.

'There's plenty of them,' said Heath, 'and they're pretty old. . . .'

But Mayweed was hardly listening. Instead he was staring here and there eagerly, fascinated by what he saw. The tunnels linked a series of chambers and the further into their gloomy depths he went, the more fascinated he became.

'If you don't mind, Mayweed, I'd prefer not to come with you. . . .'

Heath's voice receded in the distance behind him, echoing strangely among the ancient corrugations and scribings on the wall of the chamber he was in. The tunnel was curiously contorted and confusing, and Mayweed had to pause and focus fully on where he was before he realised he had taken a turn left and gone down a level and had to retrace his steps very carefully to get back to where Heath was.

'Ah! I was saying,' said Heath, relieved to see him, 'that I don't much like the tunnels you're going into now. They make strange noises at strange times – I know because I could hear them sometimes. So I just stayed up near the surface in the tunnels where we came in, and very comfortable they were too.'

'You never explored, helpless Sir?' said Mayweed.

'No way,' said Heath. 'It's the simple life for me, no complications. Anyway you'll get lost, *I* nearly did.'

'One thing, Sir, one thing only, is Mayweed certain of: humble he does not get lost. Mislays himself occasionally, scares himself rigid often, but lost never. So hesitant Heath had better stay here while Mayweed goes exploring. He will return.'

'Well, let's hope he does. Heath won't hesitate to bugger off if he feels like it.'

Mayweed smiled unctuously: 'Heath, Sir, will do as Heath must, Mayweed will do as he must, but if all moles did likewise moledom might as well not exist. Pathetic Mayweed suggests Heath thinks about that before he leaves, as Mayweed would like his companionship on the way back!'

With that Mayweed disappeared into the tunnels while Heath, grumbling now and then about freedom and liberty, settled down to wait.

Dusk came, and with it the sounds of ancient moles singing down in those tunnels. Night came, and the sound of females laughing. Early dawn came and youngsters called, anxious. Morning came and a tired female's paws dragged among those chambers as if she was making her final journey to the birth burrow. Heath felt hungry, but he waited. Late morning came and a mole's pawsteps came out of those tunnels and then, a little later, Mayweed finally reappeared.

'Mayweed is grateful to Heath for waiting, Mayweed is tired, very; Mayweed is moved, very; Mayweed thanks Heath because this is not a time Mayweed wishes to be alone. Mayweed is very tired. He is.' And with that Mayweed settled down, and with a devotion and care astonishing for him Heath stayed exactly where he was, hungry and restless though he felt. While from out of those tunnels, over the sleeping form of Mayweed, came tired and restless sounds of moles from old to youngster, from youngster to newborn.

Mayweed awoke in the afternoon, ate, and slept once more. Not until the following dawn did he say, 'Mayweed must return now to the westside and tell Tryfan what he has seen and touched and heard. Mayweed may have found, with Heath's help, what it was that Tryfan of Duncton was sent here to find. Mayweed must make his report.'

But as they went up to the surface a heavy vibration suddenly ran through the tunnels, which stopped and then started again. Mayweed paused.

'Twofoots,' said Heath, '*and* yellow roaring owls.'

'Handsome Heath will explain to Mayweed now,' said Mayweed.

'North of here, saw them myself, last summer, huge roaring owls all yellow and with twofoots, big ones. Crunch in the gravel, splodge in the mud.'

'What mud, what gravel? Explain, dauntless Sir!' demanded Mayweed impatiently.

Since words seemed inadequate, Heath showed him, though it took them a good time to get there travelling north. A huge area laid waste, the grass all gone, gravel spread, and mud. A roaring owl, huge and yellow and with pale gazing eyes, and the cries of twofoots. The two moles peered about a bit before Heath said, 'They're nearer than they were last summer. Coming in this direction.'

'Mayweed wonders if Heath can surmise what all this is about,' said Mayweed.

'Bloody obvious, mate. It's a roaring owl way, or will

665

be. Twofoots make them, roaring owls use them. They all go into the Wen don't they? This one will as well. These yellow ones come and pup ones all colours. Must do.'

'And you think this way will go straight over the tunnels I've got to tell Tryfan about?'

'Over, through, one day. Won't be any of those old tunnels left at all. Though the rate they're moving Heath here feels that there's a couple of summers to go before they clear him out of the way. By then, what with Starling making her demands and one thing and the next, Heath will be so knackered that Heath won't care much.'

Mayweed laughed appreciatively.

'Heath Sir, you are making Mayweed laugh by speaking like him; Mayweed prefers you not to do it, Mayweed's sides will ache.'

Heath grinned.

'You know what I missed all those years I've been alone? A laugh. That's what a mole's usually missing when he feels he's missing something but doesn't quite know what: a bloody good laugh.'

'Humble Mayweed, who is more of an explorer and route-finder than anything else, will think hard and come up with a joke for Heath so that when he is alone he can tell it to himself and laugh. That will be Mayweed's gift to Heath for the tunnels he has helped him find.'

Heath looked quite touched, and said rather gruffly, 'Come off it, you silly bugger, you don't have to think of a joke to make me laugh or smile. You're one of life's naturals as it is. Now let's get you back to Tryfan.'

* * * * * * *

Tryfan was only too glad to hear Mayweed's news, and willing enough to come with him since Squail assured him that 'Yf povre Feverfewe (blessid may she bee) yaf nat ypuppe by none wil nat pup thise dayspringe afore.'

'Brilliant Sir,' said Mayweed, 'what did the cronish Madam say?'

'We've to be back by dawn. Feverfew will not pup before then.'

666

'Then, harried Sir, Mayweed will take you to see what he has found, and will guide you back again before day breaks. Later on, perhaps, you will have more time on your paws and you and scholarly Spindle may return to look at those strange tunnels and chambers again.'

But scholarly Spindle, who had an unerring sense of when he should be at Tryfan's side, appeared just then and, learning where they were off to, joined them.

It was just as the afternoon sun began to thin and glance weakly across the grass of the eastside an hour or so before disappearing over the brow of the west, that the three moles descended into the tunnels Mayweed had found.

'With respect, expectatious Sirs both, I suggest you stay near me and avoid wandering. These tunnels are deceptive, very, and in my modest judgement were made by a mole wise and clever who wished to disorientate and misdirect prying snouts without harming them. Let me demonstrate. Now where, towering Tryfan, do you imagine we go from here?'

After a steady plod along an old tunnel they had reached an intersection of three routes.

'This one,' said Tryfan confidently, pointing at the tunnel that continued the way they had been going and slanted downwards. 'You can hear it goes deeper and these other two carry surface noise and must go up.'

Mayweed, grinning, went the way Tryfan suggested, and in moments, as it seemed, they were back on the surface and decidedly confused.

'Worse is to come, deluded leader,' said Mayweed. 'Try going back the way you've come.'

Which Tryfan tried, only to find himself, after a very confusing run, underground somewhere quite different to where they had been before.

'Mayweed has made his point,' said Mayweed, 'abject though he is. Mayweed has a feeling that his entire life has been a preparation for these very tunnels here, and, as he has already recently observed to that unkempt mole Heath, lost he doesn't get. But that requires skill and concentration so if your splendidnesses could refrain from talking he will attempt to get us back to where we began before Tryfan offered us this exploratory parenthesis.'

Which he was forced to do by taking them back to the surface and starting the descent from where they first began all over again. But once down they travelled quickly enough, using marks which he had left from his previous journey.

The tunnels were dry and dusty, and here and there had fallen in, but then they deepened and were untouched. The echoes in them were strong and very confusing, making it seem that there were moles ahead coming towards them, and moles behind running away.

Then they came to a chamber, lit gloomily from a shaft, and they could see scribings on its walls. In places they were thick, in others there were none; altogether it looked as if the chamber was in some way incomplete, as if the scribemole making the marks had not finished his work.

'Try them, Tryfan Sir,' said Mayweed.

Tryfan reached up a taloned paw and touched the scribings lightly. A strange confusion of sounds came, like a hubbub of moles, as if all were talking but one was trying to be heard most of all. The sounds stopped as the scribing stopped, and Tryfan went to another on the same side of the chamber. They heard the sound of muttering and mumbling, a solitary mole. They might almost have fancied that he was behind them, and Spindle even looked around nervously in the gloom as if expecting to see him there.

The sound receded and they moved on, coming soon to a second chamber, the same size as the first. Once again the walls were scribed only in part, and Tryfan touched the first one he reached. Again an old mole's voice, and still unclear, calling; then another scribing and another voice, but old again. Unformed.

Spindle touched the first scribing Tryfan had sounded and though the sound that came out from it was similar it was not quite the same; nor was the second when Spindle touched it.

'It seems to me that whatever mole made these was trying different scribings out,' said Spindle.

Mayweed, nodding his head eagerly, looked at Tryfan for confirmation of this.

'Or perhaps he was searching for something,' said Tryfan. 'Do these chambers go on a long way, Mayweed?'

'Inquisitive Sir, they do. They branch off. They split and they divide. There are some deeper, perhaps, more than limited me has found. And I can save you time and energy by telling you this: they become more complex, the sounds become more distinct, and they become more absorbing.'

'Is there a pattern to them?'

'Mayweed is not sure. The tunnels become younger, if Mayweed can put it like that. From old mole voices to youngster voices, and then on to pups.'

'Take us there then,' said Tryfan, 'for we can't stay here too long. I want to get back to Feverfew by dawn.'

They travelled on, but were waylaid sometimes as the chambers grew ever more completed and rich. In some, they discovered that Dunbar –they assumed it was him – seemed to have tried to carry the theme of age to youth in a single chamber so that a mole, by touching the scribings in a spiral around the chamber's side from the roof to the floor, could bring forth sounds of ever-increasing youth. The scribings did not work the other way, from floor to roof, sounding only harsh and conflicting when they tried it. Which was strange since moles start young and grow old. What was Dunbar trying to describe or achieve with these scribings?

In some burrows it seemed that Dunbar had worked on scribings for a particular age range, as if trying to find the perfect expression in sound which he might then have intended to incorporate with other such developed sounds into a completed chamber.

So they continued as night fell and the tunnels became lit by the lights of the Wen reflecting in the sky above, and the chambers and tunnels echoed with its rumbly nightsounds.

It became clear that their early guess that Dunbar had been experimenting with sound-scribings was correct, and that he seemed obsessed with the passage of age to youth. But why? They could not tell.

There had come over them all a kind of urgent fascination, as if they had to find the answer to that question, or at least find something, before they left. So they searched on into the night without rest, sounding walls continuously until by the gentlest touch they could tell it was 'just' another wall of try-outs. While Tryfan and Spindle were sounding and listening, Mayweed was searching and, gradually, leading them to tunnels where the sounds were becoming clearer, as if the voices of the moles enscribed were becoming more individual. Which they were, for gradually at least one voice emerged, which was clearest of all in the more aged versions though uncertain in the younger. Dunbar's voice perhaps? A mole in search of what he was before?

At the same time, as they travelled on, they found evidence that Dunbar, if it had been he, had aged as he made these great lost works. The scribings were no longer as high up the walls as they had been, and the talons were rougher, and the scribings less deep. The style changed as well, becoming freer and without the detail of the earlier chambers. Yet the sounds improved, as if Dunbar was beginning to find the very essence of what he wanted.

Still they were only voices sounding: not song, not spoken words. Nor was there any Dark Sound, as Tryfan understood it, which is to say sounds that wither a mole's heart. The sounds they found were all good, all searching, all light.

'Perhaps he was searching for the sound of Silence,' Spindle surmised, 'though I wouldn't have thought that was a sound moles made!'

'Or perhaps these scribings are part of his prophecies, that the Stone Mole is coming and so on,' said Tryfan thoughtfully.

Then, quite suddenly, things changed. They came to a

chamber of pup sounds, and mingling with it was a female voice. Soft sometimes, then harsh, even in the same scribing as if Dunbar did not quite have control over his own talons for these sounds. Weepings came then, and screams, and the sounds of comforting. And through it all the mews of pups, soft now, calling now, then softly beautiful.

Then a strange phenomena. As they moved on the scribings became increasingly subtle, and perhaps the chambers more perfectly shaped to their purpose, so that they no longer needed to touch the scribings before they started whispering their sound, as if picking up the pawsteps of the three awestruck moles, and transmuting them to the sounds Dunbar had ordained.

It was soon after this that they heard their first Dark Sound. Heavy, threatening, and travelling their way like filthy water surging down a tunnel. They held each other in fear as it passed.

Tryfan took the lead now, telling the others to stay very close. They could see that ahead of them was a portal, over it dark carvings, beyond it a chamber. They went towards the portal, the Dark Sound mounting mightily around them as their pawsteps travelled ahead and then were echoed back at them, but malformed and vile, seeming to seek them to turn on each other, to hate, to fear, to punish, to . . . and then Tryfan charged forward, pulling Mayweed after him and Spindle too and they fell through the dire portal of Dunbar and into that chamber he had made the portal guard.

Silence, nearly. Not much scribing. Light dull in a high shaft, the light mellowing from lurid to nearly dawn.

'Tryfan Sir . . .' began Mayweed, seeing it was later than they realised.

'Sshh. . . .'

But that brief exchange was enough to sound the scribings around them, and make that burrow seem as if it was at one end of a tunnel, at the other end of which was a mother and a pup calling, mewing, comforting, soft; the

671

sounds just after birth; and then that faded as a dream might fade on waking. At the far side of the chamber was another portal, blocked, most strangely blocked with flint. Black and shining. The soil around it was impacted and hard and it did not crumble to a talon touch.

Tryfan touched the flint and from beyond came a hollow sound, so he touched it again, and they all heard it, or thought they did: a fleeting sound, very distant, making a mole think he could almost hear it but not quite. Like the running of pawsteps down a far distant tunnel that a mole fancies he hears but never hears again, and wonders after if he heard at all.

It was alluring, and again Tryfan touched that flint, and again could not quite catch the sound. No, sounds. Calling, running, calling . . . and then, returning to the chamber they were in, were echoes, very faint, of that first mother sound they heard. Then a solitary roaring owl, distant as well, circling above their heads in echo form, where the light of dawn was beginning to brighten.

'We must go!' said Tryfan.

Even as he said it he turned as if barely thinking of what he did and sounded the scribing on the wall. Down its sinewy length his talon ran and, even as it did, with gathering force that last work of Dunbar outside the flint-blocked chamber sounded clear. A scream, terrible and long, the scream of birth; yes, and the scream thereafter of a female battling for her young, fighting for it, desperate to preserve its life. A scream redoubled and eightfolded all about them and the cry of a pup, mewing and desperate like its mother.

Then the strangest distillation of much that they had already heard: pups to youngsters, to young adult and that mother's scream with other females too. Then that old male voice, so old and tired, calling, seeking, crying out and travelling through time to youth again, and puphood, and before even that to the briefest and most lovely moment that they heard; so brief that they barely knew they heard it: the sound of Silence.

672

Then roaring owl again, echoing around above their heads, so far off, and that Silence gone.

With its passing the screams returned and to the three moles it seemed they were filled with terror: pup cries, birthing, life and death sounds; and such sad loss.

'Feverfew!' cried Tryfan.

Then with that cry which joined the screams that shook the chamber all about, he turned for the entrance, seeming to enter a hundred tunnels, all scattering, seeming not to know, and seeming, as the others followed him, to hear all the sounds they had heard before but no longer distilled and simple. Dark Sound: of old moles and of young, of good and of bad, of females and of males, of darkness and of light, so that the tunnels were a confusion, and their passage a chase into its depths and all the long time that each step seemed to take they heard still that birth scream and desperate mews, and cruelties just beginning.

Nomole but those three can ever know the agonies they felt, or the panic that came over them.

Never lost, Mayweed?

He was lost; and each of them as well, lost in sounds that mounted more and more, as if the whole of moledom was sounding about them, in all its light and all its darkness as they ran.

'Silence!'

Tryfan had stopped, and pulled both the others short, his great talons on their shoulders, his strength their strength.

'Be still,' he whispered, caressing their shoulders, looking at each with gentleness, 'be still now. The way out is not this way.'

Then as dawn light filled the tunnels, and grey shadows replaced the lurid lights' seeming brightness, the sounds stilled about them and the tunnel or chamber they were in seemed to stretch before and above and behind them, hugely, as if whichever way they looked they were receding into smallness.

'Silence!' said Tryfan, but it was not a command, it was a description of something nearly there.

Then that first voice they had heard, the aged mole, sounded again nearby, muffled as it had seemed but clearing as the silence grew, until they knew it was speaking, saying a word, a name, their names. And afterwards each said it was *their* name they heard that mole speak.

And each knew what mole it was.

For Spindle, it was Brevis once again, calling him to safety. And he wept.

For Mayweed it was the mole who had nurtured him when he was a pup sealed up in a burrow, whispering him out of the burrow once again, speaking him down tunnels of darkness towards the distant light of Slopeside. Humble Mayweed wept.

But for Tryfan it was Boswell, old beloved Boswell, calling him forward now, Boswell in the shadows just ahead, asking him to come now for it had been long, so long, and Tryfan was ready to come now.

'Come to me now, come . . .' said old Boswell, his face so lined and wan in those grey dawning shadows which lay beyond the edge of Silence where they were.

'You're in Whern now, you're there now,' whispered Tryfan.

'Yes,' called Boswell, 'and you're ready to come here too. You're strong enough. So follow me out of where you are now, lead the others with you, follow me . . .' and those shadows moved, that great chamber lessened about them, and, still touching his friends, Tryfan urged first one and then the other on beyond their tears, out of that nearly-Silence they had found, away from those dying cries with, 'Come now, Boswell will show us, come. . . .'

Later, dazed and tired, the three moles emerged out of Dunbar's tunnels at the point where they had started, and the sky over the Wen streaked with the birth blood of the sun. And Tryfan knew his young had been born and that

he was late, almost too late, to reach Feverfew and aid her
. . . and he knew the Stone had so ordained it.

Yet then he ran, fast and urgent, across the real world of
the surface now, the dawn-red sky breaking behind him as
he ran on; down then, down and along, back the way he
had come, fast and faster from eastside to westside.

'Tryfaaan . . .' he left Spindle and Mayweed far
behind.

'Tryfaaan . . .' he passed by Heath without a word and
ran on towards the darkness that he knew he would find.

Tunnel walls rushing towards him, darkness ahead,
and:

'*Tryfan!*' screamed at him, and she was there. His
Feverfew.

On the tunnel floor before her a single bloody male pup,
mewing. Upon her fur, about her mouth, smeared brown
and red across her flanks, was blood. And she stricken
with weakness yet driven by instinct; she maddened with
fear, yet fighting to the end.

'*Tryfan!*' she screamed, picking up her last surviving
pup, taking him mewing in her mouth and running past
Tryfan towards where Mayweed, Spindle and Heath
came, and leaving him, to face alone, the crazed moles that
chased her.

No words exist that can describe that scene, the final
scene perhaps in a system's ancient history. Old moles,
moles of a dying kind, aged and lost, embittered and frail,
their mouths and talons bearing the only living thing
about them: the blood of the pups that Feverfew had
borne, pups they had destroyed. And at their head,
hateful, filled with the venom of a sterile bitterness,
Squail. She the mole deputed to watch over, she the mole
who decreed that pups from diseased flanks are better
dead, every last one of them.

No words can describe the sounds that mob made, the
sounds of a decrepit superstitious rage.

No words for cruelty brought alive.

Tryfan did not kill them, he had no need to. Perhaps

675

such moles are already dead. Though he advanced on them but slowly, yet they broke before him as dead trees might break before November winds. Broke, splintered and cracked, a mob becoming individuals too pathetic to sully the talons of a good mole. Then they slunk, looked back, sought vainly to groom the blood from their guilty mouths and talons, and were gone, back into the tunnels where they would soon die.

Feverfew survived that murderous assault. Tryfan survived. Their pup survived, for a time. And the system pretended none of it had been, but for whispers in the night.

Sunshine came, but Tryfan saw it not. His eyes were bleak, his spirit low.

Starling pupped, four healthy ones, and Heath was watching over them nearby. Good news those pups, laughter in the tunnels of the Wen, laughter that hid shadows they all knew.

It had happened. It *had*.

For a time their pup survived. And poor Feverfew fed it as best she could from scalpskinned teats, accepting no comfort until the day came that pup was gone. Always weak, then weaker, finally dead. After that it seemed too late, for where it had been was a great silence, unknown, sterile, on one side Tryfan and on the other Feverfew, and no words between.

Why?

'Why me?'

But what could Spindle say, or Mayweed, in those beautiful days of May? Nothing but wait; nothing finally but leave.

'Not me!' said Starling, 'I've got young. And anyway, this place isn't so bad, really. Also, surprise, surprise, I think Feverfew will need me.' Starling smiled, a caring adult now.

'But she'll come. . . .'

Starling shook her head.

'She's not ready, but you probably don't understand. She's not yet said goodbye.'

'But magical Madam. . . .'

Starling touched Mayweed tenderly.

'I'll not stay here forever, silly. Just while my pups mature. Just to see them safe. Just to teach them everything I can. And then, I'll make my way back home to Duncton Wood. Really! And I'll bring Feverfew with me. Honestly! There's Lorren to find and Bailey . . . Really!'

She was right, Feverfew would not go. And Tryfan felt guilty that he felt relieved.

'The scalpskin, Starling. . . .'

'Mayweed survived it, and all he's got are a few scars.'

'Yes,' whispered Tryfan, 'yes that's all.'

Then Tryfan went to Feverfew and tried to speak, but no words came. Then she came close and snouted him gently and they dared look at each other; still no words came. Between them there was silence where their young had been, and it seemed their young was all the pain of moledom, all its hopes, and their death was all the cruelty and all the fear. Just empty silence there.

'What can we make there now?' asked Tryfan at last.

'Lat the Stane putte quat it wyl,' she said. 'Der Tryfan, mowle, wyl we togeder be agayne?' There was longing in her sweet voice yet Tryfan did not know why they were parting, nor have words to stop it happening.

'If we are faithful and true I think the Stone will bring us together once more,' he said.

'Myn der, yow are moche biloved. I desyred puppes with yow.'

'You are the only mole I loved or ever can,' said Tryfan.

But Feverfew touched her talon to his mouth as if it might be better to say nothing than to tell what one day might be a lie. His eyes travelled over her flanks, ravaged now by scalpskin, and he touched her there.

She smiled at him, 'Have nat fer, I shalle nat dye. The Stane may heille me welle. Have nat fer myn luv, have not so.'

677

Yet between them was a silence they could not cross for all the words they spoke, of love, of hope of better times. And they parted as if it was a relief, each to seek what it might be that would fill that silence and make them one again.

Soon after Tryfan left the Wen, with Spindle at his side and good Mayweed making a third, to guide them northwards to the place from which old Boswell had called, north past the Dark Peak, north to dread Whern.

Heath said a quiet goodbye, touching Tryfan and Spindle as they went and pausing a final moment with Mayweed, whom he liked.

'One thing importunate me, Mayweed, would like to ask,' said Mayweed.

'Go on, mate, I'll do it if I can.'

'Watch over the magical Madam with love, and when she says she wants to go home, you help her.'

'Heath won't forget that. Now off you go else Heath'll start to cry, and that's not Heath's way,' said Heath.

So Mayweed did, to guide Tryfan and Spindle northward from the Wen.

While down on the eastside of that dying system Starling played with her young, with Feverfew nearby. The other moles stayed clear, scared of Feverfew's scalpskin now.

Yet often Starling's pups played at Feverfew's flanks and Starling let them. She had been protected too long by a mole called Mayweed, who had the scars of scalpskin, to fear it for her young. And, too, as Feverfew sang to them, she saw a healing there, and knew from some ancient wisdom mothers know, what is right and what is wrong.

It was right that her young learnt what Feverfew would teach them. It was right that Tryfan had gone for now.

Yet it was wrong that Feverfew and Tryfan were separate, quite wrong. But Starling kept her silence on that at least, and knew that one day she might, with the Stone's help, right those wrongs she saw.

'Feverfew?'

'Myne der?'

'Will you tell my pups about the Stone when the time's right, and me as well?' Feverfew nodded gently, thinking then of a great silence that was between herself and Tryfan, and she smiled; for there must be a way to fill it, and the Stone would find it, and Tryfan would know that too, he would!

'Will you?' repeated Starling.

'I wyl.'

'Can I listen too, or is it just for pups?'

'Yow can, my luv; yow can.'

Chapter Thirty-Seven

Dissent breeds its own community, which in turn makes its own burrows and finds its own meeting places. So it was now all across moledom among such followers of the Stone as remained willing to give voice to their faith.

In some places, as in Caradoc, long abandoned Stones had become the meeting points, finding new life and ritual in the secret meetings those few brave followers held. But in Stone systems taken over and occupied by the grikes, such Stones became dangerous places to be, for they were often patrolled, and moles found there were under threat of snouting.

So followers in such systems had to choose places which were less obvious, yet which could be found by moles who perhaps had only heard of them by word of mouth, whispered quickly by one believer to another at some hurried meeting where the Stone's wonder was remembered, and its purpose praised. Often such places had to be abandoned, or went for long periods without a visit until suspicion had passed by and they could be used again.

Naturally in the seven Ancient Systems, or at least those ones like Avebury, Duncton, Siabod and Rollright which were occupied by grikes, patrols and watches over the charismatic Stones were always vigilant, especially at times like the solstices when followers like to visit the Stones. Indeed, it is said that even at times of greatest curfew or abandonment many Stones were visited by a believer at Longest Night and at Midsummer. *The Book of Martyrs* contains several names of followers who were led by their faith at such times to such Stones, knowing that their lives would be forfeit. So did the revered Herbert of Avebury die in the dark age of Clayne in that system; and

Ferris, who gave his life at Fyfield in evil Lewknor's time; and more recently beloved Brambling, who suffered martyrdom at Seven Barrows at the talons of the grikes.

But now it is to Rollright that a mole must go, hiding amongst the stand of oaks and ash that lie a little to the south east of the Stones there, to learn of the true beginning of Tryfan's mission north, when in courage and humility he would seek to tell allmole of the Stone as it had been taught him by Boswell himself.

Rollright has a circle of Stones as Avebury has, but naturally in Henbane's time the circle was heavily guarded lest followers should attempt to enter at the surface to gain the healing such circles are said to give.

Yet there are other Stones at Rollright and ones the grikes overlooked, perhaps because their name makes them sound ominous and an unlikely place for dissidents to meet.

These strange Stones, which stand to the south east of the circle, lean strangely together as if protecting each other, and perhaps a superstitious mole in the past felt they were like stoats whispering to each other before taking prey. For local moles call them the Whispering Stoats.

The wind reaches only softly into the enclave they make, for they lie in the lee of the hill where the Rollright circle rises. There, secretly, dissenters met in those days, almost within earshot of the patrolling grikes, and whispered their rituals, asking that the Stone might bring its light back to moledom and grant its Silence.

Sometimes only two or three moles met beneath the Whispering Stoats, for the followers' numbers were hard-pressed by grikes and the spies of the sideem, and many disappeared or died. Yet always others came, whose heart had been touched by the Stone's light and who dared speak out their faith.

A watching mole in those days when Tryfan seemed lost to the followers might well have sensed a longing in such moles; for the way of dissent is a hard one, and lonely, and such a mole finds his paws taking him through the tunnel of dark night when only hope, and faith, and love may lead him on.

Is it any wonder that at such a time, when to followers the whole of moledom seemed like a dark night, that that longing for the Stone and its Silence should find its expression in a need that then of all times, *now*, the Stone Mole might come? Oh, now, Stone, send him that he might help us . . . such was the prayer a watching mole might have heard spoken in the shelter of the Whispering Stoats. . . .

* * * * * * *

Tryfan, Spindle and Mayweed found, as so many travellers have, that the return journey is the swifter and easier of the two. Mayweed had taken a northern route out of the Wen and it proved a wise choice, for though the obstacles and dangers were many yet the routes were fast, and before many days had passed they were back to wormful soils and safe halts while Mayweed decided on the next stage.

They had left in May, and by mid-June were clear of the worst of the Wen and able to veer north west towards Rollright. It was Tryfan's hope to reach it by Midsummer for he believed that though the meeting with Skint and Smithills at Longest Night was past, and it was unlikely that they would have waited for so long, yet it was probable that they had arranged some message for them knowing they might themselves go to Rollright then or, like themselves, send a messenger.

But though they had started swift they began to slow as June progressed and by Midsummer were still some way outside the environs of Rollright. But at least Tryfan knew of the Whispering Stoats from Boswell, for such knowledge is part of the lore that scribemoles traditionally learn as part of their training in the lines of the Stones themselves, so they had an objective.

Spindle and Mayweed had both noticed that Tryfan, who had been quiet ever since his mating with Feverfew

682

and the terrible events of her pupping, had become even quieter since leaving the Wen, though 'quiet' is too passive a word for the state he was in.

If they had expected grief and a sense of loss in him for what he had left behind, they did not find it. Nor was his silence a matter of fatigue after the rigors of the Wen period. It was, rather, the nervousness or doubt that a mole may experience before embarking on a course for which he or she may not feel quite ready, but which circumstances dictate must now begin.

Spindle, who knew Tryfan so well, gave his support in ways few moles would easily have understood though he often seemed to go his own way and followed his interests. Yet when Tryfan needed him he was always there, as he had promised Boswell he would be, and though he never said as much in his own chronicles of his life with Tryfan, we may guess he understood that as Tryfan travelled nearer to that Silence that he sought, the demands on Spindle would become greater and more difficult to fulfil. So perhaps Spindle's reported irritability on the journey between the Wen and Rollright reflected his own unspoken nervousness of the trials that lay ahead; and his growing realisation that they would be great indeed.

For though it is true that Tryfan was continuing with the journey that started at Boswell's behest on Uffington Hill – although some would say that it began at Duncton's Stone when he first left for Uffington with Boswell, and *others*, subtler still, would say his journey began before even that – what Spindle must have realised was that with the start of Tryfan and Feverfew's love the nature of Tryfan's journey had changed and deepened, and its physical direction and objective had, in a profound way, become less important than its spiritual goal.

Tryfan had loved and he had mated; and he had seen his young die. He had felt a silence between himself and his love, great and empty, and he desired to fill it, yet he knew not how but by seeking a way that would for a time take him away from where his heart desired to be.

But was Boswell's call from Whern real? Had he imagined it? Was he running from a reality that stayed where he had left it in the Wen? And was that the way to understand the meaning and purpose of Dunbar's scribings? Was it wrong to leave them behind rather than to go back to them, and sound them once more? And what of his dead young, whom he had failed to save? What of that?

Such questions might do more than slow a mole's paws as he makes trek to Rollright; they might take him into his own individual dark night and leave him troubled and confused, and doubtful of his faith, or its purpose. And coupled with the passage of moleyears that had seen the loss of Duncton Wood, and the death of so many he might have loved and for whom he felt responsible, it might make that dark night seem much more than just a night, but enbleaken his whole life, and numb it. So, yes, Tryfan did slow in his progress towards Rollright, as if he sensed that once there demands would be made on him that he must fulfil, or he would finally be seen to have failed. And, yes, Spindle did grumble and complain, for he was as confused as Tryfan was, and, finally, as afraid.

Yet, it is one of the wonders of the Stone's ministry over moles' lives that when they strive to reach beyond the darkness towards the light, it sends them the means to do so; as if purpose and the courage of faith, especially in the darkest times, brings forth from the Stone its special and most active grace.

Active grace demands practical means, and *that* usually requires the right mole at the right time. It is a truth too many moles forget, or never even know, that the Stone will put them in the way of moles who can most help them when they most need them, even if such moles may not be of the Stone, or especially seeming of worthiness. But then how is a mole in darkness to make such a judgement, even assuming he has the right to do so? He had best trust the Stone to do it for him!

For Tryfan, and for Spindle too, Mayweed was such a

mole. Found by them on the Slopeside of Buckland, accepted by them openly and with love, and increasingly discovering his own purpose through the help he was able to give them. But if he believed that his whole life had been a preparation for his guidance of them into the complexities of Dunbar's chambers and tunnels, he did not know the task the Stone had ordained for him. For his puphood on the Slopeside, and his subsequent helping of Tryfan, was a preparation for something greater even than his technical mastery of the heritage Dunbar left.

There came a night of crisis for Tryfan, after many days when he had said little, when they were but a day or two's journey from Rollright. Tryfan was stressed and silent; Spindle angry and discontented. Yet not so much so that he did not have the sense to tell Mayweed, 'You talk to him, for there's nothing I can say at all. He's morose and ill-tempered and has been contemplating the night sky for hours now and seems to have no intention of doing anything. *You* talk to him, Mayweed, and make him smile again.'

'Trusting Sir, Mayweed will do so, but Mayweed doesn't happen to think that a joke or a laugh will serve. Tryfan needs something more substantial than that!'

'Well, I don't know what it is. Just that you might be able to help.'

'Humble me will try, Sir, yes Mayweed will. He remembers that courageous Tryfan was in a tunnel under a river once, and that Tryfan was afraid. He remembers he was able to comfort Tryfan then. He thinks that perhaps Tryfan is in a tunnel again now, but a darker and longer one, without hope of light or memory of comfort. Mayweed will try to give him hope and comfort, though Mayweed is not worthy of much, so he can only do his best. He would only ask before he tries that wise Spindle blesses him, for he is very frightened too, and sometimes, like now, he shakes with fear that he might one day have to go back to the tunnels of darkness Tryfan helped him be free from.'

Then Mayweed lowered his snout and Spindle said, 'Well, I'm not much of one for blessings, but I think perhaps if Tryfan was his normal self he would put his right paw on your own like this, and I think he would say . . .' Then Spindle fell silent, thinking of the blessings he knew and seeking to find one Tryfan might say.

Then he spoke these words softly:

> Stone, bless thou this mole fearing:
> By flank, by snout, by talon,
> By eye, by heart he's fearing.
> Stone, guide thou this mole seeking
> By flank, by snout, by talon,
> By eye, by snout he's seeking.
> Stone, help thou this mole loving
> By flank, by snout, by talon,
> By eye, by heart he's loving.
>
> Stone bless and guide and love
> This mole, trusting.

Mayweed found Tryfan on the surface 'contemplating the night sky' just as Spindle had said he would be, and he took a stance near him without a word. He saw by such light as there was that Tryfan's eyes were empty and desolate.

Mayweed said nothing, but crouched still and close to Tryfan so that he knew he was there to share the night with him. He stared at the darkness around them, so rich in its change and variety, and he heard the sounds that share the surface with a crouching mole. He did as Tryfan had taught him to, as Boswell had taught *him*, which is to breathe slow and feel each paw upon the ground one after another, one after another, as if in that rhythm a mole may become grounded again, and find his way forward.

So Mayweed felt that dark night come into him, and the dark earth beneath, and the presence of a mole he loved near him, and he whispered, 'Help him, Stone, help him.'

Much later Tryfan sighed, and turned a little towards Mayweed, and said, 'I am not worthy, Mayweed, although I know you think I am. But I have failed so many and come no nearer to the fulfilment of my task.'

Mayweed said nothing.

Later Tryfan said, 'There's so much to do and I know you and Spindle are waiting for me to decide where we are to go, and what we must do first. I know that. . . .'

Mayweed said nothing.

'But I don't know what I can do, or how I can do it, or where. I just feel I have to go to Whern, but I don't know why. I feel Boswell must be there. But the further towards it I go, the further it takes me from Feverfew and I feel I must be there too! Moles do not like a scribemole to be in such doubt.'

Mayweed asked a question: 'Troubled Sir, whom Mayweed has grown to love and trust, how do you imagine humble me finds my way in tunnels where others lose themselves? How do I choose between one way and another?'

'You must need to be very quiet to do it, very listening. I spent much of my time with Boswell learning to listen, and yet I sometimes think I never learned a thing! Which is what I told him often enough. And you know what he said? He said "Don't try so hard. Enjoy life!"'

Mayweed laughed.

'Mayweed sometimes wishes he had met Boswell, and he hopes one day he will, since he sounds like a mole after his own heart. In fact, battered Sir, Mayweed thinks Boswell would know how to find his way through tunnels very well.'

Tryfan smiled and said, 'He would be pleased to hear you of all moles say that, Mayweed. How *do* you choose between two routes when both seem equally attractive, or equally difficult?'

'Striving Tryfan has asked Mayweed a question which he has often thought about and will now try to answer. Humble he learned something very useful when he was

687

small and frightened, which Tryfan may have lost sight of in the darkness he now finds himself in: a mole faced by two choices of action may forget he always has a third, which is to do nothing. Mayweed has discovered that while he is quietly doing nothing moledom shifts and changes, and the choices he faced shift too so that one that seemed difficult becomes very easy. Mayweed suspects that Tryfan has forgotten Boswell's advice to him to do nothing and enjoy life. Mayweed humbly suggests to Tryfan that he forgets all about the choices he has to make and concentrates instead on putting one paw in front of another enjoyably. He may then find that the correct route finds *his* paws, leaving him free to snout about towards the light a bit more.'

Mayweed fell silent and Tryfan relaxed. Eventually he said, 'Would you like to make any other suggestions, Mayweed, since that one seems to me very sound?'

'Satisfied Sir, I will make a statement rather than a suggestion. It is this. This mole, me, Mayweed by name, has found much happiness in the company of Tryfan, and he is sad that Tryfan is beset. He does not intend to leave Tryfan or scholarly Spindle, nor withdraw his guiding services from them. He is aware that both those courageous moles wish to get to Whern, and though he has never been that way he will take them there by a route that may meander somewhat since, in his view, fast is not always best. If he, modest Mayweed, guides, that leaves Tryfan and Spindle free to do what together they are best doing, which is the second part of Mayweed's statement.

'The second part is this: Mayweed repeats what he said once before in different circumstances, namely, that when Tryfan found him he was an unhappy mole, yet today as a result of being in Tryfan's presence he is a happy one, very happy. He humbly suggests, in fact he boldly avers, that if Tryfan would let himself be guided through this dark period by humble me, while permitting those dark visions that pass before his snout to, er, *be*, then in the freedom that will give him he may usefully talk with other moles we meet as he has talked with this humble mole, through which process trusting Tryfan may find he is terrific again.'

'Talk of what?' said Tryfan.

'Mayweed is not the mole to advise on *that*. He can only say that what may be important is not what you say but that you, Tryfan, are trying to say it. That's what humbleness here thinks anyway.'

The two moles were silent almost to dawn when Tryfan, sounding more peaceful, said, 'And what about *you*, Mayweed? What do you hope for now? A mate at last, as you told me when we were in Wen? Are you going to find one?'

'Meek Mayweed is not much to look at, but he cheers himself up with the thought that nor are many females either. All in all, humble he is quietly confident on this subject. He has also concluded from observation of others that love comes when a mole least expects it, a point the troubled Sir should remember in the continuing context of striving to get somewhere when he is not sure where. So: Mayweed expects to fall in love with the mole he least expects to love. When that happens, Mayweed will try to put into practice all he has learned and hope his friends will help him as best they can.'

'We will, Mayweed!' smiled Tryfan. Then they both noticed that Spindle had quietly joined them, and Tryfan said, 'Won't we Spindle?'

'Yes!' said Spindle. 'Mayweed in love would be a remarkable sight.'

'Sparkling Spindle was not there a moment ago,' said Mayweed.

'Sparkling Spindle was feeling in need of a stretch,' said Spindle.

'Well,' sighed Tryfan, 'I think we all need that. So, Mayweed, where are we going today? You are now our guide north.'

Mayweed grinned.

'Rollright first,' he said. 'Mayweed will snout about and

ponder the point and then proceed. He suggests that Tryfan and Spindle follow sharpish as once Mayweed sets off in a cheerful mood he doesn't like to stop!'

'Yes, Mayweed,' said Tryfan.

'Indeed!' said Spindle. 'Indeed it is so!'

* * * * * * *

It was with a freer spirit that Tryfan arrived at Rollright some days later, knowing that from now on Mayweed would take all responsibility for guiding them, and feeling that in this the Stone was directing.

They made their way cautiously into the system from the south west and reached the Whispering Stoats without a mishap. There was nomole there, but they decided to stay quietly among the trees nearby in the hope that a St one follower might come who could give them news of the friends from whom they had parted so long before. They settled down for a long wait.

It was three days before they made the contact they sought, and in that time they saw several patrols and a couple of individuals, but none of them came near the Stoats. But on the evening of the third day a mole approached cautiously from the west, snouting about the area with great care before advancing into the enclave of the Stones. There he crouched for a little, and then said a rough prayer, looking up at the Stones and touching one of them.

He was of good size and strong, but it was clear that he had been in a good many fights because his flanks and snout were scarred, and he seemed to have lost a talon from his left paw. There was something familiar about him, but none of them could quite place him.

They waited until he came out of the enclave before addressing him, and, after a moment of stancing in which he left them in no doubt that he would have fought for his life formidably, he came forward with a mixture of surprise, relief and pleasure on his face.

'Why, 'tis Tryfan and Spindle the Cleric if I'm not mistaken, and both alive. And you . . .' He looked at Mayweed but obviously did not know his name.

690

'Before you, fearless follower, is moledom's humblest, moledom's least: Mayweed by name. But what we wish to know, and in double quick time before the gormless grikes hear us, is who you are and what news you have for us.'

'Mayweed too, eh! Well, bless me, there's a lot more moles than me will be glad to see you three alive. I'm Tundry, and I expect I've changed a bit since you saw me last, Tryfan Sir. Skint's group, the Marsh End Defence, Duncton Wood.'

Tryfan suddenly remembered. This mole had been a last-minute replacement in the Marsh End group.

'So what news of Skint?'

'Safe Sir, and well so far as I know. Smithills too. They waited here at Longest Night having damn near broke their necks getting here to meet you, and then hung about a bit after. But they decided to travel on and as I was the one deputed to stay at Rollright under cover of following the Word, they trusted me to make contact with you and tell you where to find them should you want to . . . But I know a better place than this to talk, and a mole who would like to see you, so follow me now.'

He took them downslope away from the main system, at first through dry runs but later into damp soil, and then into downright wet soil.

'Not pleasant but grikes never come here,' said Tundry.

As he spoke a couple of youngsters peered out at them from a side tunnel, both filthy, their faces as begrimed with mud as it is possible to be. Mayweed stared at them hard, a look of puzzled recognition on his face.

They went on a little way and a third youngster popped her head round a corner, as muddy as the first two. All silent, very.

'Mayweed suggests that there is something very familiar about these tunnels, and requests permission to go ahead.'

'You're in charge anyway,' said Tryfan.

'Mayweed goes ahead hopefully, into tunnels whose cut and whose general air of untidy order and muddy filth warms his heart as much as it besmirches his paws.

Mayweed's heart is suddenly *full* of hope that not far from here is a mole he feared he might not meet again. Mayweed. . . .'

But Mayweed said no more for as they rounded a corner into a communal burrow, as messy as the tunnels that preceded it, they found themselves face to face with not one mole but two. The cleaner of them was a female, though she was grubby enough, yet cheerful and well rounded, with fur that went this way and that in a carefree way and an eagerness about her that reminded them of somemole they had met before. But it was at the male next to her that Mayweed stared in delighted disbelief.

'Mayweed cannot believe his eyes,' said Mayweed.

For the mole before him, who stared with wide eyes and said not a word, was Holm. Silent Holm, whose fur was still mud-covered. Mute Holm, who was almost as good a route-finder as Mayweed himself. Speechless Holm, who had first showed Mayweed the way out of Duncton Wood.

And Holm said not a word, yet what he did do could not have said more for what he felt. For he stared at Mayweed and tears came to his eyes and his snout lowered and his little marshy body heaved and puffed with emotion. Then he turned to the female and made what was, for him, a long speech: 'I'm happy,' he said. And then, 'I'm happy, Lorren!'

Lorren! Starling's sister. Lorren?

But she was tubby, she was dirty, she was. . . .

'Happy!' said Mayweed, speaking for them all. As he spoke the three youngsters they had seen earlier poked their heads out from the tunnel at the back of the chamber and stared in awestruck silence.

'Sirs,' began Mayweed, 'Sirs, all five of us, Madam, all one of you, alias large Lorren, and wondering youngsters, Mayweed repeats the only word worth saying twice on this occasion: Happy. And he says it a third time, because seeing these two before him, once helpless Holm with once pupless Lorren, should give Tryfan here and Spindle too the encouragement they need, and moledom too, so he pronounces: Happy.'

Lorren laughed in a rounded generous kind of way, looked serious, and immediately asked about Starling. And then she was in tears as they told she too had pupped, and she was safe, and hoped one day to return to Duncton Wood.

Then those moles told each other their news, the youngsters asked by Tryfan himself to stay, for the future of moledom would depend on such moles as them, and they must learn of their past and the moles that fought for it so that one day they would know what it meant, and how much of the past a good future holds.

When news of each other was done, the three travellers turned to Tundry, who, with due solemnity, told them what happened to Skint's group in Duncton Wood after Henbane took the system over, and how it was they left.

★ ★ ★ ★ ★ ★ ★

The first molemonths after Duncton moles' departure went exactly as Skint and Tryfan had planned it should: the grikes were harassed, several were killed, they were forced to patrol in groups of two or three but even then Skint's moles succeeded in picking off a few.

It seemed to have dawned only slowly on the grikes that covert moles were lodged in tunnels in the wood, and when it did searches were started and patrol upon patrol tramped about the Marsh End seeking them. But they were never successful and, indeed, in all the time they were there, the Marsh End Defence was never found. Though whether it had been subsequently Tundry did not know.

Then towards the end of September they noticed a change come over the system. For a start there was a long period when no patrols appeared at all. The atmosphere became as eerily quiet as the autumn mists that drifted from the marshes in among the trees. Then there were scurryings in the wood, and secret comings and surreptitious goings. Screams, sometimes of violence and of terror. Skint's moles heard these things and yet, when they ventured out on to the surface, they found nothing and saw nothing in the mists and rains. The wood seemed deserted, and there was even a day or two they began to think that Henbane's grikes had left altogether.

Yet an atmosphere of fear and horror had overtaken the once peaceful wood.

'I cannot put it into words, Tryfan Sir, not having your way with them, or Spindle's here, so I can only say that with the grikes about a mole knew what he was up against,' recalled Tundry. 'But when that change came you knew there was something else, and it hid. It didn't show its snout, and you knew it was dangerous and clever. Lurking, evil, very dangerous.

'Naturally we decided to find out about what had happened to the grikes, and Skint himself and two others set out one day to head up south to the Ancient System's tunnels. Well there were grikes there all right. No doubt about that: thick as fleas on an old mole. And evidence of occupation in tunnels on the east slope, and hiding moles . . . but we could not have guessed what was going on.'

Then, in October, they found out. One wet day they heard a commotion on the surface near their defence and investigated. Moles fighting, to the death. Big moles, desperate moles. They heard the death blows and the dying screams but as their orders had always been to stay covert they did not interfere. When all was quiet they went out on the surface and found a dead mole.

'Never forget it,' said Tundry. 'He was dead from talon-thrusts all right, but you might as well say he was dead from disease. His sides were eaten raw with it, and there was maggots in there, and must have been there when he was alive. He was big, that mole, muscular, and whatever mole or moles had killed him would have been strong. Skint ordered that we didn't touch him and it seemed owls wouldn't either, though we heard them investigate. Didn't like the scent, and don't blame them. Stunk our tunnels out because he rotted where he was. And that was only the beginning.'

'Of what?' asked Spindle.

'Of an invasion the like of which nomole has ever seen, and one which nearly took us lot over and killed us. Well, it did, some of us. . . .'

Skint and his group were in the perfect position to watch the tragedy that unfolded across Duncton Wood as Henbane's policy of importing all the misfits, miscreants and diseased moles who were near enough to make the journey to Duncton Wood. Part of her unpleasant genius was to order that such moles were not forced to come but, rather, were offered the opportunity of a better life, a freer life, somewhere where they could dictate their own destiny, subject only to the rules they created for themselves; along with certain rules laid down by Henbane and enforced by her successor Wyre through his representative in Duncton Wood. The rules were simple enough: nomole to set paw in or on the Ancient System, nomole to attempt (therefore) to visit the Stone and, finally, nomole to leave the system.

The grikes effectively isolated themselves from the newcomers, releasing them northward into the system immediately on arrival at the cow cross-under over which the grikes and Duncton moles had fought so bitterly. The new arrivals went one way, the grikes another, their routes to the Ancient System being clear of the other tunnels.

What happened in the lower tunnels the grikes neither knew nor cared, least of all Beake, the eldrene in charge of them. She was as bitter a mole as ever lived, and was happy to kill with her own thin talons anymole from the lower slopes who transgressed the rules. Some did early on, simply for lack of knowledge of the system, but the others soon learnt from their deaths and the sight of their torn bodies which the guardmoles dragged back into the lower slopes were a terrible reminder. Others were too ill, physically or mentally, to know where they were, and they were killed if they trespassed. And a few, outcast for being Stone followers, strove to reach the Stone in the belief that it might take them out of the torment which they gradually began to realise they had been brought to. Such moles too were killed.

Slowly, Skint and his group came to understand what was happening, and for a time thought that they might be able to organise the new arrivals into a force that could overthrow the grikes. But that proved impossible. There was no order to be found among the newcomers, and the more that arrived through October and November, the more chaos and anarchy reigned as moles formed packs and began to kill each other in an effort to establish dominance.

Tundry made them shudder at his memories of the torments he witnessed, of the cruelty of the maddened, diseased and mentally ill moles who settled in Duncton and created a murderous and foul community of their own. They heard snoutings and mutilations, they saw killings and violence, they saw groups of males torment and destroy females, and they found evidence of groups of females retaliating against individual males. The stronger and the fitter began to emerge as leaders, and formed groups of moles which were violent parodies of the groupings that had been in evidence in Bracken's young days. For just as then the strongest moles were the Westsiders because that was where the wormful soils were, so now the stronger took the Westside, and places there were won hard, with talon and tooth. The chalky Eastside became the place to die, for the diseased moles lived there, and moles ousted from other parts were driven there, or would flee there before they were killed.

Barrow Vale, the traditional centre of the system, became an area where nomole went alone but, rather, went in groups to protect each other. While inevitably the Marsh End became the place for secretive survivors, physically weak moles who had intelligence and resource, and could tolerate the damper conditions and the poor soils of that low part of the wood.

So, quite quickly, a kind of order came to Duncton Wood and Skint decided it would be best to evacuate his small group. The decision was hastened by the loss of two of his moles, Fidler and Yarrow, when they were caught by some of the rough Westsiders and killed. Skint made attempts to parley with those moles, but after being taken he, too, was nearly killed, escaping narrowly and having to lie low for two days before being able to rejoin Tundry and the other three.

November was passing by and Skint wished to get to Rollright in good time to meet Tryfan there. So, using one of the small conduits north of the cow cross-under, the party had left Duncton Wood, unsure whether their stay there had been successful or not. But to the last their tunnels were not discovered, and when they left they did so privily, blocking up the entrances down into the tunnels in which they had successfully hidden for so long.

'The journey to Rollright proved a slow one, Sir,' concluded Tundry, 'because the grikes were thick on the ground and we passed more than one party of moles who were being taken to Duncton, judging by the state of them. I tell you, that's not a system which will be occupied again in our time and I pity the mole who tries it. Nomole would go there now, and by the time those moles started breeding last spring, it must have become a terrible place indeed. To think, Duncton Wood occupied by such poor, tormented and plain ruthless moles as that and no traditions of their own but the violent ones they make! The word we have now is Beake is dead and the grikes have retreated back to a garrison this side of the cow cross-under. She died of disease, and the grikes will not be shaken from that strong point they have reached, nor by the disorganised rabble that those moles must be. And still moles are being taken to Duncton and forced through the cross-under to whatever foul life lives beyond it now.

'As for Skint and those of us who survived, we came here, and, Stone be praised, good Smithills was waiting, and Lorren and Holm too, and told us your news, bad and good. Of the tunnel collapse and of the escape. Skint and he waited for a time and then, as I've said, journeyed north, saying that they had a mind you would be doing the same once you heard the last thing I have to tell you which is this: Henbane has gone north to Whern and that mole Weed with her; and we've heard that Siabod has fallen and the grikes finally victorious.'

'No word of Alder or Marram then?' said Tryfan.

'None.'

'Nor any other moles who survived the tunnel collapse on the Duncton side?'

Tundry shook his head. Grim news indeed, most of it.

Tryfan was silent for a little until he roused himself and asked again after Skint.

'Aye, he said he'd leave word of where you could find him, at Beechenhill, a system in the heart of the Dark Peak, too small for grikes to bother with. There are worthy moles up there and Skint reckoned that by the time you got there they would know what he was up to.'

This was most of the general news Tundry had, the rest being about his own decision to Atone bravely and admit of the Word and live among the grikes until better days came and his talons would be needed inside the system he had infiltrated.

'Not talons I think, but faith and belief in the Stone,' said Tryfan quietly.

'Yes, well, maybe,' said Tundry. 'But talons is what won grikes their territory, talons is what will lose it.'

Perhaps Tryfan saw a look of admiration for Tundry in Holm's three youngsters' eyes as they listened to this adult talk in fascinated silence; or perhaps some inner shock and disgust with the rule of violence which seemed to descend finally to everywhere that had lost touch with the Stone, whether it was Duncton Wood or Rollright, Uffington or even the Wen.

Whatever it was Tryfan seemed to grow purposeful then, and powerful, and though he spoke softly nomole doubted he meant what he said.

'The way of the Stone is not the way of the talon; and nor will that be the Stone Mole's way. I have seen too much violence, and inflicted some myself, with intent and by accident, to wish ever to inflict more. The ways of the Stone will be quiet and mindful, for they are the ways of Silence and of light.

'But they are harder ways, Tundry, than the talon and claw. And demand more courage. . . .'

'More?' said Tundry, flexing his talons and the light catching the scars of battle that coursed across his strong flanks.

'Yes, more,' said Tryfan. 'A talon-thrust is easier to make than a piercing thought, a thought is harder to absorb than a talon-thrust. It is easier to make an adult mole scream than to comfort a mewing pup; it is harder for a mole to admit a fault than to assert what he thinks may be a right. The way of the Stone is by thought, by listening to another's cries, by changes which starts in each mole's being. These will be the Stone Mole's ways, and they are the hardest.'

'And what of Skint, Alder and Marram, and moles like me?' said Tundry, suddenly angry. 'Such moles use talons for the Stone – are they wrong? Will you tell them they are wrong?'

'I know not what may be right for them,' said Tryfan, 'or whether I shall myself ever be able to hold my talons back when I am threatened, or those I love are. I know that if you attacked Spindle here now, or Mayweed, or any of these moles I would defend them to the death. That I know.'

'We were given talons for fighting,' said Tundry.

'No, we were given them for delving, we *choose* to fight with them as well. We choose to believe that talon should fight talon. But I have travelled a good part of southern moledom and I have seen only sadness and loss. I see moles who long for peace, harmless moles like Holm here, forced to hide their lives away for fear of others' talons. Are there not worms enough for all moles? Is there not earth enough for all their tunnels? I think the Stone Mole will show there is a different way.'

699

'Is he coming then, and soon?' asked Lorren quietly.

'I think he is. And I think the more moles long for him, and need him, the more certain he is to come. I think Boswell is part of his coming. I think we all are.'

'Well I hope he asks us to attack the grikes when he does, for there's plenty of moles willing to do that, and many a Stone follower to be made that way!' said Tundry.

'He will ask us to hear the Stone, not attack the grikes.'

'And what if the grikes attack us as they will – as they do – when they find us meeting together?'

'He will ask us to listen harder!' said Tryfan.

'There's not a mole will follow him if that's all he really says, Tryfan Sir; and there's precious few will accept what you say either.'

'Then I must learn to speak with more love, Tundry, and that, I assure you, is a harder thing to learn than using talons more effectively. Now, I think our group is tired and we must eat and sleep. Tomorrow we will go to the Whispering Stoats, and we will give thanks to the Stone that we are all so well met, and ask that we may so meet Skint and Smithills on our journey north to Whern, even if it is to tell them something they may not wish to hear!'

Tryfan and the other two were given food then, and shown a place to rest. While Lorren and Holm watched over them, their pups stared in awe at the great mole and his two companions who had come to their tunnels and spoken of things that in all their long lives those youngsters would never forget.

Whatmole knows how the Stone's will journeys forth, and where its grace may be felt? Perhaps it is in the longing moles have for such light and peace. But Tundry went abroad later that night, and Lorren too, and whispers went out to followers that here, in Rollright itself, a great mole slept, a mole who knew of the Stone and would give moles a blessing by it. A scribemole no less, and one whose very name it was dangerous to speak, for was he not turned against his own kind, had he not accepted the Word? Was he not captured by the grikes, had he not betrayed his friends? Lies, grike lies, all of it.

The next dawn Tryfan and the other two were quietly led by Holm back to the Whispering Stoats, and there they found others, hushed and waiting. And even as they began their meeting, more came, old moles, young moles, moles in fear for their lives, moles who had heard, and who wished to make witness, so that the enclave around those leaning Stones was thronged with hushed moles as Tryfan said his quiet prayers, and went among them, touching them and blessing them as Boswell had taught him.

Again and again moles asked him, 'Is the Stone Mole coming?'

And to some Tryfan said, 'Yes, he is coming now, be patient, have faith, the Stone's Silence will be heard.' While to others he whispered, 'If it is the Stone's will you will know of him and he will make blessings on you. Trust the Stone.' Then he spoke to all of them, saying what he had said to Tundry, that the day of talons was done, the way of mindful peace was come; and before its armies the Word would die.

Then Tryfan took his leave of the moles of Rollright and was led forward by Mayweed of Buckland, who had promised to guide him north and began now to do so. While among the moles they left behind, modest courageous moles of faith, some, just a few, said, 'Where he touched me is healing, this mole Tryfan is sent by the Stone! He has healed me!' And so, through those moles, and many others Tryfan was to touch on his long journey north, the Stone spoke its heralding of the coming of the Stone Mole, and spread word of the wonder of which Tryfan of Duncton spoke, and which *would* come.

Chapter Thirty-Eight

The heart of a mole travelling north can soon begin to die. For though sometimes his route turns east or west and he finds the sun across his face, yet finally he must always leave the sun behind him, so that only his shadow stalks ahead, pausing and stopping on the many rough rises that approach, as if to warn that a wise mole should turn back.

Yet as far as the Dark Peak there is enough to scent and see to believe it is worthwhile, and wormful, to continue, and though a mole likes not the prospect ahead yet somehow the ground underpaw is rich and good; and if the sun shines not, at least the rivers and streams that flow in those parts babble him an accompaniment, and hint of good life thereabouts.

But then the Dark Peak comes, those high and worm-less moors which have deterred moles through the centuries from venturing further for lack of an easy route or friendly moles to act as willing guides. Friendly? Willing? A travel-wise mole does not say 'Dark Peak' and use such words as those in one breath!

There the grey sky darkens with the turn of a sad rook's wing, and tawny owls hold a sway they have lost in southern moledom, where roaring owl and twofoot spread their fume and noise.

So, surrounded by high moors whose peat is claggy and difficult and leads easily on to a wormless death unless a mole knows his way well and keeps his courage bold, a mole slows down and is liable to attack by creatures whose eyes slant meanly and whose mouths whisper cruelties and tell lies.

Yet a bold mole heading north must go on beyond the Peak and try to find a route through valleys where the last great, bleak spread of twofoots goes, and roaring owls, whose ways there are smaller and light up the country lurid through the night. Narrow those ways, and dangerous, and fox roams and owls sweep and bank rats kill, if roaring owl fails to take a mole first.

The air is chilly, the sun more rare, the rain colder and more heavy, rolling in dank swathes across from the west: this is the rain that drowns the worm. Here a travelling mole sees strange and desperate sights, of black slugs roaming, of moths dying and of bleached worms floating. Warnings all of them. Warnings to turn back, warnings to retreat, warnings whispered in the thick stenchy grass as the wind conspires among it to confuse a mole, and make him better prey.

Tired now, bleak of heart, whatmole would journey on, but one with great faith, or one whose heart is dark indeed, willing to turn from the sun, willing to flee towards Dark Sound?

No need even for moles to make the scribings of Dark Sound to hear it, not *here*. The very rocks have been contorted by a dire fate, rock of grit, rock of burnt rock, rock of slippery shale; rock that catches Dark Sound and sends it forth so that a mole may think the very earth itself attacks him.

Which, perhaps, it does.

No wonder then, that for centuries past none but the scribemoles of doomed Uffington travelled north, taking their courage in their paws and seeking knowledge to scribe into the Rolls of the Systems, that great testimony to a tradition that became sterile, which collected facts of systems and of mole, but finally forgot to listen to the longing in poor moles' hearts.

Until no more scribemoles came, and that fastness beyond the Dark Peak became unknown to moles in the south, the source only of legend and story, myth and fear, as unexplored shadows always are.

Then from that unknown northern place came plague, like the stench of badger, dead, slow, and sure. Creeping on, unstoppable. And in its dire wake came grikes, unknown, faceless, feared, who spoke the Word and cowed moles and then killed them.

Of that we know. Of that we have seen. With that our hearts have withered, too, and wondered why, when the sun can shine and across a springtime field of grass a scented wind can run, *why* such darkness came and wheretofore.

But now, you moles who once said prayers for Bracken and Rebecca, and repeated them for Tryfan, travel north with him, go by the tunnels he follows, watch over him with your love, whisper blessings on him and those who travel with him: Mayweed, mole of courage, and Spindle, strange mole, wise mole, nervous for the moles he loves. Yet the one who witnessed Tryfan's ordination to his task, and pledged himself as companion and helper, friend and follower.

Go with them beyond the Dark Peak, be fearful for them, and if your courage fails as they reach the very edge of Whern and you are afraid to travel on then wait for them, be ready for their return, for surely they will need your prayers and your good help for the completion of their task.

★ ★ ★ ★ ★ ★ ★

Yet while Tryfan pauses staring north at the fearsome rises where Whern begins, and before its darkness must finally descend, remember with him something of that journey north from Rollright in which, almost without knowing what he was doing, he put a hope into the hearts of many moles, and made them believe that soon now, not so long but that they could not wait for it with patience and forbearance, the Stone Mole would come.

Many are the systems that claim today Tryfan passed their way then. Many that tell of the healings he made. Many that feel they were once blessed by him. 'Tryfan was here!' they say. They saw a mole afraid, who felt the loss of all he had seen and heard till then. They saw a mole humble, whose wisdom came out slow, and spoke only of peace and mindfulness, who asked the followers he met to hold back their talons from attack, to let the grikes be what they were. They saw a mole who was separated from his only mate, one he had hardly known at all; they saw a mole who understood the failures they had made because he suffered for his own.

They heard a mole who spoke of a system he loved, a home lost to him by plague and grike as theirs had been. They heard a mole speak of Boswell, the White Mole, who he believed was now in Whern and waiting for followers to show their faith. They heard a mole who knew the rhymes and rituals of the past, and who spoke them at their Stones, or their secret places, or simply in their burrows, simply and direct, as if they were sharing his private prayers with the Stone itself.

They knew a mole ordained at Uffington, the very last of his kind, a scribemole who taught scribing to those who would learn and did not make it a secret, mysterious thing at all.

When Tryfan passed their way followers flocked to him, and he spoke to them softly so that each felt it was to him or her he spoke alone. Yet when they asked what they should do he told them he was not worthy to tell them that, but that one worthier than he would come and he would be the Stone Mole; *he* would tell them.

Always while he spoke, Spindle the Cleric crouched nearby – a clever mole he! – and Mayweed, who made the youngsters laugh, and whose scalpskinned body and balded face could not hide the love and awe he felt for the scribemole he led north.

'Why don't the grikes attack us?' Spindle asked, often enough. For they did not, although many moles came to the supposedly secret meetings the followers held with Tryfan on his mission north.

'They *must* know,' Spindle went on. 'They've done everything else so efficiently, I can't believe our coming is a secret to them.'

'Sensitive Spindle, humble I agrees,' said Mayweed. 'Perhaps it is a plot! A thing the grasping grikes are good at. Perhaps they want us, or Tryfan here, to go north.'

'I'm sure it is,' said Tryfan, 'but since we have not been harmed, and nor have any of the followers so far as we know, then we may as well continue as we are. Remember, while the grikes may need to plot, the Stone never does! If I was in favour of images of strife I know which side I would prefer to be on.'

So they had progressed, news of their coming stealing ahead as rumour does, with followers coming to the sites they found and listening to Tryfan's words, and taking comfort from his prediction of the Stone Mole's imminence.

'But how do you *know?*' said Spindle worriedly. 'Suppose he doesn't come? We'll look rather foolish. Perhaps that's what Henbane wants. And then, even if he does come, she can have him killed so that finally the Stone will look weak and helpless and the fight will go from the followers.'

'Well, perhaps that is what she hopes, and it helps explain the grikes leaving us alone. But I'm afraid I can't tell you how I know he'll come, because I don't really know how I do. Yet I feel it is in Whern that the secret of his coming lies, and for that reason it is to there we must go.'

'Humph!' declared Spindle.

'Trouble with you is you want it in a text, Spindle, then you might believe it.'

'As a matter of fact it *is* in a text – Dunbar's prophecies. But they're so vague that they don't really justify you gallivanting about the countryside telling moles. . . .'

'Hardly gallivanting, Spindle! I'm exhausted.'

'You're not the only one,' Spindle said irritably.

There is another memory we may share before we follow Tryfan on into Whern itself. . . .

It was as they entered the Dark Peak, when they were feeling at their most beset, that Mayweed, in the way he had, found a better route for them to take. One not quite

706

north, which veering east caught the morning sun. There the land was deep incised with meandering rivers, and though the soil was poor and acid for the most part yet, in places, it was rich and good, and among its flowers stayed the sun, and birdsong fluttered.

Mayweed had confirmed that a few Stone followers lived high and undisturbed in those parts, in a place called Beechenhill. A name Skint had asked that they remember, for there he would leave news for them. As they climbed up among its dales Tryfan had felt a great lifting of his heart, for those flowers they saw were good and fresh, and the sounds of the country were all about them as rivers tumbled in the vales below.

On the third day there, before they met anymole, Tryfan decided to wander off alone.

'But . . .' began Spindle, dubious.

'Beloved Sir,' said Mayweed, 'we both prefer to keep you in our sight!'

But Tryfan laughed and said, 'There's something good about this place, something that fills my heart, something – ' And they were astonished to see tears in his eyes, such tears of joy and sadness that an open-hearted mole may weep when he feels renewed the beauty and the possibility of life.

That day Tryfan wandered far, seeing, as he had not since a pup, the good earth all about him in all its colour and sound, its texture and its scent; in its great glory.

It was July, when the trials and tragedies of breeding and raising young are done, and the darker stresses of the winter months are still far off. July, when the earth holds moisture well, and turf springs under a mole's paws and is full of warmth and maturing content.

July, when the sky is full of whiteness and blue, and beneath it moledom stretches forth, filled with the scent of honeysuckle and the sweet delight of rowan trees, and the hare stops upright to stare, its front paws dangling.

July, when moledom's finest flowers bloom, and woundwort rises by the stream and rosebay where the fire

707

has passed, and there, where Tryfan went, tormentil offers a yellow to brighten a mole on his way, and thyme a scented place to rest; while across the vale, not far for a mole to go nor so far that he cannot hear where he watches from, the green woodpecker starts and stops across the wood, knocking. Whilst nearby the insects buzz.

It was such a day in July that Tryfan roamed, the kind of day a mole desires to be alone unless a lover's near. And if she's not, or he is away, then when they meet again it is the day a mole remembers to ask what his lover did, to affirm they were thinking only of each other then.

Tryfan roamed that day and thought of Feverfew, and knew that if one day, by the Stone's grace, he was with his love again he would ask her if she remembered *that* day, and what she did. And he knew what her answer would be: that she *did* remember, for the sun had shone, and the darkness of the past was gone, and she knew *that* day Tryfan thought of her.

Alone then, yet feeling he was not alone, Tryfan wandered up those vales to Beechenhill, and found a place that would forever be beloved in his heart. High enough to feel the sky was near, yet low enough for the vales below to still be real. High enough that rock outcropped and gave the hills a majesty, low enough that streams ran well, near and far, giving the air the life of water-sound; and warm enough that a mole less full of life than Tryfan felt that day might have stopped nearly anywhere, and crouched, and stared, to watch the rich life of that season wander by.

Until, finally, he did stop, the sun upon his back and then warming his snout as he extended it along his paws to contemplate nothing more than the good scent and sights about him.

'Ssh! He's asleep.'

'Are you sure!'

'Mmm. He's big.'

'He's old.'

'No he's not. He's just a bit wrinkled.'

'He's scarred. He doesn't look frightening at all.'

'Are you sure it's *him*?'

'Ssh! Keep your voice down. It must be him.'

Youngsters! Tryfan stirred slowly, not wishing to frighten them.

'Hello!' he said.

They stared. Two of them, a male and female.

'Are you the mole come to teach us?'

'The mole from the south?'

'I could be,' said Tryfan. 'How did you know about me?'

'Everymole knows you're coming here. They've been expecting you for ages. What have you come for?'

'I wish I knew,' said Tryfan.

'Isn't it to teach us?'

'Teach you what?'

The youngsters looked uncertain.

'Don't know,' said one shyly.

'About the Stone,' said the other.

'Have you a Stone in Beechenhill?' he asked.

'Of course we have. It's the best in the whole of moledom. Didn't you know *that*?'

'Well I do now,' said Tryfan. 'Would you show it to me?'

'Come on then,' said one of them. And off they went, leading Tryfan in the way youngsters will, by places they like, by things they want to show, through time that is their own.

'There!' they said much later. 'That's our Stone.'

Tryfan stared up at it, and then at the views beyond the pastures in which Beechenhill's Stone stands.

'Well? It is the best, isn't it?'

Tryfan went to it and touched it with his paw. It rose proud and golden in the sun, warm and a little rough to his touch, and it seemed to him that day that the whole of moledom radiated from it.

'Today it is the best,' he said.

'Not always?'

'When you've touched other Stones and prayed by them, then you must decide that for yourselves.'

'You don't really think it's the best, do you?' grinned the female wickedly.

'I'll tell you what I do think,' said Tryfan confidentially. 'I know a Stone that I think you would like as much as this.'

The other youngster nodded his head knowingly.

'You mean the Duncton Stone, don't you? Everymole says that's a very special one, but how could we ever go *there*?'

'Why not?' said Tryfan.

'Too far and dangerous,' said the female.

'Grikes,' said the male.

'Well, I got *here* all right.'

'You're an adult.'

'So will you be one day, and anyway I don't think it makes much difference.'

'You would if you were us!'

Tryfan laughed.

'Would you like to see our tunnels?' asked one of them.

'I would,' said Tryfan, 'but it seems a pity while the sun's so good. I seem to have been in shadow for a long, long time, and today I found a way out of it.'

'We can wait till the sun goes in,' said the female.

Tryfan nodded and said, 'Meanwhile, you can tell me your names.'

'I'm Bramble,' said the male.

'And I'm Betony,' said the other.

'What are you going to tell us?' said Bramble, settling down with pleasant expectancy.

'Yes, what *are* you?' added Betony, impatiently.

'Well, there's lots of things to tell you about, but perhaps I should start at the very beginning,' Tryfan said.

'That's a very good place to start,' said Bramble, making himself even more comfortable.

So then Tryfan did, and told those two youngsters about things he thought he had forgotten which seemed so long ago now. And as what he told them went on, he only gradually became aware that other moles had joined them, adult moles, old moles, searching moles, moles who had lost their way as Duncton Wood had, as he felt he had; moles with a longing to hear, and a longing to hope.

But it was to Bramble and Betony that he spoke, for they were young and still had so much to do, and he thought that if they thought it hard to get to Duncton Wood then they might never try to go anywhere, and *then* they would make a great deal less of their lives than they might have done.

Tryfan spoke to them until the sun was setting on Beechenhill, and the grass was cooling, and only the Stone that rose among them retained the day's warmth, and a hint of the beauty it had had.

Spindle and Mayweed were among those moles who heard Tryfan that day, and while some would call it a teaching, most would remember it differently than that, as a day when a true mole of the Stone opened his heart to them, and told them his hopes and fears through the troubled story of his life, and made his testimony.

As he reached the end of what he had to say his voice grew quiet and all there sensed that he spoke like a mole who feels he might not have the opportunity to speak of such things again. All grew close to him then, sensing he needed the promise of a future that their hopes might give. Until, at the end, he led them in prayer to ask the Stone that the Stone Mole might come and show them how a mole who feels he has lost his way may find it once again, whatever he is, however humble he feels, wherever his failures may have taken him.

Then Tryfan blessed the moles of Beechenhill and they quietly dispersed to their burrows and to sleep.

Morning came, grey weather, the journey onwards once again, and news of Skint.

'Grassington,' whispered a mole. 'You'll find him there with Smithills. In the very shadow of Whern. May the Stone's Silence be with you, mole, and remember: you and yours will always find sanctuary here!'

711

The mole's gaze was direct, his manner cheerful. He was large of girth, but strong and there was something about him that made Tryfan ask his name, and Spindle to record it.

'Squeezebelly I'm called. Bramble and Betony are my young. They and I, as all moles here, are enemies of the grikes and therefore forever your friends. Remember us in your prayers, Tryfan of Duncton, for we shall always remember you in ours.'

Then, with that friendship affirmed with a touch, Tryfan turned to Mayweed and said that they must leave.

'Sirs both, Mayweed will get you there! To elusive Skint's burrows and good Smithills' laughter he will take you, and himself as well. So follow, and find!'

And he did! Crossing the Dark Peak in safety, getting confirmation of Skint's message from the moles of Kinder Scout, puzzling still that the grikes troubled them not, pressing on through August and into September before they reached Grassington, the last system before dread Whern itself.

* * * * * * *

Skint had aged, and Smithills too, and in seeing them again Tryfan realised that he must have aged as well, and all his friends.

But what a greeting they had, what news to share, how tempting to stay in Skint's clean tunnels (or even Smithills' grubby ones) and pass the time in idleness or chatter! A temptation to which they yielded!

They found time, too, to travel a few molemiles to see the burrows where once Willow had been a pup, and to honour that old mole's memory, whose death at Henbane's command they would never forget. There Skint recalled the anger that he felt, and Tryfan observed that there was a stronger feeling among them now, of pity and of anguish. Perhaps anger is a young mole's emotion, and anguish something only older moles can bear. They turned from Willow's former burrows and stared on north to where the ground rises towards Whern and felt that anger was not now enough.

'When do we leave?' asked Skint. He was as brave as ever he had been, but now his voice had a tremor in it, and they could see he did not want to leave his home again. Nor Smithills, though he offered his help too, and would have come and faced Henbane's talons straight.

'We three will travel on alone,' said Tryfan. 'Spindle and I led on by Mayweed here. You have said you knew we were coming. . . .'

'Aye, there's been talk of nothing else for weeks now. Allmole knows you're going into Whern, and the guard-moles have instructions to leave you be,' said Smithills. 'They say Henbane wants to talk to you, and even Rune himself, but nomole knows what to make of it, but that things are changing when moles of the Stone can visit Whern unharmed.'

'Changing or not changing, I don't like it,' said Spindle.

'Nor I,' said Skint. 'A mole that snouts old females like Willow doesn't change, and don't you forget it!'

'We won't,' said Tryfan. Yet Spindle silently shook his head and fretted his paws restlessly, as if troubled by more than he could find words to say.

Then, as Spindle and the others talked, Skint took Tryfan to one side and said, 'But what are you going there *for*? To talk with a mole who commanded the cruelties Henbane did? The mole I trained in clearing at the Slopeside of Buckland has more sense than that.'

'To seek Boswell,' said Tryfan. 'He *is* there, and he is waiting, and our coming has been long waited by him, so very long. I don't know, Skint, why we must go, nor why I know that Spindle and Mayweed will be unharmed, but so it is; so worry not of them. . . .'

'But you, mole? What of you? Eh?' said Skint softly, touching him.

'I don't know,' said Tryfan, shaking his head. 'I think I don't matter now. I think that all those moleyears ago Boswell trained me for this, but I don't know how or why. I think the Stone knows and I hope in time we will.'

'You're shaking, mole! Let us come with you – an extra

713

few paws may be useful. We're not so old yet there's not a use for us!'

'No, Skint,' said Tryfan, 'not this time. It's not with talons that we're fighting now. I have the best defences I shall need in Spindle here and Mayweed. They'll know what to do.'

'Well . . . if there's any way we can help. . . .'

'Pray for us,' said Tryfan.

'In my own way I will, every day until I know you're safe. You come back to us and tell us you spat in the eyes of Rune himself! You will, won't you?'

Tryfan smiled wearily.

Then after a moment's thought he said, 'We will return this way, and perhaps when we come we will have need of help. Be ready, Skint. Have strong talons at your command, but remember they are not for killing but for authority. Watch out for us and if we come not ourselves then news of us will.'

Skint nodded.

Then after a moment Tryfan added, 'There's a place we visited on our way here, a place you know. Beechenhill.'

'Aye, what of it?'

'Remember it, Skint. Remember that for one day of my life I was happy there. The moles there have great faith and trust and gave me courage to come on. Remember it!'

'I will,' said Skint, much moved and troubled, 'I'll not forget.'

Then Skint and Smithills accompanied their three friends on the last part of their northward way, with the moorlands that precede Whern beginning to rise darkly to their left and right, and the river flowing past and away downslope behind them towards the sun, and all the life they had ever known.

Until a great overhang of dark rock loomed on their left and Skint and Smithills muttered that it was as far as they would go.

'What is this place?' asked Tryfan, as Spindle looked

714

doubtfully about, and Mayweed narrowed his eyes and peered into the shadows there.

'Kilnsey,' said Skint. 'The start of where the grike moles breed. Ahead across the river Wharfe you see Whern rise.'

'But it is not so dark and miserable looking a place as I thought!' said Spindle.

'Aye, it has a beauty of its own,' said Smithills looking up, as they all did, at where the evening light was cast across the flanks of Whern, and lit up pale the limestone scarps that run its length.

'Pretty enough by some lights! Lethal by others!' warned Skint.

Certainly, beyond those lines of pale rock the moors rose grim, steepening off into a sombre distance. As the moles stared at the great scene the air grew cold about them, for Kilnsey casts a shadow black as night as evening comes.

'Your business, mole?' said a voice, and a grike appeared out of the scree and grass. 'Speak quick, scarper, or get killed.'

'Snub-snouted, Sir, we go – '

'Him, not you, I spoke to,' said the grike. He gave the impression of strength and confidence, and he had a sneer to his voice. It was clear that others waited near him, and suddenly those gullies all about seemed the last place a mole of the Stone should be.

'We come to Whern in peace,' said Tryfan.

'Tryfan are you?'

Tryfan nodded and the grike came and thrust his snout into Tryfan's face and stared at him in satisfaction.

'Took you a bloody long time, however you've come. Been waiting for you, and I don't like to wait, nor do my friends. We don't like it one little bit, you scum of the Stone!' He spat a gob of cuddled worm among them as dark snouts appeared all about, and eyes stared malevolently as if expecting a reaction from Tryfan. He made none.

Instead he said a brief farewell to Skint and Smithills and saw them safely away. Then, when they had gone, he stared one last time after them feeling a great sadness and shadow on his heart and turned back to the grikes.

'Where are you taking us?' asked Spindle.

'Shut up, move, and ask no questions. You'll find out if you've the strength to climb that far.'

Then they followed a grike ahead while the others circled around behind saying 'Move it, scum!' and taloning them to make them travel faster.

While below them, Skint and Smithills watched them disappear into the long shadows of Whern.

'Don't like it, Skint,' said Smithills with a shudder.

'Those moles have courage, but they may need help,' said Skint. 'But not the help that talons give, not here. We'll stand by for their return in case they need us. But they'll need something else.'

'What then, mate?'

'Don't know, Smithills,' said Skint, staring north where Tryfan and the others had gone. 'Stone knows!'

Smithills grinned, but even on his kind, lined, generous face the grin was a sad one.

'We should try something, *anything*,' said Smithills.

'Praying,' said Skint sharply.

'Come off it, you never prayed in your miserable life.'

'Well . . . I'm going to now,' said Skint angrily, and before he betrayed the emotion he felt at that moment, which had him close to tears, he turned from his old friend and hurried back down the way they had come; and Smithills lumbered after him.

Chapter Thirty-Nine

Whern had loomed so dangerous and grim in the minds of Tryfan, Spindle and Mayweed for so long that it would have been suprising if, as they set off with the guardmole grikes towards its north-west flank, they had not felt an awesome dread descend upon them. And they did.

The sense of grand darkness which Whern gave out was increased by the fact that as they left Kilnsey to cross the river Wharfe by a twofoot way, the light began to fade and the colours slowly to drain from the approaching trees and rocks.

Above them in the gathering gloom hung the rising terraces of limestone which ran north as well, defining the Wharfe's course below, and rising out beyond sight towards the high mass of Whern itself. These terraces – the first of which they began to climb towards – seemed almost luminous in the dusk, full of crannies and hollows in which a nervous mole might imagine all manner of ill-natured creatures to exist.

From open pasture they climbed to overgrown scree among which old stunted trees grew, and there was life of the kind moles avoid: owls, roosting rooks, and bats. Somewhere an old badger scratched; while far below, in the pastures, cows moaned in the valley mist and their shapes loomed above its low thin veil like rubbish surfacing across a river's reach by evening light.

The leading grike set a fast pace and seemed disgruntled that not one of them complained. But to them, who had travelled so far and climbed hill and dale and crossed the Dark Peak, and now wished finally to confront whatever it was that Whern would face them with, his pace was not fast enough.

Mayweed looked here and snouted there as he always

did, and more than once was reprimanded by the other-wise silent grikes and told not to wander. Tryfan took the pace easily, moving with strength and grace and feeling fitter than he ever had. Even Spindle, whose gait was ever awkward and untidy, had no difficulty keeping up, so that the only moles who were breathing heavily, and pausing now and then to get their breath, were the grikes, from which Tryfan concluded that this was not a route they often took.

Eventually they reached the first of the terraces. It rose palely above them, and they saw that there were many faults and clefts in its sheer edge, many places a mole might hide; and many routes inside.

Tryfan had the feeling that they were on the edge of a system vast and strange, and that even the guardmoles felt it, looking nervously about them and then up at the limestone scar.

'Where are we cutting through?' asked one eventually.

'North Flats,' said the leader.

The first one nodded briefly. Silence reigned and after a brief pause they pressed on.

They passed a point where a spring came out from just below the scar and gushed down to the Wharfe far below. Above that the ground was very dry, and the only sound of waterflow was downslope of them.

Eventually even the sound of the spring they had seen fell away and was gone. Then the shrubs and trees they had been among thinned to nothing, and they found themselves on exposed grassland. The cliff's line seemed to break up, and all about them were scars and castellations of limestone, shining mauve with the last of the western light. Across the valley they saw the distant gaze of a roaring owl and watched it run far below them, until it was gone, though whether into ground mist or trees was impossible to say. Two footlights twinkled on over the dale and dusk drew in.

A tawny owl called sharply nearby and they heard the scrape of claw on a dead branch. Somewhere far above dry rocks fell, rebounded, and the echoes seemed to sound forever across the dale.

They sheltered then, among some scree, and food was found. Whichever way they looked a grike had taken stance in shadow and seemed to stare impassively at them. But the strangest thing was this: the ground seemed reverberant with sound, so distant that at first they did not notice it. But as night fell and the grikes dozed, the sound seemed clearer and it came from out of the limestone cliffs above them. It was not specific or identifiable, but rather a dull roaring made of many things, running water perhaps, and echoes.

Morning came, and the ground was dew-sodden, and a mole could not move without tangling a spider's web in his talons, and water dripping from his snout. But sun came and the ground steamed, the sky was a rich blue.

As they were west-facing, the scars were not in sunlight, and the air beneath was cold; but on the far side of the vale the sun struck hard at the limestone scars that were twins to the ones they were ascending, while in the valley below white mist slowly cleared.

But as 'cutting through' turned out to mean climbing, they soon found themselves back in the sun and looking down on the way they had come. It was a strange landscape made of grass and limestone, chasms in the rock, deep clefts through which a mole scrabbled, paws cut by the sharp frost-shattered fragments, snout bruised by the steep slope ahead.

It felt like a landscape in which death hid waiting to be discovered. In one place they found a scatter of rabbits' skulls, in another the torn and dried wing of a rook; in a third was the rotting carcass of a sheep and in a fourth a dying hedgehog, its snout pale and its flanks shivering.

Only Mayweed seemed content, always peering about him, snouting at the rock and its welcoming fissures which ran into darkness, and turning back sometimes to check the way they had come.

'Wondering Sir,' he managed to whisper to Tryfan that

morning, 'humble me is excited by this. My paws tingle with magnificent expectation. Mayweed makes the observation that it is not Whern that a mole should fear but the moles who live here!'

'Shut up and move on, you little turd,' said one of the grikes, buffeting Mayweed. They were probably an unpleasant, taciturn lot in any case, but as they climbed higher they grew increasingly irritable and, as it seemed to Tryfan, scared.

'Who's liaising?' said one as they reached a terrace of turf with yet another cliff of limestone ahead.

'Lathe of Arncliffe,' said the leader.

'Shit,' said one of the grikes. 'Him I don't need.'

'You're a silly bugger – '

'I may be, but him I *don't* need right now. I'll lie low when – '

'Lie where you like, mole. The Word will always know. Lie how you like, lie as you like, the Word will tell the truth!'

The voice was smug and cold, and it was hard at first to say where it came from. Behind them? In front? They all froze.

'Here, fools!'

The mole was there, ahead of them, his head seeming to peer from the limestone cliff itself. Grey fur, aquiline face, cold grey eyes, and a mouth that seemed to sneer. Then it was gone, and there was a quick touch of talon on rock and the mole reappeared nearby.

'Lathe,' said the mole to Tryfan.

'Tryfan of Duncton.'

'Dismiss,' Lathe said to the grikes.

'But Lathe, Sir, there's three of them and. . . .'

Lathe smiled thinly, showing his obvious contempt for them.

'These are southern moles, they have come a long way and I doubt that they intend to flee or harm a humble mole like me. So leave us now and. . . .' He waited long enough for the grikes to think that he had forgotten what one of them had said before saying, 'You!'

'Me, Sir?'

'You, Sir. Here.' The mole who had mentioned his dread of Lathe came near. Though he was big he trembled. Tryfan noticed that Lathe's muscles flexed. There was something vile about the power he wielded, and it was made worse by the fact that he evidently wished to demonstrate it to the strangers.

'So, you don't "need" me "right now" as you put it.'

'I didn't – '

'We know why, don't we?'

There was a lifetime – no, centuries – of judgement and punishment in those words and the 'we' had all the nauseous piety of the strong over the misdemeaning weak. Despite his size the grike looked wan and frightened.

'Yes,' he agreed, lowering his snout.

'Thrust or confession, mole?' asked Lathe.

'Thrust,' muttered the grike.

'So be it,' said Lathe. He darted a quick glance at the three of them, as if to make sure they were watching. Then he talon-thrust at the grike's shoulder with astonishing power and grace, so fast that the blow seemed over before it had begun. Yet the grike spun back with a cry, and blood poured from a shoulder wound.

'May you be at peace with the Word, mole. Now go!' said Lathe dismissing them all. Then he turned to lead Tryfan and his two friends through the portal of limestone he had emerged from, and as he went Tryfan saw a scatter of blood from the talon-thrust spotting and dripping on the limestone cliff. Tryfan shuddered, and felt that it might be a long time before he and Spindle saw the light of a good day again.

* * * * * * *

The tunnels they found themselves in, and the chambers that they led to, were, and remain, some of the most extraordinary in all of moledom. Although no doubt they saw only a small part of Whern, it was enough to make them understand that moles who lived in that place might easily think of themselves as special and select.

The tunnels were the size of the twofoot-made tunnels of the Wen but had none of the filth or regulation. They were tall and sinewy, towering away above, their passages undulating and curving with a sensuous beauty beyond the experience of a woodland mole used to earth and stones, and the roots of tree.

Their striking size and shape was enhanced immeasurably by the nature of the light they attracted and gave out. There seemed to be innumerable outlets overhead – though what had made them was not immediately clear, since nomole could possibly reach so high or delve rock so hard.

The air was clear, the windsound good, the light excellent, and it seemed as if the very walls of limestone that rose so sinuously above them caught the logic and grandeur of the passing sky.

'But . . .' began Spindle, wondering what agency ever made such tunnels as those if mole had not.

'Questioning Spindle,' said Mayweed with a delighted smile, 'you see a power greater than the talons of miserable moles. You see the power of water's flow.'

'But there is no water!' said Spindle.

Which seemed true, for the floor of the tunnel was sandy and dry. Mayweed pointed to the deposits of sand and gravel along the tunnel floor, and the deep undercutting erosion of its walls.

'Sirs both, humble me guessed that we go up a passage down which an underground river once went,' said Mayweed, awe in his voice. They realised that water must still come sometimes because some crevices had small dark pools of water in them.

'Listen, amazed mole! Hear, staggered Spindle! Enjoy, cultured Cleric! The sound of the liquid that makes the rivers that carves the tunnels that us moles are in! Water! Hear its drips, see its encrustations, suffer its damp, celebrate its power!'

It was true, they could hear it. Everywhere. Above, below and about: the movement of water. Distant-seeming, rumbling, the echoed splash, the drip in a cavern dark as night. The rush of water through a crack of rock, but far? How far? They turned a corner, and there it was, Mayweed dancing about in excitement at the sight of it. A force of white water making a sound like thunder, spurting out of a cleft in the rock and then gone again into a sucking pool, a flash of white spuming water, ugly and yellow in its foam, right across the path they trod. *Under* it they went.

'Wet Spindle! Splashed Spindle! Humbleness has proved his point, has he not?' shouted Mayweed over the din.

'Humbleness has!' said Spindle

'Humbleness usually does!' said Tryfan, more to himself than anymole else.

The arched watershoot safely behind them, a corner turned, and its sound seemed as distant as the far side of a dale, and near them they heard as clear as a pup's cry the single drip of water that fell from the point of a dropping encrustation from the chamber's roof into a pool, so still that without the ripple of the drip they might have thought it was not there. The underground waterfall might never have been.

Where light fell ferns grew on the damp ground, and in them delicate spiders, pale as a weak sky, moved.

'Correct!' said Lathe to Mayweed, his voice echoing in a staccato half-shocked way among the stalactites that hung now above them, his body seeming to slide among the stalagmites that here and there rose from the floor.

Some of the thinner stalactites trembled as they passed, and gave the chamber a kind of ringing that sounded their passage by.

Then they turned up a cleft filled with stone and mud, their paws filthy with it and their bellies too, then on following Lathe's rapid ascent until they came to a portal, and a short tunnel that levelled out to the edge of a deep pool. Beyond that was a great light chamber in which several moles crouched like dead things among the stalagmites.

723

'These moles are novices and must reach such a state of peace that they notice not the moles who come and go,' said Lathe. 'This is the start of the Whern of the sideem, and this the cleansing pool through which all novices must pass. It is cold, cold as death, and you three so far as I know are the first moles who have not professed the Word who have ever passed this way. It is by the WordSpeaker's command you come.

'Swim slow in the water until the cold feels mortal and be warned that currents suck at a mole's paws and belly and would drag him down if they could. It has happened. Such moles are lost in the Sinks and are beyond redemption of the Word. So pass across confidently though not so swiftly that you are not cleansed. Each mole must learn his own time.'

Without more ado Lathe slipped into the pool and swam slowly across, the ripples from his passage dragging to his left and showing there was indeed a current there. Though no exit from the pool was visible, the water lapped and seemed to suck in a final way where the current met the wall and where the water was as black as night.

Mayweed went first and once in did not dally, climbing out on the far side with a fixed dripping grin that signified his extreme cold and discomfort.

Spindle let out a moan as he went in, and reached the other side shivering and deathly cold.

Tryfan went more slowly, looking to right and left, and letting the bitter water flow into his fur and take the grime and dirt of their recent passage out of it. He felt good when he came out, and shook himself dry. The water glistened on his body and he contrasted with Lathe strikingly: both were fit and graceful, but while Tryfan had warmth and good humour to his body the other seemed ascetic and cold, his eyes unblinking and his gaze at once earnest and vain. He was not a mole who smiled, and nor, looking about at the novices, did the other moles seem to be.

Mayweed went near to Lathe and offered him one of what he hoped was his most endearing smiles, every single one of his yellow teeth showing, and said, 'Most impressive and knowledgeable Sir, awed me would like to know what the Sinks are.'

Lathe looked indifferently at Mayweed, and then back at the pool, and finally deigned to answer.

'A place of doom, mole, where moles go who are not of the Word. Cold it is, and eternally wet, and there a mole drowns forever, lost in darkness that never ends, suffering for the wrong of his failure.'

'Terrifying Sir, you mean this pool we have crossed is one of many leading to the Sinks?'

'All water flows there, down to that eternal darkness where no Word is heard or scribed, and where sinning moles suffer without end.'

'Humble I, named Mayweed, is aghast at the horror of it, lissome Lathe.'

'Good, mole. Respect and awe are worthy feelings. Now. . . .'

And as the meditating sideem continued to pay no attention to the visitors, which appeared to please Lathe, he led them on towards where sun came down into the chamber, and then up to the surface once more.

It was a relief to be in the open again and to feel the warmth of the sunshine and see far below the prospect of Wharfedale, now quite free of mist. Kilnsey Crag lay far below them, massive still, but with the sun upon its eastward face it looked more benign. Across the dale the sun caught other limestone scars. From this vantage point Whern did not seem so bad.

Yet as they turned back from where they had come and faced again where they must yet go, they sensed again the higher glowering mass of Whern. No bright warm sunshine anywhere in moledom would have been warm enough to change the chill they all felt in their hearts as Lathe, turning north east towards where the ground sloped inexorably upward towards an unwelcoming moor, said, 'Now, I shall take you to the WordSpeaker, who will talk with you.'

'A moment, mole,' said Tryfan taking a firm stance. 'You mean that Henbane's tunnels are not here but higher up?'

'We do not use the WordSpeaker's personal name,' said Lathe sniffily. 'Few have that privilege. But to answer your question: her tunnels are indeed much higher, for that is where the High Sideem is and you are lucky to be allowed to see it. Some sideem never even get asked before they leave for their missionary work, others go there only for ritual, and only a very few of us are allowed, in the line of our work, access when we need it.' Lathe smiled smugly, and looked most insufferably vain.

'Esteemed Sir, mole of calibre and cleverness, may I ask a question of trivial importance?' said Mayweed. It was hard to say if he was being sarcastic, but he probably was: his normally smiling eyes were cold and wary, and both Spindle and Tryfan could see that he was acutely aware of his surroundings and the lie of the tunnels and the surface. But Lathe seemed unaware of Mayweed's humour, or his continual observation and took at its face value his grandiloquence.

He inclined his snout in haughty acknowledgement of Mayweed, and to signal that he was prepared to answer a question.

'Wonderful Whern is very large, and I wonder whether anymole is clever enough to know all its tunnels and ways?'

'Nomole is so clever,' said Lathe, 'nor so foolish to try. We believe that only Scirpus himself had a spatial intellect vast enough to absorb and remember his chosen system. Even such an area as that . . . ' He waved his talon at what seemed, from where they had taken stance, a low cliff.'. . . could not be encompassed by a single mole, let alone the system as a whole. Indeed it is one of the disciplines that novices must face: to learn part of this area I point to.'

'Doesn't look much to me!' said Spindle. 'Just a cliff.'

Lathe smiled in a condescending way and Mayweed, as

726

if to get himself on Lathe's side, said, 'Asinine Spindle, mulish mole, I am sure that likeable Lathe here will say that that "cliff", as you put it, is much more than it seems! Is Mayweed right, or is he wrong? Sir, you adjudicate.'

'Oh you're right, mole, very right,' said Lathe.

Diverted for a few minutes at least from his morning's task of taking them to Henbane, as no doubt Mayweed had hoped he might be, he led them the few moleyards to the low cliff, found a way up a cleft of the kind they were getting used to, and with a clear instruction not to wander if they valued their life, found a way that brought them on top of the cliff itself.

It was but a distance of a few yards and yet, suddenly, they found themselves looking on a world nomole could have imagined. It was a plateau of limestone dissected by dozens of deep clefts like crevices in ice, which plunged down into a gloom in which ferns and shrubs grew. Here and there across this limestone plateau trees grew up, the lower half of their trunks quite buried in the limestone. The area stretched ahead on either side of them so far that the rising ground beyond was hazed by warmth, and the sheep that wandered there seemed small.

'What is this place called?' asked Spindle.

'Bycliffe Ground is its formal name,' said Lathe, 'but sideem call it the Clints, and like it not. You see, this is a testing place for young sideem.'

'How so?' asked Tryfan.

'I'll show you . . .' He led them back down to the cliff's bottom edge and took them some way along it, past several deep and shadowed entrances into one that seemed more worn than most.

He turned to them: 'Now follow me close and do not wander.'

They went in the entrance and the cleft's sides rose above them, and ahead the path ran turgidly among ferns and the pink flowers and reddening stalks of herb robert.

The line of the clefts above, where they opened to the sky, seemed to bear no relation to their line at the base, so that as a mole travelled along the world above seemed to move in a different way than the path he trod. Then the path divided, then again, and again after that and they were dizzy and confused with it.

'If I left you here,' said Lathe, 'I doubt that any of you would ever be seen again.' They looked around at the shadowed walls, and at the hart's tongue fern that rose above their heads and whose leaves reflected dark light. Whichever way they looked seemed different and as they turned they had the strange sensation that the sky was turning as well so that even the way they came seemed obscure. To make it worse, high cloud drifted in the sky, but down there inside the Clints it seemed that the walls were in a perpetual state of falling down.

Tryfan did not doubt that Lathe was right and instinctively looked over at Mayweed, who was not a mole to get lost easily.

He was staggering about, with one paw to his eyes and muttering, 'Sir, Sir, take us from here. This totally unimportant mole is confused and turmoiled by this place. Please, good Sir, help him escape!'

Lathe smiled broadly at the other two and, ignoring Mayweed's apparent distress, said, 'For the novices the Clints becomes a final test of learning and trust. Each sideem must cross through the Clints and to do that he must know the way, and he can only learn to know the way by rote: left paw, left and right, right, right, and left and left and left, right, right, and so on.' His voice assumed a strange sing-song tone as he said these directions. 'But if the novice makes a mistake well . . . he is lost. Each year a few are lost.'

'As a test of learning I can understand it, but as a test of trust?' said Tryfan.

Lathe shrugged.

'The novice must hope he has the right directions, and even at moments of doubt on the way – and there are many – he must trust. I fear some are misled, but that is the WordSpeaker's right. Sometimes moles became too familiar, and must be taught a lesson.'

'You mean,' said Tryfan, 'they are deliberately misled and sent to their deaths?'

'I mean ,' said Lathe coldly, 'that erring moles must be punished by the Word.'

Spindle and Tryfan looked around in horror, while Mayweed had collapsed against a wall and was moaning to himself and again asking to be taken out.

'You only mention males, and we only saw males. Are there females?'

'Of course, some very senior ones. Why one of the closest to the WordSpeaker is a female, and one who has travelled to the parts you come from. Sleekit. *She* had no trouble with the Clints! I always knew she would go far!' He smiled, a little wanly, and for the first time they saw from the wrinkles around his eyes that he was older than he seemed, much older in fact. Tryfan remembered Boswell telling him once that some moles, those who live a life of austerity and freedom from the pressures of life, develop such a youthful fur but a certain emptiness of feature which moles who have lived more fully do not have.

Lathe led them out again, and once there, Mayweed seemed to recover himself.

'Loquacious Lathe, what happens if a mole finds a different way through the Clints?' he asked, his paws restless. Tryfan could see he was longing to go exploring on his own, and did not believe for one minute that his distressed behaviour was other than an act.

'A mole doesn't find another way through. He gets lost and he dies. If he comes out on this side, which is where he started, he is killed, so he doesn't come out here.'

As Spindle asked him some more questions Mayweed took Tryfan to one side.

'Dear Sir, good Sir, who has done so much for Mayweed over the years, dejected he is and sad, and has no time to be. His paws itch, his chest expands, his heart aches, his mind races. All his instincts say he must leave now, and es cape, and he does not know why. But here, brave Tryfan Sir, is the only place he may go. Here, Sir, now, Sir. . . .'

Lathe looked around at them, the Clints rising behind him, and the three moles, who had travelled so long together, seemed instinctively and without word to know how to behave. Tryfan and Mayweed yawned and looked a little bored while Spindle, at his most earnest and intense, asked Lathe another question in the answering of which he could display his knowledge and general superiority.

Mayweed continued: 'So, Tryfan Sir, I will shortly leave. No doubt they will search, but they will not find, not Mayweed, not he. But he will be near, Sir, because strong Tryfan will need him, and if he seems not near he will be – believe it, Sir. Mayweed has told Tryfan before and he tells him again: Mayweed loves Tryfan . . . ' He spoke these words urgently and if Tryfan had been lulled a little by the warm day and Lathe's calm and unprotected guiding of them, he felt lulled no more.

Of all moles, Mayweed knew of the tunnels of darkness and of ways through them. On the long journey since the Wen, Tryfan had come more and more to appreciate that the Stone had sent Mayweed to be a guide through more than just physical places. He was in some mysterious way an unknowing guide into spiritual places too, and now must leave Tryfan from an instinct that told him if he was to be of further use he would need to make preparation by learning the tunnels and ways of Whern, unseen and unknown.

'Mayweed suggests that Tryfan and Spindle take this last opportunity of escape, which he senses is now. Trust humble he, let yourselves be guided into the Clints, and he is confident he can get Sirs both away from this place that makes him tremble. Not nice here, Sir, moles' eyes are cold. Please leave, please come. Now is the last chance, Sir. Trust Mayweed, Mayweed knows. . . .'

'I know too, Mayweed. I know,' whispered Tryfan, 'as you know, I must go on. But the Stone is with us and though it will bring us together again I fear much will soon have changed. Each of us has a part to play in the coming of the Stone Mole, though how or when I am no nearer knowing. You will always have a special place in my heart, Mayweed, and I think in moledom's heart as well. You are a mole of courage, more than anymole may ever know. I know you will watch over us from the places you find, I know you will be near, and that gives me the courage to go on to where there will be no turning back.'

'Sir,' said Mayweed, his voice almost breaking with emotion and his snout low as his mouth trembled, 'if I am not near when the Stone Mole comes, will you tell him my name? Say Mayweed wanted to . . . see him. Good Sir, humble me asks only that.'

'I shall tell him your name, and when I tell him what you have done for us he will repeat it with love.'

That was as much as the two moles had time for. Lathe finished answering Spindle's questions, looked at Tryfan and Mayweed curiously, thought no more of it, and led them on. Spindle followed, Tryfan came second and Mayweed last. And sometime then, as the September sun warmed the pale limestone about them and they climbed northward of the Clints, the sound of pawsteps behind Tryfan faded and when, a little later, he looked back, nomole was there. He saw only the great stretching maze the Clints formed, whose entrances were all enshadowed, and empty.

'Foolish,' snapped Lathe, 'and stupid. Though we expected something like it.'

'He was confused by the Clints, he will surely be found.'

'He will be found, or he will die. But when the grikes take him they may kill him. Foolish insulter to the Word. Foolish to so abuse our trust!'

'I really think the Clints upset him . . . He's rather a one for losing his way,' said Tryfan, looking at Spindle meaningfully to suggest the truth of Mayweed's disappearance.

'Weakness is not of the Word. Forget that mole now, he is as good as dead.' The brutality that lay behind the easy dismissal of an entire life angered Tryfan and outraged poor Spindle, who was not quite sure of Mayweed's intent but understood that Tryfan knew more of it than he said.

731

'His loss is of no account,' said Lathe halting by an entrance a molemile north east of the Clints. 'In any case my job is as good as done. The WordSpeaker is interested only in Tryfan and I doubt if she'll have much to say to your friend Spindle at all.'

'He'll have something to say to her I expect!' smiled Tryfan, calm once more. 'Now, where do we go?'

Whern now rose almost east of them across two miles or so of steeply rising moorland, and even though its gritty western edge caught the sun, yet it absorbed light to nothingness and seemed like solid shadow. It was no country for mole. They felt they were on the edge of what would be habitable. To their left, or westward, they saw across the ground they had covered, which was a mass of limestone outcrops and clint-like areas dissected by faults. While directly north of them the ground sloped away into a deep and shaded gorge whose depths were lost to view, beyond whose furthest side over the moor was what looked like a massive canyon in the ground from which rose steam, or spray perhaps, which was blown by a steady north-westerly wind towards Whern.

'What's *that*?' asked Tryfan, pointing a talon at the rising mist.

Lathe lowered his snout towards it.

'That is the Providence Fall,' he said, 'where nomole but the WordSpeaker now goes, and senior sideem. It is the Master's place, and in its galleries Scirpus himself once lived.'

'Does the Master live there now?' asked Spindle, rather surprised that Lathe was so willing to talk to about it.

'Oh yes, he lives there, but is not often seen.'

All around they could hear the run of water, and beneath their paws they could sense a formidable world all echoing and strange. All the vast landscape they could see was grike country. It had a kind of sparse beauty and yet, never in his life – even including the worst times in the Wen – had Tryfan less wished to be where he was.

'This is the place of the High Sideem, whose tunnels

and chambers waited through the aeons for the coming of Scirpus, who discovered the Word here and made it known. The present Master was the one ordained to find a way that the Word might spread across moledom. He ordained the WordSpeaker and she saw his wishes through. We live in hallowed times, moles, and you are lucky to be here. So follow and be grateful.'

They dropped a little downslope, travelled on some way, and then took a route adjacent to a sink hole below ground. Their pawsteps echoed through darkness for a time until, suddenly, there was light again, high above their heads, and they were in a chamber of great beauty.

The echoes their passage made ran around them, redoubling, trebling, echoing all about before the echoes seemed to grow stronger and real pawsteps were heard approaching. If a mole's head went dizzy with sound, his eyes could barely contemplate the light as, advancing towards whatever mole came, it was reflected from vents in the high roof and dazzled in the still pools that glistened everywhere.

Ahead a mole stopped and waited for them. Light from a pool dappled across his face and seemed to run along his twisted snout. It was Weed.

'Welcome,' he said with a vile smile. 'Oh yes. Very welcome. Lost one have we, yes? Ah . . . it was Mayweed. We know him. He'll get further than most, Lathe, but that's not far, yes?' Weed laughed unpleasantly and nodded to Lathe, who, silently, left them.

'Your coming here was much discussed. It was doubted in some quarters that you would come. I was certain of it, of course. Boswell I think was the lure. The WordSpeaker was sure of it. Wrekin, on the other paw, decided you would not be quite such fools. No spiritual imagination, Wrekin. He could not think that a mole might be so illogical as to take such a risk as coming here is for you all. You "both", I should say, now Mayweed has gone off, yes?' Weed laughed again, his small mouth tight and secretive.

'But, well, Wrekin was getting old. You will not, I suppose, be pleased to know that his work in Siabod is over. That system is of the Word now, most of its moles killed. The WordSpeaker has sent Wrekin back to the system whence he came and others younger than he do his job better. But these matters will not concern you, yes?' His eyes smiled in the cold way they had.

'There was a time when I would have enjoyed talking to you, Tryfan. You put up a resistance of sorts to us, one of the few moles who did. But now, well, all that is done. The Word is triumphant and nomole can gainsay it.'

'Why were we allowed to come at all? Why not attack and destroy us as you tried to before?'

'Times change, Tryfan. The way of snouting is done. Persuasion is better. To kill you on your journey north would indeed have been easy, but it would have martyred you. But here, well, a mole disappears and is forgotten.'

'Like Boswell?' said Tryfan.

'Like Boswell,' agreed Weed.

'I wish to see him,' said Tryfan.

'Oh yes, yes I'm sure you do,' said Weed. 'But you must address that request to the WordSpeaker in the first instance. But why delay? You would like to see her, yes? She would *you*.'

They followed him as other sideem, all lithe and muscular as Lathe had been, and mostly male, emerged from the shadows and the bright light thereabouts, to stare at them and, as it seemed, to watch and guard them.

They went through great chamber after chamber with galleries high up and peepholes in crystalline white limestone, past droplets of water shining with light, the air chilly and clean. On they went, along ways cut and eaten into the limestone by water, across chambers large and dark. Never a river's flow, but always pools still as night sucking and stirring downwards to the Sinks. Yet somewhere water splashed, and somewhere else it seeped away.

Downslope they went, through cracks of rock to reach yet other chambers, to where the walls were scribed, and

734

Weed warned them not to touch the scribing. But clumsy Spindle's flanks brushed it at one point and that was enough for nauseous sound to overwhelm them, and their ears to ache and their snouts to run. Filthy sound, and Spindle retched.

'Warned you, yes?' grinned Weed, eyes bright. 'Do not vomit on the way.' It was a place of mounting terror where moles seemed to appear and disappear and from where, Tryfan somehow knew, moles did not escape without detection. Mayweed's timing had been good.

'Not nice, Tryfan,' muttered Spindle through gritted teeth.

'Not nice,' Tryfan agreed.

Then sunshine cut in a great shaft across a chamber they entered and ahead the tunnel seemed to run straight out into a void, for they could see purple heather across a moor where, superb, the dark chasm they had seen was cut, out of which the spray rose dramatically. It was caught by sun, drifted west, and the vegetation below it was wet and shiny with sky. It was hard to judge, but it seemed to drop down sheer to a gorge where a beck, which they could only hear, and the wind, roared softly at the opening's edges. But where they were was deathly still.

'May the word be with thee, Tryfan,' said a voice they knew, a female voice, floating among the high stalactites, tumbling to the stalagmites, as smoothly caressing as the surface of the deep dark pools between them: 'You like my den?'

They turned sharply, but in what direction to look they did not know. In that cavern direction seemed to vanish.

'Here!' said Weed, directing them to an arch, through which they found a burrow as grand as a burrow could be. Lofty, elegant, shining with light, with a pool that surged and played from some inlet underneath and then sucked softly away into the wall. There, with dried heather to make the place soft, curled Henbane of Whern.

'You really are most welcome,' she said.

She seemed bigger than they remembered, and had

aged. That she was beautiful could not be denied, but it was a beauty beyond mere form. There was something about her that made a male tremble with longing, as if he had been brought to see something he never knew he had missed; as if life before Henbane was incomplete, and away from her would never be the same.

Looking at her, Tryfan found his emotions separating from his head and the first beginning to dominate and influence the second, which hung on with increasing difficulty to the knowledge that this mole was evil and destructive. Yet his emotions, and the desires of his body, told him: 'No, no, that's a memory, *here* she is not what she was, she cannot be. I want to be near her.' But though this conflict caused a turmoil in him he did not immediately show it, only staring at her without expression and then, taking his eyes from her hypnotic and alluring gaze with difficulty, he looked at the two moles who crouched on either side of her.

To her left side was a female they both knew, to her right a male that might have been a mole.

'Sleekit you know,' said Henbane. 'A sideem I trust more than any other.'

Sleekit stared at them, unaged from when they had last seen her, and impassive. There was no recognition of them at all in her eyes and yet they remembered she had been a mole who shared with them the Seven Stancing in Buckland so long before. A mole marked by the Stone with a task no doubt. Tryfan looked into her eyes and knew suddenly they were blessed to have her there, and sensed that Henbane knew it not. It made Henbane fallible. Sleekit's presence strengthened him from whatever chaos waited so near now for him to plunge on into it.

But Weed knew Sleekit might not be trusted, and Tryfan sensed it. Which, if it were so, meant that Sleekit had much cleverness for Weed did not allow doubtful moles to stay long near Henbane. Perhaps Henbane knew after all, but liked the conflict between two moles. Yes . . . that might be it. With such thoughts Tryfan, still quite impassive, stilled his mind, finding it easier if he avoided Henbane's gaze.

He looked at the male on her right.

'As for this one,' said Henbane, putting a possessive paw on that mole's shoulder, 'I think you know him too.' Henbane smiled while she caressed the mole's plump side.

It *was* a mole they supposed, though as for recognising him that was less certain. More a creature, really. Plump to obeseness, his face puffy with fat and his mouth weak; his eyes dead in their stare at them, and his fur all pampered and falsely glossy. His flanks were unmarked, his talons weak. He smiled, and in that moment when his face moved to that empty smile his eyes changed, and in them they saw a flash of real emotion – shame and corruption – and, terribly, Tryfan knew his name.

'You know him I think, or he knows you. Tell them your name, my dear,' purred Henbane. Her talons played sharply at his neck.

'My name's Bailey,' he said, 'and I come from Duncton Wood.'

Tryfan knew it before the mole spoke, but poor Spindle did not and he started, genuinely shocked. Weed watched, watched everything.

'Hello, Bailey,' said Spindle to his only son, Henbane's plaything. Though his voice was steady Tryfan could feel him trembling and knew the shock he felt and the awful dismay to find his son had survived for *this*.

He knew, too, that Henbane knew the cruelty that she did to confront a pampered, spoilt young mole of Duncton to two of its leaders.

'You see, Tryfan, I have my own follower from Duncton Wood, my favourite whose company I enjoy and who reminds me of the simple things in life. What a sweet system Duncton must have been to produce such . . . naivety. But run along, Bailey, we wish to talk.'

Bailey heaved himself up and looked around briefly, nodding his head in a weak half idiotic way, and waddled off, his fat rear barely squeezing into the tunnel he went down.

'He keeps me amused,' said Henbane, adding so quietly that at first it might have been a whisper in the mind until a mole thought about what it really meant: 'But now you're here, Tryfan, I don't need him, do I?'

Tryfan's glance had lingered on the departure of that corrupted thing that had been a goodly youngster he once knew, and Spindle's son, and he knew the first feelings of a horror that he could not have imagined before. For he began to guess why the Stone might have sent him and what it might ask him to do.

Afterwards, witness to that moment, Spindle scribed a strange and tragic thing: that Tryfan then, there, in Henbane's seductive burrow, had never looked so strong and fit and sure before, and never did again. It was the moment of moments in a mole's physical life that he strives to reach and never knows, until the moment has long past and age has crept up unawares, that that was the moment. The moment when a mole might do anything and of which Tryfan, looking back, might yet wish he had reared up then and struck down the vile thing beautiful Henbane was.

It was Tryfan's burden: he knew, and understood that in some way the Stone wished it so, that he might be a sacrifice to Henbane so that Boswell, and Spindle too, might be free. Yes, and Bailey. It was in the knowing and the facing of it that Tryfan's greatness lay.

'My favourite' she said of Bailey, but it was on Tryfan she looked now and the 'favourite' was, as Lathe might put it, 'as good as dead'. And yet knowing that, and that such would be anymole's fate who lingered with Henbane and was allured by her, he felt again as their eyes met in that enchanted burrow, where light played like a May wind in trees about them, his sinking towards an adoration of the mole he most despised.

To make it worse, each mole in that chamber knew what was happening, for Henbane and Tryfan had eyes for none other.

Spindle knew it.

Weed, watching now, knew it well; his eyes narrow and his mouth moist, aware of the males that had preceded Tryfan and what had happened to each of them. What he now saw so cynically was the continuation of a desire Henbane had from the day Tryfan successfully eluded her in Harrowdown and made fools of all the grikes at Duncton. She had both wanted him and wanted to destroy him, and Weed knew that her desire to do both in her own way, pleasurably, was one of several reasons why she had permitted this arrogant mole's naive trek from south to north to the very heart of the Whern. So, knowing this, Weed watched and felt certain he knew what the outcome would be.

Last there was Sleekit, doubted mole, nomole certain of her; watching Tryfan struggle before Henbane's soft gaze and knowing that soon now, after so long, she might have a role to play, yes, knowing that. And feeling more alone at Henbane's side than anymole knew then. The Stone discovers moles' courage in many different ways, and yet if there is one truth a mole can speak of the Stone it is that it always gives a mole a task *that* mole can do, if he, or she, has the will to do it. It is in that choice, between success and failure, that the strength and the weakness of the Stone follower lies. Spindle, Sleekit, Tryfan, Mayweed – each with a task nearly impossible, assembled now at Whern. Oh yes, the Stone will find a way, but only if the moles who profess its faith have the courage and intelligence to act as they must to see the Stone's purpose right.

Henbane spoke, breaking across the thoughts of those moles.

'So. And why have you come, Tryfan? Some doubted that you would, but I . . . did not. No, not I. And seeing you here, Tryfan of Duncton, in the flesh and the fur, talon so strong, flank so . . . strong as well, seeing you . . . I am not disappointed. A worthy leader of an ancient belief. It is a pity it is doomed. But I ask again, "Why have you come?" It would be nice to know.'

'To profess my faith, Henbane,' said Tryfan.

'Moles here call me WordSpeaker,' said Henbane with a sudden sharpness edging her soft voice.

'They are of the Word, I am not,' said Tryfan. 'Henbane is your name, as Tryfan is mine.'

Henbane laughed, eyes glinting. She both liked his reply and hated it. In the sound of her laugh a wise mole might guess that the touch of her talons could be the sweetest caress or the cruellest torture.

'Good,' she said ambiguously. 'Call me what you will. Meanwhile, once again: why have you come? I have nothing you could want.'

'Boswell.'

'Ah! Yes . . . him. He's an old fool.'

'He's alive?' said Tryfan immediately.

'Some might wonder. But yes, I suppose he is. And you would see him, yes?'

There was a quality to her voice which demanded that a mole agreed with her, but in agreement gave something of himself away. Of course Tryfan wished to see Boswell but to say 'yes' was . . . weakness. It was most strange.

'Yes,' said Tryfan.

'Yes, of course. It will be, it will be.'

'When?'

'Soon, of course!' said Henbane, laughing. It was a dreadful thing, but her laugh was good, it was most beautiful. Not to laugh with it seemed almost like denying life itself. Tryfan had to flex his talons into the chamber's floor to recall, again and again, that *this* was the mole he saw snout Willow and Brevis, *this* was the mole who overran moledom with her cruelty, this. . . .

'Tryfan, what are you thinking?' asked Henbane, stretching herself before him, overt in her sensuality. She sighed a lover's sigh and gazed on Tryfan pleasurably, annexing something of him to herself.

'Of Boswell,' lied Tryfan, who never lied; lying in Boswell's name!

Spindle glanced at him and knew the struggle there and in a way understood it. In other circumstances nomole would have been better suited to Tryfan than Henbane. Seeing them together it was as if no other mole was there or should be there, even though Spindle himself thought her disgusting. But more than that, he saw with an appalled clarity that Henbane was circling Tryfan, and making him think that giving in might be the only way to release Boswell. But *was* old Boswell really here?

'Oh yes, Spindle, he's *alive*,' said Henbane, reading his thoughts.

'Well, we'd like to see him then,' said Spindle, which sounded so lame that the moment he said it he regretted it.

Henbane shrugged and looked irritated, and all warmth in that burrow was gone and the air seemed suddenly chill.

'Then you had both better see him, had you not?' she said, as if desiring to see Boswell was rejection of her. 'After that, Tryfan of Duncton, you and I shall talk again.' With which she turned and abruptly left them.

Her presence was such that its sudden absence had the power not only to make a chamber seem empty when she left it, but to make the moles there feel bereft as well. No wonder Bailey, only a youngster when he first met her, had found her both irresistible and confusing. But it was the same power that, when she was in a different mood, could make the very air smell of fear. Stone help anymole whose heart was hers. Stone help Tryfan who stared after her in silence.

'The othermole, Mayweed, where is he?' asked Sleekit.

Weed scratched himself and settled down before he answered.

'Lost. Made a run for it. He was near the Clints.'

Sleekit then looked at Tryfan without expression.

'He will die,' she said. 'A pity. I had heard he was a mole worth talking to.'

'Really?' said Weed. 'Now had you? I wonder why.'

'He led these two into the Wen, and got them out again. Of *that* I would like to hear.'

'He will die,' said Tryfan looking at Sleekit strongly. He meant: he will not! Did Sleekit understand that? Did

741

Weed know what he really said? Sleekit held his gaze steadily, and Tryfan knew she understood, and that if there was a way she would find it and reach Mayweed. Then Tryfan felt tired and turned to Weed.

'Henbane seemed to say we were to see Boswell. When?'

Weed laughed unpleasantly and looked first up at the roof, then round behind himself, and then out through the fissure in the chamber's wall across the moor to the place where they had said the Master Rune was in retreat.

'Now,' said Weed.

Now! New life in Tryfan's paws, new hope. Now, at last, after so many years, Boswell once again. Beloved Boswell. Half disbelieving what they did, they followed Weed from that strange chamber with relief and expectation.

Above them, somewhere high among the stalactites, where the rock arched one way into light and in another turned to some shadowed place where there was a gallery and sound stilled to nothingness, there in that bleak silence an ancient mole stirred. He had watched Bracken and Rebecca's son, he had listened, and now he followed them.

His coat, black. His eyes shining black. His mouth cold. His teeth white and sharp. His flanks as graceful in the cruel way an old mole's can be when his life has been austere and mean. His shoulders scarred, his gait slow. About him was a shadowed darkness that would have seemed to turn the tunnel he was in about and around and over into confusion for any other mole who was there. None was. That mole had watched alone.

Henbane's father. Evil Rune.

He turned, and senior sideem came forward and supported him out and away to follow where the others went.

While down in the empty chamber where Henbane and the others had been, light played and a fat mole came. A tired mole, a corrupted mole, whose every step was an effort, whose fur glistened with unhealthy sweat. Poor Bailey.

To the very edge of the fissure he went and he looked out towards Providence Fall, watching the swathes of spray that flew up and faded out across the moor.

He was thinking of Spindle. He was feeling the shame of a mole who feels worthless, utterly; and beyond saving. Helpless and alone.

Poor Bailey cried like a pup and looked across a scene that was to him so desolate. He cried until at last he dared whisper a name, the name of a place, the memory of which was his sanity.

He cried and he whispered it, tears salty in the corners of his mouth. Again and again he whispered it.

'Barrow Vale,' was the name he said. Barrow Vale, the lost heart of Duncton Wood.

And then, in the very heart of Whern, he added to that hopeless litany a simple and courageous prayer: 'Please Stone, I want to go home and be where Starling is. She's my sister. I want to go home.' And poor Bailey cried alone.

Chapter Forty

The route that Weed and his attendant sideem led them on was through limestone and in places cut into open galleries which hung, as Henbane's chambers did, over the gorge they had first seen when Lathe brought them to the High Sideem.

'The stream which runs through the gorge is called Dowber Gill,' said Weed, who seemed more friendly once they were clear of Henbane's tunnels. They crossed the head of this stream and then dropped down north westward.

'But doesn't Rune have his burrows this way, by a waterfall called Providence Fall?' asked Spindle.

'Not a waterfall, mole, a roof fall. Yes, the Master does have his burrows near here, but here too is Boswell confined. No doubt the Master wished to keep an eye on him.'

Weed's voice was both serious and direct, and Tryfan detected a difference in his attitude to Rune than to Henbane. Of the first he seemed in respectful awe, of the second afraid.

As Tryfan followed on, the sideem all about watching his every step, he felt a strange disquiet about Henbane. It was more than the discomfort a mole might naturally feel to find himself attracted to a mole he had good reason to distrust and hate. Now they were away from her he felt more able to combat her overt intent to charm him. No, it was not that but, rather, a sense of pity that he felt.

He remembered his mother Rebecca telling him once of Mandrake, her father. A murderous, evil mole in everything he did, she said, and yet when she went to Siabod and saw where he had been raised she began to understand why, despite all he had done, she loved him. She loved the pup in him, she loved the mole he might have been deep, deep down, beyond recall, perhaps he *was*.

Now, here in Whern, in the very tunnels of the High Sideem, where Henbane lived, surrounded by tunnels too grand and beautiful for ordinary mole, and quite bereft of any homely sense, Tryfan felt pity for her. Pity for a mole who had ordered so many to die! Pity for the enemy of the Stone! Yes, pity.

The ground became wet, their fur was bedabbled with droplets of water, and Tryfan realised they had reached the place where spray rose so strangely from the great chasm in the ground. But before they could see more of it they were led underground into rough-hewn tunnels which reverberated with the roaring of water. After a steep downward run, they emerged into the open almost beneath a great waterfall, which thundered down from somewhere far above their heads and made the very air recoil with its sound.

The rocks at the tunnel exit were wet with its spray and in the cracks between them, and up the broken limestone cliff face above, grew ferns and pennywort. The waterfall formed a turbulent pool at the far end of which, to the left-paw side, was a short stream that flowed into a bigger, deeper, stiller pool whose far end butted against the towering side of the chasm, and was there sucked evilly down into darkness.

Since talking was quite impossible because of the water's roar, all they could do was stare, and their gaze was drawn inexorably up the black cliffs of the chasm until they had to tilt their heads awkwardly back to see the distant sky.

Although the chasm ended starkly enough with the deep pool to their left, to their right it stretched out a long way until, in the murky distance, a jumbled rock fall and more rising cliffs marked its furthest extremity.

In the central part of this awesome place were huge broken rocks, which had once formed the roof of what must have been a cavern bigger than any they had yet seen.

In places the ground was flat, or nearly so, and there was grass and heather, and a few stunted trees.

'This is Providence Fall,' shouted Weed against the noise. 'In the galleries above us the Master lives, but down here Boswell survives.'

Tryfan looked around the cliffs above and saw a few dark fissures and clefts that must, he supposed, be outlets from Rune's tunnels. On the floor of the Fall itself, he saw no sign of Boswell or anymole. The place appalled him: it had no entrance but the one they had come down, and no exit either but for the sucking peat-stained waters of the dreadful pool, a place of certain death for mole.

Weed took them some way into the gorge where, behind a rock which gave some shelter from the sound and spray, he spoke briefly to one of the sideem who, pointing at a tree in the distance at a place where thin sunshine came down from the heights above, said, 'He's there, usually. At night he's in a cleft.'

'And food?' said Tryfan, knowing they were talking of Boswell. 'What of that?'

'Oh, there's worms,' said the sideem, 'and dead sheep, too, if you like that sort of thing.' He indicated a vile heap of white wool and yellow bones among the rocks. 'They fall,' he said shortly. 'The spring thaws take them away if there's been no flood before.'

'You can go and find your Boswell,' said Weed, 'we'll stay here. Don't bother with trying to escape, it isn't possible.' Then, pointing at Spindle, he added, 'Not you, though. You're staying with us!'

So Tryfan set off across the Fall alone, the cliffs towering up all about him, great fallen rocks looming, and the sense of being watched from above, by raven if not by mole.

The roaring of the waterfall receded as he went among the rocks and it was replaced by the sound of his pawsteps echoing all about. But it seemed to him to sound like his pounding heart, for he felt nervous and strange going forth in this dreadful place to see a mole he had once loved as he had loved his parents, and a mole lost so long. Here? Boswell? Mole of Uffington. White Mole?

'Tryfan!'

It seemed as if the rocks themselves had spoken, or that this dreadful place was the mouth of the great earth speaking out his name.

'Tryfan!'

Not shouting it, not calling, not questioning, but stating his name as he was: Tryfan.

'Boswell?'

And there, by the bole of a stunted birch, Boswell crouched. Smiling. Gentle. Beloved.

It seemed to Tryfan that his heart was open to the world, the long years of a journey nothing, and that here, before this old mole who had made his life what it was, he had come home.

'Tryfan,' repeated Boswell, coming slowly forward and with evident pain, 'I knew that one day you would come.'

But Tryfan could not speak, nor move, nor barely think. He could only lower his snout before the mole he loved and weep. So it was that Boswell came to him, touched him as he used to do, nuzzled him, and said, 'There is no need for tears, mole, not yet anyway! No, no need for those. As for my slow gait, don't worry about it. Old moles stiffen easily, especially if they meditate too much in the same position. I'm fitter than I look!'

Tryfan dared to look at him and saw that though he was older, and his fur whiter, and his wrinkles deeper, yet truly he had not changed. His eyes were bright, his stance eager, his sense of curiosity as evident as ever.

'Well, and have you lost Spindle? I told him to look after you.'

'He has, Boswell, he's here. But Weed kept him back. I think otherwise he thought I might find a way for us all to escape.'

'Well, my dear Tryfan, I hope you will! A mole can't live in a place like this forever! Now tell me . . . tell me *everything*.'

747

So then Tryfan told him, of his and Spindle's journeys and struggles, of the changes that had overtaken moledom, and of the many moles he had met, and of how the followers had dwindled until only a few survived, scattered, leaderless, waiting.

'For what?' asked Boswell finally. 'Tell me, Tryfan, what do they wait for?'

'For the Stone Mole's coming, for the Silence he may bring. For that they wait, Boswell.'

Boswell nodded and reached out and touched Tryfan once more.

'And you, Tryfan. Have you survived?'

'I'm alive but my heart is bleak and sometimes I have lost faith. Since Feverfew . . . ' And Boswell nodded, Tryfan had told him of her. And many others too.

'Feverfew, Comfrey, Alder, Tundry, Skint, Smithills, Thyme, Starling, Mayweed . . . so many, so very many,' whispered Boswell. He thought for a moment and then said, 'This mole, Mayweed. Tell me more of him.'

Which Tryfan did, leaving Boswell in no doubt about how highly he regarded Mayweed, and that, despite his disappearance near the dangerous Clints, he had no doubt that Mayweed was still alive, and somewhere nearby.

'Yes,' said Boswell, 'I like the sound of this mole. I like the sound of all of them, Tryfan. I am . . . well pleased with them.' He seemed suddenly tired, and his eye drifted away to the high and distant prospect of the sky at the far end of the Fall.

'You have done well, Tryfan, you have led them well.'

'I have led them nowhere, Boswell, and I am no nearer the Silence you used to talk about, and nor did I find it in the Wen.'

'You did, my dear, but you could not hear it. But its sound will be heard, soon now, yes, yes it will. But we have not much time. I must leave now, I have things to attend to in that wide world you know only as moledom. I may be fit but I am somewhat in decline, as I have a right to be at my age. One loses the will, you see.' He said this last

748

rather irritably, as if it was a state that had crept up on him unawares, and all too soon.

'You must be the oldest mole alive!' said Tryfan. 'But that's because you're a White Mole.'

Boswell laughed suddenly, a frail but wheezy kind of laugh.

'Oh I'm sure I'm old, but the oldest? I doubt it.' A look of real alarm came over his face, and he frowned. He glanced up somewhere at the walls about him, as if searching for Rune in the black and dripping fissures where the ravens went.

'You've said nothing of yourself, Boswell, but then I didn't get much out of you about *you* all the time we journeyed from Duncton Wood to Uffington, so I doubt that I'll get much here and now.'

'I've been living simply as a mole should, here where Rune lives. I think he hoped he might learn something from me but I have been a disappointment to him. I have done little but crouch in silence and watch the seasons pass. In Uffington we called it going into the silent burrows, and I did my share of that. Here the sideem call it confinement. But that is only a word, Tryfan, that a mole chooses to use – usually of himself. I have food, I have shelter, I have a safe place and here I have known Silence, but now I have a task for which I need the help you have prepared for me.'

'What help? I'm as much a prisoner as you.'

'Here? In Whern? No, no, the prison is everywhere. It is in moles' minds. Your help is in readying other moles for what is soon to be. At least I hope it will be! Spindle, Alder, Mayweed, everymole. They're ready now and I have one last thing to do and then I can do no more.'

'But . . . ' began Tryfan.

'Always "but". But nothing.'

'How will you get out of here?' said Tryfan. 'The place is guarded and impregnable, the sideem are all about, and Spindle and I *are* prisoners though you make light of it.'

Boswell held up his paw and said quietly, 'You have

already done all you need to get me out of here. You can do no more, and if I were you I would stop striving to help me. Believe me, you have. No, Tryfan, from all you have said, from all I know of you, you have laid the foundation for the Stone Mole's coming, just as I hoped you would. Now you must find Silence, and I fear it will be especially hard. It always is for moles who lead, for they cannot so easily forget themselves. Trust me, Tryfan, and trust the Stone, and know that Spindle will be there when you need him, know that. . . .'

Tryfan felt fear then, for Boswell's eyes were sad on him, as if he knew more than he said, or at least *feared* more.

'Can't you guide me, Boswell? Can't you tell me what I should know?'

Boswell shook his head.

'Did I ever guide you, mole?' he said. 'I think I never did. I showed you how a life should be as parents must show their pups. Being is the only way. If I taught you anything at all it was to listen to what your heart tells you, and to trust yourself, and if you have made mistakes, as you have, then others will forgive. Trust your heart in the days ahead, trust that I shall be safe, because without knowing it you have made it so, and when you are ready Spindle will see that you return home safeguarded.

'Now, I am tired, and there are things to do soon. Did I tell you about Henbane? No, no I didn't. I can't. Nothing to say. Too late, perhaps. But don't try to fight Rune, Tryfan. Your talons are not sharp enough. Leave him to her. Go now, go. . . .'

'Boswell, will I see you again?' Even as he asked it, Tryfan knew it as a strange question, but he felt its answer might comfort him in the darkness that lay before him, and of which he was afraid.

Boswell stared at him and seemed to look at him for a long moment not as if he were Tryfan, but as if he were anymole, or allmole. But it was to Tryfan, the Tryfan that he loved, that he replied: 'Yes, you'll see me, and I shall

750

see you, and I shall love you always as I love you now and as your parents loved you. For remember, Tryfan, you were much loved and such a mole shall always be loved to the end of his days. The darkness is not knowing it. Oh yes, you shall see me, by the Stone you shall see me and you shall know at last that your darkness was a passing thing. And in knowing that you shall know how to love me, that moledom shall know such love as well. You are a blessed mole, Tryfan, for Rebecca loved you, and Bracken did, and they put you on the way towards the Silence you may hear, where light is and from where the sound that touches all moles' hearts comes forth.'

Then Tryfan turned from Boswell, and made his way among the rocks, and the damp moss and ferns, past the roots of old trees and back to the river that surged and was sucked to nothingness. There Weed and the sideem waited, and Spindle too.

None of them spoke, but they turned and left that place, where Boswell waited to depart, and where, unseen but felt, an evil mole watched down.

★ ★ ★ ★ ★ ★ ★

For several days after that Tryfan and Spindle found themselves confined in a chamber somewhere above Dowber Gill, whose monotonous roar they could hear all day. The only view out, however, was through a fissure to the sky, up which nomole could have climbed, and the only way out was past a guard of sideem, all young, all tough, all without conversation.

The chamber was wormless and food was brought to them. It might have been uncomfortable but for the fact that somemole had transported heather and dried grass into the place, and there was a small deposit of sand and gravel on one side which meant that they did not have to take stance on bare rock.

The air currents were good, as they generally seemed to be in the High Sideem, and for their natural functions they were allowed, singly, to the surface, but always heavily guarded.

Both moles were better equipped to deal with boredom, which was now their main enemy, than they once were but even so after a few days boredom and its associated restlessness set in. The journeys to the surface were the only relief.

If they wished not to be overheard they were able to talk only in low voices, for the sideem were always near, and the chamber carried sounds easily. Even when they whispered, the sibilants ran harshly about the walls and drowned even the roar of Dowber Gill.

But at least Tryfan was able to report to Spindle all that Boswell had said, and express his fears and doubts about what seemed likely soon to come. After that, the two moles indulged in dreams and hopes of what they might do once they had fulfilled whatever task it was they were to do, and had set off once more to trek south, hopefully with Boswell at their side.

Of his fears for himself Tryfan said little, but Spindle saw them there and sought to reassure him by sharing a dream of a future in which Duncton would be happily occupied once more. There, both agreed, if the Stone granted them the leisure, they would do what they were best equipped to do, which was to scribe. Spindle would uncover the books he had hidden in the ancient tunnels of Duncton Wood, and start once more a Library in the hope that one distant day, long after they both had gone, their texts would tell future moles of their past.

'But differently than at the Holy Burrows,' said Tryfan. 'We'll scribe texts that tell the stories of real moles, and give accounts from which all can learn. For it is my hope that ordinary moles can be taught to scribe and read. Scribemoles must teach others as I have taught you and Mayweed, so that all moles may know the wisdom that was forgotten. Mind you, if I had young of my own I would teach them to scribe second, and to live first. That's how it would be!'

Then Tryfan smiled a little wanly, and fell silent, while Spindle would think that having young was not what a mole expected it would be, perhaps not ever. And he thought of Bailey, his own son, so close by here, so lost to him.

Then suddenly one day when they were whispering together their conversation was interrupted.

It was Sleekit, Henbane's right-paw sideem.

'You are to come to Henbane, Tryfan of Duncton,' she said, her face as impassive as ever.

'And Spindle?' asked Tryfan not moving.

'He will be well enough here,' said Sleekit.

Though she was expressionless it seemed to Tryfan that it was as well he went with her without further protest. And anyway, some action was surely better than none.

He joined her by the entrance and the other sideem moved to one side to let him pass. Sleekit said, 'The walls here have ears and it is well you have said nothing of consequence to each other in your time in this chamber. You have spoken only of dreams.' She smiled rather primly, and looked for a moment directly into Tryfan's eyes, as if to say: 'Beware of trying to say anything to me even if you believe me to be of the Stone, for others may hear.'

Casting one last glance at Spindle, who watched his leaving with frowning concern on his face, Tryfan turned and followed Sleekit. A sideem went behind and ahead of them and whatever the purpose of Sleekit's tacit warning there seemed no hope of talking anyway.

But the route they took was rough and tortuous and there were several times when the mole behind lagged a little while the one ahead went too fast, so that Sleekit and Tryfan found themselves together without others to see. But the tunnel was high and galleried and, as always in such places in the High Sideem, Tryfan felt overlooked and watched. Yet hopeful that she herself would choose the best moment, if that was her intention, he stayed close by her and watched for an opportunity.

It came as the tunnel passed by a shoot of water that cleft over the edge of some turning gallery above and thrust down into a pool where the tunnel became a chamber once more. There the route was circuitous about the pools and stalagmites that ranged over the great chamber's floor. There among that noise and gloom Sleekit stopped, turned ugently, and said, 'I have not forgotten Buckland or the Seven Stancing, nor the sense it gave me that I have some task of the Stone.'

'I know it, mole,' said Tryfan.

'It has troubled me always, and I have not known what to do. I heard something in that burrow that I never heard again. I felt a peace near that sick mole, Thyme.'

'The Stone meant it so,' said Tryfan, 'but as for your task, find comfort in the knowledge that few moles know truly what theirs is. It is in the truthful search for it that they find the Stone, but the way is hard.'

'I have sought that Silence again all these long years. I have been . . . alone. And now you are here I am frightened and know not what to do. Henbane will kill you, as she has killed all the others.'

'Others?'

'Males. She needs them. She kills them afterwards, or has them killed. And here, of all places, you could not escape. Do not yield to her, Tryfan, or you are dead. That is all I can say, all the help I can give. I. . . .'

And Tryfan saw a mole in fear, whose eyes were frightened and he remembered again that Seven Stancing, when he found the power to heal and first felt his strength. He felt it now.

'There is something you can do,' he found himself saying, not even knowing what he might say next. 'Something only you can do which perhaps the Stone prepared you for as it has prepared me for this day now . . . The mole Bailey.'

A look of pity and contempt came over Sleekit's smooth face.

'He is the son of the mole we once helped heal together. Thyme was his mother. Spindle his father.'

Sleekit's eyes widened.

754

'But Bailey knows that not. Help him and I think you may help us all. Take him . . . take him . . . ' And Tryfan remembered a young mole once, innocent as well, who went to the Stone in Duncton Wood and asked for its guidance. Boswell came. Boswell guided him. Tryfan remembered himself. Yes. . . .

'Take him to Boswell, he will know what to do. Take him to the Fall. . . .'

'Trouble, Madam?'

The sideem behind had caught them up.

'Insolence,' said Sleekit, 'seeking to persuade me of the error of my ways! These Stone followers live on hope!'

The sideem came as near to laughing as a sideem can.

'I would like to see him evangelise the WordSpeaker!'

The two moles smiled.

'Now, let us continue with no more talk,' said Sleekit coldly.

'So shall it be,' said Tryfan.

'Indeed it shall,' said Sleekit purposefully.

Soon after that they came to Henbane's den where, languidly, she waited for them.

Henbane looked long at Tryfan, and then indifferently at Sleekit and the sideem accompanying them.

'Leave us,' she purred.

'But WordSpeaker – ' began Sleekit.

'Yes?' The word was cold as ice.

'Is it wise?' Tryfan was surprised at how confidently Sleekit spoke. Clearly she had not become the sideem closest to Henbane for nothing.

'Not very,' said Henbane, 'but risks are fun. And anyway, I think it unlikely that Tryfan would seek to harm me so long as he knows that his dear friend Spindle is so safe with our sideem. They can have cruel talons in the name of the Word. Is there anything else, my dear, before you leave?'

Sleekit smiled.

' 'Tis nothing,' she said.

'Nothing is something,' said Henbane. 'Speak it.'

'I can report later what this mole and the mole Spindle spoke secretly to each other.'

'You can, but is it of consequence?'

Sleekit smiled and shrugged indifferently.

'No, amusing that is all. They spoke of Bailey, saying that in their Stone-warped judgement he is not so far changed towards the Word that Boswell, for all his age, could not revive the Stone in him.'

Henbane laughed.

'Did they now?' she said. 'Well! Bailey has always wanted to go down to the Fall and now you must give him his chance, Sleekit. But stay near them. I would hear your report of the effect on Bailey of their exciting and learned conversation. Summon him.'

Sleekit went out and they waited then in silence until Bailey, huffing and puffing, appeared with Sleekit at his side.

'Sleekit said you wanted me to do something,' he said with pathetic eagerness. Then, seeing Tryfan, he added petulantly, 'Oh! Hello!'

Tryfan nodded but said nothing.

'It's time you were educated by the wisest mole in moledom,' said Henbane.

Bailey's eyes widened in fear: 'The Master?' he asked.

Henbane laughed outright, and then her eyes turned cold.

'Boswell,' she said. 'He is to teach you of the Stone.'

'But I don't believe in the Stone,' said Bailey. 'I worship the Word. I do!'

Henbane looked pained and weary.

'A mole knows the Word, he doesn't worship it. Perhaps, Sleekit, Tryfan and Spindle are right to have faith in Boswell! But I hope not, Bailey, for your sake. Because I fear that if you are unable to persuade Boswell to Atone and profess the Word then both of you will die.'

'But Henbane . . .' faltered Bailey, sweating.

'I did not mean – ' began Sleekit.

'Thank you, Sleekit! And you, Bailey, shut up. You

bore me now. Take him to Boswell, Sleekit, and report on
what happens. I would know today but – ' She looked at
Tryfan sweetly and added, 'No, not too soon. Now, leave
us.'

* * * * * * *

For those concerned with the history of Duncton Wood,
and the events that formed the context of the coming of the
Stone Mole, what happened in the following hours
between Henbane of Whern and Tryfan of Duncton, and
to Tryfan subsequently, has been the subject of much
debate, dispute and controversy. Some attribute blame,
others pity. Many still feel anger about it, whilst a few –
and there have been a growing number of these in recent
years – express understanding and sympathy. No ordinary
mole is perfect, none blameless, none can look back on his
life without regret for some actions taken or for things left
undone.

But what a mole can do when he or she considers the
history of Duncton in those times is strive to listen to the
truth as it is known, and if judgement must be made let it
be in a tolerant spirit, and one which remembers that
Tryfan's life was lived in troubled and difficult times, and
the burdens he carried for himself and for others were
heavy. Though taken up with reluctance, and carried in
the knowledge that much he did he might have done
better, yet at least he accepted the tasks that the Stone gave
him, and did his best to ensure that there would be worthy
followers ready in moledom for the great and triumphant
change that he believed would soon come.

As for those few critical hours in the company of
Henbane, until now the truth of them has remained
obscure, and what should be the best source, and
generally the one it is the wisest to follow – which are the
texts left us by Spindle the Cleric who was witness to so
much that happened in those days – is on this one subject
not to be entirely trusted. Great historian that he was,
Spindle was, after all, but a mole like any other, and on
some things perhaps less of a judge than others. He was

fortunate to have a successful mating in his life, with doomed Thyme, and after that not to need, as others might, anything more than the pursuit of texts and learning, and the company of good friends.

So perhaps his account judges rather too harshly what occurred between Tryfan and Henbane in Whern. And, too, it was scribed before the full truth of the coming of the Stone Mole was known, and before anymole could hope to understand his purpose.

But we are now able to turn to another source than Spindle's, though some might say that it, too, is biased and uncertain, and they would no doubt be right: for that new and so-far unrecorded source is Tryfan himself.

He has left an account of that time with Henbane, though how he came to do so, and why, it is not yet our task to recount. But tell of it he did, and so many of its details are now confirmed by other sources that we have good reason to think that this version is as near to the truth – the terrible truth – as we are ever likely to get.

So, this explanation made, we who would continue our journey at Tryfan's side and help him with our prayers, must travel back to that strange and beautiful chamber that it pleased dread Henbane to call her den, and know what took place after Sleekit had so cleverly arranged, at Tryfan's urgent suggestion, Bailey's meeting with Boswell at Provident Fall. . . .

After they had gone, Henbane stared at Tryfan a long time, saying nothing but seeming to put herself into thoughts that troubled her, and made her seem weak and vulnerable. Whatever Tryfan might have expected it was not that.

For there, unprotected before him, the leader of the grikes stared at him until her eyes filled with tears and the chamber they were in seemed almost overcome with the power of her grief. And grief for what?'

'You dislike me,' she said, 'and yet I have no such feelings towards you, and nor have I ever had towards anymole of the Stone. But you *do*, Tryfan of Duncton, and I feel that dislike as a pain here!' And she thumped a paw to her chest and, as it appeared to Tryfan, burst into a paroxysm of tears.

'I am not loved!' she declared. 'I am alone!'

If there was something Tryfan should have said he did not know what it was. Whatmole would have done? Easy now, looking back, to think what might have been said, but at the time? Tryfan himself reports that such was the potency of Henbane's grief that it was like a natural force about him, and he felt it as he had felt the power of her attraction at their first meeting in Whern some days before and the confusion of his senses that accompanied it.

Her grief was real and to have denied it would have been to deny his own responsive feelings, and so naturally it evoked in him feelings of sympathy, and pity, and a desire to understand. Perhaps, too, he thought, so far as any mole *could* think in the presence of such elemental emotions as Henbane then displayed, that if he could reach out and understand, and show that he understood, he might achieve not only the freeing of Boswell and Spindle, but also perhaps some new tolerance towards the followers of the Stone; a tolerance, incidentally, that he had already thought was beginning from the fact that his own passage north had not been interrupted; and that no violence at all had been shown them in Whern. These hopes, then, combined with the natural sympathy for one who appeared so much in grief to cloud Tryfan's judgement.

Yet no doubt, too, he tried to hang on to the warnings about Henbane he had had from Sleekit, and Boswell, and the evidence of his own experience of what the grikes had perpetrated over the years. While all the time, before him then, *was* a mole in grief, and one who might have warmed the heart of ice itself.

What is certain is the extraordinary, almost alarming, effect Henbane's presence had on a mole when she wished it to. She was beautiful, she was one who held a fascination in her form whatever she said or did, as if through her body each emotion and purpose found its perfect expression. Hatred and animosity: they had been seen well enough at Harrowdown, but a mole forgets that when faced by an equally potent expression of grief and tragedy.

'Tell me,' Henbane said suddenly, seeming to move out of grief to something else as fast as the sun appears from behind a racing storm cloud, 'tell me, Tryfan, because I want to know, I really do: were you much loved as a pup?'

Much loved. The expression Boswell had used so affectingly to Tryfan in the Fall. Only much later did it occur to him that Henbane, or perhaps another mole close to her – Rune perhaps, but he never knew – had overheard that conversation and now Henbane knew well how to play on it.

'Was I much loved?' faltered Tryfan, and of course he knew the answer was that he had been, very much; as a mole should be. The love of Rebecca and Bracken for him and between themselves was at the very essence of his being.

'I was,' he said.

But barely were the words out of his mouth, indeed they were not quite out, before her quiet and beguiling query transmuted into dark and terrifying rage.

'But I was not, Tryfan! I was not much loved. My father I know not; my mother I killed.'

The chamber seemed to rumble and shake with the anger of her words.

'You cannot understand that, you can never understand that, nomole *can*,' she said. 'And yet all judge me!'

So shock was followed by accusation, but before Tryfan could even catch up with *that* Henbane began to scream, so loud, so long, so *violently* that nomole but a deaf one would not have gone to her side to seek to comfort her. Tryfan was not deaf, and he was a caring mole, and so, in the face of such a sudden outburst, he did what most such moles would have done: he sought to comfort her by touch.

760

Touch!

Perhaps from that moment, in the High Sideem, when Tryfan was driven by an elemental scream for help by a mole who in one sense was never any more than a pup, though one with fearsome power and authority indeed, he was doomed.

But he himself believed that all was not quite lost at that moment when he reached out to comfort Henbane. Comfort! *That* mole? Yes, comfort.

She turned on him, her eyes expressing a desperate agony, her yearning for comfort and love irresistible, and she wept.

'I was reared in a place called Ilkley, in a wormless place, and my mother's name was Charlock.'

There Henbane abruptly stopped what had seemed about to become a long, extended narrative and stared in great distress at nothing in particular as she thought about her mother. It was as if a wave of passionate regret had stopped inside her head where her face started and would any moment burst forth as tears more terrible than any she had yet shed. Then they came, but silently, great tears of grief that rolled down her face and glistened hugely in her fur.

Then, as if with great difficulty – and once more before Tryfan could quite catch up with her emotions – she began to talk quickly but quietly of her past in Ilkley, of her mother's cruel ways, of the lovelessness of her time on Rombald's Moor, of her longings to know more of the Word, and, by degrees, of her desire to visit Whern and give herself in service to the Master of the Sideem himself.

She told of how the mole Weed came, and in a hushed voice she justified the killing of her mother, that other moles might be safe from her sharp talons. Sometimes she paused and gulped, as if bravely holding back those tears that demanded to be wept, sometimes she came close to Tryfan and touched him, beseeching him not to leave her, to listen to her, to know the 'truth', and to understand that what she had done in the name of the Word was for the good of moledom and that now it *was* done she was forever alone and bereft.

So spoke Henbane, and outside the light dimmed and Dowber Gill's roar diminished, and it seemed to Tryfan that his world now was just this agonised and struggling mole who was not Henbane of Whern any more, but a pup who cried out for help from a desolate moor where her mother Charlock tortured her, punished her, and for whom the only hope was a distant mythical one called the Master of the Sideem, presented to her by cruel Charlock as a future lover.

Did Henbane know what she did in those hours with Tryfan? He afterwards doubted it. Could she have guessed that of all moles she was ever likely to know the one most likely to understand and sympathise with a confusion between a mate and a parent was Tryfan, whose own mother Rebecca had been ravaged by her father Mandrake, another evil, angry mole? Did Tryfan in those hours as Henbane spoke to him begin to see what she herself never had and what only Weed so far knew: that Rune, who first took her, was her father. Did he, knowing Rebecca's history, feel sympathy where another, like Spindle, for example, might not?

Perhaps. Probably. It helps explain why he listened on, and why Henbane dared say so much; and perhaps seeing his sympathy she, moledom's greatest mistress of inveiglement and evil, dared expose herself further and tell him everything.

However it was, the night came, and Whern was hushed, and those two moles talked on, coming closer as moles will with time, and feeling that bonding that all moles feel that share dark, intoxicating secrets and emotions.

Much earlier they had touched. Now, as darkness crept across the faces of the white limestone scars of Whern, and into the chambers and passages of the High Sideem, the world of those two moles came closer still. They were not Henbane and Tryfan any more but two of the many, two moles finding comfort, two moles in troubled times who find peace between themselves, and good feeling, and homecoming.

There in that darkness, with the water's roar nearby, their touching came closer yet, of flank to flank, of nuzzling teeth to caressing talon, of dark warmth and abandonment, where two moles lose themselves and make one, one unalone, and move towards a sensuous ecstasy that Stone or Word, or whatever power gives life and love, first ordained as desire and delight; and whose denial seems *if only in its own fateful hour* a denial of love itself.

There, that night, as the Dowber Gill's force and waterfall roared down, and all over Whern water roared and turned white in foam and spume and turmoiled into dark and sensuous pools, and moved silently and unseen within the very bowels of the earth itself, those two mated, time forgotten, friends forgotten, all purposes forgotten.

In mating, as in all else, Henbane was more than passionate, more than alive. Those sighs and screams she made before, those tears, that anger through the years, that cruelty, all that a mole puts into life Henbane doubled there that night. For in mating, moles may put all of their life for good and bad, all their strengths and weaknesses, and that was what she did then; and Tryfan too.

Others heard. Whern knew. Spindle, Lathe, Bailey, dark Rune smiling at the sounds of ecstasy, Boswell; oh yes, they heard. With the water's roar they heard it and if Henbane and Tryfan knew they did not care. Such matings care for nothing but itself.

Until at last all the sounds of passionate discovery and declarations between those fated two dissolved into the sighs of fulfilling peace, sighs of a male and female, and laughter such as moles who have known true mating can make.

Whern heard it, and was struck still, restless, angry, amused, shocked; alarmed too, and wary. Sad, and bereft: each heard it according to his need.

One other heard, and knew more than all those others

but Boswell himself that if there was a Stone and a Word they were there with Henbane and Tryfan that night, and being there might help others who trusted them.

That mole was surreptitious Mayweed, most clever Mayweed, who might have found the route through chaos itself, had there been one to find.

'I will be near,' he had told Tryfan, and under cover of the violent sounds and reverberations of that night's mating of two moles he made a route to Providence Fall.

No surprise will it be that since his separation from Tryfan and Spindle, he had found out many strange and curious things about Whern. Among them was the discovery such a mole *would* make, that the secret of route-finding through Whern was to know the way the waters ran. Made by water, dominated by water, follow water, have no fear of water: that was the way to conquer Whern.

Far and wide had Mayweed roamed, watching, listening, learning. Never once suspected. Missing, presumed dead, by all but Tryfan and Spindle. Now he came, by ways diverse and strange, to the Fall itself, down through fissures at its western end, and heard the sighing echoes of Henbane's ecstasy and Tryfan's pleasure. Heard them and knew they marked a moment of change, though for what end he could not guess but that it made him afraid and purposeful.

As for Boswell, Mayweed already knew he was somewhere in the Fall, that much he had learnt from listening. He knew too that Rune was hidden there as well, very old he believed, but still a mole to avoid.

So as dawn rose, and the mating of Henbane and Tryfan began to ail, Mayweed crept among the shadows of the Fall searching for an old White Mole.

What he found he could never have expected, not in a million years of imagining.

There was Boswell, even more ancient than Mayweed had expected, with, of all things, a fat mole whose flanks were so plump that they struggled with each other when he moved; a mole with the eyes of a lost pup and a body so useless that it deserved to die. This he saw before he made himself known.

He sensed other moles about and, moving on up the chasm towards where he heard a waterfall driving down from the surface above, even as grey light advanced across that dreadful place, he saw them: sideem. Lurking, waiting, preparing.

'Boswell and that Bailey have talked all night,' said one.

'Some have done more than talk,' said another. 'Filthy and vile are those who stray from the Word.'

'Silence,' ordered a third, a female, her voice severe yet not quite cold. She Mayweed could not see.

'I shall go and get Bailey now,' she said, 'and bring him here, for Henbane would see him.'

'May the Word have put sense into him,' said another. More chill laughter of a kind Mayweed had got used to in his long reconnaissance of Whern's tunnels.

Hearing the name Bailey, Mayweed was naturally astonished since the only other mole he had ever known so named was Starling's brother. But *he* had been a pup, innocent, young, eager with a pup's eyes. . . .

A pup's eyes! Mayweed's own eyes widened in alarm, and he felt then the power of the Stone, and the ways it saw its task come to pass. Bailey? That obese mole – Bailey? Did Mayweed then run back to reach them quickly? Not he. Mayweed was a route-finder, with a route-finder's habits and instincts, and he turned quickly past the group of sideem and went to the great stream's fall and stared at its deep, surging pool, and on to the sucking roaring disappearance of its treacherous flow beneath an overhang of rock into the unknown deeps below.

Then he crept back, past the sideem, and heard them arguing with the only female among them saying it was their duty to come with her, for this Bailey might give her trouble and Henbane would want to see him, and getting him back up the steps to her chambers was going to be a major task since he was so fat he could hardly move four steps without a pause.

So they all set off as Mayweed, unseen by them, ducked away and took another route and went now as fast as he could and made his plan as he went. Yes, yes! But Stone help them all!

So he burst in upon the strange conversation between Boswell and Bailey, who looked at him in blank astonishment.

'Decrepit and crumbling Sir, White Mole of Uffington, and mole of great gravity, Bailey. Time is short and words are long!'

'But . . . ' began Bailey, his eyes popping out of his plump head as he saw a mole he knew and loved and had never thought to see again.

Mayweed raised a paw.

'No buts, overweight Sir, no doubts. Listen and follow. Sideem come. Sideem will kill. Boswell to be saved. Humble me called Mayweed has a plan of startling complexity which he has not time or inclination to explain. Unbothered Boswell, will you trust me?'

Boswell smiled.

'I will, Mayweed, and so will this one here despite his protests. Now tell us what to do for we have both grown impatient with waiting to leave this place.'

'Sirs both, follow, follow *now*, and pray.'

'We will,' laughed Boswell like a pup, and doing something most ungentle for a White Mole, which was to talon-thrust poor Bailey in the rump to start him moving.

Mayweed led them along the cliffs of the chasm, and even as they left Boswell's clearing they heard the sideem arrive, exclaim, cry out to each other, and begin to snout about. High up on that chasm's walls the first light of the morning's sun stuck, and the shadows weakened, and Mayweed knew their cover would soon be gone.

But before that the sideem might catch up with them, because the ground was rough with scree and, though limping Boswell managed well enough, poor Bailey was

766

almost unable to get over some of them, and between others he got struck.

'Is it far?' he panted.

'It is a very long way indeed, staggeringly obese Bailey, so Mayweed suggests you concentrate your energies on moving not talking.'

There was silence behind them for a time as they struggled along, getting nearer and nearer to the great raging pool. Then they heard a shout go echoing up among the chasm's walls and the drumming of paws coming up behind them.

'Struggling Sirs,' entreated Mayweed, looking as patiently as he could at the moles he was trying to rescue as they did their best to clamber over increasingly slippery and awkward rocks and came within range of the water-fall's spray and neared the pool, 'do your best!'

The sounds of the shouts of the chasing sideem, and the sudden appearance of other sideem at the entrance to the tunnel by which Bailey had come down to the chasm, who began to give chase as well, spurred Boswell and Bailey on to the pool's edge.

It had no lip, but rather an ominous sinking past a few peat-stained boulders into black water, in which were the yellow, surgings of fierce currents and flows.

'Where do we go now?' asked Bailey, reasonably enough, eyeing the approaching sideem with fear and distaste, and the pool with horror.

'Sirs, we do what moles must always do if they are to progress in life! We take a leap into the unknown!'

'In *there*?' said Bailey in disbelief.

Mayweed nodded.

'But we'll drown!' said Bailey.

'Humble Mayweed takes comfort from this undeniable fact. If the oldest mole in moledom, and the fattest, survive submersion in this pool then it seems likely that he himself, pathetic though he is, will do so too!'

With that, and as the nearest sideem negotiated the final few boulders towards them, Mayweed pushed protesting

Bailey into the water, where he struggled briefly until the current caught him, turned him, began to suck him down. His paws reached vainly for the receding sky above, he let out a gulping corpulent scream and vanished from sight.

Boswell, his faith in Mayweed complete, entered with more grace, and was gone in a flash, his white fur turning grey and then his form quite lost in the swirl of currents as he was dragged rapidly underwater towards the lowering overhang of cliff beneath which the waters disappeared.

Which left Mayweed alone at the pool's edge, to take one last look back at their pursuers. A look which was as brief as the blink of an eye, and yet which took in a sight he had waited all his adult life to see.

As he stared at the sideem reaching out for him, he forgot his own natural fears of the pool he was about to dive into and remembered, of all things, a tunnel in the Wen a long time before, and a meeting with Tryfan, and a conversation about whether he would ever mate, during which Mayweed had said, 'I have not the precise female in mind . . . but when I meet her I shall know!'

There, in the chasm with two moles lost in the pool behind him, and sideem all but taking him, Mayweed knew. For behind the group of male sideem was the single female whose voice he had heard earlier. Sun shafted down at that auspicious moment and struck a sheening light into that female's grey fur, and her eyes stared at the extraordinary mole who had paused on the brink of death, or eternal torture in the Sinks. So Sleekit saw Mayweed.

A mole who stared at her with the brightest and most ironic eyes she had ever seen. A mole who seemed oblivious of all the dangers about him in that chasmed place. A mole who, to her astonishment, raised a paw and cried out a commanding, 'Silly sideem, *stop!*' And gave himself the brief space to say with a kind of exaltation to his voice, as he gazed into her eyes, 'Nonplussed Madam, Mayweed, who is me, will come back for you from death itself!'

With which he turned, and as boldly and heroically as

he could manage, dived into the pool and was sucked out of sight to the depths below.

* * * * * * *

As the first rays of sun entered that chamber where Tryfan had spent the night with Henbane, and even as he woke and understood the danger he had put himself in, Henbane disentwined her limbs from his, and said. 'You must leave, Tryfan of Duncton, *now*.'

Whether or not she meant him to be safe and to help him escape, he never knew, though he would have liked to think it was so. It would have made easier the knowledge that he had mated in the course of that strange night just passed, with the Stone's greatest scourge.

But it was all too late. The sun came in, and there crouched in its rays watching them with contempt and dislike was the mole Tryfan had so long feared he might one day meet.

His eyes were black, his features thin with age, his fur glossy but dry, his talons curved and clean. Behind him ranged moles Tryfan knew must be sideem, but they were older than any other he had seen. Older and senior, all slim, all elegantly cruel of feature, all powerful in that way that engenders surprise and fear when it is seen in a mole who should have reached an age of relaxation. A strength preserved for arid things.

'My name is Rune,' said Rune. 'And you are Bracken's son.'

Tryfan felt then the fear of death and knew he faced it there.

'I am,' he said.

'Your father nearly had the strength to kill me, but he failed. I have never forgotten that he tried. Your mother I desired, and but for Bracken that might have been. So I have reason enough to kill you. Now you come to Whern, welcomed, unharmed, and you ravage Henbane here. That is reason enough to kill you in another way.'

Despite the fear he felt, and the helplessness, for the

sideem closed in all about him and he had no way to go, Tryfan even then thought of another mole.

'Spindle has harmed nomole, nor will he. Let him at least be free. You have myself and Boswell, you. . . .'

Rune raised his left paw slightly. His face, close to, was lined, even frail, but there burned out of his eyes a black hatred and contempt for life and normal living.

'He shall not be harmed,' said Rune, 'not physically, just as you will not die. My duty is to find due punishment. You came here alive, and your weak followers must know you left here alive, as they must learn what you did here with Henbane. So very well.' He looked at Henbane briefly, and his thin pale tongue glanced across his mouth and then was gone. 'I believe your followers will feel you were deserving of just punishment, Tryfan.'

It was only then that, in some way that Rune moved or spoke, some hint in his form, that Tryfan must have recognised the truth of Rune and Henbane, and seen he was her father, for he turned to Henbane and said with a contempt to his voice that equalled Rune's, 'Look at him, the Master of the Sideem! Look close. Can you not see who he is, Henbane, and what he has done even to you? He is your father!'

As Henbane looked at Rune, and the first creepings of suspicion came to her, Rune turned from them both and said to the waiting sideem, 'He babbles. So do it, now, and well. *Do it.*'

Then as he pulled back, the sideem advanced upon Tryfan, and in terrifying silence began to bring their trained talons down upon him. And though he fought and wounded a few yet soon his paws were stilled and he slumped in his own blood beneath their blows. Before his eyes were taloned, he saw their hatred raining down upon him, and before his hearing was lost to the points of their talons he heard the vileness of their grunting breaths. And before the place was lost in darkness to him he reached out to touch Henbane of Whern, but felt instead her touch to him and knew that somewhere deep within that befouled

770

heart was a moment at least of pity. Then the pain overwhelmed him, and he felt himself destroyed and began to know a darkness inflicted by the Word, in which there was not Stone nor hope of Stone, and living death has come.

Chapter Forty-One

Rarely, in the whole of moledom's long history, can there ever have been such an outraged and protesting mole as fat, reluctant Bailey sinking helplessly down into the sucking pool into which Mayweed forced him that day.

His watery protest and anger doubled and redoubled as the bitter cold of the water knocked the breath out of his spoilt body, and he found himself being turned over again and again, this way and that, as curious colours of surging yellow and deep green, black and then mottled white came before his eyes.

His outrage increased still more as, swept along, he realised that this was not the first time such an indignity had happened to him but the second: for he had been one of those in the tunnel collapse during the evacuation from Duncton Wood. And such can be mole's sense of injustice that, even as he now began to die, he was thinking, 'It's not fair, not *twice*!'

Then as his breath began to give out, and his chest to feel exploding pain and his paws to scrabble at anything and nothing in the Sinks into which he had been dragged, he felt buffets of rock on his shoulders and painful scrapings of gravel on his snout and he knew, even as his outrage climaxed into a futile underwater cry of protest, that he was about to die.

Which, almost to his greater annoyance – for death might have justified his rage and not made him feel so silly – did not happen. Instead his chest pain continued, he reached out his paws as if to find air, the noises in his plump ears reached a crescendo of horribleness and suddenly his snout and face seemed to burst out of the terrible submersion they were suffering into the cold chill of a deep cavern's still air, and he knew he was alive.

Alive! Not drowned and dead. Alive to live! And Bailey felt a surge of relief and joy such as he had not felt for many moleyears, indeed, from the very moment that he had first met Henbane of Whern.

Splash went the waters about him, and high above, as he gulped in air, he saw a most beautiful thing, and that was a shaft of light coming down on to the water where he floated in chilly languor, his stomach a rotund shadow at each corner of which floated a paw, and at one end of which bobbed his head, whose mouth gulped and muttered, 'Never again! Not going anywhere near water *ever*! Bailey and water don't mix! I hate Mayweed because it's *always* his fault!'

But his plaints ceased suddenly when, the light above drifting slowly behind him, he heard an ominous sucking sound and water's roar ahead. Total panic overtook him and he turned over on to his front, scrabbled about desperately, felt a gravel bottom, and with ill grace and enormous speed considering his size, pulled himself on to the subterranean shore where he slumped panting fit to burst.

But he *was* alive and he would never have believed it possible that he could have felt such happiness in such a place. But Bailey did. Alive!

He heard a spluttering and splashing out in the midst of the expanse of water from which he had just escaped.

'Boswell!?' he called out hopefully.

But as the watery sounds continued, and nomole replied, the appalling thought occurred to him that he might be alone in this great cavern with a beast of the deep which, scenting his flesh, was making its ponderous way across the water to eat him.

'Is that mole?' he whispered nervously.

'Yes, yes, of course it's mole,' said Boswell irritably from out of the murk. 'Now come here and help me out.'

Relieved once more, overjoyed yet again, Bailey waded back in and helped Boswell on to the shore.

As they shook themselves dry a voice floated over the

773

water to them from the far side of the pool, whose size they only began to see as their eyes adjusted to the lack of light.

'Splashing Sirs, Mayweed hears you but cannot see you so kindly make a sound so that he may find you. . . .'

'What sound?' said Bailey, reminded by Mayweed's voice of the outrage to his dignity he felt he ought to feel. 'I'm cold and wet and very hungry and I want to know how we are going to get out of here. Henbane will be furious, and you know what that means. No, you probably don't. Well, I *do* and it's not nice. It's not!'

'Bothered Bailey, Mayweed thanks you for making a guiding sound,' said Mayweed, coming along the terrace of sand and gravel on which they had been washed by the stream, 'and now he asks you to stop complaining once and for all.'

'But – ' began Bailey.

Mayweed turned to Boswell and quickly saw that apart from being cold and wet, and having a bloody gash above his right eye, he was all right.

'I hurt,' said Bailey.

Mayweed turned on him.

'Sir,' he said, 'Mayweed also hurts. Boswell hurts. Moledom hurts. Humble me and aged Boswell here are not interested in what you have to say unless it's useful.'

'Well I suggest we get out of here quick,' said Bailey.

Mayweed smiled.

'Mayweed is sure that Boswell and he himself agree with that, and is pleased to observe once more that when moles are physically beset they are inclined to a concurrence of action rather than a discordance of complaints and protests. Mayweed is glad that tubby Bailey is showing signs of being normal.

'Now, Mayweed has come to know this type of tunnel well and has this to say. It is a killing place a cavern like this, for chill sets in a mole's flesh and mars his judgement. Movement is vital, the swifter the better. However, humble he is sure that the two escapees will be advised to stay underground as long as they can. Follow this stream,

774

there will be tunnels adjacent because that is the way of Whern.'

'What do you mean "two" escapees?' said Bailey quickly.

'Mayweed is not coming with you, dependent Sir. You are taking Boswell here to safety. It is called a task. Mayweed sympathises with daunted Sir at the suddenness of it but, noting Sir's corpulence and knowing the rigors of the days ahead he is, on the whole, inclined to think that fat Sir will benefit.'

'How?' said Bailey, rubbing his head where a bump was showing from his recent rush through the water.

'It will make him thin,' smiled Mayweed, 'and humbleness is sure that Sir will wish to be presentable when he travels south. Fatness is not welcome there as it suggests a mole is lazy and good for nothing.'

'But Henbane – ' said Bailey doubtfully.

'Henbane will kill Sir if she catches him. For now she and all the sideem will think Sir dead, and Boswell here as well. Good. Do not be found. Creep, so far as Sir's belly allows. Go carefully. Listen to wise Boswell here and rediscover your common sense! Go, Sirs both, now! Before the cold sets in.'

'You are not coming, then?' said Boswell.

'Wise Boswell, the Stone works strangely. It made me see a mole, beauteous and fair of fur. Mayweed desires to be alone no more. Mayweed will go back and find her.'

'Whatmole is that?' said Bailey.

Mayweed described her.

'That's Sleekit you mean. She's sideem, very important sideem. Closest female to Henbane, only other female in Whern. She's horrible.'

'Sir will forgive this observation but on the subject of female form humbleness very much doubts gluttonous Bailey is a sound judge. He reminds Sir that though she may be horrible at least she's not fat.'

'I don't know why I ever liked you, Mayweed. Well, maybe I didn't. Maybe only horrible Starling did.'

'Humble me trusts that one day fat Sir will be thin, and then rediscover why he liked Mayweed and loved Starling,' said Mayweed.

Boswell laughed. 'I am cold, Bailey,' said Boswell, 'and we had better do as Mayweed suggests, and go. So lead on!'

'*Me*?' he gasped. 'But . . .!'

Boswell turned to Mayweed and touched him gently with his good paw.

'May the Stone's will be thine soon, mole, for thou art worthy. Find Sleekit, engage her help for your final task in Whern. When the time comes seek out Tryfan once more for there will be a time when he needs you as you will need him.'

With that Boswell started to limp slowly downstream along the bank with the high light of the cavern shining down on his wet fur. Bailey, with one final heaving sigh of general protest, turned to follow him and Mayweed, having watched them disappear into the tunnels at the far end of the chamber, turned and snouted up the other way until, finding some cleft in the seemingly impregnable wall of the cavern, he started a slow ascent up it, and was gone.

★ ★ ★ ★ ★ ★ ★

Although Spindle had feared that something might happen to Tryfan once he was taken from their chamber of confinement away to Henbane's den, he had no inkling of what it might be. Nor was he warned what to expect by the silent and hurried sideem who came for him and, without explanation, led him southward through the High Sideem.

They stopped only once, and that briefly, and afterwards Spindle sometimes doubted his memory of that strange moment at all.

An old sleek mole stared at him from the corner of a chamber, with senior sideem flanking him protectively. Spindle remembered his gaze most of all, which was cold and penetrating, and pitiless. As he began to speak Spindle knew it was Rune.

776

'Tryfan of Duncton has been punished and he is yours to take from here. Tell moles that may ask that he was punished of the Word, which was merciful and did not take his life. He came here to Atone, but he abused our trust. He has been cleansed by punishment.

'As for you, Spindle of Seven Barrows, be grateful that our promise, even though to a flawed mole, is stronger than our judgement, which would have meted you a punishment such as Tryfan had. We have no doubt that you are and remain of the Stone, but that is of no consequence now. Faith in the Stone is all but dead, and a mole like you is unlikely to inspire confidence in its revival.'

There was a brief simper of a smile among the sideem. Spindle found himself unable to speak before this mole's gaze, unable even to think on the words he said. He knew only that Tryfan was hurt and that he desired be taken to him to help him.

'Take him to the surface now,' said Rune indifferently, 'and help me back to Henbane. She will be needing me now, very much, and desiring of my help.'

Spindle had time to see the sideem lead Rune away and to feel an overwhelming loathing which was alien to him. When he had been speaking Rune had commanded the chamber and nomole else in it seemed of significance; but as he went away Spindle saw how thin and frail he was, and that his skin was skeined and wrinkled on his flanks, and his fur thin. There was a sense of meanness about his gait, and indulgence – not of the body but of the spirit.

Spindle turned away in disgust as the sideem mole-handled him up to the surface. There he found himself on the westward flanks of Whern itself, and for a moment his doubts and fears were forgotten as he saw the great heathered rises of the lowering moor caught in late September sun and showing russet and purple. The sun seemed to ride southwards across the moor in waves where gaps in the cumulus cloud let it through, but the wind was cold.

'He's there, mole,' said one of the sideem curtly, pointing to what Spindle had taken to be no more than shadowed roots about a hag of heather nearby, 'and may the Word go with thee. Take him and leave here, leave now and be heard of no more. We shall give you no more than a few days and then if you are seen you shall be killed. Your day and that of the Stone is done, praise be the Word.'

The sideem left and Spindle moved cautiously in the direction they had pointed. Soon he saw that what he had thought was shadow was mole. The grass and heather all about was bloodied, the mole unrecognisable.

'Tryfan?' began Spindle doubtfully, feeling exposed and nervous. 'It's me, it's Spindle.'

Tryfan did not move. Spindle approached nearer, and went round Tryfan's prone body to look at his face and snout. They, too, were unrecognisable, but seemed at first a mass of blood and open wounds. Not 'wounds' but wound, a single dreadful spreading thing that started at what Spindle saw was his mouth and spread across his snout and eyes and ears to all his head. Swollen, bloody, and strangely glistening. Spindle started back in disgust, for the bloody mess they had made of Tryfan was now the feeding ground for midges, thousands of them, which had settled on the congealing blood in grey and bristling rows.

For a few moments he angrily tried to brush these off but the slightest touch or movement brought a frightening gasp and screams of pain from Tryfan who, seeming to think that Spindle was one of the punishing sideem, sought pathetically to shrink away.

If Spindle thought then that he was in a nightmare, it was one that was only just beginning. For even as he stared in horror at what he saw, and began to notice that the wounds extended to Tryfan's flanks and beyond, and then to his two front paws which had been horribly crushed and torn, a black shadow shot over them both, wheeled, hovered, stopped, and cried out its corvid hunger. Feeding raven. Then another. Then a third. They

778

fluttered, half turned in the air, and dropped like plague among the heather and rocks. Then they rose up again and as one, it seemed, attacked.

Spindle turned with talons raised and protected Tryfan from the onslought, the midges feeding on, and only when dusk came did the ravens depart, their great beaks shining with the autumn sun.

That night Spindle found a use at last for the skill in corpse clearing he had learned at Skint's paws in the Slopeside of Buckland.

He half carried, half pulled Tryfan downslope to the bank of a stream where limestone showed, and found sanctuary there under some rocks. He washed the wounds clean with his own spittle and the coolness of the rocks kept the midges at bay.

He was reluctant to leave Tryfan but had to do so to find food, which was difficult there. What little he found he brought back and masticated to a pulp for Tryfan in the hope that he might force some into his mouth.

Tryfan screamed again at this, and Spindle felt as if he was killing him and was in tears, but he persisted and a little of the food was taken. After that there seemed nothing for him to do but keep his friend warm and wait.

Nomole came that night, nor any creature, but in the morning there was the scutter of beaks on the rocks nearby. Ravens again. Then a stoat came whiffling near and Spindle crouched defensively by Tryfan, staring out from the rocks that protected them, watching back and fro and to the sides, in case of attack.

It came soon enough. Stoat claws thrusting under stone, muzzle snarling under rock, the foetid stoat breath making Spindle nauseous. But he struck back as hard and fast as he could and the attack died.

The afternoon came, dusk, then night once more. Nature seemed to sense that one of its own was vulnerable. Many circlings about that place that night: Fox? Stoat? Mole? Spindle never knew.

Dawn. Another day and Spindle knew that Tryfan must

drink to live. The wounds had congealed into one bloody swollen mess. His eyes seemed gone, his snout was crushed and broken.

Most terribly, when Spindle began to move him once more, and lead him down to the stream to drink, poor Tryfan let out an anguished nasal scream of pain and began to shake. Spindle had to force himself to continue, and got Tryfan to the water, and helped his mouth into it, watching carefully that he did not drown. After one final scream as the water went on to his head the protest stopped and Tryfan drank. He did not acknowledge Spindle's presence, and nor could he raise himself from the stream and up its bank, but had to be helped once more.

The stoats came back again; and again. The stench of fox nearby, tail whisking as it watched, Spindle defensive as before. The fox slunk about and then left.

It was four days before Tryfan again took food, and that barely enough to feed a pup. He sucked at the worm Spindle had chewed for him as if his jaw was broken or giving pain. He allowed himself to be helped once more to the water, and then, for the first time, attempted to use his front paws. They collapsed under him and he fell terribly on to his wounded snout.

His eyes were still bloody and swollen, and he showed no signs of hearing or seeing what Spindle did, but once: when Spindle moved away he managed to move a front paw painfully and, with the slightest of squeezes, to indicate that he did not wish him to leave.

Spindle talked to him reassuringly before, once more, he went off to search for food.

On the sixth night Tryfan cried, curious broken sounds of a mole in darkness and despair. Spindle held him and Tryfan fell into painful sleep.

It was several days before the predators lost interest, sensing perhaps that they had lost the opportunity for easy prey because the wounded mole was strengthening.

Tryfan had already recovered his hearing but now, as

the swelling over his face lessened, his eyes became visible. They were cut and bloody, the left far more than the right, yet if he tilted his head leftward he seemed to be able to see a little.

The swelling round his snout subsided and it was easy then to see the talon-thrusts that had so battered it: oval, angry holes in which blood congealed. It was his snout that gave him most pain.

The weather began to worsen noticeably. One day, quite suddenly, hail fell and Tryfan made a pathetic attempt to find shelter from its stinging stones.

The next day was warmer. With help at the beginning, Tryfan made a little progress on his own, climbing down to the water's edge. But the effort was too much for him to crawl back up again to the stance Spindle had taken and for that he needed help.

'We'll have to move soon,' said Spindle. 'This place is worm-poor and the soil not fit for tunnels. We *must* move because there's nothing left for us in the north and we don't want the winter to overtake us.'

Tryfan snouted round towards him and listened, then his head slumped forward on the ground, his broken paws splayed out.

Can't move, he seemed to say.

After that, each day, Spindle urged him to go down to the stream and back again, each day he resisted, but each day he made better progress.

Until at last a day broke when Tryfan went there of his own accord, and was able, with painful slowness, to climb the slope back to Spindle. Later that day the weather cooled once more and the sky turned a miserable slate grey.

Tryfan slept for a time and then awoke, and snouted up towards the sky.

'Grey,' he whispered, 'grey.'

'Can you see?' asked Spindle.

Tryfan nodded and then went still, thinking.

At last he whispered, 'Must go.'

781

It was the first positive thing he had said since Spindle had started tending him.

Tryfan turned to Spindle and did his best to rise up on to his paws. The effort made him tremble and shake and he let out little gasps of pain, yet he kept his stance. Slowly Tryfan pulled himself forward until he climbed out of the stream's cut to where the fell was smooth and grassy above.

For a long time Tryfan lay there totally exposed.

Then he snouted southwards.

'We can go a little southward,' said Spindle, 'but I think it's unwise to try to contact Skint in Grassington. The sideem warned me that if we are seen we will be killed. And in any case we would only bring trouble for our friends. But we can go southward to some anonymous place and overwinter there until you are fully recovered.'

'Sp – ' he began, and Spindle went close to him. 'No, not just southward. Sp – Spindle, take me home. Take me to Duncton Wood.'

Then he turned his hurt snout to Spindle's side as a pup might to its mother and wept.

While Spindle looked about the slopes of Whern despairingly and then turned his face southward, too, a look of determination came over it.

'One step now is one less to make to Duncton Wood. Come then, Tryfan, let us begin.'

Then Tryfan did so, taking first one step, then another, and then a struggling third, as the two moles began the long trek home.

★ ★ ★ ★ ★ ★ ★

The sudden and unexpected disappearance of Boswell and Bailey into the waterfall pool in Providence Fall caused dissension and dismay among the sideem, and brought extreme judgement on three of them.

Those were the guards in the Fall itself who, it was assumed, had somehow let in the weak and diseased alien mole who had led the two moles to their deaths in the torrent because, it was surmised, that was better than

782

allowing them to submit to the Word. The Master himself talked with the culprits, but it was Henbane who sentenced them of the Word, and decided that they should be forced to enter the Clints and let the Word decide whether they die of starvation or find a way out. The Word decided: not one was seen again.

As for Sleekit, she was closely examined by the Master and suffered the agony of Dark Sound. All moles heard her screams. Yet, at the end of it, he pronounced her blameless but listened to the warnings of Weed who cautioned him against letting her roam quite as free as she had before.

'Let her stay with Henbane,' said Weed with the maliciousness of which he was the master. 'What harm can she do there?'

Rune nodded his head and agreed. 'Staying with Henbane' was Weed-words for being made prisoner, for that was what Henbane had become. Weed had succeeded in avoiding any involvement in the actions of those days as if sensing what might happen on Tryfan's arrival would be of more than the passing interest Henbane and the Master themselves attached to it. Now, as news of Boswell's drowning and Tryfan's punishment and rejection from Whern with Spindle became known, Weed heard that the Master was on the way to see Henbane, and nomole knew better than he what that might mean.

Weed knew that it was one thing for Henbane to take young males in the privacy of burrows far from Whern, but it was another to know Tryfan in the very heart of the High Sideem itself. Weed guessed at Rune's jealousy, and that repossession would now be Rune's vile and lustful purpose, and he feared the consequences. The more so because he had heard of Tryfan's vile – but correct – assertion that Rune was Henbane's father.

He knew Henbane's character better than most, and could guess at what the consequences of the Master's desires – or their frustration –might be. Accordingly he ordered that the tunnels be cleared so that but for himself none would know what took place between Henbane and Rune.

Weed was proved right. She rejected Rune's jealous caresses, she insulted him, and so was ordered by him to meditate a while within the confines of her tunnels. Her own sideem were removed and his senior sideem took their place. And it was to mollify her rage that Weed suggested Sleekit should be sent to her, thus keeping in one place two moles who, for the time being, were suspect.

The atmosphere in the High Sideem got steadily worse as Henbane, formerly all-powerful, now found herself confined and powerless. She raged. She wept. She attacked. But all to no avail. Nor would Rune come to her, not even Weed. She had only Sleekit to talk to, only doubtful Sleekit to trust.

But as the days passed into moleweeks and October began and lengthened, a new and unexpected element entered the dark, oppressive atmosphere of her chamber. She herself did not know what it was, but Sleekit guessed and so, too, did Weed, watching as he did from the galleries above, and seeing the shifts in Henbane's moods and her growing tiredness.

Tiredness *and* sickness. The unthinkable had happened. *The WordSpeaker was with pup by a Duncton mole.*

Sleekit knew it because she knew the way of moledom and knew Henbane well. She saw her growing fractiousness, her sickness, her distress. For the same reasons spying Weed knew it too.

But more ominously, Rune knew it without once seeing Henbane, without even talking to Weed about her. He knew it because as Boswell was a mole of light Rune was a mole of darkness who sensed what might be. *That* would be. Yes, it would.

As for Henbane herself, she did not guess it for many moleweeks, for she had known males enough before to think she was not prone to having young. Discomfort sometimes, abortions occasionally, pupping never, ever. She knew only that following the destruction of Tryfan by the old sideem she felt increasingly tired and distressed as the days went by and seemed to lose control of herself in a way she never had before. She felt sick, and she felt strange, and her body did not seem quite hers any more.

Whatever it was it seemed to her that it hung over her and her den like a cloud, and one in which, increasingly, she seemed to see and hear Tryfan make his final cry to her about Rune being her father. That fact – for fact it evidently was – plagued her continuously so much that she attributed her sickness to anger, concern and outrage.

But then, one day, suddenly, turning at her stance her body seemed most strange and clumsy, and in that moment she knew.

She went to the sideem and asked for Weed. He came not.

November started and her swelling showed thick and ugly. She felt impotent with rage at the creatures that were spawned and kicking inside her. She hated them, she hated Rune, she hated everymole.

'Please, tell Weed I need his advice,' she cried out finally, slumping into misery with Sleekit in attendance as a final part of her performance. The sideem had no need to send word to Weed, he heard from his privy place.

The sideem, tired of Henbane's pleadings and rage, advised him to see her and he, flattered that Henbane 'needed his advice', went to a gallery and overlooked her. She looked submissive and tired. He consulted the Master, who granted his permission. There were things Weed might find out, questions of birthing, questions of attitude.

'The pups of course must die,' said Weed. 'It is inconceivable that a Stone follower's seed should sully the heart of Whern.'

'Is it?' said Rune quietly. 'Was not Scirpus himself once of the Stone? Might it not be that among her filthy young will be one who can be trained to succeed as a future Master? Eh, Weed? The ways of the Word are strange, and the Word may have it so.

785

'Go to her since she asks for you. Find out from her or Sleekit when she is due. She will pup at the Rock of the Word as she herself was pupped. But give orders that Tryfan and Spindle are found and killed. That *must* be.'

'I have already seen to it, Master. I have sent grikes out. The miscreants will be found soon enough and Tryfan and Spindle killed immediately so that nomole ever knows. Sleekit must be silenced too, but only on the birth of the young. She will be useful in attendance. As for the pups and the Word's purpose with them, that is the Master's own business. He knows more of such things than Weed.'

So Weed came once more to Henbane's den, entered in, and found her passive and obedient. He smiled and his snout turned with pleasure to know that he had understood her well and never failed the Master in his task.

'When are the pups due?' he asked.

'Soon will the vile things come and I shall see to them. They shall not live,' said Henbane.

Oh yes, she would say that, she might even think it, but mothers are never to be trusted before birth or after it. Before conception they will kill for a mate. After conception they wish to die. After birth they will kill for their young. Then, when the spring comes once more, they will drive out their young and murderously seek a mate once more. Trust not a mole in heat or one in pup.

'That will be wise, WordSpeaker.' Weed smiled, his old smile, and Henbane seemed to soften.

'But you sought advice, WordSpeaker, and I will give it if I can, though on matters such as pups I am hardly well qualified.'

'Not the pups, Weed,' said Henbane in a frail and beaten voice such as would soften the heart of the hardest mole. 'No . . . not pups. . . .'

She looked at the sideem nearby, and then at Sleekit, and took him away from both to the only place they might get some privacy, which was where the wind and water roared their sounds at the great fissure over the gorge at the northern side of her chamber.

786

Her frailty fled, her softness left, her weakness vanished. Henbane was Henbane once again.

'Weed,' she asked coldly, loud enough for Sleekit to hear, and in a tone that made her suddenly watchful and Weed wary, 'all these long years, have you known that Rune was my father?'

Weed's eyes had barely widened in surprise before Henbane was up and massive and powerful and her talons at his neck so hard that he began to choke as she drove him back with one mighty lunge. Straight to the fissure she took him before a single sideem had time to move. Then, as they did so, she pushed him right to the lip of the fissure, where the wind caught his fur viciously, and there she held him out on the edge with her left paw as she readied her right to strike the first sideem that came near.

'Touch me and Weed will die,' she said.

So they hesitated, as others rushed away to summon the Master.

'Did you know?' demanded Henbane, her talons thrusting into Weed and drawing blood as he teetered on the void and the wind grabbed at his paws to unbalance him.

'The Master – ' began Weed, lying.

The sideem, seeming to guess that Henbane had not the answer she sought and that Weed could cause her to hesitate and give them the chance to take her, advanced slowly.

But if that was their hope, Henbane acted with sudden and terrible resolution to frustrate it. She turned her back on the sideem to face Weed, and so huge was her rage and purpose that it seemed the fissure's whole light was blocked out and her chamber thrown into darkness.

In that moment she took Weed powerfully with both taloned paws and cried out at him to say again who her father was, and as her talons entered his snout and face and the floor of the gorge seemed to waver up towards them she whispered, 'He is my father, is he not?'

Then she smiled and said, 'I shall know the truth when you speak it, Weed, so tell it now and you shall be safe.'

At that moment Weed must have known that death faced him at the paws of Henbane if he lied and at the paws of Rune if he told the truth, but since it was only the vicious pain-dealing paws of Henbane that kept him from death at this instant, he told her the truth.

'He is,' he screamed.

But then his scream continued, arcing out over the void below as Henbane, with a cry of rage at final confirmation of what Tryfan had said, hurled him bloodily from her out into the void and his snout turned about him as he fell on to rock and from there his body battered its way down to the the waters of Dowber Gill.

All was still in her chamber as Weed's scream faded into nothing. Then she turned back to a silent circle of senior sideem, and for once their eyes showed emotion: shock, and fear, and, most terrible of all, respect. While Sleekit, forgotten for the moment, simply stared.

Henbane breathed heavily, painfully, her paws to her swollen sides, struggling with herself.

'Leave me, *now*,' she said.

'But we do not wish to,' said a cold voice, and the sideem parted and Rune was there.

He eyed her swollen heaving sides without compassion, and smiled evilly.

'*Leave me!*' cried out Henbane, distressed, and feeling the first waves of birthing coming. 'Leave me!' she screamed.

But Rune did not, but came closer with the sideem watching her every move, and began to tell her of Charlock and her vileness, seeking to provoke Henbane to a further rage. All the time the cold eyes of the sideem looked on.

Sleekit came closer and Henbane instinctively reached out a paw to her as her contractions got stronger.

'Tell them to leave,' she pleaded.

Rune laughed, and the sideem smiled. There was obscene curiosity in some of their sunken ascetic eyes, males peering at exposed females. Males whose dry talons had never known a female's love.

Rune talked on, speaking the filth a corruptor speaks, revelling in the distress he caused.

Then suddenly, and the very air in the chamber seemed to change when this happened, Henbane relaxed and took up once more the control of herself she seemed to have lost for so long. She closed her eyes, breathed deeply, and peace came gently to the chamber and the contractions slowed. She had lost blood but Sleekit attended to it. The sideem were suddenly shamed into restlessness and embarrassment. Rune fell silent.

Henbane breathed on ignoring him, deeper and deeper, and for the first time since Tryfan's departure seemed at peace. By giving up she had gained some subtle initiative in a nameless battle between Rune and herself.

Displeased, Rune left and the sideem backed away. Outside the November wind drove cold at the fissure and the Dowber Gill roared. Whern was settling towards winter. Snow was in the grey sky.

That night, deep in the night, Henbane spoke to Sleekit naturally, as one female to another.

'I felt them move as he crouched staring at me and they were not alien,' she said, and there was a pup's wonder in her voice, and an innocent delight lost sight of long ago. 'I can *feel* them, Sleekit. I do not want them to die.'

'Then we must not let them,' said Sleekit.

'No . . .' said Henbane, 'please not . . . You must help them, despite what I say or do, you must help them. Get them to safety, take them from here. You must do it, Sleekit, please do it *whatever* may happen.'

But what Sleekit could do she did not know: only hope that an opportunity would come which, with the Stone's help, she could take. She only knew that when the pups came she would do her best for them, and if that meant losing her life she would still do what she must. She felt strong and positive where most others might have gone in fear, as if after so many long years of living a lie and doubting that she had any faith, she had found her faith strong and purpose clear. It was for this task alone she felt she had been sent, and this she would try to fulfil.

A few days later Henbane's birthing movements began once more. The watching sideem acted at once.

'Come!' they said. 'Prior orders of the Master.'

Henbane looked in appeal at Sleekit who went up to the sideem and asked them where they wished to take Henbane.

'To serve the Word,' said one.

'To the Rock of the Word itself, that the pups may be judged for their mother's wrongs and blasphemies,' said another.

'Can Sleekit come?' asked Henbane, tired and distressed. Her swelling was larger and the skin tight and lumpy at her sides. She had no energy to resist.

'She's to come, all right!' said the sideem with a hard laugh.

They set off south westwards to the most sacred part of the Whern, to which few ever went, and even Henbane had only rarely been. The caverns and limestone tunnels gave way to ancient molemade ones but the way was steep in places and hard for Henbane. Sometimes she stopped and gasped, but the sideem cruelly pressed her on, and though Sleekit tried to slow the pace there was little she could do.

Henbane knew that it was at the Rock that Rune himself had taken power as Master of the Sideem with the connivance of Charlock, mate of the previous Master. Grikes and guardmoles all believed that their names would be scribed on the Rock of the Word if they acted well and true for the Word, but Henbane knew in her heart it was a place of treachery.

They followed the molemade tunnels until they narrowed back into a limestone tunnel of great height and there all but one sideem left them, he driving them from behind.

So narrow was the tunnel that there was no hope of turning back and attacking him even had they wished it. Indeed, Henbane had the greatest difficulty making passage at all and knew as she went on that if the journey itself had not brought her time nearer, this part of the passage would.

The sideem behind them said, 'Here I stop. Our orders are to kill you if you attempt to return this way without the permission of the Master himself. May the Word be praised and your actions be true. Now go!'

There seemed nothing for it but to proceed, and soon the tunnel widened on either side and got higher as well. Then round a corner and they were in the chamber of the Rock. Enormous and strange, with sloping rock down to a pool that stretched blackly out before them to where, on its far side, rose sheer the Rock of the Word. A cliff most severe, absolutely vertical, black in effect yet shimmering darkly.

The source of its light was the pool itself. High above in the chamber's roof a single opening let in a shaft of light that came down upon the pool which seemed to move and shimmer into its turning depth, cold grey, black, dark blue, and yellow. The Rock rose beyond it, seeming dark at first but then, as a mole's eyes got used to it, more grey-black and shadowed as the water reflected slow-moving light across the Rock's great face.

There was a continuous sound in the great chamber, as when thunder rolls across some distant horizon and gives the air the sense of an imminent charge of sound that will be loud and fearsome when it comes. Strange roarings, though whether of water or wind was hard to say.

Rune was there, staring, quite alone. He crouched on a platform of rock which formed the floor of a cave that receded deeply and from which flowed a stream, the source of water for the pool. At the platform's edge, just behind Rune, the water tumbled down into the pool which spread out to his right.

'Your time has come to deliver the pups,' he said, beckoning Henbane.

'They shall not be thine!' said Henbane, panting and gasping with the pain of contractions.

'They are the Word's,' said Rune.

'Mine,' said Henbane.

'Well, whatever . . . Come, my dear, you will be more comfortable here.'

There was something alluring about the way he spoke, and the platform of rock seemed a better place to pup than the bare stark shore of the pool.

Henbane dragged herself up and settled down. Sleekit looked about, searching for a way to escape.

The receding cave, down which the stream came, was more than uninviting, it was menacing. Never had Sleekit seen rock which exuded water as that place did. Above their heads a hundred thousand thin stalactites pointed down, their colours strange, and at the tip of each hung a drip of water.

Drips which fell now here, now there, now behind, plop! plip! plup! Where they fell, and had fallen through the long centuries, they formed rounded depositions, green-brown, brown-yellow, yellow-black. All ominous and strange, many bigger by far than mole, and intimidating. Of these there were many, and because they were wet and shining, and the stream flowed among them, they seemed almost alive, almost to move.

Their effect was made more sinister by the fact that they seemed almost mole-like in their shape, and for paws had rounded melted forms of rock, as if the sun had shone down and bloated dead moles up and then melted their forms and disfigured them, to turn them into huge parodies of what moles might have been.

'Welcome to the chamber of Rock of the Word,' said Rune. 'Here shall your young be born.'

His sharp voice echoed unpleasantly about them and finally lost itself somewhere in the heights of the Rock itself.

'You seem afraid, Henbane. And you, Sleekit. What do you fear. . .?' The words slipped and crept between them. Henbane sighed in obvious discomfort.

'You I fear,' she said.

'The Word I fear,' whispered Sleekit, trembling. It was not true any more but she felt she should say it, and as she did she felt Rune's dark eyes bore into her. She was trying to think and calculate because she knew Henbane's birthing was beginning and she must do her best to save the young. She looked desperately up the stream chamber to see if there was a way out there, but saw only murkiness in which other distorted forms lived their eternal lives beneath the dripping water.

'The pups need not die,' purred Rune, as if knowing both their thoughts. 'No, no I have ordained they should not. Trained they shall be, yes ..ll of them, trained and then . . .' He smiled.

'Then?' asked Henbane.

'Let me point out to you something which few moles ever see.' He waved his left paw at the stream chamber, and at the formations they had already felt menaced by.

'Here is Whern's true history,' he said.

At first neither of them had any idea of what he meant at all, and Henbane was now gasping regularly with the pain of pupping as Rune, seemingly oblivious, talked about what appeared to be trivialities. Even so she must have begun to have a suspicion of what he was leading to. The curiously shaped deposits which were all rounded and spreading seemed to menace them.

Henbane's unborn pups turned and struggled inside her as she stared and began to understand, while Sleekit sensed that the secret they were being told was so dark and unshared that she would not be allowed to leave the chamber alive. Those waiting sideem would kill her, though no doubt Rune would tell her she could return to her duties in safety. No doubt.

They stared at the curious shining forms with mounting suspicion of what they were as Rune whispered, 'Come, see them. They are the Masters of the Sideem. Here they went into their final meditation. Here the water enshrines them forever in its encrustations.'

As his words flowed out, the unreality of what they saw

came real. The shapes were the shapes of moles because they *were* moles, dead moles, encrusted moles, enshrined in living rock where they had died, or gone into some final black meditation. This was the death cell of the Masters, and this was where Rune wished Henbane's pups to be born.

As Henbane screamed, though whether in horror or pain, or both, it was hard to say, Rune waved a mean talon at the eerie shapes.

'They are all there, including even Scirpus himself. See!'

Even as Henbane's first pup began to show, and she gasped and strained, she found herself staring as Sleekit did at a huge deformation bigger than the rest because older, voluptuous in its shape, a huge high elongated form of rounded rock, glistening with water flow. At its base were projections of huge paws of rock, whose ends slunk thinly over the chamber's floor like cruel bleak talons that have grown after death, and seek to stab at the living from the place where death resides.

Many of the other forms were nearly as large, yet some nearby were smaller and a very few barely bigger than mole, but all glistened with that seeping water, lifeless yet having life, caught in an eternal crouch, snouts leaking solidly over the chamber floor. Sleekit stared at them in mounting horror, and at the veil of moisture and veined-purple colour of them, and then at the living pup that sucked in and out and in and out once more, as Henbane, screaming, pushed out her first.

It lay, the deformations all about obscene bloated copies of its tiny so far breathless shape, womb muck draped over it, still, crouched, lifeless yet. Rune stared at it, motionless, and Sleekit was quite still, instinctively leaving well alone.

Then Henbane pushed again, her body shaking and then rising obscenely open as the second showed, was sucked back in, and then pushed out again and more, and more, and then was there, across the other. Blind floppy things, and then, like light in a forbidden place, a sudden breath, a hacking mew and life came to the first and echoed Henbane's tired screaming voice as a single tear might signify a whole life's grief. Then life struggled into the second and survived.

While dripping from the stalactites above, on and on and ever more, drips fell on to those moles immured in stone which loomed about them, immobile yet in their ghastly way, growing.

'The Word has spoken to me, Henbane, and made me understand your blasphemous plight,' cried out Rune, his eyes wild before her pupping. 'You bear the pups of a Duncton mole, and one who has been close to the Stone and loved by Boswell. Boswell is dead, as dead as he will ever be, and Tryfan was close to him and known throughout moledom by those few remaining followers of the Stone.

'Yet I have fretted over the long power of the Stone and wondered what the Word might say for its final demise. Say *and* do. Weed advised the killing of your pups, but the Word said otherwise and made you the agent of *his* death. Wise Word. In that at least you redeemed yourself.

'Your young – ' At that moment Henbane sighed and then screamed and struggled to pup one more.

'Yes, release the pain, scream out their birth, for these young will be trained by the sideem and one of them will emerge as Master when I have gone. The Word has spoken that this will be so. Scream out, Henbane, let your screams be rejoicing, for all of moledom will know that we have taken the pups even of Tryfan himself and made them of the Word. So strong the great Word, so weak the craven Stone!'

Sleekit looked about the great chamber in desperation as Henbane entered the final stages of her pupping and the third began to show. Sunlight shone down into that dark place, the waters swirled and moved. Sleekit watched as the pup came, a darker thing than the first two, and small. But a pup for all that, and living, and Henbane's own.

As Henbane stopped screaming and pushing and brought her head round to look at what she had made, Rune backed away. So Sleekit alone, of any living mole, saw something no other mole could have guessed could be, which was joy in Henbane's eyes and wonder as she licked and nuzzled at the pups she bore.

They mewed and bleated and Henbane stared at them, nuzzling them, whispering at them and then looking round to Sleekit, her only support, and saying, not in her normal powerful voice but tenderly and with the wonder of a youngster who ventures out into a tunnel alone for the first time and then returns to tell the tale: 'I made them Sleekit, I made them!'

Behind them, Rune, unnoticed for the moment, moved slowly into the shadows, down from the floor of the stream chamber and over towards the entrance beyond which the sideem lay in wait.

Then Henbane, with courage delved from the very depth of her distorted and warped heart, yet none the less for that, and deserving of moledom's respect, whispered urgently and pathetically – for what hope of help was there there in that place then? – 'Take them as I commanded you, take them, Sleekit, help them. . . .'

Then as Sleekit looked this way and that in growing fear and desperation, Henbane turned to where Rune should have been, saw that he had slid away to fetch the sideem to take her pups, and heavily followed him, blood and afterbirth in a trail behind her and leaving her pups bereft, like sacrifices before the Rock of the Word.

Yet not quite so. For that sunlight that shafted down came strong and as some shimmered on the Rock, some too dappled softly on the mewling pups.

As Rune called out and sideem came, Henbane took a frightening, bloodied stance to defend her own against the vileness that gave her her own life.

'Help them!' she cried out once more to Sleekit, her voice echoed darkly by the Rock. 'Help them!'

Words that echoed among the long encrusted forms,

words that mixed now with the running drum of sideem paws, as that cry 'Help them helpthem helpth . . .' declined into nearly nothing where Sleekit, and the pups, and the Masters of the past waited in their different ways – for what none knew. Yet it was there.

It moved. It turned. Its glistening back, its encrusted snout, its elongated talons, its dead-living snout *moved*.

Sleekit stared, eyes wide. Pups mewed. Sideem, across the chamber, cried out.

Then Sleekit gasped, as near to death from fear as ever mole can be. Utterly frozen as she saw that what seemed immobile before, moved, and turned and opened its mouth.

Mayweed. Masquerading Mayweed. Many-sided Mayweed. Now medieval Mayweed come to life.

'Quite overwhelmed Madam, hello. Humble me emerges from the wet he's hidden in too long, and will be brief and to the point. Desperate us can take only two pups, so decide.'

'I don't know, I can't . . .' said Sleekit, overwhelmed indeed.

As she spoke the pups wound themselves around each other, climbing on one another, their tiny snouts vainly searching for their mother's teats, their eyes bulging blue beneath the unopened lids, their paws pink, their talons soft.

Then Sleekit hesitated no more.

'This one and this one,' she said taking one by the neck and indicating the other nearest one.

'Madam, go that way!' he urged, pointing a talon at the shadows beneath the paws of the great form that had once been Scirpus.

As she turned to flee, a pup dangling helplessly from her mouth, Mayweed stared at the other she had pointed to. It was the small one, smaller and darker than the other and he liked it not. It felt to him like a tunnel with no end, no good promise, and his instincts, subtler than any mole in moledom for routes – and was not this moment a route of

797

routes in moledom's history? – made him turn to the other.

'May humble me be forgiven if he what he does now is wrong!' said Mayweed, ignoring the pup Sleekit indicated and taking up the fairer of the two and turning to follow fast after Sleekit, and overtake her at the far shadow's edge, to lead her down tunnels at the end of which, if the Stone would grant it, there might be light at last.

Henbane saw what had happened, or if she did not see she sensed, for she let out a terrible scream of loss and found the strength to kill with one blow the first sideem that dared come and then strike down the next.

Then, as the other sideem ranked and got ready to charge Henbane took, at last, her vengeance and her birthright. She lunged massively at Rune. Nomole could have stopped her then, none would have dared, and as if by arcane instinct the sideem did not try.

They watched coldly as Henbane used her final resource of strength and purpose to drag Rune back to the platform where her last remaining pup lay. He did not even struggle as she threw him up and followed him, and as the tiny black shining pup quested its mean snout blindly up she taloned its grandfather against first one formation and then the next, on and on into that hateful place until with one final thrust she stabbed Rune to death against the greatest deformation of them all, Scirpus himself.

She stared down at his body and watched as, from above, the first drip of a million million drips dropped down, spattered into his bloodied fur and there, as it slid into nothingness, it left a tiny shining crystalline encrustation, the first beginning of the end of Rune under that immortal subterranean rain.

Henbane, knowing what she did, turned her back on him, went slowly back to her pup, stared briefly at it, and then unhurriedly, and utterly ignoring the awed sideem, stared up at the Rock of the Word. Then to it she made obeisance, and silently and proudly entered the sacred pool, darkness into dark, and there she cleansed herself in water coldly lit.

That done she emerged once more, shook herself, and went straight to her mewing pup, encircled it, and guided its mouth gently to a teat and started to suckle it.

Then, slowly, and at peace with herself, she plumped herself about it, and looked up as the sideem advanced upon her, their claws sharp, their eyes cold, their teeth white.

'What are thy orders, Mistress of the Word?' the oldest said.

She smiled and her body tightened about her solitary pup whose suckling was eager. She looked over her shoulder for a moment at the Rock, and then smiled again. Powerful was Henbane, in control once more. Utterly, at last.

'Find them, kill them.'

'And the pups?' they said.

'Oh yes,' she whispered, nuzzling her one. 'Especially the pups. Only one is needed, and this is he. One only need I train. So find the others and kill them.'

Then as some sideem chased down the way Mayweed and Sleekit had fled, and others went back out of the entrance, Henbane commanded those who waited on her, 'Bring me food. I shall stay here for some days and then go back to where I am most comfortable. Let all Whern know that the Master is dead and the Mistress is come.'

'We shall,' they intoned. 'Long live the Mistress!' they cried out.

'She shall,' whispered Henbane, smiling, and triumphant. Then silence fell, but for the drip-drip-dripping of preserving time in the chamber where the old Master lay dead, and the sounds of suckling.

'Long live the Mistress!' they shouted.

'Oh yes, she shall!' smiled Henbane.

'Long live the Mistress and her pup!' they exalted, as over them all the Rock of the Word shimmered with the light of the darkest pool in moledom, and whispered dark comfort to its newest son.

Part V

The Coming of the
Stone Mole

Chapter Forty-Two

December had come, and with it the first drifts of snow swept across the western face of Whern, whitening the lower parts to make the steep rock faces higher up seem as black as night.

Far below, south of the High Sideem, unconcerned by distant sights of darkness, or premonitions of a bleak winter finally setting in, two pups, youngsters nearly, played with the snow and delighted in its crisp whiteness.

They touched it in wonder, and they giggled and laughed, and then stared in delight at the way the snow, drifting out of a leaden sky, struck the solitary wind-bent birch that spread its leafless branches to one side of them. Soundlessly the snow buffeted and bumped its way down the trunk and through the branches of the tree to where they waited with outstretched paws within the limestone clefts from which the tree rose up.

'Energetic younglings, obey Sleekit, come and eat!' said a familiar voice, and they turned and play-tumbled over to him, and touched him and took the food their guardians had found.

None could see those moles, none guessed they were there hidden in the very midst of Whern. None.

So now resourceful Mayweed stared at them, and then at Sleekit, whose eyes met his with warmth and trust – and concern as well. Their glance was that of two moles who have come by circumstance and character to trust each other truly, and can guess by such a glance what the other thinks: time now to move, time to risk setting forth, time to flee the coming blizzards and find a better sanctuary than that they had. . . .

Courage, luck and faith had gone with Mayweed and

Sleekit that day when they snatched up two of Henbane's pups and fled the chamber where the Masters crouched in stone. Fast had they run, Mayweed never looking back but trusting that Sleekit could follow him through the tortuous labyrinthine ways of the High Sideem, and then out on to the fell beneath great Whern's last rise.

There they turned and took routes Mayweed knew among the peat hags and on downhill towards that spreading surface of cleft limestone, the dangerous Clints.

Down they ran, chased by pursuers behind, watched by sideem below who, not yet alerted to these miscreants were not as ready for them as they might have been. The two bobbed in and out of moles' view over that heathered waste until their breath came in gasps and their paws stumbled in the terrible ground.

'Madam,' said Mayweed, pausing and laying his pink-grey and bleating burden down for a moment, 'this mole me has been chased before and will be again. It is a habit in Whern. Humbleness pauses only to say this: trust him and we shall be safe. Our sanctuary will be the confusing Clints, of which Mayweed here has made a tour and decided they will have to do. He doubts that the sideem will follow us in, but if they do they will get lost since he intends to enter by an irregular route. So trust him , follow him close, and all will be well.' Mayweed gave one of his more ghastly smiles and added softly, 'He hopes.'

With this speech, which Mayweed intended to be encouraging and to save argument later when argument might not be possible, he picked up his pup once more and ran on, and headed straight for the knot of curious sideem that waited beneath the small cliff which marked the start of the Clints.

Behind moles cried out warningly, ahead the sideem stiffened in readiness to bar the way of the approaching moles who carried in their mouths – what? Things Whern very rarely saw: Pups.

Then Mayweed seemed to hesitate and waver and Sleekit caught him up and stopped. Fooled, the sideem relaxed. With a quick nod to her Mayweed charged straight at an entrance to the Clints and through the outstretched talons of the disbelieving sideem. Left he went, then right, then left and left, then right once more, on and on, as their shouts died down behind to cries of doom that said, 'They are lost! They will die! Watch the entrances lest they find a way out by the Word's grace! Or else they are dead!'

The Clints closed in upon them and carried further in by Mayweed's purpose and volition they went on, turning this way and that, coming into cul-de-sacs, whirling about, high walls rising around them and the ferns and moist plants getting in their way.

Sleekit followed him faithfully, never letting him get too far ahead, until he slowed, peered about, and finally set his burden down. Sleekit did the same.

'But nomole can know this place!' she gasped, her eyes wide with alarm as she looked up at the inaccessible sky.

'That's what Mayweed heard, Madam Miss, but Mayweed entered in and came out again! He did. The whole humble lot of him did, leaving not a limb, not a snout, nothing behind.'

'But how?' asked Sleekit.

'With, Madam, very enormous difficulty. Mayweed is not easily daunted but daunted he was, and daunted he is now.'

'Don't you know where you are?' she whispered in alarm.

'Mayweed regrets to say he has no idea. However all is not lost. There is method to his madness. For the moment we are safe. The sideem will hang about and take our non-appearance as evidence of our death. Which Mayweed takes as evidence of their inflexibility of thinking. Never assume a mole is dead until he rots before your eyes.' He came closer to her.

'Companion in mercy, let me speak to you of food in the Clints. Worms? A few. Snails? Enough. Spiders? Many. Other slithey edibles: a cornucopia. We shall not starve,

Madam, though we may wish to be sick. So here we shall stay; you shall take charge of the pups, and humbleness will begin his search for the Southern Passage of the Clints, and so be ready for the day when, these pups more grown so they can hold their own and we, given up for dead, sneak out unseen and make our way to Grassington, old friends, and new tunnels.'

'But I am pupless. I have never mothered young.'

'Ah! Yes,' muttered Mayweed, peering reluctantly at the gasping pups before looking in as winning a way at her as his balded face and ravaged body allowed.

'The good news is that pupless you are no more. The bad news, Madam, is that there are two of them. Mayweed timidly suggests you chew worms fine and spit it down their mouths, a process which he would prefer not to watch. However, if he must he will, or at least demonstrate.'

It is a testimony to those two pups' durability that they survived at the paws of two moles as inexperienced in such things as Sleekit and Mayweed were. Rarely can two parents have been as clumsy, impatient, bad-tempered, inflexible, angry, and at times indifferent as they.

Yet one quality more they had, and it made up for all the rest: loving determination. Each in their way had made a vow to help the parents of these pups: Mayweed to Tryfan, Sleekit to Henbane. So they did, hard though rearing young that were not their own proved to be. Tired, irritable, fed up they both became, but the crucial first weeks were weathered, the pups survived, and the Stone gave them all its protection.

Until at last the pups could crawl, and then carry themselves properly on their paws, and see, and laugh, and even try to speak . . . And Sleekit and Mayweed began, for the first time, to relax and know that they had learnt more of each other in that strange parenting than many ever learn.

'Madam,' Mayweed had said one day then, 'one is a he and the other a she and neither has a name.'

'Harebell and Wharfe,' said Sleekit promptly.

'Madam! So fast?' exclaimed Mayweed, amazed and delighted at the same time. Sleekit had a speed of mind, and a certainty about some things that he was beginning to appreciate now that December had come and the pups were growing up into youngsters.

'I have been thinking of those names for a long time,' said Sleekit.

'Mayweed thinks that perhaps sly Sleekit is mindful of the fact that their parents are respectively named after a flower and a place, though both somewhat redolent of darkness. Your choice is kind, clever and wise.'

'Harebell I first saw blowing in the wind high on Uffington Hill, and the flower suggested that perhaps there was another way than the Word. This young pup has something of its lightness and delight in her eyes. As for Wharfe, it is a river that flows clear and strong and does not stop, and this male of Henbane's seems like that. So have their names come to me.'

'Mayweed thinks that Madam is a poet, Mayweed is impressed.'

Sleekit sighed and said quietly, 'I have done much in my life in the name of the Word of which I am ashamed. Now I have a chance at last to go where the Stone directs. I do not know whether moles of the Stone could ever accept one such as me, trained as I have been in Whern itself, unused as I am to the ways of the Stone. But you seem to accept me. . . .'

'I, Madam? I accept you? Humbleness was thinking even as you spoke that you accept him! He only hopes that as time goes by Sleekit will see that this scalpskinned body of his hides a heart that is as good as any other mole's who trusts the Stone and does his best.'

Each stared at the other, much moved, and might perhaps have said more, and come closer, and touched each other as they then began to desire to, but the pups ran up, their eyes wide, their natures eager.

'Play?' said Harebell.

'Me?' said Wharfe.

Snow drifted down, the air felt good, but the sky above surged with cold.

'Happy Harebell and bold Wharfe, listen to Mayweed. Yes! Crouch close to Sleekit.'

The pups did so.

'Are you brave? You are! Are you bold? You are! Have I told you of the Stone? I have not. Well, I'm not much of one to talk of that, and Sleekit here isn't either, yet. But there's a Stone and it will keep you safe, for mole talons, however strong, are not strong enough for that. We two are going to take you there. The snow means winter, and winter in not the time to be in the Clints. So we are going on an adventure!'

Harebell and Wharfe looked at each other, understanding his concern better than his words. They were going to leave these high walls at last and see the places beyond. They snuggled closer still.

'Younglings both,' continued Mayweed, 'look about this place one last time and remember it. It was your first home but now we must leave. So follow me and know that Sleekit is close behind. Do as we say, trust us, and remember!'

The youngsters, whose speech had barely begun, nodded dumbly. Harebell cried, which started Wharfe. Both were comforted. Both gulped and took a touching stance that said, 'We'll try to do our very best, we will!'

Then they followed Mayweed, Sleekit reassuringly just behind, pausing only for a moment during which Wharfe stared back at the tree at whose roots and under whose bent branches they had played; stared and remembered it. Then, as he had seen Mayweed do, he eyed each turn they took carefully, and sought to remember it as a route-finder must.

While Harebell sighed hugely and followed on, with Sleekit smiling to see it. Her sigh had the touch of Henbane her mother about it, but not that dread Henbane, scourge of moledom. No, it was the female who once spoke in wonder in her den to Sleekit, of the joy of feeling her pups move inside her. Now two of those pups were here, and safe, and Sleekit, trained as a sideem, found herself a mother. But she would not forget that part of these pups' heritage, and one day would tell it to them honestly. For if a mole is to be himself and tread truly towards his future, he had best tread truly out of his past.

So Mayweed led them out of the Clints by a southward route, leaving the dark rising of Whern behind them as they dropped down the succession of limestone scars that mark Whern's western side, and sought to make passage to Grassington.

And not a moment too soon. Behind them over Whern dark blizzards gathered, the northern wind grew strong, and winter began to cast down its bleak pall.

* * * * * * *

By the time those same winds had caught up with Tryfan and Spindle, they had already crossed the Dark Peak and were travelling south over lower ground.

At first Tryfan's passage had been painful and slow, for his sight was impaired and his paws wounded and weak. But, gradually, he had regained his health and strength, and though his face was heavily scarred now and his sight still limited, his paws were better and he could move quite fast.

Spindle had decided to ease his passage by choosing routes along roaring owl ways which, though exposed and full of danger, yet provided a smoother path. The dangers were reduced because they used them at night when the gazes warned them in good time of what was coming and they could scurry to the undergrowth that lined the route.

Such ways had the advantage, too, of anonymity, for nomole travelled them but they themselves, and their only company was rook and kestrel to whom moles were unappealing prey. Especially moles prepared to use their talons. Owl were the greater danger, and the moles kept close for safety, and were always alert.

As for roaring owls, they learnt much of them. Their

time in the Wen had made them used to the noise and fumes, and they knew to avoid their gaze. They went too fast to be troubled by moles, and seemed to notice them not.

So by mid-December, when winter set in from the north and the first snows came, Spindle was able to say with confidence, 'We're more than halfway Tryfan, and you're getting stronger. That's the power of prayer for you! There's hope we'll get you home!'

Tryfan half grinned, rueful and serious, and said nothing but Spindle was used enough to that. This journey back was very different from the journey out. Then they had met many moles, then Tryfan had spoken of the Stone and moles had flocked to hear him. Now he desired that none knew of their passage, and made Spindle understand that it was a time of thinking and retreat from mole.

Yet, sometimes when they went off the ways moles did find them, sheltering in some nook of somemole's tunnels, hiding, and shivering as winter took grip.

'You look all in, you two do. Vagrants eh? You should burrow down in this weather, friend.' And then, in a lower voice, such moles usually said to Spindle, 'Your mate's a goner by the look of him. Got savaged by fox did he? He'll not last long . . . So , whither are you bound?'

'To find a healer,' Spindle would say, 'who is named the Stone Mole.'

'That's a joke and a half, mate, but I wouldn't talk like that if I were you. This system's of the Word now, moles don't talk of the Stone. . . .'

'The Stone Mole's coming,' Spindle would reply.

'Maybe, and you're off to find him are you? Well, he's the only one who'll help *that* mole. As for healers, none of them left these days! The eldrenes tend to a mole's needs and if illness comes, well, that's the judgement of the Word!'

Strangely, such moles never said a thing about their passage through, perhaps because to help a vagrant of the

Stone was, in some way, to serve a need in themselves they had half forgotten. Often such moles brought them food, and let them rest without further disturbance. And more than one, and sometimes more than that together, came to wish the two moles well, and that they might return home safeguarded.

While a very few clutched Spindle's paw, as if in him they saw a faith they could not themselves publicly profess, and whispered, 'If you find the Stone Mole tell him our name. We helped you for him, aye, that's what we did! And may your friend find peace!'

So when they were alone, Spindle could say with confidence, 'The Stone is helping us, Tryfan, it sends moles to guide us on. We'll get home, we will! It will be Longest Night again soon, and maybe we can find a Stone to pray at which you can touch, maybe it will help you then.'

But Tryfan's retreat continued as he delved into his own doubts and faith, so deeply indeed that sometimes Spindle caught him stumbling, though whether from his impaired sight, or a more profound darkness was hard to say.

Longest Night *was* near, and it seemed almost as if the driving weather wished to kill them before it came and Spindle could say the ritual prayers on Tryfan's behalf. No mole in living memory had ever seen the weather that came then. North, north the wind, so cold that some days it turned breath to ice on a mole's mouth, and froze up streams, and began to kill the worms, creeping its freezing talons down through the soil, making even deep tunnels chill.

Sometimes the branches of trees fell crackling down, sometimes the wind stopped and the landscape was frozen still, and birds that sought to roost died where they were, their bodies torn by fox and rook. Dangerous times, yet still Spindle trusted in the Stone and led them on.

They travelled on even when the wind renewed, a wild, maddened wind, from which all creatures sought protection except the few, the very few like them driven forward by some impulse that the vagrant has to wander on.

Those few days before Longest Night Spindle led them on into worsening weather until they could journey no more and had to shelter or die. Food they found in frozen carrion which Spindle dragged into the den they made. There they hid as the freezing blizzards roared, and the surface turned to wind-eroded ice and in the woods to drifted snow. Strange the surface then, because in places the wind had exposed the humus underneath, which was white with frost and made ways for mole between the icy drifts.

Longest Night came, its daytime grey and bitter cold, a day that spread its doom across all moledom, a day when winds died and a pall fell everywhere. Stone on Stone was deserted across the land, nomole mad enough to venture forth; not in Avebury, or Rollright, or Caer Caradoc; not in Uffington or Duncton; not in Fyfield or Siabod. Quite deserted. The great Stones were abandoned for the first time in the long centuries since great Ballagan's coming. Truly, the grike held sway.

Yet here and there, why *everywhere*, there were still the few who at least *thought* of the Stone that day, and a few who had dared to travel for that special night but were driven down below by the cold now, daring not to go up to the surface and tread the final way to the Stones they had so nearly reached. So the grikes held sway across the land, but not in all moles' hearts.

Perhaps a few even poked their snouts out and looked about as dusk and the time for celebration came. Spindle did. But the air was strangely heavy and cold in the copse where they had stopped, the surface cracked with frost, the sky seemed grey with death, the trees and grass and rocks and frozen waters of the earth so still and nothing moving anywhere.

Yes, Spindle was one of the few who peered out and who, like the others, came back down again.

'It'll be dangerous out there tonight, Tryfan,' he

812

whispered, his voice in awe. 'It's as if the whole of moledom is waiting and dare not move. 'Tis cold, so cold, and perhaps we should just say a few words here. Yes, that would be best. Soon we'll say something, when the night's started.'

But Spindle said no more as if even his speech was squashed from him by the cold, oppressive sky, whose death-grey changed to deep murk black with not a star in sight.

Yet Tryfan moved, snouting up towards the entrance Spindle had been to and himself peering out. He seemed disturbed and restless, and came down and went back up several times, and each time the night growing darker and more heavy. The wind had died to nothing. The cold was great.

'Better not go outside again, Tryfan. Best to stay inside. There's no Stone hereabouts so far as I can tell. . . .'

'Always the Stone,' said Tryfan ambiguously.

'What's troubling you? Is it because it's Longest Night and you want to be celebrating?'

'Moledom's waiting, Longest Night has come. There is not a follower in the land who does not seek a sign tonight. Few may be our number now, scattered and lost, yet as we wait here, many others wait as well. He is coming, Spindle, and I believe the Stone will grant us hope tonight. Now, come with me to the surface and be my eyes, for mine are not much good. See if there is a Stone here, or somemole, or any sign that will give us hope. Come now Spindle. . . .'

His voice was quiet and calm, but suddenly he reared and, seeming not to see or hear Spindle's warnings or willingness to come, he crashed up out of the burrow into the frozen night. Then when Spindle tried to slow him Tryfan summoned a maddened strength to fight him back which made his friend retreat, not from being forced to but rather because he could see resistance caused Tryfan even more distress. So Spindle let him go, out among the frozen drifts of snow in search of a Stone it seemed. And

Spindle followed lest he got lost or harm came to him, and he saw something Tryfan could not. The air was still as death where they went, and yet, unseen by them, most strange, high above them the stolid ghostly clouds began to move.

* * * * * * *

Tryfan had been right in what he said: followers across moledom waited for a sign that night, and later many would tell the stories of their waiting, and of how that sign first came to them. Many . . .

Deep in the Wen where Dunbar's moles clung on to life beset by age – many more had already been taken by that chill winter – Feverfew stirred at the surface entrance of a tunnel on the eastside of the hill. The tunnel was not her own.

Spread before her to the south the Wen was as still as ever it had been, its lights befogged and strange, its distances obscured, such sounds as twofoots made muffled and roaring owls scarce in the night, their gazes dim and slow.

Nearby, unseen by Feverfew, a mole watched over her. That mole was Heath, deputed to the task by Starling, though he might have done it anyway for Feverfew was a mole he liked and who, over the moleyears since Tryfan and the others had left, had shown their young, both litters, much kindness and taught them of the Stone, great teachings from a tradition almost dead.

For molemonths now Feverfew had been in distress, her scalpskin worsening from October on and making her restless and in pain. Across her face it had spread, blighting her senses, marring her sight, causing her paws discomfort.

'Watch over her, Heath, for I will not leave our youngsters on Longest Night,' Starling had told him. 'See where she goes, be with her and say the rituals she has taught us, be with her.'

Those two had nuzzled then and Heath had followed after Feverfew watching over her as, unknown to him, at

814

that same moment to the north Spindle did the same for Tryfan.

That night then, two searchers and two watchers were out on the surface in the bitterest cold, when the sky seemed to sink down its weight upon the earth and crush all life or hope from it. Two moles searching.

Then softly, almost magically, a wind from the east began to break the oppressive stillness, weak at first and then stronger; a good and welcome wind. Where Feverfew crouched, the rough grass near Dunbar's tunnels stirred; where Tryfan wandered, it was the trees' slenderest branches that first moved. Above them both, in their separate places, the moving clouds began to clear and as they did so they began to fill with light from behind. Over Wen the effect was striking indeed, for the fog that had settled on its lower parts had so obscured its eternal lurid light that for once the clouds and sky above was as others in moledom saw it.

Now light began to break through as the cloud cleared more and the good wind came. First one then two, then suddenly ten thousand stars, bringing brightness and glory to the Longest Night sky.

Then something more, and that which all moles remembered who saw the sky that night. It was a star, seeming solitary, big and bright and *there*. There before them in the east from where that warming wind came. A star which, however hard a mole might try not to stare at it, drew a mole's eyes back again, and again, and held him in awe.

Nomole told others what to say, no words were prescribed for that Longest Night, but all stared in wonder and whispered the same: 'It is a sign, the Stone Mole is coming.'

Heath, too, stared up in awe, and knew the same, and even whispered it in wonder, and so did not see Feverfew turn from that light and go down into the frozen tunnels and run as if she knew the route Mayweed had struggled so hard to find. Running through those dark tunnels where, as she went, the light of that brightening star shone down at entrance after entrance, casting its clear light across the scribings Dunbar had made.

Running she was, faster and faster, touching the walls sometimes as she went, sounding out the sound of age to youth, the long journey of an ancient mole back to where he first began. Feverfew running down that journey through a great age of time as, unknown to her, distantly, where she could not be, Spindle reached out to touch Tryfan, and guide his gaze skyward, and move out of the the shelter of the trees that he too might glimpse what so many others saw: a star that was a sign.

'The Stone Mole is coming !' cried Tryfan, 'see? He sends us a sign at last! The Stone Mole comes!'

His voice was joyful, as once it had often been, and his scarred face turned skyward to the east, and where tears ran from his hurt eyes the light of that star glistened and shone and Spindle knew Tryfan's retreat was nearly done, his hope to be restored, his faith renewed in the prayers and invocation they cried out in celebration of the light that came from a star of hope that Longest Night.

Then across moledom's sky all the stars shone brighter yet and moles looked up with wonder in their eyes and whispered, 'This night is the Longest, this is the turning, now does light begin, again, soon, soon, the Stone Mole comes!'

While alone and unknown, Feverfew ran on through tunnels lit bright by stars, past scribings made by a holy mole who scribed that one day the Stone Mole would come. Now she ran to the last chamber he had made, blocked by a stone no mortal mole's talons could break. And there, where Tryfan had once been, she crouched as those scribings she had sounded echoed, with the wisdom of age running back to youth, and they died to a whisper that echoed again one word, one final word: Listen!

Then in the silence Feverfew knew she heard the call of a coming mole, distant seeming but only lost in that chamber nomole could enter, sounding there where

Dunbar made his final scribing. And she knew in her agony of body and of lost spirit that it called to her.

Like many others that night, Feverfew whispered out his name, 'Stone Mole, Stone Mole, Stone Mole,' and felt a joy that made her sigh and laugh. For it was to her he called. Last of the young females of the Wen, last of her kind, and he called to her to help him, for he wished to come now and would need her soon.

Then Feverfew turned through tunnels brighter yet, and passed the sounds of moles so old, so young, male and female, calling out from the love that must precede the Silence, and felt the Stone was with her, shining its light to guide her, for she had listened and she had heard, and she was ready now to follow it.

To the surface she went as that light in the night sky was bright, eastward for all of moledom but those in the Wen: westward for them. A star, brighter than the rest, high and big, casting awe across moledom, its light making Feverfew's scalpskinned face seem white, and her fur seem good. And there Heath waited for her, to see her safe.

'Yow sek to tak me whar I wyl biginne?'

As Heath nodded, willing to go with her, she touched him and shook her head.

'Nat yet myn der, nat yet. Yow wyl cum whan moules are called, nat bifor. Staye with Starling redy to guid her out.'

'But you'll be lost in the tunnels or killed,' said Heath.

'Myn guid ys the Stane, and it is gud.'

Before she left, she went back to Starling, and she touched her by the light of stars.

'Guard yem wel!' whispered Feverfew, meaning the youngsters, and those old moles who still lived.

'We shall,' said Starling, 'and one day we shall come too. I will keep them safe, and when the time is right we'll come, Feverfew, as many will.'

Then Feverfew turned and laughed with joy, and it seemed to Starling and Heath, watching her, that the light of the stars lit the ground before her paws as she turned westwards to seek out her great task.

* * * * * * *

'Why do we have to go on tonight?' a mole had said that same night – a mole few would have recognised.

'Because it is a night many will remember, and I would have you remember it too,' said Boswell. 'And anyway we have not far to go.'

Bailey stared at the old mole with affection and even love, and Boswell knew it was the same way Tryfan had looked at him, all those years ago. How many years? Boswell could not quite remember, years and moles merged into each other; not so many, perhaps.

'It's as light as day!' said Bailey. He almost ran in his pleasure at that starry night, ran as the Bailey Henbane made could never have done. *That* Bailey Boswell had undone. That Bailey was lost somewhere on the long and arduous way behind, lost in bits and pieces as a tree loses its leaves before the winter winds until it shows once more the strong branches underneath. So had his obeseness fallen by the way, so had his weak smiles and spoilt sulks vanished, so had the unhealthy sweat of a mole un-exercised gone now, and in their place a different mole emerged on that long trek than any ever seen before. Older than he had looked and much, much leaner, stronger of paw and surer of talon, but most of all a mole who laughed now sometimes yet held still that innocence and earnest fun he had once had when his sisters, Starling and Lorren, had him at their side when they were young, when Duncton was still theirs; when Barrow Vale echoed for a little while to the sound of their excited talk and laughter.

Looking at him those last few days before they reached the object of their trek, Boswell was reminded of something too many moles forget: moles *can* change, really change, or shed at least those darknesses that have become dominant.

Yet he knew too that nomole goes through what Bailey had without some mark being left upon him. For this poor mole (thought Boswell peaceably), it was a nervousness of self, a timidity of soul, a sense of shame masked now only by a young male's new-found strength and confidence. The shame of a mole who has done those things he felt he ought not to have done, and who feels himself unworthy ever to see again the moles he would most like to see. For Bailey that meant Starling and Lorren. Wise Boswell sighed; moles wasted so much time *worrying*.

But that night at least that shame was a forgotten shadow in poor Bailey's heart as he watched, as so many others did, a star that shone. He must have been one of the very few who did not know, or guess, that it was a sign that the Stone Mole was coming, coming for them. And he was nearest to it.

'What is that star, Boswell?' Bailey asked looking up, and up again, for it was almost overhead.

'That star?' repeated Boswell trekking on not looking up. 'Why all moles know that star tonight. It tells them the Stone Mole is coming.'

'Oh!' said Bailey. 'Where are we going?'

'To where it shines, of course. It's not far now,' sighed Boswell. 'Not now.'

Bailey looked at the old mole at his side and it seemed to him that Boswell's fur was almost brighter than the star itself, brighter than the snow and frost that caught the stars' light in their crystals. Yet it seemed that Boswell was suddenly old too, so very old, and suddenly frail, so frail that Bailey wanted to help him.

'I think you should rest,' said Bailey, 'because you are very old!'

'It's all right, mole!' said Boswell irritably. 'The rest of mole may watch but we must move.'

'Look!' said Bailey, forgetting all concern for Boswell as they crested a hill and saw before them, stretching out across the east, a lurid expanse of lights still beneath the star-struck sky.

'The Wen,' said Boswell. 'I've been telling you about it for days.' The valley mists had cleared, the Wen was plain.

819

'You didn't tell me it looked like that! Amazing!'

'Better than a star?'

'Well nearly better!' said Bailey, not sure where to look.

'I'll show you something better, mole, if you'll just keep on going for once without stopping every time you see something new,' said Boswell, stirring himself forward through the night for one last effort. 'Come on!'

Down a drop, up another rise, the Wen's light fabulous to their left, the star ever more directly above them, the sky ever brighter and alive, the air cold.

'There!' said Boswell, old mole, White Mole, beloved mole of Uffington. 'Look and listen, mole; and remember, for many will ask you what you saw this night.'

Ahead of them was something shining beyond a final stand of trees, so bright the trees were in more than silhouette: some of their branches were lost in the light.

They went on, the light falling from their bodies like drops of brilliant rain, through the trees and undergrowth until they were before it: a great Stone that caught the light of the star that shone in the sky high above it, a Stone that seemed now filled with light.

'Oh it *is* better!' said Bailey in an awed voice, instinctively stopping where he was and letting old Boswell go on up to it. 'Much better. Is that where we're going now?'

'It is.'

'What is its name?' whispered Bailey.

'It has had many names through the centuries, but I think the one Tryfan called it is as good as any ever was. He named it Comfrey's Stone. Let it be so. It is the only Stone in moledom to be named after a mole.'

'But listen!' said Bailey. 'Listen, Boswell!' For there was a kind of Silence in the sky, and beyond it, coming out of it, a distant sound that made all moles that heard it reach forward.

'Listen!' said Bailey.

'I know, my dear, I know,' said Boswell gently as Bailey began to cry at the beauty of what he saw and what he heard.

820

The Stone where Comfrey died was where the Stone shone brightest in all of moledom that Longest Night, its sides were white, purer than white, and around it, and above, and from it, came that sound from Silence that seemed to fill the sky. Soft it was, and barely heard, and yet scribes say that many heard the sound that night, as Feverfew had heard it before she set off from the Wen. Then the starlight began to fade and the sound to go.

Bailey cried, the tears of anymole who had lost what once he had and still remembers it, and wishes it was his again.

'Is the Stone Mole coming to help us?' he asked Boswell.

'He is,' said Boswell, so tired now, so tired.

'Boswell?'

'Bailey?'

'What shall we do here?'

'Wait,' smiled Boswell, 'and while we're waiting you can find me worms and keep a burrow clear near Comfrey's Stone.'

'How long?'

'Weeks perhaps. Molemonths maybe.'

'For what?'

'A mole.'

'But why?'

Boswell smiled, the smile of an old mole who understands the impatience of the young.

'Because I need her, Bailey. Because I'm old and have not long to live.'

'I wish you wouldn't say that, Boswell. I don't like it!'

'Well, 'tis true. But never fear. If there are moles enough with courage and with faith then my journey is nearly done and hers, still yet to come, will not be in vain.'

'Boswell,' whispered Bailey as dawn struck the eastern sky, 'where has the light from Comfrey's Stone all gone?'

'Into the hearts of the followers who saw it to help them hear the Silence when the Stone Mole comes.'

'Did Tryfan see it?'

'Yes.'

'And Spindle?'

'Yes.'

'And Mayweed?'

'Yes.'

'And Henbane?'

'I know not.'

'Boswell?'

'Yes, mole?'

'Did Starling see it too?' said Bailey, crying.

'Yes, she too.'

'When will the Stone Mole come?' asked Bailey, almost asleep now.

Then softly Boswell told him, but Bailey heard it not, for his eyes were closed, and he slept before Comfrey's Stone with the light of a rising sun upon his face.

★ ★ ★ ★ ★ ★ ★

As Bailey slept an army of moles moved. From the Carneddau they came and on lost Siabod they advanced, the light of a star in their eyes, and the sun of a new day in their faces. They had seen a star, and taken it for the sign that Alder and their leaders had said it would be, which was that the Stone Mole was coming.

So on the unsuspecting grikes that guarded their former tunnels the Siabod moles came down. Hard. Powerful. Ruthless. Killing. To begin what Alder said must never end until the Stone was moledom's to cherish as it would and the Word was heard no more.

Hard the eyes of the Siabod moles, hard the eyes of Alder.

But troubled the eyes of Marram.

Killing? That again? He trusted it not but had argued against it in vain.

So, as the attack on the grikes was renewed, he turned east towards the distant place where that star had shone. Troubled, friendless now, alone, to the east he would go and seek guidance where it came.

So let our memory of that Longest Night end, not with

powerful moles, or fated moles whose names would be scribed in history. Their place is known. But with troubled moles who that new day, uncertain of themselves, with no training, no help, no special hope, their names now mostly forgotten, turned as Marram bravely did and made trek towards where they hoped they might find the Stone Mole and a final easing of their troubled hearts. But courage was theirs, and great purpose: to know the Stone Mole and seek the Silence he would help them hear.

Remember them.

Chapter Forty-Three

Of the days that followed Longest Night many moles would say, like Marram, that they marked a changing in their lives.

Indeed, a mole might chronicle all such memories through moledom, and still not come to their end. It was as if a corner had been turned down a long, dark tunnel and light seen at last; a light that drew moles to it and gave them confidence.

But not all moles followed it with the same simple joy and resolution as Marram showed. Some were irritated by it, some complained, some even cursed the time for what they saw as its insistence that they change their lives and seek out its Silence. Others discovered their new direction as if by accident.

Like old Skint, for example, and his good companion Smithills. Why, had he not made trek north to retire at comfort and old age in Grassington? Had he not sworn never to cross talons again with the grikes, or trouble himself with matters of the Stone or the Word, or whatever nonsense moles talked? He had.

Yet Skint was not a mole for idleness and after Tryfan's departure into Whern, and November came, he had become restless and irritable and anxious for something to do. He had quickly organised the Grassington followers into some semblance of a force against the day that Tryfan and Spindle returned, but the molemonths passed and interest waned. Well, it could be started up again if ever it was needed.

''Tis not the dream I dreamed of, Smithills, is Grassington! There's nothing to do here but dwell on memories, and I'm not much of one for that! I wish now I'd gone into Whern with Tryfan.'

'Aye,' agreed Smithills, 'he might have done with help . . .'

And so the molemonths dragged by.

But perhaps the Stone in its wisdom hears the plaints of such moles as Skint as prayers, for certainly it finds ways to grant them. . . .

One cold and bitter evening in mid-December when the snows had started to come, there had been a scurry of moles at his tunnels' entrance, and a voice came down to disturb his geriatric boredom which once he would never have believed he might be glad to hear. But now he was overjoyed.

'Aging Skint, mole who has done roaming, listen and guess whose voice this is! Yes, it is humble me, Mayweed, your former annoyance, your grateful but unwelcome servant, myself in the fur and flesh. And more!'

'By the Stone, 'tis Mayweed himself!' cried out Skint. 'Come down out of the cold and touch your paw to mine for you are welcome!'

'Sunny Sir,' called out Mayweed from above, 'I come with company, and more than one.'

'Let's start with you then,' said Skint, ever cautious.

So Mayweed came down, leaving Sleekit on the surface with Wharfe and Harebell, thinking that it might be wise to advise Skint that he came in the company of a sideem, and with two youngsters whose identities were matters for which secrecy and tact might be well advised.

But Mayweed had only got as far as explaining Sleekit's presence before the two youngsters, cold and hungry, came tumbling down, trotting into Skint's tidy burrow and looking about as if they owned the place, with Sleekit close behind.

'Humph!' said Skint. 'And I expect you'll all be wanting food.'

'Mmm!' said Harebell. 'Thank you.'

'Please!' said Wharfe who looked like a mole with an appetite.

'Humph!' said Skint again. 'You two can come and help me then.'

So it was not until night was well advanced, and Smithills had been fetched to join in the food and fun, and Sleekit and the youngsters had gone to sleep that Skint turned at last to Mayweed and said, 'Well, you've been busy. Autumn moles eh? Lucky for some!'

'Deluded Skint, greatly impressed Smithills, they are not mine, nor Sleekit's.'

'Then whose are they, Mayweed?'

Mayweed looked this way and that, drew near, looked about him again and said, 'Sirs both, even the youngsters themselves do not know and Mayweed boldly suggests that this is not the time to tell them. That decision is for better moles than I to make.'

'So . . . whose are they?'

Mayweed looked apologetic.

'Wondering Sirs, do you want the long version or the short, the full account or the brief one, the saga or the sentence?'

'The short version,' said Skint impatiently.

'Tryfan's,' said Mayweed.

There was absolute silence.

'Tryfan's?'

'Sir, you are old but Mayweed is glad to discover your hearing is unimpaired. Tryfan I said and Tryfan it was.'

'You've got some explaining to do,' said Skint. 'Now for a start, where's Tryfan?'

Mayweed sighed miserably.

'I do not know. A mole cannot be everywhere. Of Boswell I have told you and Bailey too, and if they came not here after their escape that was only because Boswell takes his special scribemole ways that even I, Mayweed, do not know.'

'Aye,' said Smithills, 'that would be likely.'

'But magnificent Tryfan and great Spindle, there I failed. The Stone guided me another way and I found his youngsters instead.'

'But what of the mother?' said Skint.

'Sirs both,' said Mayweed slowly, 'there are only two moles I could tell this to in the whole of moledom, and they are you. Mayweed and Sleekit cannot be expected to keep it only to themselves. They might die and somemole should know. The mother of those good and sturdy and loving youngsters is none other than Henbane herself.'

There was shock on Skint's face and simple disbelief on Smithills'.

'I said you had some explaining to do, and now I know you have. You better begin at the beginning, Mayweed, and tell us all you know.'

So he told them, simply and well, and for confirmation they fetched Sleekit and she affirmed that it was so. They told them everything, right to the frightening scenes by the Rock of the Word. Then when they had finished Skint said, 'Moles, I know not what to do or what to say. A mole must think on a matter like this before he says a thing. That's always been my way, as Smithills here will confirm. As for him, he'll say too much too quickly, so give him a worm and tell him to keep quiet!'

Smithills grinned ruefully, and engaged them in other things while Skint, much affected and amazed at what he had heard, went up to the surface and thought. For hours he was there, and only when dawn came did he seem to start making up his mind what to do. He believed what he had heard and that the youngsters were Tryfan and Henbane's own. That they knew it not he approved. But what to do with them he had not been certain.

But as dawn came he thought of that last conversation he had had with Tryfan, and remembered two things the scribemole had said. The first had been, 'Have strong talons at your command, but remember they are not for killing but for authority'. Aye, well, Skint had seen enough of killing to want to see no more. And he had heard enough stories of Tryfan's preachings on his way to Whern since then to know his views were the same. Peace must be the Stone's way now.

The second thing Tryfan said had often given Skint pause for thought: 'There's a place we visited on our way here, a place you know: Beechenhill.' And when Skint had asked him why he mentioned it, Tryfan had simply replied, 'Remember it . . . remember that for one day of my life I was happy there. The moles there have great faith and trust and gave me courage to come on. Remember it!'

Now, thinking of Tryfan's youngsters who had come so unexpectedly into Skint's tunnels, he remembered that conversation and decided what to do.

He went back down and joined the others and repeated what Tryfan had said to him.

'Beechenhill is as good and safe a place as we'll find for the rearing of the two youngsters. It's a hard place to get to, and Squeezebelly's a clever leader who keeps the system little noticed. Also, it has a Stone, and moles who'll remember those two youngsters' father with affection and respect. When the time comes that they learn who they are, for good and ill, it may be as well that they are at Beechenhill.'

It did not take long for the others to agree.

'We shall leave here without fuss and we'll tell nomole where we're going or why. If the youngsters can stand it we'll travel in two groups, so that if the sideem do come searching they'll hear stories of only one youngster and not easily put one and one together to make two. But of that Mayweed and Sleekit must decide.'

The day was well advanced before the two moles would agree to the part of Skint's plan that would split them up, but agree to it they did.

That same day they left, Mayweed and Skint with Wharfe, and Sleekit and Smithills with Harebell. Quietly they went, and no Grassington mole was told, but those that noticed anything saw nothing, for they held Skint and Smithills in great respect and trusted what they did.

As for the 'strong talons' Skint had got ready, they were told to watch out for Tryfan and Spindle, to say nothing to anymole, to humour the grikes and pay due homage to the

Word when it was asked of them. In short, to raise no suspicions.

Then they were gone, southward towards the Dark Peak, by hill and vale, by river and wood, trusting that the Stone would protect them all and bring them safeguarded to Beechenhill.

Both groups saw the star on Longest Night, and the youngsters were in awe and listened to what their elders said of the Stone Mole and his coming. They travelled on until, in early January, they came to Beechenhill, Mayweed's group a few days ahead of the others, but all were welcomed by those good and faithful moles and their leader, Squeezebelly, asked no questions of the youngsters' birth but understood there was more to their parentage than met his eye.

Mayweed and Sleekit decided that their task lay now at Beechenhill, to watch over Tryfan and Henbane's young, and to rear them ready for whatever task the Stone might give them. Perhaps, too, after molemonths of closeness without time for intimacy, and with spring approaching, they felt the need to have time to themselves and relax and enjoy life.

But Skint, restless as ever now the excitement of getting to Beechenhill was over, hesitated for days over his return to Grassington. Then one day, grumbling about life and old age, Smithills said, 'You know, Skint, you're such a misery you'll never be happy unless you're doing something. Has it occurred to you what Tryfan would have done if he saw that star on Longest Night?'

'He'd be away to the south, to Duncton Wood itself as like as not, whatever the difficulties.'

'Aye, that's what I think, and do you think he'd have need of two old moles if they could drag themselves there?' said Smithills.

'Smithills, you're a fool, and more than that you're a tempting fool. We'll start this very day. I've not been happy with myself since Longest Night. I'm not saying I believe in the Stone, mind – it's all nonsense as I've always said it is – but by the talons on my paws if I was ever to hear there *was* a Stone Mole and I never had a go at seeing him, why, I'd grumble about it the rest of my life!'

They would have liked to leave there and then, but Squeezebelly, a cheerful mole who liked an excuse for a feast and a song, insisted that they stay a day longer and say a proper farewell. And more than that, he made them touch the Beechenhill Stone so that, if the day ever came that they saw the Stone Mole, they could touch him with the same paw, as if that would bring luck to Beechenhill.

So it was that in mid-January, with the winter sharp and cold and more snow yet to come, two old moles with scarred bodies and wrinkled skin, but hearts as good as any mole's could be, left Beechenhill with many a message in their ears, and with stories for Tryfan, should they ever find him, that would bring tears to his eyes, and cheer to his heart.

Mayweed went a mile or two with them until he felt he must turn back.

'Good Sirs,' he said with tears in his eyes, 'humbleness is sad and will crouch down and cry his eyes out when you've gone. But before you go, and before he does, he asks that you tell Tryfan that he has not forgotten a promise he made.'

'And what was that?' asked Skint.

'Magnificent Tryfan will remember, Mayweed knows that to be so. So just tell him, Sirs, that for now Mayweed's task is here with Wharfe and Harebell. But when that is done, and Sleekit is content, then Mayweed will set off once more to do what he does best of all, which is to find routes where darkness is, and guide moles through them. So to Tryfan he will one day return, and if there's darkness about, and confusion, Mayweed will be Tryfan's mole. Tell him that, and say . . . and say . . .' but poor Mayweed could say no more. He lowered his snout and cried.

Skint comforted him on one side and Smithills the other and they said that they would repeat all that Mayweed had told them to. But as for that final thing, which he could not quite say, why if the Stone existed and had a heart then one day it would grant that Mayweed could say it to Tryfan himself!

Then with a buffet and a laugh, and a final smile, Skint and Smithills set off for Duncton Wood.

Yet in the days that followed, Mayweed was restless and discontented to think that in some way he might be needed by Tryfan in the south – for he had no doubt that Tryfan would finally be safe, and when he was that it would be to Duncton he would go.

The truth was, too, that Wharfe and Harebell were growing up and found good companionship with Squeeze-belly's youngsters Bramble and Betony who, though a little older, were young at heart. Even then Mayweed would have stayed but that one day the ominous word came that sideem and grike were about, and searching for a mole called Sleekit. . . .

'I must leave, my love,' said Sleekit the moment she heard this grim news, 'for my presence here endangers not just Tryfan's young, but everymole. If I travel privily south, and I arrange that I am seen, then that will draw the hunt from here for ever.'

'Madam mine,' said Mayweed, 'me, I, myself, agree. And if cuddlesome Squeezebelly is agreed, and the youngsters can be made to understand, then I shall come with you. You will need guidance and humbleness will give it.'

Sleekit looked relieved.

'Where shall we go to hide?' she asked.

Mayweed smiled.

'To hide. Us? We? Both? Together? As one? Romantic but mistaken. Mole should never hide for life is good! So not "to hide" but *to* Duncton Wood! Clever? See it?'

They smiled together, and agreed it was a time to travel wisely and fast. So, saying their farewells and entrusting Wharfe and Harebell to the capable, firm and kindly paws of Squeezebelly, they too turned from Beechenhill, and set off south in the pawsteps of Skint and Smithills.

★ ★ ★ ★ ★ ★ ★

A great good change came over Tryfan after Longest Night and he seemed once more to find an interest in life and living, and to notice again the simple things about him that for so long he had retreated from. Again and again he would pause on their long trek and look with pleasure on the simplest thing.

'It's a root, and the grey light's shining on it!' he might whisper, or, 'See how where the orange bracken's stem makes a hole about itself in the snow. See, Spindle! My father's name was Bracken and I wish he was here now. A mole appreciates his parents too late!'

Yet still he was often in pain, his eyes hurt and his paws grew stiff with the cold and throbbed, and on those days he felt unsociable, and Spindle, patient but wise, went on ahead and let him grumble to himself.

They came near Rollright just into January, but Tryfan refused to try to contact followers there for fear, he said, of meeting grikes. Not that they any more expected to be attacked, for their story was as good as it was true: Tryfan they said, because of his injuries, was outcast and was making for Duncton Wood to claim sanctuary there. Grikes did not touch such travellers, fearing perhaps they had disease as well as injuries.

Yet when it came to it, Tryfan did make trek to the Whispering Stoats, using the route Mayweed had led them on before, and there, having made their obeisances, they might have got away with nomole seeing them but that as they left they came upon a female watching them.

'Followers?' she asked.

'Seeking healing,' said Spindle.

'May the Stone protect you!' she replied. '*He* looks as if he was in a fight and a half!'

'He was,' growled Tryfan. 'Thy name, mole?'

He spoke with his old authority and she answered him

832

straight: 'Rampion is my name and I am not ashamed of my faith in the Stone.'

'Then, Rampion, an injured and tired mole would hear you say a prayer for him at the Stones.'

'I'll be glad to!' she said. Which she did, gracefully and well. When she had finished she asked them whither they were bound.

'Duncton Wood,' said Tryfan. At which Rampion sighed a little sadly, for only outcasts went there now. Yet she smiled finally and said, 'If you get there, say a prayer at its famous Stone for me.'

'I shall, Rampion,' said Tryfan, and he touched her momentarily and she gasped for she felt she had been blessed. Then she was gone and Tryfan said with sudden energy, 'Come, Spindle, come!'

'Well,' declared Spindle, 'so all it took was a young female to rouse you out of your pains and miseries!'

Tryfan had the grace to smile.

'Did you not recognise that "young female"?' he said. Spindle shook his head.

'We met her here in Rollright once before. She is the daughter of Holm and Lorren.'

'I thought there was something about her,' said Spindle. 'You may have the worse sight of us two now, but you've the better memory for moles. I'm better at facts. But Holm might help us, Tryfan. Could we not visit him?'

'I'm sure he would help, but too many moles have followed me to disaster for me to ever want to lead any more. So come, before Rampion tells her parents of the moles she met by the Stoats and they start wondering. Holm may be silent but he's nomole's fool. Come! That mole's prayer stirred me and I am impatient at last to get home.'

* * * * * * *

Tryfan's concern was not entirely misplaced. Some days after her meeting with them at the Stoats, Rampion found herself back at the burrow where she had been reared as a pup, though she rarely went there since she had left her birth burrow the previous summer.

But at Longest Night, making her trek to the Stoats for a vigil, she had been one of the many who had seen the eastern star. Crouched there in awe, she had found herself bathed in its light and seen not far off her mother Lorren and Holm, her father, whom she loved.

That night Holm had, as was his habit, said very little, but Lorren, her eyes full of joy, had expressed their pleasure to see Rampion again, and asked after her siblings, also long gone from the burrow.

But they were not there, and so it was only to Rampion that Lorren was able to suggest that she returned to their burrow before too much of January had passed, and certainly before mating time came and moles kept to their territories and avoided trespassing even where they had been born. Rampion, pleased to see her grubby parents once again, said she would, yes she would.

But somehow young adults say such things and forget about them, as if going home is going back too far, and life should be ahead, away, always away from the birth burrow. But soon after meeting the strangers near the Stoats, and somewhat in awe of the way the scarred one had touched her, she found that her paws led her back by the old familiar ways to the tunnels of her birth.

'Well, and this is a surprise!' said Lorren, dusting herself and trying to smarten Holm up a bit. 'Rampion no less, and we gave up any hope *you'd* come. Better things to do I said!'

'I just thought that it would be nice,' began Rampion rather lamely, 'to see you both again.'

Holm gazed at her in the way he had: a small mole, with wide eyes and an alert look, who knew more than he ever said. 'Shy' should have been his other name.

'Glad, to see you, I am,' he said.

'Thank you,' said Rampion, pleased nearly to tears.

As Lorren chattered on with many an apology for the mess and the lack of good worms, and this and that, Holm just stared until at last there was a gap in the conversation and he felt able to touch his daughter tenderly and ask, 'What is it?'

'It's nothing,' said Rampion settling down and shaking her head too much. 'Nothing.'

Holm stared some more and Rampion said, ' I saw something so sad by the Stoats. I met two moles and one of them was so *hurt*.' Then she told them and they listened and then Holm got her to describe them and he looked very serious.

'Tryfan,' said Holm. 'And Spindle maybe.'

'But they went to Whern and surely died,' said Lorren. 'Such a long time ago and no news except stories of killing. They must be dead by now.'

But Holm shook his head.

'That was Tryfan,' he said again with confidence.

That same day Holm ventured up to the Stoats, going his own secret way, for he had been Mayweed's companion once and he and that great mole knew more than most about route-finding. Holm felt sad, and knew that if it had been Tryfan something was wrong that he had not come to greet them. Some great hurt had been done him, as Rampion had suggested. Holm went to the Stoats and there he stayed for all that day, wondering. He snouted towards the south, where Duncton lay, and he asked that the Stone tell him what to do. He had seen that star, and he believed that the Stone Mole was coming. He had heard Tryfan's own teaching, and he listened to the Stone.

It told him to be still, and to wait, and to trust. Tryfan would have come to them if he needed them, Tryfan *would*.

So Holm made his way back to Lorren and when Lorren talked he told her what he believed, and that he was afraid.

'Why, Holm, that's a lot for you to say!' said Lorren going close to him reassuringly. Sometimes she liked to show she loved him. Small and grubby though he was, she had never looked at another mole in all her life. He was hers and would always be so.

'But there's two things I'd like to do, but *you* know that!' she declared.

Holm nodded and grinned. One thing was to go back to

Duncton Wood's Marsh End near where she had been raised and find a really comfortable muddy tunnel; and the other was for Lorren to meet Starling and Bailey once again because both were alive, they *were*. His Lorren would rather die than think they were not.

Holm sighed.

Lorren grinned and cuddled him.

'You believe it'll happen one day, don't you?'

Holm nodded his head vigorously.

'And Mayweed will come back,' he said, scratching his muddy flank.

'One day . . . ' said Lorren, and they both thought of a star they had seen and the sense of hope they felt. One day. . . .

★ ★ ★ ★ ★ ★ ★

Tryfan and Spindle reached the cow cross-under back into Duncton Wood a little after mid-January, at much the same time as Skint and Smithills said farewell to Beechenhill.

They had both been so tired in the latter part of the journey that they had felt little fear or even curiosity about what lay ahead in Duncton Wood. But when their route brought them alongside the roaring owl way that ran by the system's south eastern flank, and they began to be stopped by grike patrols and asked whither they were bound, the fear set in.

The guardmoles were heavy on the ground, and it seemed they had been deployed to watch more than just the main cross-under ahead. Though Tryfan said nothing, Spindle remembered him describing ways out of the system along the drainage pipes through the roaring owl way, though the routes were of great difficulty and danger if guarded on the other side.

It seemed that this was what was in the minds of the grikes now, and Spindle and Tryfan saw evidence of punishment and even snouting along the way, and were told – warned, more like – that that was what happened to moles who tried to escape Duncton.

'They know that,' a grike told them, 'but conditions are bad in there at times and maybe they prefer to chance their paw out here than stay inside where henchmoles of the leaders kill them.'

'But what for?' asked Spindle, but got no satisfactory reply. Was Duncton *such* a grim place to live in that moles risked death to leave it? It seemed so.

Except that he noticed one strange thing. The snouted moles they saw along the way were all females.

Once they knew that the two moles intended to outcast themselves into Duncton, the grikes were surprisingly friendly to Spindle and Tryfan, though in a dismissive superior kind of way. They preferred not to come too close, perhaps because of the risk of disease, and no names were asked. Tryfan and Spindle did not risk trying to find out if the grikes knew their names or if they had heard such moles might try to enter these parts, but anyway nomole could have suspected the limping and scarred mole that passed through their lines was the Tryfan who had once been the leader of the Duncton moles.

There was almost a grudging respect paid to them for coming to Duncton of their own accord, but they discovered they were not unusual in making a request to go into the system, for diseased moles had heard – as Wyre of Buckland made sure they did – that for misfits Duncton was the place to go. There they had freedom, and of that moles of the Word made proud, as if they believed that by labelling a ghetto a place of freedom where moles could believe what they liked they could claim that the Word showed a mercy and tolerance it did not really possess.

When they saw that the two moles were not obviously diseased, but that one was badly injured from fighting, and the other a follower of the Stone prepared to declare himself and be outcast in Duncton Wood but otherwise harmless, the grikes were laudably reluctant to let them through the cross-under and inside the system without first making sure they both wished to go.

'More fool you, mate,' one said to Spindle, 'though I

won't say I don't admire you. But if you won't Atone or offer yourself to an eldrene for teaching, well, there's nothing for it, is there? It's Duncton for you. But you must have known that. What of your friend, is he a believer too?'

'He is,' said Spindle.

'Mind you, I can see why *he's* come. Wouldn't survive in a normal system anyway without help.' The mole peered at Tryfan's deformed face.

'Can he see?' he asked Spindle.

'Well enough,' said Spindle, 'but I help him when he needs it. He's clumsy along a route and his worm-finding's poor.'

'Can he hear?' shouted the guardmole.

'When he wants to,' grunted Tryfan, turning on the guardmole. He could still be very intimidating when he wanted to be, though it was not now his normal way, and the guardmole backed away in alarm. For the most part moles ignored him, but that suited Tryfan's desire for peace and quiet.

'Remember, once in you don't come out,' warned the guardmole, staring ahead at the great cross-under. Spindle could believe it. The entrance looked dank and gloomy , and this side of it there were a dozen solid guardmoles, and more nearby.

'I know that,' said Spindle.

'Speak posh, don't you?' said the guardmole. 'I repeat like Wyre's told us to: you don't have to go in yourself provided you're in sound health and of the Word.'

'I was reared of the Stone,' said Spindle proudly, 'and I shall die that way.'

The guardmole grunted and showed no more interest in them. He had done his duty and now had others to attend to.

'Take them in then,' he ordered another mole, 'and warn the poor buggers what to expect.'

The second guardmole led them by a surface route to the cross-under.

'Don't mind him, it's not that bad if you keep your snouts low and don't try and retaliate. You two don't look much good for anything so nomole will want you in there. Keep to the Eastside, don't trespass, head down for the Marsh End, that way you might survive. Anyway the Marsh End's where the believers go.'

'Are there any guardmoles in there?' asked Spindle.

'Used to be. Beake herself was eldrene here. She died. A lot of the guardmoles got scalpskin and a lot of them died. Well, of course, they had to stay inside and *that* caused a to-do. Wyre's no fool, though. Sent reinforcements, and it was nasty for a time. Be grateful you didn't come here then 'cos you two wouldn't have survived a day. But things settled down. Lot of the fight's gone out of the moles in there now. They're just getting old, aren't they? Dying, that's all. It's a cursed system this one. Nomole'll ever come here willingly to live, not unless they're idiots like yourself or injured like your mate. No . . . the only real trouble we get is females trying to get out. Have to kill them or, if we can, persuade them to go back in. Depends who's on duty. . . .'

'Why is it females trying to escape?'

'Want pups, don't they?' grunted the guardmole. 'Not going to get any in there!'

With no further explanation, and quite without ceremony, Spindle and Tryfan were pushed through the lines of the guardmoles. They passed through the concrete cross-under, and found themselves on the south-eastern side of Duncton Hill whose slopes were slushy with cow-stained snow.

The rumble of the roaring owls came from high above them, and the rise of the Ancient System seemed dark and inaccessible ahead. It was not the return Spindle had quite imagined, nor perhaps one that Tryfan could ever have wished for when they and so many other moles had first left Duncton Wood long before. But it was a return, and with a heavy sigh but no word at all, Tryfan stared briefly up at where the Ancient System was and then did as the guardmole suggested, turned north along the Eastside, and headed for the distant Marsh End.

Chapter Forty-Four

The Pasture slopes that a mole must climb from the cross-under into Duncton Wood before he can turn north and head along the eastern side of the system towards the Marsh End were streaked with icy snow.

Tryfan and Spindle plodded up them and then veered over towards the first trees. They were leafless, dark and uninviting, and the ground under them felt cold and without life. Yet there was an infectious energy and purpose about Tryfan that grew all the time.

'We're here again at last, Spindle! Back again!'

But Spindle felt nervous rather than excited. He peered about the wood expecting to find aggressive moles watching them from the crooks of twisted roots, and moles he would not wish to meet. Diseased moles, miscreants, deviants of body and spirit. But there was nothing but the gloom of winter, and the only movement was the twist and turn of dead twigs as they fell from the branches high above and settled on the wood's dead floor.

The impression he had got of Duncton Wood from the grikes was that it was full of moles. But if it was they were doing a good job of keeping themselves hidden away down the tunnels whose entrances they occasionally saw, though there was little sign of passage and use about them.

'What are we going to do?' he asked, meaning what tunnels were they going to seek – old ones to occupy, or new ones to delve.

But Tryfan took his question another way entirely.

'We are going to keep our snouts low to save all our energies for scribing', was his surprising reply.

'Scribing? Of what?'

Tryfan laughed out loud.

'Of what we talked to Whern,' he said. 'I was ordained a scribemole and it's about time I started behaving like one.'

'But your paws . . . ' said Spindle, for though his wounds had long since healed, Tryfan's paws had remained clumsy for delicate work. He could travel well enough, but subtler delving or worm-gathering was hard for him, and always would be, and scribing might be harder still.

'No, they are not quite what they once were. But as Boswell so often told me, scribing comes from the heart not the talons. My script may not be as elegant as it once was, but others will be able to make sense of it and that's all that matters.'

'What will you scribe?'

'I don't know yet, Spindle. Perhaps of things we've done, things we've thought. So much was lost at Uffington, and it may be years before those texts you buried at Seven Barrows can be recovered, if they're still there, so I think we had better start scribing something for future generations of the times we lived through. Somemole's got to start, let it be you and I.

'But we may have little time, for if the Stone Mole comes then we will want to go to him and serve him in whatever way he asks us to. So we must find a place to work, and work hard. I am eager to begin!'

'But what about the dangers of Duncton?'

'What dangers?' said Tryfan, looking about the empty wood carelessly. 'I see none.'

'Well . . . they're probably watching us, or waiting to see what we do.'

'Who?'

'Moles,' whispered Spindle, now making himself thoroughly nervous.

'They told us we would not survive the Slopeside but we did. Most would have said it was impossible to survive Whern yet here we are, a bit battered, feeling rather weak, but here all the same – and together. So I think we should be able to survive in Duncton Wood well enough. Now come, we had better start for the Marsh End and see what we find.'

Yet Spindle's instincts were sound. As they moved off once more a mole followed them, her sightless eyes narrowed, her brow furrowed, her snout inquisitive. She kept downwind of them because she smelt, and because that way she could the more easily scent them. . . .

Sniff, snuff, sniffle, wrinkle and whiskery whiffle: she scented two of them, definitely strangers, strong, tired, one limping slightly with weak paws, talking of scribing, talking of the system as if they were familiar with it, one called Spindle the other as yet unnamed. See where they go and then report. Good worms were the reward for such reports. Or would have been once, might still be. Things not what they were. No. But worth a try. Follow then, quietly. The blind female went straight into a root and fell, and then lay still lest her quarry heard her. They did not. She got to her paws, gathered her strength, and wearily set off again. No, it wasn't the worms she did it for, it was the reward of company. Pleased they'd be to get news of strangers, and give her a worm or two and maybe let her stay a little and feel, once more, she belonged and that somemole cared. Sniffle, sniff, northward go and follow. She felt so weary, so ashamed of what she did.

It was when they were halfway across the Eastside and it became easier to take to the tunnels than stumble on over the surface that Tryfan and Spindle began to come across evidence of other moles.

There was the smell for a start. It reminded them of the Slopeside, foetid and unclean. Then there was the rubbish of roof-fall and litter drift, all uncleared. Then there was the scurry of paws and the snouting of snouts, not out of curiosity but fear and disquiet. Moles who did not wish to be seen, or contacted, or even disturbed.

Finally there was mole, squatted down and facing them.

'Who's there?' it said. 'It' because they could not be sure if it was male or female, so rough and wild its fur, so filthy its face, so formless its sore-ridden body.

843

Spindle was alarmed but Tryfan advanced, quite willing to talk to the mole.

'In peace we come . . . ' he began, but the mole turned and dragged itself away, muttering.

They went on, none challenging them. Moles stared at them from burrows, with hollow eyes and gaunt faces, and fur that was dry and patchy. Some of the moles seemed sightless, others utterly unaware, and more than one was dead and rotting where they crouched.

'Scalpskin?' whispered Spindle.

'Something more, I think,' replied Tryfan. 'It is murrain, a form of plague.' His voice was sad and concerned.

'These poor moles,' he whispered, staring at them, and watching as they retreated from fear or shame as they came near.

Some tunnels were deserted yet wormful, others held many moles as if in their suffering they preferred to be close together. None spoke but to themselves in rasping whispers, or groaned and seemed confused and agitated when the two moles went by.

It was only after they had passed through two such grim concentrations of suffering moles, and were nearly through the area where traditionally most of the Eastsiders had had their burrows, that they found themselves approaching a mole who did not go away.

She had her back to them and seemed not to have heard their approach. Certainly she started suddenly when they came within her view, but did not run off. She looked prematurely old and gaunt and sunken of eye but she had no sores upon her haggard body.

'Come on then,' she said, shouting as if she was deaf, 'you can take what I've got but it ain't much.' She led them down a poky tunnel to a pathetic cache of worms, which she crouched beside indifferently.

'We don't want your worms', said Spindle, repeating it more loudly as she was clearly a little deaf.

'What you come for then?' she cried, peering suspiciously at him.

'We're going to the Marsh End,' said Spindle.

At this her manner changed from servility to contempt and she reared up at them, her broken talons flailing, and said, 'From the Marsh End, are you? Well, what are you disturbing me for, then, with your do-gooding and interfering? Bugger off, the pair of you! It's bad enough in this dump without the likes of you wasting our time. I've got all the bloody faith I need, thank you, and you'll find others think the same. Promises get a mole nowhere.'

They retreated, and though they tried to pacify the mole and asked her who she thought they were she was not interested, and eventually her rage so overcame her that she began to cough in a terrible hacking way, and phlegm dripped from her mouth.

'Bugger off!' she screamed again and they did.

Others seemed to hear the female's tirade and gain courage from it. They shouted at Tryfan and Spindle and drove them off, saying they were not welcome.

'Who do you *think* we are?' Tryfan managed finally to ask one of them.

'Frauds!' he screamed, and then he laughed and was gone, his laugh a madness of sound in the stricken tunnels.

They got themselves to the surface and there a younger mole, and male, crouched waiting for them.

'So?' demanded Spindle, angered by the reception they had had. 'And who do they mistake us for?'

'Well,' he said slowly, 'you *look* like Westsiders, being fit and well and that.'

'Fit!' exclaimed Spindle.

'Well!' said Tryfan.

'It's what I said. So what if you've a bit of scarring to the face? Doesn't stop you functioning, does it? Got a brain, haven't you? Can think, can't you?'

'So if we're not Westsiders, who did you think we were then?'

'Marsh End zealots, of course. Preaching the bloody Word, going on about the frigging Stone, blathering on about what's to come and doing nothing about the here

845

and now. No thank you, not interested. I live my life and keep my snout low and bugger the lot of you!'

'We're neither Westsiders or zealots,' said Tryfan quietly.

'Who are you then?' said the mole.

'I think they call us outcasts.'

'You mean you've just come into the system?' asked the mole suspiciously.

'Yes,' said Spindle, with obvious truthfulness.

'And you came straight here?'

'The grikes said it was best to make for the Eastside and then down to the Marsh End. Suggested the Westside was dangerous.'

'Interesting,' said the mole, still doubtful of them.

'Marsh End seems sensible,' said Tryfan. 'It's not too bad down there in some places, moles from the worm-rich tunnels on the Westside never used to bother much with it and I don't suppose they do now.'

'Sounds like you're remarkably well informed, mate.'

'He ought to be,' said Spindle. 'He was born here.'

'Well, blow me and lie down and die,' said the mole in astonishment. 'You're not having me on?'

Tryfan shook his head.

'No, I didn't think you were. There's an alarming sincerity about you two that's unusual for Duncton, to say the least. Really born here were you?'

Tryfan nodded.

'Then you're the first mole I've met in this place who was born here. I thought the grikes killed off the Duncton moles.'

'They didn't,' said Tryfan.

'So you've got to be believers in the Stone, then?' said the mole quietly.

'Yes, we are,' said Tryfan.

'What are your names?' But before they could reply the mole pushed them to one side and, lowering his voice, said, 'Best to keep your own secrets round this place, let's find a quieter spot. Tunnels have ears.' He took them some way from any tunnel entrance, then disappeared for a little while and came back with worms, which he laid before Tryfan and Spindle.

'Now,' asked their new friend, 'what are your names?'

'What's yours?' asked Tryfan.

'Hay,' said the mole. 'Short and sweet. Now. . . .'

'My name is Tryfan.'

The mole immediately laughed and turned to Spindle and said, 'And you'll be telling me you're the Stone Mole.'

'Spindle, actually,' said Spindle.

'Stone me,' said Hay, breathing heavily and staring about in alarm. 'Well stone the crows!'

He looked at them some more and then said, 'Trouble is, I don't need to ask if you're serious 'cos nomole would be daft enough to say they're Tryfan if they weren't. Too bloody dangerous. Well! What a turn up! Tryfan, eh? And Spindle of Seven Barrows?'

'You've heard of *me*?' said Spindle in surprise.

'Heard of you? You're famous, mate. As for you,' he said turning to Tryfan, 'you're meant to be dead, and you might decide you're better off dead when you realise . . . but you don't, do you? I can see it in your faces. You've got no bloody idea, have you? Blimey! Wait a minute – didn't the grikes ask who you were?'

'Didn't get round to it,' said Spindle.

'Perhaps you'd better tell us how you know of us, and why you're so surprised and what we obviously don't "realise",' said Tryfan.

'Perhaps I'd better get shot of you as fast as I damn well can, except . . . ' And then his voice dropped to a sudden whisper. He signalled their silence, and turned away into the undergrowth suddenly. There was a short silence and then a scuffle and a scream.

A different voice cried out, 'Wasn't, didn't, wouldn't, can't, just passing by.'

'Passing by, my arse,' said Hay, dragging a protesting mole to the spot where they had been talking. She was as scabby and foetid a looking mole as they had ever seen, and she was blind. She was the one who had been following them.

'You'll find a lot like her,' said Hay, 'wandering about, listening, exchanging the miserable pittance of information they get for a pawful of worms up on the Westside. Eh? And what's your name then mole? "Filth"? "Vile"? Or they got a better name for you?'

The mole's snout closed and opened as she scented at Tryfan and Spindle, her eyes white and staring. 'I got a name and that name's mine to tell when I like. A mole's got to live. Others get worms quicker'n me, others aren't nice to me, so I get by best I can. Moles blabber, I report. You hurt me and they'll know who it was.'

'How?' said Hay, who did not look like the hurting kind.

'They'll know,' said the mole.

'We'll not hurt you, mole, and there's no secrets that we keep. My name is Tryfan, my friend is Spindle, we have returned to Duncton and intend no harm to anymole. But tell the ones you report to that if anymole tries to harm us they will not benefit by it. Go in peace, and remember we mean no harm to befall anymole.'

She shook herself, looked disgruntled, finally snouted close to Tryfan, and said, 'Give us a worm and I'll keep my mouth shut.'

'Mole,' said Tryfan softly, 'you need only ask.'

With that he pushed the worms Hay had brought, over to her.

'You're a good mole!' she said. 'Time was when I had no trouble. Reared pups of my own and fed them. Time was when I did that. Had two litters before disease came, but, mind you, that wasn't here, no, I don't come from here. . . .'

'Off you go!' said Hay. 'You've got your worms.'

But Tryfan raised a paw to silence him, crouched down with the blind and smelly female, took a worm himself, crunched it companionably and said, 'Where are you from, mole?'

'Long way off, long way. Long time ago now, and you wouldn't think it, looking at me, but I had two litters, a three and a four, all my own to cherish and care for.'

'Tell me, mole.'

'You don't want to hear my nonsense!'

Tryfan went close, gently made some of her food easier to reach, and said, 'Now, tell me.'

Which she did, in a rambling tearful way as moles do when none has been willing to listen to them for a long time, and they fear that if they stop their listener will go away. But Tryfan stayed, and Hay and Spindle backed a little away and were silent while the female talked as Tryfan desired her to.

It was only much later, when the mole had told Tryfan her whole life history, that she finally got up to go.

'Things to do, got to keep busy. What's your name again?'

'Tryfan.'

'Mine's Teasel and it's been a pleasure talking, Tryfan. I like a natter. Whatmole doesn't?'

'Company's everything,' said Tryfan.

'You're right there,' said Teasel, and she snouted about, scented her route away, and set off. 'Bye then!' she called out as she left, humming tunelessly to herself as she went, her blind and wandering form the only movement over the dusky floor of the Eastside wood.

When she had gone Hay said, 'So, now I know why there's stories about you, Tryfan, and you, Spindle. I got a feeling I was meant to meet you today.'

'More than likely,' said Tryfan cheerfully. 'Eh, Spindle? We've got a habit of finding the right mole at the right time or, more accurately, the Stone does it for us.'

'Now don't you start preaching the Stone at me!' said Hay with mock alarm. 'I'm not one for worship.'

'Not many moles are until they try it,' said Tryfan. 'Now, perhaps we had better find some temporary burrows to overnight in and you can tell us what Duncton has become in the time since we left it and what we should

849

know. Spindle is worried about surviving here, thinks we'll get attacked, so maybe you can put his mind at rest.'

'You're on! I'll tell you what I know and in exchange I'll find out if what they say about you is true. As for being attacked, forget it. Those days have passed. There's a few idiots about who make a lot of noise, and 'tis true they're on the Westside, but I just tell them to go and take a walk in the centre of the roaring owl way and they push off and leave me alone.'

'What have you heard about us?' asked Tryfan.

'That you're the only moles who ever resisted the grikes successfully, and that you did it in the name of the Stone and not yourselves. They say you're brave and clever and all that, but I'll judge that for myself.'

'The only way!' said Tryfan.

So two moles came that day to Duncton Wood and now there were three, and the little party set off to find burrows, and to learn what they could from one another.

* * * * * * *

The Duncton system they had returned to was but a place of quiet desperation compared to the murderous viciousness that had prevailed at the time the immigrants brought by order of Henbane first came.

Hay's account came partly from himself and partly from what others had told him before they had died, as many had. Now the population was more stable, and though disease was rife deaths were fewer, as if the moles had settled for a lower level of life which took as part of its habit disease and illness and general debilitation.

'Terrible those early times, by all accounts,' Hay told them, shaking his head, 'and moles lived in fear of their lives. For in those days most who came were miscreants or scalpskinned, and until madness or the sores set in bad such moles had strength and intelligence. So you can imagine what happened when they came here and were given the freedom of the place to make what rules they liked.

'That Henbane must have been a cunning mole to think

850

that one up! Mayhem it was, and murder. The strong attacking the weak, and the weak attacking the dying, and the dying living off the dead.

'Disease all over, like all the plagues of moledom had settled on this place. Well, knowing the layout of the system you can imagine what happened. The Westside's where the worms are, so the strongest took that over for a start. Mad bloody lot they were, and cruel, too, and used to raid the Marsh End for poor bastards to snout on the Westside wires that face out on to the Pastures.'

'Was there a leader?' asked Spindle, who always liked to know whatmole did what, and who was who.

'Leader? There's always leaders, jumped-up bastards most of them, but of course they can't last long. Diseased, you see. They weaken and others take over and then they go. I seen it so many times I don't bother to keep track.

'Anyway, the strongest among the first wave of immigrants took over the Westside, and the clever ones who weren't physically strong lost themselves down in the Marsh End where a mole with sense can hide himself. That's where I was when I first came, it's why I know the routes down here, or some of them.

'As for the new moles coming in, the ones who couldn't fight their way into the Westside, they stayed on the Eastside, didn't they? And lived as best they could there until they died. 'Course the moles of the Westside came and looked them over and took the females for their own.

'And not always females,' he added darkly. 'Males as well sometimes, because in those days we got some young ones in, gone mad mainly. Lot of *that* about.

'All this time what they called the Ancient System, which includes the so-called famous Stone of Duncton, was in the paws of the grikes garrison under the control of Eldrene Beake, as vile a mole as Fescue, her predecessor at Buckland.'

'You knew Fescue?' said Spindle in surprise.

'I wouldn't say "knew", though I saw her once or twice. I'm from Buckland originally and was one of the minions there, serving the grikes. And there I might still be but for a mole you once met, and who indirectly got me into trouble.'

'A mole *we* met?' said Tryfan.

'Aye. Ragwort. Said he met you when you came to Buckland.'

'Ragwort,' repeated Tryfan. Ragwort who had been a watcher and fought the grikes, and who had been lost in the disaster at the tunnel. 'Ragwort knew the Stone,' Tryfan said.

'Knew the Stone?' laughed Hay. 'Damn near lived and breathed the Stone after you left. Organised secret meetings, inspired other moles towards the Stone, including a friend of mine called Borage. Well I don't know what happened to Ragwort but Borage continued his good work and held a session on the Stone which I was fool enough to go to. Got done by the guardmoles for that and when they found I was ill I was sent here with Borage and a few others in the second wave of deportations after that mole Wyre took over Buckland and Beake was sent here.'

'So Borage is here?' said Spindle.

'Alive and dying of sadness,' said Hay. 'He's all right in his way, and he keeps his mouth shut about the Stone. He doesn't like the way the Stone zealots force their beliefs down others' throats. Feels he did that himself too much and got moles like me into trouble. He's got a mate, if you can call her that, but keeps himself to himself. Ashamed you see, of all the moles he got into trouble.'

'Trouble?'

'Blabbed, didn't he? The grikes threatened him with snouting and he blabbed and gave away the names of those in Buckland who were interested in the Stone. Don't blame him, mind. I would blab rather than suffer *that*. Nomole really blames him, but few talk to him now. Keeps his snout low.'

'I would like to meet Borage,' said Tryfan, 'he sounds a worthy mole to me.'

'Aye, well. Maybe. Anyway, as I was saying, Eldrene

852

Beake got sent here against her will and eventually scalpskin broke out among her guardmoles and then herself, and Wyre ordered that they had to stay where they were up in those tunnels near the Stone. So they found themselves prisoners too. Got to paw it to Beake, she held things together for a while, but then the scalpskin weakened her.

'Nomole knows what happened up there exactly but one day the grike guardmoles must have mutinied and killed Beake – snouted her up by the Stone and good riddance. Then they broke through their own lines and invaded the worm-rich tunnels of the Westside.

'Very nasty time that, but as I didn't come until a month later I missed the worst of it. That was all a cycle of seasons ago and a lot's happened since. 'Course, what it was all about was mating and that, and the guardmoles were not going to have celibacy forced on them. Naturally they wanted females, which Beake objected to and so they snouted her and broke ranks to get at the Westsiders. The females were mostly willing enough.'

'So a lot of young were born on the Westside?' said Tryfan.

'*No* young were born anywhere in Duncton, not a single living one. A few abortions, some stillbirths but no living young.'

'Scalpskin?' asked Spindle.

'Aye, makes moles pupless.'

'But not always,' Tryfan said, remembering: how could he forget? 'Though often the young are born deformed.'

'Sterile now,' said Hay. 'Of course the males blamed the females and the females the males – that's why the healthy-looking ones were popular. You could be as ugly as a lobworm, but if your fur was clear of sores then you were wanted. Well, they found out that spring that it doesn't matter: if one or other of the partners had scalpskin, that's it. Nothing. Not even the hope that being in pup brings. And not just scalpskin. There was this disease from Avebury which is virulent and turns a mole blind and then mad in the end. . . .'

'Murrain,' said Tryfan.

'Aye, that's it. Well, whatever the reason the moles here were sterile, and by all accounts they have been over a lot of moledom.

'Then in the summer months a lot more died and the guardmoles began to lose sway until by the autumn nomole gave a damn who was who, it was the strongest surviving, and the cleverest. Naturally there was hope of young in the autumn but that came to nothing, just more abortions, more failures, and not even a stillbirth.

'That's when depression set in. Moles, like Teasel you met, wandering around and going on about the good old days before they came here when they did have young. Without young a system's dying, isn't it. Naturally some tried to get out of the place but the grikes by the cross-under were strengthened and any who tried to escape got killed. Plenty have disappeared trying to get out and that's where the strongest have gone. Now it's the old and weak who remain, along with a few like me who seem lucky enough to be disease-free but of course we can't get out. Still, there's always hope, and that keeps a mole alive.

'Now January's here, the question of pupping has come up again and there's many a mole would like to have young but there's not much chance of it. Things have quietened down, though the Westside is still the best place to be, but there's no real order there. A few so-called leaders of different sections of the tunnels, plenty of henchmoles, the hardest bunch of females you'll ever meet but, well, the system – if you can call it that – is dying for want of young. Not that the overall number is down, no, Wyre sees to that. There's always new moles coming in like you, and the guardmoles are as strong as they ever were down by the cross-under. At the end of spring we'll probably get a batch of younger moles come in – diseased, trouble-makers, Stone followers and the rest and that's the time to keep your snout low! Meanwhile, there'll not be much trouble about.

'A few moles will try to get out, females mainly, in the

hope of making young. It can drive some moles mad that, not having pups. What's the point of it all if you don't make life? The moles here aren't getting any younger either, so the females particularly are losing hope.'

'It's like the Wen, Tryfan.'

Tryfan nodded.

'It's as if all of moledom's dying for want of young.'

'Well, I don't know about anywhere else,' said Hay, 'but this system is.'

'What about the zealots in the Marsh End?' asked Spindle. 'A mole thought we were two of them, whoever they are.'

Hay grinned.

'It's what I thought for a bit. Down in the Marsh End's where you find the clever ones, or the ones who think they're clever. They have to have an argument about something, so down there you either have to be of the Stone or of the Word. Doesn't make much difference as far as I can see: they're as bad as each other. They send zealots up to the Eastside to get recruits, because sometimes when a mole's ill enough he'll believe anything if it promises relief or help. Get quite nasty if you disagree with them, so what a lot of moles do now is avoid them and let them get on with it. In the end they all get diseased just the same, they all die. Where I suggest you go is on the eastern side of the Marsh End, which is moister and danker but there's a few sensible moles down there who keep themselves to themselves. Borage is down that way as well. As for me, I was due for a move so I'll try my luck down there for a time as well. I daresay you'll have a visit from the Westside moles, and others too if they hear you're Tryfan.

'Best thing is to be tough and offish with them and they'll leave you be in the end. Time was when you would not have survived at all without joining them. Now they're all too old for much fighting, except for a few of the henchmoles who fancy themselves.'

'What about the Stone? Do any moles live up there?'

'No, but the Westsiders don't let others through to reach it, and discourage approaches from the Eastside, because they say that trekking moles take worms. They're right, they do. 'Course the Stone followers, if that's what they are, don't like it, but the Westsiders can count on the moles of the Word to give them help. Bit of a do at Longest Night when the Stone followers set out for the Stone, but that all faded to nothing. Strange that. . . .'

'Yes?' said Spindle.

'Strange sky that night, stars so bright it was like day in the woods. There was a star in the east and talk among some of something going to happen.'

'The Stone Mole,' said Tryfan.

'Aye, the Stone Mole. That was the last time I saw Borage, Longest Night. Creeping about with his mate on the Eastside, heading up for the Stone. It was his mate more than anything, poor thing. She's like all the rest. Wants young and will never have 'em. Diseased as they come, and as thin as a female can be. Told me that if she could only touch the Stone by that star's light then she'd maybe have young this spring. I told her she was a fool to try, but . . . as I said, they're desperate.'

'And did she touch the Stone?' asked Tryfan softly.

Hay shrugged.

'Maybe she did. Persistent she is. But she would have got a buffeting for her pains, or something worse.'

★ ★ ★ ★ ★ ★ ★

The last time Tryfan had been in the Marsh End was many moleyears before when, with Duncton Wood already invaded at its southern end by the grikes led by Henbane, the system had been evacuated.

But now was a different time, a different season. The scrubby Marsh End trees stood still and desolate in the fading light, and the cold ground held rafts of snow in its darker parts. Dead vines trailed from the ragged trees, no bird scurried or flew, aching silence reigned and the place was drained of colour and hope.

Underground the earth was dark with moisture, and

chill, and what worms they found were withered and pale, every one unpalatable. Spindle cast his gaze about uneasily, uncertain where to settle for the night, and even Hay, a cheerful mole and one they were evidently fortunate to have met, seemed uneasy.

Yet Tryfan, though tired, was positive and glad to talk a little more with Hay, and answer his questions about Duncton Wood as it had once been.

The tunnels where they stopped were communal, or had been once, and word seemed to go up and down them that strangers had come, strangers indeed. For one claimed his name was Tryfan, and the other was Spindle the Cleric himself, whom some had heard of too.

So as night came, and Tryfan talked, others came, surreptitiously at first and then more boldly until the tunnels seemed full of moles, although in truth there were only nine or ten gathered there. One or two of the later arrivals, zealots apparently from the unyielding smiles on their faces and their eagerness to talk, were shushed, for the stranger was talking, and what he said held a mole's attention.

It was true enough, though Tryfan himself, whose night vision was less good than once it had been, seemed barely to notice the listeners. But Spindle did, and sensing there was no harm in it and might be some good, he signalled to Hay to let the listeners be.

So that night Tryfan talked and repaid Hay's account of the recent moleyears in Duncton with one of his own, which told of the time in the years immediately before he was born, when the Marsh End had as its elder a much-loved mole called Mekkins. He told of how Mekkins helped Bracken and Rebecca, of how he made trek to the Stone to pray for Rebecca's life.

But what brought tears to the eyes of many of the listeners – beset moles all of them, gaunt, sad, and ill, lost moles who were shorn of hope and brought to a system of despair – was Tryfan's account of how Mekkins' prayer was answered, and how he found a pup called Comfrey, and brought him to the teats of Rebecca here, right *here* in the downcast Marsh End.

There were females among those listeners, thin of flank and dry of teat, who cried openly at Tryfan's memories of stories told to him, of a system in which pups' cries were heard. The males, too, were restless and sad.

One or two dared ask questions: 'What was Rebecca like?' and, 'Was Comfrey harmed by his experience?' and, 'Were moles from the Marsh End normally allowed up to the Stone?' All of which Tryfan answered with such modesty and evident authority that a mole could have heard a beetle stir so silently and well did they listen.

Then at the end one or two females nudged each other and whispered, 'That'll be the day, when I hear a pup mewing down this system's tunnels.'

'Aye, that'll be something to make a mole feel good about!'

Then afterwards, when they had gone as silently as they had come, Tryfan turned to Spindle and said, much moved, 'Not until now did I truly know I had a home system where memories might live, and moles be content to go where others went before, knowing their lives succeed the deeds of others. I shall not leave Duncton again, Spindle, not even if the Stone Mole himself summons me! This is my only place now and whatever Hay may say I believe good life will come back to these tunnels again, and hope, and faith. As for the Stone, why that's somewhere we'll make trek to soon enough. If moles cannot live together in peace in a system like this, how will they ever live so in moledom itself?

'Here is our task now, Spindle, here where I began. And we shall succeed in it by word and peaceful deed, not by talon and tooth and war. We shall begin to scribe those things we know, and teach others to do so, that they may scribe their own lives down, and learn of others too. We shall meditate and we shall be quiet, and from the silence we make, little though it may be compared to the Silence of the Stone itself, something good will come to these moles here.

'I think, Spindle, that the pain I felt in Whern, and which lives with me always across my face and sometimes throbs in the night, will remind me of the pain all moles feel when they are wrenched from places and moles they love, and forced to raise their talons against their hearts' desire. But a mole cannot forever live on dreams and pretend he is not where he really is. Duncton is the home now of these many stricken moles, and quietly, without force or persuasion, we may, through our own stillness, help others love where they are.

'As for these weak paws of mine, and these talons once so strong. . . .' and here Tryfan raised his right paw and looked at his scarred skin and bent and weakened talons, 'They will learn to scribe again, and if the script they scribe is weak and falters then it will do so no more than the mole who scribes it.

'Tomorrow we begin, Spindle, and one day before too long, when we have made something to be thankful for, we will make trek to the Stone whatever moles in this place may say or do, and make obeisance and celebration.

'The Stone Mole *is* coming, and I pray that we may be granted to see him. A star heralded his coming, and many saw it. Many wait as we do now, and this time of waiting is a time to reflect and be still, a time indeed, as January always has been, of waiting for life to begin once more.

'Each mole to his own way of meditation and discovery, each to his own direction. It matters not what they say they do, or what names they give it, only the spirit in which they do it. With knowledge of themselves first, with love of others next, and with respect for the place they find themselves in last; that is the way. Which means no fighting with talons, nor harsh words without thought, nor belief that they are right without belief that they might be wrong. Tomorrow. . . .'

Yet tomorrow began that night. For as Tryfan slept, Spindle scribed down the words he had spoken, using bark he found, and so began the first of what historians call the Marsh End Texts.

859

Chaper Forty-Five

That first night that Tryfan returned to Duncton Wood, deep snow came. Soft, unheard, and gentle, it drifted through the black winter-stricken trees and settled heavily on the ground.

So with dawn there was startling light: reflecting from the white snow, deep and pure, the trees alive with its cold reflections. Across the whole of Duncton Wood the snow lay and brought with it a special silence that marked the coming home of Tryfan.

Under its cover, Tryfan and Spindle were able to move to a place only Hay was allowed to know, which was the old Marsh End Defence where Skint and his covert group had been. Nomole had found those tunnels, nor other creature either, and they lay quiet and protected just as Skint had left them.

There, for a time, Tryfan might be safe from prying eyes, while Spindle would help him as, together, they began their work which later moles would know as the first flowering of a time of great scribing for which moledom had unconsciously thirsted for so long.

White was the snow over Duncton, deep its purpose, silent its effect. Rumours went forth of the presence of Tryfan and Spindle, strange stories of two moles who came into the system, who told of days gone by and prophesied a peace to come. But though moles of the Westside searched for them, and zealots of the Marsh End hunted them, yet those two had disappeared as silently as the snows that fell that January and whose silence seemed to spread and deepen as the cold, still days of February came.

So Tryfan and Spindle found peace, and safety, to scribe as they felt they must, the one of the spirit and the other of mole: the one as a scribemole trained by Boswell himself, the other as a scrivener, not ordained by mole but certainly ordained by the Stone, who told of moles like Comfrey and Thyme, like Starling and Bailey, like Holm and brave Mayweed, so that moles of future times might know their stories and whatmoles they were.

Spindle made a library as he had before up in the Ancient System, in Harrowdown and other places too. Caches of texts that one day others might find to know what happened before and learn from it.

Unseen by the two scribes, but reported to them by Hay, that harsh February brought death to Duncton Wood and growing despair. For cold saps an ill mole's will to live, and many who had been strong before perished then. Nor did new ones come, for moledom outside Duncton seemed in a thrall, and more than one of winter.

By the end of February, when normal systems would be beginning to sigh and rejoice to the sounds of mating and of pups to come, the tunnels of Duncton were more silent than ever. Indeed, the winter seemed to linger in them, and on the surface where the snow had settled and then turned to ice. Now it was grubby with the fall of bark from old trees, and the earthy print of fox, and the spatter of spoor from winter corvid. Birds lay dead, branches had fallen, life among its trees seemed gone. If there was sun at all in moledom, it shone rarely upon the open spaces of Duncton Wood, and never in Barrow Vale, once the heart of the system Bracken and Rebecca had known.

So the system was beset by stillness and silence, and felt oppressed, with every entrance blocked by snow and debris and moles staying underground and waiting for a pupless spring beyond which lay no hope nor sign of relief.

Such mating as there was was a hopeless thing, gaunt flank to gaunt flank, cries not of ecstasy but despair, for those moles were cursed by illness and disease and whatever it was that made them sterile. Females wandered aimlessly, caring no more for the threats of the Westside, or the zealots. Not that they came much now, for among them many had died. And still there was ice above, still the chill ate deep.

So, surrounded by suffering and despair, Tryfan and Spindle scribed their work until, as February ended, they made their darkest texts which told of the filthels of the Wen, of the savagery of grikes, and of the story of Rune. Their days were lightened only by Hay's secret comings, though the news he brought was ever of a system that seemed downcast by cold and ice, and where the future was all gone.

One day he came while Tryfan was scribing, and he spoke for a time with Spindle alone. . . .

'. . . Mind you, the grikes are still there down by the cross-under because I've talked to a female or two who went there. Looking for mates, of course, but the grikes won't touch the Duncton females – fear of disease. Anyway they've got other things on their minds at the moment. Thick as mites in a weasel's nest the grikes are. Nervous, too. They're said to be under strict rulings about allowing new immigrants into Duncton because of fears about the Stone Mole. Think he's coming here! That's why there's hardly been a mole come in recent weeks, and no males at all. So if he's on his way, it's not to here!'

But Hay stopped his chatter because he saw Spindle was tired and looked ill, while the glimpse he had of Tryfan showed a mole slowing down.

'Not sickening, are you?' he asked worriedly. 'Duncton's not the place to be in this winter, if you ask me. Maybe you came at the wrong time.'

Spindle shook his head.

'It's always a hard season, but I'm tired and I need a change, and Tryfan's been very silent lately. He feels he's failed in his tasks, he feels he's let moledom down in some way, and he feels far away from the moles he grew to love.'

'There's plenty of moles here would like to meet him,' said Hay. 'They know you're both in the system now and I think a few suspect where. But we respect your silence and there's a good few moles take pride in the fact that even if

Duncton's now cursed to be a forgotten disease-ridden place of aging moles, at least there's you two scribing and making something for the future. Perhaps in years to come, in better times, young moles will come back and pups' cries be heard again where now only old moles die.'

Spindle was pleased at these sentiments and invited Hay to see what work they had done.

'Me?' said Hay in some alarm. 'A text wouldn't mean a thing to me.'

Spindle smiled.

'It didn't to me once, but now I think as Tryfan does, that all moles should be taught to scribe. Living comes first, says Tryfan, then scribing; the one for knowledge of the heart and body and the other for knowledge of the mind. Come, I'll show you. . . .'

So it was that Hay, an illiterate mole then, was the first to see and touch the great texts that Tryfan and Spindle made that dark winter. They were ranged on simple shelves in the dry soil of the deep tunnels of the Marsh End Defence, not far from where the light of day shafted down from the dead tree which rose above the centre of the tunnels and gave a little life to them.

Hay stared at the texts in awe, but only with difficulty was he persuaded to touch one.

'What's this then?' he asked.

'It's one of mine,' said Spindle. 'That's the title . . . here . . . ' And he ran his talons and then his snout over it and read out, *A Preliminary Bibliography of the Books Scribed at Harrowdown with a Memorandum on the Final Days of Brevis and his Martyrdom with Willow, Worthy Mole of Grassington.*

'Yes, well . . . you must be a clever mole to scribe that!' said Hay in wonder. Then he snouted at another.

'That's an account of my early puphood at Seven Barrows,' said Spindle, adding with a touching mixture of vanity and apology, 'I'm somewhat prolific, you know.' And then, moving on quickly as if to make light of his achievement, he took up some loose folios and said, 'This is one of Tryfan's works. This one's entitled, *The Way of Silence – Teachings of the White Mole Boswell*. Of course you realise we'll never finish all we have to do, scribes never do. I. . . .'

And then, suddenly, Spindle stopped and a look of constricted pain came across his face.

Hay immediately went to his side, but Spindle, unable to speak it seemed, waved him away. After a few minutes he began to breathe more easily again.

'Are you all right, mole?' asked Hay.

'I . . . am . . . well enough,' said Spindle.

'You don't look it to me. Have you had attacks like that before?'

'Twice before,' said Spindle, 'but please say nothing to Tryfan, I do not wish to worry him. The winter has been long, and the journey here from Whern tired me very much. Please, say nothing to Tryfan.'

'No, I won't,' said Hay doubtfully. Then, more cheerfully, he said, 'Maybe you two should have a visitor apart from me. There is a mole you can trust who'd like to see you, and that's Borage.'

'Well, I don't know, I think Tryfan. . . .'

'You think Tryfan what?' said Tryfan joining them.

When he heard he smiled and nodded his agreement.

'Spindle's always protecting me but we've spent enough time here alone and spring'll be on us soon even if it doesn't feel like it!' he said, cheerful after a long day's work. 'So bring Borage to see us.'

Two days later Hay reappeared with Borage at his side. He was a big mole and had the good stance of one who knows what he believes but no longer wishes to persuade others how right he is. A mole who lives as he believes and trusts others will live so too. Yet, like so many other moles who had been through the harsh paws of the grikes, Borage's body bore the signs of torture and illness.

Tryfan greeted him and stared at him in silence and Borage seemed in awe and said nothing at all.

'Did you not bring your mate?' asked Tryfan.

It was one of many times Tryfan, in those molemonths and years, showed that he had reached a stillness in himself that enabled him to see into other moles' hearts and minds.

'Well, I did, yes . . . ' stammered Borage.

'Then go and get her,' said Tryfan gently.

She came softly down into the chamber to them, and it seemed that with her came the light of a hopeful day. She was thin and diseased but bright of eye and looked at Borage with great love and tenderness. Yet she was not at peace and it seemed to Spindle, who recorded that scene, that she came to Tryfan as if she was searching for something that was not of herself at all.

'This is Heather,' said Borage.

Tryfan came closer and touched her paw.

'We have heard much of Borage,' he said, 'and it is an honour to meet his mate.'

Heather said nothing but just stared, and a silence fell which Tryfan did not try to fill with meaninglessness.

'Will you bless me?' said Heather suddenly. 'Will you bless me to be fertile?'

Tryfan laid his paw on hers again, and kept it there.

'Long ago I healed a mole here and a mole there, but I lost my way, Heather, and I do not know that I have found it again. Healing comes from the sufferer not the healer, who is only a way for the Stone's Silence to pass on to where it should be.'

'Please!' she said urgently, and Borage moved nearer and seemed a little embarrassed. But Tryfan only said sadly that he did not think he could make a mole fertile who was not.

'No,' she said, 'no I didn't think you could. Wouldn't be right. There's many like me and they'd all come running if they thought you could! A female starts to die if she knows she can't pup.' She smiled briefly and with terrible resignation, and yet – as Spindle noted – there was still the light of the searcher in her eye as if, already, she

865

was thinking there might be another way, another opportunity, and that she would never give up until she found out what it was.

'Why do you want young?' asked Tryfan.

'You might as well ask me why I want to breathe,' she said, 'or why I want to eat. It's a mole's way, a female's way, especially because a mole learns and a mole shows and a mole tells.'

'What will you tell your young when you have them?' said Tryfan.

How her eyes softened at that, how gentle the tears that came to them to meet a mole who used 'will' not 'might' and 'when' rather than 'if'!

'When I have young,' said Heather, settling down and pushing her flank to Borage's in a friendly, loving way, 'I'll be so happy that the very first thing I'll tell them is there's the Stone there always, and it hears you and it knows you and it feels you whatever you may do or say. Then I'll tell them that where they are is the best place to be if they make it so, and that's not hard if a mole doesn't expect the wrong things. Why there's lots I'll tell them. Like, for instance, that they're lucky to have the father they have and they're lucky to have *me*! I'll tell them rhymes and stories and I'll make sure they know the difference between their right paw and their left paw because a mole that doesn't trips up. I'll have to tell them that more than once: pups need telling!

'Then as they grow to be youngsters I'll tell them the things I've learnt, and hope they believe me! Mind, a mole learns best what he learns for himself so maybe I'll just tell them I am there if they need me. Then when autumn comes and they're nearly ready to leave the home burrow I'll tell them that soon they'll be on their own, except for two things: the first is the Stone, always the Stone, and the second is knowing that Borage here and me loved each other true, and the day they find out why that means they're not alone is the day they grow up and make me proud. I'll tell them that so they know!'

The moles listening, including Borage, were silent when she had finished, and Tryfan's snout was low. So many moles he had met, so many known, and always the Stone found another that taught him how much he had to learn.

'When I was a pup, Rebecca my mother was a healer and sometimes females came to her because they had not got with pup. I can remember something she said to them and perhaps, Heather, you would let me say that now.'

'I'd like that,' she replied.

So Tryfan touched her flank and spoke the words his mother sometimes said to such moles as she.

> *There is a charm for the lack of pup*
> *But 'tis the Stone to give it.*
> *There is a charm for the pupless nest*
> *But 'tis the Stone to give it.*
> *There is a charm to grant mother's love*
> *But 'tis the Stone to give it.*
> *There is a charm for father's rite*
> *But 'tis the Stone to give it.*
> *There is a charm for mating's joy*
> *Often the Stone will give it*
> *Aye, often the Stone will give it.*
>
> *Hear this mole's plea O Stone*
> *She is pupless and does not wish it.*
> *Hear this mole's plea O Stone*
> *She has faith, and to thee she gives it.*

Tryfan spoke the words in a quiet lilting way and Heather's eyes closed and did not open for a time after he had finished. When they did they were bright with tears.

'Tell nomole what I have done, Heather, and have faith, yet not so much that you do not continue the search you make! I'm afraid that these days I'm more of a scribe than a healer.'

He smiled, and turned to Borage and they talked for a

long time of Buckland and the changes there after Tryfan had led his party out of the Slopeside, and then later when Wyre had come.

'He's strong and dangerous is Wyre, and as loyal to Whern as it is possible to be,' Borage told them. 'So long as he has power in Buckland then I doubt if there's anything moles of the Stone will ever be able to do to establish their right once more to worship the Stone freely. The grikes are too powerful and strong. We cannot fight them.'

'Of that, I fear I have less interest than I once had,' said Tryfan, 'though I should not be popular among followers for saying so. But I believe that when the day comes for us to go out and declare our right to the Stone's protection it will be peacefully and not through fighting. I greatly fear that in sending Alder and Marram to Siabod we have encouraged mole to fight when other ways may have achieved the same more peacefully. Talons win less than peaceful hearts, but that is a lesson I have learned the hard way. May those two moles learn it more easily than I did!'

'But how will anything ever change now?' asked Borage.

Tryfan shrugged a little impatiently and said, 'I believe that the Stone Mole is coming and that only he can show us. We may not perhaps live to see him but he *will* come. Younger moles than I will follow him and show others the true way. For myself I am content to stay here in Duncton and scribe those things I have learnt that others might one day know them. Though in truth it may be Spindle's scribing they find more interesting since he scribes of other moles and recent history, and moles prefer such tales than stories of the spirit.'

Hay and Borage and the other two listened in silence, then Borage said, 'There are many moles other than I would wish to hear you speak, Tryfan, many who would find encouragement from your words. Could you not begin now to go among us and tell us what you believe? The dangers are much less than they were – there has been such death and illness about this winter, and such despair.'

Tryfan shook his head.

'Once I would have done. Didn't we do so on the way to Whern, Spindle? Remember those places we went, and the brave followers we met?'

'I remember it all,' said Spindle, 'and I've scribed a lot of it down.'

Tryfan laughed and said, 'I wonder if you scribed the place I remember best of all, or did you not notice?'

The others looked at Spindle, who frowned and thought for a bit and said, 'That must have been . . . ' And then he stopped.

'You see,' said Tryfan, 'he scribes everything but the bits I remember!'

The others laughed and Spindle grinned.

'Beechenhill,' he said. 'It has three folios all of its own.'

They saw that he knew Tryfan well, and loved him deeply, and were touched. Such love as that had been rare in Duncton Wood these past years and the moles forced to live there had missed it.

'Well, I hope you will go out when the weather gets warmer, because many would welcome you,' said Borage. 'As for the Westside, well the moles there bluster and rant but I doubt if they'd harm you.'

Then Tryfan grew tired and Spindle brought the meeting to a close. Yet after Borage had gone, Tryfan talked some more to Spindle and concluded that their seclusion had gone on long enough, and anyway his scribing paw still ached and felt damaged and perhaps some exercise would do it good. Soon they would go out and meet others again, soon now.

★ ★ ★ ★ ★ ★ ★

Just as so many moles remember the first appearance of the eastern star at Longest Night, so do many recall the strange heaviness and breathless hush that seemed to have come over all moledom in those still days in March that preceded its second appearance in the sky. And one that surely presaged a third showing, a final lighting that would mark his coming.

But in March, although most moles were aburrow and silent with winter, enough were travelling for it to be unusual and remembered.

Of those we know, Marram was still making his way from Siabod. Steadily and with confidence, going by the Stones that he and Alder had visited on their passage west. A little sad sometimes that his friend was not with him, but feeling that such was the Stone's way, and Alder's task was the ordering of resistance about Siabod and beyond, to rally moles to a call that one day might be heard across the whole of moledom. So Marram pressed on, each day drawing a little nearer Duncton Wood.

Skint and Smithills, too, were journeying, grumbling and arguing as was their way, yet making progress south, and glad, as Skint put it, 'to be doing'. What they hoped to find when they reached Duncton Wood they had no idea, but they had heard enough from grikes on the way to know that trouble was astir across the land.

Orders had gone out from Whern, and travelled fast by messenger mole, that Tryfan and Spindle were to be found. Skint and Smithills certainly heard as much, and the information hardened their resolve to continue south as fast as they could, for old and decrepit though they sometimes felt, Tryfan might yet need their talons at his side.

But there was more to make them speed. They found that grikes were being sent westwards, for there was news of a Siabod rising, and a successful one, and forces were being massed against incursions east. Alder was behind it, and the gossip was that Wrekin himself would be summoned out of retirement, or else that Wyre, based at Buckland, might lead moles on Siabod himself.

War, fighting, suspicion: a bad time and a good time to be travelling. Grikes were too preoccupied to concern themselves with wrinkled moles like Skint and Smithills, but a mole had best watch his flanks and keep his snout clean.

The sideem were about as well, travelling fast and whispering: stories of Henbane, blasphemous tales, stories of the Master being dead, stories too black even to whisper. But the sideem were searching and questioning moles, and their quarry were two youngsters, plus a thin, scarred mole called Mayweed and a traitorous sideem called Sleekit. Skint and Smithills were as silent as a seal-up.

There were strange warnings, too, of sideem searching for a mole of moles, the Stone Mole no less, whose coming, it turned out, was dread Henbane's fear. To the south she had sent the searchers, young, dangerous sideem, over-taking old moles like Skint and Smithills, and whispering of stars that shone and had a meaning that even the Word did not know.

Troubled times down moledom, and times when those few like Marram, Skint and Smithills, and others similarly moved, no doubt, had best go careful and keep their purpose and objective to themselves.

Travelling, too, was Feverfew, mole who spoke strange and suffered scalpskin. Strangest journeyer of all, with the light of that star in her eye and only her faith to see her through some of the most dangerous and tortuous tunnels of the Wen.

Yet singly she came, without guide or help but that provided by the Stone, which is the greatest of them all, to a wasteland Starling and Heath had told her of, and thence through an arched tunnel to find a waiting mole.

Old he seemed, and vulnerable, and he watched her come up the same filthel he himself had escaped from so long before. Where he had vowed to wait forever until Heath returned.

Now a female came and she spoke his name.

'Rowan,' she said, 'wyl yow guid me a litel waye?'

Which he did, with hardly a word, as if caught in a dream that now it had come made him feel his whole life had been waiting for it.

Then to fat Corm they went, and he guided Feverfew further still, and after him came Murr, who led her through the complex tunnels on the Wen's most westerly edge and delivered her to safety.

Barely a word she said, yet each of those moles, and others who later said they helped her then, told of how parting from her moved a mole to tears. And when they asked her where she went, she told them it was to where a star shone down, for there would be Silence and light and a task she had to do.

'What task, mole?' they asked.

But she only smiled and travelled on.

So Feverfew passed out of the tunnels of the Wen, helped by the Stone and by ordinary moles of whom only a few are now known. And she seemed to see a light others could not, until at last one winter's day as dusk reared she began to climb up that escarpment at the top of which rose Comfrey's Stone.

* * * * * * *

Mid-March and Bailey, and dusk. A clear sky when the stars begin to show early, first one and then another in a pale blue sky. While far across the Wen a myriad of lights slowly spread.

Bailey was worried and that look of self-concern and petulance long, long gone. Now there was care in his face, and tiredness too, and his gaze moved restlessly from the Wen's lights to Comfrey's Stone, and from that to the still, still form of old Boswell, thin now, his breathing painful, his face so weary. Restless, too, for his talons fretted at the snowy ground, and his head was not still.

'Stone,' whispered Bailey, 'I ask that you help him for I cannot seem to help him more. I know he's suffering but I don't know what to do. He won't eat or go aburrow. He's so tired, Stone, and yet won't try to sleep. He suffers but nothing comforts him. I'm just a mole, not clever or knowledgeable and. . . .'

'Bailey,' whispered Boswell, 'is she come yet? Ask the Stone to call her. Ask that.'

'I ask it,' said Bailey, looking up at the Stone and to the stars in the sky above. Then: 'Boswell, I don't know what more to do, I just don't know!'

'Keep me warm until she comes. . . .'

'Who will come? You never tell me. You've been calling for her for weeks and you never tell me.'

'You'll know,' said Boswell. 'Oh mole, you'll know.'

For weeks Boswell had been ailing, perhaps ever since they had first got to Comfrey's Stone and watched a light shine out which had died. In the days following he had gone aburrow when he should, keeping warm and eating. But he would come up regularly to the surface and face east over the Wen, whispering interminably, 'She's coming, and she needs my help to get here. She's coming now, Bailey, and I'm so tired. Moles must do it alone, they must. Can't do more. Pray for her, Bailey. Help her when she comes. That's your task, my dear.'

Again and again had Boswell said it. When the snows came the wind came too, and drifted the snow away from the Stone so that it rose out of the thinnest layer of snow, and the grass to the edge of the long slope down to the Vale of the Wen was clear as well.

'To make it easier for her, Bailey. Help her when she comes. Pray for her . . . pray for me.' Sometimes then his mind began to wander and he called Bailey by different names, confusing him with Tryfan, and Comfrey, with Bracken and Rebecca, with others, too. Old names, names such as moles hear no more. Confusing him even with Ballagan, who was the first, and struck the blow that made the seven Stillstones.

'I'm Bailey,' Bailey would whisper and Boswell would reply, 'No, no, my dear, no not Bailey now, allmole Bailey, you're all the same my dear . . . is she coming? I long for her to come.'

So had those last terrible weeks gone by, with Boswell unwilling to leave his vigil over the Wen, until he had begun not to eat, and to weaken, and to fade before poor Bailey's eyes.

All that last day he had breathed painfully, and his voice had become weaker, and yet he called out again and again, 'Can you see her, is she come?' But Bailey could not see anymole, only the steep slope down to the Vale and stretching as far as the eye could see, and those lights that were stronger at first than the weak stars breaking through but which gradually that evening the stars outbrightened.

It was so cold that night and Bailey was tired and concerned at Boswell's suffering. The Wen's lights lurid, the sky above darkening, the stars ever more powerful and striking down so that the place about the Stone was light, and Boswell's fur white, and his eyes longing for something he was too tired to go out and meet. No, must not meet. Must wait for. Yes. Must wait. That was his long suffering.

'Is she . . .? I need her now, Bailey . . . Is she coming?' whispered poor Boswell and Bailey was distraught. Staring up at Comfrey's Stone, then at the stars, then at the Wen, then where the breeze blew flat across drifted snow, then at the Stone once more.

'Help him, Stone, send your Silence for him, help him now.'

Then Bailey crouched by Boswell as if to protect him from his own ailing, which nomole could have done, and Boswell muttered confused words, his mouth barely moving and his star-struck old body seeming to grow more fragile with each passing moment of the night.

'Is she . . . ?'

'Yes!'

For suddenly Bailey saw her, coming over the rise, and she was thin and scalpskinned and like a terrible thing that came to take his Boswell from him. So Bailey reared up crying, 'No, no!' for he was afraid of what she was, and what she meant, and afraid of that sound that seemed to have struck distantly across the sky and which he had heard before.

'Yes . . . yes . . .' whispered Boswell, 'oh yes, now is moledom's time, now she is come.'

But Bailey was in fear and sought to run forward and stop her, for her body was caught with sores and her ugliness was coming to take a White Mole, a good mole.

'I love him!' cried out Bailey, and his eyes were blinded by tears and by the terrible light that came down on her, and on Boswell and on them all, a white light too bright for Bailey to bear, too bright for him to stay where he was, protecting Boswell from her coming.

'I love him,' whispered Bailey, and her voice said she knew it, but he saw only light, and then he was gone from the light about the Stone and afraid to see it where it shone down and shone out, and Boswell's voice and that mole's voice were one and beautiful and poor Bailey cried because he could not bear the beauty all about.

'Bailey, moule, yow wyl holp me nu, and tak me bak to wher you war fro.'

'Duncton?' he said not daring to look at her.

'Whar Tryfan ys,' she said.

'I will,' he said, and understood then how long and hard his training had been, and what his task. So he looked at her and asked her name and she whispered, 'Feverfew, myn der.'

Then with the star's light to guide them, and night all about, they left Comfrey's Stone. They did not look back nor need to, for they knew that by it lay what had once been Boswell, White Mole, white as the snow that lay all about, white as the light of the star that shone above and had returned.

★ ★ ★ ★ ★ ★ ★

Moledom saw the star that night, when it shone a second time, and many guessed the Stone Mole was near. Marram saw it and wept. Skint and Smithills saw it and slept no more, staring at the star which, from where they were, lay southward, high and bright, in a sky that was filled with light.

Tryfan and Spindle went up to the surface and saw it, and that night in Duncton many more clambered up and stared.

One especially is remembered. Long had she searched for Tryfan, long had she scented and sniffed, smelt and whiffled, for she remembered his kindness.

Teasel her name and that night she found him.

'Mole,' she said, 'is that you?'

'It is,' said Tryfan.

'Do you remember me?'

'I do.'

'Fancy a chat, Tryfan? Find me a worm?' But when he said nothing she said, 'You're silent, mole, not like before.'

'There's a star, Teasel, and everymole is staring at it.'

'Where?' she asked. 'Show me.'

Then with his right paw he guided her head towards the eastward sky, and then up, for the star was high indeed.

'Am I looking at it?' she asked, her sightless eyes wide and the star's light white and glittery on her old fur.

'You are, Teasel. And what do you see?'

'I – I cannot – I –'

'You can, mole,' said Tryfan softly, 'you can.'

'I feel it but I can't see it, I can't!' And her tears were caught by the starlight as they ran from her eyes which could not see.

'Have faith, mole,' whispered Tryfan, 'and you shall.'

'Is it what some call the Stone Mole's star?' she asked, her flank close to his for comfort.

'It is.'

'When he comes I would see him, Tryfan, I would!'

'Then you shall, mole,' whispered Tryfan.

So Teasel stared and hoped that what she felt in her heart that night was what she might one day see.

Then when she had gone, and while the star was still bright, Tryfan told Spindle, 'Soon now I'd like to go to Barrow Vale, and maybe after that to make a trek to the Stone itself. Soon, now, Spindle.'

Which he did, making a trek to the Stone that same night, though whether in waking or in sleep neither he nor anymole ever knew.

But there he came, and there he found an old mole, a White Mole, who spoke gently, saying, 'Tryfan, this place is where I found you when you were young. Do you remember?'

'I do.'

'And you asked if you might ever be a scribemole.'

'Yes,' whispered Tryfan, 'but I was not worthy.'

'Nomole worthier,' said Boswell, smiling. 'Nomole with more courage. Now listen for I am weary. Feverfew is ready to come now, and with her she brings the Stone Mole. Care for her, for each other are you chosen. Stay at her side and help her care for him, and teach him, and know that he is much loved.

'This is the great task for which I have prepared you, the true nature of which you have quested for so long. Do it for me. For now I am tired, and I must sleep and prepare myself in the Silence for my own last task, which is for allmole, now and forever. Pray for me now, Tryfan. Pray for me.'

Then as Tryfan went forward to reach Boswell by the Stone, he faded back into the light and was gone. Then there was Silence and Tryfan saw and heard no more, but the sound allmole had heard the first time the great star showed, which seemed like the distant cry of a pup across the sky.

Chapter Forty-Six

The exciting, warming, reviving changes of spring came close on the heels of the second showing of what moles now openly called the Stone Mole's star. They began with that moment of year all moles love, when winter's snow begins to thaw and the first flowers show.

In Duncton, Tryfan and Spindle knew it when the old hollow tree above the centre of the Marsh End Defence began to drip glistening drops deep down into their tunnels.

Then the worms stirred and, almost imperceptibly, the earth became alive. Tryfan's work became more desultory and sporadic as he touched up texts he desired now to finish, while Spindle, who had rarely left the tunnels in all the time they had been there, found himself fretful at his work and impatient.

'Well, I'm off!' he said impulsively, fed up with scribing, fed up with the tunnels and fed up with Tryfan. So he went forth with Hay to try out the spring sun.

The ground was getting warm and the snow was nearly all gone. But here and there on the surface old grey ice, as tired of the winter it seemed as the moles themselves, lay thick and shiny wet in the north-facing roots and boles of trees where the sun did not reach.

But to the east of the Marsh End, where the trees thin out and the ground runs out over wetlands towards the roaring owl way and the distant river Thames, there were welcoming clusters of snowdrops and yellow aconite and beyond them, where the ground got wetter, the first sharp shoots of yellow flag.

'This is something Tryfan should see, if I can get him this far,' said Spindle cheerfully. 'I'll go back and fetch him.'

Hay made to go with him but Spindle said he went too fast for a mole like him, and he preferred to go back for his friend alone, and take his time doing it.

'Well,' said Hay slowly, 'I don't want you to be disturbed.'

'Disturbed? Attacked you mean?'

'There's precious little attack left in Duncton now. No, disturbed. When moles know you and Tryfan are about once more there'll be many come to see you. They've heard of you, and many are proud to know you're here. I'm warning you, there's many will come.'

Barely believing him, Spindle said, 'Leave me all the same, Hay. I'm sure I can cope!'

Hay nodded and left him, and Spindle stared out over the marshy ground and shivered a little. The buds were still tight on most of the trees but the alders' yellow catkins bristled in the breeze.

Spindle went slowly, the wood seeming strange and a little alien to him. He was a mole of facts and texts and he preferred the chalky heights of Uffington and the stone-filled vales of Seven Barrows. While in Duncton it was to the high, more ancient tunnels that his natural inclination went. But that, but, b –

He stopped, a sharp pain across his chest, utterly unable to move. The pain was constricting and frightened him.

'I – Tryfan – I –' And he tried to speak, but could not. Instead he crouched near a root, the pain intensifying and stronger than the previous attacks he had had, none of which he had ever mentioned to Tryfan. He felt weak and old and his left paw ached.

The pain eased and he stumbled forward to find a spot where the sun came down, south facing and light. Another attack came and he stopped again where he was, near a rotten old branch, long fallen.

'But I have much to do,' he said, and rather irritably, as if to admit to himself that he felt he had little time and it wouldn't be fair if the Stone came and took him here and now without real warning at all.

879

'Want to know things,' he mumbled to himself. 'Want to know the end, want to scribe the end, want to know Tryfan's . . . want to know the Stone Mole came, want to see Bailey again . . .' Another pain came, worse than all the rest, and he gasped with it and fell a little to one side.

Across the sky between the budded trees above, two mallard flew, hard and fast. The sky darkened and he felt his mouth whispering as the pains engulfed him.

Then the pain eased and he felt tired and not sure where he was. He tried a paw and then another and found he was alive, just tired. Very. No pain now. He looked about him. East Marsh End. He very slowly retraced his steps and made his way back through the morning to the tunnels where he and Tryfan had hidden so long.

Such strange thoughts he was thinking, some peaceful, some urgent. That he must secure the texts they had made, seal them up against discovery, for their time had not yet come. He must get Tryfan to some kindly mole who would watch over him, for his paws were weak and always would be, and delving was hard for him now, and worm-finding too. Tryfan had once been tidy and thorough but he had grown careless and grubby, and needed another nearby to help. Tryfan did not talk much these days, but he did need company. Hay? Perhaps. Borage and Heather more like. Goodly moles they were (as Tryfan would put it). Yes.

'Spindle? You've been gone a long time!' Tryfan called to him as soon as he got back.

'I have,' said Spindle.

'Well I had thought I might go out myself but I decided to wait for you and the best of the day is gone now.' Tryfan sounded annoyed.

'There are flowers out, Tryfan, over on the Eastside and a lot to see.'

'Well, let's go and see them then!'

'Later,' said Spindle, 'I feel tired.'

Tryfan stared at him, a frown on his face, and saying nothing more stayed close by Spindle while he slept.

'Are you all right?' he asked when he awoke, and several times after that, and Spindle replied that he was, yes, just tired after the long winter, so very tired.

It was a day or two more before the two moles ventured out together. The warm weather had continued and the ground was pleasantly astir.

They went slowly at first, snouting down the odd tunnel or two, and though they saw nomole, they could sense mole about: quiet mole, wondering mole, mole uncertain and unsure, as if the winter had been so long that the first touches of true spring could not yet be believed.

'Yet it's quiet, Spindle, quieter than in my day when these tunnels would have been scurrying with pups or preparation for them. None of that now, nor ever will be again perhaps.'

A mole, thin and worried, popped her head around a corner and stared at them for a while.

Tryfan inclined his head in a friendly way, but the mole just stared and said nothing, and then came a pawstep closer.

'Hello!' said Tryfan.

The mole dashed away. But she was soon back, with two more, staring as well, and though both Spindle and Tryfan tried to get them to talk they would not.

They were a sorry, unkempt looking bunch, all middle aged, all bearing signs of incipient illness and rough treatment.

'Where shall we go?' whispered Spindle, who was not one who much enjoyed an audience.

'Why, where should a Duncton mole go in spring?' said Tryfan. And though he did not notice it, for his sight was poor and restricted, Spindle did: those watching them leaned nearer to catch every word Tryfan said.

'In spring,' said Tryfan cheerily, 'a mole of these parts may go to one of two places: to the distant Stone to give thanks that winter's over, or to Barrow Vale to acknowledge that he or she is of a community of moles, and that is a place where they may meet without fear or favour.'

The three moles listening had been joined by another and all hung on Tryfan's words, and when he paused or finished what he was saying, they turned to each other and whispered, ' "Barrow Vale" he said,' and ' "The Stone", would you believe? That's where he's off to!' And some – and now yet another had joined them – seemed deaf or short of sight, and peered and nudged others to say what was apaw and what had been said.

'To Barrow Vale he be going, aye and that other one too! You know who they are, eh? That's *Tryfan*, the one with the scars, and the gawky one is Spindle. . . .'

Tryfan, seeming not to notice the interest he was causing as he sniffed and snouted at the tunnels, nodded again to one or two of the moles, and set off along the tunnel with the confidence of one who knows his way.

Spindle followed, and wherever they went moles seemed to be gathering and watching them, some quite out of breath with running, their eyes wide, most afraid to speak.

But a few cried out greetings from the safety of their groups: 'Pleased to see you!' and , 'Watch your paws up that bit, it's muddy,' and 'Good day, Sir!' All of which Tryfan greeted with a smile or a nod as he went slowly, limping on his right paw a little.

He moved with the grace of a mole who, though aware of others near, yet makes his own way and is unconcerned and unafraid of others or of life. There was about him the gravity of a mole who has travelled and suffered, and he did not hesitate to pause and look at mole cast down or linger near one too weak to raise her snout.

These he saw, and others too, others more belligerent. Oh yes, they came that day, they had heard that Tryfan had come out. Up they hurried, along they came, around the corners they peered, yet Tryfan went on his way, with Spindle at his side or just behind, stopping once when a couple of large, distorted males gibbered and grinned and threatened not to let him by, crouching down when another shouted some obscenity from out of the wildness of his maddened mind.

As they went, a few grew bolder and dared come closer to him, whispering his name, glancing at each other with pleasure and a little awe that he had seen them, or smiled at them. A few blind moles seemed confused but others whispered to them saying, 'It's Tryfan himself, come out of his Silence and he's going to Barrow Vale like they said they did in the old days before . . . before . . . *before*! You follow me and you'll get there. Yes, he's just ahead, come on!'

Until there were so many moles behind, in side tunnels and ahead, and such general bustle and excitement that Tryfan led the way to the surface, and for the final part of their journey trod his way among the leaf mould of the autumn where the green shoots of Spring had started.

Sometimes he paused, still barely conscious, it seemed, of the many about him, and he stared up at the budding trees and over at the clusters of aconite among the surface roots.

'See,' he told Spindle, 'spring always comes in the end, and I do believe it has come here at last. Yet look, see that burnt tree? That was from the fire that caused this part of the system to be deserted, though before my time.'

'He says that these trees were marked by fire before his time . . .' shouted some moles to their aged ailing friends, as the chatter increased about the two moles and others said, 'Sh! We want to hear him speak!'

Then Tryfan paused, and many paused with him, and, looking ahead among the trees to where there was a dip in the ground and an open space surrounded by older trees, he said, 'Look, Spindle! Barrow Vale!'

Not a single mole there but did not stop quite still when he said that, and stared ahead where he stared, at that circle of trees which defines what, for so many decades, had been the true heart of the system. All stayed still as Tryfan went forward from them, his hurt paws a little clumsy, his form heavy now and his fur rough and in places grubby.

Forward to the very edge of Barrow Vale, to stare up at

the trees about him, where no leaves yet showed but much life seemed certain. Then to look across that secret place and see the shoots of dog's mercury rising, and all over the green shiny leaves that soon, when April came, would open out to frame the bluebells they still hid.

Nomole spoke, all were hushed, all seemed to understand the meaning of that moment for Tryfan.

'A mole forgets,' he said quietly, 'how beautiful his home system can be. Here to this place, when I was young, my mother brought me and she told me of the system that she loved. Here my father led me, and showed me which entrance was his favourite. Here we ventured as siblings from the Ancient System, whispering because the place was so deserted, peering down tunnels where we should not be.

'Here too,' he continued, signalling to Spindle to join him, 'a mole I learned to trust, and respect and love, this mole here, first spoke his love for Thyme, and here mated. A mole I call as good a friend as anymole will ever have.' There was a sigh among the many there, and that sense of trust and love that seemed a palpable thing between Tryfan and Spindle was among them all.

Then, as if reluctant to tread on memory, yet purposefully, like a mole who knows he must make his way, Tryfan of Duncton, Spindle at his side, passed through the circle of trees about Barrow Vale, stopped in its centre and slowly turned full circle to take in the beauty of the place.

Then softly, quietly, and looking about them as if there was a magic in the air they must not disturb, the following moles joined them.

'Speak to us, Tryfan!' several shouted out. 'Tell us of the past here, and what will happen to us.'

But Tryfan said only that he would not, and preferred to go among them, and touch them, and ask that they did the same this spring day, that they felt the ground beneath them and knew they were as one. Which they did, talking quietly among themselves as Tryfan spoke to each in turn, and met for the first time those old, despairing moles who had been his unseen companions through the long mole-months of winter.

Heather was there, and Borage; Hay and Teasel, and many others.

'Will we go to the Stone?' asked several.

'Aye, we've never been there.'

'Westsiders won't have that!' warned a mole.

'They'll talon you if you try!' predicted another.

Even as they talked they saw that the Westsiders, warned of what was happening, had come in force and had taken stance on the far side of Barrow Vale. A grim silence fell.

Although there were fewer of them than those who had gathered about Tryfan, they looked a good deal stronger mole for mole. It was plain that many were grikes, presumably the survivors among those guardmoles who had first come to Duncton and been under Eldrene Beake.

Although many of those in Barrow Vale were plainly intimidated, and backed away, or disappeared down tunnels, others took stance and stayed their ground, calling out threats on the one paw and whispering to Tryfan and Spindle on the other that they would cover them until they escaped.

But Tryfan would have none of it, and nor would he allow any but Spindle to accompany him as he disengaged himself from those who had been with him and slowly approached the front line of Westsiders.

'We are here in peace,' he said clearly, 'and invite you to join us.'

'Invite us, does he?' said one.

'Who does he think he is. Invites us!' jeered another.

'Talon the bastard!' said a third.

Tryfan moved nearer and took a bold stance.

'Which is your leader?' he said. His voice betrayed no nervousness at all, and at his side Spindle crouched firm.

'What's it to you, mate?'

'I would talk with him.'

'Oh, would you now?' said a large mole near Tryfan who seemed beside himself with rage. 'What about? This?' With that he pushed forward and taloned Tryfan in the face, a blow that caused a terrible gasp and sigh among all those who had followed Tryfan to Barrow Vale, and which made Spindle come quickly forward to attack the mole, which he might have done had not Tryfan stopped him.

'There has been enough bloodshed in moledom these past years, we have no need of it here,' he said, wiping a run of blood from his face fur.

He moved forward again, staring hard at the mole who had struck him, and said with authority, 'Your leader, mole?'

'He'll come when he wants to, mate, and meanwhile you bloody back off or you'll get more talon-thrusts like that last one.'

Tryfan shook his head and then, as the moles behind him began to call out aggressively and move nearer, and the Westsiders to rear their talons and get ready for a fight, Tryfan astonished everymole there by turning his back on the grikes. Then, facing the moles who supported him, as the Westsiders looked on and felt foolish, Tryfan said, 'I have seen enough fighting in my time never to want to see more, or to have moles raise their talons on my account. I ask that not one of you, not a single one, comes forward to protect me now, whatever may happen. My protection is my faith in the Stone. These moles that threaten me have suffered as we all have. Their anger is ours. Is there anymole among you would raise his talons if they strike me? – for if there is I would rather he strike me than hurt another.'

So strongly did he speak that there was not a single mole in Barrow Vale who did not lower his talons and crouch down peacefully, and the only sound they made were mutterings and whisperings to the Stone.

Tryfan ordered Spindle to join them, which he did most reluctantly, and then he turned back to face the Westsiders.

'Come,' he said, 'take me to your leader.'

'We'll take you to our frigging leader, chum!' said one of the grike Westsiders aggressively, buffeting and taloning Tryfan forward among them. With each buffet and hit there was a groan from the moles in Barrow Vale, and a few started to rear up in anger, but Spindle's stance calmed them, and none came forward.

Then they saw Tryfan taken, and shoved down an entrance into the Westside. As he went, many told the ailing ones what was happening and a single female voice, cracked and old, broke into a chanting song. Old it was, and of the Stone, and gradually others joined in and its rhythmic sound followed Tryfan down as a kind of comfort into the Westside tunnels.

There are several accounts of what happened that day in the Westside, and most tell of how Tryfan subdued the Westsiders and by the power of his personality alone converted them to the Stone. But sensible moles seek a more realistic version than that, and it does exist as it was recorded not by Spindle but by a mole Tryfan had perhaps forgotten, but who had reason to be grateful to him, and who was there in those Westside tunnels that day, though not involved in the initial attack on Tryfan.

There was no leader, or at least no single mole in charge. Anarchy was the Westside way by then, and it had been a mob of moles coming out on a spring day to find trouble, just as the Marsh End moles had come in a group to find comfort and peace.

They took Tryfan down, harried him along as once he had been harried in Buckland, and in a communal chamber began to berate him and ask him questions.

Some guessed already that he was Tryfan, but others sought confirmation of it from his own mouth. And when he gave it, their mood turned even uglier and rage was in their eyes, and bitterness in their talons.

'You're a bastard, Tryfan, and you're going to regret you ever came back!'

'Tryfan is he, this scarred remnant? *The* Tryfan?'

'Your moles killed my mate when we came to Duncton,' said another, coming forward and hitting him several times.

But Tryfan struck not a single blow in reply, which seemed to enrage them more, and there went up a cry, 'Snout him! Take him up to the Stone and snout him! Snout the bastard!' But even then, it is reliably said, Tryfan did not seek to fight or hurt another mole.

He was dragged up the slopes he had known so well as a pup, though never in his grimmest nightmares could he have imagined that this painful, brutal, progress to punishment would have been the way he came back to the Stone he most loved.

As he went, others in those tunnels heard the commotion and came to see what was happening, and a dreadful parody of Tryfan's earlier progress to Barrow Vale now occurred as mole after mole joined the rabble chase, and he was pushed and shoved, up those beloved communal tunnels and then out on to the surface until he was dragged into the circle of trees about Duncton's Stone.

There, long, long before, had his own father faced the talons of Rune and Mandrake's henchmoles. There had he first met Boswell. There, in the shadow of that great Stone, had he and Boswell said farewell to Comfrey and set off for Uffington.

Now he lay before the Stone, and pain was on him once more. But they say that from the moment those grike Westsiders got him there they themselves grew nervous, each one holding back from hurting him more, yet all shouting for the snouting of him, and for his blood.

They say that Tryfan turned from them and faced the Stone, and began to speak to it. Then a hush came and they heard his words.

'I was never worthy,' he whispered, certain of his coming death, 'yet I did the best I could. Let Spindle be safe. Let the others go free. Let these moles be forgiven for I understand their anger. Let nomole be hurt this day in

888

consequence of my own suffering.' Then he added what nomole heard: 'Boswell, I have failed you.'

There was silence about the circle of trees and he turned to face his murderers and stared upwards to see once more the sinewy grey-greens of the high rising branches of the beech trees there, whose buds were pointed, and whose leaves would soon be free. Sun caught them, spring was with them there, and he felt then a pity for mole and he did not want to die.

He looked at the circle of angry faces and saw the malevolence, which seemed continually to grow as others who had heard what was happening had come running to see him die. He looked slowly round that circle, whose collective voice muttered and whispered his death to come saying, 'Snout him! Snout him!' and he knew then how that nameless mole in Buckland must have felt as he was marked to death by the grikes at the order of Eldrene Fescue.

He knew, and he remembered what he had done, and how the Stone had showed him how to touch that mole that he knew he was not alone.

Then Tryfan spoke out to that mob as they came closer for the kill saying, 'Is there not one among you who can show pity on a mole before he dies, that he knows he is not alone? Of the Word or of the Stone, moles are but moles in the end. Is there not one?'

Then as the moles all about began to laugh and jeer at this last hopeless call, a voice spoke out among them and said, 'Aye, there's one, there's one will take stance by you, Tryfan of Duncton. One will see you're not alone.'

Then from out of the mob's ranks broke a mole, weak looking and frail, a mole who suffered murrain. He came slowly forward, oblivious, it seemed, of his own weakness against the mob's group strength, unafraid of the talons that were rearing up, unconcerned but with the mole he came forward to touch and give comfort to.

Tryfan saw him as a dream, and knew him not. Male, thin, broken, sore-ridden, not a mole he could remember.

Yet such was the mole's quiet courage, such his resolution, that the mob fell back a little, and even more so when the mole took stance in front of Tryfan as if to protect him and turned to face them.

'Why 'tis Thrift!' cried one.

'You're one of us, mate, stop acting daft!'

'Aye,' said Thrift, 'I'm one of you and of the Word. But before that I'm mole, and never would I sleep easy to see this mole cut down. There's others here saw what this mole did when first we came to Duncton Wood.

'Others here saw him save my life and risk his own in doing it. Others here know well enough what he did for me that day. . . .'

Then, out of his suffering, Tryfan remembered a mole he had saved, with Smithills in the fighting, northeast of the cross-under. Saved to tell Henbane that if she wished to find the Duncton Moles she must find Silence. This mole? Time and disease changed the look of moles, but perhaps it did not change their hearts.

'There's not a mole here could have stood alone against Tryfan of Duncton in his day, and I'll warrant the scars you see across his face were made not by a single mole in fair fight but by a rabble such as you.'

'By the sideem,' said Tryfan in a low voice.

'You hear that, mob?' cried out Thrift. 'These scars are sideem scars and yet he survived. So, those of you who remember what he did for me who wish to kill him now come forward and kill me first!'

As he said this Tryfan came forward and mole of the Word and mole of the Stone crouched side by side. But nomole came forward, and the mob was outfaced. Some backed away, some came forward and touched Thrift as a mark of respect, some seemed to pretend they were not even there, but most quietly left and afterwards barely remembered anything of that brave and dreadful scene but the Stone that rose up behind the two moles and caught the sky's spring light in its depths.

Then Thrift said, 'Mole, that's twice I've met you, and

twice I've stared death in the face in your presence. You make a mole nervous!'

Tryfan smiled.

'Then may our third meeting be more auspicious than these first two, Thrift. And I have a feeling it will be.'

'It'll have to be quick for I've not long to go,' replied Thrift bravely. Tryfan saw that it was so, for Thrift's murrain was badly advanced though his sight was still good.

Then the two moles made their way back down the slopes and were joined by the Marshenders led by Spindle.

'Well, Spindle, you missed the fun for once,' said Tryfan lightly, 'That was one way to welcome the spring!' And others laughed when they heard it, and passed it on, and that day the moles of Duncton Wood knew they had a brave mole in their midst and one they could trust; one who faced all moles equally and meant no harm to any of them.

'Spindle, tell the moles of the Marsh End to take their courage in their paws and mix with the Westsiders – now while moles are confused and uncertain. Now is the time before moles retreat back behind the barriers they made. Tell them! It is the final preparation. It is! The last thing we must do. Tell them, and insist on it.'

Which, with Hay's help, Spindle did, and from that day the moles of Duncton started the slow communal healing that was needed before they might become one again.

But quite what Tryfan meant by the words 'final preparation' Spindle did not at that moment guess, and nor in the days ahead would Tryfan explain. As spring advanced mole met mole at Barrow Vale, and mole began to wander free again, even up to the Stone itself.

But though in this way fear left the system, despair was left behind. Despair at the pointlessness and great sadness of a spring for moles without pups in a world busy with every other creature's young. Despair and a kind of madness as females wandered searching for what their bodies could not find. For that Tryfan knew no remedy except to pray, and not all moles were so minded.

While to those who, like Hay or Teasel or ailing Thrift, and many others who cared to ask, Tryfan could only say that somewhere in moledom soon the Stone Mole would make himself known, and then a Silence that would help each system face its troubles would be found.

Yet finally, perhaps, it was too much to hope that moles would have the same faith Tryfan had, or the same long patience.

As the days of April lengthened and bluebells replaced the aconite in swathes across the wood, and those beech buds Tryfan thought he had seen for the last time opened into spring-green leaf, the first flush of meeting between moles who had long been isolated died away. The system remained gloomy and abnormal. Moles seemed irritated and sometimes tempers flared.

The atmosphere was not helped by the fact that down by the cross-under the grikes seemed to be suddenly more active and watchful. Those moles who made a habit of going that way to see what was apaw, as Hay sometimes did, reported many more moles there and an influx of youngish ascetic ones: sideem.

Few moles had come into the system in the past molemonths and now the only ones that did were diseased females, no males at all. Those outcasts who tried to talk to the grikes got short shrift and none knew what was happening.

But occasionally a female came in who was articulate and from one of them they learnt that Duncton was being much watched by sideem who had come to prevent the arrival of the Stone Mole.

'Where is he? What his identity?' Tryfan and others naturally asked.

But the female knew not, only that the sideem seemed to be expecting him and that it would be impossible for him to pass through their lines without discovery.

So now excitement replaced the gloom, and foreboding the hope, and Duncton was a place of gossip and doubt, as well as the home of many moles too ill or too disconsolate with life itself to care. . . .

* * * * * * *

It was when Skint and Smithills reached Rollright that the rumours of change they had picked up so frequently along the way came into focus.

They contacted Holm there and heard from him, and then from Rampion herself, of Tryfan's passage through. Skint felt, as Holm had, a mixture of relief and concern, and the information only increased his desire to reach Duncton Wood where, he was now sure, Tryfan would be.

But the grikes were heavy on the ground, and Holm had guessed the reason why. Ever since the second showing of the Stone Mole's star, orders seem to have gone out to search for a leader among the followers. Certainly after several moleyears of a more relaxed regime, eldrenes in every system Skint and Smithills had come across were putting pressure on known followers, and ensuring that all moles abided by the Word.

At Rollright, and no doubt other similarly important systems, these pressures were especially severe, and while followers were being watched as if in hope of finding the Stone Mole, there was no violence or snoutings because, rumour had it, the Siabod rising had taken hold, grike reinforcements had been sent and violence of the old kind might provoke a reaction among followers which would be hard to contain.

It was in this atmosphere of doubt and excitement that Skint and Smithills now travelled on. Their hope was to find a way into the system other than by the cross-under which, they had no doubt, was heavily guarded.

The nearer they got the stranger their passage became. There were other moles about, mostly followers too, for many moles had taken it into their heads to travel eastward after the appearance of the Stone Mole's star and now found themselves converging on Duncton Wood.

Perhaps the grikes had a warning this might happen,

perhaps Wyre was as clever and far-sighted as Henbane must have hoped. However it was, it was he who made sure that there was a strong presence of grikes about Duncton, something he evidently considered as important as retaking Siabod, though he could not have had much to do with the fact that it was augmented by sideem, young moles who rarely smiled and who took ascendancy over the guardmoles.

There was no violence, nor any killing, for the sideem's solution to the flocking of moles who suddenly claimed they wished to be outcast into Duncton was to insist that all males move on. After all, they argued, any one of them might be the Stone Mole.

It was in this busily suspicious atmosphere that Skint and Smithills arrived at the cross-under.

'You're to get out of this vicinity fast, you two,' a harassed guardmole soon told them after they had been examined by the sideem.

'But we're old and can't hurt a flea,' said Skint, 'and we have come a long way to be outcast in the one system where there is freedom. That was promised by Henbane herself!'

'The only moles allowed through are females and they've got to be so far gone they're a danger to others,' said the guardmole wearily, for he had said the same too many times before. 'You ought to be grateful we're not letting you in that place.'

'But – '

'Look, mate, if you expect to find this bloody Stone Mole, forget it. You can see for yourself the sideem will take him if he so much as shows his snout round here.'

'They know what he looks like, do they?' asked Skint.

'Everyone's got a different story but I've heard he's as tough a male as they come, like that Tryfan used to be.'

'*He's* dead, isn't he?' asked Skint, testing.

'Now get along, get along!' said the guardmole turning from them to a female in the throng, 'And what's your name, mole, and where are you from?'

As Skint turned away with Smithills to ponder their next move he heard only her voice, and that almost unconsciously.

'Myn nam ys Feverfew. I wyl to Duncton go. . . .'

Her accent and idiom were strange, and most beautiful, and so he turned back to look at her and saw . . . what? A female, scalpskinned, travel-stained, obviously weary, and . . . something more he could not place. *He* felt strange, staring like that to see something he felt was there but could not see. Most strange.

Then a guardmole came and pushed them further off and they had no chance of talking to her. Instead they watched as the female began talking to the first guard-mole. Then a sideem came over and with obvious disgust curtly questioned her. With barely a nod he let her pass by and slowly, and obviously very tired, she approached the cross-under.

But what was it about her that made a mole look? Why did a hush momentarily fall on moles as she passed them by, moles who looked twice as Skint had done, and seemed puzzled? Was she not, but for the dialect of which Skint had caught only a snatch, just another diseased outcast?

Even the sideem who had let her through so quickly, broke off from the next interview he was conducting and looked round distractedly to where the female had gone and took a few steps in that direction.

At which Skint found himself urging her on, as if some inner voice told him that of all moles there she must get through. There was something about her, something that made a mole pause. Something. . . .

'What is it, Skint?' asked Smithills, who wanted to go back along the roaring owl way and find another route into Duncton Wood since they were not going to get in at the cross-under and the obvious, though dangerous, routes over the roaring owl way nearby seemed well guarded.

'Don't you see something about her as well?' said Skint lowering his voice, for there were a good many moles nearby.

'She's a female, she's scalpskinned, and . . .' said Smithills watching her as she reached the cross-under guards.

'And?' said Skint.

'I don't know. . . .'

'That sideem evidently thinks so too, he's going to go back to stop her now.'

Skint suddenly turned to Smithills urgently

'Hit me, Smithills!' he said. 'Go on, hit me.'

Smithills looked at his old friend in blank amazement.

'Make a diversion! Hit me!'

But before Smithills could make out what Skint meant a mole near them stepped forward and lunged noisily at Skint.

At which Smithills, so far slow in his reactions, came to the rescue of Skint and, turning on the mole with a mighty roar, talon-thrust him out of the way.

'Coward!' shouted the mole picking himself up and thrusting forward again. 'Hitting this geriatric mole smaller than yourself!'

'Me?' shouted Smithills in rage. '*You* hit him!'

'A liar as well!' cried the mole.

'I may be old but I'm not geriatric!' yelled out Skint suddenly, lunging viciously at Smithills.

'By the Stone I'll have you both now,' said the normally genial Smithills, almost apoplectic with rage.

Below them, the sideem who had been heading for Feverfew heard the rumpus and turned to look. He and a guardmole came running. Behind them, at the cross-under, Feverfew looked back briefly at the fuss, and then turned and hurried out of sight and beyond recall into the system of Duncton Wood.

Safe, thought Skint, even as Smithills continued the fight. She's safe, but from what? Skint did not know.

It was several minutes more before the sideem and guardmole sorted out the fuss, and sent Skint, Smithills and the third mole on their way. Smithills continued to grumble, but as soon as they were out of earshot the stranger said, 'Did she get past the last guardmole all right?'

'She did, mole,' said Skint, 'and now you had better explain what is going on.'

'I thought she wouldn't get through.'

'She's a diseased female', said Skint. 'They seem to think that anymole else might be the Stone Mole. Now, why would you think she'd not get through?'

'You didn't think her strange?'

'I thought her very strange. There was something about her that made a mole look at her and want her to get on. There was . . . Well, mole, what was it? You obviously know. Now what's your name, and what's your story?'

The mole grinned and said, 'I don't know much but I know my name. I heard you say yours and recognised them. I'm Bailey.'

'Stone me!' said Smithills.

'But Mayweed told us you were fat!'

'I lost weight,' said Bailey. Skint and Smithills looked at him with respect, and saw and liked his grin and the natural innocence and warmth of his eyes.

'There's much to discuss.'

'There may be,' said Bailey with resolution, 'but what I want to do is get into Duncton Wood. I promised I'd watch over her. I – '

'Mole, we've talking to do,' said Skint taking control as he did in the old days. 'You can come with us and tell us what you know of Boswell, of the Stone Mole and everything else. But you can start with that female. What mole was she and what was it about her made moles stare but not know why? Because there's *something* special about her, or I haven't learnt anything in my long and mainly useless life.'

'Her name is Feverfew and she is of the Wen. But more than that,' added Bailey with wonder in his voice, 'she is of the Stone. As for what is strange about her, well . . . nothing much, but these days moles don't expect to see scalpskinned females who are with pup.'

With pup! *With pup!* He looked over at where the sideem and guardmoles were stopping and talking to other moles who seemed, like them, to have converged on Duncton as if they expected something but knew not what.

'She's with pup?' repeated Smithills.

'I think the pup she bears is one allmole has waited for,' said Bailey.

'The Stone Mole!' exclaimed Skint in an awed voice, and staring in wonder towards the way Feverfew had gone.

'Yes,' said Bailey softly, 'I think that's how the Stone Mole is to come.'

'Then we must find a way in to Duncton Wood,' said Skint with purpose and resolution, 'for Smithills here and I have not travelled so far to lurk on the outside when wonders happen. Eh, Smithills?'

'Right, Skint!'

'Nor I,' said Bailey, following them.

Chapter Forty-Seven

All that day poor Spindle had been unsettled, going this way and that in the tunnels, fretful, returning again and again to where the texts they had made were ranged, touching them, thinking he had so much to do, but doing nothing.

Meanwhile Tryfan had decided to work at something he had been putting off, which was to scribe the last few folios of his book on Boswell's teachings, *The Way of Silence*, but he found it hard and his mind was unsettled. Nor was he helped by the restlessness of Spindle who went about and snouted here and there, and sighed, and seemed upset.

But though Tryfan tried to talk to him, his friend would not say much, only that he felt tired, and perhaps there were things he had left undone.

'You have time, Spindle, time for all of that. . . .'

But Spindle shook his head and his eyes wandered and he said, 'I would like to see if those texts we hid up in the Ancient System are all right. You remember where they are, Tryfan?'

'You and Mayweed hid them, you never told me where. Didn't trust me I expect!'

'No, no', said Spindle, 'you had no time, and now. . . .'

'I'll come up with you to find them,' said Tryfan.

'Today? Now?' said Spindle, glad to have something to do.

Tryfan laughed.

'There's time, Spindle! Tomorrow. Work to finish here.'

'I'll go with Hay,' said Spindle, disappointed. 'He doesn't have to come all the way, for only you should know where the texts are, and then other moles when we can trust them.'

'Well, I will come, but tomorrow.'

'Yes, yes,' said Spindle, leaving. 'I'll find Hay.'

But Hay was not to be found, or at least that is what moles said afterwards, for more than one saw Spindle going by, heading southwards through the Eastside, and alone.

'Looked as if he knew where he was going, *hurrying* he was,' said one. 'I called out to him but he didn't seem to hear me.'

Spindle did go alone, taking the surface routes, too impatient to seek Hay out and perhaps happier to make that particular journey by himself. The less moles knew about such things as hidden texts the better. He had left clues enough in the other caches he had made for moles to trace the other places where texts were hidden. Some of them would survive, and the story of those times be known.

'Yes, yes,' said Spindle, hurrying along, scarcely looking at where he trod, breathless, his chest beginning to hurt again. The pains suddenly sharp.

'I must . . . I will . . .' he muttered to himself, trying to ignore his pains. 'Please help me, Stone, I must. . . .'

Somemole later reported seeing Spindle alone and still, as if he was resting, but when he went over to him Spindle looked around as if he did not see him and then set off again. They saw him break out of the Eastside trees and on to the Pastures to the south east, below which the roaring owl way goes.

That mole followed him, worried for him, and found him staring at the distant way whose roars were muffled and slow and whose gazes, being day, were only occasional.

'Spindle, what are you doing here?'

'Waiting!' he replied. Then he said, 'See? They're just like us.'

'Who are, Spindle?'

'Don't know,' said Spindle vaguely. 'Not sure. Moles'll find out one day.'

Then, as Spindle started off again, up towards the ancient part of Duncton Wood, the mole cried out cheerfully after him, 'You won't find out up there, not about roaring owls!'

Spindle did not immediately look back, but as the mole went his own way, towards the Eastside, Spindle called back to him saying. 'Mole, go to Tryfan, tell him he must go to the Stone. I don't think I can go back all that way myself to tell him, so you do it. Hay will know where to find him. Others must do things now.'

The mole nearly ran upslope to Spindle, for there was something strange about him that held a mole's attention, but the command in Spindle's voice was strong, and set that mole's paws going back to the Marsh End.

'I shall,' he said, 'I shall.' But yet he did look back once more and saw Spindle climbing, and he looked old and went slow now.

Each step was painful for Spindle, and sometimes his thin paws slipped in the grass, as he wearily heaved them up, breathless, the pains strong again. He was muttering to himself, 'I must scribe it, moles must know, I shall scribe it. . . .'

Above him, right across the sky, the promising light of an April afternoon shone, and its best parts were caught in the shining of the beech leaves which were coming out across the ancient part of the system.

A hundred thousand shimmers of light were in those young leaves and Spindle climbed towards them now in wonder, yet in pain. He wanted Tryfan near him, close by, for he had shared so much with him and wanted now to share the growing beauty he saw ahead.

For over the Ancient System that light shone brighter yet, and it was a welcome, an honouring, and hard though each step was, yet each brought him nearer and the more he seemed to see.

'I'll scribe it for allmole,' he whispered, 'so they know, so they care, 'I'll – '

'Spindle moule, cum softly, cum and yev me holp.'

901

Her voice was of the wood's light and it seemed as he heard it that all his life he had been coming towards this moment, and to help her. Then he went among the trees, and above him their branches rose in greys and greens, and the wood was hushed and beautiful. While before him waited Feverfew, and she was smiling but tired, very tired.

'Whar ys Tryfan?' she said gently. 'Yow sem so tired to cum aloon.'

'I sent for him to come to the Stone, Feverfew, and he will, he'll know he must. So I'll help you there now myself and be with you until he comes.'

'Cum,' she said, and he went to her and she took his paw and slowly, together, they went through the wood. And he told her of the light he had seen, and of knowing without knowing that he must come here, and that he wished he could scribe it down.

Then as the Stone came into view, rising among the trees, Spindle said, 'I wanted to see the Stone Mole, Feverfew, I wanted to see him. He is the end and the beginning. He'll be your pup, won't he?'

'He ys nere nu, Spindle moule, so nere,' she said breathing heavily, a paw to her side where her own pains were beginning to come. 'But yow shal see hym, for yow he luved as he luved alle moulen. Yow shal. Holp me.'

So then Spindle led her slowly and with great care to the very base of Duncton's great Stone and there he settled her.

'He's coming isn't he, Feverfew? He'll be here soon. I'll wait with you.'

'No moule, yow yav done as much as any moule and yt ys enough. Go nu, moule, lev me her for Tryfan myn luv to find me.'

'I wanted to see the Stone Mole, Feverfew, I wanted to scribe of him. I have scribed the rest, as best I could, all that happened.'

'Oon moule aloon cannot mak that,' she said softly.

'I wanted to tell of my coming here today, through the

902

Eastside, up the slopes, the light over the trees, wanted them to know. I felt pain, Feverfew, but he called me to come on, he. . . .'

'He caled yow to holpen me, Spindle moule, to brynng me for the laste. Yow *hav*, moule, nu rest, lat me be, I am moste safe hyre . . . go nu and see youre sonne Bailey for he ys cumyng. Telle hym wat alle moules sholde knawe, that he ys muche luved.'

Then Spindle understood something of the wonder that was coming and that his task was nearly done. He left Feverfew safe in the protection of the Stone and went back through the woods towards the east, staring beyond the great trees with wonder in his eyes, and then ahead the south eastern pastures lay.

There, on the edge of the wood and staring downslope towards the distant roaring owl way from where he sensed Bailey must be coming home at last, he crouched down low. He whispered his son's name, and that of Thyme, as above him, very slowly, the sky began to darken and from out of its deepest depth a star began to shine.

His talons fretted a little as if he wished to scribe, but then they were still. He whispered Tryfan's name and, with difficulty, turned to stare through the gathering dusk to the north where Tryfan must be.

Behind him the High Wood stilled and its trees filled with the light of the brightening star. He had been witness to so much, and now he knew he was witness to the light and the Silence that heralded at last the new beginning that was coming to Duncton, and to all of moledom.

Yet even then it was finally to his friend Tryfan that his mind turned.

'I would see him once more, as I would see my son,' he whispered aloud. 'Grant it Stone,' he prayed.

His paws felt cold, and his flanks as well, and where they were the light of that star began to shine.

* * * * * * *

Then, slowly, a sense of wonder crept as subtly as starlight across all Duncton Wood and to the tunnels where Tryfan

903

scribed restlessly, struggling with the final folio of the *Way of Silence*, a hurrying mole came.

'You must go to the Stone, Spindle says it! You must. . . .'

The mole told him how he had met Spindle, and what he had said, and that he had not had strength to come and get Tryfan himself so sent that mole.

Tryfan went to the surface and saw that the sky was light with a rising star, and dusk had come, and was deepening.

'I shall go to the Stone, now I shall go. Tell Hay, tell others, for surely this night he comes. Now tell me where you saw Spindle . . .' and as the mole did so, and described how Spindle seemed weak and troubled Tryfan became deathly still and he knew this was the ending and the beginning, and that in this hour he must find his friend and be with him, just as soon he would be with the one whose coming they had waited for so long.

So Tryfan departed to find Spindle as word went out that the Stone Mole was come, and to Duncton Wood, for the star shone a third time, and it was rising above their Stone. All sensed it, all snouted out onto the surface and knew it.

But fast went Tryfan, urgently, knowing in his heart that Spindle had fulfilled his task and that now his time was coming. As Tryfan's paws raced, so his mind did too . . .

Feverfew. Yes, yes. Now she would come, as Boswell had told him. He could sense her, a mole he now barely seemed to know. Yet he knew she was here, and had been with Spindle when he, Tryfan, might have been and had touched her as he would have done. Feverfew was of him and he of her, and that had already begun. And the Stone Mole too. . . .

So in wonder and dread for Spindle Tryfan ran, by routes he had learnt as a pup, seeming not to need to see, the wood lightening even as it grew dark, that light which the stars give when prophecies and tasks enter into their moment of fulfilment.

He wanted to go straight to the Stone, but his heart and his paws led him another way, across the High Wood, towards the east until he reached the wood's edge and there, by the starlight of that great night, he found Spindle.

His friend crouched still, leaning a little to one side as if to ease a pain he felt, and though his snout was low yet his eyes were open, and expectant.

He stirred as Tryfan arrived at his side, and even tried to get to his paws, but his old friend stilled him and settled at his side.

'Bailey's coming,' said Spindle, looking downslope towards where the gazes of the roaring owl ran. 'I can feel him coming back to me, but I have not strength to wait. I wanted to see him once again, not as he was at Whern but as Boswell would have taught him to be. I . . . will you tell him of me Tryfan?'

'May the Stone grant that you tell him yourself Spindle.'

'Will you?' said Spindle.

Tryfan looked with love at his friend and saw that he was weak, and that words of promise or false hope were not what he wanted nor what he, of all moles, deserved. The truth was Spindle's only way.

'What will you tell him?'

'I shall tell him that his father was a mole of great courage and great faith, and one whom all moles might have been proud to have at their side. I shall tell him that Spindle was a mole who loved one female alone, and was as true to her as he was to the Stone in all he did. I shall say that this mole was one whose paws, though thin and weaker than some, yet held on more strongly than any other mole I ever knew to two things of which others too easily let go – faith in the Stone and truth to other moles.

'But most of all I shall tell him that Spindle was a mole who gave others strength, and one who through the scribings he has left will give strength and knowledge to moles for generations yet to come.'

The light of the star rose brighter each moment, and it seemed to shine down on Spindle from almost directly above, and in it he seemed to see now more than Tryfan could, for his eyes were alight with joy and pleasure, as if he knew what was to be and that it was good.

'Do you remember when we first met at Uffington?' whispered Spindle.

Tryfan nodded.

'I remember your courage not your nervousness,' he said, 'and I remember Boswell saying that you were a mole of faith, I remember so much . . . so much that we have shared Spindle.'

Their flanks were touching and now they were paw to paw as well.

'I'm not nervous now Tryfan, but . . .'

'Yes Spindle?'

His voice was weakening and his flank was cold.

'I'm . . . I'm curious!' he said, and even at that moment Tryfan could have sworn that in his friend's eyes there was that look that ever there had been, of a mole who with intelligence and humour, purpose and delight, is curious about the world about him, as a pup is.

'Tryfan,' said Spindle after a pause, 'I have scribed as much as I could, set it down, stored it away. I have left clues for you to where the texts are and how moles may one day find them. And Mayweed knows many of the sites. I think . . . I think I never dared tell Mayweed I loved him, but I did. Nor Bailey. But I did. I . . . was not good with words that way Tryfan . . . even with Thyme I found that hard. Remember how you and Maundy made us go to Barrow Vale?'

Tryfan nodded.

'Tryfan . . . I wanted to say to you that I did not follow you as a duty or a task, though it *was* my task. I followed you . . . because I learned to love you. The Stone is in you and a Silence you cannot always see yourself. I . . . but now you must go to Feverfew. I left her at the Stone. Go . . .'

His pain seemed to return, and yet the light in his eyes suddenly brightened, and his gaze turned eastwards and then to the sky, and his eyes were full of wonder as he whispered, 'Look! Can you not see him coming Tryfan. Look!' And Spindle's eyes seemed like stars themselves as his paw slipped from Tryfan's and his body was still, and over the High Wood of Duncton the star of the Stone Mole shone yet brighter on the moles who came up the slopes to see it.

Then Tryfan, whispering a final avocation of love and the Stone's blessing, left his friend where he lay, and did as Spindle had finally bid him do which was to go to the Stone and be with Feverfew at last.

As he crossed the wood once more Tryfan saw other moles approaching, but many grew timid the nearer to the Stone they got, and many were in awe and much afraid.

'Tell them all to follow!' he shouted at a group who crouched hesitant, for the night was strange and awed a mole. 'Tell them to come to the Stone!' Then they looked at one another and knew it was Tryfan himself who told them, and that they must follow him.

The old, the blind, the slow, the ill, the diseased; unsure moles, frightened ones, despairing and forlorn, they all came, making their trek that night of nights, up towards the Stone. From the Marsh End, from the Eastside, from Barrow Vale and the Westside they came in wonder. They sensed this was a night that would always be, it was the beginning, and the light they saw and let into their hearts was more than a star that shone a single night and then went out. It would be a light lit forever in moles' hearts, endlessly lit, endlessly there and always waiting for each mole to find the courage to make the trek to find it.

So those moles went, and at their head was Tryfan, the first to the circle of trees, the first to see that star's pure light shining down from above upon Duncton's silent Stone.

There, at the base of the Stone, where good Spindle had led her, lay Feverfew and she called out for her love to

907

come near now. He who had encouraged others to come now hesitated, watching where she lay, afraid of the light by the Stone. 'Go to her mole,' an old female said gently, and so he went. Feverfew whispered of a silence that had been between them in the Wen, not one of the Stone but one of loss; she said that soon it would be filled with the coming of the Stone Mole.

She sighed and shifted, and felt pain, and sighed again.

'Tryfan,' she whispered.

'Yes, my love?'

'Owr taske is grete.'

'Not so great that the Stone does not trust us with it.'

'Yt ys hys sonne.'

'I know it,' said Tryfan.

'Myn luv, I am afeerd.'

'And I, Feverfew, but the Stone is near.'

'Of Boswell wyl I tell myn der, he is the Stane yn moledome furste cum, hys sonne the seconde her, that Silence wyl be laste and alwey . . . I am afeerd, myn luv.'

'And I.'

What words did those two then speak. None knows. What touches of comfort did they make? None knows. What prayers of welcome and invocations of joy did they whisper? None knows.

But where they were together by the Stone moles watched from the shadows of the circle of the trees. For none but those two dared enter into the full gaze of that light.

Yet at the very base of the Stone, to which Feverfew now moved with Tryfan at her side, was a kind of gentle shadow, a softness of the light, as when on a bright day the branches of beech tree spread out and shelter from the fullest light that place directly below. So the Stone seemed to shelter Feverfew now.

There in that dappled starlit place, beyond which the full light of the star beat down, Feverfew let out her first birthing cry. A cry not like that of an ordinary mole confined to some secret birth burrow in the dark, but one that came out strong, over the pupless system of Duncton, among the trees, about the starlit vales, as wide and great over Duncton as the night sky itself.

And it was answered!

By moledom's faithful it was answered.

Starting with those females who witnessed that first cry and who had longed for young themselves. They now took her cries as their pain, her love as the love they always had to give, her strength as theirs to give and more; and as that fabled birthing at Duncton's Stone began it seemed to cast its cries across the sky, and all of moledom stopped and heard; and knew the Stone Mole was near, so near at last.

★ ★ ★ ★ ★ ★ ★

Alder knew, up in the high reaches of Siabod once again; Wharfe and Harebell at their secret place in Beechenhill, and Squeezebelly watching over them; so many knew and heard the birthing across the sky beyond the star they saw.

Starling knew, where she turned to stare towards where Duncton lay, and Heath. So many knew, and many whose names in time we will know. Moles like Troedfach of Tyn-y-Bedw, who gazed at the strange arcing skies that night and knew to where his way was set. The sideem Lathe knew, as he stared bewildered at a sky whose light seemed thwarting to the greatest beauties Whern might have. Lorren knew, and Holm; and others born since Duncton's flight, whose heritage was a system whose tunnels they had yet to know: *they* knew. Their eyes lit up to know the Stone Mole came that night.

★ ★ ★ ★ ★ ★ ★

And Henbane. She knew. And her one remaining young.

Dark he was, of the seed of Tryfan but with the mutant nature of warped Rune. His name? Lucerne.

'What is it?' he asked when Henbane took him out of the High Sideem to see.

'It is your challenge, Lucerne my sweet. It is the light of your life! Look at it. It is for that light to darken you were made. It marks the coming of the Stone Mole.'

Lucerne looked at that same sky that moles like Lathe stared up at, but he was not awed.

'I like that I like it not,' he said.

'And I too, my love,' said Henbane. 'Now come, my dear . . .', for despite his age yet still she suckled him, for so can a mole be to deviant darkness bound. Then Lucerne turned and took her teat, but his eyes turned to the sky to stare at that star while he suckled Henbane's teat with dark joy in his heart.

* * * * * * *

Skint and the others knew even as they made their way up in to the system's Woods. They knew, and came. Earlier all three had gone along the edge of the roaring owl way, but though there were ways up they were all guarded. They might have killed a guardmole or two but somehow that evening killing was not in the air, and Skint was concerned that they got into Duncton unnoticed.

So stealthily they went, too stealthily perhaps, for in staring over at where the guardmoles were they stumbled straight into the path of grike. Hiding grike. Dangerous grike.

Smithills reared up in the gloom, and the grike reared up too, large and formidable.

'Whither are you bound?' he said, which was a strange thing for a grike to say. Too polite by half.

Skint came forward.

'We travel in peace, mole – ' But if he was about to say more he did not do so because the mole ahead gasped, dropped his talons and came forward with relief and delight.

'If it isn't Skint then I'm not Marram!'

'Praise be!' said Skint.

They quickly exchanged their news and circumstance, barely surprised anymore at the wonders of that night. Marram, like the others, was trying to get across the roaring owl way.

'Well, you look like a grike, you are a grike, so behave like one. Go and order those guardmoles back to the cross-under and we'll just slip up the embankment and none will be any the wiser,' said Skint.

And so it was. The guardmoles argued only briefly when they saw Marram's size and heard that he spoke with authority, and back towards the cross-under they went. Then Marram went straight up the embankment and Skint, Smithills and Bailey followed him, to the noise and roaring owl fumes. It took a long time before they reached a place where Skint sensed they could cross. Already the owl's gazes were on, and they knew they must not stare into them as they crossed the way or they would be struck and crushed to death. Nor must they let the fumes dizzy them.

'Run,' said Skint, 'don't stop.'

Which is what they did, two by two, over that fumey way and into its central part where rubbish was. Then on to the far side with the roaring owls thundering past from the other direction, and their gazes terrible.

Then down the far side and by a pipe over the culvert and then at last on to the south-eastern Pastures of Duncton Wood.

'Which way, Skint?' asked Marram.

But it was Bailey who led them now, up the slope towards the High Wood.

It was as they reached the very edge of the great beeches that mark the start of the Ancient System that Bailey stopped and saw a thin mole, dead. But his fur caught the light of the stars and his eyes were open as if he saw beyond them all.

'Why 'tis Spindle,' said big Smithills gently.

'Aye,' said Skint, looking at Bailey.

'I know this mole,' said Bailey. 'I saw him in Whern, but he talked to me once in Barrow Vale.'

Smithills and Skint stared and said nothing. They knew the story of Bailey's parenting.

Then Bailey turned to his companions and whispered as if he already knew the answer to what he asked, 'What mole was this Spindle? He was in Whern, he was at Tryfan's side.'

It was Smithills who spoke, his great face wet with tears.

'Why lad, 'tis your father. Did you not guess it might be so?'

As Bailey nodded, it was Marram who took a firm and comforting stance at his side as that mole, lost so long, who had suffered so much, began to cry.

But it was sturdy Skint who spoke for them all when Bailey's first tears were done.

'He looked as if he knew you were coming home, mole. Aye, and he looked as if he knew he would have been proud of you. He knew a good future was yet to come, and he would have guessed his Bailey, born of Thyme, would be worthy to be part of it. So leave him where he proudly lies, mole, and come with us, for there's one born this night who will lead us all to the Silence which Spindle of Seven Barrows has surely already found.'

Then all four turned towards the wood and were lost among the trees, and made their way to the Stone itself.

★ ★ ★ ★ ★ ★ ★

So the last moles, or almost the last, came near Duncton Stone that night, and as they did one final cry rose up over Duncton as Feverfew gave birth to the Stone Mole.

So tiny he was, mucky with birth as all pups are, but born in the Stone's shadow cast by the light of his own star. A pup for allmoles' joy. A pup to pay homage to. A pup born in a dark turbulent time to bring Silence and light.

Then as Feverfew encircled him with joy, and licked him, the moles who watched dared come closer. And as they did they heard that pup's first mewing cry go up and cross the sky.

Then with joy those pupless moles came to gaze on him, and sigh as his mother pushed him to her and he sucked. The old, the diseased, the unsure; all were allowed to see, all to share. All moledom was represented that night before the Stone where he was born. Even those of the

Word were there, and those with no belief. And some near death, like Thrift, who yet lived to see the Stone Mole born. And even those who could not see came near.

''Tis I, Tryfan, Teasel. Now show me where to look.'

'But you can see, Teasel. Your darkness is gone.'

The light of the star touched the flank of the Stone Mole, and seemed to shine on Teasel's face; and so she saw and knew a miracle.

'Why he's special, he is,' said Teasel with joy, and she passed on to let others take her place and see as she had done. This was the first healing the Stone Mole made.

Hay was there, and Heather, and so many more. A pup had been born to moles who felt they had nothing. That night was a beginning indeed.

Until, when the last had seen, Tryfan spoke to Feverfew and she nodded. She took the pup up and slowly carried him out of the circle and down into the tunnels to a burrow where Rebecca and Bracken had lived; where Tryfan himself was born.

There Feverfew encircled the Stone Mole and said, 'Leve us nu, wee ar wel, and welbiloved. Lev us to slep, myn der.'

Which Tryfan did, going back up to the surface, staring at the Stone, and feeling that strange wonder and fear such as a father might feel on a birthing night. Wonder at the life that has come, fear at the beginning and change the birth marks.

Then out of the darkness beyond the Stone more moles came, and their gait he knew, and their voices he had heard before. Smithills, then Bailey, then Marram and finally Skint, who all gathered about him.

Light shone upon the group of moles and though all had their sorrows all felt joy too.

'We shall celebrate as Spindle would have had us do.' said Tryfan, though his voice was a little sad.

Above them that star shone, and in the wood and down the slopes wondering moles went, joyful and glad.

'As I remember there's as good a communal tunnel here

in the Ancient System as we're likely to find,' said Skint. 'Must be worms, must be moles, must be song.'

'Aye,' said Smithills, 'and between us we've got tales to tell!'

Tryfan thought then of the many moles he and Spindle had met on their journeys. Of them all it would have been hard to say which ones he would have had with him that night in Spindle's absence.

He was glad to see Bailey, younger than them all and a mole who had travelled far, though he might only know that in time. Glad, too, that of all moles it was good-natured Smithills and reliable Skint who had made their way back to Duncton that night. Content to see Marram, who had been one of those at the Seven Stancing in Buckland, when he had felt that something had changed in moledom and a journey was begun.

He looked about him. Four and himself made five. Five to bless the Stone Mole. It was enough and yet he wished. . . .

Just then there was a rustling among the trees to their right, a certain surreptitiousness. Then silence. Moles snouting about. Moles coming near.

'Sideem!' whispered Skint, taking firm stance.

'Guardmole!' said Bailey going to his side.

'Grike!' said Smithills. 'If it's a fight then count me in,' he added raising his talons for the third time that day.

Then out of the darkness came a voice, a much loved voice, a *needed* voice.

'Misguided and about-to-be amazed Sirs, Mayweed regrets that not for the first time, nor for the last, you are wrong. Humble he is not sideem, or guardmole or grike, but simply humbleness himself.'

Then Mayweed – and the others were indeed amazed – came out into the open by the Stone saying, 'He greets you in the fur and flesh and says, "What a night! What a time for a mole to be alive!" He asks you to welcome, too, his comfortable consort Sleekit! And saying that, humbleness finds he has nothing left to say until he is greeted and offered a worm, or two.'

'Why 'tis none other than Mayweed himself!' said Smithills.

'Agedly rotund Smithills, you are perspicacious,' said Mayweed. Smithills laughed and clapped Mayweed on the shoulder.

'Nomole would be more welcome here tonight than you, Mayweed,' said Tryfan, speaking for them all, 'and nor is there one to whom each of us owes more.'

'Aye,' said Skint, 'every word that Tryfan says is true. Nomole is more welcome to me, or to Smithills here!'

With which, with nods and smiles, both Bailey and Marram agreed.

Mayweed opened his mouth to speak, but the more he saw the moles about him, and the way they stared at him with such love and good cheer, the less did he find himself able to speak. So he turned to the Stone with the light it held shining on him and his scalpskinned flanks, and he bowed his balded head, lowered his snout before it and all he could say as tears came was, 'Stone, Mayweed is a happy mole tonight.'

Then he turned back to his friends and as they touched him and Sleekit with affection and love, so they touched the others. Then, looking about them all, Tryfan saw they were seven now, and he knew that the Stone spoke to him, and told him where that night each would know Silence.

'Come,' he said softly, 'for we have a prayer and a dedication to make, and when we've made that we shall talk indeed, to find out by what various ways we came here, with Mayweed to talk last, for surely his way will have been the most mysterious! Now come. . . .'

Then he led them to the tunnel down which earlier he had taken Feverfew, and took them quietly to the burrow she was in. Softly then they entered, and in their eyes, and on their faces, and over their paws did the light of the Stone Mole shine.

Tiny he was, and vulnerable, but he was moledom's own to protect and nurture until the day might come when

915

he would show all moles how they might hear the Silence for evermore.

Then those seven moles encircled the sleeping Feverfew and her pup and one to one their shining paws did join.

'Seven moles are we, come to the Stone and the Mole it sent,' said Tryfan. 'Seven moles to witness as guardians and friends. Whatever moles we are, whatever moles we were, whatever moles we may still be, we make a Seven Stancing and dedicate our lives to him who has come and the Silence he brings. We remember the moles we loved who had faith that he would come, we think of the moles we have yet to know, whose faith will draw us on. Seven moles are we, come to the Stone and the Mole it sent. Before him we offer what Silence we have found, and wait to hear the greater Silence he will give.'

In the centre of that burrow in the ancient part of Duncton Wood, the Stone Mole stirred, and turned, and was safe. Blind he was, and vulnerable, but nomole ever had better guardians than he as those seven who encircled him; nor a mother who put her paws about a pup with such faith, and gentleness, and trust. Then the seven left his burrow in peace, to talk into the night, and share their memories and speak of their hopes.

While above them all, rising it seemed to the very star itself, the Stone shone forth, and its light seemed to travel far across moledom. For that night of nights moles began to know themselves at last, turning one to another to say, 'He has come at last; the Stone Mole has come.' Everywhere moles knew it to be so, and that knowledge touched their hearts with love, and hope, and joy. And moledom was filled with their song.

916

Epilogue

Far have we travelled with Tryfan, and soon further must we go to know the final truth of Boswell, of the Stone and of Duncton Wood. The tale must be told of the Stone Mole's life, and the great Teachings he brought; with that, too, we must relate the story of the mole whom Boswell prophesied would come, whose knowledge of the Stone, whose wisdom, and whose courage, led her to be the first mole to know full Silence in life and so make all moles see that they might know it too. Such will be the story of Duncton Found.

A NOTE FROM CENTURY HUTCHINSON PUBLISHERS OF *THE DUNCTON CHRONICLES*

Fellow moles: The publication in September 1988 of DUNCTON QUEST in hardback resulted in many hundreds of letters from moles suffering what sounded like severe withdrawal symptoms as they unwillingly returned to the human condition. Most were wondering, sometimes desperately, exactly when DUNCTON FOUND would be published.

We are very pleased to say that we were able to persuade William Horwood to return to his burrow rather more quickly than he did last time, and scribe the new volume. Consequently we have been able to do the near impossible in mole-publishing terms and bring out simultaneously with this paperback of DUNCTON QUEST the hardback of DUNCTON FOUND.

We hope that you, and every mole like you, will much enjoy the new volume and feel, on this special occasion, that it is worth the extra worms your local bookseller will request because it is a hardback . . .

917